SWICK

CIRCULAT THIS BOOK
DATE SHOW

CLITHEROL

SEP 19
OCT 95
95
96

7

D0319825

THE YEAR'S MIDNIGHT

ALEX BENZIE

VIKING

065533600

VIKING

Published by the Penguin Group
Penguin Books Ltd, 27 Wrights Lane, London w8 5tz, England
Penguin Books USA Inc., 375 Hudson Street, New York, New York 10014, USA
Penguin Books Australia Ltd, Ringwood, Victoria, Australia
Penguin Books Canada Ltd, 10 Alcorn Avenue, Toronto, Ontario, Canada m4v 3b2
Penguin Books (NZ) Ltd, 182–190 Wairau Road, Auckland 10, New Zealand

Penguin Books Ltd, Registered Offices: Harmondsworth, Middlesex, England

First published 1995
1 3 5 7 9 10 8 6 4 2
First edition

Copyright © Alex Benzie, 1995

The moral right of the author has been asserted

All rights reserved. Without limiting the rights under copyright reserved above, no
part of this publication may be reproduced, stored in or introduced into a retrieval
system, or transmitted, in any form or by any means (electronic, mechanical,
photocopying, recording or otherwise), without the prior written permission of both
the copyright owner and the above publisher of this book

Filmset by Datix International Limited, Bungay, Suffolk
Printed in England by Clays Ltd, St Ives plc
Set in 12/14.75 pt Monophoto Bembo

A CIP catalogue record for this book is available from the British Library

ISBN 0–670–86506–0

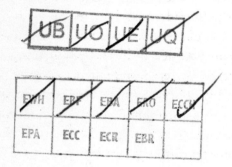

UB	UO	UE	UQ

EWH	EBF	EBA	ERO	ECC
EPA	ECC	ECR	EBR	

To many of the farmers who tended the land in the village of Aberlevin, Macpherson was the devil himself incarnate in the broad shoulders and deceptively genial manner of a good worker of the land. He was strong and confident, a wild horse never to be tamed by so brutal or unsubtle an instrument as the bit; honest and plain speaking, he never held a six-month in all his time working for any man, for it was never in him to be sweet and palliative, not for him the poisoned honey of diplomacy when the truth was there for all to see. If he had any fault, it was that he suffered fools not at all, and if the fool in question was the grieve for whom he worked, then it mattered to him not in the least that here was the man who gave him his purse for the end of his six-month, and much despised among the grieves he was for it. Like most people with a great appetite for existence, his name began to be spoken in whispers at first, at the feeing fairs up and down the county, as men and women who had worked beside Macpherson told of the many things he had done. One said he had seen Macpherson on the day that the first ploughman was sick in his bed, captaining the plough with the reins of it in his teeth and no one leading the horses from the front, his hands solid on the bars and guiding the blade as smoothly as a ship through a calm ocean, slicing deep into the earth and cutting a furrow of such precision that, after he left, the corn sprung from the ground in as neat a row as you please, and not a word of thanks or praise did he hear from the grieve for it, nor was he given any more silver in his parting purse. But there was more to Macpherson's reputation than simply his great strength and prowess in his work, for it was said that many of his jobs came to their end after a dalliance with the kitchen lass, or even the daughters of the grieves themselves, and these adventures often sealed the fate of Macpherson at his present employment, and gave rise to another facet of the legend, Macpherson the brute god of fertility, the Pan of the farmyard, the seducer of unwary young cweans, and soon enough yet more tales were told of him, dark utterances made when the sun went down on the feeing fairs and the whisky was opened and passed from hand to hand, that Macpherson kept a staff of laburnum wood to probe his way through the countryside between his jobs, and on that staff was carved a row of notches, one under the other, to represent the men who had served him ill during the long years of wandering from farm to farm. If ever you saw it in his hand, and you looked carefully so as not to catch his eye, you might see that a number were slashed across, the bark frayed under the savagery of his blade; a score settled and dealt with, a satisfactory conclusion for each of them, with many still remaining. He was a hard gambler, a player with dice and cards, lost many of his wages and gained tiny fortunes; he had never seen the inside of a kirk in all the days of his life, and among his friends he numbered men of lawless enterprise, smugglers of contraband goods, landing in unnamed beaches miles away from the harbours, rolling ashore under the cover of the night barrels of wine and brandy from France, and precious artifacts of ivory and onyx.

All of it is legend, for people will often see in the daring of others the corollary of their own reticence and failures of the spirit. There is little doubt that Macpherson was just a man, though perhaps more willing than most to speak where others might hold their tongues; he made enemies, where others worked to the tunes piped by the men who held the purse-strings, the grieves and the owners, and suffered among conditions of squalor in silence, in fear of their only livelihoods; he tasted pleasures that others could not afford, the smuggled goods sold under the noses of the excisemen, the rich meats of lawless endeavour, and damn the risks, for a wine tastes all the sweeter when gathered at midnight from the bed of a coracle; and there was not a woman with whom he had laid who had not invited him into her bed, though often he left the cweans to fatten with their burdens, and would not share the shame with

2

them when the time came to admit the act. The behaviour of no gentleman, it might be considered; but for Macpherson it was the sweetest thing about his severances, not long after being paid off by the grieve or the owner, when his boots took him far away from the farmhouse and down another road, that behind him he had left a little seed of himself to grow there in the soil of the daughter, that each day with the plumping of her belly the father would have to look on and realize that Macpherson had left his legacy, the finest revenge of the Macpherson against the chiels who would not value his work, splicing his own ragged rope to the silken cord of their fortune, and many bairns were born throughout the county with their father's cold blue eyes to stare at the grieves as if the grudge of the Macpherson had been transmitted to them in the thick and rancorous liquor which was half of their lives.

Macpherson was the least welcome sight to see at a feeing fair among the others with the sprung corn pinned to their lapels, for there was not a farmer there who did not know about him through word of mouth, and after a while he learned that the best way for him to find employment was to wait until the fair became ragged near the end of the day, when most of the workers had been matched to a grieve and a new position, for all that was left was the dregs of both. This was when Macpherson shone among all the scraps and leavings, when he stood as the most impressive wallflower at the ball, and it was at this time of the day that Macpherson found his last six-month, with a man named Angus Nevison, known far and wide as a mean bugger, an unwelcome sight for most when the sun fell to the evening; an abrupt man in every sense, walking on thick legs, his face acerbic and not easily contorted into attitudes of pleasantry. His nature at the feeing fair was entirely contrary to his workaday self, for in this dance of employer and labourer, of those with and those without, he found it necessary to present himself in the best of lights. Nevison approached the tall man, and wore a shallow smile, the faintest beacon to illuminate his intent, and said,

Fit's a fine loon like yersel deein here, at the hin end o' the fair? I'd've thocht ye'd be awa lang ere the noo, gin ye'd nae mind me askin.

Macpherson gave a shrug, for it was no matter to him, and said in reply,

I'll werk for ony man, for a guid perse, and I'll tak ony offer that's fair.

The squat man offered the usual, Macpherson would expect no less of him, soil blessed with endless fertility and a bounty of a harvest, a team of horses the like of which had never been seen, a chaumer of good construction, sound of roofing and with comfortable bedding; and Macpherson listened politely, and nodded as superlative piled upon exaggeration until the finest qualities of the farm towered to the heavens, you'd think he was being asked to farm heaven itself. The man came to the end of his description, and looked up into the face of Macpherson, who for the first time was able to see the sleekit eyes under the cap, bright slivers alive with deception, but Macpherson nodded, and held out his hand to be shaken,

I'll werk wi ye, meester fairmer, I canna richt recall hearin yer name.

The other man took the hand, his own grip moist and slippery,

Nevison's the name, my bonnie loon, Meester Angus Nevison,

and Macpherson nodded, for the name was familiar to him, and smiled himself as he added strength to his hand,

And I'm Macpherson, Meester Angus Nevison, Meester Andra Macpherson,

and Nevison's face collapsed, for each was known to the other from ballads composed by many bards of the chaumer who had known them. He did not offer Macpherson a whisky when their hands parted, but led him quietly to the cart which was to ferry him to his next employ, and of the two it was Nevison who felt the more cheated in the bargain, for Macpherson had not listened to any word of the farmer's, listening to the voice of his own experience which told him more truthfully

4

that here before him stood a rat and a liar, having dealt with many of his like in the past; while Angus Nevison lashed the horse at the head of the cart as he might have lashed himself, for he was now to give berth to the most notorious troublemaker in the county, a fool's bargain if ever there was one, seduced by the sight of so much brawn and assurance, for worse still, it was his own fault, and he determined on that ride home to the farm that he would take the best work from Macpherson that his meagre silver could buy.

The soil, Macpherson knew from the moment he saw it, was not fit to grow a thing, little more than powdered brick, dry and without cohesion, and faintly acidic, trickling through the sieve he made of his fingers; and Nevison, being of the Church of Scotland and staunch in his faith, refused to use all the artifice of agriculture to sweeten the land with lime, so that come harvest the corn stood thin and parched and with shallow roots like hair on a balding head. This as much as any reason was why Angus Nevison was unable to pay fair wages to his workers, on a point of principle, that this was the land God had given him to work, that he would play the cards dealt to him by hazard, and if its yield was not sufficient to keep the workers in decent wages, then this too was the will of God for housing such a dissolute crew. It was Nevison's meanness which finally brought Macpherson to the gallows, for fair sick were the workers of their slender meal of tattie drottle night upon night. Macpherson finally took the matters into his own hands, and said, dinna fear, my bonnie loons, we'll nae pit up wi this dert ony mair, and strode out of the chaumer and into the dark, leaving behind him fear and speculation among the bothy crew. Some thought he was away to choke a good dinner out of their employer, but he was away for a longer time than that would have taken, and so there was more disagreement, Billie MacNair suggested that he was off to see his smuggler friends, to fetch some good wine and perhaps a cask of salted beef; but Tommy Pollock said na na, he's affa far frae the coast for yon, he widna be back here till the middle o' the nicht gin he was on horseback. Two hours later, Macpherson returned, with the corpse of a sheep draped over his shoulder as easily as a stole, its head bouncing and lolling against its back as if held to the body by nothing more than cord, and he said,

Here's a feast for us a', my loons, awa tae it,

and no further urging was needed by him; in little time the sheep was beheaded and gutted swiftly and efficiently, and fleeced down to the lustrous membrane of the skin, a fleece which Macpherson kept as his own trophy for his trouble, and soon the workers were gnawing on a stew boiled in the cauldron in its broth of sweet fresh meat, and not a one of them stopped to ask Macpherson where he had got the carcass, for well enough did they know.

Unfortunately for Macpherson, there was one other who knew about the provenance of the carcass, and that was the one who had been the creature's shepherd, and in searching for his stray, James Greig had roamed a great deal of the county, following the cloven prints with the acute eye of the tracker over the soft ground. From the cover of an alder spinney, Greig saw the brute approaching the sheep he had been about to restore to the body of the flock; the sheep ran from him, but the giant was fleet, and in a moment dived and licked out his hand to grasp the beast by its trailing leg, seized in his fist as easily as a twig. Immediately the brawny man gathered the sheep in an embrace as tenderly as if to seduce it, the lone creature struggling for its life; the next moment his arms were around its throat in a hammerlock, and even across the distance Greig could hear the vertebrae snapping under the strain, and a scarlet fury seared the vacancy behind the shepherd's disbelieving eyes, as if he had been privy to the murder of his own child. It was at that moment Greig determined that he would seek the redress for his loss that was his by right of law, and so quietly he followed the big man who shouldered the corpse of his sheep so casually, as sleek as oil in the shadows, for he was a hunter of some means, no better than he in the county, and no warning did he give to his night's quarry that he was there, all the way to Nevison's farm, and he saw the man enter the chaumer from the black fabric of the farmhouse's shadow, and knew him for who he was.

The constables were at the chaumer from Aberlevin after the men had gone to bed; James Greig pointed and said, yon's the chiel fa's ta'en my sheep, and in the cauldron were the bones and skull of the sheep, the flesh parted grotesquely from it, grinning impudently as Macpherson was led away under the sheer weight of numbers, for it had been decided at the constabulary that more than two men would be needed to subdue the Macpherson, and rightly, for Macpherson made his first break at the door, and was only just held to the ground by four men who beat him soundly until the fight was exorcized from him, and he lapsed into a dream of unconsciousness, hearing from a distance the words of Nevison, tak him awa frae my sicht, for yon mannie's the deil himsel, nae but a hillock o' trouble for ony man.

The full council sat before Macpherson to hear the evidence of James Greig and the officers who had found the sheep in the cauldron; and Macpherson wore around him the fleece of the creature, which he had worn to his bed on the night of his arrest as proof against the chill of Nevison's chaumer. But theirs was not the only evidence to be heard in the chamber; for all of a sudden men he had never seen for years came to stand before the good men of the village, and swore to Macpherson's villainy. Some were men he had worked for on his travels, who testified to finding buried at their farms the skeletons of sheep long after Macpherson was gone from their employ, and Macpherson knew a number of them to be liars, and said so, earning himself the rebuke of the Provost. Some were town baillies he had crossed in his smuggling trade, and Macpherson sat passively, and knew that the wounds he had scored upon their pompous hides had finally swollen to festering, for each damned him as a murderer and a brigand, deserving of nothing but the rope, and under their sheer mass the scales keeled over beyond his retrieving, and he knew that he was to die. The Provost, wearing the gilded chain of his office, gave Macpherson his right to speech before the passing of the sentence, and Macpherson stood and addressed himself not to the men behind their oaken bench, but to the villagers who had crowded into the chamber for the spectacle of his trial, and this is what he said:

I'll taal this court, here and the noo, that I am indeed guilty o' the charge afore me, that I did tak a sheep that wisna my ain tae tak, and richt sorry I am for Meester Greig that it was his. I canna say nae tae't, for the banes were there for a' the warld tae see, and for that fine dee I ken my punishment. But I'll ask the court the noo, fit ither way has a man tae fill his belly, fan he's werkin for a crowd o' skyellochs fa'd see a man hang sooner than gie him a guid meal for the werk he's done for them? Fine wid these men afford it, am I richt?

A dangerous murmur began in the crowd, and the provost ordered silence. Macpherson continued,

There's the justice o' men, that there's nae a'body tae mak a grieve pey a guid wage tae thae fa gies him his comfort, but I'll gie them justice richt eneuch, for I curse them tae hell, ilka ane o' them, and tae thae fa'd deny tae fowk wi nae siller the guid feed and drink they'd tak for a richt tae themsels, I'd see them roast alang wi me, and hell mend them a'.

The Provost sat upright in his chair. He looked around the crowd, each nodding agreement at Macpherson's last declaration, and said, in the most sonorous voice he could find,

The fact remains that ye socht tae fill yer belly wi anither man's sheep, Andra Macpherson, and yon the court canna ignore. I sentence ye, Andra Macpherson, tae be hanged by the neck until ye are deid, at a time o' the choosing o' this court, and may the guid Laird hae maircy upon yer saul.

The crowd let out an uproar of catcalls as the council stood dismissed, and cheered Macpherson to the echo as he was led between two toun constables to an enclosed cart outside the village hall, and from there to the local gaol.

Macpherson spent his week in the cell with neither heat nor light in the evening, and nothing to use for his toilet but the bed of straw which reeked of his piss and the coiled ropes of his faeces after a short time of use. His gaolers were not at all brutal towards him, for there was no need for more brutality than he would suffer in the course of his punishment; but after a number of days, a regular visitor to his cell, a woman whom the guard let through each night, told him that the council was planning to send a messenger to Aberdeen, to the court of session, to bring back a pardon for him, overturning his sentence of execution. She told him that there had been protests and deputations to the provost, that windows had been shattered and attacks made on darkened streets upon the men who had sentenced him, that the whole village was ready to rise up in support of him, there was talk of sending for a detachment of the Gordon Highlanders to help keep order; Macpherson laughed aloud to hear of it, for he knew that his words to the gallery had struck a resonating harmony in each of them, and from the hands of his ministering angel he took a cup of wine and a soft tile of white crowdie wrapped in cloth, and a half a loaf. He asked of her,

Am I tae ken fa's been sae guid to me, or wid ye sooner keep the secret?

and the voice murmured in reply,

Ye ken the sicht o' me, Andra Macpherson, and yon's a' ye'll be tellt the noo.

It was a puzzle which occupied Macpherson's days in the cell, the remaining few before his sentence was to be carried out, and on the final day, as the young horseman rode to Aberdeen to collect the pardon, he thanked Bathsheba Nevison, his employer's wife, with all his heart for her kindness, for it was a voice he had not heard often during his stay at the farm, gentle where her husband's had been strident, filled with quiet pain for her husband's ill manners.

The burghers of Aberlevin had made one mistake when choosing young Davie Galbraith for the task of delivering their application for clemency on behalf of the Macpherson to Aberdeen, and that was in not choosing a man more willing to run a doomed errand; for Davie Galbraith was not supposed to perform his task as efficiently as he did. Davie's own father sat at the bench, and Davie knew from his father's breakfast talk that the trial was no more than an agreement upon sentence, and this the loon thought not right, that a man should fall because of minds already hardened against him, and this he said to his father, but Mr Galbraith shook his head paternally and planted a hand upon his son's red curls and said,

Davie, Davie, ye're nae affa aal yit, ye'll larn in time, that a man sic as yon has nae respect for God nor ony ither man than himsel, and sic a man has nae richt tae be in the warld wi ithers.

But this was no reason at all for Davie; and when his father returned home after the attack in the street, gathering the air into his lungs and wiping the blood from his nose on the end of his sleeve, and said,

Gin this toun disna pardon yon mannie affa soon, we'll nae keep order for lang,

Davie's heart quickened, enraged by the assault on his father, but willing to help make reparation for the injustice of the court, and his father it was who suggested him as the rider on the errand, for he was good with horses, and quickly he nodded, yes he would do it, for the sake of the brave man resting upon the mercy of the law in the village gaol, and no sooner was the verdict given by the council than Davie was saddled and given a rolled parchment, signed by the Provost, sealed with a button of wax, and off he went on the road to Aberdeen.

Davie, driving his horse as if it were an engine, had not the notion that he had been sent at the last possible moment before the arrival of the military; he threw his horse over rises and down gullies with all possible speed, and if Macpherson was not to be pardoned, then it would be through no fault of his.

At a quarter to one on the village clock, a magnificent timepiece designed and constructed by an ill-tempered Austrian mannie named Johannes Dreimann some years previously, Macpherson was taken from the gaol in a secure wagon flanked by men from the military, embracing their musket rifles to their shoulders. The village crier led the parade, the bell singing in his hand, calling at the top of his lungs a hoyzes, a hoyzes, this day the will o' the court o' Aiberlevin is tae be discharged, and Andra Macpherson will be hanged frae the neck till deid for the crime o' stealin a sheep fit did nae belang tae him, a hoyzes, a hoyzes! and behind the crier in two rows marched the burghers of Aberlevin, at one arm's width parallels, their faces dark and elemental.

The parade gained the village square, where the crowd doubled upon itself like a folded sheet, racing in from the pavement. The clock told ten minutes to one in the afternoon as the military erected itself like a barricade between the crowd and the newly struck gallows, the wood releasing its fragrance of pine into the air. The latch on the doubled doors of the cart, a simple rope and spike lanced through an iron eye, was released, and Macpherson's own eyes fluttered like a coquette's in the sudden metallic light of the sun. First into the cart was the priest, offering to shrieve him of his last sins, but Macpherson declined with surprising politeness,

Na na, Reverend, it's a lang time sin I've seen the inside o' a kirk, I canna but think that God'll hae his ain way o' dealin wi the like o' mysel.

Before he left, the Reverend smelled a foul odour, and noted that, in the corner of the cart, among a nest of straw, Macpherson had left his last defiance to survive him; a rank turd, laid there like an egg. His beard had grown thick and red during his imprisonment, stiff and crisp with neglect; but when he stood from the single bench, he held himself proud and upright, squaring himself before appearing before the crowd, an actor to the last, for his heart was sore against his ribs, and hardly another thing could he hear but the rhythm of his own pulse, as he was led towards the steps to the gallows at five minutes to one.

Now, the best laid plans of mice and men a' gang aft agley, says the bard of Ayrshire; and this was almost true of the occasion of Macpherson's hanging, were it not for a final act of duplicity on the part of the village burghers which sealed the lid upon Macpherson's coffin as surely as the nails of the undertaker. There was still the chance that the pardon would arrive on time, and the document, once received, would have forced the council to release the brigand with his feet on the gallows, an outcome they would sooner avoid. To this end, a spy was placed at the crown of the clock tower, one Baillie Dowell, a landowner as were many on the council, whose grieves had suffered greatly as a result of employing the man now standing below him. Dowell commanded the view of a god from his vantage in the belfry; the entire village was spread out before him, a community of dolls, and with the distortion of perspective came another fantasy, that he could reach down with an immense fist and pick up the Macpherson like the wriggling smout he was, capturing him in the palm of his hand, he could bring his clenched fist down upon the whole rabble who cheered the brigand to his death and scatter them to their homes, and in fact he closed his fingers around the entire gathering, just to see them held in his hands. He was searching the hills and valleys of Aberlevin, the windbreak rim cropped by sheep and cattle, when he saw the figure on a horse, racing like Tam o'Shanter chased by all the vassals of the devil, and in that moment Dowell knew that Macpherson was to be saved, that the rider was approaching with such a speed that he would gain the top of North Street before the clock struck one, and after a while of confusion he knew what had to be done.

He took the ladder down into the clock chamber itself, and hurried his eyes along the mechanism of Johannes Dreimann's clock. Baillie Dowell knew that to hurry the clock, he had to speed the weight in its fall, and this he did by sliding himself under the frame of the mechanism and pulling on the rope, so that the rocker rode over two teeth instead of only one. The train accelerated by inches, and the riot of tortured machinery squealed in the cranium of the tower, the rope burning a trough in the palm of Baillie Dowell's hand, but still he pulled, and cast a hope to God that he would succeed against the pain of the friction.

No one noticed among the ceremony in the street below that Macpherson's last four minutes were being bolted like a child's dinner; the Reverend chanted prayers for the saving of Macpherson's soul, while Macpherson's neck was placed within the collar of the noose as he stood atop a wooden dais which was to be taken from under him at the right moment. He matched the eyes of the hangman courageously before the hood was placed over them, the fibres thick enough to allow him light through the weave; and then there was a single note from the bell under the cone of the spire, and there Macpherson must be allowed the final privacy of death as the dais was kicked out from under him, his feet fell into space and found no rest, and the air turned away from his throat as if no longer welcome to tarry. There was no dignity to Macpherson's death, for it was a punishment of beasts; his penis swelled in its death erection, Macpherson's last monument to the life he was leaving, thrusting against his breeks like an obelisk, spitting its juice as he would have spat himself on those who had condemned him.

Davie Galbraith heard the gonging of the clock just as his tired horse clattered on to the surer road of the turnpike at North Street, its shoes worn down to new moons of iron, and far from pulling on the reins and calling the beast to a halt, he kicked against the belly of the horse with his heels and leaned forward into the saddle. The wind forced itself into his mouth like a cloth, as it had done throughout the journey, the beats of his horse's hooves echoed like a volley of gunfire, and he saw the crowd, pressing against a gaudy lining of militia, wrapped around the gallows like a shawl as the corpse of Macpherson was cut down from its pendant rope, and at that moment Davie Galbraith knew he had failed by the slenderest of margins to save him, for the pardon was rolled and sealed in his saddle-bag, and only then did he whoa his horse, which took long breaths through foaming lips, strolling the rest of the way to the centre.

The hangman took the corpse to the wagon from which it had come, still wearing the cowl which masked the final identity of death from the crowd which was turning to see the slightest movement around them. Davie stood down from the horse, and took the scroll from his bag. His father was standing, shielded by the militia, and Davie approached and said,

I had the pardon for him, faither. I wisna quick eneuch.

Galbraith nodded, said,

Yon's the way wi the will o' God, Davie. Mebbe he wis meant tae dee.

Then there was a sound which silenced everyone in the crowd. It was faint, and took some listening to at first, but it was quite clear; the sound of rain falling on bells, a slight crystal sound which was unmistakably that of a watch chiming the hour, and it came from the fob pocket of the Provost of the village, who dissembled with the ill timing of the amateur Machiavelli, casting around himself as if the sound were coming from elsewhere, finally looking to his own pocket as the crowd pointed straight at him, pinning him with their hatred, looking to the village clock which was now telling five minutes past the hour, and its exaggerated tale was noticeable to the eye.

No one was killed in the pandemonium which followed, for the militia had been given strict instructions by their sergeant that any discharging of the rifles had to be done into the air in warning first. The burghers ran for their lives behind the barricade of soldiers, and, a fine irony under the circumstances, took refuge in the wagon which had carried Macpherson from his cell to his final pendulum dance, and ultimately found that their only safety lay in the very cell where Macpherson had rested after the trial. Some of the crowd ran after the wagon, and beat a tattoo against its side with their fists, a drum beat which unsettled the pampered nerves inside and sent them cowering, and, so the story goes, the Provost encountered Macpherson's last testament in the corner, and reeked of it for months afterwards. For the most part, however, the crowd were in a directionless rage, and sought out the most obvious symbols of the council's authority for destruction; some cast stones through the windows of the baillies, some picked down the gallows themselves, bending it over by sheer weight of numbers as Macpherson himself had been broken by the evidence of many; but it did not take long before it occurred to the remainder, if it can truly be said that a notion can occur in the midst of a rampage, that the one prominent symbol of the council's treachery was as yet untouched. The line of the militia was sundered like a chain of paper soldiers, and cast to both sides, and the crowd bore down the door to the clock tower as if it were the illusion of wood, clambering up the helical staircase each with a will to be the first to attack the perjured mechanism.

They raged against the very heart of time in the village as if the clock itself were their oppressor, as if the corrupt kingdom of minutes and hours were lashing them with the cat of tick tock every hour on the hour. They swarmed over it like ants, taking to pieces in unreasoning moments what Johannes Drei-mann had spent his whole miserable time in the village working upon, drawing and quartering the clock as if it had willed the death of Macpherson. They tore time itself limb from limb; they severed the hempen rope of the counterweights, as if to cut down the corpse of Macpherson, and watched them fall through the core of the tower, ringing against the flagging below one after the other. They left the chamber when there was nothing left to destroy, their skins blackened by the lubricating oil and the dirt which adhered to it, laughing with glee for what they had achieved, sated for the now, leaving the clock in shreds and tatters behind them, the voiceless victim of their hate, the Judas goat for Macpherson's drop, wrongly blamed for its part.

Macpherson was buried in unconsecrated ground, the final insult to the brigand, for many thought that the pardon, as late as it had been, secured for his shell the right to be buried as any other Christian should, and from this final injustice came the tale of a man seen wandering the roads of Aberlevin, probing the cobbles ahead with his staff of laburnum, a staff on which seven freshly carved notches could plainly be seen, representing the seven men of the council who had betrayed him. When the Lord of Aberlevin, the younger lord and son of the man who had feued the territory for development, heard of the treachery of the council, he demanded that a new election be held, and this election, limited as its franchise was to those whose property in the world clamoured for a vote, returned six of the same men, excepting the Provost, who, as figurehead of the entire ship, was dashed to pieces against the reefs of adversity first of all, as is the way with corruption.

As for time, its voice within the village was stilled in its throat, for no one chose to restore the clock after its destruction, and so silent it remained at the head of its tower, a mute monument to caprice and deceit, a gravestone marker to civic trust and the health of the polity, forever telling ten minutes past one. From that day onward, time became a private affair for the villagers of Aberlevin, the sensation of a heartbeat, the morning reveille of the rooster crying at the first sight of the sun, the chiming of mantelpiece clocks synchronized by sundials in the gardens of the better off. Time belonged to no one and to everyone, measured in quarters of a year, and no longer did the markets at the foot of the tower pack up their wares and leave at the chime of five to make their way home, but stayed to gossip with their custom until the sun slanted towards its bed behind the hills, when everyone knew fine well that time it was to be leaving.

I

One minute, Jeannie Leckie was standing over her pot of chicken stew, listening to it muttering under its breath, the flesh boiling away from the carcass; the next, her waters had broken, trickling coolly down her legs, and an intolerable pain like an implosion threatening to pull her whole being through her midriff made her cry out, doubled her in two, caused the ladle she was holding to leap from her hand and spill its liquor over the floorboards. Such a sharp blade of a cry was it that Peggy, her husband's mother, who was busily darning grain sacks under the cover of the barn, recognized instantly its edge, its plea for release, and dropped what she was doing, leaving the sack she was working on to deflate and the hessian thread to worm along the mud of the courtyard, speeding as fast as her aching legs could take her to the farmhouse.

There she found Jeannie on her haunches before the stove as if in idolatrous worship of it, her swollen belly in her arms, face gashed across by the effort of will it took not to give tongue to her discomfort. She did not even notice Peggy until the calloused old hands were on her shoulders, until she said,

Fit's a-dee? Is't your time?

It was all Jeannie could do to nod in reply as the pains pulled at her from inside, as tears forced themselves through the fissures of her eyelids. From then on Peggy was the supporting pillar to Jeannie's slowly cracking world, speaking softly to her as one who understood the experience, wincing herself with every one of the seizures which brought Jeannie to a halt on the stairs, coaxing her as if she were an uncertain, frightened animal being brought to see the vet, come on my cwean, it'll nae be lang; lifting her when the pain cut her strings and left her to dangle, pressing her forward when it tugged on her and made her gasp, placing her footfalls on each step.

Only after the journey of an age did Jeannie realize where she was, sitting up on the stiffness of her own horsehair bed, her waters staining the sheets, woven through with threads of blood. Her heart was drumming against the bars of her ribcage, the very air seemed to rape her lungs, and when she sobbed, it was as much from terror as pain. Peggy stroked a hand over her forehead, said,

Ye'll be a' richt, Jeannie. I'll hae tae gang doon the stairs for a few things. I'll nae be lang.

Then she was gone, and Jeannie didn't even have the fight in her to plead with Peggy not to leave her.

Peggy brought towels with her to sop up the waters, and a ceramic bowl of warmed-over water drawn from the standpipe outside, and with a linen cloth she wiped Jeannie clean of what she called yon muck, to give herself a better view of the child's progress to the opening. She cried upon Jeannie to push lassie, push! waiting for the first signs of the baby's eviction from the womb, and Jeannie screamed and threw all her effort into ridding herself of the leaden agony buried deep inside her; finally rewarded when the tiny puckered face squeezed into the air of its own birth. But Peggy wouldn't let her stop to look down on the head marbled with her blood; as she panted like a dog, Peggy called push a bittie mair, Jeannie, dinna stop the noo, and with more effort the baby slithered into the towel Peggy held ready for him (noting that it was a he, the tiny stump of a penis jigging about between his legs). Then, after the placenta flopped on to the third towel to be parcelled up and disposed of without unpleasantness, Peggy took hold of the umbilical cable and severed it with her teeth, as easily as she might have parted a strand of her knitting wool, and coiled it up inside the towel along with the afterbirth, which she took downstairs while Jeannie held her firstborn in her arms, chanting over and over ye're affa bonnie, ye're affa bonnie. Peggy brought her a fine strong cup of tea as she lay back with the bairn. The exertion had unpinned Jeannie's long black hair, causing it to flood the pillow; pins and clasps were sown around the bed, even on the floor, and she laughed as she found another, and still another, pressing into her flesh and leaving a flagrant red memory behind, but Peggy, ever the pragmatist, said to her,

Ye'd be as weel puttin on yer nichtgoon the noo, Jeannie, for I've nae doot Wullie'll be efter seein the bairn the meenit he cams ben the hoose,

and Jeannie nodded, after all an event like a birth was no excuse for letting modesty fly into the air, and got out of bed while Peggy cleaned off the baby ready for presentation. The winceyette nightgown sighed the length of her body, and not long after she stepped back into bed she was fast asleep with the baby in her arms; and the baby too had struck its own bargain with sleep, a familiar element of blackness and enclosure resembling the fine and private place it had been forced to leave so suddenly.

Peggy crept from the bedroom, downstairs found her coat on its hook in the kitchen, and left the house, taking care not to close the door behind her with too much of a racket.

Wullie was driving the cows back from pasture when Peggy caught up with him, smacking the rump of the hindmost lingering over some appealing shoots, calling out ho Jinty, ho Lady, shaping their progress across the field. Peggy tramped along unhurriedly, and from this casual pace of hers Wullie thought himself in for a chiding for keeping Jeannie at the stove for so long; but he could only go so fast as the cows themselves, and he was ready to tell her this when she passed on her message, that his wife had just given birth to a bonny wee loon. The suddenness of it all caused poor Wullie's head to spin, he cried out,

It's a' richt? They're fine, the baith o' them?

and Peggy nodded, offering to drive the kye home for him, an offer he didn't even stop to thank her for before he was racing across the field, pounding flat the sprigs of grass not yet eaten by the cows. Once inside the house, he found the stairs and charged to the top; but at the door to the bedroom he stopped, for through it he could hear a tiny mewling cry, and he forced himself to slow down his breathing to heartbeat time, not wanting to appear in such an unholy rush before his wife, nor to disturb his son on his first day.

Both were already awake when he opened the door. Jeannie smiled as Wullie entered with his head bowed over like a penitent, his flat cap doffed and held close to his chest as if secrets were written under the rim; approaching the bed as if it were a shrine, a place for supernatural and miraculous events. Jeannie looked down at Wullie's feet, at the boots whose clattering on the stairs had shocked her fully awake, and she shook her head at the sight,

Wullie Leckie, she said, your beets are a' clarted wi muck.

Wullie ignored her. He peered inside the hood of the white towel. The eyes were closed, but he could see under the translucent lids how vividly blue they were. The tiny doll's fist punched at the restraining folds of cloth, fighting the enclosure.

He disna like bein a' wrapped up like yon,

said Wullie, and Jeannie frowned,

Fit way d'ye ken fit the bairn likes and fit he disna? He likes't fine.

And that ended the matter, for Jeannie was well enough able to fathom the needs of her own child better than any bystander of a man, even the man she called her husband. Wullie sat on the edge of the bed, looked down at the floorboards, at the rippling of the wood's grain, looked up at Jeannie.

Will ye lee me hae a look at his hands?

Jeannie nodded, parted the towel like a curtain. The baby paddled weakly in the open air. Wullie held out a thick gnarled branch of a finger; the model hand fastened on to it as if it were flotsam, and Wullie took the opportunity to study the wee hand carefully.

Aye, he said, yon's a guid ticht haud he's there.

Gently Jeannie plucked her bairn's fingers from around Wullie's.

He'll nae be a fairmer, Wullie.

Wullie sat upright on the bed, as astonished as if she had just released the stench of foulest blasphemy.

Fit way d'ye think yon, Jeannie?

He hisna the hands for it.

Wullie stood up, stared at her for a moment. She possessed the baby in her arms; while all he had in his possession with which to argue was his lifetime of study of the hands of a farmer, his own, and those of his father, from whom he had taken the farm as a present on the occasion of his wedding to this woman, who saw no such future for their son. He left the room quietly, but pained to his heart by the prophecy; which soon enough he forgot when Peggy served up the stew Jeannie had been so conscientious in preparing before she had been struck down by the pains of labour.

After dinner, Wullie invited his workers in from the chaumer to share with him his fireside and a dram or two of good Glenlevin malt to fire the tongue and lay a gunpowder trail the length of the throat. Wullie and the others sipped at their glasses with some appreciation, but his father, after whom he had been named, threw the whisky over with contempt, coughing as it detonated in his chest, holding his glass out for another and with his other hand stroking the greying fur around the ear of the Laird. Dodie Mearns left for a moment, returned with his German-made melodion of polished rosewood and brass he had picked up for the price of a drink from a previous workmate many years ago, in another farm. His arrival with the instrument meant only one thing; Andy McGrath slipped the jew's harp from his top jacket pocket, and everyone cried out a sang, Wullie my man, gie's a sang! It was then for Wullie to appear the very picture of modesty, for such was the right and proper thing to do; but such was his great joy at the birth of his first son that there was only one voice appropriate for it, and without the usual ritual of persuasion he went to the cabinet of ash he had made for himself, removed from it a protective envelope of cloth, closed over the cabinet's doors and went to stand before the peat fire he had lit against the treacherous cold of the nights close to harvest. With the sureness of touch of the born showman, Wullie peeled the cloth from around the fiddle, its coarse grained pine surface supremely polished, and looked fondly upon it, remembering the nights left over after he had worked a full day on the farm when he used to run to the shed across the courtyard and plane and chisel and polish the pieces, and when he had glued the whole together, how he had looked on the finished crafted article, surely too beautiful a thing to adulterate by playing, until Aal Wullie said to him, ye canna jist look't the thing a' day fan ye've ga'ed tae sic trouble, and took him to the hardware store in the village to buy him the reward of four gut strings and the resin with which to draw sound from them.

Wullie took the bow and held it in the groove of his oxter; with the cloth he frisked away from the liquid lacquered skin of the fiddle the dust he had imagined had deposited since last he was persuaded to play it. He drew the bow across the strings, causing the fiddle to howl, another of his little rituals which the Laird fell for every time, arrowing his ears and standing up, putting on a girn of irritation, unable to taste in the air or see with his ageing eyes the creature which was making the row, finally pacified by Aal Wullie's hand pressing along his back. Wullie drawled the introduction to The Deil's Awa wi th'Exciseman, and Dodie and Andy joined in too, Dodie's melodion wheezing like an old man reaching the top of a steep hill, Andy's harp like all the sprung beds in creation disgorging their coils and entrails; the music surged ahead like a brisk country walk, rising and falling with the hills and the drops, and all the feet in the room paced out the rhythm against the floorboards, and not long into the melody Alistair Loudon took Cathie Wallace in hand from her stool in front of the fire, bowing to her in mockery of the fine manners of those who were paid rent for land, and she raised herself from the stool and curtseyed in reply, to a patter of meaningful applause and a sparkling of grins from the company, who arranged themselves and their seats into an arena especially for the couple to dance around. So light were they on their feet that they gave the appearance of dancing not on the floor but on the carpet of music spread out before them; and they laughed as Wullie Leckie senior sang out his own version of the refrain, oh the deil's awa the deil's awa the deil's awa wi th'exciseman, the words as soft in his mouth as meal. Wrapped warmly in his blanket of drunkenness, Aal Wullie cared not one iota that he was being laughed at, nor that his wife was glowering at him for snaking an unseen hand around the neck of the bottle as it rested on the mantelpiece, emptying a generous measure into his already half-full glass. He simply beamed around the room at everyone in their turn, winking at all who caught his eye as if the picture of him sitting there with his dram should be enough to reveal to all with eyes to see that here was a man who had fathomed a purpose to his life and the mysteries of fulfilment.

The melody drawled to its finish, a mirror image of the opening, sealing the song as surely as if it were a package tied with a symmetrical butterfly knot. Alistair and Cathie sprang apart suddenly, smiled at each other, went to their stools as the silence took back the licence given to them by the music, and Peggy applauded, ignoring her husband as he reached for the ghost of the bottle and clutched on air. From upstairs, there was a thin cry from the bairn, and Peggy stopped her clapping to warn,

Dinna play ony mair, Wullie, the loon's awake,

and the fiddle was restored to its place in the cabinet, and any singing to be done for the rest of that night was performed softly, without the embroidery of music.

The child was christened William George Leckie in the Episcopal Church on North Street by the Revd James Lyle on the Saturday after the birth. The in-laws on the distaff side regretted being unable to attend, although they had visited Jeannie on the Thursday to inspect their new grandchild, with the usual polite provision of cakes and hot tea; but the Richies had their own farm to run, they hoped it was understood, and Jeannie took the disappointment well enough all things considered, being much too exhausted still from the birth to care who would be present.

Aal Wullie's face was pocked and red with its first good shave in a number of days, the rim of his collar punctuated with commas of blood. Peggy sat beside him as he hooked his finger inside the collar to release the jowls which had risen like dough in a mixing bowl; she pleated her hands over a prayer-book resting on her lap, trying not to look too ashamed to be seen in the shadow of his hangover. As for Jeannie and Wullie, they stood before the granite chalice of the baptismal font and smiled when William cried fit to fill the vaults of the kirk to the echo at the sudden shower of chilled water which rained down on to his bald head from the reverend's hand; but Wullie's brother John promised on behalf of the bairn that he would from that day forth renounce Satan and all his works, while the newly named William George Leckie howled at his untenable suspension in the hands of one entirely unused to the tender holding of children, with fingers as cold as a surgeon's, and so loud was he about it that you might have thought that the bairn was protesting in the only way he was able at the cavalier making of a promise he was in no way yet responsible for making himself.

After, when the fee had been paid and the reverend thanked for his service, it was time to return to Smallbrae, and such a fine day was it that the leather hood of the gig remained slumped over its shoulders. Jeannie sat beside her mother-in-law at the back, sharing the carrying of the baby in their generous linen laps. Johnnie and Aal Wullie sat against the grain of the journey, closer to the wheelbase than Wullie, who sat up on the board expanded with pride, steering Blackie through the village at a slow pace, the better for everyone to see the owners of Smallbrae Farm, the providers of dairy milk for near enough three quarters of a century to both high and low around Aberlevin, with the heir to the business squalling at the top of his lungs with every shock and stammer of the wheels over the cobbles. Occasionally he passed by one of the customers, and called out cheerily to them fine morn tae ye, and they turned and smiled aye Wullie, fine morn tae ye, and the wife and bairn as weel, and Wullie sat higher in his seat, sending a delicate ripple through the reins to encourage Blackie and no more.

Aal Wullie pinched his ears at the screams of his grandson, and he called over to Jeannie above the already shattering rhythm of Blackie's hooves on the stones,

Can ye nae mak the loon wheesht, Jeannie? He's far ower loud.

Peggy reserved her finest scowl for him, called in reply,

Dinna be daft, Wullie, ye canna mak him wheesht on sic a bumpy road as yon, the puir wee cratur canna get a proper rest.

She turned to Jeannie, softened her features to smile an apology,

Dinna pay him ony heed, Jeannie, his heid's dirlin efter the nicht by.

Aal Wullie borrowed the scowl from his wife and aimed it back at her, but her eyes were too full of wee Wullie to set aside any room for her husband's expressions of wounded pride, so,

Wheesht yersel, wumman; I'd sooner tak the bairn's skraikin than yours,

he said, and Johnnie looked at his sister-in-law across the gig, each balancing so elegantly on the fulcrum of propriety that the slightest tic at the corner of the mouth from either of them would have tilted them over into laughter. But the balance held true, and for somewhere to look they stared at wee Wullie's hot and flagrant face as he protested against the discomfort of the ride in the only way he could.

At the frontier of the village, where North Street stopped and the Cornhill Road began, changing its nature as well as its name to a long and subtle tapeworm of ill-maintained cobbles, Aal Wullie turned to his younger son and said,

Weel noo, Johnnie Leckie, fit way're ye nae merrit yet?

Peggy nodded agreement, much to her surprise, leaned forward.

Aye Johnnie, does Jeannie's bairn nae pit ye in mind o' settlin doon?

Johnnie smiled. He looked across at the fields of corn, just as the breeze tousled them, raising them into waves which mimicked the element he plied for his living. Finally he shook his head.

It'd tak a fine wumman, he said, to be merrit tae a fisher.

And that was all he had to say on the subject of marriage, despite the pressure of his mother and father; standing as tall as a barricade against all their questions, refusing to let their concern for him erode his immense and mysterious silence. The gig jounced over the hills towards the farm, William George Leckie drooled and cried in his wrap of warm linen, and no more was said of Johnnie's lonely existence on shore.

The workers had gladly taken up the slack caused by the family's visit to the kirk and as a reward that evening Wullie took out his fiddle and the remains of the Glenlevin, dispensing it generously even to his sot of a father, and played strongly and surely with Dodie and Andy, playing mainly to the baby as Peggy bounded and bobbed him on her lap; holding him upright as he made two good fists around her fingers, jogging him in time to the music in imitation of the cantering of a horse, even making hoofbeats in the back of her throat.

Alistair and Cathie partnered each other for a kind of polka, clattering and spinning across the floor like figures on a carousel, sometimes looking in the direction of their eccentric orbit, and sometimes boldly at each other, with the room smeared about them like a child's finger painting, nothing in focus except their own sharp presences close to one another. Wullie winked at Dodie and Andy; and soon, mischievously soon, they played their coda, stopping the couple as abruptly as if a wooden stick had been cast deep into their mechanism. The room shaped itself around them once more, and Cathie felt the fire of embarrassment touch her cheeks as she smiled in reply to the canty wee expressions of knowledge from all of those seated around; but when her hand parted from Alistair's, it was slowly and with reluctance, the contact almost lingering in the bone, radiant through the both of them.

Wullie accepted his applause with a shallow nod of the head from his centre stage at the hearth. Jeannie sat on a stool in the corner, a slight smile on her face. She was gazing over at wee Wullie on his grandmother's lap, grinning openly, basking in the attention, and a tiny embryo of resentment grew fatter inside her the more she stared across: it should have been her seated there by the fire coddling the bairn.

Wullie started up the Bonnie Lass o' Fyvie, and as the tune jaunted along, impelled by the sound of clapping, a hand entered her field of vision, a thick hand with calluses tracked across the palm.

Will ye hae a dance wi me?

said Johnnie Leckie.

She did not look into Johnnie Leckie's eyes all the while they were dancing. She felt the calluses on his hands abrading her palms, knew their pattern to be those of the trawl ropes he hauled upon to raise the netted fish into their grave of thin air; but the hand was still warm around hers, his arm about her waist brawny, guiding her along to the music. She looked at Wullie, thrashing the notes out of his fiddle, goading it to song; at Dodie, intent on siring the breath from his melodion; the spring of Andy's harp ticking against his teeth, and then the wink he passed on to Alistair and Cathie in turn as they leaned against the cabinet, a gesture which Jeannie felt ricochet from the couple to bury deep within her own heart. Her feet became slow and leaden, and she remembered the hardship she had during the last few months of her pregnancy simply to walk across the courtyard on days when the rain turned it into mire, sucking the boots from her feet and exhausting her more than any of her regular chores. Johnnie felt her dragging upon him, tried to restore the ginger to her step, tugged gently on her arm and renewed his surge across the floor; but suddenly she felt crushed by him, as much a puppet to his drive, his insistence, as she had been to the pain seeded in her belly not a week before. She released his hand, causing him to fly away from her as if on a catch, fled from the room, up the darkness of the stairs and not tripping once, into the bedroom which was lit through its window by a swollen moon. Downstairs she could hear the music tapering away to a point of embarrassment, a silence of confusion. She looked out of the window, at the byre and the outhouses plated with moonlight, and then she was staring at them through a pane of tears, not knowing the reason for them, fishing in the sleeve of her blouse for a linen handkerchief and dabbing her eyes with it, telling herself na na Jeannie, this winna dee.

There was a sequence of footsteps on the stairs, across the landing. Johnnie came into the room, his face a mosaic of black shadow and gold light from the candle he held in his hand. She went over to the pinewood crib Wullie had fashioned for the bairn, laid a hand on its railing.

Wullie says tae me, gang awa up the stairs and see fit's a-dee wi Jeannie.

Jeannie mopped her eyes quickly, tucked her handkerchief back into her sleeve. Johnnie walked a little across the room, changing the pattern of light and its absence on his face. He went around the bed, avoiding even the slightest feather of a touch against her; removed the glass from the oil-lamp on the bedside table, fired the wick from the candle's leaf of flame, crowned it with the glass.

Ye dinna ken, he said finally, fit like it is for a fisher. It's nae ony life for a'body on shore.

Jeannie went back to the window. She heard the cows in the byre lowing gently.

Ye'd've been a guid fairmer, she said.

He laughed, kindly.

I couldna be deein wi a' yon plyterin aboot in the muck.

Jeannie turned, read the irony from the slant of his lips, laughed with him; turned back to the window.

Ye'll nae dee on land.

He shrugged.

We'll a' dee, on land nor water.

He passed the bed once again, avoiding the friction even of fabric between them, went to the door; before leaving he said,

God forgie us, Jeannie, but gin I canna be merrit, then the sea'll tak me.

He didn't close the door when he left. Jeannie went over to the vacant crib, and stared inside it for a moment, just as Johnnie opened the living-room door downstairs and released as he did so the screams of her son, and she realized that he had been screaming like that for fully a minute. The sound came

28

closer, accompanied by footsteps. Wullie came in, with wee William held in an awkward father's make-do cradle of arms.

Johnnie says ye were efter seein me.

Jeannie watched him place the bairn tenderly in the crib, remembered all the nights he had spent in the shed carving the railing and planing the headboard. He looked at her for a moment, without understanding, and then she was in his arms, she couldn't stop herself, her breasts swollen and aching with milk; crying, just like her son.

II

The village saw the bairn they would soon enough know as Watchie grow from week to week, from Sunday to Sunday in the middle pews of Aberlevin Episcopal kirk. He spent his first year on Jeannie's lap, growing fatter and happier and strong enough to clutch at her lapel; but nothing, not even all her crooning and pleading, could lull him more effectively than the mesmeric rhythm of the Revd James Lyle's pulpit voice as it spoke of the breadth and depth of God's love for each of the congregation. As the weeks passed, Watchie grew stronger still, and soon enough he was taking to his legs, and using his better reach to investigate the many hats which came to his interest. Often Jeannie had to gather him to her lap and smile an apology as Watchie lifted the brim of every colourful and decorated hat in front of him, some with garlands of crêpe de Chine roses tied in a bunch with lace in the saucer of the brim, belonging to the wife of a laird, some with a simple frieze of silk bound with a butterfly knot. The colours had to be bright and vibrant, the texture irresistible before Watchie would raise himself in his mother's lap, and soon enough Jeannie learned all the signals of his curiosity, the long and quiet stare, the chubby finger pointing to the object, and she learned to tighten her hold on him, prepared to suffer his frustration more than the embarrassment of an apology.

By the time five harvests had come and gone, Watchie had learned most of the lessons he needed and foremost among these was patience. He had learned to sit still in kirk, and that the cold ash wood under his bare legs would slowly heat up the longer he sat on it. He understood nothing of what the Revd Lyle said from the pulpit, but he learned to watch him as if he did, or at least to orientate his head like the blossom of a sunflower towards the reverend while he was speaking, which he also learned liberated his eyes to suck the juice from all the things which attracted him; the blaze of gold which was struck from the chalice on the altar by the occasional slant of sunlight, the saddened expressions on the icons, reminding him of the look on his mother's face after a careless spill or fall, pitying him for his frailties, despairing while at the same time understanding.

There were many things for Watchie to investigate, but despite the great feast of things to interest him, time never ran quite as swiftly as he would have preferred, the grains of the hourglass seeming to topple as leisurely as boulders, until the whole kirk appeared to have been built from these hewn rocks of time. He began to recognize the face of Sundays even before they were on the gig to the kirk. He began to recognize them as the days when Aal Wullie would spend an age in his room, when the sound of water trickling from jug into ceramic bowl would be interrupted by the sound of scraping, not unlike the Laird's claws against cobbles, opening the door only when his face was cleaned of any shadow, dabbing at the freckles of blood with a clean towel, wearing a woolly semmit as his sole proof against the cold. Jeannie always made sure the boy had on a semmit too, which Watchie hated; the fabric was as rough against him as glass paper. Watchie liked his grandfather, for what he appeared to lack in terms of the wisdom which is supposed to crown age with dignity, he made up for in understanding what it was like to be a child, and this made Watchie feel that he was the wisest one of all.

Can ye nae see the loon disna tak tae yon semmit? The pair bairn's itchin a' ower,

but Jeannie simply looked at him out of the rim of her vision, and that was the end of it.

Aal Wullie's dressing for kirk, now, was a different matter. Once the boots were burnished to gleam like black iron, the fusty suit from the wardrobe donned and the tie looped about the collar, there was a charmed circle about him, an invisible fortress of cleanliness which no one was allowed to breach, not even the Laird, especially not the Laird after he came back into the kitchen from his morning release into the yard with his claws charged with black mud. Watchie, too, was quarantined from him by Jeannie, but the dog would always sit still and whimper when he was ordered; and when the family returned from the kirk later in the day, after the labourers had cycled home on their sit up and begs, the Laird was always the first to welcome them, his tail flaying the air, but still careful not to muddy their good Sunday clothes.

Wullie made sure that Watchie had handled all the teats of the dairy cows by the time he had seen his fifth harvest. Usually it was Jeannie's task to waken him just as the sun bloodied the rump of the Deil's Shieling; or, in the winter, to walk with her husband, balancing an empty bucket in one hand and a lantern in the other, gouging out of the chill early darkness a thin tunnel of light. But it was Wullie himself who roused Watchie that morning, the sky beyond the curtains already a willow-pattern blue, and later he ate hot porridge with his son at the table and said,

D'ye ken fit way I got ye oot yer bed sae early the morn, William?

and soon enough after being told, Watchie was carrying a pail in each hand, holding them at arm's length, having learned with his first few steps that they were bound to pivot back and strike his bare legs. At first he toddled two steps for each of his father's long strides, yawning abysmally and wishing he was back in bed; but he made a game out of printing his footsteps on top of Wullie's, causing him to flail out his legs unnaturally in order to match his father print for print as they led him all the way to the byre.

Inside, the cows lay nested in a weave of fresh straw, perking up their heads, opening eyes which always seemed to Watchie to be close to tears. Each had her own berth, and Wullie threw back the dull iron bolt on the first gate, lifted the milking stool beside it and went in, calling,

Fine morn tae ye, Elsie.

Elsie stared lazily at him for a moment, then, with an air of dignity and complaisance, raised her flanks and then her breast to such an impressive height, expanding her bulk in a way which made Watchie thrill with fear as he stood shaded by his father. Wullie saw him cower, and laughed.

Dinna be feart. Ye widna dee the loon ony hairm, wid ye, Elsie?

stroking his hand the length of her glossy back, punctuating his gesture of affection with a clap which echoed off the walls. Elsie stood still, waiting calmly; glanced around at Watchie as he brought himself out from behind his father, scanned him up and down, judged him harmless enough and probably friendly, lost interest and stared ahead again. Wullie bedded the legs of the stool in the straw, sat opposite the full pink sac, placed the bucket under the battery of teats, looked up at Watchie.

Heed weel fit I'm deein, William,

he said, then grasped a teat in each hand, easily drawing off the milk from them, firing the streams into the bottom of the bucket, causing the milk to ring from empty metal. Watchie stared in fascination as the milk filled and foamed higher inside the bucket, at the constellation of bubbles which burst crisply with each break of the surface tension; but he wished himself elsewhere, if only for the smell of dung, the same smell which cast its blanket over the yard, now especially fresh in the confined space. Haunting the portal of the byre, waiting for them to finish the milking of the kye so that he could spoon out the cakes of dung from the stalls with his shovel, was the farm's new orra loon, fee'd at Porter Fair to replace Geordie Mutch. In many ways the two were similar; both Jamie Watts and Geordie before him reclusive and preferring the quiet of the chaumer to the fiddle evenings at the fireside, but there was a difference to the message of the eyes which expressed their silences. Where Geordie's eyes had been rimmed with creases which displayed at least that he was able for pleasure, Watts's were wide and as luminous as those of the Laird, and when he smiled, it was a razor-edged weapon of a smile, honed and hardened like a blade in a smithy. Watchie was disturbed by those eyes, by the expression which you might imagine if it were directed at the milk would turn it to cheese and thin whey; but Wullie said to him,

Ye dinna need tae wait for us, Jamie, we'll be a wee filie yet,

and to Watchie's relief Watts's head bobbed at the top of its slender neck like a float on a river, and he left towards the stables.

Wullie let the loon go into Lady's stall first, and this time he approached the cow without fear, having been reassured by Elsie's cooperation in the process of milking; but a doubt began to murmur to him when Lady turned to regard him with contempt, like a pampered old aristocrat disturbed by a junior servant. Wullie rounded the beast and laughed,

Michty me, ye're affa pit oot the day, Lady,

smacked her rump cheekily; she stared about quite shocked by the presumption of it, and let an insolent moment pass before she stood herself up, subjecting herself with perfect dignity to the humiliating operation. Watchie swallowed back an annoying spike of fear lodged in his throat like a fishbone. Wullie held on to the stool,

Ye winna need yon, nae for the heecht o' ye,

he said, then placed the already half full bucket under her and stood back, nodding Watchie on; he obeyed, shyly.

The sac bulged tautly, pink and veinous, downed like a peach. The teats were as high off the ground as Watchie's head, and he reached out slowly for them. To his disgust and astonishment, they felt as warm and as tender as his own flesh, and he could barely encompass their girth in the ring of his hand. He tugged at them first of all as if they were ropes, hoping that by copying his father's actions he would somehow magically drain away the milk, but nothing happened, and he looked up at Wullie, now hoping that his failure would save him from having to try again; but no such luck, his father continued to stare at him, and he pulled again with the same result, no white piss into the bucket, and by this time Lady was growing more and more restive, faintly irritated by his cold hands, his nervous manner. He tried, again and again, tightening his fingers, loosening his fingers, and then, as suddenly as lightning, a brief spurt, an ejaculation of cream splashed into the bucket, and Watchie's smile met his father's on equal terms, a complementary sense of pride, of achievement. He remembered the exact sequence of pressures and touches, thumb and forefinger tight at the root, a slight release down the length, mimicking without knowing it the gentle mouth of a suckling calf, and soon he was able to take milk from two teats at once, causing Lady to low as her burden was drawn from her. Wullie laughed and said,

Yon's the way. I'll dee Jinty neist.

Wullie's smile was still in place when he went on to Jinty's stall, listening to the rhythm from across the wooden partition. He remembered Aal Wullie's tuition, how many clouts on the head it had taken before he had learned how to milk the herd. He coaxed Jinty to her feet, settled down on the stool, and as she filled up the empty pail he had taken for himself, he could almost see his son growing up in front of him, with shoulders broad enough to place a future upon.

Watchie couldn't even lift his full pail back to the house, but it didn't matter. He slithered in the mud behind his father, who was acting as the fulcrum to balance two full buckets, the skin of the milk trembling at the rim with each movement forward, and he went slowly, with infinite caution, in case a few drops skipped on to the ground. Once inside, it was for Jeannie to ladle the milk into enamelled flagons ready for the smaller house-to-house deliveries, while Wullie took the remainder of the buckets into the shed to fill the churns which were to be delivered to his slightly more demanding contracts, all done in time for the morning deliveries as Jamie Watts harnessed Blackie to the wagon. While Jeannie was finishing off the last of the flagons, Watchie announced proudly that the bucket she was presently emptying was full of the milk he had gathered. Wullie was reaching around his back at this time to fasten the tapes of his salesman's apron when he called over to her,

Fit d'ye think o' that, Missis L? Oor son gaed up tae Lady, had the milk oot o' her in nae time at a'.

Jeannie smiled,

Guid for yersel, my loon,

but knew only too well what admission her husband was

35

trying to prise from her; and still she knew that Watchie's hands were not those of a farmer, appreciating with all the depth of her experience the delicacy of touch needed to persuade a cow to let flow her milk, but she said nothing.

Within seconds of Aal Wullie opening the door to his room upstairs, the Laird's claws were ticking on the steps, and his yelps rang through the house, Aal Wullie having been wakened not by Peggy rolling out of the bed but by the Laird's breath on his sleeping face and the paws raking at the pillow. Now that he was liberated, he raced into the kitchen and danced around Watchie, sniffing and fussing about the boy's legs and leaping up to clutch at his jumper. Watchie laughed, then looked up at Jeannie,

Can I tak the Laird intae the yaird?

Aye, said Jeannie, but dinna lee him cam ben the hoose wi his paws a' clarted wi muck.

Aal Wullie always laid claim to Watchie's company during the fireside evenings. He held Watchie on his lap, possessing him like a toy, holding him so close that Watchie could smell his breath at once sweet and foul with the whisky he emptied down his throat while Peggy's frown carved deep and trouble-some into her brow. Jeannie had long given up her jealousy over her son, and so she sat in the corner while Aal Wullie declared Watchie his loon, clapping listlessly along to the music while Alistair and Cathie Loudon danced as nimbly as ever they did during their courting days. But what Watchie enjoyed most of all, much more than being restrained however affectionately by his grandfather, was when Jeannie lifted herself from her stool, darting over to him impulsively, girlishly almost, taking his hands and hoisting him down from Aal Wullie's lap. She always held his arms up taller than her shoulders, spun them around and around like a peerie top whipped on by the sound of the fiddle, sometimes lifting him off his feet, sometimes misstepping so that he fell into the black cloud of her linen skirt, smelling as if on a breeze how fresh it was, how pure. He trusted her completely in those moments of suspension, trusted her to restore his feet to safe ground, not to drop him or skim his knees against the floor; and never once did she fail him. But soon enough, too soon, she would say,

Awa tae yer bed, my loon, yon's fine for the day,

and he would never protest, although he might allow himself a slight downcast of the mouth as he said goodnight to them all, taking the stairs laboriously, waiting to be called back for a treat of another few minutes.

The sheets were always cold when he slipped between them in his Wee Willie Winkie nightgown, blowing out the candle alongside his bed, gathering himself together in a parcel of limbs, drawing on his own warmth until the sheets themselves became warm enough to stretch in. Wullie's fiddle etched out another tune on the air, and before he fell asleep, Watchie found himself wishing he had had a few minutes more with his mother, in the absent, mischievous embrace of suspension, in the danger of trust.

III

One night Wullie stayed awake to catch his father coming home. He stood by the front-room window with the lamp out, the room darkened and in silence, and he could hear the house moaning to itself as the timber creaked and settled around him. Through the window, Wullie saw the fat moon caught in the witch's grasp of the silver birch which grew alongside the Cornhill Road. From a distance Wullie could hear the ticking of hooves on the cobbles, the slow thunder of the wheels; and then there was Blackie defined by a frost of moonlight on his coat, laboriously dragging the cart behind him, his broad head nodding as he placed his hooves like a hopscotch dancer, one cautious step to a cobble. And there on the board, his flat cap nodding, was Aal Wullie, fast asleep and quite undisturbed by the oceanic pitch and roll of the cabin, the reins spiralled loosely about his fists, with the Laird arranged doggishly on the seat beside him.

Wullie followed the elaborate silence of the procession to the kitchen window at the back, where Blackie brought the gig to a careful halt just at the door. Wullie could see the rags of steam drawn from the pony's nostrils like handkerchiefs from a magician's pockets; and then, to his astonishment, the Laird sat upright on the board, seized the sleeve of Aal Wullie's coat in his teeth, and began to tug on it as if trying to pull a note out of a huge, ponderous bell. At first Aal Wullie rocked in his seat, paying no heed to the disturbance, but so insistent was the Laird that finally he opened his eyes and raised his head from its resting place on his chest, staring about the yard as if it were a skilfully executed painting of somewhere he knew; then, realizing that this was not a dream farm, that this indeed was home, eased himself from the gig with great care, on to the steps then on to the mud, and the Laird came round in front of Blackie to take his master to the door.

Aal Wullie brought in with him a sigh of farmyard air, sharp with the smell of dung. He ambled carelessly into the kitchen, leaving the door open behind him. Wullie stepped forward just as the old man was searching the darkness for obstacles; cleared his throat, causing Aal Wullie to start and lose his hold on his keys, which splayed out on to the floor.

Ye've been awa far ower lang at the alehoose,

he said. Aal Wullie peered through the gauze of drunkenness, opened out his hands like petals.

Wullie, he said, Wullie. Fit way're ye nae at yer bed? Ye've tae be up fine and early in the morn.

He stumbled close enough to pant sour whisky across to Wullie.

Yon's the way ye gie'd me the fairm tae rin. So's ye could gang awa and drink yersel tae the grave.

Aal Wullie bent fluidly down and clutched at the fallen keys three times before gathering them up.

Ye're takkin guid care o' the fairm, he said. Ye dinna need an aal bugger like me ony mair.

Wullie stood like a barricade against the hall door.

Ye need mair than jist ane or twa tae werk the fairm, fine ye ken that.

Aal Wullie staggered forward, stopping just short of his son.

I'll awa tae my bed the noo,

he said. The Laird padded in through the kitchen door, so suddenly and so silently that Wullie only remembered when the prow of the dog's muzzle passed the jamb that he had ever been with his father. He stood to heel beside his master, and looked up at Wullie, quite without threat, while for some reason Wullie found himself reduced by the constant doubled gaze, almost as if he had been attacked by the lour of the inquisitor, and finally he stood away from the door to the hall to let his father by.

Aye, awa tae yer bed,

said Wullie. The older man stumbled past him, still with the Laird for company, the dog's claws ticking all the way up the stairs. Wullie went to close the kitchen door, and when he looked out into the yard, there was no gig nor pony to be seen. There was a line of hoofprints placed neatly between two parallel rails in the mud, trailing to the bolted stable door. Sprinkled amongst these were the ill-defined prints of another creature Wullie couldn't properly identify, so badly smeared were they across the soil.

Wullie shook his head, and yawning like a giant, put the key to the lock.

Wullie always liked to see Watchie take an interest in the farm, and one day when the smell of the weather was right and the skies stopped louring with cloud, he asked Watchie if he'd like to come with him and help to seed the furrowed field. Watchie had seen the two big Clydesdales, Jess and Jonah, carving the earth for the past few weeks, plodding along with their harnesses chiming, shouldering the oiled and polished blade behind them, causing in Watchie the same thrill as when Elsie had drawn herself up tall in the byre; but there was Andy McGrath at the reins captaining the team over the rises and down the gentle slopes, and there was Dodie Mearns at the handlebars of the ploughshare peeling away the thick rind of the land and liberating the smell hidden underneath, and somehow seeing the power of the horses contained within yoke and harness, cooperating so readily with the hearthside musicians Watchie liked and trusted, made Watchie trust them almost by association as they loped across the field.

The smell which trailed after them was heavy and beautiful, and the whole of the farm breathed in the first opening of the earth, as rare and as rich an aroma to Wullie as any fine lady's perfume; for it was the smell of livelihood, and though he always remembered the year of his father's close brush with crop failure as a time of concern for them all, it was one of his particular satisfactions that the land had been good enough to provide him with saleable crops and enough fodder for the cattle since he had taken over the running of the farm. But all the while the family and workers saw Wullie the successful

40

dairyman, a wide swagger in his step and a high posture as he rode his sparkling gig to the kirk every Sunday, it was a humbler Wullie entirely who sat in the pew during the time of seed. Here was the man who clasped his hands together until the blood paled from the hillocks of his knuckles, and his soul abased itself before God in the cathedral of his heart, praying for the kindness of the elements.

It was to this man, to this humble farmer, that Watchie nodded when asked to help plant the seed; and trotting behind his father as he was, he could not see the breadth of the smile on Wullie's face, as another link attached itself to the chain.

At either end of the furrows, a parade of sacks, portly with grain, stood to attention. Wullie had a seed hopper slung around his neck, a huge medallion of canvas stretched around the circumference of wood, bouncing against his chest with each step. Beside the nearest of the sacks was a dented tin bucket, trodden on one day by Blackie and now useless for carrying milk. Wullie parted the lips of the first sack, picked up the bucket and dipped it into the grain, filling the vessel as if from the depths of a well, emptying it into the bowl of the hopper. The leather thong about Wullie's neck creaked and tightened with the weight, and when the sack was light enough to pick up by itself and discharge into the hopper, and when its skin was shed on to the ground, Wullie handed the bucket to Watchie and tramped the length of the furrow, filling his hand with grain from the plentiful mound before him, scything his arm from right to left, left to right, casting a generous sprinkle of seed across the parallels gouged into the earth.

Waatch fit I'm deein, William,

he said as the corn fell as evenly as any rain shower, and Watchie waded along behind him, the bucket trailing in the muck, and he stared at the expanding cloud of particles as it rose and fell above his head. At the end of the first furrow, Wullie opened the waiting sack, and allowed Watchie to fill the hopper from the bucket, which he did in small trickles, the bucket big and cumbersome in his wee hands. He even allowed Watchie to take a scoop of grain into his palms, and in a moment of playfulness Watchie hurled the grain into the air above, where it swarmed up and up, poised and held in the amber of an instant, hailing down to earth all around his ears. Wullie tsked deep in his throat and shook his head.

Na na, dinna fling it up like yon, it winna spreed gin ye dee it yon way.

So he showed Watchie the way to do it, holding the corn in a light fist, letting the momentum of his arm and the help of the breeze carry it on to the soil. With a couple of minutes' patient instruction, Watchie's first learned cast was a miniature of his father's, and Wullie walked behind his son for a little while, stooping every so often to bring the hopper within Watchie's reach.

Ye've got it noo, said Wullie, aye, ye'll mak a proper wee fairmer afore lang.

But soon Watchie was back trailing the bucket along the ground, slowed down by the careful pacing of his father. There was so much to be seen, so much to divert; birds he couldn't name planing across the sky, birds with which he was only too familiar loitering on the fences, crows hiding their heads guiltily under their cloaks of shabby silk, waiting for the attention to lapse from the fortune of corn bulging in the pockets of the field. From across the distance of the farmhouse, he could hear the Laird yapping, and after a while Watchie began to wish his grandfather's dog here, nuzzling the bucket, dancing about his legs.

The women were putting the finishing touches to the tattie boodies back at the farmhouse, stuffing spikes of straw into old coats and jackets worn threadbare by Wullie and his father. Jeannie was always grateful for the annual opportunity to clear the wardrobe of old and plainly exhausted garments, despite her husband's objection to the waste of them; faith, wumman, yon'll dee anither season yet, he would say as she held up for scrutiny a jacket which gaped at the elbows, but no no, out it went, fit only for frightening the corbies, no appeal heard on its behalf. The next Wullie would see of it, its chest would be puffed out proudly with straw, crucified on ash wood spars with an accompanying pair of his old trousers which only needed a couple of buttons repairing on the fly and a patch on the knee.

Watchie could hear the beat of the hammers across the field, knew what they meant; he had helped carry straw the year before for his mother, and when he saw the neatly folded ziggurat of worn clothes snuggled up to the range last night, he knew that today would be the day for making the boodies to help guard the young seed. Wullie had made sure that his son knew why such a task was as vital to the farm as the sharpening of the ploughshare blades, and so once the loon had learned the importance of it, he was always careful to appear tall and grown up, wise and expert in his contribution; when he brought straw by the armful across the yard to stuff the boodies, releasing it from his embrace to the ground, he made sure that each stalk lay in parallel in its bundle, and grew restless when the breeze mischievously skewed them out of pattern. Jeannie said,

It winna matter, my loon, they'll a' be jist a hotchpotch in a meenit,

as he made them stroke the right way, but,

Ye've got tae mak a proper job o't,

he replied, and went to the barn for more. Peggy turned to her daughter-in-law,

Yon's his faither talkin, proper job ye'll notice,

and Jeannie smiled, wondering if that was where it came from.

Peggy, Jeannie and Cathie Loudon had finished the six tattie boodies by the time Watchie and most of the others had returned. They lay on their backs, scattered about the yard like the victims of a massacre, and Watchie felt strangely sorry for them. Wullie approached each one in turn, staring at each of their turnip heads with eyes gouged out and zigzag mouths carved into the flesh; stood back and nodded.

My, yon's fine werk, we winna hae ony bother wi the crops this year, and Jeannie smiled, winked at Peggy,

Aye, weel we ken it's fine werk, Wullie Leckie, and mair werk than flingin corn a' the day.

Wullie took a step back as the others laughed.

Yon's nae hard werk, yon's werk for the cweans.

Cathie Loudon smiled and pointed at Wullie.

Aye, it wisna hard fan we were thinkin o' the loons files we were pittin them thegither.

She went over to one of the boodies, pointed to it.

See, I thocht o' Jamie Watts fan I cut oot the heid . . .

It was only when Cathie saw the frown slicing into Jeannie's forehead that she realized she had been talking over the lowing of cattle; and when the heavy smack resounded about the yard, she turned to find her whole self corroded by the acid in the stare of Jamie Watts as he led the straggling cattle into the portal of the byre. Even Lady, whose flank he had hit in his rage, would not so much as look round in protest at the indignity of it, but scurried into the byre to escape the concentration of hatred in the thickening air. Cathie Loudon burned with shame as she looked down at the boodie at her feet. It looked even more like Watts than before with its scooped-out eyes and its lightning strike of a mouth, but as she saw Alistair making a fist, she said,

I dinna ken a'body fa looks like yon.

For a while the silence stretched, a fibre of molten steel; then Watts moved, stiffly, towards the chaumer. At the threshold he turned and cried out,

My cwean, fine d'ye ken yersel I'm nae jist a man o' straa, and ye'll ken it frae this day forth!

crashing the door shut behind him.

Immediately the echo died, Alistair strode across the yard, his broad forearms made into vicious clubs by the seizing of his fists, Cathie pulling on his coat and no more able to stop him than if he were one of the Clydesdales gone wild with rough handling. But Wullie held himself before Alistair, said,

I'll hae a werd wi the loon.

Alistair stared beyond Wullie to the chaumer.

He widna dee yon tae me, Wullie.

Wullie put a hand on Alistair's shoulder, spoke to him quietly.

Ye'll hae tae understand, Alistair, I canna lee ye tae fecht on my property. Gin there's a'thin troublin ye, ye ken fine I'll see tae't. But gin ye lay a hand on ony ither man, ye'll be lookin for anither fairm tae fee, and I widna like tae hae tae dee yon tae yersel and Cathie.

Alistair's fury turned over like an engine, but finally he cast his head down and stood back. Wullie nodded.

Guid man. We'll hae a dram past oor supper, jist the twa o's.

Wullie walked calmly towards the chaumer, calling over his shoulder,

I'll nae be lang. Tak the boodies oot tae the field.

Everything was quiet as the company began to pick up the boodies from the ground. Alistair threw all of his strength into walking two of them as easily as if they were good companions a little the worse for too much drink. Cathie followed him with one, complaining about how she couldn't get near the chaumer kitchen for all the to-do, drawing such a look from Peggy, who was sharing the carrying of a boodie with Dodie Mearns. Watchie, too, was helping his mother, lifting the upright at the feet of the boodie and bearing it across his shoulder when they heard his father's raised voice. The window of the chaumer was open just a sliver to let the air of the spring leak into the room; and it was through that window that Wullie Leckie's fury made its charge, a hot and furious energy which passed in a tingle through Watchie's body to the ground as he heard his father's voice distorted by the power in it. Ye'll nae dee yon tae ony ither o' my labourers, nor I'll hae ye oot o' my fairm, sax months or no, and then there was a demand for an apology to Cathie Loudon at once. In a moment Wullie was out of the chaumer, closing the door behind him with great care, smiling to all around the yard; and even Alistair, his companions' arms braced about his shoulders, turned to him and nodded his thanks.

With everyone's help, the boodies were placed on guard in

the field, one at each corner and two among the furrows, and even Jamie Watts came out to swing a sledgehammer to crucify the boodies at the furthest corner, nailing the wooden spine deep into the ground. After a while he approached Cathie and spoke to her in a voice which went no further than her; and after she nodded he walked past her and went straight back to the farm, his head falling as if the effort of pleasantry had drained him entirely of sap.

This was Watchie's first sight of discord on the farm; but any confusion he may have felt upon seeing such curious tensions displayed before him was soon soothed away by his mother's hands on his shoulders as she marched him gently across the field, saying,

Ye'll hae tae gie yer hands a waash afore yer denner, Wulliam.

The scolding seemed to empty Wullie as much as the apology had his orra loon, and so during dinner and afterwards, when there was the day's paper to be read, he said hardly a thing to anyone, and scarcely noticed as first Watchie and then Peggy went up the stairs to their beds. It was the cracking of a damp twig in the grate which brought Wullie back to the room around him, to the realization that he was alone there, and that his father had not yet returned from the alehouse, and fair surprised was he that he hadn't been asleep, to let so much happen around him without him even noticing, and then suddenly he yawned like a trap, as if all the day's exhaustion had stolen the bones from him, time it was for him to be going to bed after he had taken his walk around the biggings with lantern in hand.

Once back in the farmhouse, Wullie extinguished all the lights that were still burning, the lamps left alive in the midst of the darkness, and remembered that Jeannie had taken care of the range and the fireplace before she had retired herself, working around him and asking him to draw back his legs when she had swept under the grate the black dust which remained after the peat had been consumed by flame. Wullie kept one lamp to take him up the stairs, as always at the end of the night, and crept quietly so that he might not waken his young son, who was of an age when he would be needing his sleep; and at the top of the stairs, there he saw the door to his room, a wee bit ajar and defined by a seam of pale gold against the darkness, a curious thing, for Jeannie was always saying to Wullie to breathe out the candle and turn down the wick almost as soon as they were bedded, it was the reason that Wullie preferred to do all of his reading by the fireside, since hardly a word would he have got past his eyes if he were to read at his bedtime.

Sure enough, Jeannie was awake, and lying on her side, waiting for him to come in while the candle was burning in its brass holder on the bedside cabinet. Wullie placed his lamp alongside her light, and dressed himself modestly for bed, and as Jeannie turned away from him, as he stripped himself to his underclothes, she said,

Is yon anither loon ye'll hae tae fee?

Wullie went to the straight-backed chair in the corner of the room, to where his nightgown lay like a pelt, flat and empty.

I dinna think master Waatts'll gie us ony bother, Jeannie.

He drew the gown over himself, a twin to Jeannie's it was almost, and when it lay over him like a tent, he removed those undergarments which it would not be proper for a woman to see. Jeannie spoke into the darkness, into the shadow on her side of the bed, and shook her head, though he would not see her.

Aye, weel, she said, I'm nae sae certain master Waatts is in the wrang o' it.

There was a fight inside the linen of the gown as Wullie struggled himself out of the sleeves of his semmit, which stopped when he fully heard his wife's defence of the orra loon. He half-turned, frowned,

He shid be man eneuch tae tak the werds o' a slip o' a cwean, Jeannie, wid ye nae think?

Jeannie thought how little her husband saw with his days away doing his deliveries, and it was a thought which caused her some guilt on her own account.

Gin there's nae reason tae be hurt by her werds, na, ye're richt eneuch. But gin ye're a loon nae lang frae yer schoolin, and there's a cwean ye've a fancy for fa'll be lauchin wi ye the ane meenit and lauchin at ye the neist . . .

Wullie resumed his fight with the semmit, the sooner that he might turn to see his wife.

Cathie Loudon? D'ye ken fit ye're sayin o' her, Jeannie?

I ken fit I'm nae sayin, Wullie; I'm nae sayin Cathie nor Jamie're cairryin onythin on afore Alistair. Fit I'm sayin's that yon loon's a fancy for her, and she's nae ternin him awa frae it.

The semmit came away at last, after Wullie had pulled the gown over his head, so that he appeared for all the world like the very picture of the revenant whose life had ended under the axe; and now there were only his long johns to be peeled away, a much easier task altogether, though still there was a dance to be performed as one leg at a time was withdrawn.

Then I wisna jist richt mysel, said Wullie, though I wisna tae ken.

Jeannie heard her husband's feet as he padded against the bare boards, and she often wondered what this balancing dance of his was like, though she would never have dreamed of turning to look at him.

Na na, ye werena tae ken; but it wisna richt o' master Waatts tae be hurlin thon kin' o' curse at a cwean, for a' that.

Wullie was soon enough ready for bed, and as his last act before lifting the woollen covers, he blew a breath on the candle to extinguish it, then turned the dial on the oil-lamp, which drew the wick into its collar, causing the flame to shrink to a gilded ring before it was gone, and there was a close darkness which was almost a blanket in itself. He settled in beside his wife, and closed his eyes so that he might fall into the darkness within, the night's sleep that would prepare him for another early day of milking and deliveries; but hardly was he folded in the edges of his slumber than he heard Jeannie again, turned away with her back like a wall against him, and she said,

Hae ye luiked into thon loon's e'en, Wullie? Thon's nae a loon fa's had an easy time o' it,

and Wullie, too tired to even bother to ask whether she was meaning Watchie or Jamie Watts still, gave a reply without a word, and nested himself deeper into the warmth of the sheets.

48

IV

From the youngest age he could remember, Jamie's only toy was the Bible. He remembered that there was always a man who used to take the compact black book out of his hands, admonishing him gently, telling him to take it out of his mouth when all he was trying to do was to ascertain its flavour. This he remembered happened for a while, the kindly man with his wide smile and his rough hands; and then he was no longer there, Jamie could never remember when he went away, and as he came to understand the workings of the farm, he decided that the man had simply come to the end of his six-month contract. But Jamie came to notice a gradual change in his mother, she took to sitting long hours in her straight and uncomfortable chair in front of the fire, her Bible closed in her lap, her eyes steadily on the peat tablets glowing violently in the fireplace, launching herself from her seat from time to time to shoo him outside and into the yard, just as if he had been one of the farm animals straying into the house, and as she raised her hands in threat of fetching him a terrifying blow to the head, he noticed in the last split instant before he broke and ran the tears shining on the rims of her eyes; and he wanted so much to know the cause of them, what it was that was grieving her.

Jamie's mother never seemed to accept his touch after he started to walk, of the opinion that her touch was scant preparation for a world she knew to be as naked as granite, as barren as the soil she refused to leaven with Satan's own lime. It was the greatest sacrifice she could have made, the one which demanded the most of her, because sometimes she felt the blood tingling at the ends of her fingers when he came back from school with his jacket ragged on his shoulders, his wee face grained with blood he had wiped thin across it; but by this time he had learned not to complain, he simply waited for her to tell him to clean himself up before dinner, and then later she would take bobbin and needle and mend the seams torn by the malice of his classmates, telling him aye, ye'll see yer ain o' them a', Jamie, God'll ken fine fit's jist for them, her pulse racing like hoofbeats, her head lowered over her sewing in denial.

Jamie Watts's mother was the kind of person, fairly common within her church, whose entire life was spent in the observation of evil in others, and long and meticulous practice had rendered those powers of observation to a scalpel-sharp edge. She was a rigorous surgeon of the spirit, listening carefully to the reported kindnesses of her fellow villagers before paring each one down to the bone and lights for you, and her methods were invariably radical, and quite ruthless. Present to her an example of uncalled for humanity, or a gleam of charity which might please the simple and untutored soul, and she would lay it bare in front of you so that you could see the cancerous tissue of hidden greed and selfishness, the scars and deformities of a corrupted spirit, the sweet reek of gangrenous self-deception. Especially scorned by her was the kindness of papists, being in her opinion no more than the prudence of the miser, setting aside a hoard of earthly capital with which to bribe the gatekeepers of heaven, each joyless good deed one more coin in the mattress, one more saving secreted under the floorboards. There were few Catholics in her village, but she knew each of them by name, and never replied to the smiles of forgiveness they passed on to her in the street, regarding their false concern for her welfare as the rictus of the truly damned. Only slightly more warmly than Catholics did she regard Episcopalians; for still they insisted upon heavenly reward for that most hated of falsehoods, the good work, and there was still too much of the tawdry theatre of the Church of Rome in their services for her liking. Above the Episcopalian, she next placed the Church of Scotland, honouring it as the root from which her faith had branched, while still despising it for its final traitorous acceptance of charity in the heart of God, an acceptance which had prised away from the body of the kirk all those of her own persuasion, transplanted in acid soil to flourish as best as they were able. In truth she despised them all, as her father and grandfather before her had done, carrying around with her such a burden of spite that there was no room in her panniers for compassion. In this way she kept entirely true to herself, without the need to scrutinize her motives, and in the teaching of the Bible lay her own best guide as to what it was her God expected of her, the terror of his judgements, the breadth of his fury.

Jamie found his secret places about the farm where he could sit and cry; for his mother admired strength in a man, and would not tolerate tears in front of her, sending him away from the warmth of the fire to do his crying, even in the thickest snows of winter, when Jamie imagined that the tears would curdle into beads of ice with the cold. He cried in the stables, where he learned to coil up close to the heat of the horses as they relaxed in their nest of straw at the end of their hard working day, so that even in winter he was assured of the comfort of warmth, breathing as closely as he could manage to their rhythm, and sometimes they even turned around and nuzzled him as if he were a foal, licking with their rough tongues the salt from his tears and whinnying gently to him.

To the horses he said,

Fit way am I nae guid?

but their ears only fluttered as if at the sound of a creak at the stable door.

Another of his secret places was the chicken coop, which he squirmed into through the hen-sized portal, arms first, drawing the length of his body into the fetid shade, causing no panic among the hens which were by now quite used to his intrusions. He squatted down among the nesting boxes as they paraded around him, wholly unconcerned with the reasons for his tears, and to the hens he said,

Fa'll be a freend tae me?

but they were too busy caring for their empty, infertile eggs, and passed him by like shoppers in a main street.

He went into the dark and cavernous grain store, where the

field mice scissored through the sacks of grain with their sharp teeth and sampled the barley which spilled through the holes, and to them he said,

Fit way'll they nae lee me be?

but, industrious little plunderers that they were, they simply got on with their business, filling their bellies from the sacks which his mother and the workers had laid down to rest.

So Jamie returned to the farm from his secret places, to his mother reading the psalms by the fireside, having spent his misery on those without the power to help him, and if she ever noticed the fierce redness about his eyes after his return, then she said nothing of it.

The first time that Jamie Watts discovered that he had no tears left, he was in the grain store. He had felt the sour lump of misery gathering in his throat, he was in the room by the fireside with his mother, and he knew exactly what he should do; without a word to her he stood up from his seat and left the house. Once in the grain store, sitting on the cold earth, he made the attempt to cry, and his face arranged itself into the appropriate mask of sadness in readiness for the tears to fall, but nothing happened. He tried again, for the misery was still there, he could feel it as a fist-sized ball lodged like a rock in the vaults of his throat, but still nothing came, and after a while, puzzled at this curious drying up of the source, he took to watching the field mice hurrying through the avenue of sacks, feasting on the trickle of grain they had liberated.

He watched as the tiniest of the mice scuttled closer to him by inches, and recognized it from his previous visits. It used to take the wide path around him, afraid of his monumental height, but by this time, perhaps lulled by the memory of his weeping, it had grown used to him, and indeed now ran through the archway of his huddled legs as a short cut to the grain it wanted. Jamie reached out and took a scattering of grain into the palm of his hand, held it open on the ground, and waited with the patience of a fisherman until the baby sniffed and shuffled up to the bait. Jamie's hand tickled as the mouse mounted it without fear, the whiskers vibrating like antennae; then, holding one of the grains in its forepaws, the mouse began to nibble on it hungrily, the grain as big as a loaf in the wee creature's grasp. Suddenly, without warning, Jamie closed his other hand over the mouse like a trap, shutting the palms so that the blunt head protruded from the well of his thumbs as if caught in a cangue. Lithely it hauled its shoulders out of the well, but Jamie snapped his hands together more tightly still, and it pushed and pulled against him, staring up into the giant face as if for mercy, in absolute terror of its life, and in its struggle for freedom, Jamie could smell its rejection of him, and its rejection made him furious. It was the first time in his life that he had ever held anything so helplessly in his hands; and slowly, with a detached enjoyment and the will to experiment, he crushed the life out of the mouse bairn, compacting it in his palms until he could feel the bones crack softly like the spine of a leaf, until the heart burst out of its mouth like a secret bribe of a ruby coughed up to the torturer in the victim's gravest hour of need. When he opened his palms, there was still a pulse drumming in the mouse's belly, its legs fluttered; it had evacuated itself, leaving ellipses on Jamie's palm. He raised it up to the level of his eyes and gazed at it, a suckling pig readied for the table of his hand, chewing on the glossy apple of its own heart. Bright blood cooled on his fingers, and he thought of the blood of Christ, and he tried hard to feel sorrow for the death of the mouse; but the flurry of mice as he cast the corpse on to the ground, and the fear that his display of power had engendered, filled him with more pleasure than any penitence or grief would have done, and how like God on the day of judgement he felt, casting aside those he had given to damnation before bringing life and fruit to the world. It warmed him on his way back to the house like a good hot meal to think of the other mice afraid of him, scurrying for their lives about the sacks.

What Jamie missed most about not being able to cry was the way that the tears seemed to calm down the fire crackling inside him, the clamouring heat of vengeance which followed the attacks of Alex Wallace and his yapping pack of schoolyard dogs. He even had a favourite place on the road home after the ambushes, under a dry stane dyke, where usually he would do all the crying he needed to before returning home to his mother. On this particular barren occasion, however, as he poked a finger into the lips of a burst seam which gawped the length of his jacket, there was nothing to prevent his fury from catching flame, clambering higher and further out of Jamie's control, until the heat demanded that Jamie find some way of putting it out, or, and here was an idea he found interesting and most pleasing, that he should continue to add fuel to it, that he should keep it hot and sinuously alive inside him; and so on the way home he nurtured his hatred of Wallace, he stroked and petted it like a cat until it lashed out at him with claws bared, memories of Alex Wallace's grinning moon face over his own, the strike and flail of many fists, spurs to draw angry blood from Jamie, giving the speed to his feet and a set to the face which really belonged on a much older, much more embittered person altogether. By the time he reached the farm, he had forged in the heat of his passionate anger a cold weapon with which to revenge himself against Wallace, and when he went to sleep in the pallet bed near the fire that night, it was with such a smile of incongruous innocence and peace that his mother imagined the intervention of her God, some revelation of his cool and empty essence in the brightness of a dream, and so passed her hand unnoticed across his sleeping brow.

The next day was the time for the weapon to be unsheathed; and Jamie approached Mr Hamilton with all the humility and deference due to one's elders. Jamie's face as he looked into the eyes atop the black robe was earnest and as sincere as he could compose it, and as the master listened to the loon, blood darkened his face, his lips tautened as if fastened back by pins; and by the time Jamie had finished his story, his voice echoing in the empty playtime classroom, Mr Hamilton was almost grinning with rage, his lips having ripened and split like a rind. He thanked Jamie for the information, dismissing him to the quadrangle. Jamie passed through the corridors of the school quietly, hearing behind him the sibilant release of pressure from Hamilton, and allowed himself a gentle smile.

Hamilton was waiting for the children as they arrived back in the classroom after lunch. He was seated behind his tall lectern desk, perched on top of a tall stool, his robes folded about him like wings, a black eagle perched in its eyrie, eyeing each child as he or she returned to the afternoon seat as if selecting his prey. The children waited, standing by their desks; with a silent signal, the slow drop of a level hand, Hamilton conjured them on to their seats, and once they were seated, Hamilton stood, pushing himself away from the lectern, strolling casually among the aisles, probing the desiccated floorboards in front of him with his ashen pointer like a laird with a silver-nubbed walking-stick. His eyes had claimed Alex Wallace long before he reached the boy's desk at the back of the room, and it came as no surprise to Wallace, nor to the rest of the class, when Hamilton stopped beside the offender, and brought his pointer down on the desk with such a concussion as you might have imagined would have sent farmers two miles away hurriedly driving their cows indoors with the first peal. Wallace jumped suddenly at the shock, but held his poise staring as evenly as he could at the dominie. Jamie could almost feel Wallace's heart beating in the palm of his hand, expanding and collapsing against the walls of his fist to the fleet and irregular rhythm of hoofbeats. Hamilton said,

Did I hear correct, bonnie laddie, when I heard tell from a pupil in this class that ye were publicly making fun o' the monarch o' this land?

Wallace stared along the barrel of the pointer, to the impatient fist holding it, tightening in seizures which made prominent veins on the back of his hand writhe like worms. He said,

Aye, sir, I did,

because it was true, he had once in plain hearing of many others slurred her majesty, the foul-weather aspect she wore in most of the portraits he had seen which many took for determination and resolution but which he had slandered as ugliness. Hamilton nodded, and Wallace prepared to be called before the whole class to receive a stroke of the belt for his impudence; but when Hamilton continued,

And did I also hear correctly, laddie, that ye were heard to compare the face o' the queen tae a part o' my anatomy I canna bring myself tae repeat in a classroom?

the boy began to drink down as much air as he could swallow, denying this last accusation of course, for he had said no such thing. Wallace's confusion was the sweetest feast that Jamie Watts had ever sat down to, and when the master brought down the rod on the desk again and raged,

I canna stand a liar, Alexander Wallace, nor one wha isna man enough to tell the truth efter he's been found oot,

Watts could hardly stop himself from purring like a cat, tossing its prey in the air for the enjoyment of it. Still Wallace protested even as he struggled under the claws of the lie, but Hamilton lashed the desk once again with his pointer and said,

I'll no hear your lies ony more, laddie. For the last time, did you or did you not say that Queen Victoria had a face like my hind end?

Wallace had no protest left in him when he heard the full allegation. He looked to Jamie, noting the slender and almost imperceptible bowing of his enemy's lips, knew then who had based a towering, scintillating lie upon a tablet of truth; said nothing as Hamilton led him before the lectern desk. Hamilton went behind the desk for a moment and lifted its lid, producing from its cabinet a long coil of leather which he let unfurl so that the end which was split into three tongues was released. With the ash pointer, the sceptre of his absolute rule, in one hand, and the sinuous lochgelly, his sword of justice, in the other, Hamilton commanded Wallace to raise his hands, shepherding and guiding each hand with the pointer until they were placed in the air to his satisfaction, one hand under the other and supporting it, in the same way as one receives communion. On one hand Hamilton served Wallace six strokes of the lochgelly, thrashing the boy with all his might until the hands before him were one moment as dull as meat, the next alive and bright as a torch. As determined as he was not to allow Jamie to see him cry, when Hamilton ordered him to change hands, Wallace could hold on no longer; and then and only then was the fire in Jamie Watts extinguished, by the tears of another, by a complete reduction and humiliation of his oppressor, and it was a feeling of surmounting power, better than friendship, this way that he felt now, how much more satisfying it was to dominate than to befriend, and he wondered when he would next be able to use his new ability.

In the quadrangle after school, Wallace stopped his dogs from surging on Jamie, and never any word was spoken to him again by any of the children. Now he was bothered by no one, the children walked widely around him as if he were a simply patterned snake curdled with venom; and his mother, having no more sewing to do, assumed that her God in his wisdom had sorted everything out for the better, as always happened when he was given the chance.

Jamie couldn't even find the tears to mourn for his mother when the consumption scraped her hollow and left her wearing the barest shell of pupation, the lean and excavated shape of her humanity, but the Bible was her only bequest of any moment to her son, and he spent the time waiting for her to die in reading it for any inspiration it might have to offer, so much transported by it that he scarcely noticed when she made her final journey to dust with no more than a faint culminating breath. When he turned the sheet over her, he realized that it was as much to spare himself the sight of her final anomalous well-being, the malady's last flattering of the flesh, as to accord her the respect due to his own mother, and it was with all the dispatch he could manage that he took the tin caddy she had pointed out to him from its shelf, and harnessed one of the horses to the cart with the help of Archie Tulloch, so that he might make the arrangements with the village undertaker according to her precise written instructions, also to be found in the caddy. Archie Tulloch was there at the side of the grave to help lower her into as little of a wound in the earth as her meagre saving would buy, in a plain box without ornament, tucked away with little more ceremony than a jewel casket in a cupboard, and her passage marked by a flat headstone with only her name and her parenthesized dates to tell her story. Tulloch had seen the strange unconcern of his employer's son, and he grieved to see the soil close over her head, a more proud and determined woman he had never met, prepared to captain the plough herself after the ghostly disappearance of her husband, paying out good Christian wages for a fair day's work, and for himself and for Jamie both, Archie Tulloch wept all the tears that were going to be wept on the day of her settling in the ground. The two men would have found the carrying of the coffin hard going were it not for the third pall bearer, there to pay his own respects, and his was a presence which set all the tongues in the village to clattering; the laird who owned the farm over which Andra Watts had been the grieve, Mr Macallan by name, whose presence was a tribute to the woman who was able to persuade hard ground to bear for her the best yield for the farm's small acreage of any of the lands he owned, and although he knew of her reputation through the village for severity and sourness, by her work he judged her, and found that she was deserving of anyone's respects, and especially now at the end of her life. This also left Macallan with the problem, that his lands were at the moment wanting for a tenant, and using the sleek lawyer's skills of persuasion, a skill he had scarcely required for his living since the lands had started to declare for him a profit, he spoke with Jamie on the subject of what was to become of the farm; but Jamie shook his head, and there, Macallan saw, was the absolute determination which was the only thing of substance passed on to him by his mother, aside from the palm-sized Bible;

Na na, Mr Macallan, he said, I've a mind tae gang awa frae the toun, I'd sooner be a sojer than hae tae rin a fairm.

Macallan raised his eyebrows, and looked up and down at the scant figure, clothed in the last sabbath suit laundered by his mother; but he shook Jamie warmly by the hand, and said generously,

Well, I can't say I'm not sorry, James, but if the Gordon

Highlanders'll have you, then allow me to wish you the very best of luck.

The next time he met Archie Tulloch was at the feeing fair, as Tulloch was looking for labourers to take on the vacancy left by the bold adventurer after Tulloch himself had taken on the lease. Jamie was wearing on his lapel the sprig of sprung corn, fixed there by a long pin, indicating to the mill of potential employers that here was an able body waiting to be used; but on seeing Archie across the fairground, suddenly the loon's hand dashed to his lapel, and then as if by a music-hall magician's sleight of hand, there was no sprig, so swiftly done that Archie would never be sure if he had seen the sprig there or not. They conversed for a while, but throughout Archie gleaned the impression that Jamie would sooner be away from him, as the boy told him of how he had attempted to join the Gordon Highlanders, and how he had declined when he could find there no man to match himself. Then he told Archie that he had recently discovered news of his father's heroic death, fighting for the empire in India, and this Archie knew to be untrue, for Andra Watts had died the death of a sot, drowned in the liquor of a ditch with a bottle of whisky seized in his arm, the breath frozen on open and cold lips. At first Archie decided that it would be better to err on the side of charity, perhaps the loon had learned news of the wrong man; but soon untruth compounded upon untruth, rooted in base mud that stank to heaven of their lies, and it was at that moment, when Jamie began to place slanders upon the likes of Jackie Aitken, damning for an idler the man known across the county for raising by his own hand all the outhouses on his land, that Archie Tulloch made his decision to withdraw the offer of work he had been about to make to his fondly remembered employer's son. There they parted, and Archie never saw hide nor hair of young Jamie Watts again in his long career as a grain farmer; but messages reached him across distances, rumours of a young man who never managed to see out a six-month on any of the farms he worked upon, priding himself upon his reputation for plain and honest speaking, calling the crops of barley on the farms where he worked the devil's own grain and disdaining those who lived off its harvest. Once he was given his rightful wages for the time of his employment, he always left with a word to the grieve about the manners of the workmates he was leaving behind, and especially their coarse and unjustified slanders on the good name of the grieve himself. It was easy to tell the trail left behind by this particular young man, when good working and drinking relationships became long and combative silences, and the air he left behind him would turn the milk in its pail.

Archie Tulloch heard the news at each fair, and praised God with each passing Sunday for making him hold his tongue when he did.

V

There were many clues by which Mrs Kerr could tell that the widow Jamieson had come to call at the manse. The first was the tick and clatter of polished boots on the cobbles outside, although by itself this could as easily mean the passage of Constable MacIver. The second clue was the peculiar vehemence with which the doorbell leapt and sang on its mainspring, its cable tugged mercilessly at the other end, crying plaintively for a release from rough handling. The third and most telling clue was the mosaic which formed in the stippled glass panel of the front door, a living expression of all the shades in the spectrum of black, from a diffuse grey at the frontiers of the image to a nucleus of the profoundest darkness. On this particular Sunday, all three clues were present; and so Mrs Kerr took in a breath, prepared her best housekeeper's smile while asking the Lord's forgiveness for her duplicity, after all their visitor was one of the most respected and God-fearing members of the community, and went to answer the door.

It was as well that Mrs Kerr was a charitable soul, and gave her smiles away as generously as the merchant gives alms to the pauper, with no expectation of repayment except perhaps in heaven; for the widow's deep frown was the most appropriate costume jewellery for the sober black outfit she wore. Her black hair was gripped tightly to her scalp, leaving the captured fibres no means of expressing their spontaneity before the breeze. She looked beyond Mrs Kerr, along the vestibule, then regarded the housekeeper as if she were made of glass.

May I speak tae the Reverend, if ye please?

Mrs Kerr pinned up her smile at the edges.

He's oot back tendin tae his bees. Wid ye like me tae taal him ye're here?

The widow stepped over the threshold.

Na na, I'll see him mysel,

and left Mrs Kerr tasting the wind from her as she went by, striding through the vestibule like a scissors through cloth. Mrs Kerr made no effort to catch the widow up, simply smoothed down the creases in her floral print dowdy and took in a long and patient breath, almost as if she were a mother to the woman, ashamed of the widow's manners. It was while she stood there, readying herself to go to the kitchen to warm up some water for the pot of tea she would no doubt be required to make, that Mrs Kerr saw the loon in his flat cap walking at a slow pace on the other side of the road, a thing which would have claimed none of her attention had it not been for the way his head dropped so that the round of the cap was protecting his face from her proper view, and so making certain that she could not have failed to notice him. It was his height that fixed her curiosity on the young man, after all there were few in the village of such a stature as himself, a creature of stilts and besom handles he was, if there was anyone in the congregation that he minded her of then she would have known him instantly, and then she thought of the orra loon whom Wullie Leckie had fee'd at his dairy farm. She knew him to be of the kirk, uncommonly tall and not much for speaking with anyone, there was who it might be, and Mrs Kerr found that she was about to cry out to the loon in fellowship when suddenly she realized that she had no recall of his name, as if she had it written on a rag of paper only to see it blown from her reach, held devilishly before her until she made a grasp at it, when away it went again. How such forgetfulness might have fretted at her for the rest of the day had there not been her duties to attend to; but she heard the voice of the widow calling through the house, Reverend, far aboots're ye bidin? and so Mrs Kerr closed over the front door, hoping that she had not been seen herself, that it might have been anyone she would never meet on the next Sabbath.

The Revd Walter Goodbody, having just removed the roof from the Cowie hive, was busy taming his bees with a lullaby of smoke from a bellows. He was wearing a thick coat of closely woven canvas, gathered at the waist and fastened with a rope tied in a loose granny knot, and on his head he wore a wide-brimmed apiarist's hat, his face veiled like a bride's behind a curtain of muslin. He plodded through the combs like a clerk in a filing cabinet, lifting out a file of honey every so often to examine the cells, to see that there were not too many of them committed to the wasteful rearing of drones, which would then drink too much of the precious liquor meant for human consumption; sometimes having to disturb a gathering of bees with vapour from his bellows before wiping them away and back into the hive. After a moment of scrutiny, he lodged one of the leather gauntlets under his arm, and violated the membrane of wax with his naked finger, licking away the honey which swaddled it. Once he was satisfied of the purity and sweetness of his plunder, looted in turn by the bees from the scarlet roses on the border of the garden, he replaced the triangular roof of the hive, so that once again it resembled a miniature temple of Athenian design, and offered a silent prayer to his God for what he had seen fit to provide, a prayer of gratitude also for the creation of bees which, through their industry, gave to man their great gift of honey; while inside the hive, the bees hummed drunkenly as they recovered their senses, and set to work repairing the breach in the comb, remembering nothing of the intrusive hand from the sky which had just exercised its landlord's·right to disrupt their tenancy.

The Reverend was putting the lid back on the hive just as the widow Jamieson entered the garden; immediately he held his hand up, palm towards her.

Good day to you, Mrs Jamieson. Please come no closer. I'm sure you understand.

The widow frowned slightly.

Ye're nae at yer werk the day, Reverend?

Goodbody smiled under the gauze.

I'm sorry to say, Mrs Jamieson, that my bees have no appreciation of the meaning of the Sabbath. But work is also a means of prayer, is it not? And am I not also their minister?

The widow nodded slowly. As always, she found the workings of the mind of God inexpressibly profound; and how wise this well-spoken young minister was to understand so readily. Suddenly she was as shy as a schoolgirl before him, a posture she was loath to adopt before any man unless he was deserving of her complete and accordant respect; she cleared her throat.

Can I speak tae ye for a meenit or twa, Reverend? It's a serious matter.

Goodbody nodded, causing his veil to ripple.

Of course, Mrs Jamieson. In view of your good work for the kirk, it'd be highly rude of me to refuse. Please wait for me indoors. I won't be long.

A silver teapot and two fluted china cups in their saucers were ready in the drawing-room; and the moment the Reverend came in through the door, stripped of his almost monastic garments, she had the pot in her hand, pouring a stream of tea the colour of polished mahogany through a strainer she had placed astraddle the mouth of a cup. Having given the Reverend the first pouring, she poured a cup for herself, and settled into a flabby leather armchair which was angled towards the smoking peat fire. Once the Reverend had settled himself into the chair opposite, waiting until the widow was comfortable before he did so, he helped himself to an iced fancy on the second storey of the china cake stand and nibbled a scallop from the corner.

Now then, Mrs Jamieson, this is a matter of some importance, I gather?

The widow leaned over the peaks of her knees, and lowered her voice.

I'm feart tae tell ye ower muckle aboot't.

The Reverend crossed his legs and sat back in his seat.

You can surely tell me, Mrs Jamieson.

The widow was swelling as if to burst with her intelligence, and suddenly the very seams of her split with it,

Did ye ken ony o' the villagers kept goats, Reverend?

I did not, Mrs Jamieson. Whyever would one wish to do that?

The widow leaned even further forward, capturing the Reverend's eyes in the snare of her gaze.

Tae pit tae the knife fan the muin turns fu'.

Now she sat back in her chair, to let the words diffuse in the air like a sparkling of frost. The Reverend frowned.

Killing goats by the full moon? From whom did you hear this, Mrs Jamieson?

Frae a parishioner, ye'll understand gin I nae mention fa said.

Of course, of course. This is all very serious.

The widow sipped down some tea.

But fit can we dee? He's nae frae oor congregation.

I would expect not, Mrs Jamieson. The Lord preserve us all.

The sky outside had suddenly grown darker, piled softly with ashen cloud. The Reverend stood up, went over to the bay window to gaze upon its sour and ominous aspect.

First you must tell me who this person is, before we decide on the appropriate course of action.

And so, after another cup of tea, the widow Jamieson left the manse at a full stride as the Revd Goodbody's agent. She was aware of the mockery in the eyes of the villagers as she passed them by, how they muttered to see her in the streets during the Sabbath; but her sense of mission glowed like a coal inside her, propelling her on and around all the houses she knew to be inhabited by God-fearing folk. Like a carrier of some dread infection she went, and soon all of the villagers who worshipped at the Presbyterian kirk had been touched by her virus, so that by the time night fell on that particular Sabbath some two hundred souls were being eaten away, corrupted beyond reason by the picture of a goat tethered on a solitary buttock of grassy hill, killed under a moon of the deepest scarlet by the single stroke of a knife sharpened to a whisper and held up high for the approval of a boiling cauldron of unseen, potent forces.

While Jeannie was preparing the flagons on the Monday morning, Wullie attached Blackie to the outstretched arms of the milk cart, patting his flanks affectionately to encourage him out into the grey sunless day spanning ahead.

On this Monday, there was a veil of drifting rain which moved with the wind, swelling through the open cabin and studding Wullie's overcoat with tiny pearls of moisture. Poor Blackie, exposed to the worst of it, glittered as if rolled in powdered sugar, flicking his ears as they filled up like pitchers with the water. Wullie sent a message through the reins, and Blackie picked up his hooves willingly, trotting at speed over the cobbles and grateful that he could at least warm himself with the exercise. Drawing comfort wherever he could, Wullie decided that it would at any rate be good for the grain, and pulled the wings of his collar about his neck.

The first sign of something awry came when he walked to the door of Mrs McAllister, his clothes sodden through and moulding their chill to his body. Today of all days he was looking forward to her invitation into the house, to a cup of her milky tea and a heat in front of the fire. It was a service she discharged with an almost biblical sense of duty, offering him an effusive plenty of complaints about the state of her rheumatics in the damp. Wullie began to understand after a while that accepting her tea and bathing himself in the warmth of her fire had bound him as if by contract to listening; and indeed when he tried on a number of occasions to share with her news of his crops and the health of his cows, all he received in reply was a comprehensive damage report, how she was suffering with her poor inflamed joints, how her knees had swollen like fruit ripening, showing him her trembling hands which looked like a cluster of walnuts. Wullie didn't mind too much that she never seemed to pay him any heed except as a presence, for he always respected his elders; and there was one time of year when Mrs McAllister's great age and experience would come into its own. She was always ready to tell him about the slackening of pressure on her aching knees and then she would add, Ye'll be sowin yer grain jist the noo? The first time it happened, Wullie found himself saying aye, and was away down the road before he realized that he had not told her about it; so on his next visit, he made a point of asking her how she had known, and she replied, Faith, man, ye'll hae the rheumatics yersel afore lang, ye'll ken fine fit time tae pit oot the grain then. From the next year on, Wullie made sure to ask Mrs McAllister's advice on the proper time to sow the seed corn; and while the easing of her pain was not the most definitive of signs Wullie trusted while making his decision, he realized that she was never far wrong in reading her almanac of discomforts, and often was exact enough to be the last of the signs Wullie trusted to help him come to a decision. In gratitude Wullie often poured a wee gift of an extra half pint or so into her enamel jug, and those were the only times he ever saw her smile, a weak diluted thing like the whey of happiness, and it was said about the village that Wullie was the only person she smiled at since her husband died and left her with the hardware store to sell.

Wullie always made sure that he did not crack the brass loop on the door too loudly or insistently whenever he called; for while her legs were strong enough to take her every Sunday to the Presbyterian kirk at a slow and tortured plod, she carried the weight of her devotion with the steadiness of a pack mule, and Wullie saw no reason to cause her to hurry to the door just for the sake of a wee splash of milk.

The door opened with a grind of the tongue in the latch. A slice of Mrs McAllister appeared in the slender parting between door and frame. Wullie said,

Fine day tae ye, Mrs McAllister, wid ye be for ony milk the day?

Wullie could never decide from that day until the day he died which of the two things which happened after the question gave him the most profound shock; the abrupt slamming of the door in his face, or the cry which followed it,

I widna tak ony o' yer milk, rotten cratur that y'are!

Wullie found himself at the centre of a sudden fine swirl of rain, driven towards him by the slamming of the door. He tried again, raised the brass loop again and let it fall,

Are ye a' richt, Mrs McAllister? is there onythin a–dee wi ye?

but the door remained locked for him, and while he was stepping over the lakes which had formed in the cobbles of North Street to return to his wagon, he saw the image of Mrs McAllister haunting the glaucous window, crooking the net curtain and staring at him as if he had been sent abroad from the realms below to do her terrible ill.

By the time he drove Blackie home, just after one o'clock, Wullie was confused and hurt by the way children had been guarded by parents who fired their outrage at him before shepherding their charges inside and slamming the door behind them. He was as bleak and as sour as the sky above him; and this passed through the reins he held loosely in his hands, so that Blackie, given no cause for urgency, dragged his hooves along the cobbles as if he too was lost in thought. Perhaps he had been the victim of a rival dairy farmer looking to expand his business. Perhaps something like an insect or a grain of filth from the yard had contaminated his milk; it would only take one dissatisfied customer to spread a bad reputation throughout the whole village. But the more he thought about it, the more he realized that there were no reasons for vehemence such as he had encountered that morning.

No explanation satisfied Wullie, no matter how much he stared at the facets of the problem. He worked listlessly all through the afternoon, and not even the explosions from Aal Wullie's shotgun as the old man fired above the heads of those crows which had fathomed the secret of the tattie boodies' paralysis were enough to raise his head. And in the evening, when he sat down to dinner, even Watchie noticed the uncommon slump to the shoulders, the muted thanks he offered up to God at the start of the meal, the solemnity of his expression as he stared down at his plate, as if he would never be able to take pleasure from anything ever again.

VI

Wullie still had no answer to the problem of his evaporating custom after a fortnight; and in that time, a darkness and a bitterness entered his demeanour such as concerned all who lived with him at Smallbrae. He was slow to rise in the mornings, understandable during the brittle winters, but strange for the daybreaks of the spring as the sun cast its illusion of warmth about the glens. He ate his breakfast porridge in silence, conducting the spoon to his mouth slowly as if running on rails of memory laid down over many years, and it was this which first worried Peggy, who remembered even as a child the enormous gusto with which her son dug out porridge by the shovelful, drawing out of his mouth a spoon struck to the silver, picked as cleanly as a bone. His eyes became red and inflated, and this worried Jeannie, who in sleeping beside him was often wakened by his shifting beside her, and this made her irritable in the mornings, serving breakfast to all with an ill grace quite unlike her usual rested manner. He was listless in his work, and this concerned the workers in the chaumer, used to the confident stride of Wullie the farmer, now seeing an empty sack of a creature, performing its tasks with no joy or commitment to any of them; further, no longer were there the fireside evenings to sweeten the end of the working day, and this concerned them even more, for the fireside evenings were their greatest satisfaction, when everyone had built up the ache deep in their muscles, enough to feel that the time spent in the practice of their musical talents was no indulgence. Now the chaumer was the place for Dodie and Andy to weave their songs, but there was no dancing from Alistair or Cathie under the severe and disapproving stare of Jamie Watts with his Bible open at the psalms; and the music they played was slow and almost digni-fied, a dirge to the slow passage of the hours without whisky or laughter. Even Watchie understood that there was something the matter, though he was never told as much; he breathed the new stale atmosphere of the yard, which caused the cows to piss their milk sour into the buckets and the crows to cloud about the fields with malign intent, waiting to nip the sprung corn from the bud, and his young spirit was drawn down by the new gravity of the air, the sudden and inexplicable silences, knowing that their centre was his father, without knowing why.

The only person on the farm who seemed to derive new strength from this blackening of the name of Wullie Leckie about the village of Aberlevin was Jamie Watts, for as Wullie's step became more timid and hesitant, a new jaunt came into Watts's long lope across the yard; and as Wullie's expression was drawn down by gravity, Watts began to develop a new feature, a small and secret smile like a crease in the leather of a bicycle saddle, which was what his face resembled in shape. He grew as a giant even as Wullie was diminished by every trip to the village; and he even grew confident enough to take Watchie under his command, under the full gaze of the farm, to perform the tasks which were considered the right and proper apprenticeship of the orra loon. Watchie grew to hate his days of folk-tale slavery, mucking out the byre under Watts's highly critical eye; Watts demanded that the floor be as clean as a living-room, that Watchie fill the buckets with cakes of stagnant dung, pivoting the shovel in his wee hands as if it were a rafter beam, brushing up every scrap of straw with a brush twice as tall as himself. Standing over his employer's son, staring upon the poor wee loon as he laboured over tasks made herculean by his stature, Watts saw Wullie in his stead, a miniature of his employer brought low before him as he had been brought low by Wullie's great rage not two weeks ago; and how it fattened him, to have his own personal beast of burden carrying this, cleaning that, fouled by the filth meant for his own clothes. If for a single moment Watchie fell to exhaustion, pausing in his scooping out of the muck, Watts would say,

Man, man, ye're nae ees at a', fit a big lassie, ye're jist hopeless, man!

stinging Watchie into a brief excellence of performance as surely as if a goad had been applied to his haunches, as if to prove to the father he was sure would find out about his slacking that he had the strength to move the weight of the shovel, the dead mass of the bucket of cow dung. But soon enough even this source of strength would run dry, leaving Watchie as weary as before; and Watts, by now with an eye on the clock, and not wanting to be seen by Peggy on her menial traipses around the yard, drew his eyes to slots, staring at Watchie with the judge's fury in the blue of them, and bent over to say into the loon's ear,

Ye widna like yer faither tae ken ye canna dee't, wid ye?

and the lash of those words, and the knowledge of his father's trust and confidence in his son's abilities, was enough to goad Watchie on still further, out of shame; and before the sun was up at ten, Jamie Watts returned to the farmhouse, reporting to Jeannie that the byre was now clean as a tinker's whistle, carpeted with a fresh pile of straw, that he was ready now to perform the mucking of Blackie's stable while the pony and wagon were away in the village.

The thing that spared Watchie most of the daytime repercussions of the unjust tarring that the name of his father took around the village was his first experience of learning. On the Sunday just before his first day at school, encouraged by Jeannie, he tried on the whole outfit, with the satchel looped over his shoulders by its two straps, and stood in front of the fire like a proper little model scholar, and Jeannie laughed to see him and said to her husband,

Look't the loon, Wullie! can ye nae see him gangin doon the road tae class like yon the morrow?

but Wullie barely paid it any heed, glancing up from his close scrutiny of the day's news, saying,

Aye, ane less pair o' hands tae help wi the fairm, Jeannie, but at least he'll be here tae help wi the neist hairst,

and those were his thoughts on the matter, while Watchie felt none of the urgency of transition or new passage, except a great relief that here was his escape from the drudgery of Watts's teaching; and the next morning Wullie had him awake at the usual early hour, to help with the milking of the kye for the first time in a long age, a reminder of the responsibilities he had been born to as the son of a dairy farmer.

Wullie waited in the yard in the front of the wagon, while Jeannie and Peggy both fussed over their scholar loon, settling the brim of his wee cloth cap above his eyes so uncomfortably tightly that Watchie adjusted it himself to at least give himself a slight view of the cool sky; they polished the dust from his new jacket and combed their fingers through his hair until he could still perceive their touch in the fibres, and only then, when he looked sufficiently learned, and after Jeannie had made him recite back to her a very few of the words she had taught him to read from his father's cast-aside newspapers over the course of the years, was he allowed to mount the board of the wagon to sit beside his father. It was a climb of many hazards for a wee lad like Watchie, the steps set one above the other an adult's pace high, but Watchie was allowed to do it on his own with no hands to stabilize him, stumbling not at all, kicking himself up and on to the bench, swivelling to let his abbreviated legs dangle into space. Wullie asked him was he settled before sending the order to Blackie through the reins, ticking in the back of his throat, and Blackie lurched forward, taking them out on to the Cornhill Road while Jeannie and Peggy rounded the side of the farmhouse, waving to their wee scholar to wish him luck, a wave which he returned by leaning precariously out of the cabin.

Sealed in his own troubles, Wullie had no time for those of the loon sitting beside him, who only now, as the wagon cleared the groves of tall elm and stunted sycamore to present the village to him as if on a salver, began to feel the first pains of uneasiness in the pit of his stomach as he approached the latest of his baptisms, knowing that he had learned so much about the beasts of the fields that he had never been told of the hearts of loons and cweans like himself; ill-prepared he was for it, though he was sure they would be as he was himself, and this thought he clutched as Blackie pulled the village closer to him, pace by pace.

The first sound that Watchie came to associate with his schooling was the row of children in the quadrangle in his first step through the gates; the sounds of laughter and chase, the crack like a switch on a horse's flank of a girls' skipping-rope on the paving, the click of footfalls as the rope dancers landed, the cheers of spectating loons as marbles were won and lost from a circle etched in chalk the width of a paving-stone. The sounds were so unfamiliar to Watchie that he stood just beyond the threshold, regarded by no one, his thumbs hooked through the shoulder loops of his satchel, as if the activity inside the quadrangle was simply one immense game from which he would be excluded until he had intuited the rules; he observed closely for a while, waiting to be brought in, but no one came to welcome him, until the next of the school's sounds drew the children as if on a leash, the thin ringing of a brass handbell held by a tall man in black furling robes, weaving the skein of children into lines of motley thread. Here at last was a rule that Watchie understood, the universal rule of obedience to adults, and recognizing the authority in the song of the bell, he trotted over to join the nearest ragged line and stood at the back, still not known by his peers, unacknowledged by the cruel-faced man in black as he stilled the bell's tongue and ordered the lines to thread themselves through the dark eye of the door.

Watchie often thought, for no reason at all, of the grandfather clock in the corner of his living-room at home while he was sitting in Mr Clarke's classroom; a venerable old timepiece it was which told the time with never a flutter. Its steadfast tick was the house's heartbeat, seldom regarded, sometimes referred to, and Watchie began to understand the passage of time under the single eye of its dial, the arrangement of its hands when dinner was served, or when indeed Jeannie smiled to him and ordered him up the stairs to his bed. Perhaps it was the way that time seemed to have changed its character now that he was under Mr Clarke's leaden authority; performing worthy repetitions of the alphabet, dry additions and subtractions chanted as if they were hymns to the Almighty, readings from the Bible, on and on went the process of learning, as long and as endless as the weaving of cotton in a mechanical loom. For all that Watchie found laughable in Clarke's appearance, with his robe as black as a crow and his learned man's mortarboard on which jigged the black tassel like a dancer on a platform every time he turned his head, there was no doubting the absolute rule of the man. There was his rod of ash wood, with which the master struck time against the floorboards to establish a rhythm, a for apple, or one and one are two, or blessed are the poor of spirit, whipping the class like a cruel and mean-spirited drover, and pity help the child who might find the comings and goings outside the window of more interest, for this was when the rod would fall like the lightning of Zeus on the desk, and with such a sound as you might think the sky itself would craze and topple like broken glass; and having seen this happen to Davie Lowther, whose father's farm was just on the other side of the Deil's Shieling from Wullie's, Watchie cultivated the habit of keeping his eyes to the front, even as his thoughts roamed like a vagabond. And then there was the gilded fob watch the master kept in his waistcoat pocket, chained like a dog, the only timepiece in the class, for the time of day was a pearl in the keep of Mr Clarke, the secret of his golden oyster known to him alone, and as the day crept towards four o'clock the watch would come more often out of the pocket, and a kind of torture it became in the anticipation of it, whether the watch would close over and return to the pocket, whether the master would look up and declare, you may put your books away and go home, quietly, and may God keep you safe on your journeys; and as the weeks went by after Watchie's first time in the classroom, this and not the bluster of the rod was how he measured the power of the man, that Clarke alone knew when the day was to end, and this gave him more power than anyone Watchie had ever known.

★

And then there was Anthony, the master's little seed of himself thriving among the cloddish soil of the class, the sons and daughters of farmers and merchants without grace or appreciation.

Anthony Clarke found his greatest liberation of expression within the classroom; for the rest of his time was spent in the study at home, in a library of four walls grinning with books relieved by only two windows, and with his father the teacher as his gaoler, seated at his own desk of mahogany opposite Anthony's child's desk, there was no chance of escape, no parole. By the age of five, he could recite the best-known poems of the Romantics, while by the age of seven he had defeated simple arithmetic, and was performing calculations in the Euclidean geometry with an ease which you would have to call prodigious. He came to school every morning with his father, first to be seated in the classroom, wearing a faint smile as the other children were led in by the master; for here Anthony was no longer the slowest pupil in a class of one, and here it was that he began to blossom, no longer under threat of his father's wooden ruler across his knuckles for his wilful lack of understanding, which occasionally marred his study performance. Suddenly he became the touchstone by which his father tested the knowledge of his pupils, finding them to be the purest fool's gold against the rarer metal of Anthony's achievements. He was even the voice of the classroom when the readings of Mr Clarke's favourite poetry, a later exercise in the school year, sounded like the braying of a sheep in the mouths of his children, when he would ask Anthony to stand before the class and restore the velvet to the lines, Seow we'll neow moah geow a reoving seow layte into the naight, the consonants struck as cleanly as nails, the vowels stretched like the softest fabric over the structure of it, giving the poem the shape that the master found most pleasing. It was all that most of the children could do to hide their smiles and their laughter behind their hands at the effete sound of Anthony's tutored voice, while the master closed his eyes as he sat on the tall stool at the top of his eyrie, the better to savour the clean rendition of the classic lines, and his son's mastery over the sculptured diction of the king's English.

During the course of the school year, Watchie sat in his unassuming seat near the back, working steadily and competently, pecking up from the floor the scatterings left by the master, scraps of alphabet and grammar, morsels of arithmetic, the leavings from the great banquet of learning which Mr Clarke considered adequate to feed the rough intellects of his other pupils. He learned; he wrote what was required of him; and hardly ever did the master find it necessary to administer to the back of his hand any blows from the point of the rod for answers written in haste or carelessness. Watchie grew in competence as the year progressed, and if truth be told this was much the way he preferred it, growing steadily in the shade cast by Anthony, left to his own devices. But there was one place where Watchie's reticence to advance himself, his taste for solitude and isolation, drew him into prominence far more than he would have liked, and that was in the school quadrangle, where he stood out like a monument against the swarming children with their games of tag and their skipping-ropes. He stood pointlessly against the tall granite wall as the commerce of play erupted around him, chaotic games seemingly without regulation or end, never quite losing that feeling of strangeness which he had felt on his very first day as he heard Blackie's hoofbeats softening into disappearance; a fish without a shoal, eager, fearful to join, mystified by the swirl of activity. For a long time he haunted the walls, sometimes taking cover under the cowling of the doorway, noticed only occasionally by the players during a run past, until finally he was invited to join a game of tag by James Grant, the son of the local hardware merchant, who trotted over to him as he stood under the shade,

Ye're nae for a game wi us, Wullie?

he said, and Watchie suddenly smiled and nodded quickly to the loon. James was lean but small, his skin polished clean and his eyes bright as a monkey's under the peak of his flat cap, and his smile was a quick and easy beam which immediately made

Watchie feel as comfortable as when his mother tucked the sheets in under the bed. The smile towed Watchie behind James all the way to the crowd just as they were beginning to choose their leper, and Davie Lowther was at the middle of it, pointing to each in turn as he excluded his followers one by one with his discriminating song; but the song stopped as James introduced Watchie from the edge, Lowther gazing at him before he said,

Fit's a-dee ye're aye ower at the wa', Leckie? Ye're nae waantin tae cam ower and jine us? Is it awa tae the deil wi us, is yon the truth o' it?

The other children made a secret laugh, behind their hands, and bringing a frown to Watchie's face; but he defended himself against Lowther's brief stab,

Naebody's cam ower tae me til the noo,

puzzled by the question, and Lowther laughed,

Ye're a dampt feel, Wullie Leckie, awa tae the deil wi ye,

which was the signal for the others to laugh at the shuffling boy dressed in his mother's finest clothes, and at the casual blasphemy he so readily uttered without fear of retribution. It was up to James to stand forward against Lowther, with a confidence he most surely did not feel down to his very boots,

Dinna ye gie Wullie a hard time, Davie. He disna need tae cam ower gin he disna waant tae. And yon's nae jist richt, ye ken, tae mak fun o' him like thon.

The effrontery of James's challenge caught the breath of Lowther's wheen of admirers, and Watchie began to fear that perhaps James had taken his insolence too far to escape Lowther's justice. Lowther stood there for a moment, his fists ready by his side, waiting for the quick ignition of anger to set them in motion like the pistons of an engine, and formidable little cudgels they were too; but in the event there was no spark, and Lowther simply nodded,

Aye weel, aal Clarke'll be efter ringin the bell gin we dinna mak a stert o't,

and in the following ritual Watchie found himself nominated as the carrier, and the game was on, children spraying in all directions as if from the centre of an explosion.

Watchie infected Johnnie Mathieson first with a fencer's lunge which carried him out of reach; Johnnie Mathieson in turn infected James, who had the temerity to infect Davie Lowther after him; and Davie immediately charged after Watchie, catching him with a vicious clenched fist on his upper arm before running on, throwing back the gauntlet of a stare to the loon as he gave a cry with the swelling of the pain,

Wid ye cry oot tae the deil the noo, Wullie Leckie, like yer faither wid?

Watchie glared at Lowther as the point of impact darkened into a bruise. He refused the taunt in Lowther's smile, and instead caught Tommy Crane with the lightest of touches as he passed by, leaving behind in Lowther an emptiness about the eyes. The game went on for some while, until Clarke came and rang the handbell to call them into their afternoon class; but Watchie was hardly a part of it, and found himself wondering what was the secret that Lowther and his friends were keeping to themselves, a secret that James seemed to know as well.

VII

It was after a number of months of preparation, during which Clarke wrote upon the blackboard the verses he himself found moving and excellent in their technique, that the master began to introduce his readings. Already he had made the entire class chant in chorus words he had chosen which would bring from their uneven throats the correct shine and beauty of the pronunciation which he found most pleasing to his critical ear, an exercise in which once again Anthony was cast as the paragon, the book of reference all must refer to in times of doubt; and little by little, as if by the motion of waves upon a pebble shore, the voices lost all their rags and edges, their resistance to the curious sounds eroded by continual and persistent tuition. Now, the master decided, was the right time for his treat, a chance for each child to be heard as a nearly polished example, shining on their own; except, of course, for Davie Lowther and his quite ineradicable gutter voice, no more to be trusted with the finest works of literature than his lumpen hands with a vase of fine crystal.

Watchie was spared for a while from having to exercise his speaking voice in front of the class, but he could not be ignored for ever, and on the day that the master first shone his unwelcome limelight upon the loon, Clarke had chosen to write on the blackboard a number of lines from 'The Phoenix and the Turtle', a poem which quite mystified one so young as Watchie. He was further unfortunate in that the master had abandoned his tall desk, for this had given him a superior vantage upon the class, a greater opportunity to wander among the furrows of heads, and it was from there that Watchie's low profile became as obvious as his intention to avoid conscription, an intention which to Clarke smacked of silent insolence, and therefore crying out for an example to be made. Tapping the cane into the palm of his hand to a clock regular beat, and scanning each head one by one before his choice of the inevitable, Clarke's eyes finally fell upon the withered boy as he shrank from the intrusive glare, and he said,

Master Leckie,

causing Watchie to leap up in reflex as if a hammer had been applied to his knees. All the eyes in the class fastened on to Watchie like burrs, and his throat dried slowly, like old wood.

I do not believe, said Clarke, we have as yet enjoyed a reading from you. Let us hear you speak the words of the bard of Avon, from the beginning if you please.

Watchie did not please. The blood left his face, giving him the complexion of one the worse for jaundice, and his mouth made a feast of the air as if it was not his proper element, a fish landed for sport. For a long moment he tried to make the words in his mouth, but his tongue was dry and mutinous, unable even to ask to be absolved from the task; he could see the lines accumulating on Clarke's brow as the silence became interminable, until the master could stand no more of it.

It's on the blackboard, boy. Let us hear you.

Watchie found enough breath to say,

I canna dee't, sir,

which only caused the master's face to become more inflamed, as red as Watchie's was pale, as if Clarke had received in transfusion the blood from Watchie, inflating him to twice the size with fury at this display of insubordination. He stood at the head of the class, in front of its star pupil, beating the butt end of his ashen pointer this time against the floorboards to a slow rhythm suggestive of an infinitely patient heartbeat.

What do you mean, you cannot do it? Are you disobeying me, Master Leckie?

The beat of the pointer made Watchie's pulse sound dangerously irregular and rapid in his own ears. He said,

Na na, sir, I ken I'd be nae guid wi't, sir,

but Clarke was in no mood to see Watchie escape from his clutches so easily, no more than an osprey with a trout on the end of its talons. He said,

I will be the judge of how good you are, Master Leckie. Now you will read the poem, or I will punish you for disobedience, and then you will read the poem. The poem will be read, Master Leckie, one way or the other. Let me hear your voice.

Watchie felt himself as one lashed to two millstones, each rolling in opposite directions and each unstoppable; a grand fear of Clarke and the judgement of his pointer, an equal fear of his own small abilities, of becoming foolish before the likes of Davie Lowther. A pressure built slowly within him as he gasped out the words as he saw them on the board, a balloon swelling to uncomfortable tautness, he ejected the words like spittle as soon as they were formed, as he had been taught by Clarke, let the, bird, of, loudest lay, on the, sole, Arabian, tree, he saw the gallery of eyes nailing him where he stood, the classroom became hot and cold in turns; and then there was a moment of hot release, a long white pin of agony as the tightness within him was lanced, a catastrophic release of pressure over which the poor loon had no control. Clarke watched the stain spread like a continent across the front of the boy's breeks in a disbelieving moment before he thought to say,

Stop! What is the matter with you, boy?

and the whole class laughed wickedly as the piss fair sluiced down the unfortunate loon's thighs, and poor Watchie burst into tears. Clarke walked the length of the furrow towards Watchie at the back, regarding him as if he were a mongrel stray cocking its leg, wading through the laughter towards the drip drip drip from the rim of Watchie's short pants' leg, and when he stood opposite Watchie it was to look at him in a way which heaped all the shame in the world on his head, reducing him in an instant to the meanest of beasts which had ever crept across the face of God's creation, part sneer, wholly dismissive. The pointer was impotent in his hands, for in his opinion the act was punishment enough, abasing Watchie in his eyes in a way which the application of the pointer could never suffice to do, and he said,

I will expect you to clean up what you have done before I send you home to explain this to your parents. Now go and fetch a cloth from the janitor. Anthony, please let us hear the poem as it should be read. I fear we are in sore need of the touch of civilization after this unfortunate incident.

Watchie could still hear Anthony's confident speaking voice the length of the corridor as he went to collect the cloth from Mr Mackechnie's cluttered room of hammers and nails, ripe with the smell of damp and sharp with cleaning fluids; but Mackechnie in his dungarees smiled and shook his balding head while he rooted about the forest of mops, said,

Dinna ye mind, my loon, ye're nae the first I'll've had tae gie a cloath tae, and ye'll nae be the last,

which scarcely made Watchie feel any better, being the first in his class, but the journey had dried his eyes at least, and Mackechnie's words strengthened him for the return, grovelling to wipe up the evidence of his misdemeanour with a cloth made crisp and papery with neglect, while Anthony's suave intonation swelled up fit to fill the classroom, let thee buhd of laoudest laiy on thee seoul Araybian tree, solemn, a mockery of sorts.

His trousers were dried by the wind by the time he mounted the slight hill leading to home, and his mother and Peggy took time off from their laundry to listen to the reason for Watchie's early return; but their response to Watchie's tale would have disappointed Mr Clarke in the extreme, for he was not given a sound beating, nor was he sent to bed with no dinner. Instead Jeannie shook her head repeatedly throughout the telling of her son's humiliation before the class, and at the end of it said,

Na na, yon'll nae dee at a',

and after giving Watchie a fresh pair of trousers to run about in she seized a sheet of writing-paper, a tinker-bought fountain-pen and a bottle of ink, and at the kitchen table composed an abrupt letter in her finest English, pleating the paper in thirds edged like a blade to cut the master's fingers while Peggy made the night's stew, muttering to herself all the while,

Yon mannie'll nae dee yon sae soon, nae fan he's had a read o' yon.

The next day, before Watchie left the house to climb aboard

the wagon, and after he had finished mucking out the byre for Watts, Jeannie instead of her mother-in-law settled the cap on his head, gave him the letter with instructions to give it in turn to Mr Clarke, saying,

Dinna pay ony heed tae fit they ca' ye. Ye'll nae be hurt by a name. Haud up yer heid, and dinna be feart o' them.

This Watchie did as the wagon reeled and dipped along the road, swaying by the empty cornfields and the depleted pastures; but as Blackie pulled them closer to the village, he felt his heart increase its pace just a very little, his belly eaten out as if by worms, and he thought about pulling at his father's sleeve and asking him to turn the wagon about to take them home. But his father had deliveries to make, and so Watchie kept his peace, holding Jeannie's words to himself for warmth like the stone water bottle she filled for him on bitter winter nights. He kept his head upright on a rigid pillar of vertebrae despite the best efforts of the shuddering wagon to dislodge it, and all that was left for him was hope, hope that the memory of his classmates was short, and a wish that his mother could be with him in more than just spirit, giving her strength to him.

There were many children in the playground as Watchie stepped from the wagon, skipping ropes and chasing with an early morning lack of enthusiasm. His father wished him a listless good-day, setting Blackie in motion almost the instant Watchie landed on the paving, curving around to return to the top of North Street to commence his deliveries. Watchie stood there for a moment outside the gates, looking at the back of the wagon with its painted legend and listening to the chiming of the milk churns as they rang off each other, softened by the closed doors, before turning himself to enter.

Lowther was there, and the moment he saw the figure with the elevated neck and the eyes of a hunted animal, his face bloated into a grin, he shot out a finger which made the others turn simultaneously to follow it, crying out,

Here's Pish-ma-breeks the noo!

and the cry was taken up by all the boys, pelting him with it as if it were a stone, pish-ma-breeks pish-ma-breeks pish-ma-breeks until his head dropped and he ran for the shelter of the door, but they ran after him, shaped themselves around him like a cloak, he cowered into the step and wetness came to his eyes, they were laughing like demons, and through the struggling lace of them he saw James Grant, his eyes cast to the ground in shame, not participating but neither helping, Davie Lowther changing the chant and the others following in chorus, pish-ma-breeks kens the deil, pish-ma-breeks kens the deil, pish-ma-breeks kens the deil, his shell of arms cracked open and the new name seeped in. Above Watchie's head, there was suddenly the loud and vigorous chiming of a handbell in rhythm with the chant, and there was Mr Clarke above him, causing the children to recoil and stilling their tongues,

I have never seen such disgraceful behaviour in all my days,

said Clarke into the sudden silence; then, to Watchie's surprise, he helped the loon to his feet,

Leckie, he said, who started this?

Before Watchie could answer, Davie Lowther stepped forward from the others,

I did, sir,

and the eyes of Clarke seemed to lighten at the prospect of punishing Lowther and his hard and uncouth farmer's hands, and first thing in the day, too; but so thick and impenetrable was the rind of calluses against the stroke of the belt that Lowther effectively received no punishment at all, and Watchie, after delivering his message, found that even Kate Gilfeather at the desk across the aisle from him eased herself to the edge of her seat away from him as if he were a tag leper. To crown it all, Clarke read the message from Jeannie Watchie had passed to him in the corridor silently, folding it and returning it to its envelope before saying aloud,

It would appear that your mother does not wish me to include you any further in our readings, Master Leckie. Considering your last performance, I believe this to be a sensible suggestion. From now on, you will not be required to take part. You may do silent reading instead, and I sincerely hope you will be able to contain yourself during this exercise.

And then he turned to chalk subtractions on to the board, as Watchie wiped clear his eyes in time to see all the faces in the class share the one smile.

Back at the farm, strange things were happening above Watchie's wee head, literally as well as metaphorically, conversations at adult height he was not encouraged to attend to and which loomed beyond his comprehension. On the Saturday following his playground christening, Jeannie answered the back door to Jamie Watts, who was shimmering with a fine coat of misty rain gathered during the short journey from chaumer to farmhouse. He was asking to come in and to talk to Wullie as a matter of some urgency, and Jeannie could not bear to see him stand in the steady drizzle any longer, so she widened the door to let him in, said,

Awa tae the livin-room, Jamie, he's jist at his paper the noo.

Jamie nodded thankyou, wiped his feet courteously on the straw mat placed before the threshold, wearing an expression of the highest seriousness which seemed to draw the day's chill in with him, even after Jeannie closed the door. He went to the living-room, knocked officially upon its door, entering on Wullie's invitation; the next minute, Peggy was in the kitchen, her knitting needles held parallel to her under her oxter, an oblong of knitting strung between them, her basket in her other hand heaped with yarns and her eyebrows pulled down low on her forehead in an incensed frown.

Fit way's yon loon efter a word wi Wullie that he canna tell't afore me?

she said, furious that she could be so easily displaced from her fireside armchair, even worse by business to do with the farm which the young interloper insisted on discussing in such absolute secrecy, worse still without her presence; but Aal Wullie said,

Ach, wumman, sit ye doon and dee yer knittin til they're done wi't,

and so taken aback was she at this doubled presumption that she actually obeyed him, though she made a bit of a theatre of it, planting herself on the nearest three-legged stool, clicking the needles together furiously but never for an instant sacrificing the sureness of her touch to the blackness of her mood, much to her own astonishment as well as Aal Wullie's at her reluctant compliance.

In a few minutes, the audience was over. Wullie saw Watts to the door, the latter with the nearest thing to a smile as the austere musculature of his face could offer him, a slight twist to the ends of his mouth which left his negligible lips dead level. Before stepping back out and under the swirling rain, he said,

I'm affa sorry, Wullie, but I canna be bidin wi yon kind of thing.

Wullie shook his head,

Aye, I'm affa sorry mysel, Jamie, but it'll aye cam oot sooner nor later.

Then he thanked Watts, and closed the door after him, still shaking his head and bowed over with the gravity of the intelligence. Jeannie looked up from stirring her stew,

It's nae a'thin for us tae hear, then?

Wullie stood like one at the heart of a rotting building, examining the slightest of cracks for signs of approaching treachery. He said,

Na na. Nae jist the noo,

looking over at Watchie as he did so, and left the room to return to his copy of the *Aberdeen Press and Journal*, leaving behind him an intricate mesh of glances, formless questions, uncertainties.

Over dinner nothing was said. Wullie stirred the mounds of his stew with his fork, chewing slowly and thoughtfully from time to time, finishing well after the others and not noticing how far he was lagging. And in the living-room afterwards, as Peggy knitted up reams of cloth and Jeannie read through the book of Exodus in the family Bible, Wullie defended his silence behind the great broadsheet fortress of the newspaper, from which he absorbed not one column inch of information. Even the Laird, pressing his muzzle against Watchie for attention, dared not move from his corner of the room. The grandfather clock ticked with perfect regularity, Peggy's needles gossiped and whispered to themselves like conspirators, the peat sparked in the grate, the pages of Wullie's paper turned crisply; from the room above, Aal Wullie sang a tune without words with his own drink in his hand, separated from the decisive silence below. Wullie put aside his paper, folding it in half then half lengthwise, placed it on the arm of his chair. He stood up, then went over to his cabinet, running his hands over its polished table surface, as if in imitation of the movement of a plane, the memory of his craft playing still in the tips of his fingers, unaware of all the eyes in the room, even those of the Laird. From the cabinet he took a bundle wrapped in cloth, closed over the doors and returned to his seat with it, placing it on his lap and opening out the petals from around the fiddle and bow. He stroked the cloth along the wood, restoring the shine to it, then drawled the bow over the strings, and in a moment Watchie sat upright, the warmth smouldering in his belly as the fiddle sang to him; perhaps it was time for his mother to seize him gently by the wrists and take him on to the floor, time for Dodie and Andy and Alistair and Cathie to come in and play and dance. The week of pish-ma-breeks and humiliation shrank to the size of a mote, slight and unimportant. But Wullie frowned to hear the almighty discord of complaint the creature roused at being awakened after so long a disuse, howling like a wolf and causing the Laird to leap on to all four paws as if at an intruder until shooshed by Watchie's hand between his shoulders. Wullie twisted the pegs at the head of the bridge, plucking the strings and listening as he went for harmony, but he never seemed to achieve the precise crystal sound he was after, turning the pegs as if they were clockwork keys, winding and plucking, winding and plucking, and then with the exact note he was looking for the G string parted from its stay on the body of the fiddle and lashed out like a serpent, catching his hand a vicious sting as it gave up the tension.

The smouldering in Watchie's belly consumed itself and went out. Wullie wrapped up fiddle and bow, returned the parcel to the cabinet.

I'll hae tae buy strings fan I'm at the toun,

he said, and interred the fiddle, locking the doors of the cabinet.

VIII

The term ended on a brilliant day which gave the promise of a long and clear vacation ahead; but Clarke insisted, even to the last, that his pupils should remain shackled to their desks by chains of arithmetic, in the afternoon fettering the children with uplifting saws from the Bible as a final entreaty to betterment before the end of his influence with the four o'clock bell. He chalked the sayings rapidly on the blackboard, as if the impatient breath of the children would erase it in a gust, and his watch was hardly ever in his pocket as he watched the last hours of the afternoon chipped away by the chisel of the second hand. Not soon enough, the hands saluted the hour of freedom, and with it Clarke stood before the whole class wriggling in their seats to the electricity of euphoria, and said,

My hope is that you will take my learning back to your houses, and that you will keep it in memory until our next meeting six weeks hence. I further hope that God will keep you all safe throughout the holiday, and that you will be ready to learn more upon your return. You may go now.

Outside, Watchie lingered at the door and the gates, waiting for the surge to escape properly the limits of the yard and break into the street. No longer under Clarke's protection, he feared the remembrance of pish-ma-breeks, Davie Lowther pouring the name over him like quicklime; but no one had the mind to waste any of their freedom upon him, and Watchie was left discarded behind them, a plaything cast to one side, though all the same he made sure he was properly forgotten by dragging his feet along the quadrangle, allowing the others ahead of him. James Grant looked behind himself as he went towards the hardware store, smiled over his shoulder at Watchie, and Watchie returned it, a little uncertainly. As Watchie turned to look across the quadrangle, a last glance at the paved compound, he saw that he was not the last to leave, for Anthony came out of the door, alone at first. For a long time Anthony stared at Watchie, with the same intense curiosity as he might have bestowed upon a mongrel chanced upon in the street, and for his part Watchie returned the gaze, though there was no fellow-feeling in it, as if he were staring at a child of crystal, drawn from his own imagination. Watchie was driven through the gates by the constancy of Anthony's stare, around the corner into North Street, and on the way home along the Cornhill Road, he even began to feel sorry for the poor loon, without any good reason.

Wullie watched Dodie Mearns pack away his clothing into the sackcloth bag with which he had arrived at Smallbrae Farm those many years ago, noting how fastidiously he folded the cotton shirts with their arms doubled helplessly behind them and the fringes tucked underneath, the trousers ironed thin by Cathie Loudon and layered into oblongs ready for stowing away; a bone-handled shaving brush crowned with a tuft of badger pelt, a nub of soap and a wooden-handled open blade with a strip of coarse leather coiled around it all and parcelled in a face-cloth. Finally the melodion was replaced in its square case of horse leather, the locks clipped over in a final punctuation which gouged an emptiness out of the air around him. Wullie stood at the threshold of the chaumer, looking around its single room at the gathering waiting there, Cathie and Alistair, brought together by the music from Dodie's melodion, Alistair shaking the ploughman's hand with a crushing warmth and Cathie delivering him a kiss on the cheek before letting him go, only the surface of their deepest gratitude, Andy McGrath giving his ploughmate an impeccably manly embrace with his handshake, exchanging with him a promise to write. Of Jamie Watts there was no sign, he had found some work to do during Dodie's packing, and no one could find him, and if the truth were told no one looked very hard. Before he picked his bags off the bed Dodie cast a look to Wullie and said,

Wid ye mind, Wullie, gin I see the horses afore I gang awa?

and Wullie couldn't see the harm in it, he shook his head no, he didn't mind, and Dodie smiled and left to go to the stables.

Jess and Jonah were resting in their stalls, and for the last time Dodie ran his hands the length of their flanks, appreciating under his touch the power of those muscles drilled beneath their fine glossed coats, and how gentle they were, how they each nuzzled his open palm though he had no oats to give them. He remembered the first touch upon their flanks when he was newly arrived at Wullie's farm, after they had been strapped into the plough, how easily they responded, almost their own captains steering him across the fields at a gentle pace. Dodie said,

Ye'll hae tae be richt guid for yer neist mannie, ken noo,

and Jess let out a splutter, which Dodie heard as a goodbye to him. It was only when Jonah raised his head over his stall to nudge his arm, jealous of the attention Jess seemed to have all to herself, that an unaccustomed moistness sprang to Dodie's eyes, which he padded at with a handkerchief before turning finally from the stable, saying,

I hope tae God Wullie taks on the richt man for ye.

Wullie was still outside the chaumer when Dodie went in to collect his sack and his melodion, this time to an embarrassment of smiles from the others, the vacancy left after all had been said. He smiled in reply, said goodbye again to them more briskly, and went out again. Wullie approached him, a cloth purse sealed with a drawstring in the palm of his hand.

Ye've werked affa hard tae earn it,

he said, holding the purse up. Dodie put the case on the dry ground, picked the purse out of Wullie's hand, weighed it, then pocketed it. Wullie said,

Ye'd be as weel coontin it,

but Dodie shrugged,

Ye'll hae't coonted a'ready, man,

and lifted the case again. Wullie looked down at Dodie's squat burden,

I'll hae tae fee a man fa'll play jist like ye,

and Dodie laughed,

Aye, man, and ye'll hae tae gang tae affa mony fairs afore ye'll dee thon,

and Wullie joined him in the laughter until finally the weight in Dodie's hand reminded him, and he lapsed, taking Wullie's laughter with him. Wullie said,

Gin he plays affa fine or no, he'll hae tae werk like the deil afore he'll dee as weel as yersel, Dodie, fine d'ye ken that.

Dodie smiled, disciplined by all the irony at his command.

Faith, man, he said, ye'll hae me thinkin ye'll be efter feein me back here again.

Wullie did not smile this time.

Ye ken we canna tak anither lass tae the kitchen, Dodie.

Aye, I dee that,

said Dodie, without conviction.

Watchie was in the yard looking on while the Laird tried without success to coax him into playing, rubbing his damp snout against Watchie's calves and then feinting a dash, expecting a chase at any minute; but Watchie was too busy trying to understand the conversation between his father and Dodie. He heard Wullie say,

See, Dodie, ye've landed yersel wi fit ye'd ca' responsibilities the noo,

and Dodie simply nodded, it was no more than he'd heard before; he said,

We're thinkin o' takkin on a wee holdin fan we've the time for't; ye ken, a wee place we can mebbe fairm oot,

and Wullie nodded in his turn,

Aye, ye'll dee fine, man, ye're a guid werker, Dodie.

Dodie felt the bags slipping in wet hands, hefted them for better purchase,

I'll be awa then, Wullie,

then dropped the melodion case and shook his former employer's hand with the hand now freed. He said,

I'd be affa carefu' fa's werd I wis puttin my faith in, gin I wis yersel,

and, explaining no further, picked up the melodion and went over to Watchie, who gave him a broad smile, as he usually did when he saw Dodie of a morning. Dodie dropped the case again and took Watchie's small hand in his own, giving it a good fast shake as if he were concluding a deal with the loon, then disordered Watchie's cap of hair, picked up the bag again,

Keep tae yer school, wee Wullie, he said, for yon's fit way I've tae mak my livin at the plou'.

He went to the farmhouse to wish farewell to Peggy and Jeannie and Aal Wullie; and then, glancing behind him not once, took to the Cornhill Road and was off to his next employment, thanks to a grace period Wullie had been pleased to grant him as a means to his further security and that of his cwean, and left behind him a vacancy to be filled at the Porter Fair, just before the harvest.

IX

The school holiday passed slowly for Watchie in its first few weeks, for he was under the captaincy of Jamie Watts nearly the whole time, learning with his father's permission the variety of tasks that needed doing about the farm and doing most of them himself, learning from the foundations up, so to speak; for many of the orra loon's responsibilities were scarcely noticeable to the eye, but they were the ha'pence of tar whose want could jeopardize the integrity of the whole ship. Most of them were the menial and unsatisfying jobs no one else about the farm had the time or the inclination to do, an apprenticeship in minutiae with nothing to recommend it except the experience it provided for those intending to one day run their own farm, but Wullie made sure that the wages he paid out were fair, and that the tools he provided for the job were in a good enough condition that the tasks for which they were made might be performed at all possible speed; he was never one for splicing together with a rusty nail the ragged ends of a broken shovel haft, not Wullie, for he considered it a proper courtesy to his workers to give them the best implements he could afford, in addition to the sound reasoning that the better the tool, the quicker the job could be done. But to poor Watchie, clearing up the yard under the despotic eye of Jamie, the condition of the implements was a matter of small comfort, for it was the size of them he found troublesome to his grasp, wielding them each as if they were items of weaponry as he scoured the filthy straw from the byre and the stables, brushing the muck out into the yard. Day in day out Watchie performed his Cinderella tasks without complaint, cleaning the wagon when it had returned from its deliveries, a recent addition to his chores, helping Jamie to restore the proud shine to its painted finish with a bucket of soaped water warmed at the kitchen range in Cathie's cauldron, applied by chamois cloth, buffed dry. Jamie rubbed at the body of the wagon like one fatigued, but Watchie's contribution was by far the dirtier, scrubbing at the mud which clotted the spokes and the wheel rims, and the irksome clay which gathered in the nubs of the axles, elbow deep in the bucket of water tainted with all the muck and dung of the streets. It was a thankless task, made none the easier by Jamie's continual goading and taunting, but still Watchie managed every day to bring up the wheels and fixtures to a bright polish which would do pride to his father's trade, a detail never commented upon by any of the customers but noticed with approval, like the shoes of the apprentice, inspiring trust through diligence.

Wullie never noticed this effort from his son, but Peggy drew her daughter-in-law's attention to the fact, one day when Jeannie was busy peeling potatoes at the kitchen sink, coming up behind her and saying,

Pair wee loon, look, Jeannie, he's aye deein the feels o' the wagon, files yon Jamie's at the body o't,

and almost for the first time, across the yard, Jeannie looked at what was happening, noticing the stain of tea-coloured water the length of her son's arms, his bare knees in the dirt, scouring furiously at the great rings of the wheels, concentrating his attention on each scab of muck he soaked away with the cloth. In the space between the chassis and the ground, she saw two spindly legs and a shower of soap froth drenching the earth, and it began to bother her that her son was granted the filthier of the two jobs; not particularly because Watchie was her son, although that was part of the reason, not that she considered her son above the kind of menial labour the likes of Jamie was paid to do, but more because of his age, and because she had been watching Jamie with great care ever since the dismissal of Dodie Mearns just at the turn of the half year. It was quite unlike Wullie to take any decision without hearing from his wife first of all, though usually he approached her opinion in a roundabout way, being too proud to ask her directly, casting his doubts in the air at night before the candles were extinguished like a spray of thistledown, leaving them to fall unheeded or to take root, upon which Jeannie would tell him, mebbe no, Wullie, or aye mebbe that's richt eneuch. But on this occasion he had dismissed the farm's best worker without a word to her, and this Jeannie found odd, even given Wullie's recent tendency towards silence, especially after the curious and behind doors dialogue which had displaced Peggy from her knitting place in front of the fire, and it did not take long for Jeannie to forge the link between the two events. Indeed, the day after Wullie told her that Dodie was to receive his wages for the six-month, Jeannie recalled the strange visit, and from then on tried her best to avoid him whenever possible, noticing all kinds of small proofs for her conviction that Jamie had been to blame for Wullie's sudden and uncharacteristic decision. She noticed how he kept himself separate from the other workers, preferring instead the company of his palm-sized Bible, isolating himself with prayer while staring with keened eyes at the others as they laughed and joked, and she noticed also the contempt which sealed him from them. It was on the day that Dodie Mearns picked up his melodion bag and his sacking that her conviction set into certainty, for she saw something that none of the others even noticed; Jamie Watts peering above the half-door of the byre, and the clenched smile she saw creasing his face was the same smile he had left the house with after his visit a number of weeks ago. She never said a thing to Wullie, nor to any of the others, simply returned to the house and continued to make her broth, but while she was cooking she made a decision of her own, and not a word did she say to Wullie of it.

From that day on, she avoided Jamie Watts as if he were as venomous as a nettle. There was nothing she could do about her husband's faith in the loon; in the days before the withdrawal of some of his best customers, she might even have put up some kind of defence on Dodie's behalf, told him not to be so stupid, that sort of thing had happened before and would always happen about farms. But she could not reach Wullie, especially during the days approaching harvest when everything depended upon there being no sudden floods, no long days of parching sun to scorch the risen corn, and so Jeannie resolved to say

96

nothing of her decision, but always stayed clear of Watts's very presence, never pointedly or discourteously, and every night she prayed that she was doing the the right thing, that she was not acting out of simple malice, that she had reason and purpose behind her.

It was only when she saw the loon kneeling in the dirt of the yard, shoulder deep in the bucket of water, that she felt her decision to be justified; but she held her counsel and said nothing of it to Peggy, continued to bare the white flesh of the potatoes with quick and irritable strokes of the knife blade.

The next day, after Wullie had driven the wagon out on to the Cornhill Road, Jeannie made sure she was at the window, an unobtrusive distance away from it so that she could not be seen plainly in the glass. She saw Watts and Watchie come out of the byre, Watchie struggling with a mounded bucket of cow dung and quills of straw, Watts carrying a shovel at the fulcrum of the haft and leading the younger boy to the dungheap; and immediately she leapt from the house, scurrying over to intercept them while trying not to appear hurried or driven by concern, but Watts never noticed her until she stopped a little behind them and said loudly,

My, but yon's an affa heavy-lookin pail ye've there, Wulliam.

Watts turned at the same time as Watchie, suddenly, guiltily. His eyes seemed to light up from behind with something like fear, the fear of discovery, but his voice was smooth and even as he said,

Wullie says tae me the loon's tae gie me a wee bit help tae red up the byre in the morn.

Jeannie was hearing none of it, but neither was she prepared to argue. She said,

Faith, Jamie, but the loon's lookin wore oot as weel, and his faither widna like him ower tired afore his time tae gang awa tae his bed. Na na, pit doon yon pail, Wulliam, and we'll see fit else ye can dee.

Then, staring fully at Watts,

Jamie here can dee his werk wi'oot yer wee bit help, can ye no, Jamie?

Jamie stared back at her, but brazenly he said,

Aye weel, the loon's nae been ower muckle o' a help onyway.

Jeannie smiled,

I'm affa glad tae hear ye say't, Jamie, for I can tell Wullie ye winna miss him hardly at a',

and then she took the pail gently out of Watchie's hand and held it out at arm's length for Jamie to take up; which he did, with insolent slowness, turning away once the full weight was borne by his pipe-cleaner of an arm, while Jeannie rescued Watchie by the shoulders, and led him to the farmhouse.

That afternoon, she let him play with the Laird in the yard, in full view of Jamie and despite the open blade of his stare upon her back, the same intensity of gaze he had stabbed Cathie Loudon with after her overheard playful comment about the tattie boodie. It did not matter to Jeannie how poisonously the orra loon might look at her, because she stood inoculated against Watts by her husband's faith and trust in her, and this Watts found most galling of all as his little slave disappeared behind the shed in a chase with the ageing dog, that Watchie now had the best protection in the world against him, that now he had a whole day's worth of hated tasks in front of him without his employer's offhanded permission to bring his own son low before the orra loon. As the Laird leapt and pawed at his young master, leading him out into the cleared borders of the cornfields and away from the perimeters of the farm, Jamie Watts remembered without bidding it holding in his fist a tiny baby mouse, squeezing the heart out of it, the last kicks scratching against his palm.

The Laird guided Watchie deeper into the countryside, venturing forward with his snout into troughs and runnels, led by the interest of the moment towards interesting smells and sudden movements. Especially vexing for the Laird was the mystery of the grasshopper, the loud croak which teased his curiosity away from the ochre thread of the path and into the grasses and hedgerows, no sooner found than magically no longer there, only to emerge some way distant, drawing him through the weft of grass, chasing the clue of the chirruping through the thick pile, until Watchie called out,

Cam awa tae me, Laird! Cam tae me!

causing the Laird to raise his head in recognition of the voice, then to cast over his shoulder at the unsolved mystery, staring back as Watchie sharpened his command,

Laird, cam awa!

a sudden jerk of the long leash of honour which brought the dog back to the path, to examine more static items of interest. Occasionally the Laird nosed out of the loam of the alder and sycamore forests treasures covered by dropped leaves, caged in lattices of desiccated twig. He approached Watchie with one such treasure, held gently in his mouth, coughed into the palm of Watchie's hand, though he had not been told by the loon to fetch. It was a curious structure, textured like a small fragment of wood, but fatter than any twig, and split along the middle by a seam, open to the elements. The emptiness of it, the vacancy inside the shell, put Watchie in mind of an egg for some reason he could not have tested with an explanation; but its resemblance to a fallen twig eaten out to the bark satisfied Watchie that indeed he was holding something dropped from the branches of the compact sycamore above him, and he pocketed it as a curiosity, an object found by chance, then passed his hand through the Laird's mane of black fur on either side of his head, and let him run on.

He followed the Laird further away from the farm, until all the activity was reduced to the commerce of model figures among a painted field, toy cows bent low over the grass, as the dog pulled him along the shores of Loch Bannoch on the furthest frontiers of the estate of Lord Aberlevin, along the veil of ash, elm and sycamore which modestly hid the gardens of the sleepy-eyed mansion from the impudent sight by the side of the loch. But the more curious and investigative the Laird became in the forest, turning over the soil for more unexpected prizes, the more Watchie came to realize that the dog was his only clue among the tangle of the trees, that he was being drawn deeper into a twilight of the lace of branches above him. He passed through a drapery of tiny flocking insects suspended under the oxters of the trees, whining like alarms as they skipped past his ears, he did not like the sound one little bit, with its unmistakable bite of warning, and he was about to panic like a horse and call the Laird once again to heel when he noticed the dog raise its head of its own accord and bring its ears to attention, swivelling them about to appreciate a direction for the thing which had so intrigued him, then casting back to Watchie, follow me, before prancing flat the grass in front of him. Watchie waited not one instant; he took to his heels in pursuit, not wanting to lose the dog behind a tree or in a sudden tangent, filled in a moment with the silent clamour of the dark woods, its fearsome shades and half glimpses. But the Laird made sure that he was always in sight of the young master, stopping every few paces to look behind him, and if Watchie was keeping up, he resumed his whispering dash through the crisp mosaic, until after a while he found an exit and paused once again. There was Watchie panting some way behind him, following him through the doorway in the wood between two gnarled spirals of branching and through a guard curtain of the whining insects which had propelled Watchie so quickly along the corridors. With relief, Watchie recognized almost immediately where the Laird had taken him, for while he knew nothing of the forest, he had been on many a long walk with Aal Wullie by the borders of the loch, and when he saw the easy trail of the water, and the way that the Deil's Shieling seemed to give its ground to permit the swelling of the further shore of the loch, he knew that he was not after all lost, that he had stood here before, and all comfort returned to him, he bent down and hugged the dog to himself, falling to his haunches as the dog wiped his face with its tongue, causing him to laugh without control. As he fell, he looked the length of the bank, across the growth of reeds and wild grasses and all the unkempt and profligate colours of the waterside, and there in the middle distance, poised on its knees by the rim of the loch, he saw a figure. It was much too far away for Watchie to recognize, but whoever it was seemed to have been brought low almost as if in humility before this wide and tranquil altar, bent double in worship, and if he (Watchie noted he, the hair cropped in a close bowl about the scalp) had heard any of the commotion caused by himself and the Laird, then it was of no importance to him, disturbing not in the slightest the minute focus of his attention. Despite Watchie's natural uneasiness, he found himself drawn to his feet, still grasping the Laird in his arms, but before he could contrive a stroll which would take him along the path home and past the probe of land which pulled on the fabric of the loch as if to drag it further away to claim more land for the hillside, suddenly the Laird slipped cannily out of his hold with a lithe wee twist which left Watchie's arms pinching empty air, and then he was off and bounding up and through the long grass, leaping to gain a bearing before sinking back into the tussocks, and Watchie chased after him, taking giant steps to flatten the grass in his road. The height of the grass deflected the Laird from his path to the stranger, causing him to take a wider route than was necessary; but still the stranger was not interested in the approach, ignoring the activity around him, and it was only when Watchie came closer to catching the Laird that he realized that he knew the figure, with the hard-bound notebook spread against his kneeling lap, the caps of his bare knees soiled by long contact with the earth. His interest was focused entirely on the head of a flower growing by the lochside, as concentrated as sunlight distilled through the eye of a lens, as intense as might cause the flower to ignite into a blossom of flame, raping the page of the notebook with abrupt and rapid strokes of his HB pencil. So much sealed into his envelope was the boy that even when Watchie approached within the length of a pointer from him, still he did not look up, only when the shadow of Watchie fell across his flower to obstruct his vision; and for the first time that Watchie could remember, Anthony Clarke's face split into a wide grin, a sharp-toothed and malicious thing,

Why, he said brightly, it's Pish-my-breeks!

If anyone else but Anthony had said the name, then Watchie

would have turned on his heel to lead the Laird along the path towards home, pricking tears of frustration from him which he would allow no stranger to see, raising as if fresh the memory of his bullying day in school. But in Anthony's mouth, the i of pish was pruned so far back that Watchie could almost hear the dot above it, the vowel of breeks drawn out and elongated until it almost disappeared over the mount of the Deil's Shieling; and despite himself, Watchie found himself laughing to hear such a rabble of words graced by the sophistication of the received accent, a ploughshare touched by the hand of Midas, and through his laughter he said to Anthony,

Dinna say yon,

causing Anthony to tighten and bridle,

Whyever not?

Man, man, ye canna say't richt!

At first Anthony was silent in the face of Watchie's tumbling jackpot of laughter, not understanding; then in an instant the joke turned another of its facets towards him, how strange that this peasant's son should tell him what was the proper pronunciation of his debased dialect, and without warning Anthony found himself sharing in the laughter, and in an instant they had both scared the curlews into the air and started a mesh of echoes in the forest, and not for a scant moment did each imagine that they were laughing at different sparklings of the same crystal. But by now the pane of diffidence between them had shattered, and Watchie chanced himself a little closer to Anthony, to look inside Anthony's book of illustrations.

Watchie said nothing at first, but it seemed to him a very strange pastime, to be recording the appearance of flowers you could see as plainly in front of you as the spread of your fingers. Anthony's sketches were bold and literal, the lines thick and definitive, and Watchie was puzzled by the thin threads which attached parts of the flower head to words he did not recognize. The laughter had long since collapsed under the mass of the silence, and now Watchie said,

Fit're ye deein in yon bookie?

Anthony raised it from his lap, turned back the pages on more illustrations.

I'm engaged in the study of botany. These are the flowers I've seen.

Watchie frowned, slightly.

Fit's yon, botany?

Anthony looked up to the broad awning of the sky, then down to Watchie again.

It's the scientific study of flowers and everything that grows.

Watchie understood the last of Anthony's explanation, and smiled.

My faither kens a' aboot a'thing that graas. He's a fairmer.

The laughter that came from Anthony's mouth was sharp, not at all like the laughter they had shared only a moment ago.

That isn't botany. That's agriculture. Your father wouldn't know anything about botany.

Watchie was charged with indignation on his father's behalf, and he said,

Fit's sae different aboot botany, that my faither widna ken a' aboot it?

Anthony coughed to clear his throat, his own father in miniature, as he declared,

Put simply, botany is a science, studied by men of learning. It is the science of everything which grows in the whole world. Agriculture is the practice of farming, and can be done by anyone, whether they are men of learning or not. There. That's the difference. Your father may be able to grow and harvest wheat, or whatever you grow on your farm, but he would not be able to study the growth of flowers, because he isn't a botanist.

The explanation warmed Anthony, and he gave Watchie a tight smile. Watchie nodded towards Anthony's book,

Fit ees is a' yon drawin and writin aboot flooers, then?

Anthony expressed his contempt in a snort,

What use is it? he said. Does it have to have a use? It is a scientific study. We must understand the world around us, the world given to us by God. That's why we have science.

Watchie shrugged.

Gin it's nae ees tae ye, he said, fit way d'ye dee't?

Because, said Anthony with elaborate patience, if men of learning didn't try to understand how plants grow, then men without the learning, men like your father, wouldn't be able to run his farm properly.

Watchie stood opposite the taller boy, making slots of his eyes against the glimmer of the sun at Anthony's back. The Laird nuzzled his leg, and he reached his hand down to stroke the dog's jowls absently.

I'd like tae ken a wee bittie mair, he said, and I'm nae daft.

X

Anthony showed Watchie the flowers pressed in his father's botany book, allowing him to hold them in his fingers, entreating him to take the greatest care of them, not to subject them to too much pressure; but the loon took them out of Anthony's hands with such delicacy as if a lean and colourless blood ran in their prominent veins to the rhythm of a pulse, and Anthony quite forgot to fear for his father's collected specimens, trusting them to Watchie's curiosity. Watchie appreciated the crisp dimensions of the dried petals in the palm of his hand, remembering how his father had taught him to make the lightest of fists about the cluster of seed corn and sensing how much more easy these samples would be to damage; and he felt touched by their sad beauty, bending to compare their textures with those of the living flowers on the stalk, rubbing the vibrant scrolls between thumb and forefinger for all the world like a seamster wifie testing a bolt of fabric in a haberdasher's, sad for the fragile hulls of life he held so gently in his hands. He had never seen a memory pressed flower before, and he said to Anthony,

Is yon flooer deid?

and Anthony said,

Of course it's dead, they all are. How do you expect a flower to grow without roots?

and Watchie nodded, remembering his father talking about the roots of his corn, the part of the growth cloaked by the soil, feeding and strengthening the growth above, and he found himself beginning to understand that the flowers would die in the absence of these anchors.

The next thing Anthony placed into the palm of Watchie's hand, after retrieving the flowers and putting them back in the pages of the botany book, was something he picked out of the water from the trunk of one of the rushes, and at first Watchie was quite puzzled by the form of this strange object, though he was not disgusted. It glistened a dull and deep bottle green as Watchie held it into the clear sunlight, and in a moment proved itself to be alive as it negotiated the hillocks and valleys of Watchie's hand, extruding its body until it was as thin as a strand, arching its back like a kitten and drawing itself behind, gathering its entire substance together into a small and dense lump. Watchie looked at Anthony,

Fit is't?

he said, and Anthony smiled, with the certain assurance of knowledge.

It's a leech. Once it's decided you're alive, it'll try to suck the blood from your hand.

Anthony laughed as Watchie shook his hand free of the leech as if it were a cinder, wiping it against the palm of the other to make sure that it was no longer embracing the flesh with so much affection, and fired such a look at Anthony; but the boy said,

It was only a small leech. Besides, it never touched you,

and this was true; but Watchie was now on guard, until Anthony pointed to the ruptures on the skin of the loch, where freshwater trout were darning the cloth of the water, a sight which made the loon forget all about his apprehension, netting him in the wonder of it.

Anthony led Watchie along the border of the loch, and all the time pointed to small curiosities, that is curiosities which were small and meaningless to him, with his keen eye for reduction and definition, but which to Watchie were nothing more than the opening of an entire book full of riches and wonders which he had no names for, and Anthony held close to him the power of nomenclature, occasionally tossing at Watchie morsels of information which the loon devoured with a proper will, leaving him all the hungrier and more than ever ready to play for the rest, like the kind of feeding game his grandfather played with the Laird. He saw dragonflies, their wings beating to invisibility as they maintained a pose above the surface of the water, their bodies as slender as the needles which Peggy used to seal the holes in the grain sacks, suddenly dashing away from their ledge on the air like one late for an errand, pausing again as if for breath. He saw insects dancing on the floor of the water with their legs as thin as wire, their bodies trestled above the silver, and he saw a shimmering of minnows as they ran from the shadows above them warped through the glass. It was all marvellous to Watchie, everything standing revealed as if for the first time, and from time to time he would call out to his found companion, as Anthony stooped by a flower to measure it with a calibrated cloth tape his mother had given to him from her dressmaking box, and with his father's tone of impatient authority Anthony tied a label around the object seen, connecting it to a name, in much the same way as the different anatomies of his flowers were given their correct titles on the end of a string in his reference book of botany. All the while Anthony continued with his observations and his measurements, noting breadths and lengths into his journal before nipping the flowers some way down the stalk and placing them in the pages of his book, a living mark; and in this manner they went, at Anthony's pace, the Laird finding his own amusement in the chasing of a bird into the air, no real harm meant, Anthony giving up the time promised to his father to explain the radius of concentric rings on the surface of the loch, or something else which took the eye of his slow pupil.

Watchie began after a time to approach Anthony while he was busy in the taking of his notes, and at first this irritated the taller loon as Watchie's shadow spread tar upon the object of his interest, quite obscuring it from the sunlight; he found himself snapping at the younger boy, shooing him away in the same way as he chased the Laird when the dog came searching for his affection. But when Watchie came closer still, and this time stayed out of his light so that there was no excuse for his displeasure, Anthony found himself explaining his whole scientific procedure to Watchie, using as an example the marsh cinquefoil whose outlines he had already drawn in the appropriate page of his book.

Flowers, you see, are not just made up of one part,

he said as Watchie squatted on his haunches beside Anthony, his eyes wide on the cinquefoil pressing its purple starfish shape through its competitors for an equal share of breath and light. Seeing that his pupil was stiff with attention, Anthony cleared his throat and continued,

The head of the flower is called the perianth. Say it after me, perianth,

and,

Perianth,

said Watchie, mimicking precisely Anthony's diphthong, bringing it slightly further forward in his mouth than if he had read the word in his own accent. Anthony nodded in satisfaction.

Good. The perianth is made up of a number of petals, in this case five. Say, petals.

Watchie glanced up from the flower for an instant, his eyes sparking with contained annoyance.

I ken fine fit a petal is,

he said, and Anthony sat back on his knees for a moment.

Everybody knows what a petal is. That's nothing special. However, I know the name you give to all the petals together. It's a special name.

Watchie drew his negligible eyebrows down low, hiding his eyes in the shadow.

Weel, fit name d'ye gie tae them?

Anthony smiled, a thin, superior smile.

The name for all the petals together is the corolla.

Watchie nodded, chanted in turn,

The name for a' yer petals thegither is the corolla.

That's right, said Anthony. Here.

He opened his journal at the back page, and began to scribble with the pencil. When he finished, he turned the book around for Watchie to see. He had written down in block capitals of even size, spaced apart just so: PERIANTH: PETAL: COROLLA. Watchie stared at them for a long time, the appearance different to the taste he had of them in his mouth, and he shook his head.

Yon's affa funny-lookin words,

he said, and Anthony laughed down at him from a height.

That's because they're Greek. You must learn what to call things if you're going to study them seriously.

Watchie looked at the real cinquefoil, and for a moment the breeze caused the flower to nod low on its stalk, bowing before Watchie as if in courtesy. He pointed to the crown of filaments inside the cusp of the petals.

Weel, fit's a' yon inside the co ro lla?

Anthony paused for a second or two at the sudden confidence of the loon, his demand to know more about the sexual cluster of the flower; surprised at his young pupil's giant appetite, and feeling himself to be nothing more than a lexicon from which rags were being torn whole, swallowed without grace. Anthony said, coolly,

Learning is not a thing to be hurried. I don't believe you're ready to know that yet,

and left Watchie to simmer while he unrolled his mother's tape and continued to measure, and note down results.

It was an association which never warmed sufficiently to merit the name of friendship. Watchie and Anthony walked towards the Cornhill Road which parted them, Watchie towards his farm and Anthony in the direction of the road which led him to his father's glebe, the forgotten Laird trailing a little all the way, dragged behind them by his own animal curiosity in the thickening bushes, and by the need for relief against the trunk of a thick and heavy elm. Before the boys took their opposite roads, Anthony made Watchie swear an oath before God that he would not breathe a word of their meeting to anyone, not even his own parents, knowing how speedily chance-uttered news ignited the gossip-dry village; the journey home feared him, charged him with a great dread that he may not have picked or measured enough to justify his continuing parole, and while his father was examining his work his breath was shut in his lungs, held in custody until the evidence was sorted through. Mr Clarke compared noted measurements against the tell-tale of the cloth tape, ticking them as correct, and Anthony began to release his breath slowly as he realized that, even if there was any sign of a shortfall in the standard of his work, even if his descriptions appeared at all hurried or slipshod, then such escaped the notice of his father. Anthony took his dinner without guilt, and even began to look forward to the next day, when Watchie said he might be walking the dog again by the lochside, a promise in which he found almost as much sustenance as there was in the food on his plate.

For Watchie's part, he fair skipped home with the Laird hopping by his side, his head stuffed like a laundry bag with names and definitions all in a tangle, and in the hedgerows he found flowers recognized from Anthony's book, how good it was to have a name he could call them among the tumult; and he began to revel in his observations, chanting like a prayer with every footstep he took on the way home to an infectious dance rhythm the names Anthony had consented to tell him at long last, one to a cobble; whorl, sepal, calyx, petal, corolla, stamen, carpel.

Anthony kept Watchie at the length of his arm the whole time that they spent by the side of the loch, and this confused the younger loon, who by his own lights considered Anthony as a friend, bearing with as much dignity as he could the occasional starts and frustrations of the older boy, which caused him to draw out his claws. There was much authority in the voice of the master's son, and perhaps this was why Watchie was more willing to put up with his continual punishment than he might be to accept the same from, say, Jamie Watts, mistaking it for the natural timbre of one of learning, a clean and antiseptic voice born to dispense knowledge. He took it all with the forbearance of a mule, all of Anthony's Master Leckie you're dressed like a pauper this fine day, can you not pronounce the simplest word in the way God meant it to be spoken, don't touch that flower with your rough hands you may damage it; and the goods once given to him for the price of the jibe were not to be returned, they were placed away for safekeeping, beyond Anthony's stern reach.

In the meantime, Anthony continued with his open-air classes in nature study with a bad conscience, scanning the woods and the lochside paths for his greatest fear, the one thing which chilled him under the eye of God; the chance passing of his father, to whom he was quite prepared to sacrifice Watchie in an instant as an unwelcome hanger-on unable to take the hint, a rough farmer's boy who would not go away, no matter how often asked.

One day, as Anthony was plucking and logging a specimen to be pressed, Watchie said to him,

Is't richt eneuch, yer faither has ye werkin at hame as weel as the school?

Anthony nipped the stalk, just above the second frill of leaves, with his thumb and fingernail.

I can't imagine why it should interest you.

The Laird sniffed Watchie's fingers intently, as if they had been smeared with chicken grease.

D'ye nae wish ye were ootside, fan ye're in at yer werk?

Anthony placed the bloom in the pages of his journal, closed it over gently, answering before he had the chance to stop himself.

Sometimes. Only when it's sunny.

Watchie frowned, pulled his hand away from the Laird.

Fit way's yer faither mak ye dee a' yon werk?

Anthony stood up, held the book in his hand pressed against his reference book. For a moment he looked down on Watchie, smiled wickedly.

Fit way, he mimicked, fit way. Can't you ever ask a proper question?

Watchie looked down at the caps of his boots. The breeze aroused his hair, lifted it away from his scalp and replaced it in disarray.

Dinna talk tae me like I'm a feel.

Anthony laughed.

Then don't talk like a fool.

Watchie felt the fire seep into his face, just as he dared to

look up at Anthony. Anthony shrugged, no blame of his, and
said,

I must work, because I'm going to university when I'm
older.

Watchie was puzzled.

Fit's yon, universty?

Anthony let down a sigh as if on a plumb-line.

It's where men of learning go when they're old enough to
study. I shouldn't think your father will have told you anything
about it.

Watchie shook his head.

Yon's fit way ye dee a' yon werk? Tae gang awa tae
universty?

Anthony nodded, walked a little way ahead around the
lochside.

You have to work to go to university. It's the only way to
do it.

Watchie fell into step behind Anthony, treading in his cleared
path of flattened grass.

I couldna be deein wi yon, he said, werkin jist tae dee mair werk.

Anthony laughed.

That's why you'll never go to university,

and that was all there was to it, as Anthony forged ahead
through the thick grass, leaving Watchie to tread in his steps.

After one week of meetings by the lochside, it was Watchie
who first of all found the cause of their last disagreement,
growing wild just beyond the margin of the loch, a plant he
recognized well, as would any child in the village of Aberlevin.
He cried out in joy to see it, and ran over to stand under its
thick trunk of fibres, shaded by its parasol of clustered florets,
held out from the trunk and up to the sun by thin green ribs.
Not many grew taller than Watchie himself, but the ones which
did grew exceptionally tall, taller even than Anthony, as if in
mimickry of its cousin the tree, which it passingly resembled.
Watchie stared up at the plant as if at a friend of long standing,
and announced to Anthony with a certain amount of pride,

I ken fine eneuch the name o' yon cratur.

Anthony walked over to him, slowly and without enthusiasm, in an elaborate pantomime of boredom.

All right, then, tell me its name.

Watchie drew himself tall, took a breath.

Yon's a pluffer.

The disintegration of Anthony's expression into mockery was as slow as the collapse of a glacier; his face growing top-heavy with disbelief, finally too heavy to sustain the weight of it, cracking into a grin which displayed all of his teeth, laughing and each syllable of laughter raining on Watchie's head like a slippage of shale,

That isn't what it's called at all,

and Watchie, confused and hurt, rallied,

My faither says . . .

Anthony severed it with a stroke,

Your father is not a man of learning. The correct name for the plant is hogweed.

Now Watchie stood in some confusion, because his father had been careful to tell him all about the trap the pluffers held for the unwary. They were tempting plants for many genera-tions of children, for when you carved a length of stalk from the body of the trunk, you would find it to be hollow, and an ideal instrument of mischief, ready to be packed with a charge of seed barley at one end and held to the lips, where pluff! a stout breath and the shot might rattle off the domed hat of a constable, or sting the face of any village puritan who chased you down from trees while searching for horse chestnuts. Many children had abused the power of nuisance afforded by the pluffer (or the hogweed, if we must listen to Anthony) over the years, and Wullie himself told Watchie that he had saved a young sparrow from the vicious claws of a garden tiger once with a single shot from his pluffer stem, catching the cat in the flank and causing it to leap up and yell as if it had been branded; he laughed richly to remember its face when its toy took to the wing and fled out of reach. But Watchie also remembered his father's warning, that he was not to cut the stem, or touch a stem which had been broken, because this was how many children had also been found out for their pranks; the injured trunk bled a thick milk, and where the milk touched the skin, over the course of a number of hours, there would develop a terrible sore rash, a fire and an itch almost beyond endurance, a taint of guilt seared on the lips and the hands, the crime invoking its own punishment. In point of fact, the sap was an accomplice to the irritation, and not the culprit; for blame, we must look to the invisible spectrum, the ultraviolet rays spun into the weave of sunlight, and which found the sap an ideal medium for penetration, a bridgehead through to the affected skin beneath. But this was yet to be discovered; Wullie's warning to his son still held true, that the milk of the stem was to be avoided, and Watchie had never so much as touched a broken pluffer, and was even wary approaching one whole.

Here was Anthony's mistake, challenging the wisdom of Watchie's father once too often, and for this time Watchie was having none of it.

Aye, and fit way does yer faither ken a' aboot fit he's nae had a'thin a-dee wi?

Anthony stood fast for a moment. He felt a pain, the pain of memory, a lash across his bare palms. When he next looked at Watchie, mindful of the presence of the Laird sniffing through the nearby fibres of grass, it was with the smile of the fox, his eyes as cold as twilight.

Come with me, he said, walking towards the forest. We'll see if your father has a name for this.

Anthony stopped Watchie in front of a particularly high elm tree, standing deep inside the half darkness of the lace of branches. He pointed up, and said,

There. Did your father tell you what that is?

Watchie sighted along Anthony's arm; he was pointing at a groin between branch and trunk, and Watchie's head was drawn back at an uncommon angle to follow the direction. Nesting there was a goitre, bloated to the size of a football, thick and textured as roughly as the wood it was anchored to, though not made of wood, that much Watchie could tell as he approached it from underneath. There was a strange sound in the air, one that Watchie had never heard before, a monotone of great power, contained as if in a jar, impatient for liberation.

I havena seen onythin like yon afore,

he said, and Anthony smiled.

See. Your father doesn't know everything, after all.

Watchie reached above his head, touching the cool and fluted bark of the tree, looked up at the growth.

Fit is't?

Anthony walked a little away, stopped before another elm.

Let's bring it down, where we can have a proper look at it.

He bent down and picked from the earth a number of sharp flinty stones, leaving their craters behind in the dark soil. Watchie trotted over beside him, followed complacently by the Laird. Anthony drew back his arm to cast the first stone; it reached the top of its arc far below the growth, sliding between two lower branches and coming to land with a soft impact on the earth beyond. His second stone ticked harmlessly from the trunk, dropping into the fork of the roots. The third clambered too high, deflecting off the bark, lost to sight past the mesh of leaves. Watchie laughed,

Man, man, we'll be here for the nicht gin ye canna dee better than yon.

Anthony held his hand out with the remaining stones resting in the palm,

Perhaps you might care to try, if that's so.

Watchie had the stones from Anthony's hand in a moment,

Aye, I will that,

he said, and pitched the first with all the strength he could spare. It sailed a little too far to the right; but the second was a sweeter and more satisfying cast altogether, running to the growth as if in a groove which had been especially carved in the air to accommodate it, with a perfect rainbow trajectory which was lovely to behold. Watchie turned around to claim his triumph from Anthony; but to his surprise he found that the older boy was no longer there, and that the Laird was padding away further into the forest, as if in a half-pursuit checked by the presence of his young master.

The stone fractured the crust of the growth as easily as it might have trepanned an egg. It ravaged the rooms and corridors of the wasps' nest, ending its strike in the queen's chamber, and decimating the fat and blowsy body of the reigning monarch; but in her last moments of life she signed a chemical declaration of war on the regicide, a slight vapour which was quite enough to enrage her soldiers and cause them to foam over the lip of the rupture, dancing in the air around the nest. Watchie stood and stared as more of the wasps gathered about the growth like a dark and ponderous cloud, and he realized only then what he had done, what he had been tricked into doing.

Watchie ran towards the clearing by the loch, where he remembered it to be, thrown by collision with the trees, the Laird scampering beside him and finally ahead, as the cloud followed the living scent of the only creature near enough to have murdered their queen.

XI

The doctor's counsel was that only time would diminish the grudge of the wasps' stings which had taken root inside the loon's veins, and that no liniment or vinegar rub on earth would be sufficient to help him now. Jeannie thanked Dr Farquharson for coming so promptly and so far out to examine her son, and offered him tea in the kitchen, which he refused gracefully despite Jeannie's subtlest of pressurings, avoiding with good manners any ill feeling which might have been caused by his taking to the road so soon after Jeannie had removed his fee from the tea tin and slipped it into his hand. Wullie drove him back to the village as he had driven him to Smallbrae, with his Gladstone bag perched on the seat of the gig beside him, facing the run of the journey, stabilizing himself against the roll of the carriage on the wicked cobbles.

You'd be surprised how often I'm called upon to treat victims of wasp stings, Mister Leckie,

called the doctor over the steady clatter of Blackie's hooves. Wullie replied with the correct politeness,

Aye, I would that,

but he was busy in the pondering of another problem, as the doctor continued,

Many people don't know what a wasps' nest looks like when they find it.

Wullie did not reply. Dr Farquharson shifted in his seat for a better purchase on the slippery leather, and tried again.

William will be quite all right, Mr Leckie. I cannot promise that he will have the most comfortable of nights, but rest assured, as I said to your wife, he'll be fine in a couple of days.

Wullie seemed to be voicing an answer to a conversation he was having in himself when he said,

I dinna ken fit the loon did, tae be stung by sic a puckle o' waasps as yon.

Farquharson shrugged, though Wullie couldn't see it.

It's easily enough done, Mr Leckie. As I said, not many people know what a wasps' nest looks like. William's only, what, eight years of age?

Wullie looked briefly over his shoulder before tending to the road once again.

Fit way, he said, d'ye ken he's been at a bike o' them?

Farquharson smoothed back a tendril of displaced hair.

By the sheer number of stings, Mr Leckie. He must have found a nest to have received that many.

Wullie frowned. It wasn't as if Watchie had never seen a wasp before, for there were enough of them grazing on the warm compost of rinds and clippings, enough to concern Wullie and Jeannie both into warning their son not to even point at the gaudy, fascinating insects, that their bodies held as if in a sheath a ferocious spike which hurt in the pricking; and Wullie could not believe that his son would touch or rouse one knowing what he did about them, what he had been told again and again. But the mysterious paper ball of a wasps' bike, that he could believe, seeing as if there Watchie approaching the curious object, stroking the growth with a finger; wishing himself away from the picture before he felt the need to snatch Watchie back from the angry humming nest.

As Wullie neared the top of North Street, he remembered seeing Jamie Watts in the farmyard, standing against the wall of the chaumer, and he remembered also the expression on the lean face, nothing as intense as a smile, the gentler satisfaction perhaps, like the enjoyment of a good meal; when Dr Farquharson arrived in the yard, this was the second time that Wullie had seen such a smile, the first being when Dodie Mearns turned his back on Smallbrae to find his employment elsewhere. No one else had seen the loon from behind the shutters of the byre, it seemed to Wullie, and he had much to occupy him in those days when a generous surplus of milk went souring in the churns; but now, with the time to think about the meaning of

Watts's smile, and the pains of his own son, Wullie found himself holding a fine resentment within his breast, and in silence he let the doctor out just in front of his surgery home, thanking him briefly for his time while the doctor thanked him in turn for the ride back. Wullie turned the gig around in the street, hauling a bit roughly on the reins and causing Blackie to whicker and complain at his unaccustomed rough handling, and on the way back to the farm he called to mind more and more the sneer on the face of Jamie Watts, and how he always seemed to see it at the times of the greatest trouble for the farm.

Watchie wakened from a night of feverish sleep and into a clearer realm of pain diminished, shapes forming into solid focuses and the light from the window no longer pricking his eyes as if they were bubbles in a milk pail. With Jeannie's help he was able to sit up in his bed, and the relief on her face was enough to bring them both comfort, as he grinned against the pain, shocked to see his hands doubled in size, each finger having the girth of a small sausage and the arm which held them as thick as a sapling trunk; but his mother smoothed the hair away from his face and told him not to worry, that the swelling would reduce in time, that he would soon be well enough to stand up and eat properly, she had cooked in her cauldron a hot and fortifying stew of the best beef and vegetables especially for him, to help his recovery. Peggy came in after that, to show him the warm jumper she had begun to knit the evening previously for when winter shut its teeth on the village, dropping as if so much scrap wool the recreational cardigan she had been calling forth between her needles to make this special present for her grandson, almost out-fussing Jeannie in her concern for the loon's health. There was Aal Wullie, followed in by the Laird, who together had been the day's heroes, Aal Wullie hearing the barking of his old friend across the fields as he waited by the furrows to scatter the looting of the crows with air-bursts of his shotgun. Not that this was any old shepherd's tale, told over a glass of fine malt, of faithful dogs pacing the miles to find help for the master's sprained ankle, not at all; the Laird escaped the wasps entirely without injury, his speed carrying him beyond the stricken Watchie and his dappled coat protecting him from the worst of the stings, waiting patiently by the side of the loch while his little master danced erratically on the frontier of the wood, assailing himself, not thinking to fall into the nearby water to cleanse the wasps from him. The Laird ran a little further ahead with each spurt that Watchie put on, not recognizing the game but willing enough to participate, hurling himself through the grass and waiting again to be caught up, and it was in this way, following the dog as he had done so many times before, never quite advancing far enough to reach out and touch the Laird for the comfort he needed but always stumbling in pursuit, that Watchie made gradual and faltering progress towards the farm, bringing them close enough for Aal Wullie to hear laced through the cata-strophic echoes of his shotgun the plain bark of the Laird. Aal Wullie turned to settle the fur on the Laird's back, freckled as it was with burrs, and it was only after a moment or two of the Laird's energetic greeting that Aal Wullie realized that Watchie, never far behind the dog, was nowhere to be seen. Aal Wullie did not rouse the household, as was his first inclination, but instead spoke low into the dog's ear, awa efter the loon, my Laird, awa efter him, following as the Laird found his game extended beyond his best hopes, probing through the grass until the smell of the young master drew him along to the free land between the loch and the Leckie farm, just at the rump of the Deil's Shieling, where Aal Wullie found Watchie in the thatch of the long grass, deprived of all awareness and indeed fighting against his grandfather's best efforts to lift him, hurling his fists without strength and occasionally landing them against his own body as if to torment himself.

Watchie began to feel much better, blessed by Aal Wullie's toothless grin of sheer relief, and by the Laird's uncomplicated cheer at his bedside, and when the old man said to him with not a trace of concern in his voice,

Aye, wee Wullie, ye'll soon eneuch be up and wearin yer beets and awa oot afore lang, we'll a' see tae thon, never fear, he smiled as much as his distorted face would allow, and ruffled the mane of the Laird as he mounted the counterpane just in front of him, paws on the blanket and muzzle raised to stare at the wee master.

He had a few moments to himself after Aal Wullie and the Laird left the room, during which the aching of his muscles resumed, drawn into the vacuum left by the want of distraction. Through the window upon which Jeannie had gently parted the curtains earlier that morning, he could see tiles of greying sky, across which occasional birds swam, the paths of their flight warped by the running of the glass, making them appear like images seen on water. There was a soft knock on the door, and after a short pause Wullie came into the room, stopped by the bedside. He was smiling, a shallow and distant smile, calm over a raging depth. He had a large and heavy book under his oxter, pinned to his body by the arm, enough of a weight to require effort on his part to keep it there. He stood beside the bed, about where the Laird had hopped up for a better look at Watchie, and placed the book on his son's lap, a dead mass holding the loon's weakened body down as effectively as a millstone.

Ye can hae a wee read o' thon, he said, files ye're gettin better.

Watchie ran his enlarged fingers over the surface of the book. It had a good and satisfying feel to it, even through the dulled instruments of his fingertips. The cover was thick and decorated with peacock's-tail colours grained like the veins of marble, though altogether more gaudy, and there was no title stamped on it. He manoeuvred the book into a place of greater comfort, where he could see it more clearly, and opened its heavy portal with a little difficulty, past the plain frontispiece with an inscription in extravagant fountain pen which he could not read properly, the writing flourished like a lariat. He opened the book further, and found illustrations, simple line drawings which pleased his eye; some were of solid items of furniture, reduced to dismemberment for the sake of clarity, similar to the anatomical illustrations he had seen in Anthony's book of botany, with progressions to demonstrate their assembly into cabinets and dressers, bureaux and tables; others were depictions of strange mechanisms, once again their working parts laid out into patterns, and Watchie turned the pages for more, draining each line drawing of its detail. Wullie sat on the bed,

Yon's the book I used tae mak the fiddle, and the cabinet, and yon wee crib ye slept in fan ye were a bairn,

he said, and Watchie smiled.

A' yon things in the book?

Wullie smiled in reply.

Na na, there's far ower muckle in the book for a man tae dee in his hale life. Na na, jist a few, like.

Before Watchie lost himself in the maze of fascination with the turn of each page, Wullie said,

Fit went on, Wulliam? Fit way'd ye cam across a waasps' bike?

Watchie looked up from the book.

I didna ken it was a waasps' bike fan I . . .

Wullie's eyebrows raised. Watchie halted suddenly, though why he did not know, perhaps the memory of some trust Anthony had placed in him. He looked down into the crevasses of the sheets, mumbled,

Twa big loons tellt me tae dee't.

Wullie leaned over, his voice low, insistent.

Fit tae dee, Wulliam?

Watchie looked away, towards the cream-white wall.

They tellt me tae fling a steen at the bike. I didna ken fit it was.

Wullie took a deep breath, tensed suddenly.

Did ye nae think fit way they were efter ye tae fling a steen at it?

Watchie shrugged, painfully.

I didna ken fit it was,

he repeated. Wullie nodded.

Aye, weel, ye'll ken fine eneuch the noo. It's jist a dampt feel'd dee as ithers tell him, mind ye that.

He softened when he saw that Watchie had a pool of tears

breaking its banks at the corner of his eyes. He had no handkerchief to offer, so he let Watchie use the cuffs of his gown to wipe them away. More gently this time, he said,

Fa was't? Fa were the twa loons, Wulliam?

Watchie remembered his oath of secrecy, given to his treacherous friend after their first parting. He remembered Anthony's last words before he took the road towards the village. Never tell anyone we met, not even your parents. If my father knows you've been talking to me, even if he knows that we met, he could make your time in class very unpleasant. Do you remember the time he made you read out the poem in front of the whole class? Do you remember what happened then? He could make you read out poetry every day, if he wanted to.

I dinna ken them, said Watchie, they werena frae the toun.

Wullie stared at him for a moment.

Ye've nae seen them aboot the toun afore?

Watchie shook his head. Wullie continued his stare, his brows drawn low upon his forehead by the weight of disbelief.

They'll dee't again, the loons, gin ye canna say tae me fa was't.

Watchie remembered the hot eruption before the furrows of faces; still he shook his head. Wullie stood up, feeling powerless against his son's silence.

Awa ye and read ye yer book,

he said, and turned away to leave.

Watchie was left in peace for most of the day by the work of the farm, and this gave him the opportunity to give the book a much closer examination, left as he was all alone in the room with nothing else to look at but the static contents of the window frame and the want of ornaments on the tallboy. But it was no labour for him to turn each white page, for the book proved to be a compendium of arts and crafts of all kinds; further, it was in fact a weekly magazine which had been laced and bound together with great proficiency, Watchie guessed, by the man or woman who had signed the frontispiece, and when he found a chapter on bookbinding scattered throughout the pages, one lesson to a weekly instalment, it became clear exactly where the unknown first owner had gleaned his or her expertise from. There was more in the book than could possibly have been read at one sitting, but Watchie had much time to spend, and he was speeded through the pages by the fact that the words were almost impossible for him to read, being somewhat long and technical and beyond his present comprehension. But the illustrations, they were meat for his eyes, clarity and simplicity themselves, in which many items of ornament and furnishing were shown in plan, first of all facing the reader, then in profile, their dimensions marked on a grid; designs for armoires and chests of drawers spun about all possible lines of speculation, rendered with the eye of the anatomist, wheelbarrows and ottomans picked as cleanly as skeletons, stripped of their wooden cladding. It was interesting enough to Watchie to see how these puzzles became useful structures; but what he found endlessly fascinating, and most mysterious of all, were the depictions of strange mechanisms, alive with antennae and cylinders in pirouette, parts in constant animation which thundered and blasted steam through all their apertures, moving in his imagination, great beasts breathing vapour like dragons, all there for the construction, possessed in his hands. During his convalescence, as the pain slowly left him, the book was never closed on his lap, even at the end of the working day, when all the workers from the chaumer came to visit before sitting down to Cathie Loudon's dinner, all except one. He smiled when Andy McGrath took the jew's harp from his pocket to play him a tune which had the bounce and rollick of a maritime shanty without, Watchie noticed, the wheeze of absent Dodie's melodion to root the melody firmly in the soil; his mother had always told him to smile when people were good to him, but now his impatience to be back in the solitary company of his new friend made his smile false and deceitful, and he looked secretly to the pages of his book from time to time as the song unravelled before him so as not to lose the clue among the tangle of the music, running the tips of his fingers around the perimeter of the book, as if to convince himself that it would not hide away like a traitor while he was being distracted from it.

The men rose to the voice of Cathie Loudon at the bottom of the stairs,

Yer denner's ready, awa tae the chaumer, my bonny loons!

and wished Watchie all the best for his recovery, assuring him that they would return at the same time the next day; but on their way down, it was Alistair Loudon who remarked to the others,

The pair wee mannie's affa silent-lookin, I dinna think he's richt yet,

while the others nodded, passing Jeannie on their way through the kitchen, nodding as if there was nothing the matter, leaving till the dinner table their own thoughts on Watchie's impenetrable distance.

Watchie was not deemed well enough on the Sunday to leave his bed, although the swelling was slowly deflating and the redness was calming down to its more natural pink; and Peggy it was who chose to stay behind in case of any deterioration, placing herself in front of the fire with her jumper which was nearing completion, her needles outstripping the tick of the grandfather clock.

While Watchie stayed at home with his book, and Peggy sealed the open sleeves of her jumper, Wullie was about to find out the reason for the mysterious force which had caused him to cross out the names of a number of his best customers, and the messenger was none other than the Revd Lyle, who stood at the door of the kirk as the congregation slowly teased itself into tidy skeins which spun out the length of the village. He laid a hand on Wullie's passing shoulder, and asked if he would be so good as to join him inside the presbytery for a moment, he wouldn't keep Wullie long, and Wullie nodded, pleased to be asked in to the hearth, confused as to why; but he asked Jeannie and Aal Wullie to wait for a while outside by the gig, and walked the regular adjacent path which curved into the high shaded door along beds of open rose blossoms growing in lime-enriched soil. In the living-room of the presbytery Wullie waited on his feet, and looked around him to the walls, to the oil paintings of previous residents, the edge taken from their bright colouring by years of intrusive sunlight, each face as grim and unmoving as the face of the God they had served in life. Wullie remembered one of the subjects at least, the Revd Caitlin, positioned near the window so that the light drained away from his already pale features, the last resident before Lyle, a kind and blithe man whose louring wife discouraged many visitors. He also had enough time before the Reverend entered the room to look at the display of clocks which sat on the shelving, brass carriage clocks, clocks preserved like items of taxidermy under domes of glass, ornate houses with hatch doors through which carved wooden cuckoos protruded like impudent tongues to signal the hour and the half-hour.

When the Reverend came to greet Wullie, he was transformed from his ceremonial self into a more relaxed suit of black, and he shook Wullie's hand as if they were meeting for the first time, smiling briefly in the manner of one laden with grave news. He said,

As promised, I won't hold you back, Mr Leckie.

The Reverend stood in front of Wullie, his hands laced in front of him. He took a breath.

I have recently had a conversation with the Revd Goodbody, who is, I'm sure you're aware, my colleague in the Free Presbyterian Church. Do you have any idea what such a conversation may have been about, Mr Leckie?

Wullie shook his head,

Na, Reverend, I dinna ken at a'.

The Reverend nodded.

I thought as much.

He then began to explain to Wullie the content of that conversation, which had occurred on the day of Watchie's encounter with the nest of wasps. Wullie was roused to fury as the Revd Lyle unfolded before him the intrigue which had been kept from his knowledge for so long, and for a moment he was inclined to ridicule the idea that anyone should grace the accusation with a moment's belief; but he stood before the Reverend quietly enough, and when his chance came he rooted himself firmly before the man of God, and answered with perfect truth that it was all a hillock of lies, and that anyone who cared could come to visit the farm, could even leave at that moment, and see with their own eyes. The Revd James Lyle nodded and smiled,

I must confess that I expected as much, Mr Leckie. I must confess also that I suspected even more when I learned that Mrs Jamieson was the source of these rumours.

Wullie let out a breath,

Yon wumman's touched, she's a richt menace wi yon tongue o' hers.

Although, added the Reverend, to be fair to Mrs Jamieson, I understand from the Revd Goodbody that she was merely the one who spread the rumours. I'm sorry to say that she was not the one who started them.

Wullie emerged from the presbytery a silent and much-subdued man. Jeannie asked him what the Reverend had said, but he would not reply to her, simply shook his head like one in profound mourning and mounted the board of the gig, the last to leave the kirk. He flicked the rein to set Blackie in motion, and on the way back to the farm, he spoke not one word unless spoken to, and even then gave out answers carved back to the necessary and no more. He ate his dinner in a silence different to those the family had become accustomed to, holding his counsel to himself; and when night fell, and Watchie had been left by the light of his candle to go to sleep, Wullie would not answer his wife when she asked him,

Wullie, fit's a-dee? ye're giein me a proper worry,

turning away from her so that she was speaking to his back only.

The morning after, Wullie wakened prepared for more than simply his daily rounds. Jeannie had already been dressed for some time, and was ready to serve Wullie his breakfast of porridge, which he ate quickly and without fuss, cleaning the bowl down to the glaze, pushing it aside and refusing a cup of tea. He stood up, quickly shrugged himself into his jacket, and left by the kitchen back door, to the astonishment of Peggy, whose hair was stroked by the breeze as he passed, looking up at her daughter-in-law as if she had let a stranger into the house.

Wullie knocked with force upon the door of the chaumer, and stood patiently waiting for the door to be answered by Cathie Loudon. Through the threshold he could see the workers gathered at table, eating the porridge that Cathie had boiled up for them in her black cauldron. Aloud he said to Cathie,

Guid morn tae ye, Cathie. I'll hae a wee werd wi Jamie, gin ye dinna mind.

Jamie looked up from his breakfast like a dog recognizing its name. He stood up from the plain bench after a moment's hesitation, walked over to the door; Cathie stepped aside to resume her place beside her husband, her eyes, like all the others in the room, drawn to the heat of the confrontation. Jamie stood in the frame of the door, ready, as he thought, to receive his orders for the day, after all it was approaching hairst, so much work was there to be done; but when Wullie said,

Gaither thegither yer things, Jamie Watts, ye'll nae werk a meenit langer at my fairm,

Watts's eyes became as brittle as ice in a moment, and through them Wullie saw the fact of the orra loon's guilt; but his back was turned to his fellow workers, and with a smile which flirted with insolence, Jamie recovered himself and replied,

Fit reason hae ye tae ask me tae lee yer fairm?

Wullie breathed in deeply, made himself relax the tension in his arms.

Ye ken fine eneuch, Jamie, and I'd be gratefu' tae ye gin ye'd jist tak fit belangs tae ye and gang awa wi yer ill manners tae anither fairm.

Jamie stared evenly at Wullie for a long time, then cast over his shoulders to the other workers at the table,

D'ye hear him, my loons? he canna say fit way I'm tae lee my werk.

Alistair Loudon answered for them all,

Aye, Mr Watts, fine we're hearin,

a reply so nicely poised on the balance that neither Wullie

nor Jamie knew upon which side his concern fell, nor even in which direction it was inclined. Wullie coughed gently, then said,

I can say, richt eneuch. I can tell ye fit the Revd Lyle tellt tae me, efter he had a wee talk wi the Revd Goodbody o' yer ain congregation, Jamie.

Watts was caught like a moth in the brightness of Wullie's sudden knowledge around which he'd danced for so long; but he drew himself up as if aggrieved,

Aye, and fit way does yer meenister ken a' aboot me?

Wullie struck.

Fine does the Revd Lyle ken a' aboot ye, Mr Watts. Yer meenister tellt him a' aboot fit ye said tae Mrs Jamieson, a' the unchristian lies ye tellt tae her aboot the fairm. Or would ye mak worse lies, and deny tae me that ye said it?

Watts stood his ground, folded his arms over in front of him.

Ye're ca'in me a liar tae my face, Mr Leckie.

Wullie nodded,

I am that, Jamie, I'm ca'in ye a liar, and I'm askin that ye tak yer lies tae some ither place.

Watts's sudden and startling move pulled Andy McGrath and Alistair Loudon out of their seats, and drove Wullie back a single pace with the shock of it; without warning Jamie's fists were up and out, one held before his face and one held before him, his legs crooked for suspension, and he cried,

I sweer, I'll hae ony man fa says yon o' me!

But Wullie called,

Sit ye doon, the baith o' ye,

not to Watts, but to Alistair and Andy, before they could lay restraining hands upon Jamie, who held his pose far longer than his action demanded; so angular was his posture that he began to resemble not a pugilist, but rather a bicycle frame robbed of its wheels and stood upright, with its saddle displaced to the prow of the frame instead of the handles. Wullie stared beyond the great boulder of Jamie's fist into his eyes while Andy and Alistair stood ready and tensed for the first hurling of a blow in anger; but Wullie was taking measurements of Jamie from the constancy of his stare, ignoring his leading hand, and when he had finished his assessment, he smiled at Watts and said evenly,

I'd nae mair fecht wi a craven wee coo'rd like yersel fa'd look tae ithers tae pu' him awa frae fit he sterts than I'd clart my hands wi the shite o' the kye, beggin yer pardon, Cathie. Be awa frae here in an oor, Master Watts. I'll hae yer wages ready for then.

At that moment, Wullie spun on his heel, leaving Jamie Watts standing there like a statue of pipe-cleaners behind the threshold, draining all meaning from the pose and causing Cathie Loudon to laugh at his vacuous threat, her laughter igniting that of the other workers in the chaumer. Jamie shook the creases from his work outfit, and mumbled,

I thocht he widna tak on a real man,

on his way to sit on the bed.

Within the hour, after the workers had left the chaumer still warm with the memory of Jamie Watts's great loss of face, the former orra loon had gathered together the clothes Cathie had laundered for him, as was a duty of her employ. He placed them meticulously inside a sack of tough canvas, and on top of them he placed his Bible of black morocco leather he had read so closely on the day his mother died. He was fairly quickly packed, but still he sat on the edge of his bed, staring at Cathie as she cleaned the breakfast dishes at the sink, causing her to turn every so often and fend aside his eyes while he sat beyond his time in the silence of the room. Finally he stood up, hoisting his canvas sack over his shoulder, and went to the door; but before leaving he said to her,

Cweans the like o' yersel're aye makkin trouble for the likes o' me.

Cathie's head stayed bent over the sink.

Aye, and gin I'd said onythin o' yer behaviour tae Alistair, ye'd've been awa frae this fairm mair the sooner.

Jamie laughed, a sound like an icicle loosened from its mooring.

Ye liked it fine, ye hizzie.

Now Cathie rounded on him, a butter knife in her hand.

I liked it that fine, yer heid was dirlin frae my ladle on it for a week efter. Awa tae hell wi ye.

Watts laughed all the louder,

Fare ye weel, my bonnie lassie,

he said in quotation from a ballad, then closed the door behind him.

Wullie was waiting with a cloth purse in his hand, containing all the silver Watts had rightfully earned during that portion of the six-month. Watts did him the insult of insisting that it should be counted into his hand, which Wullie did gladly, to the last penny. Watts, satisfied, dropped the coins into the purse, pulling the drawstrings in opposite directions to seal it, placing it into his pocket. Without a word, he slipped past Wullie alongside the house and in a few strides he was on to the road leading towards Aberlevin, and from there Wullie cared not where he went. Wullie let out a breath which seemed to have been pent over the course of several months; but the clouds were beginning to creep lazily across the sky, and soon enough Wullie was ready to see his good fresh milk put into pails and churns in time for their delivery. Before he left, he went up the stairs to see his son, who sat upright against the white pillows.

Fit way, said Watchie, has Jamie gaed awa?

Wullie smiled, broadly, under a deep unmeant frown.

Yon's an affa fine guess, he said, for a loon fa didna see't.

Watchie smiled too, a match for his father.

I cam oot my bed tae look oot the windae.

Wullie laughed, a sound Watchie had not heard for many a month, it seemed.

Aye weel, he said, ye're richt there, wee Wulliam, Jamie's awa. But I've my werk tae dee the noo, and it'd tak far ower lang tae taal it.

That evening, Andy McGrath came to the door at the back with his jew's harp in his hand and a wide smile, and he was welcomed in by the hearthside along with Alistair and Cathie Loudon, and before too long the whisky bottle was out, the good Glenlevin malt to fire the palate, and then from out of the cabinet and out of its cloak of chamois came Wullie's prize fiddle, newly stringed that very evening before dinner after a visit to the hardware store during his deliveries. It was never said by anyone that the sudden gathering was a celebration, nor particularly was it; but soon enough Wullie's fiddle was singing as warmly as ever, Alistair and Cathie were dancing on the floor with their lightest tread, and even Aal Wullie was tempted away from his full glass of whisky for a dance with his daughter-in-law, while Peggy clapped in time to the rhythm, and one could even forget for a moment that something was wanting in the blend, a spice which had enriched the sound of it in times gone by.

The cream of the music drifted up the stairs, through the closed door of Watchie's room, where it found the loon sitting by candlelight in his bed, his feet tapping as if by reflex under the sheets, causing them to move as if covering a trapped mouse; but his eyes were claimed by his father's open book, by the dissections of cold, denatured metal, meshing wheels, craft in motion.

XII

Wullie did his best to interest Watchie in the business of the farm in the small time he had with the loon during the days of summer; but even he had to admit to Jeannie, in the evenings when Watchie shunned the company of the fireside to run upstairs after his dinner to read more of his book, that it was becoming a struggle teaching him anything. The years had seen him sprout like corn, not much in size but in demeanour, and Wullie had no more idea how to engage the interest of this perfect little stranger than if he had been a dog to whom he could suggest but with whom he could not communicate. The Laird, too, found Watchie a sadly different creature to deal with, no longer given to riot or dances in the yard, and soon enough the Laird found himself once again companion to his real master Aal Wullie, who had never been jealous of his old friend's interest in his grandson, realizing that he had not the strength in his legs to satisfy his dog's natural fire for the chase; he greeted the Laird as if he had never strayed from his side, and said into his ear, aye, my loon, yer wee freen's graa'ed a bittie, ye'll jist hae tae mak dee wi an aal bit mannie like me, and the Laird thrashed the air with his tail, walking to heel beside the man who had been his master all along, slowing his pace to that appropriate for an old man's dog. In this way, the Laird learned quicker than Wullie that he was dealing with an entirely differ-ent loon than he had in the days before the wasp summer, for Wullie still had his hopes and his dream that in Watchie he had found his bequest of the farm, and in pursuit of this Wullie was quite ruthless. Watchie was not allowed to stay in his room with that damned book for a minute longer than necessary, especially on the clear summer days when Wullie had something to show him, when the loon trailed behind Wullie, bound to the leash of his father's enthusiasm, trying not to show the resentment at the parting which his father had never seen outside of the graveyard.

Wullie had not the skill in teaching of a Mr Clarke, which was maybe all to the good considering, but he was at least as adept in noticing all the signs of an attention which had taken to paths of its own, the eyes as expressionless as vacant glass, dimmed of inspiration, the body there on sufferance, his lectures delivered to an echoing room. But day in day out Wullie persevered with his reluctant pupil: perhaps today would be the day that he might find the light of fascination kindling in the grate, and he never slackened, taking his son on trips to the village on the board of his wagon, leading him to the fields to examine the sprouting of the grain on the stalk while Aal Wullie did his slow sentinel's patrol with the shotgun on the borders; and not once did he sense that Watchie was ever there in anything but presence, much to his regret and impotent annoyance.

Only once did Watchie show any interest in a single thing which Wullie took the trouble to show him, and that was when Hercules, Archie Wallace's prize breeding bull, was taken to the farm to fertilize one of the dairy herd, a deal which had cost Wullie a small amount of silver which Watchie saw given into the hands of the experienced old farmer. Not long after Lady began to swell with the fruit of that afternoon's coupling, Jeannie herself began to experience a great discomfort, walking through the house as if in a dream, and after a few days of it she and Peggy knew enough of her own symptoms to declare to the household over dinner that there could be no mistake, she was expecting a baby, and that evening Wullie thrashed his fiddle to song with a wild joy that Watchie had never seen in his father before; and when Wullie came home the next day from his deliveries, he was happy to bear the abundant congratulations of each of his customers, to whom he had delivered the news with their morning milk. The news delighted Peggy even more, for now she had excuse enough to produce knitting by the ream, and plenty of time in which to do it, oatmeal-coloured clothes and cozies to keep the bairn warm, blankets for the cradle, as quickly as her imagination and her supple fingers could allow it. Aal Wullie became almost as solicitous as his son, making sure the fire was ready for Jeannie when she came into the living-room and building extra bricks of peat into the grate to give her more warmth, taking the obstacles from her path before she ever encountered them, pulling chairs out for her with a screech of their paws against the floorboarding, lifting from her arms pillars of used crockery from the dinner table, fussing like a nurse; but Jeannie thanked him kindly and said,

Faith, I'm nae seeck, I can dee a' yon for mysel.

Watchie found the whole thing a puzzle to him. His first thought was to consult his best friend on the subject, and he spent many long hours in his room with his vast encyclopedia, turning pages he had not seen yet in search of a clue as to why his mother was swelling around the middle, and what would happen when the baby was due to emerge; but it contained nothing of value to him, no diagrams of mothers gravid with child, nothing about the tender mechanisms of the flesh, and this omission caused Watchie to itch intolerably with the need to find out more about the reason for his mother's growth. He put the book to one side on the cover of his bed, and made his way downstairs quietly.

Jeannie was sitting heavily and alone in the living-room, in the fireside chair. Most of the rest of the farm was at its work, polishing and trimming and readying itself for the coming year, the promise of clean skies which Wullie could taste from the wind, the only guide Wullie had now that Mrs McAllister had refused his milk and the telltale of her arthritic joints, despite the best efforts of both the reverends to assure her that the reports had been in error. Aye, far aboots was the fire a' yon smoke cam frae? The deil's nae jist like oorsels, ye ken, Revd Goodbody, he'll taal nae truth gin a lie'd suit him better.

Watchie entered the room shyly and uncertainly, his head down but peering at his mother from under his brow, as if her slow transformation had altered her to the very heart, and indeed she had become more abrupt with her husband, though she was still infinitely patient towards Watchie, carefully so. Watchie had never seen the like of her as she was now, when he could hear from his room above as he spent the fireside evening in the company of his book, the music silenced in wreckage like the unholy quiet which follows the dropping of a plate, her voice shrieking like chalk mishandled on a blackboard, the door to the living-room opening and closing with a slam and her feet on the steps of the landing irregular as she carried herself and her burden into her bedroom; and the sound of her crying, a sound Watchie found as intolerable to listen to as the whimpering of the Laird drifting through the door, he always kept his own bedroom door open just a telling crack so that the fireside music could spin a slender thread to weave into the silence. Now his book of mysteries lay open before him, with no answer to his mother's misery, and within him was the need to comfort her as she had soothed to quietness the pains which had troubled him in his short time, like the venom of the wasps. But he was also afraid of her, or more precisely afraid of this change in her temper, and he had had enough experience of sudden turnings not to attempt to come near her during this time of unpredictability, so he remained in his room with his book, and listened to her crying alone, only able to feel sorry for her and to wish her better, for her own sake and the sake of the whole house, and also for his own peace of mind if truth be told.

It was a measure of the loon's curiosity, the cast of a plumb-line into unmapped depths, that he gathered all courage and sat in the empty seat opposite his mother on that day, gazing into the hearth to see the wan blue fire of the peat as it soaked into the dark tablets. From time to time he looked up at her, glances, a finger held up to the wind; but Jeannie's eyes were not to be so easily engaged, and she kept her stare fixed beyond Watchie, beyond the chair he was sitting in, a stare which took no information, gave nothing in return. For a while, there was only the crack of the fire as it digested a dense nugget of matter; then Jeannie seemed to take notice of Watchie's presence, recovering her sight, offering him a thin but deeply felt smile.

Watchie smiled a reply, and decided now was his time. He spoke like one pacing himself by inches the length of a projecting plank, trembling as he did so.

Ken fit way Lady had a wee calfie, a filie back, efter yon Hercules cam here?

Jeannie answered him as if through sleep.

Aye, Wulliam, I ken.

Watchie swallowed.

Is yon fit way my faither gied ye a bairn?

Jeannie's eyes widened in surprise, how quickly the loon had come to realize. She laughed, lightly.

Na na, nae jist like thon. We're nae beasts, like the kye nor the bulls. Ye canna dee yon till ye're merrit. Ye hae tae be merrit afore ye can mak a bairn. Ken fit I'm sayin, Wulliam?

Watchie nodded. Jeannie continued.

Ye see, the beasts canna be merrit under the sicht o' God, but we can lee them mak a wee calfie, ye see? And gin it's a loon calfie, yer faither'll sell it at the mart for siller, and gin it's a cwean calfie, like Lady had, he'll keep it till it graas, and he'll hae milk frae't, jist like the ither kye. D'ye ken the noo, Wulliam?

Watchie nodded, much more at his ease. But there was one outstanding puzzle, and so he said, with not a trace of guile,

Did my faither gie ye ony siller afore he gied ye the bairn?

Watchie sat in some confusion as his mother began to shake with laughter, the whole house rang with it, a broad capering laugh which danced in the rafters, and her eyes ran with tears which she wiped away with a handkerchief bundled into the sleeve of her blouse. In defence of his innocence, Watchie said,

My faither said he gied Erchie Wallace siller for the bull tae breed wi Lady,

which only made Jeannie laugh the louder, mopping her eyes and drawing breath in great whoops, smacking her thighs in delight at the conceit and leaving her quite unable to talk for long enough. Watchie remembered the laughter of his classmates as barbs piercing him, and shrank lower into his seat to escape it; but when all the fuel was spent, and Jeannie could laugh no more, she said kindly,

Yon isna the way o't at a', Wulliam,

and then without embarrassment began to describe the difference between the transaction of breeding and the act of love which had caused the bairn to take root inside her. She explained that cweans folded in where Watchie jutted out, and that this was how the seed was planted, that the joining of the two made a bairn; and Watchie listened politely to her, nodding while she spoke, suddenly aware of the existence of the member between his legs in a way he had never been before when its only reason for being fixed to his body had seemed to be to make water at the worst time, an agent of his humiliation. She took the greatest of care to make sure that Watchie understood that such acts between humans were only made decent by God's sealing of the couple in marriage, and Watchie nodded his understanding; but when Watchie came to ask if it was that which had planted himself inside her, this sanctified act of love between his father and herself, suddenly she grew tired of the questioning, and sat back into the armchair, lacing her hands over her full belly, saying,

I've tellt ye a' ye'll need, Wulliam, dinna ask ony mair,

and so Watchie, fearing the return of her temper, thanked her and went to his room to wonder why books like his almanac had seen fit to tell him none of this, when surely there was much that was miraculous about a creation that did not rely upon the craft of hands, fired in the secret kiln of his mother's belly for a nine-month.

Jessica was born at the time of sowing, a much less troubled affair than the birth of Watchie; she gave her mother plenty of warning, enough for Wullie to go and fetch Dr Farquharson and speed him up the cobbled road in the gig, the hood drawn up and over the shoulders as proof against the rain. Unlike Watchie, Jessica was born into an atmosphere of carbolic soap and the latest in antiseptics, into much more professional and brusque hands than those of Peggy. She was held upside down and smacked lightly on the back to make her catch her first breath, and she let out such a howl as you might think would claw the paint off the walls, causing Wullie to smile broadly as he waited for his messenger to come down from the top of the stairs. Peggy scurried down to find Wullie already at the door of the living-room,

It's a cwean, Wullie, she's affa bonnie,

and Wullie had no complaints about that, he had a daughter now and his wife was out of danger. It happened in the evening, so the workers were out of their chaumer and waiting too, the new orra loon Tommy Fothergill and Dodie's replacement John Allison standing with the older and loyal crew, and it was sensations of the Glenlevin all round while they waited for the doctor to come out of the room to tell them that everything was well and to receive his own whisky while Wullie went to see his wife and the bairn.

Watchie was there in wait too, remembering when Jeannie told him about his own birth; he had listened to the story with great interest, and when she told him of the pain which the first few stabs had caused her, he had looked to the ground and said that he was sorry, which delighted Jeannie into giving him an immensely comforting hug for the thought of it. He had listened to his mother's cries from the foot of the stairs, the whole house heard them and wished her soon free of the pain which gouged them from her, none more so than Watchie, who remembered his own pains of two years previously, and wondered at the suffering she must be enduring to give it such a voice. Wullie took his son by the shoulders, said,

Cam on, and we'll see yer mither and yer wee sester, the baith o's,

and Watchie was not keen at first, though he was curious enough to allow himself to be led up the gloom of the stairs to the seam of light about the bedroom door. Once inside, he saw that his mother was smiling wearily, and this comforted him a great deal, that the baby was in her arms, all parcelled up in one of Peggy's knitted blankets and writhing against Jeannie's gentle restraint. Both were plainly healthy, and the blush on Jeannie's face was cooling, much to Wullie's relief. She said to Watchie,

Cam nearer and say fine day tae yer wee sester, Wulliam,

and Watchie approached the bed without any of his father's awe, peering inside the blanket as if the bairn in its folds were no blood of his, as if looking at a doll in a toyshop window. She cried volubly at the first touch of his fingers on the hot skin of her face, and he leapt backwards at the vehemence of it, withdrawing his hand as if she were made of painted shell, but Jeannie reassured him,

She disna ken ye jist richt the noo, Wulliam, yon's fit's a-dee,

and he nodded, a little hurt by the rejection. Wullie said,

We're best tae lee yer mither and the bairn tae their sleep, Wulliam, they'll be affa tired,

and Watchie nodded again, and let his father lead him from the bedroom, from the piercing scent of medication which saturated it.

XIII

There was another christening, this time attended by Jeannie's mother and father, who arrived the day before with presents of cake for the dinner as if in apology for missing the last. There were iced fancies topped by a bud of cherry in paper cups, and rich madeira cakes with alternate strata of preserves and cream, and dense fruit cakes with their treasury of sultanas sealed in a sponge which tasted powerfully of rum. Nana Richie was fair laden down with all the products of her craft and ingenuity, for which she had received many special mentions and rosettes at fairs beyond count, all packed into old biscuit tins for the shipping, and carried into the kitchen with some reluctance by her husband, who Watchie could never remember smiling in an unguarded moment. In fact, Watchie rarely saw his maternal grandparents, living as they did half the width of the country away, as busy with their farm as Wullie was with his, and when they did appear for the odd New Year's eve, he was spoiled quite shamelessly by his nana, who fed him all the cake he could eat and would have fed him more if Jeannie had not been there to stop her. But a first look at granpa Richie would be enough to tell the tale of who most benefited from the art of her baking; for while she was still in fine shape, as able to do the work of the farm as she was when she was a cwean, it was her taciturn husband who had grown fat and blowsy, with jowls which shook over the rim of his collar as he took a full draught of his plain rosewood pipe. There he sat, occupying the honour seat in front of the fire as was only but right as a guest, content and pleasured by the company of his pipe, and when he opened his mouth it was not to speak but to release the smoke which had pent up there, moving only to knock the bowl of the pipe against the inside wall of the hearth and to reach into his jacket pocket for his leather pouch, plump with tobacco, with which to fill it. The smoke unravelled slowly and lazily into the air, and Watchie felt his eyes sting as it doubled on itself and drifted like light strong fabric, as perceptible as the matter of spiders' webs, the thin blue of weak shadows. And all the while not a glance did granpa Richie give to him, not even the slightest of kindnesses, while nana Richie gave to him and no one else slivers from the cakes which would be the pride of the table for tomorrow's dinner, each mouthful flavoured with his granpa's smoke which crept sinuously around the room, even causing the Laird to cough and splutter from his lair on the floor beside Aal Wullie, who had been evicted to one of the stools.

The talk which did pass between Wullie and his father-in-law was all cattle and breeding, not in the least interesting to Watchie, and he took the opportunity to kneel on the floor and stroke the fur of his old companion the Laird, who looked at him as if they were changed friends about to pass in the street as coolly as strangers. The talk which passed like the rush of the burn among nana Richie, her daughter and Peggy was all about the arts of the household, as Peggy held up for all to see the fluent produce of her knitting needles. Only Aal Wullie and Watchie were left with no one to talk to, as Aal Wullie chose not to speak to the man he had long ago considered to be a surly bugger, though he only ever said so to his wife when they were chambered in their bedroom.

After a while, the smoke grew as dense as curtain material, draping itself across the furnishings and the whole living-room in sheets, and Watchie found his eyes smarting from the strength of it, and so he stood up and went over to Jeannie and asked if he might be excused to go outside for a while. Jeannie saw the moisture in his eyes, and looked over with a slight frown to her father installed in the guest's chair, knowing full well that she had had to do the same many times during her growing life, and she smiled at her son and said that it was all right.

The air was blessedly cooler outside in the yard, and Watchie's eyes healed after a while; even the air reeking with the dung of the horses and the kye was purer than the foul clouds dispersed by his grandfather's pipe. The lamp in the kitchen window burned in its minaret of glass, and pressed gold leaf into the mud of the yard from its long cast, black around the rims of hoof and foot prints scored into the clay. Watchie could hear the Richies' pony neighing in the stables, deep in conversation with Jess and Jonah and Blackie as all shared the hay clamped into a wrought-iron feeder, and Watchie was tempted to go and make acquaintance with the beast, a light chestnut with an easy temper which responded well to a pat on its shiny coat; but he decided against the idea, the pony did not belong to the family after all, it was still a stranger to him. He stood a little away from the window, untouched by the light of the lamp, and looked up at the sky, to a thin shaving of silver which was a new moon being polished by the clouds; he was breathing more easily now, looking around himself, untroubled by the darkness, seeing the familiar houses carved out of solid shadow against a lighter sky, and it was just as he was beginning to feel happier in the peace of the farmyard that he heard the sound of whistling, not the shrill of a shepherd's command to the dog, but a melody, pitched one annoying half-tone out of true, jaunting along with a bound which made him mind on Dodie and his melodion. Watchie pressed himself against the wall of the house, suddenly wishing himself as black as shadow and spinning with the memory of Aal Wullie's toothless tales of spirits roaming with the revenant's habitual confusion in search of a reason for its earthly death; but even when the sound of the whistling became louder, and was joined by the sound of feet on wet soil, the wet soil, Watchie realized, of the path from the Cornhill Road around the side of the farm-house, he felt not in the least threatened by the apparition, if indeed it was an apparition. There was a warmth and an openness in the melody to which Watchie found himself responding like a dog to kindness, and when a figure came round the side of the house, hunchbacked and doubled by a weight Watchie could not see, he did not run for fear, but instead stayed in place until the figure passed by the calm light of the oil-lamp in the window.

Johnnie Leckie peered into the darkness beyond the farmhouse door, to the mound of shadow which grew from the substance of the house like a wart on its face, and laughed.

Weel, noo, fit's a-dee here? Has Wullie fee'd a wee mannie tae keep waatch ower the fairmhoose, the noo?

Johnnie Leckie was always treated like the prodigal when he returned home infrequently from his long months at sea, for it was usually at those times when families are bonded by the chains of blood, when the long threads of absence demand that one should tear them finally or else submit to their pull. He was always at Smallbrae for Christmas, when he enjoyed the fattest beef roasted in Jeannie's oven range, and when the whole family listened to his tales of the mariner's life, digging out the herring from a capricious sea for the lairds' breakfast of kippers, to which they gave no more consideration than the marmalade in its pot. He roused them to laughter with the stories of those he shared time with, and the graces of captaincy of the man to whom he was responsible, Thomas Balfour by name, a swaggering chiel with all the liquor he would need for a three-day voyage secreted in his cabin and the manners of a dockyard rowdy in the drunken evenings, offering not one drop of his bottled solace to another member of the crew. Watchie laughed with the adults as if he understood; but there were silences, among all the talk of fish and farming, in which Johnnie sat in the armchair and gazed into the fire, his oceanic blue eyes fixed as if on a distance, on memories placed too far out of reach, and Watchie was suddenly made uncomfortable by the silence of his uncle, taking to his room to avoid the thought of him.

Not that Watchie did not enjoy the company of his uncle, far from it; for at Christmas Johnnie always brought him gifts made during the long and arduous hours at sea, whittled from knuckles of driftwood found on the beach, or from whalebone bargained for with a sailor in an alehouse. His last present to Watchie had been a fat picturebook whale, carved out of the very substance of the beast itself, with a sprig of water tossed out of its head and the belly shaved to a plateau so it could perch on Watchie's tallboy, an item of furniture placed in his room more for Jeannie's convenience than for his. Watchie turned the carving end over end, never having seen a whale before, hearing of them from stories of great sleek creatures hurling themselves to their own deaths in waters too shallow for them to swim in, seeing in the shape of his uncle's carving the tail and the paddles of a fish, and he said to Johnnie,

D'ye catch the beasts in yer nets, uncle Johnnie?

Johnnie laughed to think of it,

Na na, wee Wulliam, faith na, gin we had ony o' them in oor nets, the hale boat'd gang under,

and seeing the width of Watchie's eyes, he cleared his throat and began to tell Watchie a tale. It was a tale he had heard told often in the alehouse by many who swore oaths on the holy name of God that it was true, that they knew as friends the men who went down with the ship, and who bartered the story for a glass of whisky which kept their throats from drying during the telling of it. It was the story of a boat which sailed one night from Aberdeen harbour, just as the evening sun dripped blood into the sea, with five of a crew to plunder the herring from an ocean as calm as an ornamental pond. On the second night of their three-day voyage, many fish had been caught and dashed into the stinking hold, and it was the advice of the crew that the boat should return early to shore with the booty and to hell with another long evening of trawling; but the captain was greedy for more, and said, na na, my loonies, we're nae aboot tae lee a hillock o' fesh for a'body else tae steal, we'll hae anither nicht o't afore we gang tae port. The decision was made, the ship stayed at anchor for a while for the crew to take dinner, and then the anchor was lifted and the net dropped over the side as the ship drifted on a trawl course. For a few hours all was well, until suddenly there was a haul on the line which pulled the boat against the direction of its rudder, casting one man through the hold and into the reeking cushion of herring mounded below, spraying the others about the deck like the last matches in a box. The captain was thrown away from the wheel, which spun insanely like a tombola in its mountings, and when he recovered to grasp it by the handles he could not make it obey his wishes, rotating in front of him as if the boat had determined to pilot itself. The boat was now as uncontrollable as a paper model, and the crew slid on the patina of fish scales, which never usually gave trouble to their experienced legs, unable to keep balance long enough to carry out the orders their captain was bellowing at the top of his lungs, all petrified by the notion that some supernatural agency was at work pulling their craft from its course. The water alongside the boat began to boil as if in a cauldron, and the rope of the net went suddenly slack as if something had severed the line; the loosening of the tension sent the boat screaming forward as the punished steam engine once again engaged, throwing the men across the deck, mice in the paws of a lethally playful cat. Then the surface of the ocean shattered about them, and immediately they saw the force which they had reined in their net, thrashing its trapped paddles and flukes, the mesh bristling with their first catch of herring. The whale lashed hopelessly on the surface for a while, splintering the pane of the water as it tugged on the rope, and it rode them across the surface against the pull of the engine while the captain tried to cut the rope with a sharp gutting knife, a task he could not perform for the buffeting he was taking; he called into the pipe for more steam, but just as soon as the tube fell from his hand, all was still, the whale dived with a crash, out of sight under the trembling skin of the water. For a while there was silence, except for the steady pulse of the engine below, and the crew recovered their feet slowly, thankful to God that they had nothing more to show for the encounter than bruising, and one or two began to laugh like demons, and one of them even said, yon'll be werth a dram or twa o' fisky fan we mak it hame tae the alehoose. But suddenly they saw the rope once again go taut, this time dropping like a plumb, and crossing over the prow of the boat so that it dipped and shocked and sent them flying over the deck, and this time they knew, and cried up pleas to God and his saviour son to help them, while the captain, brave to his final breath, tried again to slash the hempen rope as it leapt like an eel in his hands, battered by the fists of the ocean, tasting the futility of it as plain as the salt in his mouth, and knowing that they were yoked to the panic dive of the whale, victims of the great beast's fear as much as the whale would soon drown, weighed by the mass of the sunken boat;

and doon went the boat, concluded Johnnie, wi a' its hands intae the caal caal ocean, and there's nae a'body fa's seen them frae thon day til this.

Watchie felt the deep and sinister element close over his own head. He looked at the whale in miniature he held in his own palm, imagined it multiplied in size until it was big enough to fill the byre; then frowned for a moment, and said,

Fit way d'ye ken a' yon, fan a' the feshers droont?

Jeannie, darning a sock of Wullie's by the side of the fire, smiled wickedly, said,

Aye, the loon's nae daft, Johnnie Leckie. Ye ken ower muckle aboot it, for a mannie fa wisna on the boat himsel.

Johnnie contrived a look of offended dignity over Watchie's shoulder, towards Jeannie, then looked back at Watchie.

Aye, yer mither's richt eneuch, Wulliam, I wisna jist there mysel, ye ken, or I'd nae be here the noo. But a' the feshers hear aboot a wreck nae lang efter. I tellt ye, I heard it aff a mannie in the alehoose.

But Watchie still frowned,

Fit way did yer mannie ken, gin he wisna there?

and this time Jeannie gave voice to a three-syllable laugh, pulling the thread taut to seal the parting,

Aye, Johnnie, fit way did yer mannie ken? Mebbe it was jist an ill wind.

Johnnie looked her frankly in the eye,

I've nae been tellin the loon a'thing but the truth,

and Jeannie nodded, not to be convinced so easily; but Watchie looked up at his uncle, and said,

Dinna gang near ane o' yon fales, uncle Johnnie, they're affa bad craturs,

and Johnnie disarrayed his hair with a scarred hand.

Dinna fear, my loon, I've nae seen ane o' them yit in a' my days o' feshin.

Johnnie Leckie stood to talk with Watchie for some time,

glancing to the window and shaking his head when the loon told him that he was here to escape the smoke,

Yon dampt aal feel Richie, beggin yer pardon, wee Wulliam, I dinna ken fit way he faithered a fine wumman like yer mither,

and this caused Watchie to giggle out of control, for granpa Richie was a hard man to warm to, and he laughed at his uncle's daring in even uttering such a thing as he had harboured in secrecy for long enough. Johnnie smiled, and threw the bag off his shoulder and on to the ground for a rest,

Ye're oot here awa frae the smoke, then, Wulliam? A fine wise thing tae dee, aye, affa wise,

and he looked at the boy in a way which roused the mystery in Watchie, a tender look which made him feel owned by his uncle and which disturbed him to his very roots, as if he were growing and thriving but somehow strange to the source of his true nourishment. Then Johnnie smiled, a roguish smile which quite warmed Watchie with its touch of the restless and inquisitive child, Johnnie, uncle Johnnie was home from his fishing and his life of danger, a slippery customer of scales and wet breath, and Watchie felt a profound gladness at the real sight of him, for at times he may as well have been a ghost for all Watchie knew of him, a figure who played in his dreams for a purpose Watchie could never understand. Uncle Johnnie bent over to open his canvas bag with a pull of the strings, and reached into it, and pulled out a shell as big as his hand, a shell whose substance folded in on itself, with an abbreviated spire leaning to a point; he held it out to Watchie,

A wee giftie for my nephew, the scholar,

and encouraged Watchie closer to take it from his hand as if he were a horse taking a treat of sugar. Under the thin light of the kitchen lamp, the shell gleamed as white as washed bone, and the ribs shone with the lustre of pearl, an intrinsic light it claimed as its own, a fascinating light which drew Watchie closer, mesmerizing him into taking the offered gift into his own hands; it was cool to touch, smooth to the tips of his fingers, empty and skeletal to feel. Watchie thanked his uncle, and Johnnie said,

I've nae had the time efter Christmas tae mak a'thin mysel, I ken ye'll understand,

but Watchie could not have been happier with his present than if it had been fashioned by his uncle's hands; it was beautiful in itself, needing no further craft, and Watchie found more to fascinate him in its mystery, the black vacancy once tenanted, he knew, by a creature of some kind, though he could not imagine a shape for the creature which could fit in such a doorway. Johnnie hauled on the strings of his bag to seal it once again, and sat down on his haunches, the better to look at Watchie eye to eye.

Ye'll be efter kennin a bittie mair aboot it, said Johnnie quietly, yer mither's been sayin tae me ye're aye askin her aboot a'thin under the sun,

and he told Watchie what he already knew, that the shell had once been the home of a thick and glabrous creature without bones, and Watchie said,

Aye, I ken fine that, uncle Johnnie,

and Johnnie laughed, not harshly,

O, ye ken fine that, ye dee, wee Wulliam? There's nae ower muckle ye dinna ken, am I richt?

Watchie shrugged,

I ken a wee bittie,

not wanting to be immodest, his father had told him he had so much yet to learn, and this he accepted as the truth of it, that it was all out there waiting for him like a feast in the woods, to be picked from the boughs and not hurried in a fool's greed. Johnnie nodded his head.

But ye're nae affa keen for the fairmin, noo, wee Wullie, am I richt?

Watchie's eyes widened in a moment. He looked down to the naked earth pitted by footprints, almost shamefully. He shook his head, with great reluctance. Johnnie shuffled closer to the loon on his feet with the gait of a crab, and said, in a low voice,

And fit way d'ye think I went awa tae sea, wee Wulliam, but I wisna richt for the life o' the fairm? It's nae in the blude o' me, Wulliam, and I dinna think ye hae't in the blude yirsel.

Watchie looked up suddenly. There were whole worlds of understanding in the eyes of his uncle, eyes which, he realized, were as blue as his own. Johnnie reached out, and put his hands on Watchie's shoulders.

Ye've nae the hert o' a fairmer, Wulliam. Yer mither's aye tellin me aboot yer schoolin. Dinna lee't a' tae gang tae waste, and ye winna hae tae dee the werk o' a fairmer, gin it's nae fit suits ye.

Just then, the kitchen door opened, throwing an oblong of gold across the yard. Jeannie stood in the doorway, and both Watchie and Johnnie looked up to see her. Johnnie let go of Watchie's shoulders, straightened himself to a head past her height.

I've been haein a wee talk wi yer son, Jeannie,

he said, and Jeannie stared at him, levelly, for a moment.

I was thinkin, she said, fit way's the loon nae back yet frae the yaird.

Watchie held up his present for his mother to see, walking over to her,

Uncle Johnnie brocht me a shell, look,

and Jeannie painted it with the briefest brush of her eyes before saying,

Aye, it's affa bonnie, my wee loon. Noo cam awa ben, the baith o' ye, it's nae jist affa waarm oot here.

The next day, at an early hour, so much that was new to Watchie was happening that he couldn't begin to drink in the detail of it, so much that was frantic and harum-scarum that he thought of the times when his father threw open the double door to the grain shed, the panic which set into the village of field mice at the sudden glare of the light, dashing without discipline or reason for the nearest jut of shadow, hiding from the omniscient eye of the sun. Jeannie paused only the once in her sprint from stove to wardrobe and back again, and that was to answer Watchie when he asked if this was what his christening had been like; and having been answered yes, Watchie looked around him with new interest. He found himself being dressed briskly, but not unaffectionately, for kirk by his grandmother, who parted his hair into two discrete mats with a seam on his left to separate them, polishing and pampering the loon until he shone like an ornament on the sideboard. In the kitchen, Cathie Loudon was now at the stove to keep the dinner stew at its boil, hunched over the cauldron with hardly enough time to turn and offer Watchie a smile. Johnnie Leckie came into the kitchen from his temporary bed with the workers in the chaumer, dressed in the finest clothes he had, far from fresh and newly awakened from a shallow and unsatisfying sleep without the rock and swell of the ocean to lull him in his cradle. Nana Richie was already taking the cakes from their tins, wrapped in a final tissue of waxed paper, arranging them on plates on the table, though Jeannie told her that they would only be food for the flies anyway, they would have to be moved when the stew was served; but this bothered her mother not at all, more important was the semblance of business and a contribution to the breathless chaos around her, so that she could look Peggy square in the eye and say that she had done her bit for the christening. Such a thought never entered the head of her husband, who preened himself as best he could in the mirror of the room stolen from Aal Wullie and Peggy, just as well the bed of Wullie and Jeannie was so generous and accommodating; his occasional suit fitted him like a straitjacket, the waistcoat tight about the belly and the jacket carving into the oxters so that each move seemed to take a slice from his hide, a measurement of how much he had expanded since the suit's last wearing. On his way down the stairs, he met Aal Wullie coming out of his borrowed room, and the two shared a look which for the candle's flicker of a moment joined them in agreement as Aal Wullie hooked a finger into his collar to make himself enough slack to breathe by, both men the prisoners of their outfits and longing for the release of early afternoon.

In the living-room, the grandfather clock sang ten. Jeannie gasped,

Faith, we've nae lang the noo!

and in a minute she had them all shepherded into the kitchen and ready to be on their way; the two ponies shackled to their gigs stood in the yard and fretted not in the slightest while Jeannie arranged everyone to a carriage, looking over her shoulder to make sure that the baby was in Peggy's arms, making such a whirlwind of it that all were seated and on the Cornhill Road before they knew they had ever been in the house at all.

The bairn was christened Jessica Ann Leckie, and like her brother before her she cried the rafters down at the touch of cold water on her forehead in the sight of the gathered families, and the adopted family of the chaumer, who took their cycles and angled them against the walls of the kirk while they waited for Jeannie's bairn to receive her name in the presence of God. That afternoon there was a feast such as only ever graced their Christmases, a broth thick with barley and crowded with vegetables prepared by Peggy, Jeannie's stew maintained by Cathie Loudon, the cakes removed from their store in the tins for the afters with good strong tea, and while the plates were being washed in the kitchen, the men and Watchie retired to the living-room, to the foul pollution of granpa Richie's pipe, and a cleansing glass or two of the Glenlevin to remove the taste of the smoke from the mouth for all except Watchie, who had to make do with lemonade. The women came into the living-room when the plates were safely stacked in the cupboards, and from then on Watchie's baby sister was passed from arm to arm to arm, from Jeannie to Peggy to nana Richie to Cathie Loudon; Cathie held Jessica with especial tenderness, frightened that a careless placement of her hands might cause the bairn to drop to the floor out of her constructed embrace as if greased, but her face showed the beatitude of yearning and a wish to possess which made Jeannie smile thinly, holding out her arms emptily so that Cathie could fill the space with her daughter. Aal Wullie, made courageous with the whisky, and seated away from the fire on the stool left aside for him, turned to his wandering son standing uncertainly on solid ground, and said,

Noo then, Johnnie Leckie, fit aboot ye? Yer brither there wi twa fine bairns the noo, and ye've nane yersel.

Johnnie smiled secretly, sipped his drink with restraint,

Aye, weel noo, he said, fit ane o' my cweans'd ye hae me hae a bairn by?

There was much laughter from the company, except for granpa Richie, who did however manage a slight smile, and from Peggy, who contrived to blend a smile of forgiveness for her wayward independent son with a frown of disapproval for his ill manners, surely none of her doing. But in the corner, Watchie heard the laughter, and looked to his mother as if for guidance; her eyes were owned by the sight of her daughter in her lap, at whom she stared as if a moment's lapse would dissolve the bairn in her arms to nothing, and so Watchie stood enclosed by the gathering of adults who spoke in tongues he would not understand, and listened as Andy McGrath replied,

Aye, Johnnie, it's affa hard for a man tae decide, ye ken,

causing Cathie Loudon to gasp over her small ladies' measure of whisky,

Aye, Andy, ye'll hae a guid trouble decidin yersel, ye'll be tellin us,

making them laugh all the harder, making Watchie feel the more excluded by a joke he was not meant to share. He tried to control with politeness the little eruptions and spasms his grandfather's smoke was causing him, and once again he found his eyes irritated to tears the longer he drew a tainted breath from the air in the room; and just as Wullie was being goaded to the cabinet to fetch his fiddle, Watchie found that he could bear it no longer, and slipped quietly away and up the stairs to his room while he heard his father pluck and tune the strings.

His room was peaceful, but even here the thick smoke had crept up as if in curiosity and lain its scent on every fixture, a rotten reek like the territorial marking prowl of a cat. The day was not yet fully dark, and the last milky light cast through his window and struck from the bone whale which sat quietly on the tallboy beside his huge and weighty almanac. Watchie pulled it down from its perch, and took it to his bed, sitting himself down in front of it at an angle, with one leg doubled under him. From below he could hear Wullie playing the opening drawl to The Barnyards of Delgaty, and his free foot drummed the rhythm, a regular beat like a brisk footstep on cobbles, lintan addie tourin addie lintan addie tourin ay lintan lourin lourin lourin the barnyards o' Delgaty, a chorus of nonsense syllables like the padding of rags in a knitted doll. He opened his book at random, choosing a page by shuffling the leaves and letting fall; a lathe rest, a simple construction of seven pieces laid out in diagram, all carved from wood. He traced the fixture with his finger from one stage to the next, how carved tabs fitted into gouged slots, bending closer to the book as the light faltered, perceiving as best he could the spectral line-drawings. He heard the music become louder for an instant, and then the beat of footsteps on the stairs; the door to his room opened, in a sudden glamour of bright light, and there was Johnnie, a lamp held in his hand, smiling.

Ye're nae richt keen on the music, Wulliam? Or yer gran-faither's pipe, is't?

Watchie shrugged. The lamp illuminated the book, made the drawings sharper against a golden page. He said,

I canna tak breath doonstair, uncle Johnnie.

Johnnie nodded. He looked from Watchie to the book, then back to Watchie.

Yon's the buik yer mither's been tellin me aboot.

Watchie looked up, no longer surprised by what his uncle knew.

Aye, my faither gied me't, a filie ago.

Johnnie laughed.

Fine weel dee I ken it, my loon, faith, ye're the exact same as yer faither fan he was gied the buik by the Revd Caitlin. He was aye makkin some bit thing frae yon, he'd gang awa tae the shed for oors and nae be seen hide nor hair o' till the sun cam doon.

Johnnie closed the door over. He placed the lamp on the bedside table, sat on the bed opposite Watchie, his heavier well causing the book to lean towards him.

Fit're ye readin aboot?

Watchie pointed to the page.

A lathe rest,

he said importantly; then,

But I dinna ken fit's a lathe.

Johnnie laughed.

Aye, weel noo, Wulliam, it's nae affa easy, yon learnin. Ye canna look at a lathe rest til ye ken fit yer lathe is, noo, can ye?

Watchie shook his head, feeling a little mocked by his uncle, not liking this feeling of being mocked. He sat upright, to look into his uncle's eyes.

I'll learn fit's a lathe. I'll mak a lathe, aye, and the rest tae pit it on as weel.

Johnnie looked to the tallboy, to the bone whale shimmering in the light of the lamp.

O, ye'll mak a lathe, will ye?

Watchie nodded.

I'll mak a' kinds o' things, jist like my faither wi his widwerk. But I've nae mind for the widwerk, mysel.

Johnnie smiled, a canty wee smile. He said,

Fit'll ye dee, then?

Watchie bent double over his book, and took a ream of pages in his hands, shuffling through them as if trying to animate a matchstick figure in a flickerbook, until he came across an appropriate diagram, and then opened it fully, swivelled the book around to show his uncle. It was a water pump, laid bare for inspection, a steam engine with its entrails on display, rotary wheels and cams and levers jutting in ungainly fashion, like a tall and awkward child. Johnnie turned the book slightly, so they could both look.

Faith, he said, the loon'd be an engineer! Fit's a' yon for, yon stramash o' feels and I dinna ken fit a'?

Watchie smiled.

Yon's for sheftin waater, frae a well like, or gin a'thin happens awa below groond.

The smile Johnnie had ready with which to indulge the child was cancelled on his lips. He leaned closer to the book, and read the rubric under the diagram: WATER PUMP. He looked up at Watchie, as if to an equal, just for a moment.

We've a waater pump on board oor boat in Aiberdeen, he said, jist like yon.

Then Watchie described to him exactly how the strange fixtures in the diagram were put together, piston to cylinder, wheel to cam, how the governor spun in its mountings to relieve the steam pressure at a fixed rate, and for his part Johnnie listened with surprise and a little awe, until the loon was finished with his account. He reached out a hand, as if to disarray Watchie's hair; then placed it on the loon's shoulder.

Dinna waste yer time on the fairm, Wulliam, he said. Ye ken far ower muckle for thon.

He stood up from the bed, and picked the lamp from the bedside table. Before he left, he took the glass cap from the lamp, and leaned it over the stub of Watchie's candle in its saucer of china, touching them wick to wick until the black stalk burned with an aroused flame, the heat of them both melting the collar of wax sheltering the candle. He replaced the cap on the lamp, took a final look at Watchie from behind the shield of the door, and then closed it over, sealing the mystified Watchie in a monastic silence which only the highest and sharpest notes from his father's fiddle below could penetrate.

XIV

Now Wullie had a watch made of silver, a fine big moon of a watch which fitted the diagonal pocket in his waistcoat, lashed to the final buttonhole by a chain as light as twine, and he was very proud of his watch, because it had been given to him by Aal Wullie and Peggy and bought with money he did not know they had, a surprise which he was allowed to open on the morning of his wedding, presented to him in a sturdy jeweller's box and held on a cushion of burgundy velvet, a moon rising in a pad of sunset. He opened the casing of the watch, which split along its seam upon a facing of roman numerals around its circuit, and a dome of fine glass so smooth you'd swear it wasn't there at all, and on the inside was engraved a message, in fluent script as if written by fountain pen and not etched into the shell of the casing, On the occasion of the marriage of William Leckie and Jean Richie, with fondest love from Mr and Mrs William Leckie senior, 1895. Wullie held the watch by its looped chain, removing it from its box by means of a gentle tug, and listened to its delicate ticking, like the pulse of a small animal. Aal Wullie, who smiled secretly with the knowledge of yet one more surprise for his son, said,

Weel, my bonnie boy, ye've a waatch tae fill yer weskit pooch wi the noo,

and grateful Wullie was for it, slipping it into the diagonal slash in his waistcoat and threading the pivoting anchor through the final buttonhole to secure it, grateful beyond words as the chain dandled in a parabola across his waist, and Peggy, standing beside her husband and remembering her own wedding day, said,

Ye're a fine young gentleman fairmer, the noo, Wullie Leckie, and in twa oors ye'll hae ta'en a wife,

walking forward to brush the dust from his shoulders and lapels with her fingers.

During the ceremony Wullie felt the weight of the watch in his pocket, even as he stood beside Jeannie on the dais; it was the weight of pride, of being beside this bonnie lass who smiled in her costume of virginal white, of being in the presence of God and this congregation of fine people from the village, many good customers and good friends, and he found himself thinking of the first time he met Jeannie, at the Turriff fair, where he saw her standing outside the craft tent, waiting for her mother to enter to attend to her baking which was there on display. He remembered playing his fiddle for her at the fair, at the dance on the last night, when Johnnie pressed against his brother's shoulder and said into his ear, gang ahead wee Wullie, she's had twa three dances, and nae ane o' them wi ye. He remembered their courting, when she would cycle to Smallbrae and quite charmed Aal Wullie with her pleasant gentle voice, speaking with some knowledge and the authority of experience about the rearing of beef cattle and what to look for in a good sturdy cow, and she loved the herd, and never thought twice about helping to round them up from the pasture. Now, in the echoing kirk, the Revd Lyle, newly taken over from the Revd Caitlin, sealed them together in front of as many of the village as Wullie considered among his closest friends, and in his pocket Wullie carried his precious token of this day, burning in his eyes like the beacon light of the moon while Johnnie gave to him the ring of gold and a single diamond wormed from the earth and cut to a star to ornament his lover's finger, while the weight of the watch married him to the day; he would never be happier, he thought, never so frightened for the rest of his life.

Wherever Wullie went, there was the watch, for the first three years of his marriage to Jeannie and to the farm, for this was his father's surprise to him, announced on the evening of the wedding supper held at Smallbrae, that his was now the responsibility for the running of the dairy business from that day on, the fruit of many visits to Ferguson's solicitors and notaries at the far end of North Street. Now Wullie went alone to the cattle marts on a Tuesday, while his father stayed behind to tend to the farm's more common chores, and each and every week he had the watch in the pocket of his second-best waist-coat, a freshly laundered garment which spoke of not too much affluence but neither a reliance upon mended rags. At the show-ring he slipped in beside the other Aberlevin farmers of dairy and beef cattle, Lowther, Crozier on the eclipse side of the Deil's Shieling whose cows often drank from the burn there, Wattie Keillor of few words who sometimes played whist in the village hall, though not well, and together they watched the cattle being led around the arena, judging each one with the eye of the critic, this one too flabbery about the mid-section, such and such a one as thin as a clothes-horse, another just right and bulging with fine healthy meat atop a proud carriage, haughty as a laird. But at many times during the long day, Wullie would scan the clock at the top of the ring above the entry where the beefs and the cows came into the circus, led by their owners, and reach into his pocket to lift out the watch by its chain, opening it with the slightest feather of pressure on its catch, and then he would frown noticeably, angling the face a little away from himself the better for his neighbour to have a look with him, and remark to the air,

Yon clockie's nae jist richt, look, it's a guid ten meenits ower fast,

and Lowther smiled, tapping Crozier on his broad shoulder to offer him a sip from his flask,

Ye· hear thon, Lachie? The clockie's ten meenits fast, nor Wullie's waatch's a guid ten meenits ahint the time, tak yer pick.

Wullie wore the watch on his deliveries, even though it was obscured by the apron, and on each of his stops he consulted it to see if he could find the time for a cup of tea if it was offered, wrenching his hand under the bib to draw it around the material, a fine contortion which only served to draw attention to its presence. On his way up the Cornhill Road, he looked at it many times, even when there was no one there to see it catch the sun's fire in the palm of his hand, quite taken with the notion that here for the first time in his life he had the power of time at his beck and call, and never before was Blackie so soundly chivvied as when Wullie could see how far behind the poor pony was in his journey, forced to pick up his hooves to a rare rhythm which Wullie sent through the reins, so that the poor thing hove into the farmyard panting and swaddled in veils of steam, his mouth champing on phlegm and the bit hot as a brand under his tongue.

Then, one day three years after he had been given the watch, Wullie opened it to find that the flow of time had been staunched, that the second hand in its own separate orbit around its tiny circle no bigger than a farthing was stilled at thirty seconds, that the hands on the dial signalled half-past ten, and no sound could be heard from the mechanism behind its shield. Wullie turned the ribbed winder until it could go no further in its socket; still nothing. He shook the watch and held it to his ear, listening carefully for a pulse; still nothing. From outside he could hear Blackie spluttering impatiently for attention, and he had no time to waste on the damned impertinent watch any longer; the churns were loaded on the back and clattering as Blackie lurched a little forward with each wasting minute, so he took his cap from its hanger and went to make his deliveries, with the watch pressed against his rib in its accustomed pocket, sullen and heavy under the weight of its silence.

The watch still went everywhere with Wullie, his mute companion now worn for ornament, for he had not the time to go to the nearest watchmakers' and jewellers', Strachan's of Turriff, even though he made his way to the village at least once a week; or such he told himself, for reasons beyond reason. Now the only arbiter of time in the household was the old grandfather clock in the living-room, its impassive face and its solid tick making a mockery of its smaller cousin nested in Wullie's pocket worn for ostentation, staring it down with cyclopean authority, how dare it imagine for an instant that it could replace such a distinguished timepiece rooted in the corner like an oak; and forever Wullie was going to get it fixed the next time he went to Turriff, and forever he was spending the time with his cronies in the appreciation of the beef and a fine mouthful or two of the flasked Glenlevin until the shops were closed, and another opportunity was missed, which would never have happened if the watch had been working in the first place.

Now Watchie would not have acquired his nickname if his father had not taken to leaving his watch lying on the kitchen table after kirk on Sunday after the dinner dishes were cleared away; nothing more now than an item of costume jewellery, it was a dead mass in his pocket, and Watchie had seen it sleeping there every Sunday since he could remember, never opened, secured by a leash of fine chain to its collar of silver, placed gently on the table as if relieving his father of an immense weight. Sometimes Watchie would approach it as if it might leap from its perch and snap at his finger, not daring to touch it but only tracing its circle around, stroking the river of its chain down to the pivot which held it to his father's buttonhole. Week after week, he made his approach shyly, as if this were his first love, reverent and afraid of it at one and the same time, satisfying himself with a cool touch of its chain before running up the stairs and into his room to spend some time with his book. But as the weeks drew on, the loon became bolder in his approaches, and after a time he began to follow the chain not down towards the wood of the table, but up towards its source, to the guardian loop which sainted the head of the winder like a glory in papish depictions of the Christ. Many more weeks later, and the watch itself was in the palm of his hand, as if by its own permission, and he thumbed the catch, starting a little as the shell shot open with a will. Inside, he could see his own face reflected in the glass, as clear as the portrait in a locket, lit by the oil-lamp at the end of the kitchen table and warped by the dome into the very picture of a cherub, the cheeks pouched. The hands still told their lies under the glass, half-past ten, and Watchie shook the watch gently, as his father had done before him, listening for a revived heartbeat; but still nothing moved behind the dial. Its silence was a fair puzzle for Watchie, and he put the watch down for a moment and scampered up the stairs, returning with the book under his arm as heavy as a child's headstone, placing it below the watch on the table, shuffling the lamp over for a better light and opening the book at its table of contents. There his finger found Watches, repair and care of, and the appropriate page number, which he found after a little to and fro. He read:

> The machinery of a watch is not unlike that of the human body. Every one knows some little about a watch, but only a specialist understands its inner workings, and even he, like a doctor, is often deceived in his diagnosis. Many simple rules have been laid down for the regulation of the human body, but very little is known as to the proper means of preserving the watch in the best working order. But there is no valid reason why much more may not be done by the general public, and particularly by the amateur mechanic, to increase the accuracy and usefulness of watches.

And on, and on, in long slumbrous prose which caused Watchie much incidental frustration, until he found this:

> Let us now take the most effective of the high-class methods of cleaning. In the first place, the skilled workman, inspired by a professional pride in his craft . . .

(Watchie straightened back his shoulders, and carried himself at a proud distance from the book)

> . . . carefully examines the watch before taking it to pieces, searching inductively to establish a cause for the stoppage.

This Watchie did, turning the watch end over end so that a coin of silver spun on the walls until he was satisfied that the watch had, indeed, stopped. He went on:

> Having made a number of observations – very trifling, perhaps, but yet important in the result – he proceeds to take the watch to pieces with great care and without undue haste.

This was to prove more difficult for Watchie, not having to hand the instruments required for fine work; but a look into the kitchen drawer provided him with a knife his mother had cleaned down to the steel, with a slender enough blade, half of which he wrapped in cloth to protect his fingers. The glass dome came away without trouble, secured as it was on a simple hinge, but the facing was another problem, until Watchie looked to his diagram; the hands were to be removed, all of them, even the second hand. This he did, rapidly and without fuss, placing them on an unfolded napkin where they might be seen. The face was now loose enough to work free, which he did as if taking the lid from a newly opened can, pressing down on one side of its circumference, lifting it by the raised edge. Even before he peeled away the rind from the mechanism, Watchie took a deep and almost reverent breath, as if he had just been invited to stare God in the eye, and in that moment he knew he could do no wrong by the poor sick beast; he remembered Anthony, and his lessons in the patterns of being which existed in the natural world, and he knew that this product of mechanical skill which settled so comfortably in his hand would, must, respond to similar laws of construction and purpose. Finally he raised the lid, placing it like a saucer on the napkin alongside the hands, and there it was, the whole viscera exposed to his eyes, glittering under the light of the lamp like constellated points pricked on to the sky, and though Watchie had no name for them, he could see them in their ligatures, there was only one order they could follow, and as he parted each from their anchors, he placed them on the napkin in the order he encountered them, establishing a taxonomy of primacy from top to bottom of the cloth, implying that the first to be seen would therefore be last to be returned to its place. He took an hour to dismantle the watch, from its smallest wheel to the very heart of the mystery of time itself, the mainspring coiled up in its den like a hibernating squirrel, his fingers working with a delicacy you might find surprising in one of his age; in the Sabbath quiet he worked without interruption, while the family gathered around Jessica at the hearth, until the casing was vacant and all its parts, the organs of its continued breath and existence, were laid out in all their perfection, and Watchie could see at a glance what had caused the mechanism to seize, a fine patina of farmyard dust seeping under the glass and the facing, depositing on the wheels. This done, in accordance with the process of the book, he leaned up onto the table and began to read again:

> Then, having laid out all the pieces before him, he washes them in a basin of hot water, using a perfectly clean, very soft and well soaped brush.

This task was easy. His mother kept pudding basins of many sizes in her cupboard under the sink; and with the smallest amount of water he would need for the task pumped into the clean cauldron soon bubbling on the range, and a shaving brush borrowed from his grandfather's bedroom of the finest tufted badger hair, and a tablet of Sunlight soap, he set about brushing all the filth which had mired up the workings of the watch away, heeding well the book's instruction not to simply brush back and forth, which would only shift the particles around in herds. He was unable to follow the book's next instruction, which was to bathe each piece in a solution of spirits of wine, but no matter; he dried the wheels with great care, and also the tiny screws which fixed them to their mountings, using the barest corner of another napkin, until all gleamed to his satisfaction, and he was ready to follow the book again:

> Having carefully put the watch together, the workman oils it from an oil pot which has been kept sacredly covered from dust, and with oil which has not been longer in the pot than one or two days. The process of oiling is one of extreme importance to the well-being of the whole watch, and must not be taken lightly by the man who views his work with any sense of pride.

The reconstruction of the mechanism took Watchie a further hour, being a simple reversal of the procedure which rendered it to pieces in the first place, though he had trouble in persuading the mainspring to return to its barrel since its expansion upon removal, stretching itself on release to a long spiral; but once he was finished, he now had the problem of finding the oil with which to lubricate the whole mechanism, and this was not a thing the book was able to tell him, no matter how hard he hunted. There was only one place on the whole farm he could think of; he took the oil-lamp in his hand, and left by the back door, closing it over quietly behind him.

The lamp cast grim shadows over the clutter in his father's shed, and there for Watchie to see was the evidence of abandonment and disorder, of interest slowly lost and never regained. There was a small lathe in the corner, operated by a pedal the breadth of an adult foot, and held in its pin was a length of wood skewered like meat, half worked into the shape of a lion's paw, half cubed like a brick. Watchie approached it through a bristle of chair and table legs which reared above him as he passed the lamp before him, casting hooded shadows over the walls, sly and knowing, drawn around the shielded flame as if for warmth. Watchie held out a finger to stroke the wood in its lathe, and found it grimy with the velvet of long settled dust. There was much to take his curiosity in this shed; but he remembered his purpose, and held the lamp before the shelving, as the shadows swarmed around the wall beyond, among pots of lacquer, until he found a glass jar, crowned with a membrane of Jeannie's greaseproof kitchen paper secured by a loop of thin twine, on which surface had been written carefully in bold pencil, OIL. Watchie reached up and took the jar from its place on the shelf, and he made his way back to the farmhouse.

Watchie did not have an instrument such as was shown in his book, a small metal spatula shaped like an oar with a slender stalk and a broad candle-flame blade which captured the oil more efficiently than any pointed tip; but once again the knife was pressed into service, and Watchie picked at the knot in the twine which held the membrane over his jar of oil for a long minute, holding the greaseproof paper over the mouth as tightly as drumskin, until the knot finally surrendered and unwound. When the paper came away, the jar breathed out a sharp smell which quite took Watchie by surprise, heavy and delicious, and in keeping with the advice of the book he dipped only the barest tip of the knife into the liquid amber and touched it to the holes in the chamfered inner casing, bending closely over his work and making sure that not too much oil seeped into places it was not supposed to go, guiding the slow gems of amber into the right holes, spilling none over the edges, like a good proud worker.

Watchie wiped off the knife with its sheath of cloth; took the greaseproof paper seal and replaced it as a lid on the jar, securing it with the twine; replaced the watch dial as a lid on the casing, attached all three hands to their centres; and there, it was done, and all that was left to do was to return the oil to its place on the shelf, and the brush to Aal Wullie's bedroom after a rinse under the pump and the pudding basin to its rest under the sink after a wipe with a dishcloth, all done quickly enough; and soon enough he was able to take his book back up to his room and then come back down again to announce to the living-room that he was ready for bed, with a kiss for his mother and Peggy, and a final mysterious glance at the grandfather clock in the corner, as if sharing a secret with it.

As usual before the house settled down for the night, Wullie took his ritual walk among the biggings with a lantern in his hand, passing along the byre to hear the sleeping breath of the kye, past the stables, where he could hear the snoring of the horses and the pony; past the chicken coop, where he listened for signs of foxes prowling for a free and defenceless meal; past the chaumer, where on occasion the lamp burned in the window and there were still the sounds of carousing and music which drew a smile from Wullie as he thought of the chaumer crew in the morning, ill slept and yawning through their chores; then back to the farmhouse to prepare himself for his bed.

The lantern brightened the kitchen as he placed it on the table to free himself to shrug out of his coat, and while he did so he noticed his silver watch glancing brightly in the lantern's cast, and then, only then, did he hear the steady chirp of the mechanism, which he at first thought to be the sound of an insect in the house. He left his coat to hang by the scruff of its collar on a peg fixed to the wall, listening to the house's other sounds, the range digesting its night-time fodder of twigs and small mats of peat, the slight moan of the timbers, and lifted the cap of the lantern to blow out its flame; and this brought him closer to the watch, the only other possible source of the sound in the room. He lifted the watch into his hand, touched the catch, but he could feel the pulse of the movement vibrant through the casing, holding it to his ear just to make sure, a good strong beat like the beat of his own heart, a joyful living sound, and Wullie exulted in its revival, snapping its silver door shut and holding it as if it could not be true, as miraculous as if the house had been visited by the elves who made the cobbler's shoes for him.

Wullie trudged around the house, extinguishing all the flames in the lamps before making his way upstairs, one in the kitchen, one in the hall on the ornamental table, three in the living-room, and while he was breathing on the wick of the lamp on the cabinet he had made, he remembered his fiddle, the time spent in the shed with the book, now Watchie's book, following its instructions. With a lit candle in his hand, he saw the glimmer on the flat glass of the grandfather clock, and frowned, remembering something Peggy had said, that Watchie had been gone from the living-room for an awful long time, nothing unusual in it, though he didn't seem to be up in his own room, where Wullie would have expected him to be.

The candle took Wullie up the stairs, to the door of his son's room. The oblong door was etched in gold on the darkness, not quite closed. Wullie pushed it further open, to a descant from the hinges, and saw Watchie still asleep, lying on his side under the sheets, eyes closed, breath long and even. On the bedside table a candle stood to attention in a plain saucer, the flame trembling on top of the stunted wax. Wullie sat on the edge of the bed, and Watchie rolled slightly towards the mass, breathing more deeply as if rescued from drowning, opening his eyes a very little. Wullie said, quietly,

Ye'll set the hoose afire wi yon thing,

nodding towards the candle.

I canna sleep gin it's nae there,

said Watchie, and Wullie smiled; Jeannie's indulgence, an upkeep he didn't really mind when it came down to it.

Dinna gang oot o' yer bed, Wulliam, it's nae time for school yet.

Watchie harvested sleep grains from the corners of his eyes.

I ken that.

Wullie's eyes opened wide.

Aye, and fit way d'ye ken?

Watchie looked at the candle.

It's nae burnt oot yet.

Wullie nodded. He held the watch up by its chain; the reflection fluttered about the walls like a moth.

Fit was wrang wi the watch?

he said, unsurprised. Watchie shrugged under the covers.

Jist a bittie o' dert aboot the werks. It was efter a richt guid clean.

Wullie looked at the watch, at the bright silver casing.

Ye had the werks oot o't?

Watchie nodded, on the pillow.

The buik tellt me fit way.

Wullie nodded again, remembering those skimmed chapters he had never read, which had never interested him. Watchie burrowed his face into the down of the pillow, dragged down by the weight of sleep. Wullie lifted himself off the bed and went towards the door, the watch now warm in his hand.

Jeannie was in bed and fast asleep when he went into their room, the oil-lamp turned down bright enough for Wullie to see by, dull enough not to rouse her. Wullie blew out the candle in its holder, and put it on the bedside table next to the lamp. He undressed quickly and dropped his nightshirt over himself, raised the cowl of the lamp and blew it out. The bed squealed as he went under the sheets, but Jeannie lay undisturbed as he made a nest for himself beside her. The watch was still in his hand, and that was how he fell asleep, thinking of his son of ten years of age; and of the farm, and what would become of it now.

XV

The barren years at the doon-by school, the school for the children grown beyond the authority of Mr Clarke, were made bearable for Watchie by the woodwork classes of Mr Dennis, where he spent the time making empty clock cabinets of varied designs, until the day he was able to prove himself; and that day was not long in coming, though for Watchie it might as well have been eternity itself.

It started with much hard work for Watchie; now old enough and rangy enough to pull on greater weights, he was expected to help at the farm whenever he could, and often found himself rolling the churns out to the back of the wagon before he was allowed to go to school, taking a lift to the village on the board of it. This particular day, he had been expected to help Andy McGrath load the unthreshed corn on to the back of the cart, and a hard time he had of it. The task was made no easier by Andy's easy power, and his calling out,

Cam awa, Waatchie! Ye're nae fexin yer waatches the noo. Pit a' yer beef intae it, my man, nor we'll nae mak it ower in time tae the fairm.

There was no pity to spare for the struggling Watchie, and precious little beef in his frame to help him with the work; but his father said,

Aye, my loon, yon's fit's ca'ed experience, ye ken, ye'll need tae ken fine fit way tae dee a' yon,

as he shared the carrying of a bale with John Allison, manoeuvring it with great efficiency on to the cart, a simple one two three and up, another brick was added to the structure, and not even half of them yet loaded, to the annoyance and impatience of Watchie. He had helped to load the bales into the grain store not long back; now he was shifting them out, and he was beginning to tire not just physically, but of the very sight of the woven golden things, lighter than they looked but cumbersome, and dense enough to draw his arms down to their full length.

The last of them was loaded by Wullie and John, the climb of an age atop a pyramid they had to rearrange to a level; and once that was done, it was time to go, Wullie and Watchie and Andy McGrath, on the board of the cart to Lowther's farm, where the grain was to be threshed. Strangely for Watchie, he did not need to be told twice to come with the grain, and this puzzled Wullie at first, for Watchie showed not the slightest interest in anything to do with the running of the farm; having long ago given up trying to inspire Watchie with any of it, Wullie now simply claimed the parent's right of command, in the hope that when this fad for watches had run its length, spilling out and into the great ocean of human experience along with many other of the temptations which might take Watchie's interest, then at least the loon would be sound in his knowledge of the business of farming, there was always that to fall back on. It wasn't that Wullie was any the less proud of his son for his accomplishment that long ago night; indeed, he grudged him the name not the least, and to hear the villagers calling after the Sunday service, fine day Wullie, Jeannie, aye, fine day Waatchie, it made him sit taller on the board of the gig, he felt himself somehow elevated by the achievement of his son, struck by the light of reflection and drawn out of shadow. The ticking of the watch beat in his pocket until he could feel it just under his last rib, the one purportedly surrendered by Adam for the making of Eve, a reminder of the ingenuity of his son, but also of time's advancement, and of how much the loon and his sister were growing with each day which passed; and Wullie knew that some day Watchie would have decisions to make, a day which Wullie feared with all his heart, and all he could do was to be the best teacher he could, and hope that the decision Watchie would make would be the right one, for himself and for the farm, and a fine productive farm it was, deserving of the best care, not the half attention of someone whose heart was not in it.

★

By the time their cart arrived at Hebbie Lowther's farm, the others in the cooperative had gathered and were waiting for the arrival of Wullie, as well as for Peter Millar and his engine, drawn into knots beside their carts, the farmers discussing their year's harvest, the workers telling heroic stories of their moonlight jaunts to other farms, assignations kept in the barns with farmers' daughters or kitchen maids, scarcely believable tales of narrow escapes through byre back doors. There was also Davie Lowther, now grown into a squat little gargoyle of a creature who eyed Watchie with amusement as he climbed down off the board to talk to the horses; to that day he refused to grace Watchie with his newly acquired name, but still called him Pish-ma-breeks to his face, not yet beyond the petty cruelties of childhood. But under the severe eye of his father he kept his peace, even though Hebbie Lowther himself had refused to believe Wullie when he produced the watch, beating out good time and once again declaring the mart clock to be fast, even more so when he declared his son as the one who had mended it,

Na na, Wullie, he had said, nae wi Strachan's jist there up the road, I dinna think a loon o' ten'd be fexin a waatch noo,

but Wullie's chaumer workers all swore the same thing, though none had seen it; one day the watch had been asleep as usual, the next ticking as if aroused by a prince's kiss, and there was no reason for them to disbelieve Wullie, for it was known about the village, at least by all except the widow Jamieson, the Revd Goodbody and many of the village's Presbyterians that Wullie might be a proud man, and given to prideful exaggeration, but he was no liar. Hebbie knew that Wullie believed to his bones that his son had fixed the watch, that he had it dismantled and reassembled and running fine time, and he would never call Wullie Leckie a liar, fine well did he know better than that, and he had seen with his own eyes the watch open and telling time, so there was the evidence of that too; but privately he had often been heard to say,

Aye, ye ken fit way the loon fexed the waatch, I'll bet ye? Up and gied it a dunt on the table, yon's the way he fexed it, I'd pit a sax month o' my wages on it.

This, too, was Davie Lowther's opinion, for a loner and a moonchild such as Watchie Leckie, Pish-ma-breeks himself, who still never saw fit to join his other classmates in their rough-and-tumbles, would surely never have the wit to turn his hand to anything so practical as the mending of a watch. Davie Lowther kept his eye on Watchie as he shifted about the farmyard, a guest he would never have thought of inviting but for the business of the afternoon; there was something different about him from the solitary child kicking pebbles in the quadrangle, a difference in the very air that he breathed; he seemed much more tightly bound than Davie had ever seen him, set to unravel at the slightest pull of a thread, and this made Davie wander closer to him, disguising it as business, supplying the wrought-iron feeders with more hay for the guests' horses, attracted almost magnetically by Watchie's irresistible silence. Watchie absently patted the muzzles of Jess and Jonah as they tore sheaves away from their feed, crunching them audibly at their back teeth and drawing the remainder into their mouths with their tongues to be ground to pulp; Davie placed more into the black iron trestles from a medium-sized bale he carried under his arm, laying the besom of straw flat in the cradle. He looked up at Watchie for a moment, as if only just noticing who was there, said brightly,

Ye'll've werked hard the day, will ye nae, Waatchie? Nae like yon wee bit werk it taks tae fex yer waatches, the noo?

They were separated by the horses, Davie beside Jess and Watchie by Jonah's side. Watchie was a slight half head taller than Davie. He looked Davie in the eye, then looked back to Jonah, picking out a thatch from the cradle with which to feed him.

They're hard werk, the baith o' them,

he said, holding the straw up to Jonah, who took it from his hand. Davie laughed, and raised his own free hand, palm up, for Watchie to inspect; it was boiling with calluses, lines meandering through valleys of toughened skin.

Yon's fit ye get wi hard werk, said Davie. Yon's nae like yer ain hands, Waatchie. Yer ain hands're affa saft, man, for a fairmer.

Watchie shrugged.

I dee fairm werk as weel. I've nae fexed a waatch for fower year.

Davie's grin was a trap catching Watchie's unwary footfall,

Aye, he said, and there's them that say ye've nae fexed a waatch in yer life, for there's nae a'body fa seen ye dee't, and fit d'ye say tae thon?

And before Watchie could open his mouth to reply, Davie Lowther spun on his heel and left to replenish the next trough in front of the stables, from which Lachie Crozier's horses were having a feed as if they'd never seen hay of such quality before, which rumour said they hadn't; leaving Watchie angered to the core, with no answer to give but the truth, about which Lowther seemed to care not a thing.

It was only when Peter Millar stood on the plate of his engine, controlling his beast with slight adjustments of the handle which rode the rim of the steering-wheel, turning every so often to spoon one-handed into the teeth of its furnace another mouthful of coal from the bunker, that he felt his investment to have been wholly worthwhile. Raised above plain sight as if on a dais, he could see over the mounts and dips of the road, and even though he travelled at not much more than a good brisk walking pace, and sometimes slower than even that, there was the power of the engine shuddering under the soles of his boots, sensible through the thick rubber, and the feeling of command was sometimes enough to make him giddy with irresponsibility, letting off a blast of the whistle when there was no one around to hear it, unless it was those in the distance who might hear it coming back from the hills, who might say to themselves there goes Peter Millar on his traction-engine, off on another job. The engine huffed and panted like an asthmatic, gasping on the rises and breathing out from its single trumpet of a funnel a dense spume of steam, a chalkmark on the landscape surely visible from afar, a paper-chase trail of rags which would lead the watcher back to the source of it, the engine polished to a shine and pulling at its back the closed box of the threshing mill as easily as if it were a tinker's cart. There was money in his pocket now, a sprinkling of farthings and sovereigns, an initial payment for the use of the engine, and there was a greater sum in the house, from which Nancy was taking the cost of good nourishing meat for young Robert, now on his legs and unstoppably curious; this year's harvest had been good to them, good enough that Peter could employ another young man for the duration of the season, Harry Winter by name, and with a little instruction teach him to operate the companion to this first engine in Peter's affections, as well as the second mill he had recently acquired with the windfall inheritance left to him by his old and affectionately remembered uncle Tammas, a godsend which had saved Peter from having to work at the farm for his sour old sot of a father, and which had allowed him to start the business with the traction-engines in the first place. It was a much happier Peter Millar altogether, flush with the hiring money of the farmers who were gathered and waiting at Hebbie Lowther's farm, the first hiring of either of his engines after a long and droughty summer, who navigated the road which followed the furthest borders of Lord Gordon's estate, worming close to the Deil's Shieling and around Loch Bannoch, finally turning into the thread of a path protected from sight by a grove of hawthorns which led to the farmhouse of Hebbie Lowther, and a long proud whistle he gave in warning of his approach, three pulls on the chain above his head as the engine crept closer to the yard, slotting into the gap between chaumer and house.

From the moment the engine arrived in Hebbie Lowther's farmyard, angling sharply to run parallel to the house and away from the horses' berth near the stables, it claimed Watchie's eyes. In aesthetic terms it was not a handsome brute, being a strange collaboration of pipes and grumbling pistons, venting great farts of steam from its funnel, and to call it an iron horse would be a great disservice to the poor graceful beast whose only base of comparison with this creation of the forge lay in its ability to perform tasks requiring more brawn than was lashed to the average human frame; but to Watchie it was the finest architecture of brass and iron he had ever seen, with all the power if not the speed of lightning, and its great beauty was not the comeliness of its form but its perfection of design, the complexity hidden modestly under its cowling, like the mechanism behind the facing of his father's watch. He did not move when the farmers unravelled to return to their carts, the workers doing likewise and all clambering aboard to captain their loads a good distance behind the engine for fear of worrying the horses; he followed the engine's slow progress, guided by Hebbie Lowther out of the yard and into the broad field, and only his father's cry,

Cam awa, Waatchie, tae werk, my loon!

brought him back to a sense of place, scampering alongside Jess and Jonah as Wullie manoeuvred them into third place in the queue of carts which dripped one by one through the yard, gaining the board while in motion, settling himself beside his father at the reins, seeing over the wall of hay on the back of Lachie Crozier's cart the soiled wool retched from the lungs of the engine, and his pulse sounded to its gruff rhythm in his ears.

Lowther, of course, was to be served first by the mill, by right of ownership of the land on which it stood, and he guided Peter Millar over to where the ricks had been woven, blond towers each the shape of huge cannon shells pointed up as if to threaten the sky, the best shape to defend the corn from the heaviest shower of rain. The ricks were each as tall as two men, bound together simply by the mass of the whole, and it was the task of Lowther's hands, the men who had pleated the stalks into their present form, to tear them apart to feed the appetite of the machine which would excrete grain, hulls and stalks separately into waiting sacks, the stalks for fodder, the grain to the distilleries or perhaps to enrich a crofter's broth, the hulls for no purpose except perhaps to decay in the compost. While the workers teased out the stalks from the ricks on the tines of their pitchforks, Peter Millar prepared his engine, engaging the brake with a pull on the lever, for its change of function, a simple enough operation he had performed many times now. At the foot of the plate there was a small cabinet, from which he took a folded band of tough leather, longer than the band which went in an ellipse from flywheel to the gear which drove the mighty rollers. Next, he pulled the drive band away, and replaced it with the longer band, carrying it over to the body of the mill, making sure all the time that it was taut around the flywheel, and looped the free end around a smaller wheel whose roots lay inside the mechanism of the box, not an easy task, demanding some strength on Peter's part to drag the band further than it would have preferred to stretch, releasing it to snap on to the round of the wheel and to be seized by its serrated teeth. Peter's head was held high as he returned to the plate, calling,

Richt y'are, Hebbie, I'm awa tae stert it up the noo,

and Watchie dropped from the board of the cart and walked briskly over beside the engine, waiting for Peter to throw the lever which would set the whole process in motion, his heartbeat almost unbearably fast now. When he was close up to the body of the beast, he noticed that on one pipe there appeared to be a loose seal, for water was bleeding from it at a slow and barely noticeable rate, small beads standing out on the dome of the boiler like sweat, and it didn't seem at all right to him; but Peter was quite content to take the lever in both his gloved hands, committing all of the engine's idling power to turning the great flywheel in its moorings, slowly building up the steam to pull in its turn the wheel of the mill, from whose innards there came a ragged sound of the rotation of working parts kept secret inside the frame of wood. Hebbie's workers came over to the mill with their forkfuls of grain, and raised them above their heads to fill the open hopper at the top, satisfying the mechanism's great greed; the stalks whispered through the box as they were stripped of all their grain, passing through flails and sieves which spun in time to the spin of the wheel, linked by cams and perpendicular gearings, until finally everything emerged from their proper places from the mill, the grain showering like a jackpot from the first chute in the side, the hulls scattering into their sack as light and as empty as the shells on the beach, the stalks emerging wrapped in twine and compacted into bricks, excreted from the opposite side to that of their disordered entry, droppings conveyed away from the body by a belt which stood at a long jut from the end of the box. Wullie shook his head at the marvel of such a machine, and he approached Lachie Crozier and said,

It's affa wonderful, fan ye gie thocht tae't, is it nae, Lachie? They'll aye think o' some thing or ither tae be savin ye the werk,

and Lachie Crozier nodded too. It was a process beyond his comprehension; it might as well have been the product of alchemy, for all that he knew of the churn and thrash taking place inside, caring only that its final result should be the separation of his corn into what could be sold at market, or to give him his winter feed for the beef herd.

For a while all went well enough, as Hebbie and his workers and his young son carried the stalks from the ricks to feed the mill, and Peter fed the engine with coals from the bunker, with no product for its trouble but ash and steam; but after a while Watchie, standing by the engine at the foot of the plate, began to hear a discord in the heart of the machine, a low grumbling of dyspepsia from the boiler and the merest tail feather of steam from the leak he had earlier spotted in the piping, and now he knew that it was not right, and he looked up at Peter Millar on the plate and said,

Can ye nae hear yon? Yer engine's soundin affa seeck, Mr Millar,

but Peter listened for a moment, then shook his head,

Na na, it's aye makkin a pother like yon, Waatchie, dinna fash yersel,

which made Watchie even more disturbed, unsure of his own judgement, for he knew that a contented mechanism would never bicker in such a way, at the same time as he knew that Peter Millar had been working with engines for three years now, long enough to know all of the signs of disease in them. If Peter was prepared to say that his engine was in good health, then Watchie was prepared to believe him, though the evidence of his ears told him differently; if there was one thing Watchie had learned from his father, it was that you must always listen to experience, most of all the experience of elders, but also the experience of greater knowledge and wisdom, and so Watchie held his tongue, but stood away from the boiler none the less, staring from a safer distance, and looked on the mill as it shivered under the demands of the leashed engine, rattling as if shaking the bales within it like dice.

In minutes, Watchie's doubts proved to have some foundation; for there was a sudden shriek like the last cry of a slaughtered beast under the knife, shocking Peter Millar off the footplate of his engine as rapidly as if it had turned on him. It began to shudder, shrugging its shoulders again and again as if rolling on eccentric wheels, and the drive band was called free from its fastenings on the threshing mill, lashing as the final rundown of the flywheel doubled it back on itself, writhing like a wounded snake on the moist ground and chasing the workers in a furious game of tag, spraying them to one side like lice from a soundly beaten carpet before slipping from the flywheel and on to the rim. With nothing to restrain it, the wheel began to turn faster and faster in its moorings, the entire mechanism howling in pain and causing the farmers to haul on the reins of their carts, drawing the horses back and away.

Only Watchie kept his head. He stood away from the engine, but circled around it from the back, almost as if stalking it, and keeping an eye on it as he approached the plate from the farmhouse side, away from the flywheel. When he was satisfied that the engine would continue to bluster without exploding, he pounced on the plate, grasping the lever in his hands and pulling it to its home position, and then turned quickly to find a valve tap on the pipe leading to the boiler. His first touch was unsuccessful and he drew his hand quickly away from it, unbearably hot to his fingertips, but he pulled his hand into his sleeve to wear as a glove, and tried again; this time it felt comfortable, and as he twisted the valve a long plume of steam escaped like a pent breath, and he looked for the inlet valve, finding it, covering it with his makeshift gauntlet and twisting it shut. Wullie ran to the engine, calling,

Waatchie, cam awa frae the engine, it's nae weel!

but Watchie stood there calmly as the wheel ran down to stillness, the engine breathed more easily and purred on its way to a long sleep, and Watchie turned to his father and looked down on him from the plate,

It'll be a' richt the noo, I've shut doon the waater and let oot the steam.

All around him, the farmers whoaed their horses and whispered reassurances into their ears, the workers shook their heads, and Peter Millar held his head in his hands, as if to stop it from falling, another catastrophe, with his other engine contracted out and all, with only a very little of Hebbie Lowther's harvest put through the mill, and with the terrible possibility of having to pay back the hire money staring him full in the face. His problems mounted one on each other's shoulders, laced into giant patterns like the body of the leviathan woven from many; and Hebbie Lowther approached him, a broad smile on his leathery face,

Weel, noo, Peter, he said, yer beastie's lookin affa tired the noo, is he nae?

Peter took his hands away from his head, and dropped them by his side. He nodded, emptily, unable to look away from his machine slumped and smoking beside the hayricks. Hebbie put an arm around Peter's shoulders, as much in mockery as in friendship.

Fit way're ye gowkin at the dampt thing, Peter Millar? Awa and gie't a fexin, and we'll gang aheid wi oor threshin, fast noo.

Peter was not listening. He was staring at the traction-engine as if it were insubstantial, forged out of sheets and castings of light, an illusion of a mechanism, and he fancied he could see the fields through the body of the creature as if it were made of glass; he balanced and shuffled figures in his head, running costs and refunds and the coal for the other engine set off against the profit he would make from the working machine, and only by a miraculous act of legerdemain would he manage to pay his apprentice and feed his family over the long winter and the expectation of Christmas. In a voice meant for his own ears, he said quietly,

I dinna ken fit way tae mak it run again,

and in that moment the other farmers gathered, and the sky shattered about him and rained over his repentant head, cold blue angles and splinters of stained glass, and he was the loneliest man in the world as he wondered what he could possibly say for himself that would comfort Nancy whenever she looked at Robert, growing faster as the days went by.

XVI

But Wullie Leckie had an idea.

The combined meteorological expertise of the gathered farmers came to a reckoning, that they had perhaps three days before the next rains, a decision arrived at through an appreciation of the flavour of the breeze, brisk but not chill, and only likely to drag behind it soft bales of cloud. Peter Millar admitted that he knew nothing of the mechanical workings of the great beast, for it had been a purchase of a whim, his glimpse at a future of steam seen driving a carousel of wooden horses at the county fair, the easiest way to escape working for his father, and how grateful he was that the old man was not at Lowther's farm to see his humiliation; but he offered to send to Aberdeen, where the engine had been purchased, and where he could find someone with the appropriate knowledge; though the journey would take the better part of a day, therefore so would the return, with perhaps the further waste of a day to disclose the fault and restore the engine to health. This was not to the liking of Lachie Crozier, who said,

Faith, it's nae bother tae Hebbie, his ricks'll stand the rain, oor corn's oot in the open wi nae coverin, we'd be as weel takkin the hale lot back tae oor fairms, or see the ruin o' it,

and Peter Millar stood like a man at the focus of a storm, couched in safety while everything blows in tatters around him; scarcely taking stock of it, he had no further to fall, and he wondered how much a repaired second-hand engine would be worth, if not simply for its value in scrap. The gathering was just coming to its decision, and a decision which Peter wished himself away far from, when Wullie Leckie stood on the plate of the silent engine and said,

Haud yer wheesht for a meenit, Lachie, we're nae feenished jist the noo.

Hebbie Lowther let out a laugh,

Aye, Wullie, ye're aboot tae tell us we'll be trustin tae providence? That nor ye ken fit way tae fex an engine, ane or the ither.

Wullie smiled with Hebbie for a moment, then said,

Na na, Hebbie, I'm nae richt guid at the fexin o' machines, fine weel d'ye ken that. But gin we ken a'body fa can fex an engine, fit way then?

Hebbie nodded, still grinning.

Aye, nae bother at a', Wullie my man, but we dinna ken a'body fa can.

And in the silence which followed, Watchie stood among them, wishing to himself that his father would stop at that point; for many eyes had turned to him, realization spreading among them like sparks to tinder. They caught Watchie in a gaze which was almost predatory in its intensity, forcing him to speak up,

It's nae the same as a waatch, ony feel can see yon,

but Wullie was having none of it,

Aye, and fit had ye tae dee wi waatches afore ye fexed mine, Wulliam Leckie? Nae a thing, nae a dampt thing, gin ye'll recall.

The first to laugh was Davie Lowther, a laugh edged like broken glass, as he looked Watchie up and down from the brim of his cloth cap to the toes of his wide and muddy boots. This started his father, Hebbie Lowther, and Hebbie's laughter gave the others permission to join in, though many refused from politeness, willing enough to indulge Wullie in his delusions; but all the workers considered this a fine joke of Wullie's, until Wullie said,

I dinna ken fit way ye're a' lauchin at the loon, for there wisna ane amang ye fa ga'ed forward tae pu yon lever, nor tae shut aff the steam neither,

and this was true, and the laughter stopped raggedly. But Davie Lowther would not stop; he said,

I'd've pu'ed yon lever as weel, gin I'd been near eneuch,

and for a moment many eyes were focused on him, though

without the faith in him that he would have preferred. Wullie said,

Aye, ye were near eneuch, Davie Lowther, ye were jist feart.

Davie Lowther looked to the mud and was silent. Hebbie said,

Yer son's nae aaler than wee Davie here, Wullie. We've nae werd but yer ain that he fexed yon waatch, and ye're efter him tae fex an engine, the noo. Far aboot's the sense in that, man?

Now Wullie took proper command of the proceedings, showing the mettle of one addressing a political gathering rather than one of undecided farmers, for he was not about to let that point go uncontested. He stood tall on the dais of the footplate and said, severely,

The man that says my son didna fex yon waatch ca's him a liar, aye and me as weel, is yon fit ye're sayin the noo, Hebbie Lowther?

Hebbie opened his mouth as if to answer, then shook his head. Everyone knew of Wullie's trouble with Jamie Watts, and would have hesitated to make another accusation on Wullie's honesty; but under his breath Lowther said,

I'd nae say yon, Wullie, though mebbe it didna happen as it was tellt.

Davie Lowther treated himself to a smirk; Watchie boiled to see it. Wullie, satisfied, grasped his lapels in his hands.

Weel noo, here's fit's wrang. Peter's engine isna werkin, and we're a' sair in need o' oor corn tae be threshed. He's tellt us he can gang awa tae Aiberdeen, tae ca' oot the man fa kens fit way tae fex it. But nane o' us can wait that lang, on yon we're a' agreed. Am I richt?

Some nodded, while others looked dumbly at him, Hebbie Lowther included. Watchie stared at his father with a plea within himself, a message he hoped against hope was transmitted to Wullie on his platform. All to no use. Wullie continued,

Noo then, fit hairm wid there be in leein the loon hae a lookie intae the engine, files Peter taks a cairt tae Aiberdeen tae fess the mannie? Wid there be ony hairm in yon, Peter? Fit d'ye think o't?

Peter heard his name called, and like a dawdling schoolchild looked up at Wullie, recovering himself for a moment.

Na na, nae hairm at a', Wullie,

he said, shaking his head.

Watchie stood in the middle of the crowd, suddenly and once again at its focus. He looked around at the faces, first of all at his father, who stood tall on the plate of the engine with an expression of great faith across his eyes, a faith in his son's ability that Watchie himself did not feel. Next he saw Hebbie Lowther, and his son Davie standing beside him; one kind but doubtful, the other malicious and openly contemptuous, and this stoked the furnace of Watchie's fury as he thought of Lowther's past attacks, Pish-ma-breeks, Pish-ma-breeks, Pish-ma-breeks. Then there was Peter Millar himself, looking through everyone as if all was gauze, even the monster which gave him his living, and the look in his eyes was pitiful, a willingness to trust to anyone, even a wee bit fourteen-year-old with an untried reputation and a moderate knowledge of mechanical artifacts.

Watchie's feet were slow to respond, but they carried him forward with all the appearance of confidence. He shouldered through the crowd to the fore, and studied the form of the engine, walking around it in a tight circumference, a slow examination, touching this on occasion, making note of that; and all the time he was thinking of his book at home, the illustrations which depicted the movement of piston in cylinder, the arrangements of gears and wheels. For a long time he held the breath of the gathering collected as if in his hands, a long silence as the breath of the wind itself seemed caught in the throat of the hills; he approached the engine cowling, threw its lever, opened its chest, and with one look knew what was the cause of the engine's failure.

The workings were scabbed and calloused with a coating of rust; but rather than removing the parts to be cleaned, Peter Millar had simply poured more oil into them in order to facilitate their movement, and this deposit had in time thickened until it was the consistency of treacle, stopping the workings as effectively as if indeed treacle had mischievously been exchanged for the oil in its barrel. Watchie dabbed his fingers into the glaur, and pulled them back painted in a miasma of rust particles suspended in old oil, holding up his hand for everyone to see,

Ye've nae been cleanin yer engine, Mr Millar, he said; there's a' the dert o' the day aboot it.

Hebbie Lowther looked at Wullie on the plate; Wullie took his watch from his pocket, pressed the catch with his thumb, inspected its face for a moment.

Fit time'd ye think ye'd hae't fexed for, Waatchie?

he said, but Watchie shook his head.

I can clean it, he said, but I canna fex it. Yon's nae for me tae fex. The biler's nae werkin, d'ye see, and I canna fex the biler as weel.

Wullie frowned over his shoulder, snapping shut the watch.

Fit way can ye nae?

Watchie closed over the cowling, hopped on to the plate beside Wullie, pointed to the upright boiler.

The engine's been strainin for far ower lang. Ye'll hae need o' new pipin for it, and I've nae the tools tae fex the rivets, see.

Watchie pointed to the pipe which led from the boiler to the intestines of the engine, where the steam drove the pistons. There was a collar of brass sealing the pipe, the source of the bleed Watchie had noticed earlier, ill-fitting like the collar of a fat man's shirt, worn down and curved acutely to allow the passage of steam, even permitting the leakage of water. Evidently the collar would have to be changed; there was no new collar to be had, nor did Watchie have any tools with which to pick out the rivets from their beds. But Wullie was not having this from the loon who had set his watch up and running at an age by which a wheen of composers had already put many of their finest works on paper, shaking his head and saying,

D'ye mind on fit ye said tae me the day efter ye had fexed my waatch? D'ye mind on fit ye said, Waatchie?

in a low voice, not enough to carry to the others, by now gathered around the engine as if about to witness a birth or some or other previously unseen miracle, drawn over in spite of their scepticism. Watchie shook his head. Wullie said,

It a' gangs thegither. Yon's fit ye said. It a' gangs thegither, Waatchie.

His eyes pierced those of his son, threading him on to Wullie's enthusiasm, his belief. Watchie nodded, and stepped down from the plate, once again going to look inside the exposed machinery. It was different from what he had expected, and yet it was no different, for there was at least the manifestation of a guiding order latent in the arrangement of wheels and spindles, and fine well enough did he know the theory behind the running of the pistons, the injection of the steam into the chambers; only his doubts about the boiler remained but as he gave the matter some thought, and as the eyes of the farmers and the workers fast faded into the look of ghosts with no power to affect the actions of the living, he began to think more clearly of ways around the problem, into the realms of improvisation and temporary solutions. If he could carve a slender bung from wood, not the best way to heal the sick machine, nothing more than a tourniquet to staunch the bleed, lagging it perhaps with a binding of cloth, fixing it into the widened collar, but little enough experience he had had with engines of this kind, and once again he found himself perceiving the collected gaze of the crowd, and especially that of Davie Lowther, a broad dismissive stare which touched a flame to Watchie, and determined him that if he was going to fail in his enterprise, then at least no one could say it was for the want of courage; and he looked up at his father on the plate and said,

Mr Millar, ye'd best gang awa tae Aiberdeen tae find yer mannie fa can fex it; I'll dee fit I'm able tae dee here files ye're awa. But I'll hae the need o' tools for it.

Hebbie Lowther stood forward, and looked Watchie in the eye, steadily, without malice or condescension.

I dinna ken fit way ye'll fex it, Waatchie, but I've a' the tools ye'll likely need in the shed.

Watchie nodded. Wullie came down from the plate, and said brightly,

We'd a' best mak oor corn safe for the noo, nor tak it hame wi us, file the loon's fexin the engine.

Lachie Crozier laughed, and returned to his cart, speaking over his shoulder,

Aye, Wullie, file a fowerteen-year-aal loon fexes a grand big beast like yon! Oor corn'll spile far ower lang afore thon,

and this was the final lash, the last goad Watchie needed, and he said,

I've nae said I'll fex it, Mr Crozier, I've jist said I'll hae a lookie, that's a' I'm able tae dee.

Crozier half turned, and nodded,

Richt y'are, Waatchie, ye're jist haein a lookie,

and the gathering splintered apart slowly, giving Watchie the room he needed to make a calmer assessment of the task ahead of him, having made no promises, uncertain of the kind of surgery a mechanism of this kind would need to have it running in perfect health, knowing only that its sickness was in some way related to the seizure which had taken his father's watch many years ago, and realizing that a similar kind of reasoning must therefore apply; and so busy was he at the carcass of the engine that he was quite unable to see the look on the still smoutish face of Davie Lowther, with his greedy readiness for the humiliation of Watchie. What a feast he would make of it when the time came and no progress had been made, what a fine savour of failure was in the air; he followed his father to the shed with his head lightened by the anticipation of it.

Watchie made his first acquaintance with the engine in much the same way as he had made his first acquaintance with his father's watch, by slowly eviscerating the mechanism, rummaging inside the cowling like a child in a toy-box, for he knew that the machine would yield up its order with a knowledge of how it was constructed. One part connected to the other in a blessed evidence of purpose, and for some others the connectivity of cranks and swivels might reveal no purpose other than chaos, a sack of metal thrown together and left to fall where it lay; but to Watchie it was a declaration, as clear and as plain as the description of a blueprint. When he found a strange valve at the foot of the cylinder in which the piston rode, one more than he would have expected, he knew that it must be for the expulsion of steam into the system; but so small it was that he further surmised, given the evidence, that it could hardly be a propulsion valve, and that therefore it must be there to inject a pillow of steam into the cylinder to ease it to a halt on the downstroke, since its escape seemed entirely to depend on the cylinder's downward motion, meaning that it was an essential part of the governing mechanism, the weighted calipers at the top of the boiler. In this way he reasoned himself through the engine, placing each dismantled part on to a hessian sack spread over the earth, once again following a rigid taxonomy of connection and order, a living diagram which grew root and branch as he delved into the casing. For some of his task he was watched by Hebbie Lowther, and by Tommy Kerr, Lowther's first horseman, a tall construction of brawn ready to smile but silent as a winter's night. Wullie stood near by, fretting his knuckles with his teeth and refreshing himself with slight sips from Hebbie's flask, a shaggy beast of badger hair stoppered with metal, and as Watchie began to pull out the more substantial entrails of the mechanism, heavy eccentric wheels cast in iron and the rotary cranks which bound them, he stepped forward to give his son a hand; but Hebbie pointed to his worker and said,

Tommy, the loon's efter a hand, awa and gie him a help tae tak yon oot,

and Tommy nodded,

Richt y'are, Hebbie,

and strode forward to help Watchie manoeuvre the lumpen machinery into the open air, placing it according to Watchie's instructions on the right sack, letting it down with such a row that you might think would shift the earth itself. Hebbie turned to Wullie, and said,

Yer son's takkin a guid bit time ower it, but he's nae a feel, a'body'd see yon.

Wullie smiled, at the nearest thing to a compliment that Hebbie Lowther could muster. Wullie said,

Aye, weel, I didna see him fex yon waatch, ye ken, Hebbie, but fine weel dee I ken it's rinnun.

Hebbie laughed, and took yet another sip from the narrow mouth of his flask. He gasped as the drink went down with its claws bared, tearing hotly at the back of his throat, then said,

Haud yer horses, Wullie, he's nae fexed it yet.

Watchie heard none of their conversation; but worked on, laying out the anatomy of the vehicle in front of him, and how perfect it seemed to him the more he looked into it, and quite beautiful, and a quiet outrage grew within him, that such a fine beast should have been neglected for so long, imagining the suffering it must have endured while straining against its corrosion and the broth of spoiled lubricant while its appearance presented its owner with the perfect picture of health. He was clothed in farm dowdies which now collected all the muck and glaur, the vital fluids of the engine's operation; and with the engine's anatomy exposed to his sight at the end of the day, as the light failed and the sun and the luminescence of the sky guttered like an old lantern, he turned to Hebbie Lowther, deep in conversation with his father, and said,

Yon's the last o' it, Mr Lowther. Hae ye a cairt, and we'll tak the pieces tae yer shed for the nicht tae store them?

In the burning ember of the day, at about half-past nine in the evening as estimated by Wullie with a glance at his watch, Watchie and Hebbie Lowther and Tommy Kerr and Wullie helped to load the bed of the cart with the vast and heavy organs, leaving the engine behind them as nothing more than an empty cabinet slumbering in the open air, roughing it for the first time in its life, all dignity gone from its demeanour, a pampered king now deposed from office, cared for by a loyal subject moved to pity by his silent despair. The pieces were loaded on to the cart in their proper order, the sacks lifted like hammocks by Tommy at one end and Hebbie at the other, while Wullie helped his son with the lighter items. On the way to the shed, it was agreed between Hebbie and Wullie, after some consultation with Watchie, that there would be no threshing on the morrow, and that the two would send their workers with messages for the other farmers, telling them to keep the grain safe in the stores until they were called to Lowther's.

For the final unloading at the shed, Andy McGrath was called from the farmhouse, where he had been given cups of tea and entertained by the Lowthers' kitchen maid Meggie during the long hours of waiting; he emerged with a bound in his step and a great will to work, while Meggie stood on the threshold of the farmhouse and watched the men shift the chiming metal from the back of the cart into the interior of the shed. When they had finished, Hebbie Lowther invited them into the house for dinner, but Wullie thanked Hebbie for the offer and said,

Na na, Hebbie, Jeannie'll hae oor denner waarm at the hoose, she'll nae ken a'thin o' fit's kept us, pair cwean,

and so it was arranged that Watchie should return to the farm after helping with the milking at Smallbrae to get as early a start as possible on the engine. As he took them over to collect their cart, still heavy with a tower of corn, Hebbie said,

Peter'll be awa tae Aiberdeen the noo, wi ane o' Crozier's men on a cairt: I dinna envy him ower muckle for thon,

for it was known that Crozier only hired labourers as soured as himself, and Wullie laughed at the thought,

Aye, he'll gie the pair loon a richt hard time o't for yon engine o' his,

and Hebbie kept his peace, that a sizeable part of Peter Millar's anxiety might be the notion that his livelihood was at that moment lying in a field at the mercy of a mechanic not yet old enough to shave; but Hebbie was not prepared to say that such a task was beyond the loon, not after what he had seen that day and early evening, though still he doubted that fourteen-year-old loons could fix monstrous engines of great complexity. Watchie walked in silence behind his elders, and from time to time Hebbie cast over his shoulder to look at the boy, mantled in concentration and seemingly unable to talk because of it; such an intensity of spirit he carried inside him that Hebbie wondered if perhaps Watchie did know something more than he was able to express, and for once Hebbie found himself willing the loon on, hoping that his doubts were wrong, hoping that in two days he was in for a pleasant surprise.

Watchie spent the last hour before his bed in his room, in the light of his candle by the bedside, reading the scattered chapters of his monumental book on the subject of steam engines. Most of the information covered machines which were dedicated to other purposes, engines for pumping water from mines, smaller engines which powered band-saws and even lathes, nothing there about engines which drove immense structures of iron through the countryside; but from his examination of the working parts of Peter Millar's beast, he could see the additional ligatures which gave the engine its ability to convert energy into motion, and knew fine well what he should do, though the boiler still remained a problem. He closed over the book, and returned it to its place on the tallboy, beside Johnnie's carvings and the empty cabinets for clocks he had been allowed to take home with him from the woodwork class.

While he slept, he dreamt that Davie Lowther had grown tall above him, and that he was once again a child in the byre. The tools in his hands were once again as thick as rafter beams, and demanded all of his strength to shift them even an inch. Lowther wore an expression he well remembered, and he said, man man, ye're nae ees, nae ees at a' as the shovel became slippery and clattered to the ground from his grasp. He appeared to be stoking the open furnace of a boiler, with the flames snarling at him in the greedy hearth, the riveted dome rearing above him and exhaling such a heat that called to his mind a fever, and the sweat drizzled into his eyes and gave them such a sting as he reached down for the fallen shovel.

When he wakened, the candle was burned almost to the last of its tallow in the saucer, the wick slanting without any support. Watchie turned on his side, away from the light, and took a minute to fall asleep again, this time safely, without any dreams at all.

Wullie took Watchie out of his way to Lowther's farm in the

morning, and on the loon's lap was a package of bread and cheese made up by Peggy as a noonday lunch. He was dressed more appropriately for hard and dirty work, in a pair of his father's overalls no longer used since Wullie had given up the joinery; and he had left that morning to Jeannie's solemn declaration that his previous day's clothing would never see its natural colour again after it had been painted in filth the like of which she had never seen before and hoped she never would to the end of her days, as black as tar and tenacious beyond the powers of hot water and grated soap to coax from the fibre.

Lowther's farm was alive by the time Watchie was left to do his day's work. The beef herd had been scattered to their pasture, feasting on sweet hillside grass, each marked with a red number in order of future delivery to the mart, and there was now some work in train to do with the planting of the turnips which would keep the cattle fed over the winter months when they were confined to their stalls in the byre, a sentence ending with the first signs of spring and the growth of new grass in the fallow field. Through Hebbie's doing, Davie Lowther passed across Watchie's path much humbled, glancing sullenly at the loon as he went to the shed to look at the parts of the engine; Watchie lifted their cover of sacking and saw in the full light of day the extent of the task ahead of him. Each was in sore need of a thorough cleaning, this much he had known before, but he began to doubt just then that three days, now pared down to two, would be enough to see them fit to take their place in the hollow of the casing. He had little slack time to waste in being daunted by them; and so he made his way to the farmhouse, and just like a doctor asked Hebbie and his plump and matronly wife for several essential items he needed in the preparation.

The first was a great plenty of hot and soapy water, which Mrs Lowther gladly boiled on her range for him in a fat cauldron of tarnished copper. Next he asked that the water be divided between two large buckets, which Hebbie sent Davie to fetch from the shed, much to his son's noticeable annoyance, that he should become nothing better than an orra loon to Watchie's doomed venture. Also from the shed Davie was asked to pick up a brush of steel bristles, ordinarily used for cleaning the blade of the plough before polishing, a second journey he began from the farmhouse by saying,

Could he nae say yon afore I went for the buckets?

drawing a fierce look from Hebbie which sent him away at a scurry. Finally, and more difficult to fulfil, Watchie asked if there was such a thing as spirits of wine at the farm, a request which sent Hebbie Lowther's brows plunging on his forehead, turning to his wife who shook her head slowly. Hebbie said,

Wid ye buy yon spirits o' wine at the wine merchants in the toun, d'ye ken, Waatchie?

and Mrs Lowther frowned for a moment in disapproval, that one so young as Watchie should ask for such a thing when he was supposed to be working; but Watchie said,

Na na, it's nae real wine for drinkin, ye ken, it's for cleanin the pairts efter they've been waashed, ye'll buy it at the hardware shoppie,

and both Lowthers brightened and nodded, and once again Davie Lowther found himself charged with an errand, as Hebbie said,

Davie, tak ane o' the werker's bikes and gang awa tae the toun, tae the hardware shop for yon spirits o' wine. I'll tak the siller for it frae Peter Millar fan he cams frae Aiberdeen,

leaving Davie Lowther wondering when it would ever end, obeying his father as Mrs Lowther found the money to give to him and stabbing a look at Watchie as he left to borrow a bicycle from the chaumer.

Aside from the spirits of wine, and a few rags and cloths which Mrs Lowther tore from garments fit for nothing but tattie boodies, Watchie was now ready to begin his operation; the patient stood ready in the field, none the worse for its night under the sky, and again Tommy Kerr helped to load and unload the cart, standing beside Watchie as he scrubbed at the simplest of the parts, trotting without complaint to the farmhouse at Watchie's request for fresh buckets of water, helping Watchie to bundle the parts around in order to reach new patches of corrosion on the heavier components. He said nothing to distract Watchie during his long task, and watched with interest as the slender loon worked back and forth between his diagram and the engine, replacing the slighter parts with a spanner, quite admiring of Watchie's determination, but none the less unconvinced that he was able to bring the mechanism back to its full working life, though he would never have said it to him.

Mrs Lowther was in a flat spin over her guest, and brought him cup after cup of strongly flavoured tea in the field while he worked; but once, when Mrs Lowther was too busy to come to the field, she sent her kitchen maid Meggie instead with the tea, and Meggie came brightly with the refreshments and walked fully and boldly up to Watchie, tapping a finger to his shoulder while he was bent double over the engine and causing him to turn to face her. He had seen her in the kitchen of the farmhouse, standing behind Mrs Lowther and caught in her wide eclipse, dressed in pretty florals and a long white apron fastened about her waist; in front of him now, holding a cup of tea by its rim with the handle turned towards Watchie like an invitation, she gave him a wide display of all of her teeth, and he smiled in reply, shallowly, and stopped himself from wiping the flats of his hands on the thighs of his overalls. She said,

The missus thocht ye'd be efter anither cuppie o' tea, Waatchie,

and by this time Watchie had lost count of the cups he had drunk; but he did not feel minded to refuse, and so nodded and rounded her to wash his hands in the appropriate bucket, the water now the colour of threatening cloud, soaping his hands on the cake of Sunlight resting on a cloth, bathing them in the manky water and drying them on a rag smeared grey with filth, so that his hands were not much cleaner than when he began. He said,

Aye, I'll hae a cuppie, affa kind o' ye,

and reached for it, hooking his finger through the ear of the cup; she released it after a moment, and his hand trembled a very little for the duration of her hold on the rim, he fancied because of the sudden nicety of grip he had been forced to adopt after so much heavy lifting. Meggie smiled at him as she parted from the cup; then, after an indifferent glance at Tommy Kerr, she wandered over to the open casing of the engine and peered inside, her arms fastened behind her, looking the exposed workings up and down as if she had never seen such a thing before, which of course she had not. She looked over her shoulder at Watchie, and said,

Fit a hotchpotch o' a thing; a wonder fit way yon engine werks at a',

which drew Watchie over to her side as surely as if a loop had been thrown over his neck and she had pulled on the cable of it. He said,

Na na, it's nae a hotchpotch at a', a' the pairts werk thegither, ye ken, look,

and he was away, leading Meggie on a guided tour of the vast mechanism, first of all taking her round to the boiler and pointing to the circuitous pipes which led to and from it; on the plate she contrived a number of soft collisions as she leaned over to have a look which quite drove the poor loon into a fluster, causing his explanation to fray a little as he tried to calm the involuntary drumming of his heart. On he went, next taking her to the gaping interior of the engine, to where the outlet pipes trailed to the base of the piston bearings, and she giggled as he described the motion of the piston in its cylinder in a way he found perturbing, though he had no reason for it, and he found an uncomfortable heat braising him, knowing that his face had gone as scarlet as the dawn, and next he explained how the vertical motion of the piston was converted to a spin of the flywheel which turned the great rounds on their axles, and finished with,

And yon's fit way yer engine werks. See, it's nae a hotch-potch, I tellt ye.

Meggie smiled.

I didna ken fit ye were sayin at a', she said. But fine d'ye ken fit ye're deein yersel, yon's a' ye'll be efter.

She turned from the engine, and looked at Tommy Kerr,

standing guard over the remaining parts, lying on their sacking blankets like vagabond tinkers.

Twa year younger than I am mysel, Tommy Kerr, and he kens fit way ane o' yon big craturs werks. Is yon nae a thing?

Tommy nodded, and gave Watchie an up and down look, totalling what stood between the cloth cap and the boots.

Aye, he said, nae affa bad for a fowerteen-year-aal.

Meggie burned indignantly on Watchie's behalf, though Watchie himself was pleased enough with the admission.

Nae affa bad, Tommy Kerr? And fit like were you at fowerteen, my bonnie loon? Yer first taste o' the fisky, was't, fan yer mither's eyes were awa frae ye?

She said it in all sweetness, perplexing Watchie beyond words, for Tommy stood in place, buffeted by her scorn; but at last he stirred, like a gentle ox subjected to the switch once too often, and turned his back, saying,

God forgie ye for thon, Meggie,

taking himself to the farmhouse and away from her. She smiled at Watchie, another of her broad and appealing smiles, said,

Will ye nae hae tae be back at yer werk on the engine, Waatchie?

and he nodded, at the same time sorry for poor Tommy Kerr while jubilant that she was looking on at him, and for her he put a little more of his back into it, shifting weights he thought beyond him, working with a speed and a dexterity which often led him to lose his fingering on the tools he was handling, so quickly was he able to perform the task; and never once did she laugh at his foolishness in so doing, but smiled, and in her smile Watchie found his surest touch, and he knew that he would be finished for the day after, when the others gathered and Peter Millar arrived with his man from Aberdeen, as his father had promised.

She did not distract Watchie from his fixing of the engine with her presence, but mothered him through it, speaking encouragement to him when he most needed it, helping all that she could to lift the heavier parts of the machine after they had soaked in the bucket of spirits of wine. Watchie said,

The pairts'll nae last affa lang, but they're a bittie cleaner the noo,

and she nodded as if Watchie were the wisest young man she had met, looking on as he installed yet another of the curious castings into its proper place in the whole. From time to time Tommy Kerr stood some little distance away from them, always just ready to intervene but never quite pressing hard enough on the membrane which kept him separated from Watchie and Meggie; watching like the guardian he was charged to be to the young mechanic, staying out of reach of Meggie's tongue, as miserable as if the sky were pouring all of its chill upon his head.

Meggie was the nurse to Watchie's surgeon, as the beast took back its shape under his hands; and by the time the light failed on his second day of work, it was restored to its form, each part in place, leaving him only with the stopgap repair of the boiler for the day after, and the prospect of finishing the job under the eye of Peter's expert. It was no prospect he looked forward to, while Meggie returned to the chaumer to make the dinner for the workers, leaving him to see to it that the whole construction did not want for oil, the last task before his father came in the wagon to take him back to Smallbrae. Hebbie Lowther was there to meet Wullie when he turned in to the yard with Blackie at the front, and welcomed him with a handshake,

Aye, Wullie, the loon's been werkin affa hard a' day, though I've nae had ower muckle chance tae see him at it,

and Wullie nodded, it was quite understood that Hebbie had much to do and not enough time to spare to oversee Watchie; but once in the field, it was obvious that indeed Watchie had been working hard, by the evidence of the completed engine looking almost ready to purr deep in its throat at the throwing of the lever. The loon's overalls were in if anything a worse state than his everyday clothes had been, and he was busy washing his hands and exposed arms at the bucket which had been refreshed barely an hour ago, diluting the filth on his skin. Wullie said,

Ye'll be haein a bath fan we've ga'ed hame, will ye nae, Waatchie? Nor yer mither'll pit oot sic a skraikin fan she sees ye like yon,

and Hebbie Lowther laughed to see him smeared in oil from top to toe,

Fit a plyter, he said, the loon's as blaak as a corbie!

and Watchie's teeth glittered in his face, at which he scrubbed with his hands to remove as much of it as he could, which was little enough. While Watchie gathered together all of his materials, the two buckets in one hand, one taken from him by Wullie full of water silted with aged oil even blacker, if such a thing were possible, than Watchie's washing bucket, the steel brush, the bucket of spirits of wine which he had to splash over the larger components which would not fit, and the rags now useless for anything but throwing away, he thought about Meggie in the chaumer, wondering what she had done after she had left a number of hours ago to make her dinner, what she was doing now; and he thought about the engine, quietly resting in the mud, if he had done enough to make it well again, if he would be left standing in the field tomorrow midday among the gathered farmers with a failed machine, how he would cover himself with his arms and wait to die from the embarrassment of it. But as the three took the materials back to the farmhouse, Hebbie Lowther said,

Dinna fash yersel ower yon buckets, I'll gie them a clean mysel, Waatchie, ye've had eneuch werk tae dee the day.

Watchie nodded, said,

I dinna richt ken gin the engine'll werk efter a' yon,

more to hear it said than for any other reason. Hebbie Lowther shook his head and smiled.

Fit's it matter gin it disna, Waatchie? Ye've did mair for thon engine than Peter Millar, and he's the dampt goat fa't belangs tae.

On the way home, Watchie was still a little fretful about the day after; but not as much as before, worrying more about how Jeannie would take to another filthy outfit to be cleaned. In the event she was ready for it, and boiled up a cauldron of water for a bath in the living-room, in front of the fire, while Jessica was removed to the kitchen to play with Peggy, forbidden to go in to see her naked brother. Jeannie had as much of the dirt out as she could manage, and after Watchie was dried and settled into a fresh nightshirt, she spread the overalls across a tall clothes-horse like a drunk slumped on a fence, and dropped a few extra bricks of peat on the fire so that the overalls would have the benefit of a whole night's warmth to dry themselves. Watchie went to his bed, and before the day's exhaustion gently drained away all consciousness, he heard Meggie's voice whispering through the cavern, I ken fine yer engine'll werk, Waatchie, fine dee I ken, just as he fell asleep.

Early the next day, Watchie carved out of a sliver of wood the bung for the collar of the boiler, exercising some skill in the process, for it was an irregular parting, and in hammering it securely into the mouth of the opening he took great care not to worsen the situation, only too aware that too much enthusiasm might compromise the seal between pipe and boiler even more; and when the bung was secure in its anchor, he bound it with a long ribbon of cloth once again offered to him by Mrs Lowther, torn from one of her old blouses. It was the only makeshift repair to a part of the mechanism he did not fully understand; and as he went to the farmhouse for a bucket of fresh water to fill the boiler, he hoped that it would hold, at least for as long as it took to thresh the grain, or until the man came from Aberdeen.

Meggie was not there to see him scrape out the ash from the throat of the furnace, replacing it with coke from the footplate bunker; but this bothered him not at all, since it was no more complicated a task than building the foundations of a good blaze in the family hearth, and soon enough with the loan of a match the black nuggets caught and made a good fire under the crucible of the boiler. Watchie kept his eye on the pressure gauge linked to the outlet pipe, a self-explanatory calibration which warned by the skipping of a needle when the pressure inside the boiler became a danger; once again gloving his hand in his sleeve, he adjusted valves and released the plumage into the air, only then noticing that Hebbie Lowther and Tommy Kerr and others of the workers were standing around, not Meggie, but on each of their faces was a smile, and Hebbie was shaking his head and bringing his hands together in mighty applause, approaching Watchie at the plate and saying,

Michty God, Waatchie, yon's affa fine werk,

but before he could overpower the loon in immoderate praise, Watchie held up his hand and said,

Na na, Mr Lowther, yon's jist the biler, ye'll hae tae haud on for a filie yet for the rest o't,

and without pausing picked up the leather band left forgotten on the ground since three days past, and with some effort shook free the twists and convolutions worked into it by the merciless action of the flywheel. He repeated Peter Millar's first task, stretching the band over to the body of the threshing mill, which had been waiting dutifully to the rear of the engine like the beggar king's conscientious attendant, never deserting its true master, humbly aware of its station. He attached the band to the wheel of the mill, examining the connection minutely for early signs of a possible slippage, deciding that it would hold secure, aware he was treading the same path that had led to Peter Millar's humiliation only two days ago, and then returned to the plate, from which he could gain a better view of the roads that led to Lowther's farm, hoping to see from there Peter Millar's cart and a man he did not recognize; but all he could see was a skein of carts and pillars of corn, his father's among them, each approaching on different roads, drawn to a single point through which they would take the ochre earth path to the farmhouse. Hebbie Lowther stood beside the plate and looked up at Watchie, and said,

Waatchie, wid ye be efter listenin tae a wee bit advice, the noo? Jist a thocht for ye, gin ye'd be hearin it.

Watchie looked out as the first of the carts, belonging to Lachie Crozier, turned into the path; looked down at Hebbie, whose face was kindly, and quite unlike his son's, gathered there with the workers, readying himself for Watchie's presumed failure. Watchie nodded, and Hebbie leaned closer, lowering his voice.

Pit yer engine on the noo, afore a'body cams tae the fairm. I'll be takkin first shot o' the mill onyway. Jist a thocht, ye ken.

Watchie smiled, despite himself, then shook his head.

Na na, Mr Lowther. Ye've tae wait for the pressure tae cam richt in the biler. But I'll thank ye the noo for't.

Hebbie Lowther nodded,

Aye, weel, he said, fine ye'll ken yersel, Waatchie,

and returned to his place beside the workers.

The carts gathered one by one, in the same order as they had arrived three days before, but still with no sign of Peter Millar. Wullie Leckie had finished his delivery that day at all speed, pushing Blackie to exhaustion along the filigree of streets about Aberlevin until the poor pony was heaving the breath into his lungs on the final stretch of the Cornhill Road, sounding much like the traction-engine while he was being led to the stables after being uncoupled from the wagon and blowing almost as much steam from his nostrils. Jess and Jonah had already been linked to the cart when Wullie arrived at Smallbrae, and soon enough Wullie had them on the road to Lowther's farm, giving them some idea of the urgency of their mission with each switch of the reins, to which they responded by shouldering the cart at a good pace, turning into the path just after Lachie Crozier and not far behind him. Now Wullie stood with Andy McGrath behind Lachie Crozier, and smouldered quietly as he overheard the chiel saying to his hands,

Mebbe we'd a' best hope Peter cams tae the fairm wi his mannie, afore the rain fa's doon in buckets.

Wullie could take no more of it. He came behind Lachie Crozier, and said brightly,

Aye, Lachie Crozier, ye've aye been affa quick tae look doon on ither folk, hae ye nae? Can ye nae hear the biler werkin tae some tune, my man? Far aboot's yer faith?

Lachie Crozier turned to face Wullie, and his expression changed not one jot.

Fine weel dee I hear yon biler, Wullie, he said, but I'd sooner hear yon engine werkin tae some tune, for I'd ken my corn was tae be threshed fan I'd heard thon.

Lachie Crozier's hands laughed in chorus; but Wullie refused to be roused to anger, and simply said,

Wid ye pit a wee bit siller on it, Lachie Crozier, gin ye dinna think ye'll be hearin the engine the day?

Lachie Crozier's sour face cracked in two, the first smile Wullie had ever seen from him.

Gamblin, Wullie Leckie? Yon's nae an affa Christian thing tae be deein, ye ken, nae affa wise.

Wullie's own pressure was building, as much as that of the engine's boiler, but he vented it with a smile.

Jist tae see fit way ye're sae keen tae see my son's werk fa' doon, ye ken, Lachie, gin ye'd be sae keen tae pit yer siller on it. I widna ca' yon gamblin, jist.

Crozier paused to give the proposition some thought. One of the hands leaned over to him and said,

Dee it, Lachie! Yer siller's safe, man,

and Wullie stood forward a pace, staring evenly at Lachie Crozier,

Fit's a-dee, Lachie? Are ye feart the loon'll mak it werk efter a'?

Crozier matched Wullie's pace, and stared just as evenly back.

E'er sin the day yon waatch o' yours was fexed, we've aye been hearin o' yer loon, Wullie Leckie; aye, I'll pit my siller on it, that yer loon couldna fex the harness tae a horse's cairt gin the horse himsel gied him a hand, and I'll pit a sax-month worth o' siller on it.

The hands suddenly lost their taste for the game, since Lachie Crozier had just wagered one of their stipends for the sake of his pride; but Wullie and Lachie Crozier had already shaken on it, the deal was irrevocable, and they looked to the engine with anxiety as Wullie returned to his place beside Andy McGrath, while Lachie Crozier reassured them,

Dinna fash yersels, my bonnie loons, yaise yer heids, d'ye think a fowerteen-year-aal'll hae yon grand beast werkin proper?

but by now there was doubt on both sides. As Wullie heard

the words of Crozier he found himself looking up to a faintly clouded-over sky, to what might lie beyond it, and more importantly perhaps thinking of what Jeannie would say were she here, and what she might yet say if it came to the worst.

There were three main arcs to the pressure gauge, and Watchie's eyes never left the dial as the needle slowly crept around the face of it, from zero at six o'clock to the next major calibration, when the pressure was barely sufficient to drive the engine, to the frontiers of the parenthesis in red, when the pressure was in danger of stretching the boiler at the seams, popping the rivets like the buttons of a jacket and causing a sudden and catastrophic release of steam through the first weakness in the bloated copper. Only when the needle jogged on the spot at around two thirds of the way around the gauge did Watchie feel confident enough to grasp the lever in his hands, and by then his heart was raging against the bars of his ribs like a wrongly held innocent. He looked around the gathering as the captured steam thundered in the boiler, and there, at the back of the Lowthers, were the two faces he needed to see to give him the courage to do it; Meggie Hill, his nursemaid with her cups of tea and her smile; and Davie Lowther, the tunnels of his nose distended the better to discern the scent of his kill in prospect; and then, without thought, Watchie released the trigger grip and then hauled on the lever, pulling it securely home.

For a moment, nothing happened. Watchie could sense Davie Lowther's grin brightening like the sun emerging from cloud, even without looking at him, and Wullie felt his pocket lighter already even as his heart grew heavier, even as his hand went unbidden to his pocket to clasp his watch like a talisman, feeling it cold to the touch. Then, slowly, the engine uttered a long and steamy sigh of relief, the piston reared up in its cylinder and turned the crank, and the flywheel too spun to its demand, transmitting its power the length of the leather belt and resurrecting the dormant mill with a shudder, causing it to shake itself like a dog with fleas.

Watchie climbed down from the plate and sat on its step, his legs trembling like those of a newly born foal. Immediately a carnival went into session all around him; Hebbie Lowther and Tommy Kerr and the other workers gathered around, his hand was shaken until he thought his arm would be loosened at the shoulder, and Meggie Hill came over to say,

I kent fine ye'd dee't, fit did I tell ye?

but it was lost in the warp and weft of simultaneous chatter, though he heard her say that she knew. Wullie did not wait to claim his wager from Lachie Crozier, but rounded the chiel, who was slumped dismally against his cart, and carved straight through the crowd towards his son,

Did I nae taal ye, Waatchie? Fit was I aye taalin ye?

and Hebbie Lowther said,

Aye, Wullie, the loon's werth the blaain, efter a',

a dart which ricocheted into the hide of Hebbie's own son, driving Davie Lowther away and into the yard to kick at the stones there beyond the farmhouse.

Lachie Crozier, too, was growing impatient, and came over to the gathering to say,

Wid ye hurry up and pit yer corn tae the mill, Hebbie Lowther, for the rain'll nae be ower lang in camin, mind ye?

Hebbie nodded, and said,

Aye, richt y'are, Lachie,

and sent a number of workers, Tommy Kerr included, to pitch free corn from the ricks to feed the appetite of the idling mill. Wullie approached Lachie Crozier, and kept his expression even as he said,

There's jist the matter o' a wee bit siller tae settle atween us, is there nae, Lachie?

Crozier shrugged his shoulders, and nodded.

I didna think ye were a gamblin man, Wullie Leckie,

he said, but Wullie shook his head.

I'm nae, Lachie. Gie't tae the kirk, for yon's fit I'd expect o' a richt guid Christian,

and then spun on his heel, and went over to tend to his son, who still sat on the footplate with his face in his hands, numb with exhaustion.

★

204

Peter Millar arrived later in the day to find to his great relief that his engine was in the pink of health, with the mechanic from Aberdeen whose schedule of repairs had been too busy for him to drop immediately for the sake of a distant village; but he scanned Watchie's repairs, and saw that they were by and large sound, though he proclaimed it a miracle that Watchie's bung in the collar had held long enough to thresh an entire load of corn. For his trouble, Peter Millar sent Watchie through the post a single shilling coin folded into a short letter which read, with thanks for your repairs, Peter Millar, which Jeannie received and gave to Watchie, saying that it was only but right considering the bother his engine had caused, with half a mind on the cleaning that it had caused her.

Sure enough, as Davie Lowther had feared, the news did spread through the village, that Watchie Leckie, a fourteen-year-old loon whose chin had not yet felt the scrape of a blade, had been responsible for fixing the great beast of an engine belonging to Peter Millar; and while Peter Millar himself was generous in his praise for Wullie Leckie's son, Hebbie Lowther too made sure that word of the event passed to any who would listen, in the same breath as he announced the engagement of Tommy Kerr to Meggie Hill, much to the surprise of all. The word of Watchie's prowess pricked up the ears of the widow Jamieson, who had followed the story of Peter's broken engine with unholy delight, breathing in the fragrance of a reputation in shreds and sure that this was a herald to the ruination she had known would trail him to his deathbed; but on hearing that the son of Wullie Leckie had brought the damned machine back to its full vigour in three days of hard and unstinting work, she prowled the streets of the village with a murderous tread, and stopped by Henderson's to declaim to the clientele, aye, the deil's in yon loon, certain I am o't, fit ither way wid a fowerteen-year-aal ken fit way tae fex ane o' the deil's ain craturs, answer me yon?

And so Watchie Leckie gained a new reputation for himself, no longer the skittish and awkward loon of Mr Clarke's class-room, now the name Watchie was his by right and by the dignity of his office, reported throughout the alehouses and the places of worship by those who had been witnesses; there were those like the widow who thought it a gift bestowed by the devil to bring a corrupt world to the doorsteps of all in the village, who considered Watchie a disciple of Satan's for his precocious knowledge; but they were few, and despite the best attempts of Davie Lowther, it was not long before the name of Pish-ma-breeks was tramped soundly into the mud, and left there to be forgotten.

XVII

Wullie was very much caught in two minds over his son's undeniable gift for mechanical repair; for while he viewed Watchie's achievement with great pride, he also saw the continuity of the farm deliquesce in Watchie's hands like quicksilver, slipping through fingers that were never keen to hold it in the first place. This saddened Wullie as he sat in his living-room of a night, reading the day's *Press and Journal* and listening to the tick of the clock and the clatter of Peggy's knitting needles, and hearing his old father singing from the floor above, full of the whisky and stroking the greying coat of the Laird behind closed doors. Watchie was never there to talk to him, spending as much of his time in his room with the book as he possibly could now, somehow able to ignore his grandfather's off-key voice during the course of his monastic study; the only other contented member of the household apart from Jeannie, whose pride in her son was quite unalloyed by any considerations of the business, and who had seen her prophecy concerning Watchie's future for his delicate hands come to its full and ripe fruit in the matter of the traction-engine. Wullie began to think unworthily of her as he sat across from her at the fire, that it was no concern of hers, having simply married into the family and therefore having no intimate stake in the family's concern, though he knew fine well enough that Watchie had never shown any great interest in the affairs of farming, and while even through the years he still blamed Jamie Watts for it, hearing from Jeannie how pitilessly he had used Watchie during his time as the farm's orra loon, he had still to find within himself the notion that perhaps Watchie would never make a farmer, that he was cut from the wrong material for the task, and now Wullie walked about the farm as if he knew that his tenure here at Smallbrae was to be a short one, that the family was no sooner established here for three generations than the land was to be squandered, and this was a prospect which dulled him so that nothing seemed to catch his attention for long, not even Jessica pulling on his coat for another penny to buy a playtime candy from the sweetshop. In Jessica, Wullie saw a pretty little daughter to be sure, her hair gold as the corn stalk and eyes as blue as his own, but not the continuity he was after, for most likely she would grow to be a beautiful young woman, this was his hope, working for the farm until she was able by all means, but one day she would be lost to them, like her mother before her, working for another's farm, or worse still in service to another as a kitchen maid; and for all that Wullie thought kindly of Cathie Loudon, it was not something he would soon see for a daughter of his.

Wullie remembered well the stories told to him by Aal Wullie when he was young enough to perch on his father's knee, stories that he had never told to Watchie and that he had forbidden Aal Wullie to tell, of an old woman whose croft had been built on the site of Smallbrae a long long time ago, about where the byre was now. It was a story he had asked Aal Wullie to tell him again and again, a story made richer by the heat of the fire and his father's malty breath as he sipped on a glass of whisky; sipped, mind you, for he had not yet lost his footing on his own land, and still took the drink in moderation. It was the story of how the most visible rump of a hill nearest to the farm came to be called the Deil's Shieling, long before Lord Gordon's feuing of the land, when old Nellie Fordyce in a fever dream saw the giant beast himself surmounting the hill and crying out his claim on the land for twenty miles around where he stood, and it thrilled Wullie to the marrow to hear it in the light of a single lamp, while the shadows fed on the telling of it and grew fatter in the corners, rising and baring their claws above him. Now Wullie paced the extent of his land, the land given in his name by his father as a wedding present, and stared up at the mount of the Shieling, wondering beyond reason if the cursed and venomous touch of those hooves had somehow drained into the loam, saturating the earth below with its malignancy, giving him a son with no interest in the very thing he held dearest to himself, with the curse in addition that his son should give him reason for great pride.

Wullie stared at the hill from the furthest boundary of his farm, and wondered if this was where it would all end; though there was still Jessica to be learned how to milk the kye, it was not enough to provide a succession, and he stood on his land when the weather was fine, drawing his comfort from his possession of it, vowing never to leave this land until the last breath passed him, it would always be Wullie Leckie's until his time came, and nothing would change it.

A year passed since Watchie's miracle, before the Revd James Lyle stepped in to plough the furrows for Watchie's future, and this is how it happened:

One Sunday, the Leckies made their way to the mouth of the kirk after the finish of the service as usual, Aal Wullie heaving himself to his feet in his uncomfortable Sunday clothes, followed by Peggy modestly raising the back of her skirt as an obstacle during her exit from the pew, then Wullie, as the head of the household, then Jeannie, grasping tight hold of Jessica's hand to curb her wandering, with Watchie at the rear. Tommy and Meggie Kerr were there, Meggie beginning to swell with her bairn and trailing behind her husband of three months, never smiling in his company once. Outside the kirk, the Revd James Lyle took Watchie's hand and held it captive, saying,

And you, young man, young William. I've been hearing great things about you, great things indeed. They've begun to call you Watchie, I believe.

Watchie felt the heat in his face as he nodded, smiling. Before he could say a word, Wullie stepped in and said,

Aye, Reverend, he's richt guid wi the waatches and the like.

The Reverend continued to stare at Watchie,

And traction-engines, too, I hear. Most remarkable. Most remarkable in a boy of your age.

Watchie shrugged, feeling the moisture spring to the palm of his retained hand.

It was jist efter a wee cleanin, Reverend, there was nae hardly a thing wrang wi' it.

The Reverend released his hand, opened out his own like an angler describing the measure of his catch.

I've always thought it the sign of the truly gifted, he said, that they will wait for others to remove the bushel from their light. Most remarkable.

By now, the congregation had begun to spill around the obstruction on their way to their carts and gigs and bicycles, and Watchie stared at the Reverend, who continued,

Such a fine gift you've been blessed with, Watchie. What a great pity, should it go to waste, do you not think?

Watchie nodded, in the absence of any other reply he should make. The Reverend smiled, and brought his hands together as if in prayer. The hands left behind them a fragrance of perfumed soap, a smell which intrigued Watchie, carried swiftly away by a skittish breeze.

We must talk more about this, William, he said. I'd be most grateful if you would come to the manse some time in the next week, perhaps after school, if you could. Would that be suitable for you?

Watchie nodded, turned to his father; the Reverend turned also,

Of course, I'm sure your father will be only too glad to give you the permission, am I right, Mr Leckie?

Wullie nodded too,

Aye, he can that, Reverend,

said Wullie, for he would never think of standing in the way of the man who had revealed to him the reason for his diminished custom. The Reverend smiled broadly,

Excellent, he said. Then I may expect you to visit the manse at some time during the week. I hope to see you whenever it suits you.

Jessica twisted her head to look up at her mother,

Fit's Waatchie awa tae see the Reverend for?

Jeannie and Peggy both smiled,

We dinna ken, Jessie, said her mother, but Wulliam'll be awa tae fin' oot the morrow, will ye nae, Wulliam?

She had no need to urge Watchie any more; for Watchie was by now quite curious himself to find out what precisely was to be demanded of his gift, that he could barely eat his dinner that evening for the thought of it, perhaps it was another clock to mend, and he slept lightly on the cushion of it, until he was wakened by Jeannie shaking him by the shoulder and telling him that it was time to help with the milking of the kye, and that he could dress in old clothes in the meantime while she prepared the best of his apparel for his meeting with the Reverend.

Miraculously, the outfit stayed clean for the duration of the school day, and Watchie took his satchel on his back and walked with a good confident stride to the kirk, and through the gate of the manse. It was a bleak day, not raining but bulging with threat, and the roses stood in their beds in a final defiance before shedding their petals and drawing themselves in for the long frosts of winter. Watchie stood at the door to the manse, shaded under its canopy, and stared at the round of glass in the frame, a thick lens which distorted the images seen through it. He reached around to the stirrup set into the pilaster and gave it a gentle pull; for little effort it set up quite an alarm, and Watchie hoped that it did not give the impression of impatience with all its jangling. In a moment the door was opened by Mrs Jenkins the housekeeper, with her kindly face and her froth of well-brushed hair, which refused the discipline of a bun, and her smile seemed to be made for setting anxiety at its ease, causing Watchie's bottled shoulders to fall as he was shown into the large drawing-room facing the street.

The room was empty, and smelled like the rest of the house of polish and scent, with a slight odour of peat smoke from the fire burning in its place. It was empty, but not empty of interest for Watchie, because, like Wullie before him when he went to receive word of the slander of Jamie Watts, Watchie could not fail to notice the many clocks in the Revd Lyle's possession, and immediately he was drawn over to them. Some were quite familiar to him, nothing special about the workings and only made extraordinary by some intricate detail about the casing; but others were quite beyond his common experience, such as the clock whose workings were perfectly visible under a dome of clear glass, with a mysterious escapement which appeared to depend upon the slow rotation of four brass spheres anchored to a spindle, turning first this way then that. Then there was the clock suspended on the wall which resembled more the small dormer window of a rustic wooden house, complete with carved oak leaves and acorns, with a pairing of closed shutters on the frieze above the facing, and as the clock chimed a quarter hour, the shutters fled open and a tiny carved cuckoo charged out of doors, nodding after the beat of the chime and opening its beak to let out its two-note song, cu-ckoo! before tilting back and slamming shut the doors of its house. Watchie started back on his heels at the suddenness of it, though he had heard of cuckoo clocks before, and he was just beginning to wonder what mechanism would cause the bird to utter its whistle when the door opened, and in came the Revd James Lyle, walking over to Watchie to take his hand in a firm shake.

Very pleased to see you, William, he said. I thought you might like to see the clocks before we begin.

Watchie drew his hand away from the Reverend, and pointed to the cuckoo clock.

I've nae seen a clock like thon afore, Reverend, he said, and the reverend looked at it as if for the first time.

Ah yes. Made in Switzerland, I believe. Remarkable work. Delightfully silly, do you not think?

Watchie did not understand the Reverend, but said,

Na na, it's richt bonnie, a lot o' fine werk aboot the casing.

The Reverend smiled.

Of course, he said, there's always value to be found in the most curious of objects. Please take a seat. Mrs Jenkins will be bringing us tea shortly.

Watchie made no reply, and indeed showed no sign that he had even heard. He was busy staring at the polished brass of the carriage clock on the mantelpiece, the handle which arced above the plain cube, the miniature fretwork on the points of the hands. Again the Reverend smiled, and leaned over to look at Watchie.

Or would you rather stand, William?

Watchie seemed to awaken as if from a mesmeric trance at the snap of a finger, suddenly, turning to the Reverend and blushing slightly.

I'm affa sorry, Reverend, he said, but I've nae seen sae mony clocks afore in the yin room.

The Reverend opened his hands a little, from their joining at rest.

I quite understand, said the Reverend. It's a small hobby of mine, but I do bear in mind the fact that they're more than simply a hobby of yours. Please continue.

There was also a grandfather clock in the corner, nearest to the window, in sight of the fading portrait of the reverend's predecessor, and Watchie went over to inspect it, the fine and rich mahogany casing towering above all the others, and on the dial was a sunrise and moonrise which turned to the movement of the mechanism to shine above a painted farmhouse, the moon trailing behind it a constellation of five-pointed stars glittering in a darkened sky. All the clocks in the room were unanimous in their telling of the time, so that they chimed the same hours and half-hours like a committee in agreement; but each of their beats was different, some more rapid than others, and through it all was the stately pulse of the grandfather, marking the time solidly and with a leaden stammer which sounded like the voice of authority, and the Reverend said,

The grandfather clock is the one which I use to synchronize all the others. It never seems to go any faster or any slower. I quite rely on the dear old thing. I picked it up in a shop in Edinburgh, while I was studying divinity. I used to set it to the one o'clock gun, but it's never lost time yet.

Watchie stroked the lacquered skin of the clock, felt it perfectly smooth to his fingertips, and quite cold. He said,

It'll gang faster or slower gin ye shift the pendulum on the shaft.

He realized what he was doing, and snatched away his hand as if the casing had become electrified; he said,

Ye widna be efter changin it onyway.

The Reverend nodded.

Not when it tells perfect time. I have great faith in that clock. It's the first one I ever owned. Please, sit down, unless of course you have more to see.

Watchie shook his head, and obeyed. He realized that the Reverend had not stopped him from touching the grandfather clock, and wondered if that meant he was trusted with it. The armchair sank underneath him, a flabby thing of red buttoned leather, guiding him towards the heat of the fireplace and its gentle flame; the Reverend sat opposite, and formed his hands into a temple in front of him. Watchie noticed, for the first time, how long and delicate the Reverend's fingers were. The Reverend stared evenly at Watchie, and said,

Are you aware, young Watchie, that you have roused the ire of Mrs Jamieson with your work?

Watchie shook his head.

I didna ken, Reverend. My faither says she's a wee bittie touched.

The Revd James Lyle uttered a laugh, as rich and brown as the polished mahogany.

That's a rather uncharitable interpretation of her behaviour, he said. Perhaps not touched. Devout in her peculiar beliefs, maybe, although I understand why your father might think her mad. Quite simply, she believes that all mechanical objects are products of the devil, and so you, by consenting to fix them, are in fact performing the devil's work.

He was smiling like an explorer who sees a frenzy erupt in a tribe of natives over a string of coloured wooden beads. He leaned forward to Watchie, and said,

Are you performing the devil's work, William Leckie?

Watchie sank further back into his seat, as if grafting his flesh to the leather. He said,

Na na, Reverend, I widna dee the deil's werk, nae ever. I'm jist fexin waatches, and engines fit fa' seeck . . .

The Reverend laughed, and settled back into his chair.

Rest assured, William, I do not see any blame in your

actions. The widow has a curious idea about the products of man's intellect, an idea to which I personally do not subscribe, nor does the Episcopalian Church as a whole. There is nothing sinful about relying upon the good brain that God gave you to mend and create the products of artifice which are also the invention of God-given intellect. Do you understand me, Watchie?

Watchie nodded, and the Reverend nodded in sympathy. At that moment, there was a timorous knock on the door, and in came Mrs Jenkins with a silvered and elliptical tray, smiling her apology for interrupting as she took the assembly to a chair-high occasional table placed beside the Reverend. The pot was crafted with veins and almost vegetable shoots sealing the handle to the stout body; she tilted it, pouring a generous measure into each of the cups, milking them from a matching jug, sugaring each to their fancy from a matching bowl, before modestly retiring with her back to the door, keeping each of them in her sight until the door closed over. With the flat of his hand, the Reverend gestured that Watchie should pick up his cup and saucer; which he did, drinking the tea, sweet and moderately strong, much to the Reverend's obvious taste. The Reverend swallowed his tea, then settled his cup on its saucer and rested the saucer on his lap.

Are you familiar with the argument from design, Watchie?

he said, and Watchie frowned for a moment.

I dinna ken, Reverend,

he said, and pushed himself forward on his seat to better balance the cup on his lap. The Reverend looked into the fire in its hearth.

The argument from design, said the Reverend slowly, suggests that there is an underlying order to the whole of creation, much as there is in the mechanism of a watch, or a clock. Everything fits perfectly together, like one wheel meshing with the movement of another to produce a single movement, the clockwise movement of the hands. The argument has been criticized by many, especially by David Hume, but I must admit I find it a quite compelling argument, for all its shortcomings. What do you think of the idea, Watchie? Is there a master clockmaker behind the whole of creation, a clockmaker we may call God? Have you given it much thought?

Watchie's frown deepened. He remembered his time with Anthony, the book which showed the parting of blossoms, laid out for inspection like the diagrams in his own book of artifice; and it was true, there did appear to be an order behind the making of them, each according to their function, though he said,

I've nae thocht ower muckle aboot it, Reverend,

and the Reverend took another delicate sip,

I would ask you to think about it, Watchie. The Lord God and the humble clockmaker have much in common between them. Each brings together the disparate pieces of their creation, and renders them into a meaningful order, an object of great beauty. Remember that when you next put together a clock; you are no more and no less performing an act of creation which has God's blessing, and let no one, not even Mrs Jamieson, who claims to be speaking with the voice of God, tell you otherwise.

For a moment the Reverend's eyes lost their focus, as if he were speaking to a wide congregation seated in their pews; then he shook his head slightly, and turned his full attention on Watchie, who was shifting in his seat, quite taken aback by the implications of his comparison.

I believe that I may be able to help you, said the Reverend.

And that was how Watchie left the manse with an envelope in his pocket, addressed to James Strachan in Turriff, some twelve miles west of Aberlevin, sealed with a scab of wax in front of his eyes not ten minutes previously, after the reverend had shown him the contents of the letter. He had written on the front of it, in a tightly bound and flourished hand, the name James Strachan Esq., and inside was an introduction from the reverend, a testament to Watchie's reputation in the village of Aberlevin and the witness of many who had seen him fix with his own hands the traction-engine belonging to Peter Millar at the farm of Hebbie Lowther, whose name was also invoked in reference. The Reverend had explained to Watchie, over a second cup of tea, that he had been in conversation with the Revd Dalwhinnie of the Episcopalian communion in Turriff not two weeks previously, when the name of Watchie Leckie of Aberlevin had come up during the course of it, for through the mart the news of Watchie's repairs had spread in the way that mythology will, reaching the ears of many who knew nothing of the loon, and this included James Strachan, who was looking for one to teach as an apprentice in his shop in the main street of Turriff. Many conversations had followed, negotiation and promises and all of them culminating in the Revd Lyle's invitation to the manse, and the proposition which set Watchie's heart leaping the more he heard of it; the envelope filled the pocket of his good jacket, peering over the rim, and on the way home Watchie kept his arm over it in case of a sudden break in the cloud, and a squall of rain which might spoil it, and he jigged childishly with one foot in front of the other like a sword dancer.

Back in the house, Peggy and Jeannie both ruined the loon with congratulation when he told them his news, and both insisted that he should tell Wullie himself, going through to the living-room where his father was hidden behind the day's copy of the *Press and Journal*. The fire sparked, and the clock stammered over its seconds; Wullie noticed Watchie entering the room, uncertain of himself, walking slowly over to take the seat opposite his. Wullie looked over the top of the newspaper, closed it over and folded it in quarters, placed it on his lap, and looked at his son.

Weel, he said, fit was the Reverend sayin tae ye, Waatchie?

His face was grave, as if he had just received word of an illness. Watchie leaned forward in the chair, and joined his hands over his knees, scarcely able to meet his father's eyes. Like one standing outside a locked door, he considered all the possible means of entry, unable to decide which was the gentlest; he coughed and began,

We were talkin a filie aboot clocks,

he said. Wullie's posture fell noticeably.

Aye, said Wullie, fit then?

Watchie took a breath.

He's gied me a letter for Mr Strachan, ye ken, the clock-makker mannie in Turriff. He's lookin tae tak on an apprentice, but he'd like tae hae me werkin Setterdays for him. The Reverend's gied me the reference.

The fire cracked in the grate. Wullie nodded slowly.

Ye'll be efter me tae say ye can dee it, am I richt?

Watchie sat still, and Wullie fell back into his seat. He mauled his face with his hand for a moment, and looked fully at his son. Watchie was swelling with the anticipation of his word, shivering though the room was not cold, and Wullie knew that with a shake of the head he could ensure that succession, that continuity he wanted so much for his farm, and for the life of the family on this land. He remembered his own father, in his nightshirt when the skies opened, and looking anxiously for cloud when the days without rain blazed uncommonly on and on, and he thought of his own times in the kirk on Sundays, imploring God for a good season and a good harvest. He thought of Jeannie, taking the bairn's hand gently out of his reach after it had been born and cleaned, he'll nae be a fairmer, Wullie, and he thought of the night that the loon had fixed the watch, and the pride that he himself had felt when the traction-engine had thundered into life in front of all the sceptics of Aberlevin who had laughed at him in the mart when he showed them the watch telling the time once again. He remembered most of all the respect of Hebbie Lowther on that day, how he had shaken Wullie warmly by the hand before they left the farm and said, Ye werena jist blaa'n efter a', Wullie Leckie, yon's a richt guid wee werker ye've there.

He looked to the floor and said,

Will ye be stertin wi James Strachan Setterday neist, Waatchie?

Watchie's eyes lit like beacons, though his face was calm.

The Reverend says tae gang along for seeven o'clock.

Wullie nodded.

Aye, weel, he said, we'll a' be up early yon day onyway, for the milkin. We'll jist hae tae fex Blackie tae the geg fan ye're feenished, and we'll hae ye there for aboot seeven, richt eneuch.

Watchie sat upright in his chair as he realized, and he was about to thank his father, knowing how much it must have cost him, when Wullie held his hand up, the blade of it out towards him, causing Watchie to hold peace for a moment. He said,

I'll nae tak yer thanks, gin ye'd sooner, Waatchie. It's a richt fine thing the Reverend's done for ye, I'll tell ye that.

Watchie left the room with a lightness of step, and at the very least Wullie gave thanks for his son's happiness as the room was sealed behind him. The only two sounds in the room were the rhythm of the clock and the sparking of the fire, brief snaps as if the seeds of flame had taken momentary root in the thick loam of the peat, and Wullie sat in that almost silence for a long time until the readying of the dinner, damning silently the day he had gifted his book to Watchie, opening eyes which might have remained closed during the years; and yet wishing well for his son in these new days of invention, caught in the dilemma of the age, and hoping that there was enough of a living to be made in the contingency of mechanical failure, as his son so obviously thought there was.

XVIII

The week passed, and the farm saw more of the man who had emerged during the crisis of slander so many years ago, as Wullie became more taciturn in the presence of others, even Jeannie, his wife. But it was Aal Wullie who walked to the furthest frontiers of the dry stane dyke which limited the fields, and stood with his son as he cast his eye on the great mound of the Deil's Shieling, turning to regard the land fall away from the swelling, and shaking his head to see the farmhouse beneath him, the biggings squared like a fortress as the land flattened. But Aal Wullie was having none of his son's moods, knowing fine well what was the cause of them, and he said,

Wullie Leckie, I gied ye the fairm tae help ye pit the feed in the mou's o' yer wife and yer bairns. Yer ain son, noo, he'll hae tae think o' the same for himsel. Far aboots is yer pride, man? Ye ken fine he's nae for the fairmin, and there's nae ane o's fa could fex a waatch, nor an engine neether.

Wullie breathed the cooling wintry air from the hillside. It would soon be time to call the cows in from pasture for the rest of the cold season; this he knew from the glass edge of the wind. He said,

I've pride in my fairm as weel.

Aal Wullie placed a hand on Wullie's shoulders.

Tak pride in yer son wi it, Wullie Leckie, for I'll hae ye ken, I tak pride in mine.

They walked down the hillside together; and Aal Wullie found all sorts of remembrances of his younger days, when he saw Johnnie Leckie revolted by the very idea of touching a cow, and Wullie smiled to remember it, the faces his younger brother made as he was pressed near to the cow, his hands formed into the right shape around the teats of the cow by Aal Wullie, and still he could only bleed a little from it; aye said Aal

Wullie, fine did I ken oor Johnnie wisna richt for it, but still he helped till he was ca'ed awa tae sea, and Wullie nodded, how right his father was, though it made the loss of Watchie's hands no easier to bear.

On the Saturday appointed by the Reverend's letter, Wullie drove the cart with Watchie by his side on the board, making the pony take stretches of the journey at a trot, giving the poor old creature a rest periodically before gingering him into an energetic bound again, and the journey was just long enough for Watchie to feel the envelope as a momentous weight in his pocket. A chill breeze disarrayed his hair, and he flattened it down with a nervous movement of his hand; he looked at the hand and found it to be shaking, his stomach was as cold as if he had swallowed a drift of snow, and he turned to his father and said,

D'ye think this'll be richt for me, this job?

Wullie kept his eyes on the road ahead, as if there would be any obstacles to be found there, not looking up at his son.

Dinna say ye're haein doots the noo, Waatchie.

Watchie shrugged.

It's nae the same . . .

Wullie held up a hand, with the rein lashed around it in a spiral.

Wheesht, my loon. Ye were sayin the same aboot the engine, and ye went and fexed yon, did ye nae?

Watchie nodded, for it was true, and fell into a contemplative silence, keeping his eyes like those of his father on the road in front, and after a long and twisting passage, the village of Turriff was visible in the middle distance. There was an increase in the leisured Saturday commerce as they approached, many wagons making deliveries to the main-street shops, and Wullie was once forced to swerve the gig a little to escape a guddle of children, up with the lark and frantic, playing a game of chase which led them dangerously close to the wheels, which made Wullie cry out,

Awa, ye wee buggers ye!

quite unlike his usual self, and Watchie turned to see that his father wore a taut expression of something like grief on his face, a thing that Watchie had never seen before, not even during the time of slander. He was now more like the driver of a hearse, delivering the corpse of a cherished old drinking companion to the kirkyard, performing a last duty for the sake of binding ties; as if he bore the corpse of the farm itself through the town. He approached the plain canopy of the watchmaker's shop, a cap drawn over the legend of square black writing, JAMES STRACHAN, WATCHMAKER AND REPAIRS, JEWELLER, as gamely as a prisoner to the gallows, and left Watchie at the door with not a word of good will or encouragement, turning the gig about almost the very moment that Watchie's feet were on the ground, promising to return for him at six o'clock that evening, and so without ceremony he was away.

Watchie stood in front of the shop for a while, and went over to the shaded window. The clocks behind the glass all told five minutes to seven, and such a fine expression was each of the clockmaker's art that Watchie was held captive by a frank admiration of their beauty and form. Some were fine examples of architecture, rococo and gothic and baroque, temples and cathedrals raised in worship of the blessed mechanisms that each held, and some were simply whimsical, carved from all manner of woods, depicting painted rural scenes with caricatures of lairds and gun dogs on the friezes. Watchie was especially taken by the dignity of the grandfather clocks, which rose above the entire display, keeping a magisterial eye upon the activities of the others, polished to a severe shine, with faces of sleek golden metal, eternal as headstones above the black velvet array of fob watches slanted for the prospective customer's inquiry. The other window across the parting of the doorway was of little interest to Watchie, being another black velvet cloth of gold and silver and platinum rings and items of ornament for the wives of the lairds; it was the clocks and the watches that drew him to the door, forgetting for a moment his profound disquiet, as if the watches had been set to a spin on their axes, mesmerizing him into a confident stride, giving his hand the strength to pull on the rococo handle which released the latch.

When the door opened, it struck a tone from a bell placed on the jamb, tripping a hammer which hit the upended brass bowl, and Watchie nearly jumped to hear it, a sudden strike above his head which made him turn abruptly as if at an unexpected shot from Aal Wullie's gun in the farmyard. The shop was empty, but alive with the smell of linseed oil, a fine perfume to Watchie, and he took the time to look around at shelf after shelf of more clocks than he had ever seen before in his life, each with a label tied to the pedestal on which the prices were inscribed. There was a waist-high counter to his left paned with glass, in which many of the more expensive clocks and watches were kept alongside small cloths of rings; to his front there was a plain counter of wood, and more clocks out of reach behind that, and at the corner of the counter, where the right angle sent another counter towards the opening of the window display, there was a hinged trap which folded down upon a bolted door, the only way through to the other side. Three brass stems sprouted from each wall, flowering into reservoirs of brass and glass tulips cupped around an oil flame, all sending out a generous golden light, giving an extra polish to the clocks which ordinary daylight might have denied them. Watchie approached the fold in the facing counter, which stood opposite an open door in the wall from which he could see a thin light emerging; from behind the door, he heard the whisper of feet, an infirm gait, and after an age an elderly man appeared, passing through the door and over to the counter, taking his time, silent until he was perfectly in place and standing before Watchie like a figure from a weather house, and only then did he start up, bracing both of his hands on the top of the counter and raising his head the two or so inches that Watchie had on him, the expression on his pale and seamed face balanced nicely between gravity and professional necessity.

Aye, my lad, he said, and fit can I dee for ye? Ony clocks tae be repaired, waatches nae keepin the time o' day, a present for a wumman mebbe?

Watchie only then remembered the letter, which he delved for in his pocket, producing it clumsily and putting a crease in it as he made to pass it on before it was ready to come out. The old man let the envelope stay in the air between them for a moment before lifting a hand to take it from him. Watchie looked on as the old man pulled the envelope closer to his eyes to make out the writing on the front, and it occurred to Watchie that perhaps this was not Mr Strachan; but the old man read the name, and slipped a finger under the fold and tore open the flap at the seal, and almost painfully released the letter and opened it out, holding it once again close to his eyes. He read the contents with great care, during which long time Watchie stood as still as he could, aware that he would soon be put to a test of some kind; Strachan nodded and reduced the letter once again to its folds and put it back into the envelope, then looked at Watchie with a much more critical eye, the kind of vision he might have brought to bear upon a faulty watch. He said,

Stand awa frae the coonter, Mr Leckie, gin ye'll please, twa-three steps jist.

Watchie obeyed, taking three short paces back. Strachan leaned a little over the counter, and looked Watchie up and down, then nodded.

Ye dinna look like ye'd fex an engine, Mr Leckie, he said. But the Reverend says ye did, and I'll nae say ither than that. I'd nae tak on a man fa didna hae a pride in his craft, mind ye.

Watchie swallowed hard. He was a man in a courtroom, judged by the timepieces themselves and all that he held dear, standing before a jury of clocks with Strachan as their final instrument. He said,

I've nae been efter ony ither job, Mr Strachan.

Strachan gave him a thin smile, faintly amused.

Ye've nae had affa lang tae be efter ony ither job, my loon. Ye're, fit're ye, fifteen the noo? Fit way am I tae ken ye'll be at it for ower lang? Ye're still at yer schoolin, are ye nae? Fit way am I tae ken ye'll nae be efter anither job afore lang? Eh, Mr Leckie?

Watchie had no answers to Strachan's questions, for he had not expected to need them. The old man's grey brows settled over his light blue eyes, and Watchie felt himself coming apart under the scrutiny, but he said, mildly,

Mr Strachan, I've been lookin at the inside o' clocks for half o' my life. Yon's nae an affa lang time, fine dee I ken that, but I'd nae be richt guid at ony ither thing the noo.

Strachan stared around the room, as if to derive his judgement from the community of clocks on the walls. For a moment he held Watchie suspended in doubt; then he ambled over to the trap in the counter, slowly raised it like the roof of a jack-in-the-box, unbolted the door, and held it open, gesturing with his head that Watchie should go through. As he closed the door and bolted it and snapped shut the counter trap, he said,

Ye're on fit ye ca' a trial, Mr Leckie. Ye'll be peyed weel for yer Setterdays, but ye'll be here at seeven exact, nae later, ither than it's snaain, nor some ither reason ye canna be helpin. Yon's yer conditions, Mr Leckie. Cam awa noo, tae the backshop.

Through the small door, barely taller than Mr Strachan's head, was a perfectly clean and windowless chamber panelled in oak, a little shabby perhaps; there was a low table at the far corner, and there were a number of watches in a queue for repairs, each labelled with a name and a collection date, tied to the loops of the fob watches, and clocks with the labels fastened to their feet. Evidently Watchie's arrival had interrupted one of his repairs, for there was an eviscerated watch lying passively on a scroll of black velvet, and in a small cloth pouch several tools designed for minute and finicky work bristled, restrained in their pouch by a simple girdle not much bigger than a thread which caught the tiny screwdrivers by their more substantial handles. There was one of the screwdrivers waiting on the scroll of velvet, no doubt where Strachan had placed it. There were also a number of miniature lathes on the table, each regulated for differing degrees of finesse, doll's-house copies of the one he had seen in his father's shed, for what purpose Watchie did not as yet know, though he guessed that they might be used for tooling metal to the appropriate shapes for replacement. Strachan led him over to the table, and pulled him out a seat, sitting beside him, and looking all the time at the expression on Watchie's face. Watchie stared in wonder at the dismantled mechanism in front of him, and he recognized like a gathering of old friends the pieces he saw on the velvet, seeing also beside them the empty shell of the casing, discarded like the shell he had been given by his uncle Johnnie. Strachan stared at Watchie, and said,

Fit's yer expert opinion o' yon waatch, the noo, Mr Leckie? D'ye see ower muckle wrang wi't?

Watchie bent over closer, shadowing the light of a small spirit-lamp in the corner of the table, eclipsing his own view of it; Strachan pulled on his shoulder, causing him to straighten in his seat, and look at the old man in puzzlement. Strachan said,

Mindin, ye ken, at a' times that ye darena breathe on the pieces o' the mechanism. Weel, noo, fit tools hae ye got, Mr Leckie?

Watchie looked into Strachan's pale disconcerting eyes, and felt as if he were trying to outstare the sky. He said,

I've nae tools o' my ain, Mr Strachan, there's nae ony shop in Aiberlevin fa'd sell me them.

Strachan nodded, understanding, and said,

Aye, weel, fit tools hae ye in front o' ye? Mind ye as weel that ye canna touch the pieces wi yer fingers, nor they'll be a' creeshie and winna werk richt fan ye pit them a' thegither.

Watchie looked to the instrument pouch, and saw held there a pair of tweezers, a slender wishbone of steel, with long and delicate prongs. He made to pick it out of the pouch, then checked himself and looked at Strachan, interrogatively; Strachan nodded, go on, and Watchie slipped the tweezers from their restraints, and with them picked up a small wheel. Before looking at it properly, he said,

Is it jist efter a cleanin, Mr Strachan? For gin it's jist yon, ye'd be as weel tae tell me the noo.

Strachan shook his head,

Na na, it's a bittie mair serious than jist a cleanin. Hae a lookie wi the glesses, Mr Leckie.

He picked up a construction that Watchie had never seen before; spectacles forged from brass wire, the frames circular tiny barrel of a watchmaker's lens and invited Watchie to try them on. Watchie took the device from his trembling hands, and eased the question-mark legs of the spectacles over each ear; immediately the wheel leapt into focus in front of his enhanced eye, as large as the wheel of a toy wagon, and Watchie could see that it had been forged from tin, seized in what now appeared to be the mighty clamps of the tweezers, and it glittered with a patina of mica. Watchie held it closer to the naked flame of the spirit lamp, drew himself further forward to see better, careful not to cast his breath on the other pieces, then straightened and said,

There's nae a thing wrang wi yon feel, Mr Strachan; but I think it's needin a cleanin, efter a'; and they'll a' be needin a cleanin, gin yon is.

For the first time Strachan's smile warmed, and this made Watchie feel better. The old man said,

Aye, mebbe I didna see thon the ferst time. Ye're quite richt aboot yon feel, Mr Leckie; there's nae a thing wrang wi it. Hae a lookie at anither.

Watchie toured the mechanism one piece at a time, from smallest to largest in order as it had been laid out by Mr Strachan on the velvet, revelling in the clarity of vision the watchmaker's lens granted him, now better able to appreciate the great craft and design which had gone into each of the parts of the watch. He was just in the middle of the array when he caught sight of a pattern of tell-tale bites taken from each of the teeth of a medium-sized wheel, and he cried out,

Yon feel's affa badly pocketed, Mr Strachan, ye'll hae tae replace it wi anither.

Still holding the wheel seized in the prongs of the tweezers, Watchie took off the watchmaker's glasses one-handed and offered them to Strachan. For a moment the glasses, like the letter before them, were suspended in the air between them, and Strachan gazed at them for a while, into the bloated image of nothing distinct formed around the lens. Then he took them from Watchie, and placed them on the table, beside the square of velvet; and then he began to laugh, a dry sound which took Watchie as much by surprise as the shop bell, and as the old man shook in his place, it was as if his professional demeanour cracked through and fell away, and by now he was reaching across the space between them which one moment ago had been the distance from Turriff to Aberlevin, putting a curled old hand upon Watchie's shoulder and saying,

Aye, I'll be listenin tae fit the Revd Dalwhinnie's sayin tae me the neist time! But I'm nae sae certain ye'd be pittin the waatch thegither sae easy, Mr Leckie, unless ye'd care tae prove me wrang there as weel.

Over the next hour, this Watchie did, first boiling a small amount of water in a tin pot, using a spirit burner on a tripod, and cleaning the mechanism as he had done many years ago, this time with the proper spirits of wine, of which Strachan had many bottles; and Strachan was able to give Watchie a replacement wheel of exactly the right size to fit into the mechanism. Strachan's trusted regulator clock, with its eternally constant telling of the proper time of day, chimed ten o'clock exactly when Watchie came from the back shop with the watch fully assembled and oiled, and Strachan took it from his hands and listened to it, a fine healthy beat for a watch of cheap tin such as this one. Watchie said,

Is the mannie fa's waatch it is camin by tae tak it the day?

and Strachan paid him with a smile and said,

The mannie fa's waatch it is, he's pecked it up jist the noo, for ye dinna think a waatchmakker jist has the ane waatch, dee ye, Mr Leckie?

Watchie stared at Strachan for a while, the crafty old goat that he was; and Strachan stared unashamedly in return,

I'll be yaisin yon burner tae mak mysel a cuppie o' tea in a meenit. Wid ye hae a cuppie wi me, Mr Leckie, and then we'll fin oot a' ye ken aboot clocks?

There were many movements for Watchie to learn about, but he was eager to learn, and once again James Strachan had models for demonstration that he was given to try, some the simplest variations on the theme of rotary movement, some quite curious and different, but Watchie worked through them all speedily and with great efficiency. Of course, Watchie's wages were paid for other kinds of work not related to the craft of watchmaking; his were the menial tasks around the shop, freeing Strachan to fix the watches to be collected on the Saturday. He kept the shop as free of dust as he could, with birch besoms and shovels and damp cloths on working surfaces, but he understood the necessity for these tasks, and every week Strachan gave him another lesson on a strange and antic mechanism alien to his eyes, stretching the muscles of his intellect just that little bit more each week so that the range and depth of his knowledge grew. With a small deduction from his wages each week, he purchased his own set of watchmaker's tools, in their own strapped purse of cloth, and a pair of watchmaker's glasses, and soon enough Strachan was trusting him with his simple watch repairs. And with the wages he was given, Watchie made the first purchase of his adult life; a bicycle, to save his father the long journey there and back of a Saturday, which only served as emphasis that Watchie Leckie of Aberlevin had his own roads to travel, with no help but his own, and that for several hours on a Saturday he was lost to the sight of Smallbrae, no longer in need of even the smallest of favours.

XIX

It was a measure of Watchie's great patience, and his will to learn at the pace set by Mr Strachan, that his brushing of the floors and wiping of the counter was never considered by him to be any more than a test of his dedication rather than an abuse of his willing labour, that he was never heard to complain to his employer about anything he was given to do. At midday on every Saturday he unwrapped the parcel of bread and matured cheese given to him by Jeannie, and Strachan brought through to him from his sanctum a chipped enamel mug of hot tea bleached almost white by a generous addition of milk. Strachan dragged over the dustless floorboards a small chair and sat down into it, a long process of arrangement of his limbs into appropriate and comfortable positions while his frame cracked as much as the limbs of the chair itself, and both sat to enjoy the tranquillity of the closed hour after Watchie turned the sign in the door.

It was during one of these breaks, many months into the apprenticeship, that Watchie, standing at his customary place behind the counter, decided to broach the subject of his greater involvement in the business. He gave a slight cough to make a tear in the silence which gathered around them, and said,

Mr Strachan,

to draw his attention, and Strachan looked over the horizon of his mug, through the loops of his glasses, and waited patiently for his apprentice to continue. Now that Watchie had gathered his courage together, he said quickly,

Did I taal ye I've been makkin clock cases in widwerk?

Strachan looked at his charge for a moment, then took another sip of tea, thick with sugar. He placed the mug on the counter top, just within reach, and said,

Na na, nae a werd, Master Leckie, ye've nae tellt me onythin aboot yer clock cases afore; na na, I canna recall ye sayin onythin aboot yon,

then pierced Watchie with a look, as if Watchie had made him an offer for his business with sixpence in his hand. Watchie nodded quickly, and broke a rag of bread from his mother's lunch, holding it in his fingers.

Aye, I have that. There's nae ower muckle tae dee in widwerk. Maist o' the ithers jist mak chairs and tables and the like.

Strachan reached out for his tea, drank it casually.

Fowk'll aye hae the need o' chairs and tables, he said. Fowk dinna need clocks fan they've the sun tae taal them fan it's day, and the muin tae taal them fan it's nicht.

The mug rang once more on the counter top, and this time Strachan gave Watchie a glare of open incitement, against which Watchie had no defence. Watchie had seen his employer at work, and had a fine regard for the craft of old man Strachan, having often taken for his model the senior man's patience and dedication in hunting down the least noticeable of faults and the time spent over the lathe, tooling to perfection a piece for replacement; but many were the times that he returned to Smallbrae, to his close chamber of a bedroom, and looked upon the top of his tallboy, where the vacant cabinets gazed emptily in return, a mockery of their purpose, disturbing in their blackest depths where the candlelight would not shine, mute, demanding to be given life and meaning. This had been on Watchie's mind for some time now; and he said to Strachan,

Fowk'll aye need their clocks as weel; fit ither way wid they ken the time o' day or nicht?

Strachan smiled, mysteriously. He said,

Man, man, fit way did fowk ken the time afore there wis the clock, years ahint us? God makt the sun and the muin for yon, and there's still fowk that'll nae hae a clock in their hoose, for they've windas tae see oot o', and doors gin they've nae windas. They gang awa tae their beds fan the muin's oot, and they gang oot o' their beds fan the sun gangs up; fine dee they ken the time o' day, and nae mair wid they hae a clock in the hoose than they'd hae the deil tae sup wi them.

Watchie looked to the pale tea shimmering in his mug. He said,

Mr Strachan, ye're sayin tae me there's nae ees in the warld for a shoppie like yer ain. Ye're sayin there's nae ees for fowk like yersel and me as weel.

Strachan held himself upright in the chair, and looked severely at his apprentice.

I didna say ony sic a thing, Master Leckie, if ye'd but hear fit it is I am sayin. I'm sayin, dinna fex a' yer thocht on the makkin and fexin o' jist the ane thing, for yon's nae a richt guid thing tae dee wi yer life.

He gripped the chair under the seat, and carefully and painfully raised both it and himself closer to Watchie. He laid the flat of his hand on the top of the counter and used it to beat out a gentle rhythm in time to the words he spoke, and this is what he said:

Fine dee I ken that they cry ye Waatchie in Aiberlevin, for yon's fit the Revd Lyle tellt me, and d'ye ken fit that taals me, Master Leckie? It taals me ye're a loon wi jist the ane mind, and yon's nae the way tae mak yersel happy in life. D'ye ken fit I'm sayin, Master Leckie? I winna cry ye Waatchie, nae in my shop, for there's a hale week fan I dinna ken fit ither thing ye're deein, and there's but ten oors fan I see ye fexin clocks and waatches, and a richt fine learner ye are, I'll taal ye that jist the noo.

Watchie looked to his feet, the shine of his boots bright and mirrored thanks to the ministrations of Peggy the night before, and took a brief and swollen breath.

Thank ye, Mr Strachan,

he said, in all modesty, but Strachan raised his hand from the counter top to present a seamed palm to the loon, halting him,

Aye, it's nae mair than yer due, Master Leckie, for ye've proved tae me wi yer time here that ye're a guid werker. But ye're nae affa aal jist yet, and gin there's a'thin I canna abide wi, it's a loon o' nae verra advanced years makkin his mind on jist the ane thing. Fit'll ye dee, the noo, gin ye lose the ees o' yer hands, or the sicht o' yer een, and ye canna fex anither clock, eh,

Master Leckie? Wid ye hae a wee corner tae yersel, and nae see a'body, and waste a' the time that was left tae ye jist in weeshin? Wid ye noo, Master Leckie?

Watchie looked once again into the elderly eyes, and remembered when he had first arrived punctually in James Strachan's shop, some months ago. Old Strachan's will was once again to test his charge; but Watchie had no idea whether or not this was a test of faith in his vocation, and for a moment he stood confused. He looked away from Strachan's magnified gaze, trying to find his strength in the judgement of the clock jury which stared him back evenly, and he said,

I've nae thocht o' yon, Mr Strachan. I've a fine strang pair o' hands, and nae bother wi the sicht o' my een.

Strachan nodded, then reached to his glasses, and plucked them from his ears by their wire legs.

Fit way d'ye think I hae the need o' my spectacles, Master Leckie? Ye canna luik at sic a sma' thing as a waatch and nae ruin yer sicht, I'll taal ye thon.

He replaced the glasses, one hooked leg at a time; in front of his eyes, they appeared to Watchie like the lenses before the faces of the clocks, and for a moment it seemed as if all time were incarnated in the ageing face of the watchmaker himself, an old and weathered aspect, the features blank and somehow carven, and Watchie gathered himself together and said,

Mr Strachan, I've tellt ye aboot the cases I've been makkin at the school, and ye've nae said gin ye're minded tae tak them in or nae.

Strachan stared at his young assistant for a long time, suddenly wearied; then gave a broad smile, the lifting of cloud and the sheerest light through the gloom of it, and said,

Ye will persist, Master Leckie. I'll see yer clock cases neist Setterday. But jist the noo, it's affa near the time tae be gangin back tae yer werk. Fit'll ye be larnin the day, Master Leckie, eh?

Upstairs in his room, Watchie spent the next week sorting through the cabinets which had by now displaced almost every other ornament from the surface of the tallboy. Only the ivory whale carved for him by his uncle Johnnie remained in full sight, blessed by an improved vantage, perched on the roof of a clock whose frieze, appropriately enough, depicted the hunting of a stylized whale. Even the book, which he now had less need to consult after the lessons learned during what he still thought of as his apprenticeship, had been removed from its privileged place to make room for the empty cabinets. Watchie stared each cabinet in its single vacant eye, and for the six days which preceded his next visit to his employer, he tried to choose his favourites; quite inclined towards the decorative friezes, though there was an integrity to the plain hutches with the slightest of ornamentation inspired by architecture which also moved him. With the candle burning in his room when the light began to fail, some days he preferred the clocks which were more ornate, walking around them to appreciate a new shadow which sprang from a detail he had never regarded when applying the chisel to the wood; some days his preference lay with the simplicity of a cube of oak, relieved by Doric columns and the triangular geometry of a temple's crown, or a spire which mimicked that of a house of God. One day he might be a sculptor, the next an architect; and when Friday evening forced a choice upon him, he decided that he should take one of each kind.

On Saturday, Watchie clambered aboard his black-frame bicycle at an early enough hour to reach Turriff, with the two clocks in their hessian resting comfortably in the basket lashed to the handlebars.

Watchie arrived at Strachan's with five minutes to spare, drawing comfort from the acute angle of the minute hands on the plethora of displayed clocks which he had come to know as friends over the months. James Strachan turned the key which was settled inside the brass escutcheon, and opened the door enough for Watchie and his bike to enter,

Aye on time, Master Leckie, he said, nor wind nor hail nor snaa'll keep ye awa,

and he guided Watchie and his bike through the dock of the counter flap to its stable in the back-shop sanctum. The canvas sack sat in the basket, and Watchie almost reached out for it the moment the bike was angled on the banister; but Strachan said,

Ye'll be stertin yer werk the noo, Master Leckie,

and looked behind his shoulder, to where the brush and pail were standing shiftlessly in the corner, layabouts waiting for the word before they would turn a hand to their task. Watchie's gaze fell to the floorboards, how clean they seemed to be, but he went to the corner and took the instruments into his hand, and just before he left the back shop, Strachan said,

There'll aye be the time fan we hae oor lunch at midday, master Leckie, never fear o' that,

and Watchie nodded, chastened into silence.

Now, Watchie understood perfectly that time loses its meaning when something must be waited for; each second, sharpened against the strap of anticipation, drags across the flesh. During his long wait, Watchie found himself comparing the craft displayed before him to his own, the beaten and forged metals of some, and some made with great care and a wider access to better materials than he had ever seen before; and already tattered by the waiting, Watchie began to wish that he had never taken his clocks from their tallboy, that he had not said anything to his employer.

The noontime chorus of all the chimes in the shop had no longer faded when Strachan came out of his room, the door squalling like a bairn as it opened and closed, and went slowly over to the counter flap, raising it slowly and opening the latch, shuffling out and over to the shop door, turning the sign in the glass to show closed, padded back to the counter. Watchie fretted his lower lip with his teeth as the old man returned to the inner room, and came out with the usual two mugs of tea, placing Watchie's on the counter top near to him. Watchie swallowed hard, said,

I'll jist awa and tak my clocks frae the bike . . .

and almost instantly Strachan held his hand up, palm out, and said,

Efter tea, Master Leckie, dinna be in sic a rush.

It is to Watchie's credit that he pushed no further while Strachan drank his tea at his leisure, insisting on telling Watchie of his latest repair, a fine golden fob watch belonging to Mr

Macandlish, a laird known to Watchie, living in grandeur near
Aberlevin and sociably close to Lord Gordon of Aberlevin
himself. Only when the last of the tea had been drained to the
leaf was Strachan prepared to turn to Watchie and say,

Richt y'are, Master Leckie,

nodding towards the door of his room, and for a second
Watchie quite failed to understand what he was being asked to
do, until, feeling quite foolish, he remembered suddenly, and
stood upright from his leaning posture against the counter top,
and went in to collect the sack from the basket. He did not
dither, so much excited was he at the opportunity, but snatched
at the sack rather suddenly, causing it to rattle from the mesh of
the enclosing basket, and took it with him, placing the sack in
front of his employer. Strachan would not give his approval
so readily to Watchie, who stood back starving for it; he let
the sack rest before him on the counter top for a while, as if it
were a dog panting and breathless returned from fetching a
stick for its master, and only when he was quite ready did he
part the lips of the sack and reach for the bundles inside. He
placed them side by side on the top of the counter, and moved
the sack away from his sight; the parcelling cracked and settled
once out in the open, and Strachan looked to Watchie in some
amusement,

Aye, he said, ye're nae a loon tae tak ony chances, are ye,
Master Leckie?

and nodded that Watchie should commence unwrapping,
which he did, as carefully as he had sealed them, so as to
preserve the paper for their return home. He released the petals
of newsprint from round the first of the cabinets gingerly until
the naked rosewood was exposed, passing it over to Strachan
and smoothing out the paper as best he could on the top of the
counter. Strachan held the cabinet before him, looking at it this
way and that to begin with, passing his fingers over the grain.

A fine bit wid, richt eneuch, aye, verra smooth,

and then gave focus to the frieze capping the piece almost
seamlessly. At the first, he was looking for signs of defective
craft; finding none, he examined the frieze itself, and as he did

so his face went as smooth as the wood itself, passive and almost entirely without crease, and he held the clock closer to the lenses of his spectacles. He raised it higher, the better to catch the two lights which came into the shop, the invited guest of more penetrating and critical sunlight, and the oil glow which oppressed the shadow the sun carved out of the corners; and in both lights the tableau on the frieze, in which a man in a rowing-boat on the open ocean was holding a harpoon over a distant whale arcing in a dive, gained a sense of motion and urgency, as if the whaler had been poised at the very instant of casting his wicked spear, as if the whale had reared from the water to sacrifice its supple back to death. Even the ocean itself was caught in the act of arranging its fabric around prey and predator, glittering with the borrowed light of the day outside the window as if the sun had consented to weave gold thread through it. Strachan put the cabinet down on the counter, turned it this way and that and finally made it stare him in the face. He leaned back in his chair, and let out a long breath, and said to Watchie,

Gie me the ither clock, Master Leckie.

Watchie's hands began to tremble slightly as he parted the paper from around his kirk. This time Strachan held it close to his eyes, and with a free hand raised the spectacles to his brow, at the same time pressing his eyelids tightly together, as if narrowing the focus of his concentration, the better to see the flaws in the execution. There in his hands was a miniature kirk awaiting a congregation of dolls, with vaulted doors on either side of the window in which would sit the face of a clock, and a steeple crowned by a belfry of latticed woodwork, carved in imitation of stone, as were the cruciform walls, roofed by a slanting forgery of slate.

I thocht, said Watchie into the silence, I'd mak a clock face o' tin, wi enamel tae mak it luik like stained gless. And I thocht as weel the strikin train wid ring a wee bell in the tour, jist like in a proper kerk.

Strachan placed the kirk on the counter, alongside the whaling cabinet. He replaced the lenses over his eyes, and then raised them again to wipe his eyes with the crook of a finger, as if to free his sight from a gathering of dust. James Strachan was by no means a frivolous man, having had the frivolity tapped from him by pragmatism; a plain speaker, and known for it, he now raised his head and turned to the young loon who stood waiting for his word, and said,

Master Leckie, fan'll ye be leavin yer schoolin?

Watchie's tea was cold in its mug. He said,

Three-fower month, jist aboot.

Strachan nodded. He stood up from his seat, the wood of it complaining underneath him, and looked levelly into Watchie's eyes.

Yon's affa funny, he said, for yon's jist aboot the time I'll hae need o' an apprentice. Wid thon be jist aboot the time ye'd be efter an apprenticeshep?

XX

Watchie was allowed to work on his clocks in the back shop of
Strachan's whenever there was an hour or so to spare, filling his
cabinets with parts he bought from Strachan himself, at a
modest deduction from his week's wages; but most of the time
he worked side by side with the old man in the clock surgery,
separated from him by the width of the table, using his own
instruments to tend to all the maladies to which the realm of the
mechanical was heir. By now he was even trusted enough by
Strachan to venture his own diagnoses, opening the offered
timepieces before the very eyes of the anxious customers, holding them as gently as if they were mice, and if a first look
revealed no obvious clues as to the nature of the condition, then
a description of the symptoms was usually enough to set off the
alarms of memory and allow him to pronounce a flaw which
could be the cause of such a fault.

Watchie found this work enjoyable enough; time's own
surgeon, he made well the injuries wrought by time itself, and
derived much satisfaction from the pleasure of the customers as
they returned after a number of days and found their best
possessions whole again and beating healthily in the palms of
their hands, restored to their full vigour as if the little beasts had
been for a week at a spa. His experience at the shop was fine
and pleasant, and he was always learning something new in his
vocation at the attentive hands of his employer, gaining rapidly
a wide and comprehensive knowledge of all means of driving
the hands of a clock, and more importantly of the varied
mechanisms used to strike the chords of time, the trains which
operated many different releases to sound out the bells and set in
motion the tableaux which decorated the crowns of some of the
clocks given to Strachan for repair. Watchie's breath was fair
taken by the ingenuity of the constructions which gave life and

pulse to such simple arrangements as the kissing couple of the clock which Strachan went up to his room to fetch, just to show him, opening the front door of its cabinet to allow Watchie a better look at the mechanism which made them take their hourly promenade; wheels rotating in countervailing movement, one under the other and moved in opposing directions by a single release, drawing the couple together pace by pace. The man was wearing a suit of rather loose design and articulated at the hips on a pivot, the woman in a flounced dress of shining scarlet and also articulated, her torso drawn in at the thorax and pinned to the wide bell of the skirt, both attached to wires so that when they met in the middle of the decorative crown, in front of their house of alpine wood, a chalet whose roof was folded in an abrupt and acutely angled slant, another mechanism drew them one to the other, the wires pulling on each and causing them to meet in as many kisses as there were hours being struck, their wooden mouths clicking shyly together. At first Watchie saw only the vignette as it was being enacted, and he laughed and said,

Yon's affa daft, the twa o' them deein thon afore a' the warld,

and Strachan laughed with him and said,

It's a Belgian clock, Master Leckie, naebody kens fit yon foreign mannies and cweanies dee afore a' the warld,

but after he opened the clock and let Watchie see the intricacy of the mechanism which made the two take their deterministic hourly appointment, Watchie lost all objection to the propriety of the scene, and became lost in the beauty of the construction, and over midday tea Strachan told him that the clock had once been in the window,

jist for display, ye ken, Master Leckie, for I widna sell a clockie like yon, nae for a' the siller in the warld. Weel, the neist thing, the meenister frae the kerk alang the road, the mannie frae the Presbyterian Kerk, ye ken, the Revd MacPheter, he cams intae the shoppie ane day, and fit a pother he maks! Losh, like oor Laird in the temple he wis, ragin at the mannies fa were lendin fowk the siller, and he says tae me, Meester

Strachan, tak yon clock frae the winda this instant, for it's deein ill tae the guid God-fearin fowk o' my parish. Weel weel, master Leckie; I'm here ahint the coonter, and I says tae the Reverend, weel, sir, I've nae the will tae dee ill tae ony fowk, God-fearin nor itherways, but gin ye'll taal me jist fit's a-dee wi yon clock ahint the winda, we'll see jist fit can be done aboot it.

Strachan laughed at the memory of the confrontation, and continued:

Fit a luik he gies me! Daggers it wis, and he says, Mr Strachan, I'm richt sure I dinna need tae taal ye fit hairm a clockie like yon, depictin (yon wis the verra werd, depictin) a loon and a cwean makkin luve afore the hale o' the toun, wid dee tae the morals o' the young fowk o' Turra. Weel, Master Leckie! I dinna ken jist fit tae dee; I says, weel, Reverend, I'm nae efter hairmin the morals o' the young fowk o' Turra, I widna wish ye tae think yon o' me, but I'm efter the sale o' clocks at my shoppie, and I doot nor my clock'll pit the young fowk o' Turra in mind o' onything they widna dee, whether it's in the sicht o' God nor in the sicht o' the hale toun. Noo, Master Leckie, I ask ye; fit hairm dis a clock like yon dee tae yer ain morals, eh?

Watchie shook his head.

It's a grand bit werk, Mr Strachan,

and Strachan nodded vigorously,

Yon's jist fit I says tae the Reverend, and I gangs ower tae the winda and taks the clock oot, and pits it on the coonter afore him, and I says, Noo then, Revd MacPheter, wid ye jist tak a lookie at yon clock and taal me that it wisna werth the craft that wis pit intae it, and d'ye ken fit he dis, Master Leckie? he ca's oot tae the Laird himsel, and in the sicht o' God cries oot for him to punish a' blasphemers! Blasphemers, is't, and I says tae him, Revd MacPheter, I gang tae my ain kirk ilka Sunday, I'll nae hae ony man ca' me blasphemer, and I'll tak the clock oot o' the winda gin it'll mak ye a happier man, but I canna help but mind that the Laird has ower muckle tae dee than punish a man for a clock depictin (aye, I gied him his ain werd as weel, depictin) a loon and a cwean kessin afore their hoosie.

Weel, he turns awa and gangs oot o' the shop, but d'ye ken fit he dis then, Master Leckie, eh? He terns aboot afore takkin his lee and says, it widna be sae bad gin the twa were merrit.

Strachan's eyes strove upwards behind their own thick windows, and Watchie laughed at the culmination of it, remembering his father's own experience at the hands of members of the old kirk, and looking at the clock as it ticked innocently before him, the cabinet closed now and the couple returned to their opposite berths beside the chalet. He wondered how anyone could find fault with such a delightful execution of mechanism and the theatre of innocence and courtship which enacted its unresolved drama on the hour, never claiming any more than a kiss the pair of them, waiting patiently for the time to make their appointment for them once again.

The strangest days of all for Watchie to go to his work were the market Tuesdays and Thursdays, for there was always the possibility that his father might be there of an afternoon, after his milk deliveries. Often Wullie went to see the cattle being paraded through the ring and to meet his old cronies, a veritable forum in addition to its commercial purpose, and the scene of some excitement in recent years, when Wullie Patterson was forced to sell his cow by the local authorities in order to pay for his workers' National Insurance, a practice which the old bugger abhorred to do, and a *cause célèbre* which resulted in a minor riot, the abduction of the cow from the ring by supporters of Patterson's tough stance against the government's claim on his money, and its eventual sale in an Aberdeen mart to a consortium of farmers who restored the cow to Patterson's possession. Quite a famous disturbance this was, which Wullie Leckie was not witness to, though the story spread for miles around, and many with little interest in cattle farming came from miles around to see the culmination of Patterson's act of defiance against the law, his refusal to lick Lloyd George's stamps for him; Wullie saw no heroics in Patterson's action, and happily gave his workers the benefit of the extra money for their comfort in older age, and to those farmers who stood behind

Patterson's principles, claiming that enough care was taken of their labourers with their meals paid for and their board provided, Wullie said, aye, yon's fit ye're sayin the noo, but fit're yer werkers tae live on fan they've nae their ain fairms tae keep them, and a' their sons and dauchters have ga'ed awa tae their ain werk? and he refused to buy the commemorative plates struck with the image of the cow painted in enamel in their centres, angered by Patterson's betrayal of responsibility, though he had never met the mannie, and never would he hear the farmer's name spoken in conversation without spitting, ach, yon aal myser!

By and large, however, the Turra mart was a quiet affair, and often Wullie took to staying behind after the purchases had been made and the crowd melted from the fairground, talking the business of farming to this one and that one, and from time to time, as he passed by Strachan's shop on the main street of the town, glancing into the twin windows on either side of the doorway to see if he could catch sight of his son working behind the counter. He took his watch from his pocket to see the correct time, if it was near to the six o'clock that Watchie finished work each day, but rarely was it, for the mart was always finished in good enough time to allow those farmers who lived a good distance away from the town to return home for their dinner, and Wullie rode past the watchmaker's shop, where under another man's tutelage his son was learning his chosen trade.

Then one day, a Tuesday it was, he met Geordie O'Donnell hawking for trade at the Turra mart. Geordie was dressed fit for the weather, for crisp and cold it was, with a pair of fingerless gloves sheathing his hands and leaving him still free for the delicate manipulation of silver he gathered into the pocket of his waistcoat, wrapping his end-of-the-day takings in a white linen handkerchief embroidered with the initials of another man, the only wallet he possessed. Many enough times had Wullie seen the tinker at the marketplace, calling the trade closer to himself with the confidence of a fairground barker, his Irish voice as colourful and as prominent as a painted sign, standing in front of the scarred old cart which had served him for many years and for untold miles, drawn by the redoubtable mare he called Maisie and who seemed now as loose as the canvas sack in which he carried the implements he had fixed. Often Wullie had nodded to the tinker mannie, for they were after all from the same village, it was only but politeness to do so, but Geordie was not a man to be so easily distracted from his trade, though he never made Wullie feel that his interruptions were unwelcome, granting the dairy farmer a smile that seemed to be quite branded into Wullie's attention before once again raising his voice to cry out,

All the repairs ye'll need, household goods fixed in a trice, good quick clean service I'll promise, all at fine prices, bring me yer wares, Geordie O'Donnell at yer beck and call!

Now, this particular Tuesday, Wullie was lingering a while after the mart, talking as usual to this one and that one, finishing off a conversation with Lowther and Crozier and accepting a draught from the hip flask of Lowther's, and the conversation turned to the subject of Watchie,

I've been hearin, said Lowther, that yon loon o' yers is werkin at Strachan's shoppie here in Turra, is yon richt, Wullie?

and Wullie nodded,

Aye, yon's richt eneuch, Hebbie,

stopping the flask with its deerhorn bung and passing it back into Lowther's hand. Hebbie nodded to the same rhythm,

Ye'll be richt pleased wi yon, Wullie, the loon'll mak somethin o't, will he nae?

Wullie composed his mask into one of pride in his son's achievement,

Aye, richt pleased I am, Hebbie,

he said, but the untruth soured on his lips, even though he would admit nothing but pride. Faith, even Davie Lowther, as thrawn as he was, had accepted that he was born to run a farm, and was now casting himself into the grain business with a will that claimed Wullie Leckie's admiration, now grown into a strong and stocky young man, determined to pull what weight he had. Crozier took the offered flask from Hebbie Lowther, and drew out its bung, and said,

Aye, Wullie, ye ken I had my doots, but the loon's gied us the proof o' the gifts God gied tae him lang ere the noo.

Before long it was time for the farmers to set off along the road and just as Wullie prepared to mount the board of his own cart, there came from behind him a soft voice which none the less made him turn,

Mr William Leckie, I'm sure, and how are you this fine day?

and there was Geordie O'Donnell, a sack held in his hands stretched bulbous by all manner of irregular shapes, smiling as if in competition with the sunlight, a smile Wullie could not ignore and to which he responded as generously as he could,

Aye, fine day yersel, Geordie,

looking him up and down and deciding that he was ready for business, holding himself as tall as he was and not bowed down by the awful weight of the sack. Some distance behind him was the poor mare, standing faithfully and waiting for her master to return, not once pressing her muzzle into the curious crowd for a handful of oats. Wullie said,

And fit can I dee for ye, Geordie, standin there?

and Geordie took a quick pace backwards, looking down at boots which were impeccably well polished for a tinker mannie, though Wullie would never be the one to make such judgements, and said,

William Leckie, sir, would ye say now that I'm lookin like a man who wants something done for him? I ask in all fairness,

and Wullie could not help but laugh,

Na na, Geordie, nae at a', man,

at which point Geordie shuffled closer, before Wullie could ascend the board of his cart, and looked evenly into the farmer's eyes,

Though I will say, William, that I couldn't help but hear ye talkin about yer boy, a fine hard workin lad, yes indeed.

Wullie stared deeper into Geordie's eyes, for the tinker would not let him loose from them, a stage mesmerist trapping his victim within the genial lariat of his will; and Wullie was held there by his curiosity as much as by Geordie, and he dropped the reins on the ground, and said,

Aye, he is that, Geordie, fine dee I ken.

Geordie took another pace, something of a shuffle, a parody of reticence.

And fine in love with his watches, so he is, nose never out of his work, so I hear. Sure, isn't it a fine thing when a lad has an interest like that, a fine thing indeed.

Geordie's flattering tongue was not playing the kind of music that Wullie preferred to hear, not when his mind was turning to thoughts of employing another worker to make up for the lost pair of hands working only a half mile away from where he was now standing. He presented Geordie with a dam of granite against the gentle flood of compliment, frowning only a very little, and said,

I ken a' that, Geordie,

abruptly, and once again Geordie looked down to his boots as if to attract Wullie's attention to them; and when he looked up, there was a lopsided expression to his mouth, slight and ironic.

Makin right good money as well, so I hear, though tis sure I am that he'd always find the use for a bittie more.

Now Wullie's frown deepened, though with puzzlement this time.

Yon's affa like a proposition, Geordie O'Donnell, tae my ears onyway. Wid I be richt tae think yon, wid ye say?

Geordie O'Donnell stood back as if at the shock of a discharged shotgun, his eyebrows clambering high to meet the brim of his cap.

Mr Leckie, he said, my, but ye're a forthright man indeed! never did I say such a thing, though I'd be a liar if I were to say that such a thing were not on my mind.

Wullie looked the Irishman up and down slowly once again, himself taken a little aback by Geordie's admission, and said,

Taal me fit's on yer mind, Geordie O'Donnell.

So, on that particular market Tuesday, it was something of a surprise to Watchie to find waiting for him outside the shop as he wheeled his bicycle through the door not just his father, calming the impatient Jonah whose head nodded as if against the discomfort of the bit, but also Geordie O'Donnell in his ramshackle cart, smiling broadly and reaching over to smooth his hand over the chestnut flank of Maisie, who was leading the cart backwards and forwards as if to make better acquaintance with the other horse, then thinking better of it. Geordie aimed a wink at Watchie, and touched a finger to the brim of his cap as a greeting; Watchie nodded in reply as his father said,

It's the Tuesday for the mairt, ye ken, I thocht I'd spare ye the need for yer cycle the day, jist pit it on the cairt and I'll gie ye a ride hame,

which Watchie did, hoisting the heavy machine with difficulty on to the bed until it was partly rested, leaping on to the back to place it wholly and settle it down for the journey on its side, climbing over and on the board beside Wullie. Before Wullie made the click in the back of his throat to give Jonah his start, Watchie looked behind himself to Geordie, who was busily smoking a clay pipe. Watchie had seen Geordie O'Donnell about the village often enough to be greeted by him, a man Watchie liked by instinct, for he had a leathery trustworthy face which wrapped itself around a pipe well, creating an emphasis of the lines which signified bonhomie and good humour whenever he drew on the stalk of it, and more than once he had called upon Smallbrae looking for something to fix, tin goods coming to the end of their useful lives, teapots with loose handles perhaps, baths which had sprung a leak; well enough known was he to Watchie, and now as he caught Watchie's backward look, he winked once again, an action which called upon the participation of his whole body, inclining his head with his eye and giving the simplest gesture of fellowship the intensity of a lighthouse beacon, and breathing out a ream of smoke to be shredded on the breeze.

On the way home, Geordie's cart took the road abreast of Wullie's, for there was just enough room for them, the wheels creaking and shuddering in their axles and the whole frame of the old cart loosened by the continual punishment, scaring into their paths many rabbits on the journey, alerted by the wailing. There was much talk of cattle and business passing between the two drivers, very little of which Watchie was moved to comment upon; Geordie appeared to have some knowledge of cattle farming, for he talked confidently about the yield of cows and the richest grasses and the winter feeds, talk to which Wullie responded by nodding in agreement. Watchie began to sight along the rises and falls in the road before them, taking refuge from a conversation which held little interest for him. After a while, however, there was a long silence, and from the corner of his eye he could see that Wullie's face was turned towards him; he heard his father's voice with sudden clarity,

Waatchie? The man's speakin tae ye, noo,

and altering his focus he saw that Geordie O'Donnell's face was also towards him, smiling patiently, a redundant hand on the bowl of his pipe. Geordie repeated his question,

I was just sayin, Watchie, ye're not a man for the farmin yerself, so I hear.

I've aye had a mind tae be a waatchmakker, Mr O'Donnell, yon's true eneuch,

and Geordie O'Donnell smiled and nodded energetically in agreement.

A fine ambition for a young man like yerself, Watchie, where would we all be without time, I ask ye? Eh, Wullie? Is that not a fine thing for a young man to be? And such hard work for a lad so young, so much to learn, I'd put silver on it.

Watchie found himself engaged by the tinker's interest, despite himself, despite the presence of his father beside him. He said,

I've a bittie tae ken aboot clocks and waatches yit, Mr O'Donnell.

Geordie laughed richly, and reached out to slap the flank of Maisie as if she were a table, causing a detonation which echoed from the hills.

What a fine modest lad ye have, William Leckie, sir! A lad who takes the measure of a traction-engine, in two days, no less, and still he says he has more to learn about watches and clocks!

Wullie's face was turned to the road, but his eyes were still sideways held on his son,

Aye, he said, he's nae a loon tae blaa aboot it, he'd aye lee yon tae ithers.

Watchie by now was quite red about the face with all Geordie O'Donnell's immoderate praise, and he shifted in his seat as if it had suddenly begun to sprout thorns.

Mr Strachan's an affa fine teacher, he said, I've larned mair bein his apprentice than gin I'd done it mysel,

and for the next two minutes, Watchie was in his element, describing for them the intricacies of the many continental movements which may be contained within the mysterious oyster of a watch to complicate the fixing of it. Geordie was encouraging and attentive, nodding as if he understood completely and drawing Watchie further into his confidence, while Wullie now distantly settled on the road ahead, suddenly interested in the obstacles Jonah might have to face, gentling the horse around the rises of the cobbles with a slight tug on the rein. Finally Watchie came to the end of his explanation,

Yon's jist the dear waatches, mind, waatches frae abroad and the like,

and Geordie gave a last nod and said,

And what about the cheap watches, Master Leckie? Easy to fix, are they?

Watchie nodded.

Aye, Mr O'Donnell, much o' a muchness, ilka ane o' them, nae affa difficult tae fex at a'.

And that was the last they spoke about watches and mechanisms for the rest of the journey to Aberlevin, much to Wullie's evident relief; and when they parted at the wishbone of a road which took them in separate directions to their homes, Geordie O'Donnell halted his cart for a while, calling across,

Well, thank ye kindly for the company, gentlemen, and thank ye for the talk, for it's a long road back to my croft, so it is, and I always think a good talk sets the miles to flight.

Wullie touched the brim of his cap, as Geordie had done earlier, a courtesy to a fine companion,

Aye, weel, richt pleased tae see ye, Geordie,

and Watchie too leaned out of the shade of his father to say,

Aye, richt pleased, Mr O'Donnell,

in echo; but Geordie leaned forward too, his eyes catching the loon's own, spinning that net which had captured Watchie's father so effectively before, and said,

Well, now, Watchie Leckie, I've enjoyed our talk; so much to know about watches, so there is, I can't say with hand on me heart that I even know the half of it meself, though like yerself, I'm eager to be learnin.

Watchie smiled, saying nothing, for one small arrogant moment in his life wondering at the ambition of the Irishman to master what he himself knew by instinct. But Geordie continued,

I'm thinkin, would ye be interested in carryin on our wee talk some time in the weeks to come? Over a cup o' tay, perhaps, if ye'd like?

Watchie looked to his father, as if for his advice; but Wullie's eyes, too, were on the tinker, his head turned away from his son, so that Watchie felt a sudden abandonment of guidance, that here was a decision he had to make on his own. There was a strange scent in the air, and Watchie sensed a wordless complicity between his father and the tinker, with no evidence other than the currents which played around him.

It was Watchie's fathomless curiosity which made the decision for him, and he nodded slowly,

Aye, Mr O'Donnell, fine pleased I'd be tae cam roon tae yer hoosie, fane'er ye'd like,

and not long after, the two carts went their separate ways, Geordie's lost to sight behind the lattice of a grove of elms; and Watchie looked to his father, who was staring ahead between the ears of Jonah as if along the sight of a shotgun; not a word had he to say about the bargain which had just been struck, though Watchie knew within himself that Wullie could tell him much more about it if he chose to.

XXI

Well enough was the story of Geordie O'Donnell's dissolution
and eventual resurrection after the death of his wife known to
Watchie Leckie, for the tinker had been coming to the farm
ever since Watchie was a loon, putting to rights the contingent
ills of his mother's cooking utensils; he had seen Geordie before,
when Ailsa was still alive and ruling her realm of hearth and
homestead, when his work was of such a standard that he
guaranteed it till the end of his own life, and he had seen
Geordie after, held together almost by the patches on his breeks
and on the elbows of his jacket, his face raw with ill shaving
and a permanent rheum about his eyes. He remembered Jeannie
looking at one of Geordie's repairs which had freshly come
apart, tutting to herself and saying to no one in the kitchen,

Michty me, it's awa again, fit's Geordie deein wi his time at
the croft? Yon widna hae happened a file by,

but Wullie drew himself upright, and fixed his wife with a
stare which implored her understanding, and said,

He's nae ower Ailsa's passin yit, Jeannie, he's nae the same
mannie at a' that he was afore thon,

and Jeannie nodded, the circumstances forgotten in a moment
of inconvenience, for which forgetfulness she lowered her head
and took the pot back to its bed in the cupboard, and she said,

He'll jist hae tae fex it fan he cams here the neist time.

Watchie remembered the long doldrums of Geordie O'Donnell's reputation, for it was the subject of discussion in nearly
every house in Aberlevin among those who saw him emerge
from the alehouse on uncertain legs, and Aal Wullie, no stranger
to the alehouse himself, brought back with him stories of
Geordie's meetings with Johnnie Deans and the others of Andy
Grant's labouring crew,

Ach, fit a scoundrel thon mannie is, said Aal Wullie, sittin wi a mannie fa's nae lang lost his wife, takkin his siller tae drink the drouth frae himsel, they're makkin a richt feel o' the man, and he's nae the wit aboot himsel tae see it,

but Peggy at her knitting interrupted,

It's nae lookoot o' yer ain, Wullie Leckie, and fit're ye deein yersel but makkin a wealthy wumman o' Kate Maclennan, in the alehoosie ane nicht efter anither? Dinna ye taal me aboot Geordie O'Donnell thraain awa his siller, fan it's jist fit ye're deein yersel,

which silenced Aal Wullie as effectively as if she had created a vacuum about his head from which no words could escape, and he passed an affectionate hand through the greying mane of the now infirm Laird, the only companion who might understand his concern, and dropped his head before falling asleep in the warm air of the fire.

Watchie had heard all about Geordie O'Donnell when suddenly, one day, he was back at the farm in a suit of clean clothing, and the wounds on his face had begun to seal up, so that he no longer seemed like a drifting ship crusted with scabrous barnacles, but a man who had once again been polished new and bright as a schoolboy and sent on his way. His fingers were long and sure, and he turned the stricken pots end over end, his eyes unclouded by the stale air of a sour morning's awakening; now he placed the cross-hairs of his attention firmly upon the fault which had caused handle to part from pan, and promised that it would be back in their hands by the morrow; and there it was, as if nothing had ever happened to it, sound to the touch and promising silently never to fail its mistress again, the handle anchored firmly on to the basin, rooted as deeply as an elm in the earth. And once again Geordie's disposition was cheerful, his sight cleared where once it had been troubled and milky, a fine transformation it was to see, and with a year's hard work and dedication Geordie once again built up the good will which had made him welcome at most people's doorsteps, restoring it like a painting which had grown dull and sepiaed with age and neglect, now attending to each fine brushstroke until it was brought back to vibrancy and its full pride. He was another uncle to Jessica, lifting her to the height of his shoulders whenever she scampered out of the farmhouse to meet him, o, a darlin lass she was, he teased her and made coins appear from air, minted behind her ears, and gave her them to keep, and he always asked after Watchie, usually at his work with Strachan.

Geordie's emergence from his time of adversity was complete within the year that Watchie learned his trade with Strachan; and now he was ready to open his wings, to take to the light and face the world in sobriety. It was the knowledge of this that drew the loon towards Geordie O'Donnell's croft, a walk of three miles up the road, to keep his promised appointment.

From a distance, Watchie could see that the land around was well tended and cared for, and he saw a single old horse gently mowing the grass, chewing unhurriedly on flagrant growths which sprouted at the borders of the dry stane dyke containing the fields. How different to the story he had been told of the property as it was when he was hardly on his legs as a wee loon; barren as chalk the land around, and hardly able to sustain the least growth, but Geordie O'Donnell had come past it with his wife and newly born cwean, at a time when Geordie would have captured the moon in a ring for the woman he had stolen from the islands, and seeing the wreck that the elements had made of the croft which stood at the heart of the scrub, Geordie had decided that he must take his lesson from the hermit crab, and claim the shell that had been abandoned by another. It was this tale he had been told by Aal Wullie, heard in the alehouse and therefore not considered by him to be as womanly as gossip, which made Watchie cautious of the tinsmith, for anyone who was able to win the lands and the croft in the manner of Geordie O'Donnell, for a song it was said, and from a harsh bargainer such as the laird Macallan in his doll's palace, not just rent or tenure mind you but the deeds and all, would be one to look out for in business, and the thought slowed Watchie's pace as he neared the gate as if there were traps before him, carved under the cobbles and set for the unwary.

Once beyond the pillars of the elm grove, he could see that

there were figures in front of the croft, at work in the early evening air, and as he lifted the rope securing the gate to his post, he recognized them as two young women, dressed in plain linen, and these he realized must be Geordie O'Donnell's daughters, hardly seen in the village but to buy meat from Baird the butcher's and household goods from the hardware shop. There was a sound on the air, drifting as finely as mist, and at first Watchie thought that it might be birdsong, the same piercing quality that carries over great distances, beaten thin at the fringes the further it goes from source; but coming closer to the croft, he realized that it was the voice of the cwean standing by the table set in front of the croft's door, singing as she was washing at an old tin bath, lavishing soap upon a pair of woollen long johns, coaxing the dirt out with strong and capable hands, drawing the sodden garment along a corrugated washboard angled into the bath. The water was unfurling flags of steam into the open air, rich with lather which she wore on her arms like a glove, and all the while she sang a high bright song that Watchie did not recognize, not from his shores at all but from somewhere across the sea, exultant and mournful all at once. In the plot in front of the croft, among the close furrows, another cwean was uprooting potatoes from the soil, and coating her hands in a thick glaur in the process, hauling on the sprigs and digging away the filth with her hands to reveal the earth's treasure of growth. She too was singing, the same melody as her older sister, but it was mostly all breath and accident, the notes coinciding rarely with those her sister sang, though she was not in the most natural posture for the ordered breathing that singing demanded; the cwean, whom Watchie knew must be Mhairi, shook the earth from the potatoes and held out her apron of floral design like an awning, in which she placed each tattie as it passed the test of her glance. In looking up for this task, she noticed the stranger on the periphery of her vision, and looked round at Watchie suddenly, and smiled,

Fine day,

to him, to which he replied with a nod. The washer cwean, who as the elder of them Watchie knew would be Kirsty, paused in her work to look quickly up at her sister, then to where her sister's eyes were aimed, to the awkward-looking loon with cloth cap and heavy prominent boots, and for the first time Watchie got a proper look at her, the luxurious drift of black hair secured at the back with a wooden clasp, a thick loaf of hair risen tall above her scalp. She left a long silence, which she filled by busying her hands once more, before saying as if to the bath,

Gin it's for fexin, my faither's oot at the shed.

She appeared to be troubled, as if Watchie had caught her in a shameful act of defiance in a land where singing was forbidden by law. Watchie drew his tongue over his lips, which he suddenly realized were as dry as paper, and said,

I'm nae here tae hae onythin repaired. Mr O'Donnell asked me ower the week gaed by.

Still she did not look up; her hands gathered the material in pleats, abraded them one surface against the other.

Aye, and fit for'd he ask ye ower?

Watchie shook his head. The eyes of the younger sister were still on him, and she stood poised like a statue, the potatoes held in the hammock she held taut at the length of her arms.

I dinna ken. He jist asked me ower. He didna say fit way he was efter seein me.

Just then, the door to the shed opened, and Geordie O'Donnell came into the fresh air. He smiled broadly at Watchie as he approached, the same smile he had given to Watchie's father at the mart, and he held out before him a hand to be shaken; Watchie saw that the skin was glittering with tinsel, the slight shavings of the material of his trade, and after the two had shaken Watchie noticed that his own hand was sprinkled with flecks and freckles like shavings of the moon. Geordie O'Donnell said,

Why, young master Leckie, a pleasure it is to see yerself now; but I'm afraid you catch me unawares, in the middle of a repair it'll only take me a moment to do. Kirsty'll see to a cup o' tay for ye, won't ye, Kirsty, while I do me work for a little while, and then we can have ourselves a wee bit talk.

He turned towards the shed, as if in genuine regret. Kirsty had not the look of one upon whom an imposition has been trusted, but she gave a mighty sigh, and sloughed the soap from her hands and into the bath as if it were the skin of a lizard. She looked up at Watchie, said,

Ye'll cam awa ben the hoose for yer tea,

and Watchie followed her into the croft, all the time aware of Mhairi's eyes upon him like burrs on cloth.

The first thing that occurred to Watchie the moment he went inside the croft, once his eyes had become used to the shade of the place, was how clean the interior was, and how slanderous the rumours he had heard were, that Geordie O'Donnell lived in a perfect state of degradation and squalor. Every surface shone brilliantly enough to hurt the eye, and even compared to his own farmhouse home, Watchie considered this to be a fine place to be living in, warmed and cheered by the peat fire sparking in the grate. There were jugs held up by the lug on hooks above the fireplace, and on either side of the hearth were two copper bedpans, which shone like coins as if never used, though it would have surprised Watchie to find out that they were, especially in the cold winters. Watchie sat where Kirsty told him to sit, at the bench in front of the table nearest to the fire, and there she went to look inside the copper cauldron, to see if there was enough water on the boil for a pot of tea. She brought a plain cylindrical tin to the table, and a squat tin pot, and spooned leaves from one to the other; but Watchie shifted in his seat, for from her he felt the cold radiance of a perfect observance of hospitality, and for a moment Watchie felt his presence resented by this taciturn cwean with her wealth of dark hair gathered to herself like a miser's fortune. He wanted to look at her, but undetected, and he so desperately wanted her to sing again. He began to look at his knees, and became suddenly aware of a number of creases thrown up by the shifting of the fabric, which he smoothed down fussily. He took off his cap, realizing too late that this would have been expected of him as soon as he walked in through the door, and held it on his lap like a well-behaved, silent cat, kept for the sake of ornament. He searched the inside of the croft again, and as he did so his eyes passed by Kirsty, but he was frustrated by the partition of hair, and so for the want of anywhere else he looked towards the mantelpiece shelf, and on top saw a thing he had never seen before; a wooden crucifix, the trunk of it kept upright by a small plinth, with a tin representation of the limp corpse of the suffering Christ nailed to the spars, above him a metal scroll with the mocking initials written by the Roman soldiers. Watchie thought it a grim and morbid kind of an ornament to have in a room, though well enough did he know the story of the Crucifixion; no more would there be such a thing in his house than there might be a portrait of a hanging, and to be presented with this most famous of deaths made him turn away from the fire. Kirsty finished with the tea, replaced the lid of the cylinder and took it to a ledge beside another tin bath, then went to the hearth, and picked the cauldron from its hook after wrapping the arc of the handle in a dish-towel, taking it over to the teapot. Steam tumbled out of the cauldron like sheets from an overfilled laundry basket; but Kirsty was deft about it, despite the cauldron's great mass, and poured the precise amount of hot water from the cauldron's gargantuan maw into the pursed gawp of the teapot, allowing just enough water out and no more, before righting the huge vessel and returning it to its perch. From outside the croft, Watchie could hear the sounds of industry in miniature, a ringing of hammer on metal, and there was a pleasant intrusive smell to the air which he could not identify, but which reminded him of linseed oil in the way that it pricked up the hairs in his nostrils, and Watchie wondered just how long it would take Geordie O'Donnell to finish the repair.

Kirsty sat an enamelled mug on the table in front of Watchie, still without looking at him. Watchie thanked her quietly, which she did not seem to hear, for she stared into the depths of the teapot until the water was stained to her satisfaction, setting the hinged lid down over the coil of steam, and brought the pot over to the mug, pouring him a thick stream the colour of polished teak. She offered him milk, and he shook his head, for his taste these days was for tea without, and he tasted it; fine and strong, and so dark that he could not see the leaves which had escaped in the pouring. She went to sit on the stool by the hearth, and Watchie followed her with his eyes as furtively as if he had been sent to spy upon her, as if sanctioned by some greater authority than himself. She dressed forbiddingly in black linen, with a tight bodice, so that she appeared to Watchie a being in two articulated sections, like the kissing doll on top of Strachan's Swiss clock; she moved crisply, succinctly, the pleats of the linen daring to whisper to themselves, and when she sat down it was with a perfect awareness of her own grace, a fluency which Watchie thought must be self-confidence, and which diminished him the more he thought about it. Watchie tried to find within him the right thing to say, as the silence grew around him and became dark and fearsome; and then, just as the silence began to crack beneath its own unbearable mass, Geordie O'Donnell came into the croft with Mhairi, the potatoes weighing down her apron, scattered among carrots the size of her fingers.

Well, now, Watchie Leckie, that didn't take too long, did it? he said.

Kirsty poured him a mug of tea, and he sat down beside Watchie on the bench, swallowing down a draught the moment it was handed to him with such a thirst that Watchie was surprised he didn't scald the flesh from the roof of his mouth. He gasped with pleasure as the heat suffused him, and he sighted along his shoulder to look at Watchie.

A fine thing is a cup of tay for a workin man, Watchie, yes indeed, a fine drink for a thirsty man, so it is,

and Watchie smiled and nodded, not knowing what else to say. Geordie nodded with him, choosing the same rhythm as Watchie, and said,

Now for a workin man such as yerself, Watchie Leckie, I daresay a cup of tay's every bit as welcome as it is to me, would ye not say?

Watchie nodded more vigorously this time, having a question to answer;

Aye, Mr O'Donnell, I like fine a cuppie o' tea fan I cam hame frae Turra ilka nicht,

and Geordie laughed as if this were the wittiest thing he had ever heard, a huge detonation of a laugh. Geordie said,

Aye, take yer tay when ye come back from Turriff, Watchie Leckie, and ye'll come to no harm, mark my words,

and held his mug in both hands to draw the warmth from it, and for the first time Watchie took a good look at Geordie O'Donnell's hands; the fingers lean and long-jointed, but strong with it, a small risen muscle for each joint, as hard as the muscle on the arm. The door to the croft was still open, for it was the weather for it, airing the house with the brisk cloth of God's own breeze, and Mhairi stood with her mound of vegetables still, leaning against the jamb. She was looking openly at Watchie, and there was a perpetual smile upon her face, as if not yet turning the corner of adolescence and retaining the strategies of childhood, blessing every stranger with the same smile in the hope of winning concessions for her age. Geordie looked up at her finally, said,

Mhairi, darlin, ye'll tire yerself with those tatties loadin ye down, take them over to yer sister, there's a darlin girl,

and with her pinned smile she did as she was told, passing by Watchie's side of the table as she went. Geordie turned to Watchie, and straightened himself in his seat; his face, never wholly serious, lapsed into a businesslike expression, and he said,

Well now, Watchie Leckie, I'll go to the heart of it as soon as I can. Ye know that I'm a worker in tin, and there's them that'd go so far as to say that they'd come to me afore trustin their repairs to another livin soul, which is very kind of them.

Watchie nodded, led like a child by the hand, not knowing where. He said,

Aye, Mr O'Donnell. My faither widna lee ony ither mannie tae fex oor pots nor pans, nor my mither neether.

Geordie smiled; grateful to Watchie for eliding the word tinker before mannie.

And there's the problem, Watchie, there's the heart of it, now. Sure and it's a fine thing to be known as a man who does good work in this world, but peyple come to expect terrible much of ye. Have ye ever found that, Watchie Leckie? peyple always look to ye for miracles, and it's no easy thing, to be givin them miracles when they aren't in ye.

Watchie remembered the threshing season, Peter Millar's engine succumbing to its malady before his eyes; with feeling he said,

Aye, Mr O'Donnell, fine dee I ken.

Geordie laughed,

I thought ye would, Watchie Leckie, for a watch is a little miracle all to itself, is it not? I can't understand them for the life of me. But here's the rub of it; Geordie O'Donnell, they'll say to me, ye're a worker in tin, are ye not? Here's my watch for ye, and it's made out of tin as well, so why can't ye give it a good repairin for me, when tin's the very thing ye can repair with just a look at it?

Watchie roared with laughter at this, and Geordie joined in, spilling a little of his tea which Kirsty wiped up almost immediately with her cloth, giving him a look of admonition which he didn't even notice. He said,

Ye see the matter now, Watchie! A simple thing like a tin watch, Geordie O'Donnell, and ye can't even fix it, what kind of a worker in tin d'ye call yerself?

Watchie nodded agreement and said,

Aye, Mr O'Donnell, there's nae a waatch on God's earth fit's easy tae fex, nae matter gin it's tin nor gowd nor siller.

Geordie leaned closer to the young man.

That's so true, what ye're sayin, Watchie, o, the custom I have to turn away for the want of knowin how to repair a watch, it'd break yer heart, so it would, I'd be doin not a thing else if I had to fix all the watches handed to me I've had to give back.

And still Watchie could not see where it was he was being led; he shook his head in sympathy with the tinker's plight.

Yon's nae richt guid for ye, Mr O'Donnell,

and drank another sip of Kirsty's cooling tea, and wondered why it was that Geordie O'Donnell shone the lamps of his eyes upon him, and leaned further in as if to gather him into the heart of a conspiracy, and lowered his voice to say,

But of course, yerself now Watchie, not a thing about tin d'ye know, other than as a metal for makin things as well as watches; but what ye don't know about watches, why, if it were paint, ye'd only be coverin the littlest corner of the table with it, and maybe not as much as that, is that not true, now?

It took a while for Watchie to realize that he was being paid a compliment; and in the puzzling, the door cracked open a seam and the fresh light of day came through a sliver, as Watchie understood for the first time why it was he was here, and what Geordie O'Donnell and Wullie Leckie had been talking about at the Tuesday mart at Turriff. He sat a little back from Geordie, suddenly aware of how close he had let him creep across the bench, and sealed himself in his own thought for a moment. He frowned for a while, bringing his brow down low as a shield over his private considerations, before saying,

Wid I be richt tae believe, Mr O'Donnell, ye're efter me tae fex the waatches ye canna dee yersel? For I dinna hae the time at Mr Strachan's tae dee't.

Geordie shook his head, laughing.

This is what ye call a private arrangement, Watchie, I wouldn't be expectin ye to do such a thing on Mr Strachan's time, no indeed, that would be fair to neither of ye. Just a couple of hours at home a week, that'd be all, no more than that.

Watchie narrowed his eyes a little.

And fit'd be the rate o' pay for yon, Mr O'Donnell?

Geordie burst into another fit of laughter, like the laughter of God himself, a wide encompassing sound of generosity and bonhomie.

A fine question to ask, now, the very thing I'd be concerned about meself! How does nine pennies the watch sound to ye, Watchie Leckie? Is that fair enough payment for yer time and trouble? For if ye don't think so, we'll shake hands as gentlemen, and ye're welcome at me house any time for a cup of tay, aye, and yer father as well.

Watchie considered the offer. He made a sheet of paper of his thoughts, and scored on it a number of sums, and found the rate to be fair and comparable; then over his shoulder he glanced, and there at the hearth was Kirsty, waiting for the use of the table to slice the vegetables, Mhairi to the other side of it just out of the reach of clear sight. Watchie turned again to Geordie O'Donnell and said,

Yon seems fair eneuch tae mysel, Mr O'Donnell, I'll fex yer waatches for ye, for ninepence a waatch.

Geordie O'Donnell beamed his luminous smile, and held out his hand.

Ye'll not regret this, Watchie Leckie, and here's my hand on it, we'll shake like gentlemen anyway.

Geordie O'Donnell asked that Watchie should wait a fortnight before returning to the croft, for he still had the custom to inform of his new line in repairs, and to this Watchie readily agreed, for it was a sensible enough period of time to leave to gather together the broken tin watches of Aberlevin, with one condition to which Geordie agreed reluctantly; and that was that he should not hawk for such a custom at the market in Turriff, this being Strachan's town and Strachan's concern. Geordie shook his head at the thought of all the business he would lose by this, but most of the farmers who went there on a Tuesday and a Thursday were within reach of his rounds anyway, and so there was a further shake of the hands on this, Geordie understanding Watchie's position, and with that and another cup of tea, it was time for Watchie to leave for home, a simple brisk walk along the cobbled road. Long since Kirsty had abandoned the notion that she would ever have the table for the slicing of her vegetables, and when Watchie went outside the croft and turned to wave to Geordie, there she was at the washing table constructed by Geordie out of plain rough pinewood, with a fresh bath full of hot water, still not looking up at him, and Mhairi was by the side of her father at the doorway, waving in unison with him at the young loon who had dropped by to talk business. Watchie fairly breasted along the road to the farmhouse, and all the while his thoughts returned to the croft and to the sweet and high voice of the elder daughter of Geordie O'Donnell, and to the mystery of her face, grim and cheerless to the stranger, a mystery he longed to open to his sight as if it were the face of a clock.

XXII

Watchie Leckie busied himself in preparation for his first new
task since his apprenticeship with Strachan as meticulously as
ever he faced any new problem, and in silence away from the
hearthside. He was in the shed for most of the fortnight, and
there he made for himself a worktop from his father's offcuts,
which Wullie granted him with a lack of resistance which quite
took the loon by surprise. Wullie had smiled, and said,

Werkin frae hame, Waatchie? Weel, I canna see the hairm in
yon,

and even offered him the use of the lathe, which Watchie
used to turn the legs of his working desk until they were fine
structures resembling eggs balanced on bricks, turned so elegantly that you might imagine them to be a defiance of the
laws of geometry and gravity themselves, that perfect ovals
such as they were could never hold poised on edge between the
stability of the cubes; but there they were, and within the
fortnight Watchie had his table, slanted towards the bottom
from a straight batten in which Watchie had carved a crater at
the exact centre. The table was taken into the farmhouse by
Wullie and Aal Wullie and Watchie, while Peggy and Jeannie
opened the doors for them and laughed at the pantomime the
men were making of it, having to turn the beast on its side to
cajole it through the doorways, and the comedy of them
wrestling it up the stairs.

Finally the desk was installed in Watchie's room, in the space
in front of the window, and Wullie clapped together his hands
and said,

Fine werk, Waatchie, affa fine, ye're as guid wi yer hands as
ever I was in my day,

and Aal Wullie patted the loon on the head as he went to his
own room for a crafty lie-down which he had talked himself

into deserving after his exertions, a dance soon scattered by Peggy who raged through the door,

On yer feet, Wullie Leckie, ye aal idler! There's mair werk tae dee, and ye'll nae be gied the lee tae gang awa frae't.

There was one more item required by Watchie to complete his work, a luxury item, or so it was thought by most folk, to be purchased from the spinster Cairney's drapery shop on South Street.

She was busily reading when Watchie Leckie came into the shop, triggering the bell upon opening the door and recoiling from the sharp brazen notes as if he had never heard one before, and she saw immediately from his expression that he seemed to be a little ashamed to be there; she closed her book over and put it to one side, but she could tell from Watchie's demeanour that he was making a purchase which might cause him some embarrassment, and so she composed her face into a limpid understanding which was designed to set the loon at his ease, and said,

Fine day tae ye, Waatchie, and fit can I dee for ye?

Watchie approached the counter, looking around at the bolts of fabric in their proper grids like scrolls in an ancient library, then smiled at the spinster standing opposite.

I'm efter a wee bit cloth, gin ye hae't.

The spinster canted her head to one side, and honeyed her eyes to indicate complete discretion.

A wee bit cloth, noo, and thon widna be for a cwean o' yer ain acquaintance, wid it? A handkerchief-size bit o' cloth?

Watchie closed his eyes for a moment, as if he had been readying himself for this all along.

Aye, weel, it'd be aboot the size o' a handkerchief, ye ken, but it's nae for a cwean, Miss Cairney, it's for mysel.

Miss Cairney frowned, her head now to one side in puzzlement.

For yersel, Waatchie?

Watchie nodded.

Aye, a wee bit handkerchief size o' velvet, gin ye hae't, black velvet. I've the siller for it wi me the noo.

Miss Cairney was mildly outraged, that the fabric of kings should be turned to nothing more than wiping snot from the nose, and she said,

An affa dear handkerchief, Waatchie, wid ye nae say? I can cut ye a piece o' linen for thon, it'd dee ye jist as weel,

but Watchie laughed suddenly, piling outrage upon outrage, until at last he said,

Na na, Miss Cairney, for my werk, ye ken, for waatchmakkin. It keeps the pairts o' a waatch far aboots I can see them, efter I've ta'en it tae pieces, ye ken.

The spinster nodded, and went to find the shop's only bolt of velvet, measured it against a calibrated brass rule fixed by screws to the top of the counter, handkerchief sized, a foot by a foot. From a ledge under the counter, she took her sharp scissors with their long scythe blades, and snipped the air a couple of times before introducing them to the edge of the velvet, carving from it an exact square, and after she had returned the bolt to its place, she folded the velvet down and wrapped it in an ironic parcel of brown paper, telling him the price of it. Watchie thanked her in a small voice, and left the shop, and the spinster behind him, poor confused woman, finding out late in life that there was more to velvet than she had ever imagined.

His first trip to collect the watches Geordie had reaped from his regular custom yielded him not a single glimpse of Kirsty, for Geordie gave him a laden canvas sack at the croft's door, and apologized for not being able to stay with him for a blether, but he had much to do, what with the cracking of a number of the roof slates and some repairs still in hand to be returned the day after; and so Watchie returned to the comfort of his mother's good hot stew, and then went up to his room to see what there was in the sack. He removed each watch one by one, and found them to be very much of a muchness, the same design of fob as if a single organism had propagated itself by division, nothing as special or as elaborate as he had come across in his daily work with Strachan. He turned them each end over end in his hands, plain tarnished moons closed like the shell of a mollusc, springing open as his father's watch had done many years ago, revealing glasses scored and clawed by dirt, and ordinary white faces with a circuit of black roman numerals, blood relations one to the others, nothing there to intimidate him in the least. Before starting on the first of them, Watchie lit the oil-lamp, which stood in a recess he had gouged in the desk, from the candle which burned in its holder on the bedside table, replacing its clear glass dome over the mitre of flame he had roused; turning, he saw his own shadow grown black and tall behind him, grown to the size of a giant like Vulcan at the forge, shrinking as he returned the candle to its place. In his cloister, Watchie started his work, choosing the nearest of the watches and placing the rest in the canvas bag carefully so they would not injure each other in their jostle for position, then unrolling his pad of velvet flat upon the counter of the desk and placing the watch in its exact centre, so that now even more than ever it appeared like a polished full moon in the sky of night. Beside the velvet, he placed his canvas purse of watchmaker's tools, the fastening strings undone and the purse open like the surgeon's instruments waiting to be chosen; and beside the purse, he placed his watchmaker's spectacles, the single barrel of the lens secure in its brass wire frame, the other vacant lens staring at the array of tools in surprise.

The first watch was opened without fuss or ceremony, the face removed with the simplest twist of the minute screwdriver to loosen the anchoring hands; and there it was, through the looking glass which brought the duplex escapement into closer relief for him, the age-old enemy of the watch and the reason for his first-ever repair; neglect, ill lubrication, dirt blending with the oil and seizing the workings, and Watchie almost laughed to see it, though he held his breath for fear of misting up the mechanism and introducing unseen droplets of vapour which might corrode the simple metal of its construction. This was a task he could perform while his thoughts reached out beyond himself, to the croft up the road, and as he took the watch to pieces he heard the music of Kirsty's voice again as if she were singing to him over the distance. From below, Watchie could hear the tuning of his father's fiddle, the drawl of the bow over the strings, and he smiled at the memory of fiddle evenings gone by, in the days before and after Jamie Watts; such a rare happening it was now, with his father's strange silences about the farm returned to sour the days, silences that Watchie escaped from in his room atop the stairs, that Watchie wondered whether there was an occasion he had forgotten among a ragtag of other concerns, though nothing came to his mind. Watchie heard the voice of the latest of the crew, stout John Allison, the first ploughman, a rough thing like wheels of granite milling the corn into flour, crying above the strands of Wullie's fiddle as the two of them together interpreted the ballad Half-past Ten, a coincidence which brought the smile to Watchie's face as he thought of it, the song of a young man and his lover who alter the hands of the clock which belongs to the cwean's father so that it always reads the same time, half-past ten, the time by which she is supposed to be home.

With a cloth of linen given to him by his mother, he wiped the last of the spirits of wine from the parts and laid them out in their order, on the pad of velvet, so that the watch in its entirety was in front of him. He rested back in his seat, his eyes wearied by long and painstaking concentration, and gratefully unhooked his glasses from his ears and placed them on the counter of his desk so that they stared blindly out of the window, the barrel of the lens and the empty loop, the lamp striking a light of gold from their brass frame. He ground his fists into his eyes, through his closed lids, causing metallic after-images of red gold to blossom and unfold after he released the pressure. He stared at the wheels and gears and bushes on the night of velvet, constellations and galaxies, then looked out of the window just above his table, on a clear and dark sky laid out as if to invite a comparison; he was struck by the similarity, and remembered the words of the Revd Lyle in his clock room, explaining the nature of the clockwork world, and in the flickering candle flame of a moment, Watchie saw the metaphor and the object in conjunction before him, and the tumblers were jus about to fall into their places as each became a proof for the other, *quod erat demonstrandum* laid before him like a feast of enlightenment, the nature of godhood on velvet, on a table of his own making; and the last tumbler was just about to fall to this treacherous key when suddenly the door to his room charged open, and Watchie turned to see his sister Jessica bounding in, capering to the music from below, ruining his concentration, the fine ear it takes to hear the opening of the vault of numinous mysteries. Jessica by now was of an age to help her mother and her father with the milking of the kye in the byre, and a gentle touch she had with them, sitting on the milking stool that Watchie remembered himself. Being the younger of the two, and also being more dependent on Jeannie's indulgence and kindness at a time when Watchie was trusted by his mother to take to his legs, she was inevitably pampered and encouraged, more confident than her brother; and the two grew up as complementary mysteries, one to the other, Watchie locked in his room and needing nothing more than the companionship of his book, Jessica now becoming playmate to the Laird, though not so much now in his declining years. Quite why she should have chosen this particular night to come into Watchie's cell is another matter; perhaps made curious by the lifting of the desk into the house, perhaps magnetized by her brother's concentration, but she strayed into the room as aimlessly as a cat, avoiding a look at the business on the desk as if it were the least of her concerns, touching instead the wood of the bedside table as if to claim it as her own. She said, in no direction,

Fit way're ye here fan we're haein a sang doon the stair, Waatchie?

Watchie turned in his seat to look at her, resting his arm over the back of the seat, sitting on it sideways. Her hair fired up proper gold in the light of the candle, braided into two ropes by Jeannie, fastened at the ends by red ribbons each tied in a butterfly bow.

I'm at my werk, Jess, yon's fit way I'm nae doon the stair.

Jessica nodded, without understanding, approached him with

her arms fastened behind her, one wrist manacled in her other hand, swinging them from side to side. She arrayed herself over the frame of Watchie's chair, leaning against it and supporting herself on one leg, her free foot resting against the instep of the other. Watchie sighed, thankful that she had come in while he was resting, still passing a hand over his eyes. She looked over his shoulder, at the pad of velvet, and said quickly,

Fit're ye werkin at?

though fine she knew; she looked down upon her brother from her better vantage, and he frowned suddenly.

Fit's it look like? I'm fexin a waatch, can ye nae see that?

Jessica pushed herself away a pace or two, as if from the unexpected ignition of a flame, the first sprig of a roman candle. She said, her voice thick with hurt,

It's a' in bits.

Watchie laughed, a laugh sharpened on his knowledge, a cruelty he knew was quite wrong.

Ye canna fex a waatch gin ye dinna tak it tae bits first.

Suddenly Jessica came forward, darting her finger out to touch the velvet beside the biggest wheel in the mechanism,

Fit's yon dee?

and Watchie turned away from her and took her hand, flinging it away from him, crying out,

Dinna touch yon! Daft cwean that y'are, I've jist been cleanin a' yon, ye'll mak it a' dert again!

Jessica leapt back now, burned savagely by her brother's inexplicable vehemence though fine she knew that she was pressing herself into the heat of his obsession when she first came towards him. Her eyes were as angry as the tiger's as they matched with his, inflamed with pain and the force of his rejection; but then she smiled, and said as sweetly as any inquiry made in innocence,

Aye, and the sooner ye'll fex it, the sooner ye'll be seein yer fancy cwean again,

and then turned to the door and left Watchie to call behind her,

Dinna ye cam here file I'm at my werk, Jess,

as if to reassure himself that she had left at his command rather than by her own will. He turned back to his desk, to the sparks of a mechanism which blazed on the velvet before him, picked up his watchmaker's spectacles from their lookout, and passed the question-marks behind his ears; but his fingers shook with remembered rage at his sister, the glass magnifying his slight tremor into an immense vibration which he judged would damage the engine of the watch, and so he put down his instruments for a while, and breathed into the darkness of the shadow he cast behind himself until his heartbeat became slower, until he had separated thoughts of Kirsty from the work he was about to perform, and he was ready to work with an unclouded judgement, examining each part as he seized it in the points of the tweezers under the watchmaker's lens.

XXIII

Watchie had been working a year for Geordie O'Donnell when the sealed letter arrived at the step of the front door, long after he had left for Strachan's on his bicycle. It was picked from the floor by Peggy, after the new Laird had barked his warning to the entire household that someone had come along the path, and it was the only postal delivery received that day. The envelope was thick and respectable, a fine quality of paper, smooth to Peggy's touch, immediately arousing her curiosity, for it was heavy on one side, and she turned it before looking to see to whom it was addressed; there on the back, fixing the triangle flap to the envelope, was a scab of vermilion wax, printed in bas-relief with the coat of arms of the village of Aberlevin, and she ran a finger over it before turning the envelope once more to see who was to be receiving this communication from the council. It was addressed, in a wide and cursive script which coiled as fluently as rope cast aside, to Master William Leckie of Smallbrae, which could only mean Watchie, and she took it into the kitchen, where Jeannie was standing over the sink and mopping out the remains of the morning's porridge, and said,

Fit way, d'ye think, oor wee Waatchie'd be sent a letter frae the cooncil?

and she held up the envelope for Jeannie to see. Jeannie turned and wiped her hands on the fabric of her apron, and took the offered envelope, investigated it in precisely the same way as her mother-in-law, running a finger over the scab of wax as if to determine the contents by force of will, and frowned when no further sign could she tell of its importance. She said,

Yon's gey funny, a letter frae the cooncil,

but shrugged, as she always did when faced with simple

mysteries soon to be resolved, and placed the letter on the kitchen table, at Watchie's accustomed seat, and that should have been an end to it, but for the fact that throughout the day, the letter radiated a quiet demand to her to be opened and read, and she found her eyes drawn away from her work and towards its silent secret message. When later she carved the vegetables for the night's dinner on the table, it sat brimming with a content which was denied to her, and for a moment she considered that she was the mother of the recipient, and after all the content would be known to her sooner or later; but she shook her head and refused such thoughts the power to move her, for her son was now a young adult, with an adult's right to his own affairs, though the envelope seemed to grow fatter in front of her as she fed it on her unrequited curiosity, bidding upon it some accident which might open it without her will.

The family gathered for dinner at a time adjusted to account for Watchie's later arrivals these days from Turriff; Aal Wullie as the paterfamilias at the table's head, Peggy at the next right angle down, Jeannie's seat vacant beside her as she fetched the stew from its pot, Wullie at the opposite edge of the table, book-ends with his father for seniority in the farming, and Jessica opposite her grandmother, risen for the moment to help her mother carry the plates to the table. In Watchie's place sat the letter, in promise of his arrival, and Wullie picked it from the table and looked at it for a moment, first the address, then the back, with its seal, and he said,

Fan cam thon for the loon?

Peggy spoke across to her son,

This morn, I took it mysel.

Wullie nodded, his thumb playing with the edge of the flap as a child might play with a razor-blade, and tearing the paper around a little of the seal, but Jeannie saw him, and called out,

Dinna ye open thon, Wullie Leckie, it's nae for ye tae open, can ye nae see? It's for Wulliam, nae for yersel,

for she was damned if an afternoon spent on the rack was to be wasted by her husband's assumption of a right she had not granted to herself, and so Wullie let her see him replacing the

273

envelope where he had found it, and brought his hands forward to lace them one into the other on top of the table.

Watchie arrived in time for dinner, as usual when the weather was fine; nodding to all, he sat in his seat and scraped it closer to the table, and only then did he notice the envelope with eyes wearied by close examination of minute workings. There was a lid of silence pressed tightly over the table, and he looked around to see that all the eyes in the room were upon him, even Jessica's; he turned to his mother at the range, and said,

Fan'd thon letter cam for me?

Jeannie was elaborately casual as she scooped a ladle of stew on to his plate.

This morn, she said; then, Are ye nae openin it?

Watchie noticed the fractional tear around the rim of the seal just before he ripped it. He took out the letter, razor pleated in thirds, and unfolded it; written in fountain-pen script upon a council letterhead, he spoke its message aloud:

Frae the desk o' Provost Thomas Macpherson (and here he uttered the date and the year), Dear Master Leckie, Further to a cooncil meetin o' (another date, some weeks previously, was mentioned), it has been decidet tae restore the toun clock tae werkin order, in time for the anniversary o' an event o' significance in the history o' the village o' Aiberlevin. It has been brocht tae my attention that yer ain expert eyes in the repair o' clocks wid be verra valuable tae the cooncil in makkin the final decision, and tae this end I wid be gratefu' for yer presence at my office tae discuss the matter further. I am free on the Setterday o' this week, atween the oors o' midday and three o'clock, and may see ye ony time then. Trustin ye are weel, I remain, yer maist obedient servant, Thomas Macpherson.

The signing off brought a snort from Aal Wullie, who declared,

Macpherson, noo, anither man's servant, I canna see thon mysel,

but Jeannie stood puzzled by the content of the letter, and said,

Fexin the clock o' the village? Is thon fit he's efter ye tae dee, Wulliam?

Watchie shrugged, scanning the letter in his hand.

I dinna ken. He's jist efter me tae hae a luik at it, I think.

Wullie looked down into his plate of stew, as if suddenly afraid.

Nae ony a werd o' siller, ye'll notice,

and his father laughed and pointed,

Aye, ye're richt there, Wullie, sooner the siller'll rain oot o' the sky than cam frae the hand o' Macpherson,

and Aal Wullie next focused on Watchie,

Mind yersel, my loon, for a' that he's a guid name as a makker o' sheen, for he cherges affa dear for it, and thon's his way wi business as weel.

So many opinions for Watchie to heed, and the work to do on Geordie O'Donnell's tin watches as well; he ate his dinner in silence, answering only the briefest inquiries, and when everyone was finished, and had settled down to a cup of tea and a slice of Nana Richie's substantial fruit loaf, he announced,

It widna dee ony hairm tae gang tae hae a talk wi Meester Macpherson, for we dinna ken jist fit he's efter, and I winna ken gin I'll ne'er see him.

A reasonable response, to which Peggy and Jeannie nodded in agreement, while Aal Wullie regarded his grandson as if he were a loon once more, the loon who had cast a stone at a wasp's nest because he had been told to, and Wullie Leckie sat like a man in a falling house, hearing the first sounds warning of collapse; and as for Jessica, it was a subject fit for those overhead adult conversations she was never made privy to, that is to say, it interested her not at all.

Provost Thomas Macpherson was a slave to the good living which came with a successful business, enjoying as he did the pleasures of a fine malt whisky, the Glenlevin of course, being the best of the locally produced distillates, and the smoke of a good rich pipe, which against all the advice of his wife Henrietta he inhaled down to the pits of his lungs. Such indulgence, of course, would have been anathema to his most famous ancestor, one more example of how comfort and excess corrodes men of property, insulating them from those who must work for meals and their keep; but this took no part in the present-day Macpherson's considerations, for he could not help but think that if he were able to walk up to Andra Macpherson, if the stories were true and the spirit were still roaming the cobble strings, and if he were able to meet this troubled man in the ethereal flesh, then Thomas Macpherson had no doubt at all in his mind that the elder man would appreciate the irony of it all, that a Macpherson of the tainted blood would cock a smile at the very notion that one of the past-notorious name had ascended to the heights of respectability in the village which had once execrated the Macpherson and all of his deeds. It was something of a coincidence that Macpherson shared a surname with his ancestor at all, for his great great grandfather through marriage had been an entirely unrelated Macpherson, whose love for a woman seeded with the bastard of the brigand transcended the prohibitions of the times, so that though Thomas Macpherson's name was that of the man who started the line, it was not, in the strictest sense, the name of the Macpherson, the Andra Macpherson who died on the gallows in the Aberlevin village square, that he bore. No matter; for every child in Aberlevin was weaned on the tale of the brigand, and Thomas Macpherson was no exception. He sat on his mother's lap as a loon, and heard from her as vividly as if she herself had witnessed it the dignity with which Andra Macpherson submitted himself to the caress of the noose, walking through the door into that dark room of annihilation as courageously as he had walked the roads for his keep; and from those days, when his mother encouraged him to be proud of his blood, Thomas Macpherson knew he was a breed set apart from the others who catcalled at him in the streets, mimicking his fat little stride of straight and open legs which looked like the gait of calipers. He became haughty beyond his years, not an attractive trait in anyone, answering only to the memory of his ancestor, and from this he drew his strength, plummeting his roots into the soil of the Macpherson's reputation and growing all the fatter for it; and as he grew into adolescence, Thomas Macpherson decided that this was to be his mission, to honour the man who had allowed him to walk through the spite of them all, who had made him impervious to all the darts cast at him tipped with the poison of jealousy, for that was all they were, jealous mean-minded individuals unrefined by the blood of the brigand charging through their veins. His trade was in the making of shoes, and a fine shoemaker he was, of that there was no doubt; he made the shoes of Lord Aberlevin himself, and there was a sign in his shop to celebrate the fact, a tin oblong of black ink on cream enamel, BY APPOINTMENT TO HIS LORDSHIP, LORD GORDON OF ABERLEVIN, which raised the smile on many faces, faith, there wasn't another shoemaker near to Lord Aberlevin, but many owned that it would be a small matter for the lord to send away for his footwear if he found any cause for fault in Thomas Macpherson's product, and so his pride was not without justification. He made shoes for all purposes, from hard-wearing working boots for the farm hands, armoured creatures of thick leather which wouldn't even bend under the careless hoof-fall of a Clydesdale, to elegant shoes of the court variety for the fine wives of the merchants and the lairds, slender beasts decorated with redundant buckles and bows and frills of soft pliant hide, with heels of a good and modest length. The quality of his work in leather was known the width and breadth of the county, as were the king's ransoms at which he valued it, but as he himself said, ye'll nae pey for yer sheen verra aften, there's a hillock o' werk ga'ed intae ilka ane o' them, and gin there's ony need for repair in a year in ony o' my sheen, ye'll hae't back tae ye wi nae cost, a pledge he had never had to redeem in all his years.

Such a reputation had won him the trust of the voters – or rather those who qualified for the vote – for good work always seems to mistakenly find its way into the same parcel as morality; and soon Macpherson was modestly disclaiming any intention of running for the position of provost, even as he stood with roses for the pauper's grave of his ancestor, ready in his heart to redress the great wrong which the village of his birth had done to the man whose blood and breath were immanent within him.

★

There was no fuss about Watchie's appearance as he readied himself on the Saturday to go to the village hall; he was smartly dressed, to be sure, but there was none of the sense of urgency and impression from either Jeannie or Peggy that had accompanied his first visit to Mr Strachan two years previously. For his own part, Mr Strachan had accepted Watchie's reason for being unable to come to work on this particular day, smiling slyly when he was told. Ah, Waatchie Leckie, ye'll hae the business oot frae under me in nae a lang time, is that it, eh? But there was no rancour in him over the matter, and he wished Watchie luck in his interview, and that was the end of it, for well did he know that the purpose of every teacher is to watch the back of a pupil when the time comes.

Watchie rode the three miles to the village on his bicycle all the way along the pleasant spring road, until at last he gained the rim of the Cornhill Road and saw the village before him. There, above the low houses, was the striving tower of the clock, a lightless beacon cast up by the village hall, and Watchie cycled closer towards it, suddenly and for no good reason feeling a chill in the depths of his stomach.

The bicycle was safe enough angled against the granite wall of the village hall building, at the side of it away from the tower, and Watchie looked up at the clock in passing, seeing freshly a monument known to him since childhood. From the trunk of the tower, there was hardly anything to be seen of the clock, except for its facing of blue opaque glass, and the brass hands telling the hour of the clock's final destruction; and immediately Watchie felt drawn to it, fascinated by the hidden mechanism, willing himself already beyond the door and into its cloistered workings. But there was the appointment to be kept first and foremost, and so Watchie went into the side door, where the council met and the Provost's office was to be found, and found the appropriate door at the end of an abbreviated corridor, with a wooden plate fixed into the panelling by two obvious nails, painted with the words, THOMAS MACPHERSON, PROVOST OF ABERLEVIN.

The voice called to him to come in after he had planted two

uncertain knocks upon the door; and there, behind an oaken desk, sat the Provost Macpherson, wearing the gilded chain of his office around his wide shoulders. He stood up, drawing his lips over teeth which hung distinctly in his mouth like herring in a curing shed, yellowed by the pipe uncoiling its rope of smoke into the air, and came round to the public side of his desk to shake Watchie by the hand, a grip which was tight and businesslike and moist. The fingers which made compliant fabric of tough hide were strong and inadvertently hurtful, and Watchie was glad to be released at the end of it, unable to match him.

Fine pleased I am tae see ye, Master Leckie, said the Provost, tak a seat, gin ye'd be sae kind,

and he nodded to the spindly creature of leather and uprights positioned in front of his desk, returning to the official side. He sat at the precise moment as Watchie himself, as was only courteous, and leaned forward.

Noo then, Master Leckie, he began, ye'll be familiar wi the sad story o' my ancestor o' mony years ga'ed by, will ye nae? The hingin in the square, that is tae say, and fit folla'ed frae yon.

Watchie nodded, knowing it by rote, as did all the children of Aberlevin. The Provost was satisfied, and continued,

Weel noo, this year's fit ye'd ca' the anniversary o' the event, that is tae say, Master Leckie, a hundred year ga'ed by sin a guid mannie wis pit tae his death by the ill manners o' a puckle o' sleekit craturs nae fit tae dig oot his grave for him, and it has been the decision o' the cooncil, in this anniversary year, tae rid up the clock in time for the date o' the hingin.

Again Watchie nodded, saying nothing, for nothing needed to be said; except, perhaps, that the anniversary of a hundred years is properly called a centenary, but he held his peace while the Provost drew on his pipe and coughed liquidly to one side, then went on.

Beggin yer pardon, Master Leckie, I'm a fair martyr tae my lungs, ye ken. Noo then, yer name was mentioned at the cooncil meetin by the Revd Lyle as a mannie fa kent a deal aboot clocks, and fine things I've been hearin aboot yer werk, Master Leckie, fine things, nae doot aboot it. I'd like tae hear fit ye've tae say on the werk o' buildin the clock again, for the Reverend wis speakin affa weel o' ye, and I've brocht ye here the day tae accompany me tae the tour o' the clock, tae hear yer opinion on fit there wid be tae dee tae it, gin we were thinkin o' bringin a'body here tae fex it.

There was a long silence, during which Watchie realized that he was expected to speak. He said,

Aye, Provost Macpherson, I can dee thon for ye, nae bother at a',

and the Provost smiled broadly,

Capital, Master Leckie! We'll awa the noo, for I've the key to the tour on me the meenit,

and raised himself with difficulty from the plush leather seat which, in his own eyes, his office deserved.

The key was of dull iron, one end of it a wide metal loop, with a square filigree at the other, a puzzle to trip the ancient and scarred door's cunning array of tumblers. Watchie grimaced a little as the key turned in the lock, with the help of the application of strength on the part of the Provost, to the sound of nails dragged down the slate of a blackboard, a harsh shrieking which echoed inside the tower. The door opened to the squeal of untended hinges, and Macpherson and Watchie entered, Macpherson first by assumed right of seniority, to hear the dying of the door's agony within the corridors of the tower, and Watchie entered with a sense of trepidation, as if the tower were still a vessel for the spirits of the dead hordes which had wronged it so many years ago, as if the light of day would send them scurrying from the door like field mice to escape; but there was only the long-settled smell of neglect, a stir of dust which made a shining tablet of the daylight, and Watchie's first sight upon entering was of the two cylinders of iron which had been the weights of the old clock, resting upon their sides at the foot of the central well sunk through the body of the tower, now rusted beyond use. Two of the stone flags were cracked across like cheap ceramic, the fissures striking radial patterns from where they had landed, and from the weights two ropes, aged and weathered and flayed unrecognizably, coiled around like snakes. Watchie approached the weights as if they were corpses, the first victims of the rage, and touched the frayed ropes, causing them to splinter in his fingers like thorns; to the provost they were nothing more than debris cast off from above, and he walked past them without knowing, but to Watchie they were his important first clue as to how the mechanism above had been regulated, even as his fingers touched the roughened barrels of the cylinders he knew approximately what he would find at the head of the stairs, and already the breath came more easily to him, for he was quite familiar with this kind of balance, and he stood up as the Provost held out his hand flat and said,

We'll gang up the stairs the noo, Master Leckie, but nae sae quick, mind, for I'm nae richt guid wi stairs, on accoont o' my lungs, ye ken.

Watchie followed the Provost on his long and laborious climb up the spiral, their boots displacing the dust which had eroded from the walls and on to the steps, and used the time to consider the arrangement he would find upon gaining entry to the chamber. Once during their journey, Macpherson held up his hand and stopped to lean against the casement of a window, a bevelled slot like the archer's vantage in a castle turret, drawing in breath uneasily through a turmoil of phlegm; but a determined character he was if nothing else, and after his moment's rest he turned his face towards the summit of the tower, and made sure that each footstep was sound, denying the weakness of his body with the strength of his resolve, and soon they made their way up the remaining height and gained the clock chamber at the top.

Macpherson walked simply into the chamber without a care, grateful for the respite of flat ground under his feet, but Watchie felt a curious dread just upon the threshold, a strange awe in being faced with the skin of the ages stretched taut across the portal. His sight altered just then as the dust roused by the stumpy feet of the Provost caught the light which came in through the hatch to the belfry, as shapeless as spirit. With this new sight, Watchie saw the walls with their blight of lichen as those of a tomb which he was about to desecrate with a thoughtless step; he was a child before the dead generations, and like a child he quailed before the thought of it, as if history itself had charged him with the clock's redemption. Like a house of granite which keeps hidden under its roof the trial and anger of a bitter marriage, Watchie showed no signs of this to the Provost as Macpherson turned to look at him; but it rooted his feet to the threshold as time itself reared up to face him, and all his courage and confidence melted and ran in the heat of this numinous fear.

Macpherson was not touched by the sight of the chamber in the same way as Watchie. To Macpherson, the chamber was simply intolerable chaos, nothing more than dust and filth and a scattering of rusty metal, and the kind of decay that needs hard work, restoration, and so the look he gave Watchie was quiet and expectant, and it was the insistence of his gaze which brought Watchie down to earth, as it were. Watchie took a deep breath of the rotten air, and felt better and steadier for it, and then he was able to take his step forward; for a clock is just a clock, after all, no matter how meaningful, and a surgeon can perform the same operation on a pauper as on a monarch, though the cause of the malady may differ between them.

The mechanism of Johannes Dreimann's clock had been cast in iron, which explained to Watchie's satisfaction the curious red dust which swirled about the floor among the sparkling mica and the meaner particles of soot. A single cast around the flags revealed the wheels and gears, badly corrupted by the weathering they had received through the open hatchway, until they were nothing more than fit matter for archaeology, curious relics to be pondered at leisure. But to Watchie, there was a story being told before him, and Macpherson kept his silence and stood in the corner as Watchie established a taxonomy of function before his eyes, muttering to himself all the while, I ken fit ye dee, thon's far aboots ye gang, putting the skeleton of the clock back together, until the structure was apparent to him, as he had thought upon seeing the weights below. Finally he turned to Macpherson, noticing him as if for the first time, and said,

I canna see ony ither pairts for it, Mr Macpherson, they'll a' hae risted awa, ye ken.

Macpherson nodded. With more respect, for he prided himself upon recognizing application and diligence when he saw it, he said,

I see ye'll be needin mair werkins for the clock, Master Leckie, for yon winna dee at a'.

Watchie laughed, not unkindly.

Na na, yon pairts'll nae werk in their lives, they're nae ees tae a'body the noo.

Macpherson strode forward, and looked at Watchie as the loon squatted down on his hunkers to look at his assembly.

Fit wid ye be recommendin, noo, Master Leckie? For yon's fit way ye've been brocht here.

Watchie lifted the brim of his cap a very little, as if the tension across his brow were unbearable. He looked not at Macpherson, but at the remains of the clock, as sadly as if it were the corpse of an old friend.

Ye'll be needin a hale new mechanism, Mr Macpherson. Brass, mind ye, nae iren, for brass winna rist like yon. A hale mechanism cast oot o' brass, aye, and the weights as weel, yon'd last a lifetime.

Macpherson nodded. He paced the chamber around Watchie for a moment, and said,

Wid it be easy tae mak, yon mechanism?

Watchie shrugged.

I dinna ken. Ye'd hae tae dee the draa'ins for it, and pey a foondry tae cast a' the feels for ye, it wid a' tak a bittie o' time, ye ken.

Macpherson continued to pace, his footfalls deadened by the cladding of lichen.

Aye, but for the anniversary, Waatchie, wid it be done for the anniversary?

Watchie thought for a moment; they were in spring just now; one week to design the workings, perhaps, a further week to ready the chamber and free it from dust, the delivery, putting it all together; finally he nodded,

Aye, it could be, Mr Macpherson, but it's an affa wheen o' werk, ye ken.

Macpherson stopped, with his feet on the rim of the aperture, the well through which the huge weights had fallen nearly a century ago. His breath came and went rapidly, like an accordion playing an idle note, and he looked down upon Watchie, his small height grotesquely tall to Watchie's squatting vantage. His face pleaded with the loon, but his voice was strong and sure as if addressing a meeting of the council, without fear and without doubt, and he said to Watchie,

Ye'd be weel peyed for yer time, Waatchie Leckie, gin ye were tae agree tae be the mannie fa'd dee't, and mysel, and ane ither fa dee'd by thon hillock o' rist at yer feet, wid aye be gratefu tae ye.

XXIV

Watchie brought the news home with him and over the dinner table it was the only subject of conversation for the evening. Aal Wullie still counselled caution to his grandson, and suggested that the Provost should be asked to state plainly what it was he meant by well paid, no good way it was for a canny businessman to open such negotiations, and all nodded agreement but Wullie, who sat gathering all the silence in the room, as impassive as an ornament, hardly touching his meal. Jeannie said what a good thing this would be for Watchie's reputation, and Peggy spoiled the loon with her pride, so much that Watchie smiled in the middle of his dinner, lowering his head to avoid it. But finally Wullie at the head of the table cleared his throat, and this was the signal for the conversing to stop, and Watchie met the eyes of his father in a manner which quite disturbed him; for Wullie was almost shaking himself apart in his seat with the effort of control, and his voice was quiet, leaking from him,

And fit aboot yer mendin for Geordie O'Donnell? Gin the clock'll be as muckle a werk as ye're sayin, ye canna dee the baith o' them.

Watchie had considered this on his cycle ride home, and so he wiped his mouth with his tongue and said,

I'll jist hae tae gang tae the hoose and taal him I canna fex his waatches ony mair.

Wullie nodded, slowly, as he was presented with this, and began calmly,

Weel noo, Master Waatchie Leckie, Master Wulliam, I'd've thocht mysel that ye'd've larned a wee bittie frae yer helpin Geordie wi his waatches. Are ye nae content wi werkin frae yer hame for him?

Watchie nodded into the space left for his reply,

Aye, I can dee the werk at hame fine weel . . .

Wullie leaned into the table, his face hot and red.

Aye, Master Wulliam, ye can dee the werk at hame, can ye nae? Ye can mak yer siller at yer trade, can ye nae, and ye dinna hae tae gang frae the hoose for a meenit, am I richt?

Watchie almost heard the creaking of the trap released by a careless step. He shook his head, opened his mouth to say no, no, but his father was ready for him,

Fit way can ye nae werk at the fairm by the day, and dee yer trade at nicht? Fit's tae stop ye, answer me thon? Fit way can ye nae dee the baith o' them?

Jeannie raised her hand just then, and said,

Wullie, that'll dee, the loon's eneuch werk afore him, dinna fash yersel ower it,

but Wullie was impelled beyond all hope of recall,

Aye, werk for ithers, fan he'll nae tern a hand tae help his ain faimily, yon's the werk he'll dee, can ye nae see he's jist as able tae dee his waatchmakkin at hame? Are ye blin tae't, wumman, fit's a-dee wi ye? Can ye nae see he can dee them baith?

The trap shut around Watchie, and caught him in its bite. He realized why his father had agreed so readily to Geordie O'Donnell's proposal that day in Turriff, and the food in his mouth turned. Around him, the table was animated by his mother, his grandmother, his grandfather, all speaking at once, pointing their fingers at Wullie, and Jessica, puzzled by it all, looking through the gap between herself and the edge of the table to her feet dandling off the floor, for the voices striking against each other were harsh and angry, the way her mother sounded when the cwean went too near to the fire, and she could not bear to look at their faces.

Watchie stood up from the table, and went over to the lattice of hanger pegs fixed to the back of the kitchen door. He found his jacket and his coat, and put them on, stilling the argument as effectively as if he had brought a gavel down on the table. Wullie looked at him over the head of Jeannie, demanded,

Far aboots wid ye be gangin the noo, Master Leckie? ye've nae eaten yer denner.

Watchie went towards the door. He was suddenly weary,

and filled with an anger he knew he could not express towards his father, though he felt as corrupted as the iron wheels in the tower, betrayed by a sorry trick. He did not turn, but seized the handle to the back door, and turned it in its socket, and said nothing, and closed the door gently behind him despite his great fury, as his mother had always taught him to do.

Parents, said Geordie O'Donnell, are a funny thing right enough, Watchie; though I'll say meself, it was surprised I was when yer father agreed to me little proposition, for well known it is throughout the village that he'd sooner have ye runnin the farm than lookin at the insides of a timepiece, and that's the truth of it.

The whole of the inside of the croft was buttered by the warm light of the peat and twig fire constructed inside the shallow hearth, and for once Watchie found himself entirely at peace, for in comparison to his own home, the croft was as snug as a womb, a single chamber livened by the smell of cooking. Kirsty was seated by the hearth, stirring the nucleus of the fire with a poker as if it were a stew, making certain that all the morsels of wood were being evenly consumed by the flames, and only once did she look up, and that was when, at the end of Watchie's story, Geordie O'Donnell made his declaration concerning parents, and Watchie saw, without her noticing, that her face had become an ironic mask, and this caused Watchie to hide a smile behind the appearance of careful consideration.

He did not know why it was that his legs took him in the direction of Geordie O'Donnell's croft after he had left the farmhouse; for a while he had not been the captain of his own actions, for there was much for him to think about, not the least his father's outburst at the table, and he began to realize that much had changed about Wullie since he had taken on the job at Strachan's. Watchie had been something of a lodger in his own house since agreeing to work for Geordie O'Donnell, every night in the studious half-darkness of his own room, conducting a parallel life with the family below. He remembered his father's ambivalent joy in the discovery of his son's talents;

and there was always the farm, the farm above everything else, Wullie Leckie's proof of his worth in the village, and the will which demanded that such a gift should pass along from father to son, from father to son, served into unready hands. Watchie thought of the shed, his father's lathe motionless for many years, carpeted thickly with the dust of forgotten ambitions. Soon into his long walk, Watchie realized that he was being taken away from the village, and knew where, and continued none the less, for there was always a cheer at the end of the journey he was making, and Geordie was always right pleased to see him whenever he came, a cheer of which he had great need at that particular time.

Ye understand, Watchie, said Geordie O'Donnell, I had not the faintest idea what it was yer father was after me to do when I put my proposal to him about a year ago. But I'll tell ye this much, if ye will; whatever he was doin, I'm sure so I am that he thought he was doin best for ye, for it's right hard for a father, aye and a mother as well, for to see their boy or girl goin the wrong way without tryin to push them back on to the right road.

Watchie uttered a short ironic laugh.

Aye, Mr O'Donnell, but I'm nae gangin the wrang road, nae for mysel, ye ken.

Geordie shook his head, and stuffed his clay pipe full of tobacco from a leather pouch.

Ah, well now, Watchie, tis sure I am that ye're not, for tis fine work ye do, all the custom I have says so, and is the customer not always right, so they say? But yer father now; I'm thinkin, there's a man who's spent his whole life makin somethin o' his land, and who's wantin to pass it down to yerself, the only son he's got, and there's the road he wants ye to go down; and there ye are yerself, stubborn as the cuddy loaded down with messages, ye're not movin an inch for him, and begod, why should ye? If he wants his watch fixin, he'll come to yerself, and if ye're after a pint o' milk, ye'll go to himself for it, and that's just the way of it.

Watchie smiled, and looked to the fireplace, beyond Kirsty,

to the mantelpiece above. He looked to the representation of the Christ standing there between two vases of freshly picked flowers, and it reminded Watchie that it was soon to be Easter, and the O'Donnells were celebrating the time of Lent by denying themselves of that which was their dearest vice, a perversity that was quite beyond Watchie's Protestant understanding, to be endured until it was time for the Christ to rise again. Mhairi's greatest indulgence was the sweets and hard candies which her father brought from the village when he went there to shop for Kirsty, and it was these she had chosen to deny herself for the duration of the Lenten festival; but still Geordie had insisted upon buying them for her, and so Mhairi had taken to keeping all of the sweets in a glass jar perched beside the vases on the mantelpiece, to one side of the crucifix, so that whenever the will came upon her to damn her fast and reach for one of them, there would be the suffering of Jesus to remind her that she was not to do so, and there would rest the jar, filled with brown candy balls which tasted of dark cane sugar, until Easter Sunday, when she would gorge herself in fact on this feast whose sweetness had only been known to her eyes until then. There was Mhairi's sacrifice made; but Geordie and Kirsty had their own decisions to make. Geordie declared, one night after returning from the chapel in Banff,

I think I'll be givin up the whisky for Lent,

to which Kirsty laughed, a rare sight and enough to cause her father to regard her curiously,

Ye dinna drink the fisky, daddy, mind ye thon? Nae for a lang time, onyway.

Geordie placed a hand upon his breast, as if on the site of an arrow wound jutting from him, a mortal loss of blood,

Kirsty, Kirsty, ah, ye're not to know, lass, and a good thing it is, it never leaves ye once ye've drunk it. Ye'll never know, bless yer heart, how much the taste is with ye all yer days, and so it's not as easy a givin up as ye might be thinkin. I've been givin up since the day ye brought me to me senses, ye might say that all me days are days o' Lent, so think of it as me penance goin on, for the sake o' yerself and Mhairi there, for I'm not certain I'd have cared for me own sake.

Kirsty approached her father, and laid a hand on his shoulder, willing her own strength to him as he sat in a rescued chair before the peat fire. He reached up, and stroked the back of her hand, a great comfort to him, for it was as much Ailsa as his daughter who was forgiving him for that drunken self which the whisky had shelled from him, leaving the hull of a decent man in the grave beside his wife. He said,

And yerself, Kirsty me own, what'll ye be givin up yerself for Lent, if ye don't mind me askin?

Kirsty smiled, and looked down into the eyes of her father, and said,

I'm giein up nae bein able tae read for Lent, daddy, for I dinna ken fit way the grand ladies can dee't and I canna.

Geordie laughed, not to dismiss his daughter's ambition, not that at all, and this Kirsty knew, and laughed with him as he said,

A fine thing to be givin up, Kirsty me own, and ye can be teachin yer daft owl father to be readin while ye're about it, if ye'd be so kind.

This was the galvanized household Watchie entered in seeking rest from his own problems, with Lent turned inside out for the O'Donnells, a time of preparation and fierce study, as Kirsty picked her way through a book bought by Geordie in the village shop, an alphabet book with pictures from a for apple to z for zebra, this last a puzzle to her, being a cuddy with striped long johns the like of which she had never seen. Strange to say, she was thinking about the zebra as she turned over the fire in front of Watchie that evening; for it occurred to her that Watchie might know something about this antic creature woven from like and yet unlike fabric to the horses in their fields. Once she almost asked him aloud, d'ye ken a'thin aboot zebras, Wulliam, for she thought Watchie to be too familiar an address to be calling him; but she saw that his face was troubled, the lines of care eked out by the gentle light of the fire before him, and she heard her father talking to him about roads and watches and milk, and then, with her head turned away to the fire, heard Watchie reply,

My faither'll nae be pleased til I've tellt him I'm rinnin the fairm, and thon I canna dee. Nae efter the provost's gied me the clock tae fex.

Geordie nodded.

It's a chance, right enough, Watchie, and if there's a thing I've learned in all me years, it's never to let a chance go by ye.

The pipe was unlit in Geordie's mouth. He inspected the end of the stalk, yellowed and stained by many smokes, replaced it between his teeth, then said,

I'm thinkin, though, that your good fortune in gettin yerself the job'll be meanin an end to our wee arrangement, is that not so, Watchie?

Watchie was about to speak, and raise his eyes to meet Geordie's, his face ashamed, when he noticed a sudden movement on the edge of his vision, and when he turned his head he was staring for the first time full into Kirsty's eyes; and more, for the suddenness of her turning had caused the entire gathered weight of her hair to shift, too much for the binding of her wooden clasp, which sprang apart, releasing the full wealth of her black hair down below her shoulders, now unstructured, lavish, defined only in the room's dim light by the polishing it received in the fluttering rag of flame. For a moment, a channel of wordless honesty was opened between Watchie Leckie and Kirsty O'Donnell, carved into the air between the meeting of their eyes, and Watchie was sure that she was communicating a plea across the distance, though for what he could not guess, nor even hope; but Watchie's were not the only eyes upon her, for both Geordie and Mhairi were staring at her openly after the tick of the hair clasp on the floor, and she looked from father to sister, and hurriedly, as if caught in a moment of unguarded nakedness, rooted the iron poker in the overlapped slates of peat, and darted down to a stoop to find both crafted sword and shield, building the whole structure again until the hair was as close to her scalp as filaments of black wire, binding it with care and stabbing it through with the sword, and patting it to make sure that the fastenings were sound.

Watchie said,

I canna dee baith, Mr O'Donnell, I'm affa sorry,

as if nothing had happened; but Geordie looked at Watchie with a small tilt to his head, replying slowly,

No matter, young Watchie, no matter at all, I wouldn't be wantin to be the one to stop ye doin yer work, now, though I'll miss ye comin to the house on a Monday, sure and I will,

and here he cast a look over his shoulder, to Kirsty resuming her stirring of the fire, her face in eclipse from his sight behind its full shadow of dark hair, and evenly he continued,

and I'm thinkin I'll not be the only one,

binding Watchie and Kirsty together along the taut line of his gaze, though neither looked at the other. Mhairi it was who made Watchie his last tea before he went along the road, but it was Kirsty who took it over to him, and this time she looked at him as the enamel mug passed across, a brief stroke of a glance and a warmer smile than ever he had received before; and when he left the croft, with all of Geordie's wishes for good luck piled high on his back, again it was Kirsty who opened the door for him without the need for Geordie to ask her, saying to him softly,

Guid luck wi yer clock, Wulliam,

before closing the door over quickly, facing Mhairi's deep frown, and her father's inclined head, and his look of curiosity.

The last person to be told of Watchie's good fortune was James Strachan, the man he worked for by day, and strangely enough this was the man he most dreaded the prospect of having to tell. Watchie took to his bicycle on the Monday morning, having endured the glacial breakfast-time atmosphere of his father's presence, and throughout his journey to Turriff he cast the news into different frames. Strachan had spared no lesson for the fear of nurturing a rival beyond his own expertise, and it was this that caused Watchie's feet to drag on the pedals of his bicycle when approaching Turriff, the feeling that, in accepting Macpherson's contract, he was being treacherous towards the man who had given him his instruction, and as he hopped off the bicycle, to bring it to harbour inside the doorway of the shop, there was Strachan, smiling at him, his hand on the key, unlocking the door to his apprentice.

Fine morn tae ye, Master Leckie, eh? A bittie caal in the air, but it's spring jist the noo, finer weather tae cam, eh? Yer faither'll be pleased at yon.

Watchie gave him a thin smile in return, feeling most undeserving of the old man's good humour. Strachan led him, as usual, into the backshop, to berth his bicycle against the stairway railing, and there was work for him to do almost immediately, a watch which would not go no matter how tightly it was wound, a watch of gold and delicate embroideries of gravure. He sat down to work, and determined that he would use this time to find the courage to tell James Strachan when the shop closed its doors at midday. But his fingers were inexpert liars for him; a handful of thumbs they became, and more than once he applied a deal more pressure on the tweezers than was required, causing a wheel held in its grasp to skip away and spin across the floor like a top on the point of its bearings, lifting him from his seat to search on hands and knees. The third time it happened, Strachan looked up from his own work, sighting Watchie through his magnifying lens which he wore in the same kind of frame as Watchie used himself, curiously doubled over his own spectacles so that Watchie felt himself scrutinized by three pairs of disapproving eyes, examined as closely as the watch opened for surgery in front of his employer through a great orb of a pupil that was as wide as a black world, and James Strachan said,

Fit's a-dee wi ye, Master Leckie, eh? Are ye nae up tae yer werk this morn, is yon yer trouble?

but Watchie scanned the floor through his own magnifying eye, traversing the landscape of ravines and contours of wood grain which his watchmaker's glass made of the planking until the escaped wheel was in front of him and captured in his tweezers, and he rose to his feet and said to Strachan,

Here it's here, Mr Strachan, I'll gie't a guid clean afore I'll pit it back in the mechanism,

and Strachan gave a long sigh, and turned back to his own

work, leaving Watchie to return to his, breathing slowly as the clocks sang at the top of their voices, from above as well as below in the shop, and yet another hour had elapsed before the midday closing.

Trapped in the one place where he could not help but be aware of the time, Watchie heard all the hours that passed, the clangour of agreement from the council of clocks, until at last Strachan put aside his instruments and dropped a fine weave linen cloth over his work, and said,

Nae lang till midday the noo, and it's affa quiet, eh, Master Leckie? We'll jist lock up for oor lunch the noo, gin ye dinna mind.

Watchie looked up, and realized that the execution of his intent was, like that of the brigand, to be brought forward. As usual, Strachan made his leisurely pot of tea at the spirit stove in the corner of the room. Watchie made another promise to himself, that he would tell Strachan after the making of the tea, when they were seated behind the counter; and this, too, elapsed, just as every clock in the shop rang out its midday message, the longest chime of the day, a riot of time erupting around Watchie as he sat on a stool beside Strachan, resting his enamel mug of tea on the counter. He waited for the final laggard chime to trail away into silence, tasted the sweetened tea before opening his lips to say,

Mr Strachan, I've tae taal ye somethin the noo,

and waited while Strachan drew his own tea from his mug, putting it down patiently on the counter beside Watchie's, and stared at him through the lenses of his spectacles.

Aye, Master Waatchie, and fit wid thon be noo, eh? Somethin tae pit yer mind aff yer werk, I'm thinkin tae mysel, nor ye widna hae been sae cack-handet earlier on.

There was a gentle smile on the old man's face, for he knew his apprentice by this time; Watchie looked to the floor, as if in shame at being caught out by the telegraphy of guilt, and said,

I've been askt tae fex the village clock in Aiberlevin, Mr Strachan.

Strachan nodded slowly, and took his mug into his hands,

resting it upon his lap like a shiny beast comforting in its warmth to him. He said, slowly,

And fit hae ye said tae that, Master Waatchie, eh? Fit hae ye said tae them?

and looked down into his milky reflection on the surface of the tea. Watchie found it easier with Strachan's eyes away from him; he let a moment pass, gathered all the courage he had to himself, and said,

I've said aye, Mr Strachan.

Again Strachan nodded. He would not look at his apprentice, and Watchie needed the guidance of his eyes, but the old man's words were firm as he said,

And d'ye think ye'd mak a fine job o' sic a grand clockie as yon, Master Waatchie, eh?

Watchie drew in his breath.

I dee, Mr Strachan.

Strachan looked up suddenly, and the lines about his face lit as he smiled,

Aye, I thocht as much mysel, Waatchie, yon's fit I was sayin the ither week jist tae the Revd Lyle. I says tae him, reverend, I says, it'll be a muckle big job for a'body, he was sittin jist far aboots ye are yersel, Waatchie, but I says tae him, I'm an aal mannie mysel the noo, and I ken guid werk fan I see't, and fine dee I ken that Waatchie Leckie's yer man for the job, and ye can taal yer cooncil thon as weel. And d'ye ken fit, Master Waatchie, eh? He left my shoppie, and says he'd taal them thon, and neist ye're camin tae me and sayin tae me ye've tae fex the clockie in yer village; aye, richt guid fan a man o' stature like thon listens tae the advice o' an aal bugger like mysel and does richt by himsel by it.

Strachan raised the mug to his lips, resting as it was in the cup of both of his hands as if its weight were too much for him to bear, and took a giant sip from it. Relief spread through Watchie in that moment, he could have fixed every timepiece in the building before having to go home; but Strachan held him to his seat, and spoke advice to him, words which Watchie never heard, for now he was ready, armed with the certainty that, despite his father, he had the will and confidence of the one man who knew him in his life away from the farm, and that soon he would restore time to the village of Aberlevin, the gift it had rejected a hundred years before.

XXV

Watchie's first job was to establish his measurements; and so, on the Wednesday evening of the last week of his apprenticeship to Strachan, he went to the village on his bicycle and knocked on the door of the provost's house. The basket of his bicycle contained the fat little bundle of a canvas bag, in which was a lantern, and he looked quite ready for business; for also inside the canvas bag was a folded pair of dungarees, bought for Watchie by Jeannie after a visit to the village clothiers in readiness for the dirty job ahead. The Provost was enjoying a cup of tea at the time, and it was his wife who answered the door, the Lady Provost herself, and she led Watchie inside the house, casting her eyes to the floor, for she was not a forward woman at all, enjoying none of the attention that her husband's position brought to the household, but bearing it all quietly for his sake, and she even poured Watchie a cup of tea for himself as Watchie explained to the Provost that he was needing entry to the tower to start his work.

The Provost's house was finely arrayed with decorations and ornaments, touched by a woman's influence. There were soft cloths on all the tables, fine linens dyed in pastel shades like the petals of flowers, and every wooden surface in the house was polished to a shine which was almost metallic in brightness. There were vases of crystal from which sprouted flowers without roots, carved from the garden and drinking from a small pool of water, and in the exact centre of the longest wall was a reproduced portrait of Queen Victoria, over which was twined a black ribbon, a mark of respect for the old monarch's death.

A fine wumman, d'ye nae think, Waatchie? The aal queen, aye, a character she was, richt eneuch, a character,

almost toasting her with his china cup of tea. Watchie nodded without thought, having none to offer, and he said,

I was affa young fan she was queen, Mr Macpherson, I dinna mind affa muckle aboot her.

Macpherson nodded, his eyes distant and tributary, snared in the past.

She was a grand wumman, Waatchie, she was aye here in Balmoral, ye ken, her hert was in Scotland richt eneuch,

and Macpherson's eyes now filled with a glaze of tears for his dead queen, and he said,

Enterprise, Waatchie, ken ye the werd? Yon's fit yon queen was a' aboot. Enterprise, aye, and confidence as weel, for files she was oor queen, we makt guid Christians o' fowk fa'd ne'er heard o' the Bible in a' their lives, and brocht oor ways tae ither lands. Aye, we'll ne'er see her like again.

Watchie shuffled in his seat, his trousers squealing against the glossy leather which was the colour of freshly cut steak. He finished his tea, and said to the Provost,

I'll hae tae be gettin stertit the noo, Mr Macpherson, for I'd sooner be hame afore nine; I'm still werkin for Mr Strachan till the end o' the week.

Macpherson nodded, and went to the sideboard cabinet, a blowsy architecture of oak rooted in the carpeting by lion's paws. There in a drawer he searched among keepsakes and sundry items until he found the key Watchie had seen opening the great door to the tower, thinking nothing of keeping such civic property in his own possession, a fact which gave Watchie some pause, though he said no more about it than,

Thanks, Mr Macpherson,

when Macpherson handed over to him the key, and thanking the Lady Provost for her hospitality, he left the house, with Macpherson's words from the threshold,

Aye, guid werk, Master Leckie, there's nae affa mony fowk'd dee't at thon time o' nicht, and ye can keep the key for the noo, gin ye'll need it.

At the foot of the tower, Watchie reached into his canvas bag for the lantern and a box of matches, and lit the flame which would carry him up the stairs, after several attempts while breath after breath of wind snuffed the dancing light on the end of the matchsticks one after the other. With the lantern settled and the flame glowing contentedly inside its bulb of glass, Watchie opened the door to the tower, taking several turns of the key to loosen the rusted tumblers inside, and then took his first night-time visit to see the mechanism. The lantern was a comfort to him on his way up the stairs, for he could see something of the journey ahead, the spiral close enough that he could reach up and touch the ceiling with its ribs of as yet unencountered steps; and when he finally gained the clock chamber itself, he placed the lantern on the barrel of the old mechanism, and it was no more fancies for him, no more of his imaginings, it was time to work.

He measured the remains of the wheels, still constructed upon the floor, though not all of them were present; but what he could not see, those wheels which had rotted to dust, he was able to intuit, and through calculation, formulae taught to him by Mr Strachan during his time as an apprentice, he was able to deduce the radii and circumferences as clearly as if the red dust had flown together from the flagging of the chamber and cast itself into a wheel before his eyes. He stood back for a moment into the corner, and used his pencil as a pointer down the pages of the notebook; all the wheels were accounted for to his satisfaction, and for a while the entire mechanism took shape before him; he looked up and there he saw it, meshing together into a pleasing whole, both the going train and the striking train, a cable lashed to eyes set in the wall of the chamber and extending to the bell above, he saw it complete and ready to strike the hour, and it was all the work of Master William Leckie, Watchie himself, the brass of the wheels glinting like the metal which it resembled, like proper gold in front of him.

Before he left the chamber, he looked at the castle of mechanism he had made of the old workings, scattered as they had been across the floor. Macpherson had told Watchie of the work of the Austrian gentleman many years before his ancestor's fall, and it was with respect for the work of Johannes Dreimann that Watchie took from the construction a single rotted wheel, rough to the fingertips with the accreted oxides of age, and put it into his canvas bag, a keepsake of the elder mechanism whose design was still sound enough for Watchie to consider as the foundation of his own. When he returned home that night, he placed the wheel at the head of his work table and from it came his inspiration, for in the whole tale of the brigand Macpherson, Watchie's sympathies lay primarily with the clock, which had never loaned its support to the tampering of the council, deserving none of what happened to it, cursed for its part in the sad happenings; time's own town crier, slaughtered without pity for the deceitful news it was given to tell.

XXVI

Watchie awakened from an angry sleep, coiled in the corner of the chamber, and the moment he did he was furious with himself; he had no excuse for himself, he had laid himself down for a minute, there being nothing more for him to do but wait, and then the air itself had drugged him, a thief which put all awareness in a bag of sacking, leaving him quiet, inert, until he heard the footsteps from below. Instantly he stood up and shook the dust from himself, and looked guiltily into the single opaque eye of the clock face, the iris of blue glass which stifled the light of day, and through the well in front of it he heard the sounds which had woken him up, the pacing of great muckle boots on the flagging below. Before he approached the well, he composed his face into a wakeful mask of efficiency and assurance, for you never could tell who it might be, perhaps the provost himself − God forbid that he should find Watchie wasting the good silver he was being paid in a treacherous slumber − and then, slowly and when he was sure he was ready for it, Watchie took himself over to the lip of the well and looked down.

There was a man at the bottom, his head tilted up so that Watchie could see the generous twill of a scything moustache. He was busily peering up and through the spiral into the opening high above him, and for his part Watchie matched the gaze; underneath the foreshortened stump of his body, the wee man (or wee so he was from this height) wore boots of highly polished black leather.

A'body aboot?

he called, and his voice was divided into an uneven chorus, rattling keenly from the walls. Watchie called in return,

Aye, I'll awa doon tae ye,

and took the steps at a good run, proving to no one but

himself that his sleep had been the lapse of a moment, fleeing down the coil and almost coming to grief twice on the worn-down rims of the stairs. He stopped in front of the beef-fed man, and stood face to face with him, and then found that he had to take a long breath and hold it against the laughter which came naturally to him upon seeing the antlers of the energetic moustache, preened to needle points, but Watchie was not a cruel loon, and so held his peace as best he could while the man studied him carefully. The man stared at Watchie in return, then raised his flat cap an inch, lifting the shadow its peak placed over his eyes, and Watchie saw that the man's cheeks were red and alive with ruptured capillaries, the complexion of a drinker.

I've a delivery o' clock pairts, said the man, for ane Wulliam Leckie.

Watchie nodded, and broadened his smile, which seemed to make the man uneasy; he nodded, shuffled, said,

Aye, weel, ye'd best be awa tae taal yer clockmakker the noo,

and did not understand when Watchie found the release for his laugh, catching a shallow breath to be going on with,

I'm Wulliam Leckie; I'm yer clockmakker.

The man studied Watchie even more closely after that, a strange specimen he was under anyone's glass; fairly slight, shyness bringing the smile easily to his lips, too young surely to be putting together the monster he had carried for so far. He tried to find some hidden sign of greater age or experience than was at first apparent to the eye, but there was nothing to be seen, no honourable shine of wear about the overalls, no lines about the face. It was a genuine mystery why anyone should trust such a young worker when greater age and greater experience would surely be much more desirable. He said,

It's a' ootside for ye, Mr Leckie,

and led the way through the door at the foot of the tower.

The doors at the back of the pantechnicon were wide open, and there was a tall man standing guard, his musculature filling almost to bursting the seams of his tough canvas dungarees, and the shadow he cast behind him was nearly as solid as himself; his cap was settled on his wide head, and underneath the brim of his cap were two whiskered sideburns, each shaped like a hatchet. Watchie offered him a smile as he approached the back of the pantechnicon, and the huge man smiled in reply, immediately revealing him to be as open and as innocent as a bairn. Inside and through the gloaming, Watchie could see what he had been waiting so long for; a vast coinage of milled wheels and balances, like the thievings from a giant's treasure chest, each packed inside a structure of planks and battens for their own protection during the rough journey, some lying irregularly on their sides like tinkers in a byre, others propped up against the sides of the pantechnicon like drunks in an alehouse at the calling of time. Watchie studied them from the distance as closely as he himself had been studied by the little man, seeing no immediate blemish about the brass of the wheels, and after a while he became lost in the looking, he was one in a travelling gallery, meditating almost on their perfect circularity of form and the beauty of their craft, and he was making the smaller man impatient with his looking. So much time Watchie spent in the appreciation of his delivery that the horses at the front of the pantechnicon, big Clydesdales with braided manes and hooves as big around as soup plates, began to whicker impatiently.

Far'd'ye hae us pit them?

said the smaller man; Watchie turned suddenly as if shocked awake a second time.

Tak them tae bide at the fit o' the stairs, gin ye please.

The man nodded, and called to his side,

Rab, man, time tae dee a bittie werk, the noo, ye can hae a taalk wi yer freens a file efter.

The small man smiled at Watchie, as if begging forgiveness for the giant's slackness, and Rab the giant came humbly around the side of the vehicle, stung to it like a pack animal. Watchie was surprised to see that Rab's eyes were globed and swollen, as if hurt physically by his senior's lash, and he looked gently, strangely apologetic, towards Watchie, as if the loon might think the less of him for the switch brought across his shoulders by the smaller man. Watchie remembered a thing told to him by his father, when he was trying to interest his son in the workings of the farm; to look out for the horses, for by this means might you know the master of them, and though Watchie had hardly ever been to a fair since his apprenticeship, he had had experience of enough of them to understand what it was his father had meant, the poor creatures bowed under the weight of their harnesses, the leather polished to a fine trim, while the animals inside looked out with gentle liquid eyes, their flanks bearing lattices of scars.

The two men were used to the business of lifting, and like genies brought forth from a bottle were Watchie's to command for the day, but he was not a one minded to abuse the privilege of silver, and so left them to lift the load as best they judged; they grasped the wheel by the jut of the battens and rested it upon the racks of their collar-bones, the difference in heights causing the wheel to tilt badly out of true, and Watchie saw Rab's muscles distend with the effort into spheres each as big as boulders, while at the other end the senior man was making such a palaver of the lift, puffing and blowing down the unfolded steps, bearing the weight as dutifully as if it were a prince in a sedan chair, blustering it out of the pantechnicon and towards the door of the tower. Once inside and at the foot of the well, it was Rab's work that settled the wheel, hurling the smaller man around with his impetus, straining enough for two while the other released his end with a clang which sounded out as if in mockery of the bell at the crown of the tower, and Watchie flinched his eyes to hear it as if it had struck him on the foot, and said mildly,

Dinna let it doon sae hard, gin ye please,

and Rab heeded his words, and lowered his end carefully and sensitively, settling it on the stone with barely a sound, as gently as thistledown on a bed of earth.

During the hour it took to unload the pantechnicon, Watchie was much preoccupied with drawing the teeth of the nails which bit tightly upon the battens and held the wheels in place, and so he was quite irritating the senior man with his silent pointing to spots at the foot of the tower underneath the well, for the senior man was certain that there were better places for them, for example each upon a step so that they would be easier to carry to the top, more easily picked off on the way up to the chamber. It was all a matter of greater experience, and long years spent shifting many houses, he might as well have been one of the Clydesdales for all that Watchie cared, but the senior man kept his peace, reminding himself that the job was all that mattered, all that was important was the silver.

The unloading finished with a crate which Watchie cracked open with the fork of the claw hammer; it was the heaviest of them all and the reason was because it was filled to brimming with bearings and pinions stacked in battery order of size, as well as a number of straight iron poles and bolts with which to fasten them together; Watchie took one of the pinions and parted its paper swaddling, peering inside the hood, and replaced it, satisfied. The crate occupied the centre of the well, and after Watchie had nailed the lid gently into place again the senior man took a welcome seat on top of the box, removing the cap from his head, revealing a pate as bald as his moustache was luxuriant. He puffed and blew like an engine and said,

Michty God, yon pairts're affa heavy,

and Rab stood behind him, his arms buckled across his chest, nodding in agreement with the older man, who looked up at Watchie from his perch.

Is't here yer pairts'll bide?

Watchie shook his head, treated himself to a slight smile,

Na na, I'll nae be makkin the clockie doon here.

The senior's eyes hardened, detecting the gentle irony of Watchie and considering it to be rich indeed: how dare he talk to one of the senior man's experience as if he were feeble in the mind. He looked up the spiral, through the centre of the well, and he was dizzied by the distance, losing his perspective the longer he looked through the aperture above, so that after a while the structure made no more sense than a fairground illusion, and when he looked back at Watchie his head was fair spinning with the reduction of scale,

Yon pairts'll nae gang a thon heecht, he said, nor they graa legs and gang up theirsels.

Watchie's smile broadened until it became an annoying thing to the senior man,

Aye, jist wait ye,

he said, and the next thing he was dashing up the stairs as quickly as he had come down, driven by all the doubts he had seen in the eyes of the senior man, and once inside the chamber he shouldered through the web of ropes and lacings through the eyes of the pulleys he had arranged in preparation for the arrival of the wheels. He lifted a smaller pulley on the end of the long coil of rope, approached the square opening with it like a poacher ready to cast a line through a hole carved in winter ice, and called down,

Mind yer heids, the baith o' ye,

and when he was satisfied that Rab and the senior man were in no danger, dropped the sinker down the well, where it fell to the limit of the rope, bouncing and dancing like a hanged man when the rope tautened, until Rab reached out a hand to still it.

Tak ane o' the begger feels,

called Watchie, and it was Rab who took the lead, hoisting the biggest wheel he could see on top of the crate and fastening the rope through the spokes of it, securing it with a convoluted knot he sealed with opposing tugs of his brawny arms. The senior man shouted up,

Ye're a' richt the noo,

and then the wheel soared into the air, spinning and catching the meagre light and burning proper gold like the sun in the firmament, and Rab and the senior man followed its progress as far as their necks were able for it, a miracle it was almost, they could see it falling up towards the aperture as if all perspective had been reversed like a coin dropped into a well to buy the donor a wish, a bribe for the forces of chance. Watchie gentled the wheel through the opening, fearing that the wheel might ring against the edge, warping the wheel slightly, tellingly out of shape; but none such happened, he held the rope tightly wound around his fist while he reached out with the point of his boot and imparted a small swing to the wheel, inch by inch releasing the rope and letting the wheel down when it had cleared the opening at the apex of its pendulum motion, landed upon the flagging, suspended on its edge. Next, he loosened the rope in his hand, mindful of the delicacy of the weight on its end, and coaxed it to fall on its side on the floor, lulled to sleep by his play on the rope, making no sound as it came to rest, and it took a good two minutes before he could free the ends of Rab's solid knot and spin the wheel on its edge over to the corner of the chamber, angling it against the wall, and when he was finished, he was aware of a dreadful ache in his forearms, which he soothed away by rubbing each in turn, as he approached the opening and dropped the sinker down once again.

Tie anither on,

he said, with confidence.

When it became obvious even from below that Watchie was struggling to raise the heavier wheels in their order, without needing to be told by the senior man, Rab came plodding up the stairs of the tower, and strode into the chamber just in time to catch Watchie rubbing his aching forearms, and smiled, though not at Watchie's frailty; but none the less Watchie released himself almost instantly upon realizing that he was being looked at. The big man spoke not a word to Watchie, but simply went over to the opening and took a hold of the free end of the rope as if it were nothing but twine, and then in seconds, as Rab applied a hand–over–hand grip which seemed to Watchie's eye to be as graceful and as musical as dance, the next wheel shot through the opening and hung there, suspended like a medallion while Rab lashed the rope around the angle of the ladder which led up and through a hatchway to the belfry platform above. He reached out and over the opening, bracing his legs in an impressive architecture of strength and stability, loosening the knot he had tied about the wheel himself as if it were the merest fankle of knitting, then plucked the wheel out of the air and carried it tenderly to rest against the wall alongside the others.

I thocht ye'd be efter a wee bit help,

he said simply, and Watchie nodded in gratitude. The work
now progressed quickly, with the senior man tying loose and
careless knots below, and even the massive crate Rab persuaded
into the air, charming it against the last word of gravity and the
reluctance of its own weight, though he needed Watchie's help
to hold the rope tight in case of accidents.

It winna dee, he said, gin yon affa box fa's doon.

Everything about him was understatement and modesty; but
the crate gained the opening, up and on to solid ground as
easily as if it were a jewellery chest, and no sign there was of a
frosting of sweat on the big man's brow, even as Watchie was
drawing away buckets on the sleeve of his jacket.

My thanks tae ye,

said Watchie, and Rab shrugged immense shoulders.

Ye'll aye hae't done the sooner wi twa deein the werk.

He spoke gravely and resonantly, reciting an article of his
deepest faith, and Watchie nodded in reply, having no answer
for the man other than his agreement. Rab looked around the
chamber, at the complete gathering of the clock parts, arrayed
around the rim of the chamber like bracelet ornaments waiting
to be strung on a common thread, and he turned to Watchie,

Ye'll be pittin a' yon thegither yersel, will ye?

Watchie shrugged as if it were no matter at all,

I've a filie yit, twa-three month tae feenish it.

Rab nodded slowly, and gave Watchie a look from the sides
of his eyes; not quite doubting, for everything is possible,
questioning perhaps, uncertain at least. He could tell that the
loon was inventive, for the pulley system was the product of a
good practical intelligence, but in his own silent way Rab
wondered if that inventiveness would be enough to perform
such a muckle task as that which was ahead of the loon. He said,

Nae a'body else tae help ye at a'? Jist yirsel?

Watchie went to the first wheel he had pulled up himself,
stroked its coat of brass as if it were a pet.

There's nae a'body else aboot the toun can mend a clock.

Rab lifted the cap from his head, a lid to press down the

seething curls of red hair which lapped at the brim of it like flame at the roof of a house. He replaced the cap more firmly, adjusting it with both hands, said,

Ken, Mr Leckie, I hope ye'll be peyed weel for't, ye'll be earnin ilka farthin o' yer siller.

Through the well, the voice of the senior man reached them at a boom, a note of air compressed in the horn of a trumpet:

Rab, are ye nae feenished the noo? We'll hae tae be awa, nor we'll nae gang back in time.

Rab listened for a quiet moment to the echo, and closed his eyes to rest them. Watchie could almost see the big man gathering all his giant dignity about him, it was the only armour he possessed against the stings of the ridiculous little man who was his senior by right of earning and experience. Rab was half turning to go to the door, and then he looked at Watchie with his gentle sideways look, and said,

Heed weel fit I'm sayin tae ye, my loon. There's nae the ransom o' a king in this warld that's werth a hillock o' shite for yer health's sake,

and then, dropping his head to avoid the lintel, he was gone, and Watchie could hear the voice of the senior man all the way down the street towards Macpherson's shoemaker's shop, where the Provost was to pay them for their services.

Now the minute work was to begin for Watchie; but for a long time he could only look upon these castings from the foundry with admiration, that such beautiful objects were to find their places in a mechanism of his own design, and it was a thing which quite took his breath the more he gave it thought. He held the rule in his hands for some time, readying himself to measure each wheel for its task; he was the midwife of time in the village, and he knew that it was a responsibility, that so much could still go wrong, that there was much that could be miscarried in the last seconds. But he had given his word, everything was there and ready to assume its proper place, and so he unfolded the rule, holding his arms at their fullest length apart, and began to examine each piece in turn, carefully.

XXVII

It soon became apparent to Watchie on further inspection that the wheels would need to be prepared before they could possibly assume their place in the mechanism. At an initial glance, they had appeared to him perfect in their form, and from the other side of the clock chamber they did seem perfectly round and well cast; but a closer look revealed that they were very slightly flawed in the casting, bristling with surplus metal. It would be minute and painstaking work, but this was where Watchie excelled, and soon enough he had his watchmaker's glass held against his eye by an unnatural grimace, roving around each wheel in its turn, noting in a little journal notebook for later attention where the faults were to be found. Watchie knew that a slipshod worker could have assembled the wheels as they were and a tinker's damn for the consequences; but he also knew that such flaws, if left untreated, would only become apparent during the long years of the train's operation. He had seen the same thing happen in many of the watches he was called upon to fix; one wheel fitted out of true could bring the whole mechanism to a halt as it wore down the teeth of the adjoining wheels, biting into them in such a way that you could see upon opening the watch how the culprit wheel had gnawed curvatures into its companions, halting the movement of the hands as the resistance of the wheel in opposition was worn to the point where the bite taken out of its substance could comfortably accommodate the entire rotation of the greedy, erratic wheel which had fed on it for so long. Such was the stately process of a clock tower's machinery that decades might pass before the mechanism would suffer visibly; but Watchie trusted nothing to chance, and so now was the time for the wheels to be treated like patients, prevention always sooner than the cure; and he passed the tip of his finger carefully over the surface of each of the wheels, a violation he would make right once the job was done, feeling gently for pits and cracks.

He was quite lost in the detail of the work, and such was his concentration that he heard nothing which rose through the stairwell from the street below, not the clopping of the horses' hooves nor the footfalls of heavy morning boots. He was distracted for a moment by a voice which he recognized as that of Baird the butcher, his bright Guid morn tae ye, Mrs Gil-feather, echoing through the whole of the tower as if through the horn of a gramophone. Mr Baird often stood in the doorway of his shop just opposite the clock tower if business was slow and the weather was fine, his hands carried behind his back the better for the world to see his white linen apron shocked with red, the tails of a comet of blood, and the voice which carried in the kirk in praise of the Lord carried his greetings across the street, causing Watchie to look up and smile as if the big hearty man had come into the tower to offer his greetings to him in person. On most mornings, Mr Baird was opening up his shop just as Watchie arrived at the vaulted door of the clock tower to begin his work, and he called across to Watchie from the other bank of the square while hooking out into prominence the canopy of red and white canvas his shop wore.

Guid morn tae ye, Master Watchie! Fit's the clock like, the noo? Camin alang, is't?

There was, as yet, no blood on the fabric of his apron; but Watchie could hear, not long after the opening of the shop, muted sounds of distress from the shed at the back of the premises, screams such as might have been uttered by any animal in fear of its life; and soon enough, as the village wakened at its accustomed early hour, there was Mr Baird the butcher, standing at his door, calling out his fine gentlemanly Guid morn tae ye, the apron worn clean that morning now painted with the blood of fresh meat, the window of the shop now filled with perfect steaks, and stewing meat, and fresh tripe glistening like coral.

★

Watchie heard the percussion of the steps roam around the tight spiral of the stairwell, and he had by now learned by the quality of the sound who he should expect in the doorway. If it was the Provost Macpherson, then the steps would begin like a sudden shower, at first heavy and slow, quickening to a patter around the waist of the tower as the Provost fancied he could use all the strength in his stumpy wee body to carry him up the swifter, petering out as he approached the crown to a slow horse's plod, dragging as if lashed behind him the full weight of the unacknowledged years and the consequences of a comfortable living. If it was his father, there was no hurry about the footfalls, each one measured carefully as if demanding his full concentration, each sounding full in echo, with hardly any way to tell his progress inside the tower.

The footfalls Watchie heard were slow and steady. He continued his work.

When he turned, Wullie was there at the threshold, dressed in the apron of his trade. He seemed uncertain to be standing there, as if he had been invited to stroke the beard of God. In his hand was a stiff paper package, folded like a present. There was a moment of silence, as Wullie stared at the girdle of wheels around the chamber, at his son as he stooped to their attendance. He said,

Ye're nae at yer werk proper yet, I see,

and immediately Watchie straightened, and looked severely at his father. In an instant he was explaining to Wullie why the work he was doing at that time would be essential to the wellbeing of the whole mechanism, and Wullie for his part did his best to understand, nodding when required and dipping his head to one side; but soon enough Watchie was using words as far removed from Wullie's comprehension as algebra, the explanation reared above Wullie like a wave and left him floundering and gasping for breath as it fell upon him and shattered about his ears, he kept nodding until Watchie finished, and added,

Yon's fit way I canna pit the feels thigither the noo.

Wullie looked around the chamber once again.

Ye'll hae a wee bittie werk yet, then?

Watchie nodded, gravely.

Aye, jist a wee bittie.

Wullie walked a little into the chamber, and was immediately bitten by the chill. He said,

Ye're nae affa caal in here, wi yon thing open tae a' the winds?

He nodded up at the trapdoor in the wooden ceiling leading to the belfry, at the tile of willow-pattern blue sky held in its frame. Watchie shook his head vigorously.

Na na, ye dinna feel the caal files ye're at yer werk.

Wullie pressed a pace forward.

Aye, at nicht though.

Watchie bent down to resume his examination.

It waarms ye up, the werk, day nor nicht.

Wullie nodded. He heard doors slamming all around him. He held out the package.

Yer mither says ye've tae tak this for yer denner.

Watchie looked up, one eye bloated in the meniscus of the lens which he had fixed there after bending down. The flecks of hazel around the pupil were perfectly visible to Wullie, against the lightning blue which had shown through his son's lids as a bairn. Watchie said,

I've breid and cheese wi me. I winna hae the time . . .

Mind, said Wullie, she's affa worriet for ye.

Watchie stared at the offered parcel, the neatly tucked down envelope ends; for a moment he saw his mother folding them down, sealing the parcel with care. His vision was divided into windows of clarity and nonsense, one eye sharply on the parcel, the other tearing and blending all the colour in the chamber, one the painted image, the other the palette. He reached out for the parcel, taking it reluctantly, leaned over to place it in his canvas bag of tools.

I'll mebbe hae't efter.

He turned to resume his work. Wullie stood awkwardly for a moment.

Aye, weel, he said, I've the milk tae deliver.

Watchie nodded, not looking up. Wullie turned to the threshold.

I'll tell yer mither ye winna be hame til late,

and then was gone, spinning his echoes through the circumference of the tower, leaving Watchie in an emptiness without comfort, with a taste in his mouth like milk turned under the rays of the sun.

At night, Watchie performed his work by the light of an old oil lantern which printed vast shadows on the walls of the chamber, and sometimes their motion caught his eye and spun his head around; sometimes he hoped it would be someone to visit, he didn't know who, but it would only be the movement of his dark twin on the wall, a slight reaching or adjustment magnified by the shielded flame. The air was cold enough to draw mist from him with every breath, even for early spring, and he often paused his work to curve his hands around the lantern to capture the glass's warmth, scaring the chill from him. This evening, the evening after his father's visit with his dinner, he felt more than ever before a sharp emptiness, a deep want of companionship which the absence of light he caused by the cupping of his hands about the flame seemed to emphasize by gouging space from around him; there were faint glimmers from the wheels caught in the penumbra, as cool and as distant as the messages of the stars, a spark which could as easily have been caused by unimaginably far heat or nearby frost, and it was no comfort to him. From the belfry above, through the open trapdoor which guided the winds through and into the chamber, Watchie could hear the chirping of his family, the pipistrel bats which roosted under the dunce's cap of the spire for their daily shelter, hanging like beef from a butcher's hook.

Watchie worked steadily against the cold and wishing himself a hearth in which he could construct a good fire of peat and kindling, and every so often he would stop and explain into the air what he was doing just then, informing the bats of what tools he was using and the problems facing him; and then, when the light drained away from the wick of the lantern and he had not enough oil left in the can to replenish it, he put everything away in his canvas bag, and wished the bats a guid nicht. He saw his way down the spiral in the lantern's remaining light and, once out and on the street, he locked the heavy door behind him with the bold iron key given to him by the Provost Macpherson; after pulling on the ring twice to make sure that the antiquated lock had taken, he went on his way, passing no one on the almost curfew-quiet streets.

XXVIII

It took two days to complete the frame for the mechanism, but in the end it was ready. It was late into the second evening, and through the hatchway overhead he heard the pipistrels rustling their capes while on the foray for moths, chirping as vividly as the sparrows in the morning. The lantern cast a calamitous shadow upon the tower's single eye of blue glass, and at the time Watchie was conducting a debate with himself, whether it was too late to think about beginning the work of placing the wheels within the frame, or whether he should start again in the morning, when he heard the footsteps at the stairs, their echo faint, no labouring of breathing such as he might have expected of the Provost, nor as purposeful as he might have expected of Wullie. The footsteps came as questions in the darkness, courageous and regular with a whisper of cloth against the spiral of the wall; and it was only as he wondered at the intent of the owner of the gentle steps that he began to see the figure assuming form in the darkness, becoming more real to his eyes.

She wore a black linen dress tight about the waist, and underneath, and around her ankles, were the petals of a white petticoat he had never seen her wear before, a startling ornamentation of broderie anglaise against the trusty leather of her high boots. She wore a cape of wool about her shoulders, also in black, so that when she finally assumed form out of the dense blackness of the staircase and into the light of the lantern, Watchie felt a strange charge through him; and when they saw each other, both leapt in shock at the recognition, and both laughed at the same moment, for this was not quite how Kirsty O'Donnell had expected to see Watchie Leckie, as a silhouette against the glimmer of the lantern.

Michty me, said Kirsty, still on the other side of the threshold, I thocht ye were a ghost, Watchie Leckie, and Watchie laughed with her, and said,

I dinna ken fit I wis thinkin,

and stood to one side to let her by.

She was carrying a pannier on her arm, the contents under a disguise of white linen, which she put down on the flagging beside Watchie's canvas bag of tools. She looked around in fascination at the wheels and mysterious parts of the huge mechanism, slouched aimlessly against the walls, and then at the frame into which they were to fit, and no purpose or conclusion could she see to them. But Watchie explained to the best of his stammering ability, how one piece meshed with the other, what each turn of such a wheel did for the progress of the whole train, and not hardly a word did she understand of it, nodding to Watchie's voice rather than his words; and this she took from his explanation, which otherwise she couldn't make head nor tail of, that it was the presence of the clock in pieces that stirred the passion of him, that here stood the heart of the taciturn loon who came to her croft each Monday evening with his sack of watches cured of their ills, and there was nothing more important to him than seeing his colossus of a timepiece restored to the fullest dignity of its office in the village. Week in and week out, Kirsty had seen him in the croft, and such a silent job he had made of it, tramping through the snows in winter and regular as the unregarded beat of the instruments he mended for his silver, nothing to mark him from a hundred like him; and now here he was, in the silent tower, consorting with these pieces from God's own carriage clock. As if to make emphatic to her his lordship over these scattered pieces, he took a seat on the brass weight he had told her would be lashed to a rope of braided steel, and motioned her to sit beside him on its companion, just beside the lantern, but she feared for the muck that might rub on to her skirt, and shook her head. An unseasonably chill breeze breathed through the hatch to the belfry, and Kirsty's whole body shook against it; she gathered her arms to herself suddenly, clasping the wings of her cape to herself and drew it around in a wrap, causing Watchie to smile suddenly and declare,

Ye're lookin affa like the bats fa're livin at the reef, pu'in yon thing aboot ye,

and for a moment her face went serious as she suspected she was being mocked by him, though she could find not a trace of it in trawling his eyes, realized that it was not so; then said,

Bats? Ye've nae bats in the reef,

her expression as distasteful as if one of the creatures had lodged in her hair, as bats were known to do, captured in the net by their claws and tangled such that they could only be cut free with a pair of scissors; Kirsty walked quickly by the lantern, beside Watchie, but he only laughed and said,

Dinna be feart at the bats, Kirsty, they'll nae dee ye ony ill, they're jist awa for a flee tae theirsels.

Kirsty nodded, though she felt no security by it. She cast around Watchie's chamber, and saw there only desolation, in which Watchie performed a task of almost penititential gravity, without relief. She said, holding the fabric of her coat to herself,

Ye'll be affa lang, fexin the clock, oot in a' weathers,

but Watchie shrugged, the merest water off his back.

It'll nae be lang the noo. A few weeks, nae langer mind, for it'll hae tae be ready for the anniversary.

Kirsty pulled herself even deeper into her cocoon.

A few weeks in a wee bittie tour fa's caal as charity,

she said, for herself to hear, resonating around the enclosed walls like a sentence on his head.

I'll hae the werk tae keep me waarm,

said Watchie, for he would not let her see his task as a thing to be endured, nothing laborious or herculean about it. She said,

Aye, nae tae pey ye. My faither says ye're nae tae be peyed the siller till the clock's werkin again,

and this was true, but Kirsty's words reminded Watchie of the old worker in tin, and he said,

Yer faither noo, fit's a-dee wi him? Is he weel, and yer sister Mhairi?

and she said that Geordie was fine as could be expected, though missing his weekly visit from that honest hard-working lad,

Aye, and his handkerchief is missin it as weel,

said Kirsty, which made them both laugh without malice at the memory of Geordie and his handkerchief of silver from which he paid Watchie for his trouble, and Mhairi was fine, if a little quietened of a Monday evening, which brought the blood firing to Watchie's face and a smile to Kirsty's. She turned to the pannier, resting just beside her, and said,

Ye've brocht this tae mind,

reaching down to the blanket of linen covering it, lifting it away and revealing half a loaf of bread and a white cake of cheese.

My faither says, ye'll hae tae gie thon fine hard-werkin loon a bite tae eat, for he'll be affa hungry werkin at a grand thing like yon. I makt the breid mysel, new oot the oven for ye.

For a while they sat and ate, and a pleasant time they spent in each other's company, and Kirsty even learned to ignore the chirping of the bats overhead, given courage by Watchie, who seemed not to fear them in the slightest.

They shared a road in common to their separate homes, and so Watchie gathered the tools of his trade into the canvas bag, and they made their way downstairs with Watchie at the front, holding his lantern by the loop out to the side so that its wide circle would light the steps for Kirsty, who took them with great care one after the other, pressing herself against the wall so that she was always on the widest rim of the steps as she came down the spiral. The journey down was a great relief for her, now she could see that she had not missed a crack in the stairwell, nor the lack of a step which may have invited her to fall to the flagging below; but there, at the foot of the spiral, was Watchie's bicycle, leaning patiently against the wall just in front of the first step, gleaming blackly in the lantern's cast, and a miracle it was, or so she thought, that she had not met it on her way to see him, waiting to snatch at her clothing on the way past.

Watchie locked the door to the tower behind him with the iron key given to him by Macpherson, the tumblers grinding in their casing with the unoiled effort, and he kept the lantern burning as they walked through the unlit streets, the bicycle coming like an interloper between himself and Kirsty. There was no one about in the evening silence, and their voices and the beat of their paces came back to their ears from the buildings on either side, and while they were within the precincts of the village they spoke in whispers which carried no further than to each other. Once North Street was behind them, Kirsty began to talk about her father, and his days in the shed, repairing the pots and pans gathered from the farmers around the village,

He's aye on his ain, ye ken, she said; at nicht he's fexin for the morra, and he cams ben tae the hoose at late oors, he's aye settin afore the fire, he widna merry efter my mither dee'd. He's a smoke o' his pipe afore he gangs tae his bed, and he says his prayers afore pittin on his nichtshert, ilka nicht, nae a puckle o' defference frae the ane nicht tae the ither.

The lantern was now hooked on to the handlebar of the bicycle, on Kirsty's side of it, swinging this way and that to the irregular meter of the cobbles. It lit the road immediately before them, so that they appeared to be on a treadmill, their paces taking them no further than the end of the visible stretch, offering them the security of its luminous bow wave. The motion of the pendulum light brought Kirsty into Watchie's view, first as a figure picked out in gold leaf, applied to the prominent contours of her face, then denied her, reducing her to a trick of the shade, Watchie's own shadow cast on the other side of the bicycle. Her face was dull, and greatly sad, and Watchie said,

My faither tellt me aboot Geordie's wife.

Kirsty nodded, and her face hardened.

Aye, and she wis my mither as weel. She didna care ower muckle for gangin awa frae oor hame, ye ken. Yer faither was at the hoose, twa-three times, he met her, fan she bocht his milk frae him. He was at her funeral as weel, I seen him there.

Watchie nodded, remembering. The swing of the lantern brought her face once again into light; her eyes were dark and tearless, and Watchie sensed that there was more sorrow to her than anyone he had ever met. Her paces on the cobbles were steady and regular, she was not to be hurried through the night, and Watchie found himself falling in with her rhythms, the time she set for them both, placing his own feet so that only a single pace could be heard above the whisper of the bicycle's wheels on the road. The lantern continued its to and fro, to and fro, creating miniature dawns and sunsets around her, and Watchie looked at her through the brief days and nights, as if the geology of her would alter in the time that he could not see her face, that she would smile or frown and he might miss her doing it, but her expression was steady, without even a fractional change. To return the life to her he said,

Aye, affa kind o' yer faither, richt eneuch, tae say tae ye tae bring me a feed,

but Kirsty's face remained unaltered. She said,

Aye, he's aye kind tae fowk he disna ken weel,

and Watchie was puzzled at this, at the sharpness of her reply. Watchie suspected that she was still heavy with thoughts of her mother, and so left her to her silence for a while, not looking at her but at the road ahead, as the light followed the river of cobbles and breasted their path for them. Finally he heard Kirsty's breath beside him, and looked to see her; her face was still set and troubled, and she said,

My faither wisna the same at a', efter my mither's passin. Ye widna ken him as the same mannie at a'.

Fine dee I ken, Kirsty,

he said, remembering the talks around the kitchen and the hearthside, how Geordie O'Donnell was keeping, one more tale of his long fall into the abyss of his own great grief; but Kirsty shook her head with great vehemence, as if to warn him of the impossibility of grasping the change in the small fist of his understanding, said,

Ye dinna ken, Waatchie. Ye couldna ken, nor ye had the hale o' yer time in the warld tae think o't. Ye widna trust a'body in yer life, gin ye kent.

The lights of Smallbrae came into view beyond the grove of

trees just then, a sight which Watchie would find cheering were it not for the presence beside him of Kirsty, gathering the darkness to herself like the cloak she wore around her shoulders. Now she had taken to walking with a good distance between them, as if the glass which Watchie imagined surrounding her were still alive and molten, pressing him further out and away from her; but he respected that distance, and promised himself that he would not breach it, and so they walked, separated by the width of Kirsty's sudden reluctance and solitude, until the farm was beside them, and Watchie drew to a halt beside the path.

Weel, said Kirsty, I've nae affa far tae gang tae the hoose,

and Watchie nodded, the invitation to hospitality dying in his throat, suddenly glad of her distance and the bicycle between them. He said,

I'll awa in then, for my denner,

and was just about to turn the bicycle from the road into the path, when Kirsty said,

Ye'll be affa hungry the morra nicht, nae doot.

She stood at the furthest influence of the lantern, and she was smiling, no betrayal to her silence of before, but a thin smile in its despite. Watchie pretended to be uncertain, but it was a device which Kirsty saw through easily, he nodded long before opening his mouth to say,

Aye, gin ye'd nae mind keepin me company at my werk,

and so it was decided. They parted just where the road surrendered to the path, and Watchie wheeled his bicycle by the side of the farmhouse, into the night-time harbour of the shed; sitting down to his dinner, he presented all with a silence which quite concerned Jeannie and Peggy, that his work was exhausting him such that he showed all the signs of sickening for something, though not a word did they say of it. He left half his plate to Aal Wullie's new dog, who ate his windfall meal with tremendous gusto.

XXIX

Kirsty returned the next evening, as she had promised, laden down with rounds of soda bread in her pannier, baked for him that afternoon, and once again she brought the crowdie she had made, which Watchie thanked her for as if he had never seen crowdie before, leaving what remained of his lunch inside his canvas bag, not wanting to appear ungrateful to her. She spread the cloth of linen which had covered over her bread as if they were sleeping bairns upon the flagging, and they ate as if on a picnic in the open, and not in a chamber raised high above the village. Each circular loaf of bread was as big around as a paving stone, and Watchie found its smoky flavour of peat to be right delicious, baked as it had been on a griddle pan placed in the heart of the fire at the croft, and this he said to her, which made her look away and smile modestly, and say,

Jist a wee bit for yer feed, Wulliam, it didna tak ower lang tae dee.

The chamber was different from the last time she had visited. Some of the wheels had been taken from their places around the chamber, and now she saw them cast in the frame, in their pins, and just before she arrived Watchie had been using the pulley, hauling on the ropes to drop a wheel through the cradle of iron, delicately, to make sure that there was no chiming against the bars; on Kirsty's arrival, Watchie took the rope to the hatchway ladder, asking her to stand back for a moment, lashing the end of the rope to the third rung to suspend the wheel above the frame, where it spun lazily around as if it were no more than a bauble on a lady's neck chain. It stayed suspended there while Watchie and Kirsty enjoyed their picnic under the ceiling, catching the lantern light with each rotation like a mesmerist's watch, so that a leaf of gold struck from its bright surface chased around the walls of the chamber, illuminating them both for an instant like the beacon of a lighthouse, while Watchie explained that he would lower it through the top of the buttressing when it had lost its spin, and pointed out to her the place for it in the mechanism; Kirsty sighted along his arm, but still could not see what was obvious to Watchie, and nodded nevertheless, for she could not bear to be seen by him as ignorant.

After a while, Kirsty began to sing. She sang in the same voice that Watchie had first heard at the croft when she was thrashing the dirt from the house's clothes, for many things seemed to move her to song, and Watchie sat back on the barrel of Johannes Dreimann's clock, which he had kept for himself as a seat, and closed his eyes to listen. Some of her songs were from the old country, that is to say songs from Geordie's native Ireland, from a country she had never seen but had heard much of, and some of those were melancholy verses of love tasted and lost, drowsy ballads which swelled the breast to hear them. She gave no warning that she was about to sing for Watchie; one minute, there was only the chirping of the bats on the wing, a song which served them in place of eyes; the next, Kirsty was resonating like a tuning-fork, and she was away on the journey before she knew it, brimming with the music of it, and for the duration time was suspended like the wheel, spinning on its axis. She sang more expressively than she could speak; she threw back her head, and for a moment Watchie could almost hear his father's fiddle in accompaniment, for the fiddle in the hands of Wullie Leckie was just as able to weep as it was to jaunt, a fine touch he had with it and no mistake. But Kirsty needed no instrumentality to tap the music from her; she sang of love doomed, of men presumed lost in battle returned incognito to test their loves, and finding them strong and grieving for their memories, trysts kept in the face of all opposition, illicit unions and loves never to be consummated; she sat on the cloth she had spread for their meal, having deemed the barrel to be dirty, and closed her eyes while the music poured from her, losing all sense of time or place in the world. Watchie thought of the kind of mechanism he had seen in the book his father had given to him many years ago, in which was described the workings of an intricate fakery of life and breath peculiar to German craft, animated dolls which danced to a musical scroll driven by clockwork hidden in the plinth; but it was a thought he let away as soon as he had coined it, for there wasn't the least artifice about her.

She brought her own lantern after her second visit, for she fretted greatly in the darkness of the spiral, and feared that Watchie's bicycle might paw at her clothing on her way up the stairs; but Watchie had taken to leaning it at the bottom of the well, away from the steps, and this she saw when she opened the unlocked door, giving her a little of a start when she saw its shadow bloated grotesquely by the light.

The arrival of another lantern gave Watchie more light to work by, for which he thanked her all the while he manoeuvred the wheels into their positions. By now a number of other pulleys had been added, so that it had become a problem from a child's puzzle book for Kirsty to find the origin of the rope by which Watchie drew the wheels along, a miracle it seemed to Kirsty's eyes, how he lifted the great golden weights and then by playing on another rope dragged them like a sun across the sky of the chamber, settling them inside the frame by varying the tensions of the two ropes which bound them. Time and again he clambered through the frame when each of them was above its place, plucking at the knots to both ropes, taking the mass on his arms as it dropped and bearing it on to its proper arbor, an exhausting effort Kirsty saw, for all that he would not show the exertion on his face, arching his back against the doubling of the strain with his hands on either side of his hips. She remembered her father in the days of the bottle, how he would awaken with no memory of his previous night, before starting his morning with a breakfast of whisky; how he would declare himself fit for work when unable to place one foot straight in front of the other, tripping over the ruined floor-boards and remarking, I must fix them some time, not the now mind, I've my work to do yet. She remembered how, even then, she had told him that he was in no state to be working, but this raised further questions her father would not discuss with her, such as the way he spent his evenings, and so his work became shoddy and no better than that of the other tinkers who came to call in the village, and Kirsty soon realized that she had no power to stop his fall, for when Geordie looked into the shaving mirror he saw no fault in his scabrous face, none of the alterations wrought by despair, none of the changes apparent to those who stood outside and saw the slow erosion from day to day. The one thing she remembered from this time was that her father would not be told, and now she saw Watchie bent over by the sheer weight of labour, climbing out of the frame and avoiding her eyes as he did so in a pretence of nothing amiss, nursing the small of his back especially and striding across the chamber more for her benefit than his own, the rope in his free hand, lashing it to the next wheel in order, returning to the frame to pick out the other trailing rope to be fastened; and for a while Kirsty considered whether to tell Watchie to slow down in his work, that he was heading for an injury if he persisted. But her experience with men told her that she would not be listened to, that he must find out for himself, and so she waited patiently with her soda bread under its cover in the pannier for Watchie to find his own limits, when he would decide to come for his dinner himself, saying to himself that this was all he could do for now.

The going train had less than three weeks' work in it when Kirsty came to the tower and found Watchie doubled over the frame.

Work had been progressing to Watchie's satisfaction. Every night Kirsty came with her dinner for him, and stood to one side while he moved one more wheel by his pulley arrangement, his last before stopping for a feed, he said, and in this she indulged him, spreading her cloth over the ground while he landed his wheels. It was a gentler way, she had decided, of bringing him to a halt than the harsher methods of fussing and bothering, which she knew from her own experience with her father to have no effect, but she had also noticed that he was beginning to wear down from the activity, that his hands were slippery on the rope, and this, she understood, was almost certainly the fault of his continual and unrelieved work during the day, and therefore his own fault, for he was determined to fulfil the contract of the council with no help at all, and this began to worry her during her days, when she was housewife to her own croft. She looked at the cauldron as it boiled above the fire, and wondered was there any way to bring the hot stew to Watchie; perhaps it could be heated for him once it was brought, for she had heard tell that Watchie barely picked at the dinner kept warm for him by Jeannie on the farmhouse stove, and there was surely plenty to spare in Kirsty's own cauldron for him. She immersed the blankets in the tin bath outside the house, rubbing them clean in the cream of the soap, and wondered if she should take to Watchie a jumper such as was worn by fishermen as protection against the gales of the ocean, for it could become cold in the tower in the evening when the sun fell and the granite released its chill as if it were fire's opposite, radiating a searching cold. Suddenly, as she reaped the vegetables from the plot in front of the croft, she decided that this was what she would have to do; she would have to be a mother to him, and like a mother she would have to become more insistent upon his welfare, even at the risk of turning into what her father called an owl nag. She decided that this was the night that Watchie would dine on cold stew, which surely was better than no stew at all, though perhaps there was some way that the lantern flame could be exposed to provide a make-do hearth, especially if she brought it in an enamel bowl.

Once at the tower, she took the lantern from her pannier, and the matches given to her by Geordie, and lit it before going through the gullet of the stairs, for the miserable light of the evening was diluted within, and there was still the danger of falling over her own feet on the way up. She took the climb gradually, holding the lantern out as her guide, placing each step with care before she would trust her entire weight to the ancient stone, and wondered if Watchie feared its treachery as she did herself, scarcely able to trust the flame of the lantern and the golden sight it gave of the few steps above her.

Finally she reached the chamber; and only when she was at the top of the stairs did she hear the sound that she had not heard on the way up for the papery rustle of the bats in flight. There she saw Watchie, bent low over the frame of the mechanism, not quite fallen on his face, but in among the wheels he was from the belly up, held there by a cross bracing of iron bars while the toes of his shoes touched the flags outside of the assembly, while inside the trap of it there was a wheel canted just short of its mooring, resting against the floor on its circumference. He did not look round at her, but said weakly,

Is thon yersel, Kirsty?

Immediately Kirsty dropped the pannier on the floor, and went over to Watchie's side, resting the lantern beside the frame. The light it cast upon him striped his face black with shadow and gold from the flame, so that he wore the mask of the tiger, and when Kirsty fell to her knees she saw that Watchie was smiling at her, a lost smile which made her wonder if he was in any discomfort. It was only when she pulled upon his arm that she realized Watchie was caught in the frame like a mouse unable to resist the bait of cheese. She said,

Aye, it's mysel, Wulliam, fit's a–dee wi ye?

and he grinned broadly as if he were a loon again, caught thieving cake from the tin, though he could not turn to look at her.

My back, Kirsty; I canna rise tae my feet, I think yon feel wis jist ower muckle for me,

meaning the wheel canted on its side among the others. For a moment Kirsty was struck dumb by the wealth of curses she was minded to visit upon him for his stubbornness, but instead she said,

We'll jist hae tae pit ye on yer feet.

The first thing she discovered was that he would be no help at all to her, having no strength in him to add to hers, and so she was just able to pull him from the heart of his workings and kneel him on the ground in front of the mechanism, bent before it as his mother had been before her stove when he was born. From there she tried to raise him to his feet, embracing him from behind and caring nothing for the intimacy of it, rooting her feet against the ground and pulling as hard as she was able; but this caused him to laugh all the harder,

Dinna dee thon, Kirsty, I canna tak it.

She stood over him for a moment, and found herself wondering what there was to be done. There was only one person in the whole village to whom she could turn, and so she bent double over Watchie, close to his ear, and said,

I'm awa for the doctor, Wulliam, I'll nae be lang.

Watchie made a brief sound, which seemed to be an agreement; and so she stooped to pick up the lantern she had dropped beside him, and then took the stairs outside the chamber at all speed, approaching each step sideways and leaning against the walls, for there was no sense in the haste which leads to less hurry, giving the doctor two patients instead of just the one, and soon she was out on the street and casting around the village for the proper direction to Dr Fairley's surgery, the same street as the widow Jamieson lived on. She did not notice in her flight the black heavy curtains at the widow's parting to see what was the matter, the sudden splinter of light in the perfect darkness, nor the eyes behind it, narrowed, bright, aroused.

As little as Kirsty had known of the extent of Watchie's exhaustion, the truth of it had been suspected by all at Smallbrae for some time, as Watchie returned to the farm on legs wearied by their pretence of strength in the presence of Kirsty. The signs were apparent to Jeannie, who saw her son falling asleep over the dinners she kept hot for him while he was sitting at the table, his hand formed around the spoon while his eyes closed and locked their gates, and she said gang awa tae yer bed Wulliam, nor ye'll nae be fit for yer werk the morrow. Thus Watchie fed on no other banquet than a surfeit of sleep, and when he wakened to the cry of the rooster at the first appearance of dawn, it was never enough, and his sleeps were thick and dreamless, as if he had been wrapped the whole time in close black fabric like the velvet he used for his watchmaking. He descended to his breakfasts as if at another's command, he ate like an automaton, and answered questions about his progress with the clock briefly, his head lowered over the bowl as if drawn down by intolerable weights. Jeannie and Peggy both said nothing of it at first, for they knew that the work was hard, and that the same could be said for the work of the farm; and Wullie, who had been warned by Jeannie that he was to say nothing to discourage the loon from his job, looked firstly at his son and then at Jeannie, and noted that she was growing more worried by the day. He had heard her say to Peggy, on their way to bed one evening, that she had had a look at Watchie's hands as he held them out to receive his dinner plate, as raw as meat they were with the scars and rope burns across the palms; this she had said to Watchie but he had told her there was no pain, and looked at his own hands as if they were strange five-legged beasts on the ends of his arms, with their own will, so that the pain was their own as well, no discomfort of his. Wullie listened to this, ye'd hae thocht they werena his hands at a', yon's fit way he was luikin at them, and remembered entering the room of Watchie's birth, how Jeannie had laid claim to the hands of her son before Wullie had had the chance to educate them in the touch of the plough, and most appropriate it seemed to him that Watchie should not see those hands as his own, that they had somehow been subverted from the task to which they had been appointed by blood, and he hoped with all his heart that here was the first sign of wisdom shown by his son, that the loon was beginning to understand they were instruments cast in the mould of the father and the father before that, and soon he would know the land as his provider. It was only a matter of time as the work became harder for him; soon he would return to where his blood lay.

The friction burns were not the only injuries to Watchie's hands, as the rope skidded out of his grasp many times while he was placing the wheels, causing him to seize it all the tighter to prevent the catastrophe of such a weight falling on the already placed parts of the mechanism. There was also the cold which often sighed through the chamber, through the seams of the hatchway, and through the narrow slots of the windows in the spiral, which drew the blood from his hands and made them blue, giving him no grip, no control. He had to manoeuvre the wheel by mooring it in the air with the rope tied to the hatchway ladder; and as the mechanism came to fill the frame, he could find no means of access inside, so that every time he released a wheel from the ropes he was leaning across and through the cradle, throwing his legs out widely and taking the full weight upon himself as he lowered them the last few delicate inches to crown the wheels already assembled. Each night, when Kirsty arrived, she saw Watchie putting on his finest performance of competence for her, wearing the mantle of assurance, as tireless as a mule and as stubborn, and then there was no pain in his hands, he stood squarely and told her how much further ahead he was in the construction. He ate reluctantly of her bread and crowdie as if this might have been in itself an admission of weakness, and so well did he fool her that she thought that all he was needing was woollens and more substantial food to sustain him during the work. But on this night, a curious dissipation of focus suddenly came rushing to meet him as if he were being carried at great speed on the surge of a wave towards a wall of granite. It happened when he bent over the frame to untie the rope from the wheel; the wheel became a bright star in a mechanistic sky, a glory such as surrounded the head of the statuette of the Christ in the O'Donnells' croft, casting out thorns of light, and Watchie stood as one entranced. He perceived another presence in the tower, and turned to face it; but it was nothing more than the shadow he cast behind him once again, a being of sheer darkness, raising itself above him against the far and opposite wall, and he began to laugh in its face, diminishing the power it assumed over him; but it persisted in its growth, and Watchie stared deeper into it the better to understand what the shadow demanded of him, why it refused to shrink away. The shadow became a tear in the fabric of the chamber, a rent which led to nothing but deeper blackness, and through its cavern he heard a laughter which he recognized; it was the dry laughter of Jamie Watts, long gone from Smallbrae, and he remembered it as the laugh which the orra loon uttered when he worked Watchie as his own personal mule, ye're nae ees, man man, ye'll nae dee a' yon werk afore yer faither cams hame, fit'll ye hae me say tae him. Watchie could not bring to mind the orra loon's face, but the laughter whipped him across his flanks and drove him to reach through the crossed bars of the frame, his raw fingers plucking furiously at the knot securing the wheel in suspense. It was just as he took the full weight of the wheel on its release that the strings of his back snapped as if he were a fiddle, and he was pitched forward into his own workings, pulled down like a plumb by the brass round.

Watchie's first thought was for the wheel and the mechanism as he tipped over the fulcrum of the crossed bars, and so he embraced the wheel to himself in both of his arms as if it were a child falling down a precipice, and in this way gentled its landing so that it did not crash into the pinions already in place. It dropped through the latticed mechanism, and dirled like a coin on its edge on the flagging as Watchie let it go; and this was the first time that laughter came to him, for he understood that his strange posture, balanced on his midriff with his head and legs both in space, was something to be laughed at, graceless and ungainly. It was the moment he tried to right himself that the pain severed him in two as if he were a gingerbread man, and then he did cry out, for he was unable to draw himself to his feet or even just upright without suffering, and found it more comfortable just to hang over the bar, unable to gain the leverage from his arms against the ground. In its own way, it was a worse suffering than he had endured when the venom of the wasps' nest burst over him, for much of that time he had spent without consciousness, in the cradle of delirium; and now here he was, awake in a nightmare of suspension, in the cradle of his own frame constructed as a vessel for his clock, held in paralysis for fear of moving and rousing to its full torment the jagged glass which seemed to have bedded in his back, slicing him with every move. That way he rested for what seemed to be an age, and sometimes he laughed, for he deserved the fate of the clown for his stupidity, or so he thought, not minded to forgive himself for thinking he could mend the pocket watch of the gods through his own slight effort; his face was reflected in the brass of the wheels, an imperfect image in the alloyed metal, and he wondered what Wullie would have to say when he finally returned home bent over like an old mannie, and Kirsty, too, when she arrived.

XXX

Elizabeth Fairley had not spent long as the wife of a village doctor; but if there was one thing she knew from what little experience she had, it was that at any time the bell might ring and draw Edwin from his seat before the fire, away from his newspaper and his single glass of watered whisky on the occasional table by the side of the chair. While it could hardly be said that she was by now used to the idea, reluctant to lose their evenings as ornaments in the delicately furnished room appointed so as to be a pleasure to her eyes, she had at least accepted that a doctor must be prepared to relieve immediate suffering whenever such a thing can be done, no matter what hour of the day or night, and this he had explained to her at length when he first assumed the practice in Aberlevin from Dr Farquharson, to which she nodded without acceptance. It made her feel that their moments of peace were leased from the contingency of others, though some injuries were of a kind which made her feel mean and petty for grudging her husband's time, for more than a few of Fairley's farmer patients had lost fingers and sometimes limbs to the blades of a thresher inadequately cowled against carelessness; such things never happened in the gentle comedies of manners of Jane Austen, her favourite reading of an evening while Edwin was at the newspaper, but then, neither did young women of leisure marry doctors in her books, and when Mrs Murray knocked at the door to the living-room, having already studied Kirsty with as practised a diagnostic eye as that of the doctor himself, separating the wheat of genuine distress from the chaff of drunken discomfort which was so often the cause of a late interruption, Elizabeth Fairley knew that once again she would be in the company of a vacant chair, the whisky resting on the table half drunk, the paper folded in quarters and left on the seat which by rights belonged to her husband.

The very assurance and calm of Dr Fairley as he stood in front of Kirsty made the breath come easier to her; concerned but not given to panic, he took the story from her in pieces, nodding encouragement to her, drawing more information as she went, and finally he said,

It may be nothing more serious than back strain from the sound of it. Is the young man in the tower just now? Can he be moved, do you think?

Kirsty swallowed over a sudden surge of breath.

I dinna ken, doctor, I wisna able tae dee thon.

Fairley nodded. He glanced at Elizabeth, who did not look up from her book, then made past Kirsty towards the door.

He'll have to be taken to the surgery. I may need your help. Will you come with me, please, Kirsty?

The last was uttered through a breeze which drew across Kirsty's face like fine cloth, and he took the stairs in the same way as she had taken the spiral of the tower, though they were lit by oil-lamps on curved standards and not by the wavering lantern she had brought with her. At the bottom of the stairs, in front of the door, there was a free-standing coat rack, decorated with two sprigs of deer antler on either side of a square mirror, from which the doctor seized his coat, a warm and encompassing twilled woollen coat he shrugged himself inside while Kirsty pattered down the last of the stairs to catch up with him, and they were out of the house in a moment, walking briskly down the road, so briskly that once again Kirsty did not notice the parting of the curtain at the widow's on their way past, so absorbed was she in explaining to the doctor for the second time how she had found Watchie in the chamber.

Watchie was still there, held in a posture more appropriate to the expectation of an undignified punishment, his arse up in the air with the tips of his boots resting on the flagging. Dr Fairley approached Watchie from the side, through the frame of the clock, and said,

How are you feeling, Watchie?

and while there were times when such a question sounded naïve to the doctor's own sensibilities, hardly any one of his patients missed their opportunity to answer, and so it was now, as Watchie replied,

I canna lift mysel, doctor, my back's fine sair the noo.

Doctor Fairley nodded.

We'll have you out of there first of all, then.

Fairley ordered Watchie as if he were a lay figure, standing behind him and grasping him as Kirsty had done, about his waist, taking great care not to strike Watchie against the bars of the frame, until Watchie himself was able to drop his feet to the floor and achieve his own stability; but so overwhelming was the pain that he fell back with his first attempt to stand upright, into the arms of the doctor, who lowered him gently to the flagging, taking the sudden dead mass of the patient and resting him on his arse. From where Watchie sat, he was able to look up and see Kirsty standing over him, her hands busy in front of her, joining in a clasp, then raised to touch her lips, and it occurred to Watchie, though he did not know for sure, that she was uttering a silent prayer, for Aal Wullie always said that Catholics were right buggers for troubling the Lord whenever they were in trouble themselves; but Watchie found himself hoping that she was praying for him, though he wondered what worth her prayers would be to one who wasn't of her communion. The next thing he knew, there was a pushing against the small of his back through the fabric of his dungarees, and a curious sounding thing he gave voice to, howling at first like the wolves and ending in laughter; he said,

Dinna, doctor, dinna, yon's affa sair,

and Fairley raised himself from his haunches, and said,

I'm sorry, Watchie, but we have to find out what's wrong with you. I'd much rather do a proper examination in my surgery. Do you think you can walk?

Kirsty released her hands just then, and stood forward, but before she could say anything Watchie spoke up,

Aye, I'll dee it, doctor, dinna fear, my back's sair but my legs are fine, and without help gained his feet as awkwardly as the calves he remembered being born to the kye in the byre, the acute curvature of his back forcing him to bend his knees as well to maintain the least uncomfortable position that his muscles would allow. But he was able to walk without help, it was true, though his gait was not graceful, and Fairley stood to one side of the loon, taking his arm and throwing it over his shoulder. Kirsty with the lantern became their guide down the stairs and into the street. Their progress was slow, for Watchie was perched on each step with his balance thrown over as if on the edge of a cliff face, taking one at a time, with the doctor casting all his weight in the other direction: and Kirsty descended in front of them, taking the steps sideways, and holding the lantern in front of Watchie so that he could see each of his footfalls, her other hand ready in case the doctor himself lost his grip and all tumbled to the ground through the spiral. At long last, with Kirsty telling the remaining distance as far as she could see, they were at the bottom of the well, and once there Watchie insisted upon locking the door. It was just as she turned with Watchie and the doctor to walk slowly and painstakingly towards the surgery that Kirsty first saw the figure on the opposite bank of the street.

The widow Jamieson was wearing her crocheted black shawl about her head as proof against the cold, clasped by no pin other than the slender pins of her lean exposed fingers, and as they passed her by Kirsty's lantern illuminated her seemingly ancient eyes, though there appeared to be a fire already burning, a furnace to which she consigned them all three. The shawl gave her the appearance of a judge already dressed for condemnation, and she surveyed them each in turn as items in a tableau, cartoon allegories each reduced before her to labelled figures representing three of her most profound fears and hatreds. There was Kirsty O'Donnell, the daughter of Geordie O'Donnell and a believer in the papish church, leading the way with her lantern held high, the foul and filthy and duplicitous light of the church of the Antichrist. There was Dr Fairley, with his blasphemous potions, mending the physical shell of dirt and stench and corruption, the base vessel which presented so much opportunity for ill works, removing from God the wisdom to determine the allotment of a span, delivering unworthy life back into the hands of humanity. And then there was Watchie, a healer of a different sort, brought low and bowing before her, a minister to the needs of the realm of mechanical creation and artifice, and all the creatures of metal brought into being to ease the rightful burdens of labour which God had decreed upon flesh ever since the days of Eden. And then the widow threw back her head and began to laugh, for this she understood was how God had chosen to punish Watchie, and the council too, the very idea that they should celebrate the death of a chiel like Macpherson, and this was how they suffered for it, though she had no notion of how his hurt had been caused; once again God had revealed himself to her, in the manner of his chosen punishments for those who dared to defy him, and no compromise was there in her, damnation was her whole business. Her laughter echoed around the street, and finally Kirsty's anger found all the focus it needed; she knew little of the widow, other than her father's tales of the demented woman who refused his services, crying at him through her door that she needed nothing from papists, that he would roast in the fires for his religion, and so it was as much for her father as for Watchie that she raged,

Awa tae hell wi ye, ye dampt aal gowk!

which made the widow laugh all the harder at the irony of it, for it was not herself who was to be pitched into the slough of damnation, of that she was certain; and she followed them all the way along the road, laughing as God reduced them all to fools and jesters, giving up all pretence that she had simply been an accidental audience to the little drama while out for a walk. She laughed like a crow behind them and waited to see them enter the doctor's house seven doors further down the road, and she was still laughing when she settled herself down on her black chair, giving thanks to her God for the best joke it had been her pleasure to observe in many a long time, a spanner thrown deliberately in the workings wrought by the hand of man, and much would she have to tell the customers at Henderson's the morrow when it opened its doors.

★

338

While Watchie rested on the couch in the doctor's downstairs surgery, Fairley lit the oil-lamps, muttering all the while that she was a demented old crone, angered still he was by the meeting in the street. But once the last lamp was lit, his anger was forgotten, and he blew on the flame to extinguish it from the stalk of the taper, and turned to Watchie, sitting bolt upright on his couch, and to Kirsty, staring around the now bright room and struck dumb by the sight of it.

Much of what Kirsty saw disturbed her, for reasons that she did not understand. Around the walls were a number of unscrolled anatomy charts, each of them secured to the picture rail by a parabola of chain from a hook. There were mannequins with their arms held open as if denying an accusation, with flesh as transparent as glass in each of the depictions, so that in the first chart Kirsty saw the fat pillows of offal which were the mannequin's organs, some cut apart to reveal others behind them. Kirsty had never seen such a thing before, although she was minded on the entrails which spilled from the carcass of a chicken, and assumed them to be the same. The next chart along represented the heart, but no other organ, for it was there to show a fuller map of the system by which blood was driven around the body, blue veins and scarlet arteries, which Kirsty thought was like a tree. Next she saw the ropes of muscle anchored to the bone by tendons, and even the striated musculature of a face without its mask of epidermis, from which she turned away in disgust towards another transparent man, this time poised to show off the skeleton. She turned to see Dr Fairley smiling at the look on her face, though she herself had no idea of what he was reading by it, and he said,

What a work is man, is that not so, Kirsty?

Kirsty nodded while the doctor went over to Watchie, and sat behind him on the couch. She said,

Is yon in ilka ane o' us, doctor?

and the doctor probed Watchie's back.

Yes, Kirsty, though there are differences between men and women, wee differences in the way they're put together,

339

and Kirsty nodded once again, and said nothing more as the doctor continued to feel Watchie's back, alert to his every slight spasm as his fingers read the injury as if by braille. She heard the doctor say,

Can you try and straighten up, Watchie? The injury may not be as bad as you think,

but the shout and the following laughter told Kirsty that it was; and she joined her hands once again, this time looking up, even though there was nothing to see but the charts; she faced the man in outline and prayed hail Mary, who art in heaven, and imagined that the base heart at rest in its cage was the sacred heart of Christ himself.

Fairley drew a curtain around the couch while he wound a girdle of bandage around Watchie, a strapping he called it, and pronounced that Watchie was suffering an over-extension of the lower lumbar region, which confused the loon until it was explained to him that all it meant was a straining of his back muscles. The strapping lifted him erect against his will, and caused him more pain, and also forbade him to bend forward, for it was tight around his midriff, a constricting belt; Watchie took shallow breaths, and Fairley said that he should rest over the weekend to give him a chance to heal. He drew back the screen once Watchie had struggled back into his shirt, and Kirsty turned to see Watchie sitting among the tatters of his dungarees, grimacing like a gargoyle, and the loon's first words after the doctor stood and went to his desk were,

Fit time'll I be stertin werk, doctor? For yon clockie'll nae hae the patience tae see me healt.

Doctor Fairley withdrew from the top drawer a small envelope of tissue, folded in thirds like the provost's letters of importance, and smiled, first at Kirsty, who raised her eyes to the ceiling, then at Watchie, shaking his head emphatically.

No, Watchie, I'm afraid the clock will have to do without you for a few days while your back gets better. I'll be back in a minute.

Fairley left the room, and Watchie looked at Kirsty and smiled uneasily.

Ye ken fine I'll hae tae dee the werk, Kirsty, it's nae ower lang till the date it'll be needin fexed for.

The concern swelling within Kirsty for so long was lanced by Watchie's apparent carelessness about his own welfare, and without the witness of the doctor, she rounded on Watchie and said,

Ye're a feel, Wulliam Leckie, a dampt feel yersel, can ye nae see it was the clock that pit ye in yon state tae begin wi? And ye'd werk yersel tae yer grave for it, jist like a feel, for the sake o' the cooncil and yon mannie Macpherson fa a'body says is nae tae be trustit.

Watchie met her eyes levelly, the strapping holding him upright; he remembered how severe she had been when first he had come to the croft to hear her father's proposal, and there it was again, her face as composed as if she had never smiled nor ever had a thing to smile about, and this time, while before in the croft she had avoided his eyes, now she turned her severe aspect upon him, and he realized that he had never seen her smile while she was in the croft either. She stood with her back to the chart depicting the musculature, and Watchie broke her gaze and looked at the gallery around her; new soft mechanisms he had never dreamt of, the fitting together of parts, as recognizable to himself as they had been to Kirsty, from his mother's dissections of snared and freshly killed rabbits and chickens prepared for the pot; and he said simply,

Clockmakkin's my job, Kirsty, nae the cooncil's, aye, nor Macpherson's neether. I'll hae tae dee my job. I dinna ken fit way the noo, but I'll hae tae dee it.

Kirsty turned away. Quietly she said,

Ye'll nae dee yer job wi thon back,

and then the doctor entered the surgery with a whisky glass of water in his hand and an envelope in the other, looking from one to the other as if unaware of an argument between them. Fairley smiled, and went to the flat of his desk, and began to prepare his potion, unfolding the envelope and tilting it like a chute until the powder turned the water into milk, stirring the mixture with a teaspoon he had also brought with him, offering the glass to Watchie,

Here. I'm afraid it isn't a cure, but it'll help relieve the pain.

XXXI

The effect of the laudanum was not instant; but in a short time
Watchie began to feel leaden and drowsy as the drug exacerbated
his exhaustion. It was a feeling not unlike exhaustion itself, so
that the pain became extrinsic to him, as the pain in his hands
had become, another's pain, another's burden. He shared the
pain as if it were his own, for there was no doubt that it was
still fretting at him like a dog at a hare; and he took to his feet
at the command of another, or it may have been himself, he
could never be certain, and there was discomfort to be sure, but
it was no longer troublesome, and he held himself proudly, as
upright as a tower of granite, or so it seemed to him. He could
put names to the faces before him, there was Dr Fairley and
there was Kirsty, and they had their hands around him on either
side, he could feel their shoring taking the support of his legs,
and he told them that it was not necessary, he was perfectly able
to walk, but the words were milled in his mouth and turned to
a fine powder of sound which told them nothing. From the
light of the surgery, they entered a bleak long room which
Watchie neither understood nor recognized, and the doctor left
after telling them to wait for a while, through a door paned
with glass which reduced him to fragments, and there was
Kirsty standing beside him, her arm around his shoulder, and
there was something important he wanted to say to her, something urgent and which had to be said now before it was
forgotten; but it was away from him like thistledown, blown
further away by the current set up in the catching, a transient
seed which would fall eventually and he would know what it
was when it was properly rooted. Kirsty was asking him was he
all right, are ye a' richt Wulliam? and he was answering her, he
was certain of it, he knew that his lips were moving and he was
telling her that there was nothing to worry about, they'd be all

right after a good long walk home, for this was the kind of exhaustion he was used to shrugging off, he would feel all right after a good sleep, when Jeannie would come into the room and part the curtains about the window, he would awaken in the scarlet light and he would ready himself for another hard day; but she was asking him, fit're ye sayin Wulliam? I dinna ken fit ye're sayin, and so he told her that he was tired, and she let out a breath beside him which he felt cool about his face. The door opened, and the doctor came back into the room, the long black room, and said that the gig was now ready and waiting outside; Kirsty waited until the doctor had Watchie about his waist, and said she would run ahead and gather together all the things which had been left in the tower, and the doctor promised that he would meet her with the gig at North Street, and then took all of Watchie's mass on one shoulder and guided him into the street. There was a mare lashed into the forks of the gig, and it was as black as the night itself, no Clydesdale bred for power, but a fine pedigree with legs elongated like a dancer's for the sprint, and her shape was only defined to the eye by the gloss to her coat, and Watchie said that she was a beauty, though Dr Fairley did not reply to him. Watchie decided that both Kirsty and the doctor had suddenly become deaf, for the doctor spoke to him as if he were saying nothing at all, and gave him help into the hooded cabin of the gig as if he were in need of it; right insensitive he was, for he bundled Watchie as if he were a package of irregular stumps and protrusions, poising him to lower his head below the risen canopy, lifting his legs for him and bearing him into the front facing seat. It was a small gig driven not from a board like Wullie's but from the occupants' cabin. The doctor then climbed in beside Watchie, causing the gig to pitch and roll on the storm of sudden movement, and Watchie was tossed from side to side as the doctor retrieved the reins from a hook in front of him, and passed a ripple through the leather cords. The gig started with a jolt, the hooves of the horse, whom the doctor called Diana, sounded crisply against the cobbles, Watchie settled into the leather upholstery of the seating, comfortably supporting his sore back, and the journey

343

along the road was short, though he could focus on no single detail of it, and was only aware of Kirsty clambering into the cabin beside him, setting the pannier and Watchie's bag of tools and their two lanterns at her feet, her legs squeezed unnaturally to give them room. He laughed, and thought he said to her, aye, we're gangin hame in grand style the nicht, Kirsty, are we nae? but she was still deaf to him, and after a while, when the cart had passed the tower, the lids of his eyes became intolerably heavy, he was possessed by a numb euphoria which stole away all awareness of where he was and even of the pain, and he fell fast asleep, his head nodding to one side and striking Kirsty's shoulder gently as the gig took the uneven and weather-displaced cobbles of the Cornhill Road, one two three, one two three, one two three.

On the road home to Smallbrae, Dr Fairley told Kirsty that he would like to purchase a motor car, such as he had seen driven through the streets of Aberdeen, though this he qualified by explaining that he was not dissatisfied with Diana in any way; she was a good obedient horse, he said, but there was all the business of lacing her into the straps and girds of the harnessing before he could get started, when all he needed to do with a motor car was to crank the handle under the radiator, a much faster process, and much more efficient too. He would be quicker to see his patients, he said, and there was a fortune to be saved in veterinarian's bills, not to mention shoeing, though there were hardly as yet any places to purchase the spirit that such a vehicle would need for its running. Kirsty nodded all the while, having never seen a motor car, though she had heard all about them from her father, who had often seen them on the road in Turriff; noisy metal beasts, he had said, capable of charging over a man and killing him as dead as a stone, they snorted and rampaged like bulls along the roads, and there farted from the arse of them such a foul vapour as you'd never smelled before in your life, and Kirsty wondered if the doctor would be so quick to laud the creature's benefits if he found himself treating some of the innocent passers-by caught in its unruly stampede; but she held quiet, and raised Watchie in his sleep to extend the wing of her cloak around his shoulders, the mother hen's concern over the hatchling, and this brought Watchie's head closer to her, and she sensed his regular breath against her face, warm and somehow comforting. She had not understood why Watchie began to act like a drunkard after swallowing over Dr Fairley's potion, and she had turned to the doctor and asked him had he given the loon whisky, for this was the only drink that she could imagine would cause such a curious slurring of the voice; but no, said the doctor, it was a drug, which he explained was a preparation which would bring Watchie relief from the pain of his injury, and this made Kirsty feel easier, for she was afraid that the doctor had given Watchie the same elixir as had stolen her father from her for so long.

There was cloud overhead, obscuring all sight of the stars, and after a while it released the weight of rain which bore it to the ground, a fine needlepoint rain which slanted through the cabin of the gig and stitched the cold to their skins. From time to time the doctor looked to his side, as if to say something to Kirsty; and sometimes she caught him smiling, a slight indulgent smile, as if privy to a secret knowledge beyond her awareness, which would be made known to her as well in good time. She told herself that she had no idea what the doctor's smile meant, and replied to it as guilelessly as she could, causing him to turn away and keep his eyes on what little of the road he could see through the cast of the warning lanterns and the sting of the shower; but the smile remained on his face as if he had seen a sight which gave him warmth through the coldest of weathers, and here was a fine doctor, Kirsty thought to herself, whose heart was lifted by the relieving of the suffering of others, and she brought her cloak more tightly around Watchie to protect him from the intrusive wind, and the sharp rain drilling through his flesh.

The rain was properly on by the time Kirsty helped to guide the doctor into the gable-end path of the farmyard, and now the wind was asserting its displeasure, shaking at the portal of the byre as if Wullie had stolen what belonged to the elements by right, and the kye were stamping and lowing in alarm at the insistence of the unseen chiel who was disturbing their sleep. Fairley picked up the collar of his coat, and stepped from the cab, asking that Kirsty do the same, and between them they had Watchie down from the gig with a great deal of difficulty; for the stop and the manhandling roused him from his laudanum stupor for long enough to complain as once again he became an item of luggage, his head slumped between his shoulders as they half-carried half-walked him the little distance that the doctor had brought the gig to the house. Now and again his feet failed him, and his shoes pointed and became ploughs to furrow the kirn of mud; he was borne along unevenly with his arms around the shoulders of both Kirsty and the doctor, lopsiding his gait, though he did not know where he was. Once at the door, the doctor rapped firmly on the wood with the points of his knuckles, and it was answered by Jeannie, who took a step back when she saw her son in such a state.

Good evening, Mrs Leckie, said the doctor. Don't worry about your son, I had to give him a draught of laudanum to relieve him of his pain.

Jeannie helped the doctor to install Watchie in one of the chairs in conference around the kitchen table, and then dropped to one knee to bring her face level with his. Watchie's head fell and rolled around his collar like a turnip on a plate. Quickly the doctor said,

I'm afraid William's had a wee accident; strained his back while fixing his clock. He's in some pain, which I decided he was better out of as soon as possible. Please don't worry about him, this is not the effect of the laudanum, I think he's suffering from exhaustion. He'll rest comfortably tonight, you can be sure of that.

Jeannie had never seen anyone, let alone her son, in such a waking trance before. She called out his names, William first, then Watchie, and he appeared to recognize them, raising his head both times, and her calling drew from the living-room all the family at once, Wullie first through the door, then Peggy, and Jessica darting in front of Aal Wullie. Wullie said to the doctor,

And fit wid be the cause o' Waatchie's ill, noo, doctor? The clock, I'd say, it's nae richt guid for him tae be fexin it, I've tellt him afore, ye ken, but nae a werd he'd hear frae me.

Fairley was ever sensitive to the currents playing around him, for many times he had been called upon as arbitrator to quarrels, as one considered to be trustworthy and whose opinion was worth coinage in the bargaining of disputes; and such he sensed now, and he said,

Not the clock precisely, Mr Leckie, I wouldn't say it was that. Perhaps the way your son chose to work on it, that I would say. He's a very hard worker, Mr Leckie. In my opinion, he worked himself too hard. That's the reason.

Wullie nodded, knowing well enough from Watchie's experience with the traction-engine that this was so. There was a long silence, which no one thought to interrupt; Jessica stood in front of her grandfather and eyed Kirsty steadily, and after a moment Kirsty became aware of the gazing of the young cwean, and remembered Watchie talking about her as if she were a mystery to him, like a doll which danced pirouettes in a musical box, a construct with no seeming motivation or reason, though to Kirsty she appeared to be a perfectly ordinary cwean at first sight, more outgoing than Kirsty had been at Jessica's age, for Jessica dared to look longer than Kirsty had ever done herself at a stranger. Kirsty attempted a smile in return. For the duration of that smile they were two innocents, both children in the presence of elders and betters, afraid to step wrongly or do anything to bring attention to themselves.

Wullie was taken aback by the presence of the doctor in the house; he appeared to be slightly bowed over in his posture, in deference to the doctor's greater learning and his powers of healing. Such were the concessions to be had by doctors in a village practice, though it was not a position that Fairley was minded to abuse in any way, a man of liberal inclinations he was, never a one to see his own trade as anything other than just the kind of work that Watchie performed, though the mechanisms he fixed back to working order were more complex in their failings. Fairley was keen that he should not be set above other tradesmen or women, for often he was powerless where others were expert in their trade; but Wullie's shoulders had fallen as if in shame, to compare his own poor learning with that of the man before him, and this was a thing the doctor would sooner not have. Fairley said,

If I might be permitted to make an observation, Mr Leckie?

Wullie looked up suddenly, and nodded, being able to refuse nothing to a man who was able to use such words adroitly and without self-consciousness. Fairley stood as upright as if to attention, himself respectful before the man of the house, in whose realm he was, after all, an intruder, and said,

I would be failing in my professional duty, Mr Leckie, if I did not point out to you that Watchie should not have been working alone on his clock. I understand that his experience until now has been with pocket watches and the like, apart from the time when he fixed Mr Millar's traction-engine.

Wullie nodded, surprised that Watchie's reputation should have reached the ears of the doctor, and once again the embers of his pride were kindled by the memory of that day, and the doctor's mention of it. The doctor continued,

Since then, he has had little experience of fixing heavy machinery, and I think that it's fair to say that your son's injury was caused by his pride in his work, not by the work itself. I've strapped his back so that he won't move it for the next few days; but while I was doing so, he was most concerned that his work should continue. I intend to visit the provost tomorrow, with your permission, and tell him that the work must stop for as long as it takes for Watchie's injury to heal.

Wullie nodded, for this tune was much to his liking, and he said,

Aye, doctor, yon's affa kind o' ye, I'll gie ye my thanks.

The doctor went over to the range, beside Kirsty, to warm himself in front of its heat. He said,

I would be failing my duty if I did not do so, Mr Leckie. Watchie is simply not fit to work on the clock without help.

Wullie shook his head.

Aye, a richt peety yon,

he said, as Jeannie and Peggy returned from the bedroom after undressing and putting the loon finally to his sleep. Wullie turned to Jeannie and said,

D'ye hear thon, fit the doctor's sayin? Waatchie's nae tae gang near thon clock till his back's weel.

There was a look which passed between them then, which Kirsty found difficult to decipher, a frown from Jeannie almost of anger at her husband, an answering frown from Wullie to parry her, then a softening across Jeannie's brow, capitulation, defeat, and Wullie's authority exerted. It was all mysterious to Kirsty as a stranger, unaware of the family struggles involved, but Jeannie's voice was small as she said,

Fit can we dee tae mak him comfortable, doctor?

The doctor declined Wullie's offer of a whisky, and Jeannie's of a cup of tea, for he was thinking of Elizabeth smouldering quietly by the fireside, with only Jane Austen and his folded newspaper for company; though he accepted a modest payment for the bandaging and the laudanum. He offered Kirsty a ride back to her croft, but Wullie said,

Na na, ye've been brocht far eneuch for the noo, doctor, I'll see the cwean hame, dinna ye fash yersel,

and it was decided. The doctor bid them all a good-night, but before he opened the door he turned and said,

I think Kirsty here might appreciate a good strong cup of tea, after all her efforts to help Watchie. Good night once again,

and left to attend to his impatient mare, prancing on the spot as if for warmth in the penetrating rainfall. The moment the doctor was out of the door, Wullie turned to his wife and said,

The mannie's richt, ye ken, Jeannie. Pair Kirsty's nae been offert a drap o' tea sin she cam ben the hoose,

and Jeannie frowned once again, though she was careful not to aim the frown at Kirsty, and placed a kettle on the range to boil while Wullie led the cwean across the hall and into the living-room. Aal Wullie and Peggy stayed with Jeannie in the kitchen, while Jessica was held by her grandfather, watching Kirsty's back as she went. Wullie placed Kirsty in front of the fire, and all the time he spoke about her father, what a fine mannie he was, a good friend to him, right sorry he had been when he had heard about Ailsa's death. Kirsty felt the heat of the fire pressing against her back, an almost physical presence. She said,

Ye're nae affa worriet aboot Wulliam, Mr Leckie?

Wullie looked directly at her, as if anticipating the question and delighted to give it an answer. He sat down on the seat angled towards the hearth, gestured that Kirsty should do the same on the seat opposite, which she did, and settled himself, a king on the throne, before saying,

Weel, noo, Kersty, yon's nae the ferst time I've seen oor Waatchie brocht tae the hoose in a state like thon, na na. He wis brocht in here fan he wis a wee loonie, a' stung wi waasps, efter he'd flung a stane at a waasps' bike, stung tae the deil, he wis, and we a' thocht he'd ne'er be weel frae it. Has he nae tellt ye thon afore?

Kirsty shook her head. Wullie smiled, tightly.

Aye, there's ower muckle ye'll nae ken aboot Waatchie. Fan ye've seen yer ain son in a state like yon, like efter he'd been stung, ye'll ken fine eneuch fit a body can tak. Fine dee I ken he werks affa hard, losh! Ye widna see him for days fan he wis fexin the waatches for yer faither. I've seen him werkin hard, Kersty, and thon's fit way the doctor'll nae gie me a fleg fan he taals me my son's the iller for it.

His words were calm and reasoned, but Kirsty saw that he was rigid with concern. He crossed his legs over in his seat, as the tea was brought in by Jeannie. Before leaving she said,

He's restin the noo. I've sat him up in his bed, and pit a few pillas under him; he winna be able tae tern aroon.

Kirsty nodded, though Jeannie did not look at her as she closed the door silently behind her. Wullie sipped his tea; he had refused cake. He said to Kirsty,

Ye've been at the tour affa regular like, hae ye, Kersty?

The fruit cake was delicious in Kirsty's mouth, and she held up a hand to excuse herself while she finished eating it, for Ailsa had told her time and again that it was not the manners of a fine lady to talk and eat at the same time. She swallowed it over, and said,

Aye, Mr Leckie, my faither thocht I'd tak breid and crowdie tae Wulliam, affa hungry he'd be fexin a big thing like yon clock.

Wullie laughed,

Faith! I widna taal yon tae Mrs Leckie, my cwean, for she's thocht that Waatchie wisna eatin ower muckle o' her denner fan he ga'ed hame. And, has he been seein ye hame yersel, like, Kersty, efter ye've been sae kind tae gang tae the tour wi denner for him?

Kirsty shook her head,

Na na, Mr Leckie, I widna hae him gang three mile ony farther, fan he's tired oot wi the werk.

Wullie nodded to hear it, and sipped on his tea. He leaned forward before the fire, and Kirsty caught a profile that reminded her of Watchie; the prominent bounty of the nose, though there was something different about the sculpture of it, which she did not understand. Wullie'e eyes darted, and caught her stare; she smiled in reply, a little in alarm, and then Wullie stood and went to his cabinet, for what purpose Kirsty did not know, for the opening of the cabinet and its contents were obscured for her, thrown into eclipse by him. When he stood, closing the door of the cabinet with a careless cast of his hand, it was with a bundle of chamois in his other hand, wrapped over in an envelope, and he returned to his seat, placing the bundle on his lap, unfolding the petals of the chamois, and there it was, Wullie Leckie's fiddle, still polished but silent and untested for an age, the bow resting alongside the strings. Wullie said,

Hae ye e'er seen a fiddle like yon, Kersty?

and Kirsty shook her head, wondering what this meant; but Wullie's abused and callused hands passed over its smooth surface as if it were the skin of a lover, and in this Kirsty saw the tenderness and delicacy that had been transmitted down through the generations, that had given Watchie his skill with mechanisms. Wullie said,

I made thon mysel, ye ken, oh, mony a year afore I stertit rinnin the fairm.

Kirsty said,

It's affa bonnie, Mr Leckie,

for it was a beautiful instrument, as finely crafted as anything that Kirsty had ever seen; the blood charged to Wullie's face with the compliment, and he said,

I was aye guid wi my hands, Kersty, aye, I was aye makkin furniture and the like.

He guided her around the room from the comfort of their seats; showing her the cabinet, his too, and the tripod stools, all of them of sound craft and well wrought, and mentioning to her the carpentry of the kitchen, where he claimed the tables and chairs and the cabinets there as his own, but all the while his hands were stroking the fiddle on his lap like an especially cherished pet, and finally, as if in expression of its own affections it nuzzled under his chin, and he drawled the bow over the strings to let her hear the sound of it; but Kirsty said,

Aye, it's a grand-soundin fiddle, Mr Leckie, but ye widna waant tae wake Wulliam the noo, I'd nae think,

and Wullie dropped the fiddle back on to his lap and nodded.

Aye, ye're richt, Kersty, neether I wid.

and sadly returned the fiddle to its bedding, wrapping it in the wings of the chamois, and went over to the cabinet again and placed it inside while Kirsty put the last bite of cake in her mouth. When he sat down in his chair, it was no longer as a king, but as a worried parent, a much smaller station for Wullie to occupy, and he wondered why this moment, the moment when all of his warnings and doubts had found their realization and had brought him closer to his own wishes, should be sullied by his fear for Watchie, and he felt petty and low suddenly, without vision, as if understanding that from the stilling of his own craft and dexterity rose the bitterness that had led him to stifle his son, and in his own victory he felt like a conqueror troubled by the memory of his atrocities, and he could look no one in the eye, not even Kirsty after that.

★

Kirsty stood in front of the bed, and looked on as Watchie rested in the light of the candle in its holder on the bedside table. He was not at peace; like a man in a tailor's fitting room, in front of a private mirror, he tried on a succession of faces, one after the other, and he never seemed to be satisfied with any one of them, a fussy customer he was. First he was elated, and grinning like the cat in *Alice*, then he was almost weeping, and then he was inflated suddenly by rage, animated from moment to moment like a flickerbook, from grief to delight, and it unsettled Kirsty to see him this way, she began to wish she had never asked Wullie if she could enter the bedroom in the first place; it was the profoundest mockery of all, that a face should be as changeable as the weather, and it disturbed her to the core to see it, but she approached the bed nevertheless, and sat on the edge of it, a much softer mattress than her own. There was a tumble of hair over his brow, and without thinking her hand reached out and stroked it back into place; and she saw how vulnerable he was, only one ill at ease within himself would need to present the peacock's display of competence to her in his tower, but it was the first time she had seen him as a bairn, a creature of raw needs and transitory responses, and she wanted to expand around him like blown glass around a flame, to protect him from the elements and to let him be seen by the world, she would be a transparent bushel to him under whom his light would not be hidden, under whose guidance he would burn brighter. She thought of the stories her mother had told her when she was old enough to listen, of the princess sleeping in a castle, and her asking what was a castle, for she had never seen one, her mother explaining that it was a big house that kings and queens and princesses lived in, like Queen Victoria herself, and Kirsty imagined it to be a vast croft, a granite building piled as tall as the palaces of cloud she saw in the sky. There was Watchie on the bed, as she imagined her princess during her long and suspended sleep, the slumber of a century, waiting to be wakened by a kiss; and for a moment the fancy came to her that perhaps this was all that Watchie needed, the slightest brush of her lips against him, though she knew that it was a remedy from a story for children; and then she heard the voices from the bottom of the stairs, for she had left the door a little ajar, voices in conflict and quiet argument, and Kirsty recognized them both, Wullie steady and rational, Jeannie high and querulous.

Fit's thon cweanie deein up wi Wulliam the noo, Wullie Leckie? Can ye nae see he's needin his rest; tired oot he wis,

but Wullie's voice suddenly became predominant, and for once masterful, unseating his wife for a moment,

Ach, wheesht, wumman, the cwean it wis fa brocht yer son hame, dinna grudge her a meenit or twa wi him, Jeannie.

There were no more voices after that, though there was a release of held breath, and Kirsty knew she had been privy to a conversation which had carried from the living-room to the hallway, a clash of wills with herself as the dispute. Soon enough there were heavy footsteps mounting the stairs, and then the door widened, and Kirsty shot to her feet, a little too suddenly, leaving behind her print upon the mattress, a deep well in the blankets, and she looked up, her face light and guileless, as if having learned from Watchie how properly to wear a mask.

Richt ye are, Kersty, said Wullie Leckie. Time it is for me tae tak ye hame.

XXXII

Jeannie Leckie tolerated the frequent visits of Kirsty O'Donnell for the sake of Watchie, for hers was the first name he spoke upon waking up from the sleep of the dead, and Jeannie was there to hear it, sitting on a stool she had brought from the living-room and placed in the corner after milking the kye. She heard it distinctly from his lips, though his eyes were not yet open, and he made as if to sit up in his bed, his eyes opening then with pain as many realizations came all at once, with the girdle of the strapping around him tightly like a memory knot around the finger to remind him of the doctor's surgery, Kirsty waiting there and looking at the charts depicting the human anatomy, the poisoned cup which granted him relief from the pain; beyond that, he remembered the tower, and his final grapple with the wheel that threw his own mechanism out of balance; and then there was a parade of images, as if from a succession of particularly vivid dreams, none of which he could call to mind in their entirety. He saw Jeannie in the corner of the room, and saw that the curtains had been thrown aside, and that the light of the day was brighter, the sun ascending higher in the sky than on his normal waking days. His posture was more erect than was normal for sleeping, and this he realized was because of the pillows upon which he was resting, piled high behind him, rearing above him like mountains, which he understood were there to support his injured back, and in a moment Jeannie was by his side, sitting perched on the side of his bed, and he felt his body stiff all over because he had not moved from this position all night, and he tried to sit up to escape from the bed. He said,

Fit time is't? I'll hae tae be at my werk this morn, I'm affa late,

but Jeannie was hearing none of it, she rested a hand on his chest and gently pressed him back, and he had no power to resist, being weak from healing and having moved not an inch during the night, and she said,

Ye'll hae yer breakfast in yer bed, Wulliam, yon's fit ye'll dee, and ye'll nae be werkin at yer clock till the doctor says ye're fit for it, and yon'll nae be for a filie yet.

Watchie allowed himself to fall back into the embrace of the pillows behind him, a tender cradle which gave him the best of support, and he felt no pain when he was lying on them, only discomfort, that is to say a continual shiftlessness in which no posture could be said to be comfortable for him, but which sent him none of the agony which had overpowered him the day before. Jeannie's face softened as she looked upon him; he was a loon again in her eyes, needing his mother's care, and she spoke to him in the melodic soothing voice that a parent gives to a suffering child as balm and liniment to all ills:

Fit were ye deein, liftin heavy weights like yon, ye daft cratur? Did ye nae think ye'd dee yersel a mischief?

Watchie shook his head.

I'd been yaisin a pulley, I didna think I'd pit my back oot yon way.

Jeannie shook her own head, fancy that, her bairn imagining he was not heir to all the weaknesses of common humanity, a sensible adult would know better, and without knowing it herself, reached over to replace a sprig of hair from over his brow, the way that Kirsty had the night before; then she lifted herself from the bed, and said,

I'll awa doon tae the ketchen and mak yer porritch for yer breakfast.

Before she left the room, Watchie said,

Fit aboot the clock? I'll nae hae't fexed in time for the richt date, nae frae my bed.

Jeannie made no reply, but shook her head, what curious priorities her son had.

There was another reason why Jeannie Leckie tolerated Kirsty's presence in the house, and this reason was Wullie, who had told

Jeannie, told mark you, not consulted nor advised but outright commanded, that Kirsty was to be made welcome whenever she chose to come calling, and this was not to Jeannie's liking at all, for she had no time for brazen hizzies who threw themselves at the feet of her son, visiting him at the clock tower indeed when Jeannie herself was not even permitted there, or more appropriately would not grant herself the permission to go there whenever her worries began to prowl around her like a hunting pack of wolves, fretting her down to the bone the more she thought of what might happen to him. It was not that Jeannie was ungrateful to the cwean for finding her son in the midst of his distress, not that at all, never that, right glad she was that someone had found him and made sure that he was brought back to her; but she had heard all kinds of stories about the O'Donnells, most of them from Aal Wullie and from the alehouse, of Geordie O'Donnell's drinking and the bottles of whisky he bought over the counter, and while she had pitied him before, for men like that were to be pitied for their slavery to their appetites, and while Geordie had been a gentleman in business, dealing fairly with Watchie for the services he rendered, she could not forget that her husband had brought the two parties to the arrangement together, for his own purposes as it turned out, and how she had felt herself when Wullie made obvious his reasons over the dinner table, that the whole deal had filled her nose with the corrupt stench of conspiracy, hidden purposes and hands shaken away from her eyes, so that she began to imagine that Geordie O'Donnell himself had another good reason for giving Watchie the work. But Wullie had usurped her judgement on that occasion, she wasn't to upset the cwean in any way, the cwean was to be given tea should she come, could Jeannie not see that Kirsty was the tonic which would bring Watchie out of his illness? And then he exercised his biblical prerogative, I'm yer hisband, Jeannie, and ye'll dampt weel dee as I say, for ane time in yer life, and I say the cwean's tae be seein Waatchie ony time she cams tae see him, and there's an end o' it. It was after Wullie returned Kirsty to her home, and soaked through he was despite lifting the hood over the shoulders of the gig; Jeannie stared at her husband in stark fury, for she had not the words to express it, this sudden laying down the law as clearly stated in the good book itself for which she had no answer, the foundations were called out from under her and left her standing in ruins, and she turned on her heel and said over her shoulder, I'm awa tae my bed, ye'll nae hear a werd I've tae say tae ye, Wullie Leckie, passing a slight glance to Peggy and Aal Wullie in turn as she went by, for now more than ever she felt herself to be the intruder among this family, in a house that was hers only by marriage, and the only thing which prevented her from making plain her disapproval with heavy footfalls was her thought for Watchie, that he should not be wakened by the row simply because she had a point to prove.

Even Jessica noticed that a silent kind of war had broken out between her parents, though she had no idea of the terms under which it was being fought; for she had been seen to her bed by Peggy not long after Watchie was retired, and so heard none of the arguments over Kirsty which followed. The first she knew was during Kirsty's first visit to the farm after Watchie's injury, the day following, when she heard a knock at the door, slow and timid, as if whoever was on the other side were uncertain of their right to be there at all; Jeannie was preparing dinner at the time, stirring the stew in the cauldron, and she wiped her hands on her apron and answered it, and it was Kirsty, wearing her hood and cloak once again, for a spell of wet weather had settled over Aberlevin, not enough to give Wullie concern for his crops since they had hardly rooted yet, and Kirsty's head was bowed within its shade once again when she saw who it was, for it was Wullie who had told her after leaving her at the end of the path leading to the croft that she was welcome to visit Watchie any time. But then Jessica saw a strange thing, a smile coming to the lips of her mother, not that this was strange in itself, but rather the kind of smile it was; as if it was a flat courtesy offered to any guest, like the tea and cake of the night before, and Jeannie widened the door to let Kirsty through, all done as if at the will of another, as if none of it was her own volition,

Cam awa ben, cwean, she said, I'll mak ye a cuppie o' tea, and ane for Wulliam, ye can tak it up tae him.

and then there was silence in the kitchen, Kirsty was seated on one of the kitchen chairs and no more words were spoken while Jeannie put an enormous copper dome kettle on the range to boil and gave it her full attention, not even looking over her shoulder. Jessica caught Kirsty's eye again and smiled at her, and the smile she received in return was friendly and grateful, as if Kirsty considered Watchie's sister to be her only ally presently in the room, though Jessica did not know why; and Jessica had come to understand her brother's feelings more and more even in as little as the past day upon seeing this woman, for woman she was to Jessica, older than herself and grown to her adult form.

When Kirsty took the tea to Watchie, he was upright in bed, and reading a vast book not much smaller than his torso which rested on his belly and was angled up so that he could see the pages, and fine pleased he was to see her, closing over the heavy door of the book and placing it on the counterpane beside him while she fetched the stool from the corner of the room and placed it beside the bed nearest the door, sitting down easily despite the volume of her skirts. She passed him over his tea; he thanked her, and sipped from it while Kirsty explained that his mother had made it for her to take up, and he nodded, and for a long moment there was silence between them, for Watchie had never seen Kirsty in the house before, and he needed the time to place her there, an unfamiliar conjunction. He said,

Thanks for makkin sikker I ga'ed hame,

quietly and simply, and she shook her head, there was after all no need to thank her, and she drank her own tea and put it on the bedside table, beside his. She said,

I wis affa worriet aboot ye fan ye were camin hame. I thocht thon medicine o' Dr Fairley's had made ye gang tae sleep.

Watchie nodded, for he remembered his dreams, convinced that they were dreams and not visions. He said,

Aye, weel, I'll be oot o' my bed in nae time at a', fexin yon clock for the provost's anniversary, ye'll see.

Kirsty shook her head, and smiled,

Na na, ye'll nae dee thon sae soon, Wulliam. Ye're fit they cry an invaleed the noo, ye're nae weel, and ye're nae meant tae dee a'thing that'll mak ye werse.

Watchie stared at her. At least Kirsty, he thought, would see the necessity for his fast recovery; he frowned a little, and said,

There's nae affa lang till the day, Kersty. I canna lie here a' the time, the clock'll nae fex itsel.

Kirsty became stern, all of a sudden, a transformation Watchie remembered among his last memories of the doctor's surgery, a silver hook of a glare that left him to squirm on the end of it, and she said with a voice which matched her stare,

Ye're nae tae touch ony mair feels, Wulliam, yon's fit the doctor said, he's the mannie fa kens a' aboot fit ye can and canna dee wi yer back like yon. Nae wi nae help at a', Wulliam, his werds, I mind on them fine.

She was as stern as a nurse for that moment, and Watchie subsided, fell back on the bed and his pillows, for the agitation had lifted him from his helpless posture to the limits of the girdle of bandaging, tight now about him, and he fell back as much to give himself breath as because the battle had ended in his defeat. Kirsty wielded the power of a queen just then; she was determined, and would take no reply, and she was here to visit, and this together silenced Watchie as effectively as any gag, but she leaned forward and took her tea from the bedside table, and said,

Ye'll be efter a bit help, Wulliam Leckie, yon's fit way ye'll fex the clock, and it's nae afore the time, neether.

The rest of the visit was spent on talk of Geordie and Mhairi, in whom Watchie expressed a polite interest, and heard all about the shoeing of the now aged Maisie, which had cost Geordie dearly for leaving it so long until the poor mare was virtually tiptoeing on the roads; Kirsty herself was reading books now, whole words, though she still had never made the journey through the Bible, too convoluted for her at her present stage of learning, and Watchie offered to help her in her reading when he was better, and she would like that, she said, for Geordie himself was only good for recognizing words, the words themselves meant nothing to him, simply markers on his road to what he wanted, and so it was agreed. It was no matter for shame, there were many others who could not read in the county and had never needed to, and Watchie offered her his hand on it, which she took lightly, without the hard shake of the canny bargainer, though her hand stayed with his longer than there was the need for. And then she had to be getting back to the croft, much work to be done, Geordie's and Mhairi's dinner to be fetched from the garden and made, she stood and returned the stool to the corner, she would come back tomorrow to see him, he hoped that he would be up on his feet in a few days; she gave him a look to the side that promised, playfully though, all manners of hell should he be on his feet sooner than he needed to be, and then she was gone, and Watchie raised his book to rest on his lap once again, shuffling through the leaves until he found the place he had left, engines, internal combustion, the anatomy exposed in ghostly transparencies, for which he had a distant curiosity since he had heard it was to be the coming thing, though no one in Aberlevin as yet possessed any such vehicle.

That evening was the first that Jessica saw her mother take up silent arms against the alliance between Wullie and the personable cwean who came to see her brother. It was fought across the table over dinner, when Jeannie rather sourly asked should she be setting another place, she's nae oot o' the hoose, she'd be as weel sittin wi us for oor denner, but Wullie let her shot pass him by, after all it had been broadly aimed and would only draw blood if Wullie presented himself before it, and took an uncommon interest in the news of the day, shielding himself behind his *Press and Journal*. It continued into the living-room with the cups of tea, when Jeannie settled to her knitting beside her mother-in-law, asking the air if there was any news of Ireland, an issue much in prominence at the time, then proceeding to

descry the whole nation as a shower of drunkards and para-
sites, nae a'thing but bother ilka ane o' them, tinkers and layabouts, and fair silenced they all were as Jeannie's overruled fury
curdled in the heat, Romish traitors the lot of them; Peggy bent
low over her own knitting and hoped that Jeannie would not
look for her agreement, while Wullie bore it all behind his paper,
now unfolded into a mask of current affairs which kept him
from the need to answer her. She was an unguided engine of
war trampling over all alike, and she said to Jessica, who knelt
beside her playing the harp strings of wool which resolved themselves into patterns by the magic of the needles,

Aye, heed me weel, Jessie, ye'll nae trist the Irishman, wid
talk the hin legs frae a cuddy, he wid, affa sleekit chiels,

which left Jessica none the wiser, no idea had she that Kirsty's
father was from the land so maligned by Jeannie, but she
nodded anyway until finally Wullie could take no more, he
lowered his paper on a taut face alight with anger and said,

Yon's faur eneuch, Jeannie, fine d'ye ken there's jist the ane
Irishman aboot here, aye, and he has a dauchter as weel, a guid
cwean fa I'll nae hear a werd said agin, noo wheesht and dee yer
knittin in peace.

The paper soared upright again, and Jeannie glared at it as if
she might cause it to burn in his hands before she did as he said;
and Jessica wondered why suddenly the Irish peoples were not
to be trusted, a curious battle it was to her, the first discord she
had witnessed in Smallbrae, but she tended to the wool as
quietly as ever, and earned for her troubles a smile from her
mother, which she banked and set aside, for in the past few days
it had been a rare coinage indeed.

XXXIII

The Provost Macpherson's visit on the second day of Watchie's time of recuperation was unannounced and unexpected, and he came on a boneshaker bicycle, seldom used, for he had no stabling for a horse and certainly no room for a gig. It was a strange and undignified way for a man of high office to travel, and many times on his road to Smallbrae he thought of dismounting the creature whose spindles and bearings were badly in need of oiling, walking it on the cobbles like an exhausted horse, but his shop was closed and therefore earning no silver for him during the time he was away from it, and besides this was not the spirit which had seen the country's mulberry birthmark of an empire staining the map of the world, and so Macpherson endured his discomfort, hacking loudly and bringing a flood of mucus into his throat to be swallowed over, for he would never consider disposing of it in the manner of a farmer, or even of his ancestor, though he would never have owned that such brute manners might be in his blood.

When he finally gained the farm, it was to sink in a kirn of mud, which lopsided his bicycle and drove him off the saddle to land heavily on one foot in the muck, and the perfect shine of his boots was lost to a coating of the foul clay as he walked his mount along the path to the courtyard, and this displeased him, for his wife spent a long time making sure that his boots were as bright as black metal, as was only fitting for the master shoemaker of Aberlevin; all her good work had gone to waste as if he had worn them for a week in this state. There were bothy men going about the usual business of a farm, a business he could not begin to fathom, and they looked up at him with a curious indifference, though the more Macpherson gave it thought, the more he realized that there was no franchise for them, and therefore no reason for them to know him from any other visitor to the farm, other than of course the slightly more prosperous cut of the clothing which was bound to mark him out from the sort of visitor who might be approaching on common farming affairs. Though there was no advantage to it, he gave them each a smile anyway, for he was keenly aware of his own proud origins from this salt-of-the-earth stock, they were for better or worse all God's creations it had to be minded, and he was gratified to find them nodding in reply.

Jeannie knew the moment she heard the knock that it could not be Kirsty at the door, for she knew Kirsty's hand by now, a reticent interrupter of chores the cwean was, though for a while the thought passed through Jeannie's mind that perhaps she had become bolder with each day that went by, now she thought it her right that the door should be answered for her, and so it was in a small temper that she wiped her hands on her apron and turned the handle in its collar almost as she might have wrung the neck of a chicken, until she saw that the visitor was the Provost himself, stepping into the kitchen as if it were his own and forcing her to sway to one side to avoid him.

Guid morn tae ye, Mrs Leckie,

said the Provost Macpherson, trailing the words like a banner behind him into the kitchen,

and hoo's the loon the day? Richt sorry I was tae hear frae the doctor that young Master Leckie wisna weel, isna yon jist the way o't the noo? Guid werk he wis deein, and neist he's on his back, aye, an affa place the warld is, gin ye'll ken fit I'm sayin.

Jeannie smiled, with nothing to say in reply to the Provost's unstoppable sympathy, and nodded, and asked would the Provost be after a cuppie of tea, and the Provost saw himself to a kitchen chair and settled himself upon it,

Yon's affa kind o' ye, Mrs Leckie, he said, efter thon journey, sic a lang way it is tae the fairm frae the village, a cuppie o' tea wid be grand, I'll thank ye verra much for it, aye, I will that.

In truth Jeannie still had nothing to say to the Provost while the kettle was on the boil, and listened instead to its murmuring while the Provost told her, without being asked, how his business was coming along, slower now with the onset of the summer and the sheltered weather that the village enjoyed, its winds and storms broken by the hills to the far south,

Ye ken, Mrs Leckie, said the Provost, fowk'll nae hae their beets fexed in the summer, for it's nae sae caal and damp then. Gin their beets are torn they can suffer it affa mair easily than fan it's rainin doon, and the muck gangs a' ower the place. Mind ye, I can aye tell fa bocht their beets at anither toun, d'ye ken fit I'm sayin, Mrs Leckie, for gin they're torn, they didna purchase them frae me, and yon's the truth!

and he invited her to laugh at this slight puff of the chest, and she did so, for his very presence made her uncomfortable and childlike, he was aware of his power and arrogant with it, and this she did not like; but he was doing his level best to be affable, and he was also aware that there were votes in this house, she treated him with the deference due to an emperor though she trusted him not in the least, knowing that were she entitled herself to place a mark on a ballot then this was not the man she would choose to be Provost, but she was polite to the man who employed her son, and gave him his tea once the kettle shrieked its readiness. He complimented her on the keeping of her house, and this made her nod and bow a very little in reply, thanking him for it and continuing the chores which made the range gleam dully as if for inspection; and he stood with his tea, and said,

May I see the young mannie, if yon's tae yer pleasin? For I winna gin he's sleepin, nor gin he's nae weel eneuch tae see me, I widna be efter disturbin him ye ken,

and Jeannie nodded,

I'll awa up and see him the noo, Provost,

not so much jumping to his attendance as to preserve Watchie from the curiosity of this small mannie and his strange questions.

She found Watchie reading his book in bed; he was never doing anything else when she went to see him. She told him that he had another visitor, and the start he gave told her that he thought his visitor to be Kirsty, but she said quickly that it was Mr Macpherson, and this caused Watchie to attempt to sit as upright as he could manage against the pillows, much easier it was after his two days' rest, putting the book to one side and helped by Jeannie's supporting hand on his back, and so Jeannie left the room to lead the Provost up, leaving Watchie behind to wonder what would be said, though this was not his greatest concern at that moment. His book was not the comfort to him after two days that he had at first considered it would be, no more than a cookery book would be to a man deprived of food and starving for the want of it; he had not the fever dreams of his previous illness to distort time for him, but sat instead in an awful silence during which the hands of the clock revolved in leisurely manner around the face. Now once again he was time's prisoner, though on this particular occasion the face of his gaoler had changed; a sullen and uncommunicative sort this sort, leaving him in a bleak mire of speculation, giving him glimpses of the world through the bars of his cell, allowing him his visitors, of whom he had had a few so far, Kirsty of course, Alistair and Cathie Loudon, by now both of them in with the brick of the farm, John Allison with his rough good humour, not Hugh Dodds however, the latest of the farm's orra loons, for the two had never much to say one to the other, unless it was fine morn tae ye at the first blood of the dawn.

On the stairwell, he heard the familiar slow footfalls of the Provost Macpherson, as well as the long-drawn breaths as he made his way to the top, and Watchie waited for him to arrive, composing himself and slamming the lid on all of his uncertainties, pushing them away into the corner and into dark, unregarded shadow for the now.

Macpherson sat himself down after placing the stool exactly in front of the bed, so that he was a stubby silhouette in Watchie's eyes, lit around by a glory of daylight from the window. He had Jeannie's cup of tea in his hand, and he drank thirstily from it as he inquired after Watchie's present state of health; Watchie replied that he was well, though in a little pain, as was to be expected, but he was growing stronger by the day, which was also true, and Macpherson nodded satisfaction and said,

Fine pleased I am tae hear it, Master Leckie. I've nae doot ye'll be on yer feet in nae time at a', it's nae richt easy tae pit ye awa frae yer werk, a hard-werkin mannie like yersel, fine dee I ken yon.

There was a short silence, during which the Provost took another draught of tea, and Watchie felt the cords of his back tighten a little, causing a slender needle of pain to rise through his back, knitting him together. It made him remember his promise to Kirsty, and he said,

I'll be needin a week yit, Mr Macpherson, afore I can stert the fexin again.

Macpherson nodded, and placed a hand upon his knee, a strong posture of buttresses and supports, much as when Watchie first went to see him about the clock. He said,

Aye, weel, Master Leckie, I widna wish ye tae gang aboot yer werk gin ye werena fit for it, but mind ye, yon'll nae be lang afore the clock's tae be ringin, ye ken, it's affa near the noo, and I widna be efter disappointin a' yon fowk fa'll be at the denner tae hear it . . .

This last fell upon Watchie all of a sudden, a weight he had never seen above him, released at a critical moment, and he sat upright in his bed, the shock of the pain ignored, and he said,

Fit denner wid thon be, Mr Macpherson?

The Provost frowned suddenly, then leaned forward, stroking his forehead with a powerful hand;

I've tellt ye aboot the denner, Master Leckie, dinna say tae me I've nae.

Watchie shook his head,

Na na, Mr Macpherson, nae a werd o't.

Macpherson looked at him for a moment, a stark accusation, then laughed,

Man man, is yon jist nae like the thing? I believe ye're richt eneuch, Master Leckie, for I'm a busy man, ye ken, I canna ca' tae mind a'thing I'm deein, frae the ane meenit tae the neist. I'm affa sorry for yon, Master Leckie, for ye'll ken I've affa muckle tae mind on, I should hae tellt ye aboot the denner sooner.

★

It was to be a grand occasion, held in the Memorial Hall which was the home of Aberlevin's clock, in front of which the brigand Macpherson had been wrongfully hanged all those many years ago. The invitations had been sent out, and most had been replied to, though there was as yet no response from Lord Gordon, a matter of some little regret to the Provost, though he was expecting a message from the stately home soon. The shopkeepers and the lairds and the gentleman farmers, in short the voting public of Aberlevin, or more accurately those whose opinions mattered most to the Provost, had already agreed to be present, and there was also to be what the Provost described as an orchestra to provide the music for the occasion, and there would be a dance after the meal, and then, the reason for the whole affair: the first chimes of the village clock in one hundred years, signalling midnight, the beginning of the first hour of a day which, a century before, had seen the brigand, Macpherson's honoured ancestor, hanged for a crime that was worthy of pardon, wrongfully executed by a council past. The Provost Macpherson was animated by the joy of anticipation as he described the occasion to Watchie. The loon had never seen so much energy in the man before, his arms were all a-flail as if they were mill sails in a good breeze, his eyes were full of the juice of life and bulged from their sockets like ripe fruits; he held his arms open wide to encompass the tables and the spread he saw in front of him, inviting Watchie into the embrace of his vision, but Watchie shrank away from it, for now he had many people to disappoint by indulging his infirmity, or so he saw it for the moment, carried along by the vast tides of Macpherson's enthusiasm. He saw another picture, in darker hues than the Provost's, long and unremitting labour, the clock unready for the hour of midnight as he struggled the last of the wheels into place, too late, just too late. But there was no way of stopping the little shoemaker, and Macpherson finished and settled himself on the stool, his hands and arms ceasing at last to become expressive instruments and returning to their previous purpose, that of shoring his posture; now he sat solidly on the stool like a carved statue of himself such as he might have imagined would grace the village square, the Provost in his most characteristic pose, resolute and determined, and finally he said,

Weel noo, Master Leckie, I'll ask ye; d'ye think ye'd be weel eneuch tae be fexin the clock for yon date, and yon denner? For gin ye'll nae, ye'd be as weel tae say the noo, and I'll send for anither tae dee it, that nor I'll hae tae write tae the fowk I've invitet, tae taal them they canna cam efter a'.

Poor Watchie, without the sense or the will to contest so able an opponent as could charm the votes from even those who considered him a chiel, manoeuvred around the wide hills of Macpherson's argument like a sheep fleeing from the dog, and he had nothing to say to Macpherson other than what the little man wanted to hear,

Ye'll see yer clock fexed, Mr Macpherson, and ye'll hear it ringin for yer midnicht, and yon's my promise on it.

Politeness demanded that Macpherson stay to talk of other things than the clock, but Watchie heard none of them. The rest of the Provost's time in the bedroom was spent by the loon thinking of the task ahead of him, the promise made, and wondering how he was to live up to the words which had been so easy to say. He had not tested his back for two days, and while he was prepared to trust the word of the doctor that he had to rest for a week, he knew also that it was now imperative that he should be ready at the end of that week for the task ahead of him, and now time was against him in this. The Provost stood at the end of his visit, left the stool where it was, and said,

Richt pleased I am tae see that yer injury's nae affa serious, Master Leckie, and I'll be seein ye afore ye gang back tae yer werk, tae see that a's weel wi ye,

and then he said goodbye, and left Watchie to listen to the caution of his footsteps down the stairs, as hesitant as a drunken man, while Watchie rubbed his lower back with his hand; and still tender it was, how much it annoyed Watchie to be at the mercy of the healing processes of his own body, how frustrating that he could not will himself better. Perversely enough, rather than blaming the Provost for the demands placed upon him, he began to blame himself for not being able to bear the weight of a wheel, a weak man he must be to fall so easily under it, how unworthy such a man must be, though of what he could not say.

Wullie met the Provost as he came into the kitchen, for he had just returned from his deliveries, and was removing his apron to hook it on the lattice along with his jacket. The provost placed his cup on the kitchen table, and greeted Wullie with a broad smile and an air of hail fellow well met; Wullie for his part replied to the smile, shallowly, and asked him how he had found Watchie. The provost laughed,

Aye, Wullie Leckie, yer son's a guid wee hard werker, ye ken thon yersel, canna wait tae be gangin awa tae fex his clock, man, jist canna wait, it'll tak mair tae haud him awa frae his werk than a sair back,

and Wullie passed over to the hanger lattice and pegged his apron there, nodded, said,

Aye, weel, Mr Macpherson, the doctor's tellt him he'll hae tae wait jist, anither week, and I widna jist say ither than thon mysel.

Macpherson nodded, emphatically, in complete agreement,

Aye, Wullie, fine dee I understand, and I widna say ither mysel neether, I widna hae him dee ony werk on the clock gin he's nae weel tae dee it.

Wullie looked the provost up and down for a moment, and decided that there was more to this visit than just to wish his son well. He held much the same opinion as his father on the subject of the Provost Macpherson, that here was a slippery wee man of dubious trustworthiness, and being a man of certain qualifying means he was entitled to vote in the election of a Provost, and in his own consideration it was not right that neither his workers nor his wife had the franchise, after all they had opinions as well as himself and therefore the right to express them by the means of the ballot. Wullie was a quiet Liberal, and this, in part, explained the antipathy he felt for the known Tory Macpherson, for the Provost had been loud in his decrying of this new custom of national insurance, fit way, the Provost had been heard to say, should a guid hard-werkin mannie hae tae leck Lloyd George's stamps for him, fan he taks fine care o' his werkers the noo? And this had infuriated Wullie, that a man who employed no workers himself should deny those employed by the unscrupulous the right to have their health taken care of.

Wullie stood opposite the Provost as he thanked Jeannie for her tea, and squared himself before the little man. He said,

A meenit o' yer time, Provost, afore ye lee my fairm.

The Provost touched his fob pocket, though he did not withdraw the silver watch nested inside it.

A meenit ye hae, Wullie Leckie, for I'm an affa busy man, my shoppie's a' locked in the toun.

Wid I be richt tae say that Waatchie's back wis pit oot file he wis werkin on the clockie, the noo?

Macpherson nodded,

Aye, Wullie, yon'd be richt.

Wullie nodded, in time with the Provost.

And yon wis durin the cooncil's time, wis it nae? His back wis pit oot file he wis werkin for the cooncil, am I richt?

Macpherson saw the walls of Wullie's labyrinth being raised around him where he stood, and so with one bound he threw himself clear while he was still able.

Mr Leckie, he said, I'm affa sorry the loon's hurt file he wis deein the werk the cooncil askt o' him. I dinna ken fit else ye'd hear frae me, ither than he's bein weel peyed for the time he spends werkin on the clock.

Wullie shook his head.

I dinna mind ye sayin that ye'd be giein him ony National Insurance, Mr Macpherson, nor dee I mind on Waatchie sayin sic a thing himsel. Wid ye taal me the noo gin ye'll be giein the doctor peyment for fit he's done for Waatchie?

The two men were rams cast into battle, clashing brows, and Macpherson's eyes were now dull steel, how different from when he was telling Watchie of his memorial dinner. He said,

Mr Leckie, yon wisna pairt o' oor wee arrangement, oor contract o' werds. I wisna tae ken that Master Leckie's werk wid be done in sic a way that he'd dee himsel ill. Noo, I'd sooner ye'd lee me gang by, for I've my shoppie tae open, and I've the business o' the cooncil tae dee efter thon.

Wullie stood, powerless and angered. He went to the table, and picked from it the cup which Macpherson had left there, and simply pressed it into the little man's hand, and said,

Wid ye tak yon cuppie wi ye fan ye gang awa, Mr Macpherson, for I doot nor a'body'll be efter drinkin frae it fan they ken fa had a drink frae it afore them.

Macpherson stared at Wullie for a moment, and Wullie had the satisfaction of seeing that Macpherson's fury at this gesture was at least equal to his own. The little man took the cup with him, as if too shocked to release it, and it stuck to him as if glued to his hand, until he was able to let it go against the bark of an elm tree which grew on a grove some halfway towards the village, a downhill road which led his bicycle faster along, and he heard the fracturing of the china behind him, the music of its splintering, though there was little satisfaction in the sound of it.

But Macpherson's visit had something of the desired effect, for when Kirsty came to see Watchie, she found him much more fretful, and eager to be up on his feet, the very thing that everyone with his welfare at heart was counselling against. He told her what the Provost had told him earlier, and he seemed to be fidgeting about the bed, this she noticed, that he could not keep still for a moment, his feet drummed under the blankets and rippled through the bedding, and she laid a hand upon his arm to stop him, and felt the tremors through her own body; not the tremor of fear, but impatience pure and simple. Kirsty shook her head as Watchie told her that he must be up, and soon, and strong enough to resume his work, for she had no reply to him, and silently she damned the provost for whom she had never voted; sleekit and clever she had heard him to be, and she wondered how long the Provost had known of this occasion, and why he had chosen the now to declare it to Watchie, though well she knew the answer, and in herself she damned his cleverness, for there would be no talking to Watchie now, she could see the determination in Watchie's eyes, fear of the kind which had caused him to work too hard. She wanted to be furious with Watchie at this weakness of his, that he should be so easily influenced by one so cunning as the provost, that he should be so transparent as to be manipulated across the board of the Provost's intentions as easily as a draughts piece, that his main strength, his will to hard work, should be turned around and made into a weapon for the Provost, but she found that she could not remain angry with him for it. It spoke much for his determination that he should not be defeated by the frailty of his own body, and this she found admirable in its own way, for she had seen her own father's determination drained away after the death of her mother to irrigate the wants of fools, and how angered she had been to see it.

Can ye nae see, Kersty, said Watchie to her, there'll be fowk ready for the clock tae strike, thon I didna ken afore, I'll hae tae mak it ready for them, and for mysel, for I widna hae a'body sayin that the clock wisna ready in time,

and then she knew that all hope of persuasion was lost, she looked into his eyes, she mined the seams from them which glittered with their own hopes among the dross of the fears, and she thought back to the time when she had first taken courage to look into them, the evening that Watchie announced that he would not be coming back to the croft. It had been an act of great faith for her, for she had ill been able to trust the eyes of strangers, not since the eyes of her own father had first become those of a stranger years ago, made strange to her by the drink. In truth, she knew that Watchie was all that her father had not been after her mother had died; he was not a drinker, he was not flamboyant with his words or his deeds, he was not moved to pick her up in his arms and swirl her around as Geordie had done, but nor was the drink his fuel for a great and uncontrollable engine of grief and joy and intolerable rage, and she sensed there was a skin like the hide on a drum over all the tumult of his passions, and much more did she prefer this to her father's perpetually open box of a heart. Kirsty looked in the eyes of Watchie for any sign that he was prone to the same desires as her father, the same appetite for the milk of the barley, the same bundled passions waiting for their expression, and to be sure, yes, there were the passions of one who could be moved to tears, but his hands were firmly on the tiller of them, and she had often enough heard him say that na na, I'll nae be gangin the same way as my grandfaither, and he laughed as he said so, not without affection, but well enough was it known about the village that Aal Wullie was a frequenter of the alehouse and a carouser with the best of them, despite his advancing years. She was as good a reader of eyes as anyone else, for a lifetime's avoidance of the eyes of others, held within her quiet devotion to her mother's house, had made her especially sensitive to the way that eyes spoke without words, and as little as she knew of the language of the written word, she knew much much more about the silent language of intention as expressed by the capturing of a gaze.

So now, she saw in Watchie strengths kept from normal sight, and no will to destruction, though there was a will to test and prove, to place in hazard, which could be calmed by the right influence. She saw doubt over the Provost Macpherson's latest imposition, natural enough, she considered, given the sleekit way it was lowered upon him. She read him by his eyes, and even his inability to sustain a gaze for long, looking aside to the marbled cover of his book which rested on the other side of the bed, she saw as significant, though she had no idea why as yet, but that would come, too, another secret she would divine.

All the advice he had been given, he ignored; and so on the third day Watchie threw aside the bedclothes, when no one was around, and pivoted himself until his feet reached to the floor, and then tried to stand. To his surprise, he found it very comfortable, there was no pain at all, even when he slowly drew himself upright, but there was tension around his lower back, nothing agonizing, and the strapping seemed to be holding him together, as if he had been broken in two and wrapped in binding until the glue had the chance to dry properly. He experimented with a walk around the room, in the clearing around the bed, and found that he could manage, though without much speed, and with a slight stoop; he was definitely getting better, in his own judgement, and he ambled towards the window and looked outside, to the Cornhill Road, to the silver birch and its greenery, to the cobbled road and the dry stane dyke beyond it, another farmer's land, the corn rising like his father's, still green and unripe. The farm beyond the dyke belonged to Malcolm Carltoun, and Watchie could see the scurrying and striving of the workers over the distance, and he thought he could even pick out farmer Carltoun himself, his dour and unneighbourly presence, his empty and purposeful stride. On Carltoun's land was a tree, a birch like the one which Wullie let grow in front of the house, and Wullie had often remarked on what a strange thing it was that such a determined man as Carltoun left it leave to grow, but for one thing; it was a lightning tree, severed by a knife of lightning some years ago, whittled down to the naked wood by a single strike, too saturated by rain to catch fire from it, and for those many years the stricken branch had held by a strap of bark, refusing to leave go. Perhaps it was superstition which made Carltoun leave it rooted where it was, and now Watchie felt a curious sympathy with that tree, brought low by the action of contingency, and on looking upon it he felt an old man's twinge in his back as it began to punish him for seeking to rush the processes of healing; but he ambled around the room a few more times until the pain died, and he could hold himself upright once again, and then he dressed himself as quickly as he could before anyone could come to the room to stop him, and then took to the stairs, one at a time, down and into the kitchen, where Jeannie was subjecting the range to a vigorous cleaning at the sink. The water was ink black with the collected soot and she could have written a ballad on paper with her finger; her arms were deep in it. She turned to see who was at the door, and saw that it was Watchie, and in a moment she dropped the grate pan she was cleaning, and said,

Wulliam, ye're nae tae be up yit, the doctor said so! Awa
back tae yer bed, and I'll tak ye a cuppie o' tea, dinna be sae
daft . . .

but Watchie shook his head, he was not to be ordered so
easily with so little time before the completion of his clock, and
he said,

Na na, it's a' richt, weel I'm able for walkin aboot.

Accepting his word was not easy for Jeannie, for still she
thought she had all the authority of parenthood at her command,
the rights conferred to her by a lifetime of concern for his
welfare, and she raised her voice to urgency,

Wulliam Leckie, I'm sayin tae ye the noo, ye're tae gang
back tae yer bed, and I'll nae hae ony arguin aboot it,

the black water dripping from the ends of her fingers and
shattering on the floor; she looked down and thought she
would have to clean that up later, then stared at her son as he
stood at the frame of the door, a portrait of determination if
ever there was one. His eyes were not sullen or unkindly but
there was a stubbornness that she had always known to be there.
He drew himself to his full height as dictated by the pain that it
was causing him, and said,

I'll hae tae be takkin tae my werk, and I'll hae tae be able for
it.

The next two minutes Jeannie spent in a protracted scolding,
to which Watchie was the sole and intended audience; she called
him a fool, and told him what would happen as if she had the
power to call from crystal the certain images of the future, that
his back would break under the strain of more work, that he
would be nursed for all the rest of his days and he would never
walk again, that he would have to be carried from his bed to
the kitchen table for his dinners and all because he would not
listen to her, all this while scouring the grate pan of the range
back to a fine polish under the opaque water in the sink, and
while she was not looking Watchie allowed himself a slight
smile at her apocalyptic concern for him, and all the imagined
consequences which she predicted would follow if he ignored
her advice; but his face was perfectly serious whenever she

turned to look, and he thought her very much like Kirsty in her expression of this concern, in the way that she was roused to fury when he presented the contrary argument, and he wondered at the relationship between their intense angers, for on his mother's part he knew that it was her love for him that stoked such a fire as burned constantly in her own hearth, and this set him to thinking, and hoping, that perhaps this was what made Kirsty so vehement, though he could never be certain, and if there was one thing that was his guide and rule through life, it was that undertakings should not be considered until you were absolutely certain, for in that way you avoided causing greater damage than you were meant to be fixing; and so in the love of his mother he saw no correlation to his friendship with the daughter of Geordie O'Donnell, though he knew that he could expect to receive the same at her hands.

How true this was; for the first sight that Kirsty O'Donnell saw upon entering the kitchen, apart from the even face of Jeannie as she opened the door to the cwean, was Watchie Leckie sitting on a kitchen chair and he was laughing in much the same way as she remembered from the tower, a careless and slightly defiant laugh to see her astonished face, the unbelieving gape of her mouth, and she exclaimed,

Wulliam Leckie, fit're ye deein oot o' yer bed the noo?

to which Watchie shrugged and said,

I canna be deein wi lyin on my back a' day lang, Kersty, and my back's nae sae sair the noo.

There was a strange alliance at that moment between mother and son, for Jeannie's prickles rose like a hedgehog's at the presumption of this stranger to the family, coming in indeed and daring to talk to her son like that, so that no matter how much Jeannie found herself in agreement with the cwean, and it surprised her just how much she was in agreement, it was the blood that spoke as she said, coolly,

Wulliam says tae me he's better, and I canna say ither than yon mysel.

Kirsty lapsed into silence, for this was not her house. She

allowed herself the little insolence of a frown, being unable to voice her disapproval in the way she would have preferred, and suggested to Watchie that they should go to the living-room rather than interrupt Jeannie at her cleaning, which was evidently a time-consuming task. She was aware of Jeannie's eyes on her until they were out in the hall; and it was a relief when the door closed upon them, and she helped Watchie to settle himself in the armchair beside the fire, which he protested that he was quite able to do himself, though he landed with enough force to dislodge the dust from the cushion underneath him, a mist which rose and which she found at the back of her throat as she sat in the chair opposite, causing her to cough drily, away from Watchie, as was only manners.

For a long time they stared at each other, and this discommoded Watchie, uncertain as to what Kirsty was thinking. He tried smiling at her, but she was having none of it; her brow remained steady, and he remembered such a look before, from his mother, a look which told him that he had committed some unimaginable wrong, and so he broke and looked to the fire, to the mystery of flame, more fathomable than any speculation he might have advanced upon the thoughts of another. Kirsty finally took in a breath, and said,

Ye're a man fa kens his mind, Wulliam Leckie, and yon's the truth. Ye winna heed ony werds a'body'll say tae ye, and ye'll jist be hurt the mair for it.

Watchie had no reply for this. He looked back to her, and saw that her look was not unaffectionate; he said,

There's nae ony ither thing tae dee, Kersty. I'll hae tae fex the clock. I gied my werd on it, and yon's the werd I'll heed.

Kirsty had expected no other reply, and she nodded slowly, though not with agreement.

Ye'll nae dee't on yer ain, fine d'ye ken.

Watchie was silent. With anyone else on earth, he would have argued the point, that he was as fit as anybody, of course he was capable, he was young and strong and would not be brought low a second time by an insensate mechanism; but this was Kirsty, who had seen him hurt by his own stubbornness and had not been convinced by his laughter, who had wrapped him in her cloak and had run for help when he had not been able. Her eyes said as much, that she was not going to listen to him no matter how much he protested; they hunted him no matter where he ran to ground, no matter what earths he might find to shelter in, and he admitted silent defeat before her, there was nothing he could say that she would accept, and so he sat as limp as the strapping would allow him, resting his head in his hands. When he next looked up, Kirsty was leaning forward in her seat, and her eyes were this time searching for a connection to his own, which he granted to her, and she said, in a low voice,

I dinna ken fit way ye pit thegither a clock, ye ken that. But I'm as strang as a'body, and gin there's a'body there fa dis ken fit tae dee, I can pu' on a rope as weel as ony man. I'd dee thon, for I'll nae see ye hurt yersel ony mair for yon affa mannie Macpherson, and I'll dee't for fite'er peyment ye see fit tae gie me for it.

Watchie had his mouth open to say no the moment she suggested it; but the flame from the hearth was reflected in the blacks of her eyes, and he thought briefly that it was a fire which they contained within their own dark hearths, burning of their own accord and within a slender corona of ice green as if to melt it. He had no argument to serve back to her against her sudden offer. He looked into the source of the fire in her eyes, burning in the grate; and while all his instincts cried against it, he pursed his lips and held his hands together, having few choices, with his back playing hell with him at that moment, a reminder that he was no longer able for it himself.

XXXIV

Kirsty had no need to worry for her croft in her absence, for
Mhairi proved to be every bit as capable as herself in running
the business of the hearth, as young as she was; she knew well
enough how to cook a fine meal, having helped her sister and
seen her do it often enough, and also having seen her mother at
it, too, and she threw herself into the task with a determination.
She was ruthless with a duster, and she too punished the
clothing for having the temerity to contain as much dirt as it
did, and though she had no songs to sing during the job in
hand, her attack was every bit as fierce as Kirsty's, showing a
fine hatred for muck and disorder.

In fact, on the crisp and sunny afternoon of the stranger's
arrival, Mhairi was outside the croft washing the clothing in the
tin bath while Kirsty was away at the tower, and she was
thrashing the silver out of her father's work clothing, that is to
say the curls and shavings of his trade, the slivers pared away
from a tin patch carved to fit an ailing bath or a kettle. Mhairi
remembered that he used to tell herself and her sister that they
were shavings from the moon; where d'you think yer owl man
goes while the two of ye're asleep, me darlins? O, an awful load
o' fixin the moon needs, and I'm just the boy to do it, me and
me tin; but Ailsa was there to scowl at her husband, not a single
lie would she bide with even if it were nothing more than a
story-book fancy, enough of them she had heard in her time
without the children's eyes becoming broad caverns of absolute
belief in their father, and Mhairi remembered her mother's
hand on her shoulder, the other on Kirsty's, a roof across them
both, how soft were the hands, forgiving them for the gullibility
of their age. Mhairi remembered that at the time her father's
stories made her shine like the tin plate of his repairs, privileged
to hear him tell his tales to her; and then she remembered the

day that his story-book became nothing more than a repeated list of excuses for not doing his tinkering in the workshop, uttered so that the air itself might give them belief and substance, and there was no Ailsa to hold his horses of fable, to pull on the reins of them and draw them into their stable, there was only herself and Kirsty. The days of Geordie's dissolution were gone, however, and now Mhairi pounded the shavings of the moon from her father's work clothing, and not once did she see that she was as much her father's daughter as Kirsty was her mother's, that it was the same will to fabrication which made her wrap herself in her sister's airs which had led Geordie to paint the picture in their heads of himself as the moon's own trusted tinker, and no illusions now did the sparkle in the dirtied water rouse within her, even as she saw her sister's serious face reflected in the mirror of the water.

Not only were there her father's garments to wash in the open, but the week's soiled garments of the house, her own and Kirsty's, and grateful she was that her father was away on his touting and delivering, for this was a lesson that Mhairi had taken from her sister, that it was a matter of personal dignity that there should be not the slightest of a blush of their monthly flow on the cotton to reveal to any man, not even the man who was their father. Mhairi was more than especially conscientious in her examination of their clothing as she drew it time and again over the corrugated washboard; and this was how the stranger was able to approach her so closely without her remarking on the whisper of his feet among the grass, or hearing any other sign of a footfall. One minute and he was a shape on the Cornhill Road, nothing more than that, certainly not a thing to pay close mind to any more than a rabbit in the field; and then there was a cold radiance which caused a shiver to pass through Mhairi's frame, a sudden chill like the occlusion of the sun, and then she thought to look up to the presence she had sensed before she had seen, the whole substance of him appearing to be nothing but shadow, an utter absence of light which caused her to start, to draw her wet hands from the water and place them over her heart in an attempt to suppress its headlong leap.

For some curious reason, perhaps pressing the shape of her dearest and wildest hopes into the unfocused clay of the figure before her, Mhairi's first thought was that she was looking at Watchie Leckie just on the frontiers of the vegetable plot nearest to the door of the croft, returned from his work on the village square clock without her sister by his side, and Mhairi had even considered in her uncertain moment what accident or anger had parted the two of them before she understood that the man was too tall to be Watchie, too far up for her eyes to travel from the bright and hard glitter of the boots, footwear, she realized, more appropriate as protection against a fall of hooves or the runaway blade of a plough. His trousers had the gloss of long wear about them, as indeed had the weskit and jacket of dark wool, and it was as if he were wearing garments fashioned from tar, over a lean frame of sticks and kindling, contriving to appear at one and the same time shabby and dignified, at once deserving of pity and worthy of respect, and carrying a sack of hessian in his fist, his only luggage.

The eyes of the stranger, Mhairi knew from her first look at them, were wide and tired by long experience, and yet vibrantly like those of a loon, frozen around his youth. The age of him was not written in lines upon his face, and so Mhairi squinted at him to make a judgement for herself and decided that if he were a day old, then he should at least be thirty years, though he could have been less, for the face was not quite as weathered as Mhairi would have expected from one with labourer's boots such as she had seen at the beginning of her eyes' journey, and he could have been more, for the longer she peered into the blacks of his pupils, the further she seemed to tumble into an opaque depth which drew her in as certainly as gravity, catching glances and glimpses of darker shapes the longer she fell. It was only through an immense effort and all the discipline that she was able to gather together that she managed to reverse the pull of him and come to her senses, enough to see that the stranger was now smiling at her, a smile to which she responded as openly as she could, and it was with great relief that she understood that he was a man with a capacity to smile, a thin and watered bowing of the lips. But as her sister was with eyes, so was Mhairi with smiles, she could read to you the print on the label of any stranger who smiled at her, man nor woman both, it made no difference to Mhairi, as clear as any beacon it was to her, she could tell you if any smile were grudged or effortless, brimming full of kindness or as empty and meaningless as the expression on the face of a plaster bust; and between her sister's knowledge of the tongue of sight, and her own understanding of the unsaid words of the mouth, the two of them had the measuring of any stranger who came to stop at the croft, and there was a thing about the smile of this stranger which caused Mhairi to raise her guard as suddenly as a sentry at the drawbridge. It was as if she had no more dimension before him than a painting of herself, somehow emblematic, as if only through his sight, his continual understanding and appreciation of her presence, would her existence be made valid; as if the very breath which raced through her body had the stranger as its cause, the action of his hands pressing upon a bellows. With a sudden shock, Mhairi realized that her time of the month clothes were there on the table, to the fore of the pile on one side of the tin basin waiting for her attention, and if they were not for the sight of her father then they were certainly not to be seen by a man unknown to her, and quickly, she hoped unseen by the stranger, she fetched a dress over to hide the bloomers and the faint seeping of a stain which had touched the petticoats, and frowned openly at him, daring him to make remark if he had laid his prying eyes upon them before she had seen him standing there. The smile remained constant, an ambiguous smile with two sharp edges to it; perhaps he had seen the soiled garments and was simply amused by her unease, perhaps nothing at all had he seen, but the edges could have drawn a line on the pad of her thumb no matter which way the blade was turned, and still she felt as if he had placed her in the limelight of his present scrutiny, to make her a small and more shameful thing before his sight. The stranger cleared his throat just then, and held out before him in his free hand an envelope, on which Mhairi could see a name, Mr George O'Donnell Esq., and an address, both of which she recognized as a brand carried by all the messages received at the croft; and she was about to demand the business of the stranger, as was only fair, she considered, after nearly causing her to take flight like a corbie at the barking of a gun, when he spoke to her himself,

Yirsel'll be Mhairi O'Donnell, will ye nae?

Profoundly unsettled she was, that he should have a label to fasten around her arm before she herself had the naming of him, as if she were a chair in an auction, that there was no accord between her purest response of the moment and the fury which rose along with her lighter relief, that there appeared to be no harm to him, and she said in reply,

I'll ken mysel fit way ye can taal my name tae me, aye, and I'll ken fit way ye couldna mak mair honest noise aboot camin tae the hoose, nor I'll ca' my faither frae the shed far aboots he's werkin, my bonnie loon, and fit d'ye think o' thon?

The man's eyes widened at her bluster, but there was no fear in him, a simple curiosity as if she were a farmer's mousing cat striking out pettishly with claws no more threatening than barbs, and said,

Can ye nae read the letter, my cweanie? Yer faither tis I'm efter. Ca' him frae his shed the noo, gin yon's far aboots he'll be.

Never once did his eyes waver upon her, and now his smile showed a serration of teeth as Mhairi looked from him to the shed, and knew that surely this stranger had more knowledge of her father than one with no rightful business with him should have been entitled to possess; a small comfort to her, and yet she heard the murmuring of her worst fears, that this knowledge may have been gathered for no innocent purpose, and she wondered for an irrational moment if there were anyone about the village who had nurtured a long resentment from the days of Geordie's drunkenness, someone her father might have offended without a thought in his head when out with Johnnie Deans and his cronies in the alehouse. But the shame leapt to her face just then as she realized that he had seen through her untruth, and she said,

Gin ye ken as muckle as tae taal me my ain name, sir, ye'll ken that my faither's oot on his roon's a' efterneen, and winna be back for oors yit.

That, she had hoped, would have been enough to have the loon shaking his head, damnable that he had missed the gentleman of the house, sending him on his way and cursing his luck which had surely been touched by the devil himself, so far for no glimpse of the man he had come to see. The stranger shook his head, but Mhairi felt her heart drop in her chest to see him put his sack gently on to the ground between his feet, and then spring upright like a jack-in-the-box, planted squarely on the spot and with no intention of moving from it, posting the letter into his pocket while he was standing there,

Jist, I widna weesh tae disappoint Meester Macandlish gin I were tae taal him Geordie O'Donnell wisna here tae read the letter I've here for him; yer faither kens Meester Macandlish affa weel, does he nae?

For a terrible moment, Mhairi took careful stock of the stranger, because the thought occurred to her that if her father was receiving a letter from Macandlish, the original owner of the land upon which their croft stood, then it was bound to contain nothing of any comfort to them. She looked again at the man before her, to see how likely it was that he would be the messenger for Macandlish's sudden reversal of his whim of many years ago, his act of unthinking charity, which perhaps in his dotage he had now come to consider as an untenable indulgence, a home for a tinker family which was at least able to grow grass for the feeding of sheep or cattle. Mhairi knew, as well as anyone in this part of the world, that those who laid claim to the land had never thought twice when the husbanding of sheep or cattle was put into the opposite pan of the balance from the housing of poor tenant farmers, for there was an unseen weight of silver behind every creature under consideration to rig the scales against those who ploughed and reaped the soil for the bounty it returned, and this was never far away from the thoughts of any laird alive, nor was it indeed far from the thoughts of every farmer in tenancy. She thought of her father once again purposeless and drifting at a sudden eviction, out they might go to house the sheep or the kye, and then how would she and her sister ever stop him from going back to the bottle, his false friend in trying days? Once again, the more she gave it thought, the more she studied the man in front of her, the total of him, a little meat evident on the bones, taller he was than many, including perhaps Watchie; and there was an expression about the face that she could not quite understand, as if he had never had a taste of sweetness or joy in the whole of his life, regarding her with as much indifference as if she were little more to him than a monkey capering on a barrel organ, and now it was anger which pressed from the mire of her confusion, ready she was to take him down to a size she could pocket, when suddenly the man leaned forward and across the table, placing one hand flat before the fankled clothing to hold himself from her at a closeness she could hardly bear, and in a calm and even voice said,

Ye ken, my cwean, I'll hae tae wait for yer faither; and waitin's aye mair pleasant wi a cuppie o' tea, d'ye nae think yersel?

and then Mhairi had no more resistance to offer to him, not when he was as close as she could almost feel the heat of his breath, grateful she was to turn from him and find a reason for entering the house, wiping her hands on her apron as she went and leaving behind her the water in its basin with its blood and tinsel, a mirror of the sky into which, she saw from the hearth through the open door, the stranger peered as if there were something more profound in the depth of it than simply the reflection of his own face.

He came in to accept the enamel mug of tea that Mhairi had made, sitting at the table and placing the sack on the floor by his feet, and he drank slowly and appreciatively, with all the more enjoyment for the gift offered with a grudge, as if the grudge itself gave his tea its sweetness. Mhairi busied herself at the table in front of him, she would not allow the settled routine of the household to be thrown out of its symmetry by the presence of this chiel, of that much she was determined; and with a bone-handled knife she began to draw parings from the potatoes for the evening's dinner, long, unbroken spirals of the skin taken from stem to stern, for this had been her help to Kirsty through her years of assistance, she could peel down to the flesh as cleanly as you please and leave the hide of it to fall away like a coiled spring, and then with two neat slices at right angles quarter the potato ready for boiling, no harm would it do, she considered while working, for this interloping loon to see that she was perfectly able to handle a knife with a delicate touch, especially when she thought of how little she knew of him. Occasionally she cast a glance to him, to see where it was that his gaze had settled, for this she remembered about Watchie with some affection, that he had looked around himself as rapidly and as nervously as a sparrow, as if he had never seen a place the like of it, and this she found to be an admirable and trustworthy uncertainty the watchmaker had about himself, that he had the good grace to be deferential within the walls of another's house, respectful of the rhythms to which they ate their meals and took their tea and sat in the sheltered and rested silence after the washing of the dishes, determining where best he might fit in the mechanism which caused the house to run from day to day; but not so this stranger, imposing himself on the house without annunciation or welcome, not one gesture of humility from him, no proper respect in the way that he carried his shoulders, tall and proud he was when all the rules of propriety demanded that you be hosted into a house and not carry yourself as if you were its owner, and after a while of swift touches with her eyes to see what the stranger was up to, Mhairi saw that he was looking over her shoulder, to the mantelshelf, and so she followed the string of his gaze to find that he was engrossed in the tin Christ hanging on the wooden crucifix. Mhairi returned to the last of her potatoes huddling in their ceramic bowl, skinning it as quickly as possible, warmed that he should regard the family ornament as worthy of his interest, and for a wee moment she wondered if she had been perhaps hasty in her judgement of the stranger, that anyone who held the cross of Our Lord in the slightest esteem was bound to be fair and decent themselves, no matter how bristling or arrogant they appeared, for there was always in their thoughts the memory of Christ's execution for the sins of the world to keep them from harming others; but then the stranger spoke for the first time, a low voice meant for his own ears, and he said,

Fine werk, yon on the mantel, for a bittie o' blasphemy, ye ken,

and the knife slid at an unintended angle and through the hinge of Mhairi's thumb as if it were still carving the flesh of the potato; holding her thumb clenched against her hand to staunch the flow, she declared,

Fit ilka man wid ca' the cross o' Oor Laird blasphemy, noo, meester I dinna ken fit's yer name?

The smile again, how complacently it came to him, to the eyes of Mhairi, stirring her as if she were broth in a cauldron, as deliberately provocative as a child with a fallen branch, raping an open hive of bees and having a fine laugh at the alarm and confusion he was causing among creatures for which he cared nothing, and into the cup he said,

Ah, noo, yer Cathlics, richt eneuch oor meenister was fan he said, yer Cathlic wid sooner hae a picture o' the Laird hingin in his hoose than read his Bible tae ken fit it wis he says tae dee. D'ye nae ken yer guid buik, Mhairi O'Donnell, thou shalt hae nae ither God but me, the verra werds he gied tae Moses, aye, and thou shalt nae wership graven idols, d'ye hear? Nae, graven, idols, and fit wid ye say yon crucifix wis but a wrangfu' image o' oor Laird; fit wid ye say, Mhairi O'Donnell, will ye taal me the noo?

The iron taste of her own blood was in the mouth of the cwean as she saw the eyes of the stranger light up with the fire of possession, and for a single instant Mhairi felt more wholly judged herself than ever she had before then, subject to the comprehension and justice of an altogether harsher God than the one to whom she prayed on her knees at the altar of her bedside night after night, and this was the mask which this pitiless God wore, the false face of his earthly disciple

388

contemptuous of all representations of piety, an austerity and a starkness which turned her bones to ice. But there was the pain of her self-inflicted wound of distraction to remind her of how much this stranger's presence was resented by her, no instrument of any god was he but a chiel who would insult the faith of another with his ill intentions, demanding an answer when the question itself had no meaning to it, and so she replied to him as she thought was his desert; no theologian was Mhairi but well she knew manners from damned presumption, and so she recovered herself and said,

I'll taal ye the noo, fite'er ye ca' yersel, that yon's yer last cuppie o' tea, and I'll thank ye gin ye'll mind yer ain faith in anither body's hoose, and lee us tae mind oors.

There was no time to be wasting with him, nor with the wound, now raw and bloodless. Mhairi picked the knife from the floor, and wiped the edge of it on her apron, and began to gather the other vegetables for her evening meal of stew, aware of this gaze of the stranger's that rendered her before him to a toy of clockwork, and try as she might to deceive herself, she was a clearly visible lamp of curiosity, wondering just what his business was with her father.

XXXV

Geordie O'Donnell was very near to his croft when the glorious smell of his daughter's cooking reached out to take him by the hand almost, and for a moment the thought came to him that Kirsty had cooked up another fine stew with which to feed her old da after a long and troublesome day before he remembered that there was no Kirsty in the house, and it was a rueful Geordie O'Donnell who opened the door to go in, why yesterday it seemed that Kirsty had been squalling like a hinge needing oiled for a dinner he could scarcely provide, and now his younger daughter it was who was readying the evening meal for him; and this brought him to a meditation on time, and how swiftly the clock was racing for them all. He entered the croft, with his own sack ringing with pots and pans and enamelled flagons, unmusical bells cast for a devil's appreciation, declaring,

A hungry man it is comin back to his house, darlin girl, and a fine smell it is that meets him,

and it was only after he closed the door behind him that he saw the shape of a man seated at the table, and Mhairi with her back set as squarely as a defending wall against everything behind her, stirring with a wooden spoon the cause of the delicious aroma, hooked above the fire in its cauldron, and there was something mean and driven about her attention to it, grateful she seemed to be for a distracting task, not even paying a mind to the arrival of her father. The man rose, the stool on which he had been sitting giving out such a screech as if it were a cat on whose tail he had trodden, and immediately took Geordie by his free hand, shaking it firmly in his first act of deference since his arrival, this of course unknown to Geordie, and a tall one he was, rearing up like a horse above the tinsmith although a starveling of a horse he seemed to be, and said,

Meester Geordie O'Donnell, I've heard affa muckle aboot yersel, and fine pleased I am tae mak yer acquaintance. A letter I hae for ye here, gin ye'll be sae kind as tae read it.

The hand which was not seizing Geordie's as if he were a man on the edge of a precipice reached into the stranger's pocket, and withdrew the envelope, holding it out for him. Geordie politely relaxed his grip, indicating his wish to be released, which the stranger obliged, and stooped to let his sack of tin land on the floor without any unholy clangour. He looked at the envelope, and after a moment took it from the stranger unwillingly, recognizing on the face of it a coiled and inflated hand he knew was the way that his name was written, though not at all did he recognize the style of the writing as being that of the name on the foot of his title deed until the stranger said,

Frae the laird Macandlish, ye ken,

and then he began to take an interest in the content, entertaining the same notion as had first occurred to Mhairi upon discovering the identity of the sender, that here at last was the laird come upon his senses after a faltering attempt at largesse, after all these years of forgetfulness. The stranger held the envelope out for what seemed to be a long time, until Geordie quite forgot himself, finally shaking his head and saying,

I wonder if ye'd be so kind as to read it out to me, for I'm quite hopeless without me readin glasses, so I am.

The stranger smiled, and for the first time Geordie saw the twisting at the join of his lips, a cruel and knowing smile it seemed to be, and said,

Mebbe yer dauchter'd read it oot for ye, gin she'd be sae kind hersel, jist sooner than hear it frae mysel, ye ken.

Mhairi started, and Geordie remembered that she had not turned to greet him in from his work, and still she would not turn, but began to agitate the stew more vigorously with the spoon, as if the fire were boiling herself along with her cooking. There appeared to be more to her silence and her hiding than had first met the eye of Geordie on entering the croft, and this caused the tinsmith to frown, straining almost to see what would not render itself obvious to his present eye, imagining what might have caused the man before him and his daughter to begin their introduction on the wrong foot. Perhaps, he thought to himself, it was nothing more than she was bristling like a hedgehog after being asked to read the letter when she knew she could not, and if that were so then a quiet word after dinner with his pipe in his mouth and a cup of tea in her hand might bring her calm, the man wasn't to know, darlin, he wasn't intendin to make ye feel stupid.

Perhaps ye'd rather read it yerself, sir, since ye know what's in it and we don't.

Sure enough, the letter began by calling to mind the favour that the laird had done Geordie those many years gone by, selling him a good sound bigging that had served him and his family well; and the stranger proved that he had some small talent as a mimic, for Geordie could hear in the voice the blustering cadence of the laird himself, the tone of it as rich as a glass of port, and he let out a low chuckling as he heard the very portrait of the laird before him in sound; holding the letter open by the top and end of the leaf and reading the message aloud, the stranger was like a town crier, and Geordie felt low and ignorant before this young man's confidence with parody; only one who could read from the page so easily would have the audacity to change his voice in such a way, but at the same time he felt a complicity with the loon, that both of them understood the dryness and the arrogance of the laird for what it was, and so he was better disposed towards the visitor as he read more of the laird's request to Geordie.

The laird wrote that the bearer of the letter had been taken into his employ in the position of gardener, with fine references from previous men and women of standing who had paid for his services, but with not the room in the laird's house to lodge him for the present; and this finally caused Mhairi to turn from her cauldron as the sound of it stank like rotten meat, holding her wooden spoon in a tight fist as if it were a weapon, dripping it was with the juices of the stew, and looking beyond the shoulder of the stranger to her father she said,

Aye, a bargain wi hooks thon laird gied ye!

which caused Geordie to say to her,

Not so hasty, now, Mhairi me own, leave the fella carry on while I'm fillin me pipe,

and this he did, from a leather pouch, his own mysterious envelope, taken from his pocket, wondering what would cause Mhairi to turn as suddenly as milk in a thunderstorm, unless it were the time that his old debauched father called holy week, the time of strife in their poor household when Geordie's mother was no more approachable than a slavering dog, or so it was told by Patrick O'Donnell, who never thought he made any contribution to her ill temper himself. But Mhairi seemed to have escaped the legacy of her old grandmother, never up nor down under normal circumstances, and so Geordie thought that she must have had a disagreement with the loon before his arrival, for this time it was the turn of the laird to furnish a proposition for Geordie O'Donnell, a proposition that Mhairi seemed feared her father would accept, and which the stranger read in the words of the laird while Geordie finished packing the bowl of his clay pipe, and went to harvest a flame from the depth of the fireplace with a wooden spill.

The proposition was that Macandlish would pay his new gardener an addition to his wage, to be paid directly to the household of Geordie O'Donnell, if he were to be provided with temporary lodging in some appropriate room of the premises, which it was understood by both the laird and the bearer of the letter would hardly be the crofting itself, and that this was acceptable for the duration of the more temperate summer months. Geordie suckled the stem of his pipe as Mhairi had her cut thumb before he had arrived, though perhaps with more of an air of deliberation about it, conducting the smoke the length of the stem and causing the tobacco to kindle under the flame of the spill, a small hearth in itself to warm Geordie's hand and sweeten his thoughts for him; but the smoke did not appear to be much to the stranger's liking, though not a word would he say about it while so much was still undecided, other than the unspoken messages of a telling lengthened gaze at the chimney of the pipe as it spun a clue to the ceiling, a single thread pulled from the skein of the burning tobacco.

In conclusion,

read the letter, and read the loon in his mockery of the laird,

I would ask this of you as a favour, for I would not dare to suggest that the release of my property should entitle me to any more than merely a sympathetic consideration of my request,

at which Geordie found himself smiling, for the silver already offered towards the board of the stranger had made him inclined towards the view that more profit was there to be made from a sympathetic consideration than from an unconsidered refusal, and the smoke began to issue from his pipe in thick, almost industrial columns, as if from a factory, as if the wealth and richness of it were enough to tell the tale of his thought. The letter ended pleasantly enough, trusting that everyone in the croft would be found in the best of health, and for a moment Geordie blazed like the fibre in his pipe, no respects had the laird Macandlish paid by the side of Ailsa's grave, for all that he made his polite inquiries, and how dare this man of property imagine that all favours were there for the buying, that his crumbs of copper would buy him a housing for this man whose only purpose was to keep the laird's wasteful, abundant grounds as pretty as a harlot. But Geordie knew as well as any that there was no real choice to be made. The croft would never again go to the devil as it had during Geordie's time of grievous uncertainty, when every sleep after the bottle had been an endless drink of death and nullity, a welcome extinguishing of awareness, and when the croft's many flaws had opened untended before him like running sores, this was a promise he made to Ailsa every night in his prayers before he took to a gentler rest; and so, as the stranger folded his letter and put it back into its envelope, and held it out to be taken again by the man of the household, Geordie O'Donnell said,

Mhairi, be so good as to be settin out another bowl of yer stew, will ye, darlin, for I'm sure that our lodger has a power of a hunger on him.

Mhairi was still facing her father, still holding the wooden

394

spoon like a club, a curious and unreasoning posture which threatened the house with a display of her temper if she were not to be heard like the children in the Victorian adage; but only partly seen she was by her father, half-hidden in the shadow of the tall man, her head barely reaching the shoulder of this strange gardener of Macandlish's, though the scowl she aimed at her father could be seen well enough by him, a scowl which, for all that she put the heat of her long stoked rage into it, was not one of Kirsty's, which could raise within Geordie fearsome memories of her mother's searing disapproval. Geordie was not to be troubled by this display from Mhairi, especially when a fair rent was to be delivered for the housing of this man, no matter how much of a tax he might draw upon Mhairi's patience, for the silver was surely more than enough to cover the deficit of harmony about the house.

Mhairi obeyed her father with the spirit of his law, setting before their stranger a shallow bowl of enamelled tin with a wide brim like an ornamental hat, and making her fine displeasure known to all in the croft by the briskness of her actions, and the way that the bowl spun in place on its edge, causing the spoon on the table to fly away from its irregular placing at a careless angle. The oil-lamps were lit to provide more light than the evening sun would consent to pay into the croft, and placed on the mantelshelf at either end, so that the tin Christ was loaned their fire and shone as if incandescent, as if the glory surrounding it were its own by right; and when the gardener took his seat, it was the seat beside that of Geordie O'Donnell, a presumption which kept the anger of Mhairi on as much of a slow boil as the stew at the hearth, for it kept him facing away from the crucifix that she had spent the later afternoon polishing with a linen rag while the chiel had been outside for a stretch of his legs, a waste of effort it seemed to her now. The stew was doled out as fairly and as generously as Mhairi could manage, the cauldron testing the soundness of the table's construction, so heavy with stew it was, and Mhairi burned with a determination that Macandlish's gardener should not feel himself able to declare that your Catholics gave lean measures of hospitality, even to those who made slight of their faith, and so heaped his plate in spite of her guilty, private wish that a string of mutton might catch in his throat. She gave herself the last measure, and placed her cauldron on the stone ledge beside the hearth, sitting at the table opposite her father, making a point of arriving at her seat around his side; and Geordie smiled at her, tilting his head the way that she remembered from when she was a cwean, whenever she came crying into the house after a fall, promising his understanding, casting no judgement on her, and this made her smile briefly for him, quickly showing that she was able, before she stamped the last guttering of the match out and looked fully at the gardener with a deliberate want of expression, to her surprise noting a gentle satisfaction on his face, as if he had already finished the meal she had made. Geordie asked that Mhairi should lead the table in a grace before their evening's dinner, and she nodded, pleased to do so, lacing her hands together in front of her and dropping her head devoutly so that she might focus her attention on the prayer, so that it might be felt and meant and known to be so all the way to the highest vaults of heaven; and then, suddenly, there was a movement from the gardener, which Mhairi saw only as a darkness passing across the dulled screens of her closed eyelids, causing her to open them quickly to see what had happened. The gardener was holding up his hand, palm out as if to whoa a horse unsettled and ready for bolting, and he said,

Meester O'Donnell, I'm sair sorry, I canna lee yer grace tae gang ony ferther, ye ken, for I'm nae jist o' yer ain communion, and I canna be bidin wi't gin I canna say it's richt.

Geordie looked at the man he had chosen to lodge, and saw into bleak, abysmal pupils, as deeply sunk as well holes, drawing from a certainty beyond the fallible power of humanity to question. For a moment, the croft was a tableau of astonishment, and Geordie felt the eyes of his daughter from his other side fair crackling with fury as if she were filled with lightning, but he would not be drawn into an argument when a compromise would be more to the advantage of them all; if he had learned anything from his time in the exercise of trade then it was this above any other, and he said, evenly,

Admirable, I'm sure, me boy, to be strong in yer own faith; but I'm thinkin too, are we not all praisin God in this room, for makin the food we're goin to eat, isn't he worth praisin for that? Or d'ye have yer own thoughts on the matter, would ye be one of these that aren't believin in God, now?

For a moment, there was a blaze about the man, as if he had been heated to a temperature which just invited combustion and no more, leaving the smoke to coil off him, promising fire if further provoked.

Mind far aboots ye pit yer feet, Meester O'Donnell, for I'll nae tak the name o' a derty atheist sae kindly. Na na, yon's nae fit way I'll nae hear yer grace, sir; ye gie yer thanks tae the Laird, like the feed was fa'in doon frae heaven like manna, and ye'd nae tae dee ony werk for it at a'. The fa' o' man, Meester O'Donnell, mind on it, for yon's fit way we've tae dee hard werk for oor livin, and a' for the vanity o' a cwean fa'd ken mair than was guid for man tae ken.

It was said to Geordie's face, but it brought the blood to Mhairi's, though she held her peace while her father thought about this.

Are you sayin God isn't deservin o' praise for makin the food here before us? For that's what it sounds like to these ears, my boy, though I'll do ye the favour o' listenin harder to what ye've to say.

The man took his spoon and gouged from the bowl a helping of meat and vegetables, which he ate quickly and before either Geordie or Mhairi understood what had been done; and then he said,

I'm nae sayin yon at a', Meester O'Donnell. I'm sayin God didna mak yon feed, in the boul afore ye the noo, yon was the werk o' man fa gied it tae ye, and yer ain werk was it that brocht it tae yer table, for gin ye dinna werk hard, there's nae eneuch prayer in creation'll gie a feed tae ye, and yon's the truth o't.

Geordie played with the head of the spoon among the stew,

and now it was a silent contest of temperaments, with only Geordie's companionable nature to serve him as armour against this loon, who almost seemed to know by instinct where the chinks and joins were in even the thickest hide. He said,

Ah, young man, young fellow, that's a terrible unforgiving thing ye've said there just the now, and I'll tell ye for why, sir; for the home of my childhood was the great city of Glasgow, and I lived among the poor, and every one of us a family of farmers, sir, who would've taken a living out of any land ye'd care to find, only no work was there and no land to be tilled. And work! By God, sir, ye'd've worked like the devil himself if there had been any to be found to be payin the grocer's with, for there's where ye'd find all the crops o' the day, young fellow, more than ye could afford.

The gardener's head was nodding,

Cities, aye, I've ne'er been tae a city afore, I'm pleaset tae say,

he said, quietly, before raiding another spoonful of stew and eating it. To see him flout their grace in such a way, feeding himself like the swine at his trough without the slightest of blessings, was more than Mhairi could stand, and as patient as she had considered herself to be in the presence of her father, she could no longer contain her rage as this least welcome of house guests once again treated the faith of those whose roof it was above him with no more thought nor care than as if it had been a feather, light and slender and driven by the winds. She said, loudly and boldly, with her eyes only on her father,

He widna hae oor Laird on the mantel he says tae me afore ye cam hame, and noo he winna hear oor grace; ye widna ken him for a Christian at a', faither.

She stabbed a glare towards the gardener, a long and pointed iron reddened by the coals of her anger, and waited for him to speak to the accusation; but instead he drew another spoon of her stew to his mouth and ate, with neither worry nor concern, and indeed appeared to be deriving a continuing strength from Mhairi's plain fury, driven like an engine by the outrage he provoked in her. Geordie frowned, and looked into his bowl, shaking his head sadly.

Our crucifix offends ye, now, is that so, sir?

The gardener by now was half finished the stew, and nodded,

Yon's nae the practice o' my kirk, Meester O'Donnell, tae be prayin tae a wee bit wid and tin fan the warld's nae tae yer likin; yon's fit we'd ca' papism aboot my kirk, and I'd sooner nae hae ony o't, gin it was my hoose.

Geordie O'Donnell heard the word papism from the stranger's mouth, the guileless chasm into which his daughter's stew had been disappearing without a blessing on its substance, and for the first time wondered what it was, what force on earth, he had agreed to give a harbouring to. Again he felt the charge of his daughter's eyes, the will she loaned him to be telling this stranger in no uncertain terms what bounds a guest should never cross lightly; but he was aware that he was in no position to do so after accepting the silver of the laird Macandlish, a tainted purse it had been and no mistake, and the constraint of it was like the circling bite of a collar, reminding the tethered dog of the post to which his leash is fixed, and the futility of an escape. The gardener laid his spoon into the bowl, and reached under the table, and when he straightened himself, it was with the square sack he had placed there as soon as he had arrived, and with a swift few strokes of his fingers released the knot in the twine which throttled the neck of it, unbinding the sack and casting the soiled string to one side, on to the table in front of Mhairi's bowl, much to her obvious distaste, where it squirmed as if living itself. He delved his hand inside the open sack and among the folded contents, and there was a curious air of the theatrical about his sudden movement; but he let drop the sack to the floor with hardly anything to show for it, and Mhairi and Geordie looked at each other, puzzled, until they saw that in the gardener's palm, where it rested as if it had been there all along, was a small book of moroccan leather, the material of the cover pebbled like the skin of a black reptile, and he lifted it before them so that they might better see it, as if the very appearance of it might serve to edify their heathen souls, the rood cross tooled upon its cover in leaf of gold, which he exposed to the oil-lamps so that it might burn itself like the stamp of fire upon it, a brand of truth to reveal as worthless and shabby the papist sculpting of the form of the Son of God, and he said,

Yon's my Bible, Meester O'Donnell, the buik o' the Laird himsel, gied tae me by my faither afore he ga'ed awa tae fecht and dee for the aal queen in India, far aboots broon mannies fa dinna believe in God are livin. They fa' doon on their knees tae pray tae statues o' weemen wi mair than twa airms, and men wi the heids o' beasts ye winna see ither than oot o' a cercus, an affa sicht for a Christian mannie tae be seein, fowk wershippin likenesses, jist like yer, fit d'ye ca' it, yer crucifix on the mantle. D'ye nae think, Meester O'Donnell, yon's nae richt guid for fowk fa'd ca' themsels followers o' Christ, tae be deein fit heathens dee?

Geordie O'Donnell knew the behaviour of tin as well as anyone alive, the strengths and the flaws of it, how malleable it was so that a plate of it might caress any gap that needed repairing in any vessel you might think of; he knew what it could bear for its thickness and what lay beyond its ability to endure. It was his whole expertise, and it was the great joy of his profession, that he had the knowledge which allowed him to make whole what had been parted by the action of wear and contingency, and more than anyone else on earth, he fancied, the conscientious tinsmith should give all rightful praise to God for the creation of imperfections and the tendency of all matter to split and be flawed, because in details such as this were entire livings to be made, and so he felt that his very livelihood was to be scavenged among the interstices of the great structure, and that God revealed his existence more purely to folk such as Geordie, who knew the ways of mending, understanding deep in his bones that misfortune for one was silver in the purse for another, that this was the purpose of accidents of matter, and not a proof of the intervention of devilish agencies that some chose to see in their inconveniences of the moment. If there was some virtue in Geordie's special knowledge, it was that flaws and partings were as much in the nature of God as joining and harmony, and so he listened with the patience of a reasonable man to the gardener's explanation, and humble at least he was in his own knowledge to assume that the man knew confidently of what he spoke, and shook his head at the end of it, and avoided a look at his own daughter who was now seething beyond the expression of her antipathy; he heard the chiming of the silver in the stranger's hand as clearly as if it were being brandished as a taunt, and this is what Geordie O'Donnell said, in as firm and as calm a voice as he could manage:

Well, now, sir, I don't know what yer folk do in other lands, and I couldn't rightly say who's a follower o' Christ and who's not; but I'll say this to ye, sure and is there not just the one Christ for all of us, and doesn't he have just the one pair of ears to be hearin what all the faiths are sayin to him? To be honest with a plain-speakin man like yerself, sir, I don't know what it is that the folk o' Protestant faiths'd have us do about the faith we're born with, for wasn't it the first of all o' them? And I'll beg yer pardon to be differin with a strongly principled gentleman like yerself, sir, but for yer lodgin I'm afraid ye'll have to be puttin up with our crucifix and our grace, for we're not ones for changin our ways for the sake of a lodger, and I hope, sir, that I'm explainin meself to ye in a manner ye'll respect as a gentleman o' principle.

The man looked at Geordie, from the side, in some surprise, though not much disturbed in his composure, and appeared to be satisfied that he had tapped the very spring of Geordie's spiritual self, like heart's blood it was, a rich flow of pride and sanctimony. Geordie nodded to his daughter, and while she said the most fervent grace before meals that she had ever delivered, the stranger opened his Bible with no particular lesson in mind, allowing the pages to fall where they would, as he drew another spoonful of stew and ate it, and read to himself to hear the voice of his mind obscuring the faithless words of the papist grace, for thou dost show thy strength when men doubt the completeness of thy power, and dost rebuke any insolence among those who know it; and then, having drawn nourishment for the spirit as the tinker and his cwean started to eat their cold stew, closed over the palm-sized book which had never belonged to any father of his. He looked at the pencilled name on the endpaper as if to remind himself, a square and confident script which imposed itself on the word of God for many pages underneath, the deep impression of an overbearing hand which could be seen from Genesis to the end of Exodus, written upon the printed pages as if in trick ink made visible only by thin fibres of shade on the rims of the carved trenches; and this Geordie saw from his side as he ate, that a fierce hand had driven the pencil through the papers, and he shook his head a fraction as he thought of what a task it would be to bear for the time of his stay this stranger whose name he only knew from the reading of Macandlish's letter, and would never have known from the writing on the Bible alone, to be James Watts.

XXXVI

When Kirsty first reported for work at the tower, it was to find Watchie already engaged in fixing something to the roof of the chamber with bolts and a screwdriver; and she was about to give him a scolding for being hard at work after all his promises to let her help when she saw that he was not moving any wheels, but instead was putting in place a further block-and-tackle pulley alongside the one already present, and this, he explained, was to be her help to him, for with another pair of hands to share the work, he could now set the wheels within the mechanism with greater delicacy and less expenditure of effort than before. It relieved Kirsty to hear it, but in another sense she was even more frustrated than ever, for now she understood that Watchie's injury might have been prevented but for his own damnable pride, the legacy of his father – that this could have been done earlier had she only had the wit to open her mouth sooner – and she cast him a frown that missed him, busy as he was testing the firmness of the pulley's bite in the ceiling, grasping it and shaking it from side to side, nodding at the result though grimacing a little as he taxed his extended back. She said,

Wid ye be strang eneuch tae be pu'in yit?

and Watchie turned and nodded, he had answered this question already several times over in the morning. Kirsty knew that she had been wrong to suggest it, that now he would be willing to test himself as he had before, and so swiftly she said,

Fit'd ye hae me dee?

as determined as Watchie not to allow him to do something that she could just as easily do herself. Under his direction, she threaded rope through the runnels of the pulley and through the second pulley, which was to spread the load borne by its fixed brother on the roof, a task she performed with all possible speed, for Watchie was now infected by urgency and gave instructions quickly and efficiently, which she much preferred; the rope coiled around the twin pulleys and dandled through the eyes of them, and to her own eyes there was no sense to their arrangement, so much tangled yarn they were, but once she was finished Watchie chose the next wheel in order, and Kirsty noted that the wheel which had forced Watchie double over the bones of the frame was now in its proper place, he had used the time before her arrival to fix it on to its arbor, and she was about to say something to him about this, surely the first violation of his promise, when he was spinning the companion to it along the floor on its edge and then he was fixing the two ropes to its rim, through the spokes of it, asking her to take up position at the other end of the chamber, which she did without argument. He said,

Pu' on it fan I ca' tae ye, Kersty,

and she nodded ready and waited; Watchie grasped his own trailing end, and wound it several times around the bobbin of a fist, and this time, she saw, he bent himself into a posture better suited to dealing with the strain of it, taking all of the weight upon his legs and keeping his back low and his centre above his heels, so that he was much more able for the mass he would have to bear. He said,

The noo, gin ye please, Kersty,

and together they hauled on their ropes, and to Kirsty's surprise there was no weight at all, or at least the weight was well within her ability to bear. The wheel took to the air and under the play of tensions that Watchie called out to her to maintain it floated towards the open frame like thistledown in the breeze, rising and traversing the chamber as gracefully as if it was no weight at all, you might imagine that you could place it where you wanted with no more than a breath, and sooner it was inside the frame, and here the ingenuity of Watchie's new pulley arrangement became apparent, for with the new pair of hands offered by Kirsty it now became possible to use the puppet strings to manoeuvre the wheel with much greater delicacy, so that with Watchie's command and Kirsty's cooperation it fell into its place, with a slight tug on Kirsty's rope it tilted until it became level, so that it came in to land exactly upon the arbor which was meant for it, so that all Watchie had to do once it was settled was to approach it in the frame and loosen the ropes and secure it in its place with a straight pin of iron. Kirsty looked on, astonished that such a heavy weight had been so simple to raise and move, and she said,

Could ye nae hae done a' yon afore, ye daft loon, ye?

but Watchie made no reply, nor even any sign that he had heard her, but went to the next wheel in order, and said,

It'll nae be lang noo afore we'll mak a stert on the coonterbalances, Kersty, yon's fit maks the hale clock gang, ye ken,

and she decided that he was not to be challenged over this, and went quietly back to her rope, for she would be the last one at this time to halt him at his work.

It was during the installation of the immense brass counterweights which were the real heart of time in the clock tower of Aberlevin that Kirsty O'Donnell first understood that the work had become its own reward for Watchie, for his pleasure it was to see his designs come together before him, taking substance from their spirits upon the drafting paper, when their only existence had been in the abstract realm of calculation, in formulae which were even more of a mystery to Kirsty than the opaque explanations that Watchie gave to her of rotation and circumference, and, as he now did, the purpose of two such massive cylinders apparently cast from pure gold, or so she at first thought, which made him laugh,

Losh, Kersty, he said, gin eether o' them was gowd, I widna hae need o' werkin at the clock for my fees, I'd be awa doon the road wi them mysel!

but she knew it was only for devilment he had said it, and so she said,

Fit're they, brass, aye?

to let him know that she too knew a thing or two, was not entirely ignorant though little capable she was of reading, and then wished she had not. The next thing, Watchie was away and running like a hare from the hounds, really it did not matter in the slightest that she was there before him as a supporting presence to his efforts at restoring the clock, for he spoke to her as if she were the air itself, in the manner of those in public office, like the Provost Macpherson. It was in this manner that Watchie gave her his explanation of how the brass counterweights, capped with eyes of iron and lashed together by a fastening rope of spun and braided steel, were to be wound on to a barrel in such a way that exalted one while the other depended down the well, so that the exchange of their stations with almost biblical certainty, one rising as the other fell, would be converted to mechanical rotation to drive the hands of the clock,

And richt queer, said Watchie to her, that we're markin the centenary o' a hingin wi a clock that turns like yon.

Kirsty shivered to think of it, and saw her own silhouette in the dull shine of the brass as they stood one of the cylinders on its edge. Watchie continued to explain almost as he had done to the family of bats in the tower above before Kirsty had begun her evening visits to him, that the counterweights would have to be manoeuvred in such a way that each of them stood on opposite banks of the aperture, so that the long coil of steel rope could be unwound to straddle the drop,

Yon's oor werk for the day, Kersty, he said, it'll tak us lang eneuch, ye ken,

and right he was, for delicate work it turned out to be, much to Kirsty's surprise. The weights were as heavy as bulls each of them, and all the while they moved together under Watchie's orders, gang this way Kersty, mind the frame noo, with Watchie taking the end of the counterweight with the eye and the steel rope fastened to it, Kirsty taking the blind end with nothing raised to grasp, and frustrating it was for her to be continually changing her hold, stopping to adjust her embrace around its girth; and on Watchie drove her, and if he did not notice her complaints as the weights came gradually with them towards their place for the moment in the frame, it was because his back was beginning to tighten in a manner he thought to be familiar, and perhaps he was hoping to bluster Kirsty in such a way that she would be too busy feeling sorry for her own stretches and strains to be occupied with those of another.

It was the longest day that ever Kirsty had spent, for now she was beginning to understand time in the subjective sense, when a laborious and hated task can cause the sense of passage to be engaged more slowly than usual; for most of it was spent in merely removing the weights from their first placement, and standing them to Watchie's satisfaction at the position where their connecting rope might be spooled on to the bobbin like thread in a giant's sewing box. When this was achieved, Kirsty sat fully on the ground beside the squatting frame, caring nothing for the soiling of her clothes, too exhausted even to notice, and laboriously she drew air into her lungs and said aloud,

Fit an affa deal o' werk yon wis, Wulliam, I'm fair pecht oot,

and she thought at the least that Watchie would be smiling his encouragement to her; but there he was, in the frame among his wheels, caged like a beast in the travelling circuses of which she had heard tell, poor creatures from other lands who paced their same tracks time and again and of which she had heard it said, aye, nae beasts frae oor lands ye ken, but beasts I ken fine mysel frae keepin them, and nae beast that's contentit wid gang back and to like yon, this she had heard in the butcher's shop while buying meat at the time of the circus's coming to the village from someone or other, hardly did she know a body in the town, but this she remembered and thought of it now as she saw Watchie padding among his own workings, but most important of all, he appeared not to have heard her nor even to recognize her presence, attending as he was to the weights as they and their coiled steel rope straddled the aperture, and so she shrugged and took more even breaths, prepared to wait for him to thank her for a job well and efficiently done.

The wait extended for longer and then longer, when they began to pack the remains of a dinner that had been made for them the evening before by Mhairi into Kirsty's pannier, Kirsty decided that she would wait for his thanks until the end of North Street, and when North Street became the Cornhill Road she decided that she would have to wait until reaching Smallbrae; and upon reaching every one of these points in between, landmarks on the homeward journey, not a word was exchanged, and a wee bit more impatient did Kirsty become, for surely it was little cost to him to walk his bicycle so that it did not come between them, though he said that hooking up the lantern on the handlebars gave them both light by which to see their footfalls, but only if the bicycle were to be steered so that each of them was on opposing sides of it, and Kirsty nodded that she understood his reasoning, and went silent. This was not the kind of treatment that she would have expected for her offer of help, and so on the way along the Cornhill Road, in the gloaming of the near turning of the solstice when the fires of sunset and dawning burned in the sky with hardly an interruption between the dying of one and the birthing of the other, Kirsty found herself angered and puzzled and hurt by Watchie's continued talk of work and solutions to this conundrum and that; and so she reminded herself that she had made the offer without condition and for pity's sake, after seeing how devoted he had been to the fixing of the mechanism, and surely preferable it was to have him take her work for granted than to break his back without the help. She scolded herself for being as selfish as to need to hear his thanks expressed to her, and so listened with all politeness to his thoughts and his explanations, and nodded whenever it seemed to be appropriate. Only when they arrived at the farmhouse, however, did Kirsty realize that, as pride was Watchie's first and foremost payment for his work on the clock, so his gratitude was for her, and at no time previously did this make itself known to her until it was dashed from her hand like a cup of water, when Watchie turned to her and looked briefly at her, so briefly that she was quite unsure of whether or not their eyes had touched at all, and said,

Aye, weel, we'll be feenishin oor werk on the coonterbalance the morra; guid nicht tae ye, Kersty,

and away he went, his back turned on her, the bicycle was

heaved about so that the wheels spun in the rut left by his father's wagon, and all there was to see him by was the fire of the lantern suspended from a handlebar, now dancing and oscillating like a glowworm and intimating depths of blackness beyond.

On her way along the road to the croft, Kirsty O'Donnell thought of her day's labours gone by, and how dry and unfulfilled she was feeling, and how she could find no good reason for it.

In the ambiguous night of midsummer, when the sky became a crucible of dark blue steel for the molten light of two days, Kirsty walked the distance between Smallbrae and her home, and placed her feet according to the path revealed by the thin light of her lantern and its shy flame captured in the glass, and her discontent with Watchie filled her thoughts, as much a paving by which she walked home as the cobbles underfoot. Little was there to be seen with clarity in such a light, though little was there to interest Kirsty in any event, but there were motifs of the gnarled reach of hawthorns and laburnums printed against the sky, and there was a savagery in the scarlets and dull golds which seemed to consume the earth, and which quite moved her in her present rage, for swollen and resonant colours they were to her, the colours of fire devouring wood; and in such a light, Kirsty knew, there were many things to be seen, for her father would come back from the alehouse in his days as a sot with tales of known drunkards swearing that they had been met in forests and the open roads by all manner of apparitions. A practical cwean Kirsty considered herself, not given to seeing the capering spirits of the air for herself as much as she might believe in powers unseen; but on this of all nights, she looked above herself to the familiar grove of elms with their branches colluding overhead, and she remembered a thing that Watchie had told her about his first entry to the tower's spiral, how like being in the belly of a serpent he had imagined it to be, the fancy of a moment for him, and a recounting which had caused Kirsty to shake her head and say, fit thochts ye hae,

Wulliam, fit queer thochts; and yet here was Kirsty looking above herself and thinking at that moment of the story of Jonah, and of things she had heard of whales landed mysteriously on beaches, immense black fish you might believe would swallow a village let alone a single man, and how like the ribs of a vast beast were the trunks of the elms and the meeting of their prominent branches, that Kirsty began to feel once again the suffocation that always came whenever she thought of ascending Watchie's tower in utter blackness, the sensation of being smothered in the folds of an eternal black cloth and which she endured only by the knowledge that there was a chamber above where she would find Watchie, and it was only this faith in his presence at the head of the tower which made her perform the mechanical repetition of step and step and step. The summer's opening of leaves meant that little of the sky's fire was seen in this orderly forest of parallel trees, and so another step of faith was this for Kirsty, albeit one she knew would lead to her home and a good hot meal, furthermore in the presence of her lantern, and so hardly could her present trepidation compare to her previous fears in the stairway of the tower. But she found herself greatly comforted none the less when she saw the moon caught between the branches like sixpence in a drain, for the night's own lantern she felt it to be, and a sign that this was not as complete a cloth of black as that of the tower, that somehow this was its merest imitation, the paler darkness of the sleep of dreams in opposition to the annihilating darkness of enclosure, at the top of which may be found either a place to rest or a step into eternal loss of being, and so it was the moon and its promise to emerge from the belly of the elms with her that guided Kirsty on the path towards her familiar gate in the dry stane dyke, causing her once again to breathe as regularly as if she were newly awakened.

It was only when she saw the stranger's form as a silhouette against the burning sky, standing against the stone of the dyke like a breed of centaur half flesh and half mineral, that Kirsty wondered if perhaps her fear of engulfment by the woven trees had in fact been a prescience of him, an awareness that there was a thing to be feared beyond the neck of the grove; and then she thought of warnings she had been given by her mother, long ago, even before she had come to her first blossoming. There were men, her mother had said, who waited for young cweans to come near in dark and forbidding places, and some were of higher birth who assumed what they considered to be their blood's right to take whatever they fancied, and others were simply chiels of no exalted birth, with no intent to make right what they had subverted, and though Ailsa had not seen fit to tell either Kirsty or Mhairi what it was that these secretive mannies were after, what honey it was that they possessed to be attracting so many bees, Kirsty understood that it was a prize that no man should be encouraged to take lightly from their claim, and so the sight of a loitering man, for man she could see that it was from the peak of the flat cap crowning the shadow, placed her on her guard as she approached the gate, though nothing had she by which to defend this prize of hers. The lantern daubed its light of translucent gold on the stones of the dyke as she came steadily nearer to the man, and she realized that the lantern would betray more of her to the stranger than it would illuminate of him for her inspection, as to see anything properly by it, it was necessary to hold it at the level of her eyes, thereby showing her nothing for the dazzle of its flame; but two curious things she heard before she saw anything of him, the first of them the strange crooning of a creature she was unable to identify, for it was not the stranger's singing voice but a bird she would have surmised, and this she knew because of the second of the sounds, which was the voice of a man, the sound of rich laughter it was, amusement rather than broad hilarity, and as she came nearer then the shadow proved itself able to speak as well as to laugh.

Affa late, are ye nae, Miss O'Donnell, even for a busy cwean like yersel?

Still Kirsty was not quite able to see the man properly, but for a reason which was no reason, intuition more likely, she thought him little of a threat, although she was cautious enough to declare,

Aye, sir, but nae sae late as I widna wake my faither in the croft ower yonder gin I were tae cry oot tae him frae here,

just to let it be known; and now that she was near to the crooning, she knew it for certain to be a bird's, though from where it came she had not the slightest idea. The stranger laughed anew, but with a difference in timbre, now he was mocking admiration at her boldness, as if she were a cat lashing at him with open claws for his presumptuous stroking of her pelt, he said,

Dinna fash, Miss O'Donnell! For yer faither and mysel are acquaintit, dinna fear o' it, and fair hurt I am that ye'd think me sae ill mannert as tae tak ony liberties yon near tae my fine new lodging.

At first, Kirsty O'Donnell was lost in the contemplation of the image which the circumference of light from the lamp afforded her, and so did not properly understand the implications of what the stranger had said; and so the most obvious thing that came to her initial notice was that he was on the side of the dyke that belonged to her father by right of purchase, and not on the side she was on herself just now, on which side anyone had a perfect right to stand. He was leaning against the irregular stone as casually as if he were the laird over the land, as much at his ease here as he would be leaning against any furniture of appropriate height he might possess in his own drawing-room, and it was the presumption in his bearing that touched the flame to Kirsty, and dry as tinder she was and ready for burning until she remembered what the stranger had said,

Lodged here? Sin this morn, my loon? Yon's affa quick, widna ye say yersel?

For a moment Kirsty imagined a strange thing, that the longer she stared into his eyes, the more she felt that she was being delivered into the generous chamber of an oven, there to roast like a chicken in the heat, so much was she gathered into it, and what an effort it cost her to remove her sight from this glimpse upon damnation which the stranger seemed to have offered her.

Aye, I suppose ye could say yon, Kersty O'Donnell, but ye'll ken the man I'm werkin for, Meester Macandlish by name, likes tae see his business done affa quick,

and then, to Kirsty's suddenly raised eyebrows and opened mouth, so much like her sister's disbelief that the source of it could only be the same, the suspicion that his presence could only be linked to their claim from Macandlish upon the land, the stranger laughed and said,

Na na, Kersty O'Donnell, I'm nae here tae tak yer croft frae ye, and fine dis yer faimly ken yon as weel; na na, here jist tae live amang ye as a lodger, til Meester Macandlish can gie me a place tae bide at his ain hoose, for fit favour I'm giein yer faither a rent for his stable.

Now Kirsty frowned, despite the constant honesty of the stranger's gaze, which for a reason she could not name caused her to believe the man's story. She frowned because she had little to guide her in the matter of the stranger's trustworthiness, other than her own instinct, and herein lay her difficulty, for little could she tell in such an unfavourable light other than what the lantern consented to show her, and precious little was that on the late evening drought of fuel after its long day's burning. Just as she was thinking that she would rather be more sure of this stranger before she was minded to enter by the gate which was her own, this he appeared to notice, as if he were able to divine the very thoughts from her head, and he leaned forward so that he was struck more fully by the light that remained, subjecting himself to her lantern's scrutiny so that no whisper of a shadow was there to obscure him from her view, nothing was there hidden from Kirsty at all, and he said,

Gin I were o' ill intent, my cwean, wid ye nae ken it by the noo?

as plain a proposition as ever she had heard, and as far as she could tell a claim with a certain degree of truth, for there would be no need for such a story as he had told if he had been loitering for an ill purpose, and the reasoning behind his statement did much to comfort Kirsty the more she gave it thought. The man smiled to see her pause, the triumph of his logic over her unreason, or such it conveyed to Kirsty, who, now moved to annoyance by this end to a frustrating day, two damnable men who played her for their amusement as if she were a thing of wood and string like Wullie Leckie's fiddle, declared in a sudden bravery,

Then wid ye gie me lee tae pass, sir, and nae keep me here fan I've airly tae be up in the morn?

and away she went towards the gate, some yards away from where the stranger was standing, expecting to be allowed to enter without obstruction; but towards it he followed, if followed may be said of a movement which matched her own so precisely as to have been conducted simultaneously, and stood before her, behind the gate of weathered pine that Geordie had fashioned before Ailsa's death, one of the few artifacts from that time which had lasted through the degradation of the household. He was holding in front of her, so that she might see by the light of her lamp, a curious object so fat with life that it appeared to Kirsty to swell and diminish before her eyes, and he said,

Na na, Kersty O'Donnell, I widna hae ye thinkin afore ye'd walk by me that I was a mannie wi nae freens tae think weel o' me, gin ye'd wait jist a meenit,

and such a tiresome thing it was for Kirsty to have to stand there after her day of hard work that she was inclined to shout the stranger to one side, and to hell with whatever his business might have been with her father. Just as she was about to reach for the fastening rope that held the gate to, the stranger held the object closer towards her in one hand, and then she could hear where it was that the curious trilling had been coming from all the time, perched on the palm of his hand as if there he held all of the world's tranquillity and contentment, and he said to Kirsty,

Hae a luikie,

and gestured with his head that she should look more closely with the lantern's gold; and so, at his invitation, Kirsty approached more boldly, and raised the lantern so that she might see better.

The cock pigeon with his proud collar of feathers pecked from the grain which the stranger held in the cup of his hand, and Kirsty came closer in wonder, for the bird seemed little disturbed by the shining of her lantern.

Yon, said the stranger, is my freen, and afore ye cam alang the road, he wis up in yon elms.

Kirsty stood before her home gate once again, and said calmly to the man, who still held the cock pigeon for her inspection over the wall,

Aye, weel, sir, yer freen frae the trees disna hae the tongue tae taal fit way ye're tae be trustit, mair's the peety for yersel.

The stranger was not in the least offended by her, and this caused her some surprise, for though it had not been her intention to offend him, she had meant to drive some distance between them; but instead he laughed, and drew his hand over to his own side of the wall,

Ye'll hae need o' a wee bit faith, I'd say, Kersty O'Donnell,

he said, and then began to sing as freely as a bird himself.

The stranger began to speak in a curious avian tongue of clicks and whistles, a veritable babel of the feathered realm with all the sounds of which every bird in the world was capable, or so it seemed to Kirsty, uttered one after the other, all pouring from him as if he were scarcely able to contain himself from speaking in the many tongues of the birds themselves, and then, to Kirsty's surprise, the pigeon before her stirred in his hand, and with a suddenness that tore the breath from her, the cock bird took to the air, its wings striving and labouring so much that one applauded against the other like a pair of open hands, as if the pigeon were giving its due appreciation to the one who had made it to assume its proper flight over the mundane drag of the earth.

The cock bird oared about the burning sky with the sense of freedom that Kirsty had always associated with the journey of the spirit to the realm hereafter, for surely there would be no leaden tramping for such a generous soul as her mother had been, no boots in the mire for the road to glory, but a soaring and a planing for certain, joy in liberation from the bonds of troublesome flesh. As much as Kirsty understood that this was only a pigeon in the sky, no harbinger of the world to come, still she exulted to see the evident pleasure that the cock bird took in pacing and measuring its freedom, places now within reach of a flex of its wings, and Kirsty began to wonder what it could see from its height, now higher even than the tower. From the cock bird on the wing, she looked down to its master, for the stranger most definitely stood in such a relation to a bird so apparently free, and smiled at him despite herself, for she took pleasure in the flight of the bird as if she had been as newly liberated; but a peculiar thing, that the stranger seemed never to have taken his eyes from her for a moment since lifting the pigeon to the sky, and Kirsty felt that she had been studied by the stranger while her eyes and her thoughts had been diverted, though she found that the notion offended her less than she would have considered. She said,

A freen tae ye, sir, fa canna wait tae be fleein awa frae ye?

but she was smiling as she did so, and it was a smile that touched the face of the stranger as well, like a candle giving its flame to the wick of another; and instead of an answer, the man shook his head and said,

Wait ye,

and then once again began to speak in his bird's tongue, chattering and whistling and caw-calling and fluting, and invited her to look to the sky, to where this puppet of his, his kite almost, was swooping to test its wings and to smooth away the creases of disuse gathered in it as if it were an item of folded clothing airing itself in the wind. It was a wonder to Kirsty O'Donnell what happened next, for as soon almost as the pigeon heard the commands of the stranger, it was as if it had been reeled in towards him on the end of a cable; and then, as she began to understand that this was one of the gentlest creatures ever put together by God, a strange thing she saw, for rather than take its perch on a natural place which would remind it of the branches provided by nature for its rest, such as perhaps the shoulder or a raised arm, or the mount of the dyke itself, the cock bird came down in such a way that for an instant it stayed motionless in the air, apart from the wings that thrashed and applauded mightily for its cleverness in executing such a manoeuvre, an immodest acrobat soliciting the appreciation of his audience by himself leading it, and this it did before landing on the flat cap which surmounted the stranger's head which was as fine a slate roof as ever it would find, a place for its slim talons to find a purchase and hold it secure. For a while, the cock bird stood upon the man's head as if to confirm the crowning triumph of nature over those who would seek to tame it, and the stranger came closer to the gate to lean over it, encouraging Kirsty it seemed by replying to her smile and presenting the pigeon for her to stroke and pet should she wish by dipping his head in a nod, and so she approached, taking her lantern in her pannier hand awkwardly so that the plinth of the lamp should not touch the cloth which bedded the pannier's contents, and reached her hand out, uncertain that it would make response to her stroking and slightly fearful also that it might fetch her a peck on the finger for her trouble. Then, as her finger neared the cock bird to smooth the feathers of its round head, suddenly it raised itself and began to beat its wings, and the stranger stood upright so that Kirsty thought it her fault that the bird was so suddenly startled, and was about to apologize for bringing panic to its breast when, wonderful to see, the pigeon sent a thrill through its plumage as if shaking loose the folds of a cloak, and then opened out both of its wings at their fullest stretch, and there it held them for a long while that quite forced down the breath in Kirsty's throat like a bolted meal.

The pigeon, the cock bird, had become a glory for the stranger's head, and Kirsty thought immediately of the tales of the saint of Assisi, of his great kindness to gentle creation, and this she saw in this stranger, the kindness which drew the cock bird back to earth to bless him with this tribute, and despite knowing nothing of the stranger she found herself inclined to give to him her own tribute, that is to say the benefit of her now growing doubt.

Finally, the open span of the pigeon's wings caught a flow of air, and up it was raised once again, and Kirsty gasped at the suddenness of the lifting, and then laughed at her own surprise. There seemed to be no good reason for her laughter, for it was in the nature of birds to fly, this was after all the way they had been made by God; but then she understood that she would have laughed similarly had she been presented with any show of good training, as touched with the dust of miracle as this particular example seemed to be. As the pigeon sought its own course in the sky, there was a smile on the face of the stranger, and Kirsty realized that once again the stranger had been observing her all the while her attention had been with the cock bird, and though it was no violation, Kirsty was unsettled by his habit of catching her when all of her doors were thrown open; but forward he leaned once again, and opened the gate for her like the finest of gentlemen, standing behind it so that she might fear no lunge nor liberty taken during this most vulnerable and disadvantaged of moments, when she was treated as a guest on her own family's croft, albeit a guest of some privilege, and off came the cap into the other hand which was not seizing the gate, a gesture which was not accompanied by the stooping of a man of lesser station to a finer lady, though this may have been an irony doubled, this respect shown to her. Kirsty took her lantern once again into the hand accustomed to holding it, raised to light her way, and if there was any disrespect intended by the stranger, then the failing flame under the globe showed not the faintest of traces in his smile, burning more constantly this smile than the oil in the reservoir.

As they walked back across the small distance to the croft, Kirsty looked up at the flight of the cock bird in the sky now that the fires of the evening were being extinguished with the lowering of the darkness, darker itself the silhouette than the night above it; and this the stranger saw, and so, for the sake of a conversation, for little else had each said to the other once the gate had been opened, he announced,

And fit d'ye think, Miss O'Donnell, o' the mannies fa've ta'en tae the air, a few year ga'ed by?

No mockery was there in him to be seen, but still she said,

Sir, dinna mak sport o' me, for man disna hae the wings for it.

The stranger laughed.

Richt y'are, Kersty O'Donnell, neether he has! But brains he has, and a' ilka beasts o' iron ye can mak wi the ees o' yer brains, wid ye nae say?

Kirsty was approaching soft and bare ground, dented by the hooves of Maisie and rutted through with troughs and runnels by the wheels of the cart, and so she dropped the lantern so that she might better see the nearing dangers, and choose her footfalls with caution. She wondered if Mhairi were keeping the plots safe from excessive irrigation while she was at her work, for little could she see but her own lantern's light plating the surfaces of the gathering pools, and then she said to the stranger,

Aye, richt y'are yersel, sir; but a muckle cratur o' iron widna gang aff the groun, wid ye nae say?

The stranger nodded, unseen by Kirsty,

Yon I'd've thocht mysel, ye ken, but twa mannies frae America did it, brithers they were, and it didna gang up affa far, and it didna gang awa affa lang, but flee it did, for I read it in the papers wi my ain een.

Not a word had Kirsty heard of this great miracle, or this damnable presumption, whichever she considered it to be as she turned the thought about like an object found in the mud, now seeing one face to it and now another. She wondered if Watchie had heard of this, and if so what he himself thought of it, for the more she gave it contemplation the more she realized that she had no means by which to picture such an engine, other than by recourse to images of birds and creatures that flapped their wings; but what a width of a wing would be needed by a flying engine, and so she wondered again if she were being played for a fool by this strange lodger, though he had the look of a man in earnest. She said,

Fit does yon fleein beast o' iron look like?

to test him out, but he shrugged and said,

I dinna ken, Miss O'Donnell, I've nae been tae America tae see. I've sin heard tell they're makkin them ower here the noo,

419

and again she read no sign of mockery from him; but the very idea of a flying engine she found to be curious, and she said as much to herself as to the stranger,

Man thinkin himsel like the inejels; yon's nae richt, jist,

and shook her head, not knowing in truth what to make of the notion. The stranger looked to the sky, to his pet, the cock bird, which made its flight as was intended by its maker, and said,

Aye, weel, yon's the way wi a' yer mannies fa're nae content wi the warld as the Laird gied them it. Fit mair're they efter, wi the kye for oor meat and oor milk, and the grain for the kye and oorsels, and waater tae drink and the sun risin in the morn and settin at nicht for oor clock?

This was clearly a passion of the stranger's, for Kirsty could sense the swelling of a fine voice the more he spoke of it, and he continued,

Na na; yon's fit's-a-dee wi yer mannies fa'd aye be makkin a'thing they've thocht the Laird's forgotten. Gin he thocht it was richt for men tae gang aboot in yon cairts wi ingines, fit d'ye cry them, motor cars, is't, wid he hae gied us legs or feels?

Kirsty laughed to hear the argument, fine true did it strike her, indeed it was, and the stranger extended his logic still further,

and gin we were tae flee aboot, aye, weel said, Kersty O'Donnell, like the inejels themsels, wid we nae be gied wings tae dee it wi?

and harder Kirsty laughed, for unlike a flying engine this she could picture, a man with the sweeping wings of one of the Lord's servants, and a ridiculous sight it was to her mind's eye, a man in the garb of a labourer with a pigeon's dull feathering on two wings folded under the oxters, a picture which, she realized in time, was the very image of the man by her side, walking at his respectful distance apart from her, and so engrossed was she in this image that she missed her footing in the mire of the ground, a slight tilt away from her balance which caused her to fall towards the man. There was little danger that her clothes would be ruined by a fall in the mud, no more than they were already by her perspiration from the day's work, and she had had no intention of wearing them for a second day to the tower; but none the less she was grateful for the steadying arm of the stranger as he caught her pitching to the side, setting her right again and making certain that she was standing upright and ready to walk forward, for which help she thanked him, grateful also to the workings of providence that he would not see her reddening in the darkness at his touch.

They were nearly at the croft when the stranger asked Kirsty why it was she was returning to her home so late at night, a lateness that made her mistrust any shadow or incomplete glimpse she might see; and at first she saw no reason why she should deliver the truth to one who offered no name to her while airing hers as if they were cousins to each other. She looked into the sky for a moment, and there saw the cock bird, and then she thought of the bird's instant return to the stranger's side, and wondered why she should not give him the trust that was so readily granted to him by the gentlest of God's creatures, and so she said,

I gied a promise tae a freen, that I'd gie him a wee bit help wi his werk.

The stranger raised his eyebrows, slender as they were, and said,

Nae affa muckle o' a freen, gin he'd lee ye gang sae late tae yer hame, nor gin he'd gie the wifies o' the toun a deal tae taalk aboot.

Kirsty O'Donnell stood upright with pride, and said,

Aye, they'll taalk, mebbe, in their ain thochts'll be fit they're taalkin aboot.

The stranger laughed in delight,

By heaven, he said, Macandlish wisna wrang fan he says, aye, luik oot for thon cwean o' Geordie O'Donnell's, a cwean o' speerit, ye ken,

and the compliment fair served to mollify her as she stood before the croft, though she wondered now if perhaps the stranger had heard more of her than he was allowing. She said,

I'm at werk on the clock o' Aiberlevin toun haal, wi the waatchmakker Wullium Leckie, for he's awa and did sair hurt tae his baack, and I gied him my promise I'd help wi the liftin and cairryin, I dinna ken ower muckle o' clocks, ye ken . . .

but no sooner had she explained than the stranger's brows were dropped in a frown, and he said,

Yon clockie o' Macpherson's, the brigand's, ye're werkin tae fex yon affa cratur?

Kirsty nodded, and said that was the very clock, and little further did she say, for immediately the stranger said,

Faugh! I widna be affa serprised gin yer waatchmakker's baack was brocht doon by the Laird himsel, my cweanie, for an ill clock is yon, wi ill ahint it, aye, and ill afore it, gin e'er it gangs werkin again.

For such a strong judgement, it was spoken in a remarkably calm voice, as if it were nothing more than a statement of fact, and Kirsty replied, evenly,

Fit way's it ill, sir, fan a' the ills done tae it were done sae lang ago?

The stranger looked her plainly in the eye himself, quite bold about it though the lamp revealed little of the face in which the glimmering eyes were set; and this he said to her:

Fit ither way wid ye care a farthin for the clock, ill or nae, gin there wisna ony ither puckle o' interest for ye aboot thon tour? Or am I wrang, my cwean?

Kirsty held the very breath at her throat after it was said, for it was so like an accusation that she felt the welling of the rebuttal before she had the opportunity to swallow back the words, from the spring it came and under the great pressure of the stranger's observation,

I care tae keep the promises I mak tae my freens, sir, tae guid freens wi nae ill aboot them.

The stranger shook his head; his stare was constant, and without compromise.

Heed me weel, Kersty O'Donnell. Yon fa'd dee the werk o' the deil serves him, jist like the mannie fa's ga'ed tae the deil; and ye widna keep a promise tae the deil, noo, wid ye?

Kirsty shook her head from side to side, slowly, but all the while her eyes were on those of the stranger, for his never left her, a continual stare it was, like the cat's before a leap, judging the measure of her, how frightened of him she might be, how ready to bolt from his presence.

I'm nae werkin wi the deil, sir, though mebbe I'm taalkin wi him the noo, for a' I ken.

The stranger threw back his head at that moment, severing the link their eyes had cast between them, and let out such a laugh as Kirsty had never heard before in her life, a pure tone of delight such as she imagined may be struck from the bell in its tower, and yet coarse with it, like the sound of feet never raised from a walk on shale, far too plentiful a sound the whole of it to be contained within the slight body. At last his laughter fell to a stop, and he drew a hand over his eyes and said, as evenly as now he could manage,

Na na, my cwean, the deil I couldna be, for I'm nae the mannie fa's raisin monuments tae freens o' the deil, deid sae mony years. Forgie me, Kersty O'Donnell, for I thocht the guid buik says we're tae be glad fan a wicked mannie's pit tae death, nae makkin clocks tae remind oorsels o' him.

And then, suddenly, and without ceremony, the stranger turned on his heel, and went towards the stable, and there was a curious elegance about his movement as he did so, for there was not a suggestion of rudeness about such an abrupt departure, and over his shoulder he said,

Guid nicht tae ye, Miss O'Donnell, here's hopin we'll meet the morra nicht as weel.

Kirsty found that despite herself she was smiling when she said to his back,

And here's hopin I'll ken yer name afore then.

He left her with much to consider, and little time to consider it before it was time for her to go to her bed. She ate the stew that Mhairi had made for the dinner, continually watered in the cauldron so that it would not boil dry, and found herself subjected to as fine a scolding from her younger sister as ever she had dealt herself in her time as the house's keeper, which Mhairi ended by leaving the dried stew before her sister in its bowl, and declaring with a scowl,

Wis it yon chiel o' a lodger keepin ye frae yer denner?

which made Kirsty deny such a meeting, with a silent prayer asking forgiveness from God along with her grace. Much to her puzzlement, she found that there was Geordie pacing the floor at such a late time, drawing the smoke from his pipe as if it were the last he would ever taste, the embers rising from the bowl as if to seed the rafters with their fire, and minded he appeared to be to talk of men and women, and the satisfaction to be taken from a sound and happy marriage. He spoke once again, like Ailsa before him, of those men who were after the one thing, a thing that he did not see fit to explain, and Kirsty, tired after her thankless day of shifting the counterbalances, could barely endure this strange and confusing talk before her eyes were closing as if she were a child's doll with the lids drawn down by weights. She excused herself from the table, leaving Mhairi to clean the dishes after her, and drew the curtain over while she prepared herself for bed, washing the grime of the day from her skin with a brick of rough soap thrashed to a lather among the waters she poured into the washstand's bowl of porcelain from its matching jug, a recovery made from the midden of a graceful home by Geordie; and once she had towelled herself dry, and changed into her night-gown, she fell to her knees by the side of the bed to utter her evening's prayers, blessing as usual the shade of her mother before all else, and only then her father and sister, and then Watchie, as had become a habit during the time he had lain in convalescence.

By the time she realized that she had quickly included among those for whom she had petitioned before the Lord the name of the lodger, she was in bed and striving for comfort on the palliasse, and so there seemed no reason for taking back her intention. From the other side of the curtain came the spiteful percussion of Mhairi, a clash of plates and pots meant to keep her thoughtless sister awake, and which was stilled by a murmuring from Geordie, an admonition that Kirsty could not hear behind the curtain, so gentle it was. She wondered, as the last thing before she went to sleep, what had brought such a curious rage to the house, other than perhaps the imposition that the stranger's arrival had represented to them all, and then, with a final smile before the sleep came upon her, she thought that it was at least a pleasure to have a God-fearing man about the croft, and she remembered how he had introduced himself, by taking from the pocket of his jacket the Bible of black moroccan leather given to him by his father, and with shame she remembered having to ask him what was written in capital letters on the flyleaf, scarring the pages as far as Exodus with the depth and heaviness brought to bear on the pencil, and he told her, it was his name, as told to her father earlier, though a name, this Jamie Watts, that was not known to her as well as to others in Aberlevin.

XXXVII

It was during the fixing of the counterbalances in their well, work that took a number of days, that Kirsty O'Donnell most thought of the stranger, for so she considered him despite that he had given his name to her. She had no reason to think of him just then, and her reasons were abstract at best when finally she did give thought to them; for there was Watchie, across the chamber from her and on the other shore of the well, and he was sitting on the flags with his jeweller's glass held against his eye by a curious one-eyed frown, his attention journeying over the surface of the cylindrical brass weight to see the minute flaws in the casting, and so apart from her he was, parted by the detail of his work, that she began to take her lesson from the power which drove the clock, no one weight did it need but the two of them in concert, and so she thought of her previous evenings whenever she was in need of company. Now and again she laughed as she thought of a particularly amusing story told to her by Jamie Watts, and little response did her laughter draw from Watchie, bent over his weights as he was; and if ever he did take notice, and asked her fit's sae funny, Kersty? then she frowned and said as if to herself, nae a thing, for it was not to be shared like the soda bread that Mhairi now made for them, this company of an evening after her days at the tower, days which now caused her some dread as she wondered if perhaps the clock were not better left in silence.

And then, at the end of the day, on her return from her promised work, there was her meeting with the stranger.

She had come to expect it, the welcoming of the pigeon crooning in the roof of the grove, his appearance by the side of the road in the exhausted drapery of gold from her lantern, and then it would be, waalk wi me for a wee filie,

Kersty O'Donnell, as the pigeon came to hover above his head, a fleshly form to a spiritual blessing it seemed to Kirsty; but at last it took to its own flight, and then it was, and fit like's yer werk been the day, Kersty? more concern than ever she heard from Watchie, and so she told him if it had been strenuous or merely long and dull with waiting, and the head on its stalk would shake to hear it, a sad waste o' a young cwean's time, aye, yon it is, and this infuriated Kirsty at first, until Watts said, na na, I'll nae be misunderstood by ye, Kersty, for the Laird widna froon on a cwean fa'd dee her duty by a promise, but fine displeased he'll be wi the fexin o' yon tour, and a richt waste o' yer time it'd be gin ye were tae folla a thing pleasin tae the Laird wi a thing that raised his wraath. To hear concern for her uttered at all, even in such terms as she felt were intended to distract her from the matter of the clock's restoration, the core of her promise, was an almost spiritual relief of a suffering that tainted her so, more than the simple balm of needing to hear a thought for herself, and she opened herself to this man who had the beginnings of distinction marked upon his features, lines scored with the promise of depth and character and into which the shade of her lamp was rubbed like the suggestive darkness of a charcoal sketch, with less definition to the deepening furrows. They were trustworthy lines, Kirsty imagined, lines about the mouth which pulled the thin lips down so that his smile was a curious conflict against the natural set of the bow, and which made smiling an act of defiance against the nature of the mask he had been dealt by God, a courage which Kirsty found herself quite admiring whenever she first gave it consideration. There were pinched lines around the eyes, not the radiance with the eye as its centre which denotes happiness as clearly as the sun in a child's painting, but a narrower gathering of lines which pointed to the eyes' corners in the pattern known as crow's feet, and which gave Kirsty the impression of a man who had taken these lines as the harvest of a lifetime's deep and concentrated thought, perhaps, as he was so fluent in the speech of it, in the contemplation of the nature of his God; for he declared to her on their second night of meeting, quite openly, that his faith was not hers, and that indeed his church and her own were the most implacable opponents one to the other, though he added, yon's the kirks, ye ken, nae the fowk that gang tae them, and she nodded her head in more than understanding, thinking of the sour old widow Jamieson and how she had stood on the corner of the village square, not even enough manners had the old biddie to make a pretence of sympathy for Watchie.

On this second night, Kirsty asked Jamie Watts how he should find himself here, in Aberlevin, and though he said nothing to her of his last passage, nor of his departure from the dairy farm of William Leckie, he told her his story of his younger years, and the story it was of his years gone from the village.

According to the tale that Jamie Watts told to Kirsty O'Donnell while they walked to the croft, how constricting he had found the small life of a farmer, how narrow it was for a spirit as free as his, for many were the dullards he had encountered in his time working as an orra loon for many who had not the sense of a cuddy, and how ironic it had seemed to him that he should be a mule for those with hardly a mule's brains, and this it was which had led him to enter the service of the king as a soldier in the Gordon Highlanders, where he hoped that one of his great initiative might be put to better use than in scouring the manure from a byre; and he apologized to Kirsty for the use of such a word, manure, as if there were dirt festering on the very sound of it, not appropriate for the hearing of a lady. How great a disappointment to find that he was as much in the power of fools and, as he put it to her, chiels fa're like stanes in a dyke, ilka ane o' yer sojer loons, fighting amongst themselves and, worse than fighting, swearing appalling oaths against the names of the Lord and the saviour which he found himself unable to abide, nae sooner wid I stay amang sic a throng o' the godless than clart my hands wi dung. He told of the night that enough was enough, the night that private Norrie Yuill declared in the barracks that the Son of God himself would be welcome to take a drink with the company during their next time in the town, and this had raised the blood of Jamie Watts to such a boil that he could not have prevented himself if the Son of God had been his commanding officer ordering him to drop his fists, and Kirsty listened to his description of how he drew blood from the nose of Norrie Yuill, a nose that was reddened like a beacon by the drink in any event, and had to be pulled away by the sergeant before he sent the blasphemous private to the parade-ground hospital, I'll fecht ony man for my faith, said Jamie to her, and fit an affa thing for ony man tae say, and in the glimmer of the lantern he saw that Kirsty was shaking her head in a manner that was intended to demonstrate to him her divided understanding, disapproving of his means, approving of his reasons. This, he explained, was his last act as a Gordon Highlander, for he was brought to discipline as a result of his forthright defence of the Saviour's honour, and at the first opportunity Jamie Watts took his purse and left, and it was then that he decided it was time to use the growing hands that he had been given by the Lord, for rare is the talent that can bring life from the soil, but scant opportunity had he been given to display these talents to their best flower, so to speak, and so now was the time, with his discharge papers kept in hand, to look for another horizon to be explored.

No horizon on the map was it that Jamie Watts chose to set out for, not towards the setting sun, but the furthest reaches of his own talent for growth and fertility, a talent which he considered had lain fallow during his days as the poorly paid servant of unworthy men, slow of wit the whole crew of them, hardly inspired by their sparse existences. It was an interest he had cultivated during his while in the ranks of the Highlanders, for a great shame it had been to Jamie to see the waste that good soil and beds were going to, a subtle eye for the medium of growth he had bred into him, and there he had volunteered to make a growth that was the pride of the regiment, as fine a courtesy to whomever of importance might choose to visit as a carpet laid to soften their steps, serving to give a favourable impression of the barracks; and now, with so large a world at his disposal, he was inclined to make his way in it using the talents that were truly his own, discovered under the soil after years of neglect, no discovery in point of fact since there they had always been and there they would have remained had not circumstances, in the shape of private Norrie Yuill, forced him into searching for other seams to mine.

A gairdner, noo, said Jamie Watts, yon was fit the Laird made me tae be, for a gairdner's werk is mair pleasin tae him than a fairmer's, and mair like his ain, as weel.

Kirsty did not understand, not because she was slow of understanding, but because there appeared to be no reason why a gardener's work should please the Lord before anyone else's, for it was always the assertion of Canon Collins that any work done with sincerity was a pleasure to the Lord as well, and so surely this made no difference to the Almighty no matter whose work it was, whether the baker's nor the gardener's nor even the clockmaker's work, all should be equally pleasing, and without favour in his eyes. Jamie Watts shook his head in pity when she said this, and said,

Na na, my cwean, for yon's nae the case. Ye ken, there's thon fowk as wid werk at things the Laird's nae created, and that think theirsels affa clever, mebbe mair clever than the Laird himsel, for makkin things he's nae made for us. D'ye ken fit I'm sayin tae ye?

Kirsty shook her head, not understanding, for she had no comprehension of the kind of arrogance which would place itself above its maker, and so Jamie revelled in his greater understanding as he declared,

Answer me this, Kersty; wid ye trust yer makker afore ony ither mannie nor cweanie?

and naturally, Kirsty, being devout in her faith, said aye, and from there Watts went on,

and wid ye nae think the warld roun aboot ye wis made the way it was for a purpose, and gin the Laird didna mak a thing, he didna mean us tae hae it?

and this seemed to be reasonable, given that Kirsty's conception was of a benevolent maker who would place all that was required for existence within easy reach of a good amount of toil and a fair passage of time; she nodded, it seemed to her that the proposition held as soundly as one of her father's repairs, and so Watts continued,

then ye'd say that a'body fa'd mak machines, like say fleein machines fan the Laird didna gie us the wings o' a berd tae be fleein wi, thinks himsel better than the Laird, and surely ye'd nae say that it's richt tae be thinkin thon?

It was a squall of words that threw Kirsty around and left her without direction, a sudden bluster that searched to the bone for a doubt, and though it was just midsummer Kirsty adjusted her clothing as if there were a draught to be kept away, and again nodded, having little to say and not willing to allow Jamie Watts to see her confusion. She held the shawl fastened with the fingers of the hand which grasped the ring of the lantern, taking the light from Watts's face, and found herself hoping that he did not think her an ignorant cwean of the land, for clearly a traveller was this man, and also one who was not feared to follow a road until its ending; and more, for his courage had taken him from the ranks of a deeply respected institution in the county, and not much minded was she to disagree with such a self-willed man as this, strong in his faith and in his convictions. Jamie Watts was already nodding, anticipating her agreement, for little room had he allowed her for difference or question, and he went on,

I'll taal ye noo, Kersty, I'd think o' mysel as a maist privileged mannie, for werkin wi the warld as it was created by the Laird, and fine contentit I am mair than the fairmer, for the Laird, himsel was a gairdner, was he nae, fan he made the gairden o' Eden? and was it nae man himsel fa brocht it tae ruin, and efter yon ilka mannie had needs o' bein a fairmer, yon's fit ye'll read in yer Bible, will ye nae?

His logic was as subtle as a serpent, so that poor Kirsty saw only the mesmerizing winding of its coils, and not the threat of a strike; but no Eve did she consider herself, falling to the seduction of a honeyed tongue, and no serpent was Jamie Watts with his pleasantries at the end of her long day and a smile which never failed him, and which was more heartening to her than the forgetfulness of the one for whose sake she had given up her continual mourning presence at the croft, her young life of tribute to her mother. She listened as he told her how he came to gardening, and left to fall the matter of her reading the Bible, hoping that in her fascination he would find a fine and solid pavement across which to guide her on the journey to his past, and never stop to see the colour on her face which sprang from her deepest embarrassment, as fiery her cheeks as the sky overhead, and God forgive the omission that she knew the story only from hearing it as one of a flock, not from any reading of her own, a small sin she would unwrap in the confessional when the time was right, when her maker would expect her to disclose it.

If only Kirsty knew, then this negligible sin of hers, which she considered to be as pernicious as an absolute lie, would be as the mote in the neighbour's eye in comparison to the beam of an untruth cluttering the vision of Jamie Watts; for so little of the truth was there in the story he had told, other than his discovery of a new calling in his time of trouble.

The truth was that Jamie Watts found himself unable to work with any farmer in the county some four years after his experience with Wullie Leckie, and not because Wullie had spread tales among colleagues met at the feeing fairs of this surly worker, but because Watts's temperament became evident to all who gave him the work to do, and the tales passed from one farm to the other of their own accord, so that soon the name of Watts was known for the same word as liar, and not a day would anyone have him as a labourer, other than perhaps at the time of harvest, when men were taken on as they were needed. It was this dearth of work, and of the purses that came with it, which forced Jamie Watts to cast himself on the charity of the parish for a period of time, and it was this period that he now claimed as his time billeted with the Gordon Highlanders, when in truth his billet was a stinking barn of a chamber with none more regimented than the sort of chiels which he personally considered to be the refuse of the county as his company.

During this time of want, he slept alongside men who whimpered like brutes if they had no whisky to sip for their breakfast, and men who had lost every possession they had to some ill circumstances, and men known to be idlers across three counties; but most pitiful of all were those who, through tragedy or no fault of their own, found themselves in a chamber without mercy, among men who gave no concessions for whatever flaws may have led these poor creatures to their breaking, placid as the kye they were and as like as not inclined to piss in the clothing they stood up in if they were frightened, skittish as calves. The chamber itself was foetid with waste and old scraps of bread, and it quite turned the belly of Jamie Watts to see the sad old men gouging at the seams of the room, where the floorboards met the skirting, for some old morsel of food on which spores had begun to bloom, for they wouldn't touch the slops brought to them at the proper time for feeding by the brusque caretaker, and what a perversity it appeared to be to Watts that they would sooner choose their own time to eat rotten fare than submit to the routine of the parish, as disagreeable as such a submission might be to him in a home which was maintained under the auspices of the Church of Scotland.

Jamie Watts soon came to realize, during his tenure at the mercy of the parish, that he was in an earthly chamber of hell, and if ever he needed proof that man was the corruption that drew to mockery the perfect creation of a perfect maker, then here it was before him; for the sheerest apes from a circus cage were these strutting men with their hierarchy of the brutes, ensuring that the pride of those who considered themselves least worthy to be in this stink and filth and dirt was kept, at least the monkeys of the world outside may be the lions among dross, and the devil take the hindmost, those slow of wit in the slough of sobriety, or those whose madness rendered them dull and uncommunicative, all of them at the arse of the heap. The moment that Jamie Watts was released into the chamber, he was a new beast in the cage, with his sack of perfectly folded clothes washed in the burn and left to dry with the smell of summer in the fibre, the only man there with a single possession in the world, and so for his first few days he was left to himself, and spoke to no one, aware only that he was the cynosure of all eyes, for none knew what to make of him, and were content for just now to engage in small provocations, indirect talk of men in fancy clothing, known to them from long since, and talk of how thin men could be hard to beat in a brawl; but for one such as Jamie Watts, long practised in the art of fomenting discord, the bait was so obvious that he could see the gleam of the hook, and so he ignored it and settled on the plain bunk to which he had been shown by the caretaker, and took his Bible from the sack, which he placed under the crackling pillow of straw and hessian, and opened it to read.

All through the first days of his stay with the parish, Jamie Watts took his succour from the Book of Psalms, most especially Psalm 75, whose words he found right appropriate to the predicament in which he found himself; and more than ever he knew that he had been sent here to fulfil the Lord's purpose, not just sent into this world but also to this particular chamber of damned souls, for here he was to be their example of a soul touched by the saving grace of its maker, and further than this, now he stood more convinced than ever he had been, even as he brought low his enemies, who were also surely the enemies of the Lord if they opposed one of the Lord's servants, that he, Jamie Watts, was one of those elected before the world's very creation to spend eternity in the company of the Almighty. It was a privilege which only those who shared in Jamie Watts's faith would ever be accorded, for, as his mother never failed to remind him whenever she could, there was a man many years previously whose name was Calvin, and this brave man it was who challenged the right of the foul church of Rome to speak on God's behalf, for the sins that these chiels that would call themselves men of the cloth would forgive in their confessionals, the murders you could do and be forgiven for as long as you had the silver to give to the Romish kirk, Mrs Watts choked to describe the iniquities of the Catholic communion to her son; ah, but then there was Calvin, and he was the one to understand that there was what men thought the Lord was saying to them, and then there was what God himself was saying in the Bible, and to the fire with those who would limit the power of the Lord by their own intricate theologies, a cat's cradle of words which would only shackle the foolish. It was the sheerest folly and vanity on the part of man, more especially the vanity of those men arrogant enough to interpret the Lord's own word for him, to believe that God would disallow himself the fore-knowledge of what was after all his own plan, for the world and all that was in it were his from the beginning, and the world was saturated in the living presence of God within all creation; and so not unreasonable was it to believe that the eternal fate of all the souls in his world had been decided at the very seeding of the whole process, a belief for which there was scriptural evidence, for after all, were not many called but few chosen? This had been the childhood comfort of Jamie Watts, the only suckling of warmth his mother had to offer him, that he, by virtue of the faith into which he had been born, was more likely to be saved than those of other kirks, who had nothing but a purging by perpetual flame as their expectation for daring to wilfully misinterpret the scriptures, or more precisely for following a kirk that encouraged them so to do; and here, in a place that was nothing more than a gaol for all the vanities and absurdities and deformities of the day, it became apparent to Watts that this was to be his earthly trial, the means by which the man who walked in the grace of the Lord would be proved like steel in the fire, cast out by a world of corruption which had no room for the righteous, and here was the reason for his present ill turn of fortune; now he would rise again by the strength of his own character and through long and detailed meditation on the scriptures, for even a lair such as this could be the monastic cell for one who was staunch enough. As far as he had fallen, there was nowhere low enough for those who were the elect of God which could not be considered as the bottom-most step on a climb to glory, and so for the duration of his stay, Jamie Watts devoured the contents of his pocket-sized black Bible as food for the spirit, and rested himself until he had built up his strength sufficiently so that he might begin his ascent from hell, which not for a moment did he ever see as a hell of his own making.

By his many days of quiet observation, and the grace that his presence as a quantity unknown won for him, Jamie Watts saw that the man named Norrie Yuill was the senior among them, and not by virtue of his being the longest tenure, which it was not, but by the simple exercise of brutality, which won him the perverse admiration of those with the sense to recognize one greater than themselves, and this gave him three of a fawning retinue of men sleeker than ferrets, and a chamber of peace to himself upon which he imposed his will as he saw fit. Yuill was a man who would have inclined to fat if there were any fat to be had, for little moved was he to raise himself from his bunk that Jamie could see, and little did he do apart from telling the air of the times when he was able for working, and of the men that he provoked to brawling and then took to their final slaughter by means of the fists he held before him to elicit the admiration of all, and those who were his sincere admirers, sitting around him on the bunk, would fair gasp like fish aground to see these hammers of Norrie Yuill and declare, aye, a muckle fine pair o' fests, richt eneuch, Norrie. Yuill finished every tale with the same words, and I hit him on the heid like a nail, and had him flat in the groun afore ye'd cough, at which his sincere admirers would bay with laughter and say, has there e'er been the like o' the man? Aye, fit a man y'are, Norrie, fit a man richt eneuch! And such immoderate praise touched the flame to Jamie Watts, whose fury was kindled to hear this open veneration, and the devil's own arrogance from such an empty sack of a creature, an arrogance that was crying out to heaven to be brought low.

At last, Jamie Watts came to the notice of Norrie Yuill; not that Yuill had paid no mind to the presence of the stranger in his kingdom of abjection, reclining on his assigned bunk and wrapped around by the silence of the scholar, a loon who could read no less, not that at all, but such a self-containment was the dearest challenge to Norrie Yuill, whose position at the crown of this hillock of discarded beings had been established through destroying their sense of having a right to a self that was not qualified by Norrie Yuill's approval. It took a number of days; but once it was discovered that Jamie Watts's reading matter was the good book itself, then Norrie Yuill was made bolder by this knowledge, and so one evening after dinner, or such a dinner as it was considered that men in these straits deserved, Norrie Yuill called over to the new loon,

Ye're aye with yer neb in yon buikie, man, and fit buikie wid thon be the noo?

Jamie Watts chose his moment to look up, after he had finished a sentence, so that the answering of the question was at a time of his choice, and he said,

The Haly Bible, sir, yon's the buik,

and then returned to it, as if his reply were no more significant a gesture as the parrying aside of an insect. The success of it, throwing Yuill back with his honesty, was in large part due to Jamie Watts's ability to act against the current of his feelings, for the very heart of him was striving in his chest as earnestly as ever it had whenever Alex Wallace and his pack stopped him on the way home from school as a child, of which he had been sore frightened; for now there were no higher authorities to whom he might turn for help, other than the one authority who insisted that suffering was to be borne in his name, and whose deeds of bringing low the unholy were past in the time of the prophets. It brought Jamie Watts some satisfaction to see that his masquerade of utter confidence caused Yuill to sit more upright on his bed, and made the thin beasts who formed his guard soften like candles near a blaze, given the prospect of one unafraid of their numbers and knowing none of their reputation; but Yuill frowned, and said,

Aye, yon's affa grand, tae be a believer, ye ken, man man; thou shaltna steal, affa grand gin ye can afford nae tae steal, gin ye'll ken my meanin.

Jamie Watts frowned in his turn, and this time would not even look from the page.

The Laird's commandments, he said simply, are tae be kept; nae taalked aboot.

It was as if he had recounted to them a fine story over a glass of ale, as if he would; but first Yuill, and then his men, laughed at his reply, and then Yuill stood from the bunk, swivelling his broad body to one side using his arms as formidable levers, and approached Jamie Watts's bed, stopping at the bottom so that he would not be so easily ignored. His entire matted being was rank to Jamie Watts, from the hair that grew in tails, like a nest of rats brought to light, to the clothing that had not been shown the look of water since the day it had been woven, and a stink it put out that would have told you he was damned before ever you had seen him; but Jamie wouldn't let on he had seen or even sensed him, and turned the page in his book as Yuill stood between Jamie and the light by which he was reading, draping his presence over the Bible.

Heed me, my loon,

said Norrie Yuill, and his voice was as pale and desiccated as an autumn leaf,

in here, ye'll nae think yersel better than ony ither man; for here, ye'll pray tae me, ken fit I'm sayin?

It was fear, of course, that caused Jamie Watts to make his lunge, the determination that never again would he be a victim to anyone; and the suddenness of it took Norrie Yuill back a couple of steps, and further drew his men to their feet, to come to his protection. For an instant, the heads of the other destitutes on their bunks turned with languour, for there was to be no more happening in the chamber than the visiting of discipline upon a new loon who had not yet learned his place in the hierarchy. It was an initiation that each of the spectators had suffered as they arrived, this experience of being made to know their place more completely than ever, and of knowing that the humiliation was not to end with their reprobation in this scuttle for men abandoned by the world, that there was one further rung down which each of them must fall; and so the heads turned, and from this performance would come the night's only amusement, and the relief that at least they would spend the evening without the attention of Norrie Yuill and his sincere admirers.

The surprise came for Norrie Yuill when the new loon did not appear to be making his lunge towards him, and so the arms that were raised in momentary defence were held stupidly there, before his face, as if he were staring into the heart of a dazzling apparition, an angel taking the form of light perhaps; while Jamie Watts propelled himself to the corner of the chamber, to where sat one of the poor ruminant creatures who had been in his place almost since the day that Watts had arrived. Norrie Yuill's arms remained where they were, for, from the fury with which Jamie Watts conducted his business, Yuill found himself needing to be shielded, as if he were faced by a conflagration built from the sticks up to the very point of the flame by his own hand; and so astounded was he that he called his sincere admirers back, making them stand in place by the force of their loyalty to him, freezing them as if they were children in a game of statues at the halting of the music, and all watched together as Jamie Watts approached the cowering man, gathered as he was like a bairn in the womb, wrapped like a gift in his own limbs, quailing even at the proximity of another, and away from him flowed on the careless and irregular boarding of the floor a lengthening stream of piss, running in the canals between planks, strained like whey through the fabric of his breeks.

At first, Jamie Watts beamed a smile at this childish man, whose name never needed to be uttered by anyone, for none knew, and it was of no importance to him; Watts bent over him and said, I'm affa sorry, so softly that none but the bairn man could hear; and then, he grasped the man by the lapels of his ragged sark and drew him to his feet, stronger was Jamie Watts than he looked though not much of a weight was the bairn man, a man of twigs and thin flesh he was, and once the soul was upright, Jamie Watts looked over his shoulder, a constant stare into the eyes of Norrie Yuill, and then commenced to beat the bairn man, one blow for every verse of Psalm 75, from the first of them, unto thee, o God, do we give thanks, unto thee do we give thanks, for that thy name is near thy wondrous works declare, through until the seventh verse which he spoke with special zeal, but God is the judge, he putteth down one, and setteth up another, until came the tenth and final verse, all the horns of the wicked also will I cut off, but the horns of the righteous shall be exalted, and only then, when the psalm was at its end, would he let drop the bairn man to the floor, and turned without a thought to face Norrie Yuill, and said,

I ken fine a' my psalms, sir. Can ye say the same yersel?

He left the bairn man where he had been dropped, issuing blood from nose and mouth and squalling like a child left as a foundling, and much to the surprise of all who watched disinterestedly, Norrie Yuill sent his sincere admirers to tend to the wounds of the bairn man, using handkerchiefs clarted with filth to wipe the blood from his face and perhaps inadvertently causing hurt with their kindness. The bairn man lashed like a fish in their grasp, weeping for fear that this was to be another gentle approach that might end in a dreadful beating; and all the while that this was happening, Jamie Watts took part in none of it, and went to his bunk, and there he lay, caring as little for the wounds he had caused than if the loon had been a mouse bairn choking on its own heart, and returning to his meditation upon the scriptures, to Psalm 144, blessed be the Lord my strength, which teacheth my hands to war, and my fingers to fight. No harm had he done, in his own thoughts, to the imbecile, for it had been the corrupted cladding of the body to which the damage had been dealt, not the spirit which was God's own, and thus was inviolable, and so no lasting harm would come from his demonstration of the beating he would gladly serve upon anyone who came to impose their will upon him. In any event, it might be said that this example he had provided for their consideration of the strength which the Lord gave to those who walked in his grace had the effect that was intended, so that for the rest of his stay on the parish, he was approached by no one, and that not even Norrie Yuill, nor even his sincere admirers, would pass Jamie Watts's bunk without a look to the side, as if to draw a reading from the sight of him as to the depths under the deceptive surface; and this was exactly how

Jamie Watts preferred it, for hardly could he understand the notion entertained by those of other faiths, that the Lord would care for the love of his creations, or even that the Lord might love them in return, when surely a being of such boundless power would demand respect and fear from those he had fashioned from the basest of materials, the fear that a parent might demand for his discipline to be effective.

There was another way in which Jamie Watts considered himself to be a different breed from the dulled creatures without the will to raise themselves from the parish's menagerie, and that was his interest in cleanliness, and his obsession with the laundry in his sack.

With what little money he possessed, Jamie Watts made certain that he was never without a bar of thick white soap, and never did he enter a town without examining the rise and fall of the land for the threads of water that would provide him with a periodic wash for both himself and his clothing, should the farm he had come to prove not to be blessed with such amenities as a water supply of its own. The soap rested on the other side of the sack from his Bible, so that it could be said in truth that cleanliness was indeed next to godliness, at least in the sack of Jamie Watts if not the world at large, and there was his open razor and the nub of shaving soap in its wrap of waxed paper sealed into a pouch of its own by a length of string to complete his toilet; and so once in a while he would absent himself from the stink of the parish house and go to the burn he had seen during his desperate arrival. There, in the cold waters which tumbled like a fall of crystal from the heights of the hill, Jamie Watts looked about himself out of the same kind of modesty that made Adam blush for his nakedness, a righteous modesty which understood the carnal shame of the unclothed state, and once he was satisfied that there was none to see him, there he conducted a thorough wash of himself, and of his clothing, which he placed in the interior darkness of a spinney of alders where his sarks and his breeks would never be seen to be stolen, and there they would always be whenever he returned, the pelts of his respectable self, dried by the wind and as fresh as the pollen which reeked in the pores of the fabric. In this way did Jamie Watts set himself apart from the others in the chamber; caring enough for his earthly self and of the impressions it engendered, while nothing but disdain he had for those who judged the worth of another by no more than an appearance, for grace was not an easy quality to apprehend with the less subtle senses, and to his knowledge there were many within his own communion who had fallen into error in this way, assuming themselves deserving of the Lord's salvation because of their false rectitude which stank to high heaven of performance, awareness of unseen observation, when at least Jamie Watts was humble enough to consider that the chosen grace may be bestowed upon the least of men, the least of women, indeed among any within the parish house who might be from the Presbyterian kirk, though to his almost certain knowledge he was the only one there belonging to this communion, and so only one candidate would there be among them all for the Lord's elevation of the humble, which made it all the more imperative that the world should be able to see clearly which among them was the one deserving.

It had been a minister of the Church of Scotland, or more correctly his wife, who had first given Jamie release from his earthly hell; an ornamental minister's spouse, she enjoyed the harmony of a fair-proportioned garden, but lacked the knowledge of how to tend the earth to persuade it to give up its fruit and blossoms, and this was the time that Jamie Watts's appearance mattered the most, for the overseer of the parish was a man of the kirk, and spoke to Mrs Fairbairn of the young man in his care who was not much like the others in the hostelry, sealed in his own meditations upon the text of a wee black Bible and not at all molested by the other idlers in their bunks. Once he had tended to plants it was thought, although he kept very much his own counsel; and this sounded fine for Mrs Fairbairn and the ill-kempt plot of their glebe, throttled by weeds, for to encourage a young man out of the stew of the parish and into gainful work was surely in harmony with the will of God, and Mrs Fairbairn was a one for her harmony, with her very laughter a light music of three rising notes, and her gait under the volume of her black skirt a dance in itself. For her faith in him, Jamie Watts made her husband's glebe a pleasure of colour and grace for her eyes, bedded with all the tints of a burning evening sky, scarlet roses and flaring orange tulips, and there for Mrs Fairbairn was the harmony she sought, so that in the fine evenings of summer there was her garden in descant with the sight of heaven above, and this she said to him, why Master Watts, you have brought heaven down to earth, quite quite beautiful. She was the salvation of Jamie Watts, bringing him from the parish to his first taste of comfort in many a long year, after a while of persuading her reverend husband of the need for a gardener, for if she was the music then he was as plain as the paper upon which her music was written, he would have been straight without her, and monotonously silent.

The arrangement worked well for a time, with Jamie in the room which was there for children, a blessing as yet not visited upon the Fairbairn marriage, and which Margaret Fairbairn confided to Jamie was a blessing never in all likelihood to come to them; he breakfasted with them in the morning before the Reverend made his way to the adjoining kirk to announce the first of the day's services, and he took dinner with them in the evening. All would have been well for him had it not been for the housekeeper, Mrs Caulfield, who had not the least liking for the loon for the way he scowled at her whenever she presented herself to her mistress to tell her of someone at the door, or to ask was there shopping needed for the day or for the week. And this was Jamie Watts's first mistake, to use this sharp weapon of long and trusted service to poison the regard which the Fairbairns had for Mrs Caulfield, and once again he was back to his old ways, telling Margaret Fairbairn that the housekeeper had dealt out a lash of a slandering upon the good name of the reverend while in his company, when he had come in to the house through the kitchen's door, that the lady of the manse was considered by the elderly woman to be frivolous and lax in her duties as a minister's wife, and that the Reverend himself had the need of a good woman who could run the house with efficiency and the correct sense of pride, and I thocht it my duty tae yersel, Mrs Fairbairn, gin I were tae taal ye o' it, and Margaret Fairbairn's brow drew together like a disturbance on silk, and she went to see her husband immediately to pass on the message, finding him in his study, deep in meditation on the scriptures, and in little mood to be roused from it.

Jamie Watts was given a while to find himself a new position, during which time he was still employed and paid as the manse's gardener. He performed his duties conscientiously by day, and hawked his labour in the evening with a letter of reference in his hand that Margaret Fairbairn considered to be a courtesy to the loon rather than a lie to an employer to come; and when he finally did gain a position, this time tending to the garden of a doctor not seven miles down the road, it was only Margaret who felt able to face him to give his leaving purse into his hand. She was as distressed as a mother puzzled at the behaviour of a disruptive child, shaking her head, Jamie, I do not understand what made you tell such a terrible lie about Mrs Caulfield, and I don't know what made you think my husband would let it go unpunished, but Jamie interrupted her, aware that the house was filling with the aroma of the housekeeper's cooking as swiftly as Margaret's eyes were filling with tears, and he said, I'll taal ye the noo, missis Fairbairn, thon's nae a hisband tae ye, and thon hizzie Caulfield's mair suited as a wife for him than yersel, and that was how he left her, picking up his sacks from the floor with a last thrust of the knife at the young woman he had loved as if she had been his mother of preference. Behind him he left a garden never better cared for, with all the colours of the sky settled and taken root on earth, and a great comfort to Margaret Fairbairn was this sunset garden, as she began to call it after a while, and so pleased was she with it for the way that it resonated within her melancholy heart that she began to learn how it should be tended for herself, and so it might be said that Jamie Watts had left behind him the seed of an interest, as Macpherson in days gone by was wont to leave behind him a bairn in the soil of a farmer's cwean, though no bairn screaming for its suck was this garden, but the purest child of Margaret's fancy, with time as its father, all the time she had to spend while her husband was composing his sermons in his study for days before they were needed.

This was the only time that Jamie Watts ever left behind him so bonny a bairn in the charge of an employer, most of the time soiling the doorsteps with his discordant whelps, no new tricks for this old dog. He had been the length and breadth of many counties before it occurred to him that his path was leading towards Aberlevin once more, just as his trail as an orra loon had led him away from the village, and that he was retracing his steps among a new clientele who had never heard of the name Jamie Watts before, and who had no cause to ever hear it. Some day he might own a farm to himself, and then he would work as he wanted, among God-fearing folk of his own communion; but for the moment there was his life among the tinker tribe, and his stories to tell, and he was content to picture Kirsty in the darkness, seeing her man of honour who would never work on the devil's clocks.

XXXVIII

The final installation of the balance which drove the mechanism in its entirety meant that the last construction of all could be attempted, and this was the striking train, which derived its power from a single point of contact from the rotational array and which would give the bell in its belfry the means to announce the first midnight in one hundred years of silence. It took several days of hard shifting and placing, during which Watchie became more absorbed than Kirsty had ever seen him, and on the last full day of work Watchie had to endure a visit from the worried Provost, his brow gathered heavily over his eyes so that hardly a thing could be seen of them, and it was all Kirsty could do to maintain her poise and keep from laughing as she lifted the lesser wheels of the striking train with Watchie on her opposite side, both taking them by the rim and not pausing as the Provost asked, and d'ye ken fit time ye'd be feenished for the denner, Master Leckie, eh? And right comic it was to her to see the glistening of a dew of sweat on the forehead of the little man, while Watchie made his replies as abrupt and as confident as politeness would permit, and giving the Provost small reason for staying in the chamber longer than was necessary for his reassurance.

It was a determined Watchie she saw this day, a loon pressing himself against the limitations of his craft and the limitations of the injured flesh which defined those tasks for which he was able, and this was a Watchie that she had seen rarely since the mundane work of simple construction had begun, only this Watchie could have been so abrupt with the Provost without giving actual offence, aye, Meester Macpherson, but it'll be done mair the sooner gin I were left tae dee it, and then there was the smile on the broad and fleshy mouth and a shaking of the jowls as the shoemaker took his eyes to Kirsty and said, aye,

Master Leckie, and there's some'd say it's nae a' werk that's a-dee here ilka meenit o' the day, though I'd nae be sae ill-mannered as tae say it mysel, mind, and then away he went so that Watchie had no means of rebuttal.

Kirsty laughed to hear it, though little could she express her laughter with such a burden to be carried, and she wondered if perhaps she should have argued with Watchie when he had made the apparently reasonable suggestion that it would be a waste of effort to use the pulley to carry such portable weights about the chamber when one of them on either side could move them sooner and with less fuss. She shook her head and declared,

Yon Provost's an affa chiel o' a mannie! Nae a' werk indeed, he's been listening tae thon widda wumman and her rumours,

but then they were approaching the mechanism with the wheel, and so Watchie would say no more of the village's darkest speculations, and would not meet the eyes of Kirsty for any length of time, but delivered his instructions to her as succinctly as if passed through telegraphy wires so that the wheel might be settled on to its arbor, a long spindle that accepted the wheel as closely as a ring on a finger, and then, smacking an imagined dust from his palms like his father cleaning the fiddle of dust which had not gathered, brought her to take the next wheel in the sequence, so that Kirsty almost began to wish for the return of the brief little man with the lungs of a grampus, for no other reason than to see a rage from the loon.

The truth of the matter was that Watchie had much gratitude to give to her; but he had himself told, as if he were a parent to himself, that here was a task that must be completed with no distractions, and so he had his moment chosen when he would give to Kirsty the thanks that were no more than her due, and that was as soon after the completion of the work and the sounding of the clock as he could find her. Of the arrival of Jamie Watts in Aberlevin, Watchie knew nothing, or else perhaps his hand would have been forced had he learned that this taskmaster of years gone by was for now resident at the croft of Geordie O'Donnell; as matters stood, however, Watchie had no means of understanding the shortening of Kirsty's patience towards him, nor in particular the reasons for her strange enveloping silences that caused her to be as remote from him as if she were in a room of her own without communicating doors nor visible windows. For the duration of the work, Watchie had reasoned that his best chance of success lay in his standing far apart from the concerns of the world, needing his clarity of perception most of all, his power to see the connectivity behind the meshing and the bite of many wheels, for this was not the same exercise as the simple fixing of a watch, he was now walking among the relations between moving parts as if he had been reduced to nothing but dust in the workings, and yet there were the same relationships to be seen, all of it familiar to him in much the same way as once he had seen the relations among the parts of the traction-engine, so that here he was not just grit in the motion of the train but the one who had called this monstrosity into dear existence. And yet there were the differences in size and the grand scale of wear that would cause him worry in the years to come, his was the ultimate responsibility for this gargantuan beast that ate gravity for its meat; and such a reduction in scale it was to return to the world of sunrise and sunset, to the realms of flesh and breath and miracles of no consequence, that if truth were told he found the return to such cares a bewildering loss of depth, as if he were to be bothered by the whining of an insect during contemplation of a particularly domineering and institutional building. In some sense, this immense scale was a peculiar comfort to Watchie, for at least the mechanism and the effects of wear were calculable quantities which responded to certain equations dealing in the wheel's perturbation from a true centre, and so despite the seeming complexity which was laid before him there was at least the chance of reasoning the gross effects of a mistaken placing of a wheel, more likely a shoddy casting which may have pressed the centre to one side or the other; and in his consideration of such great forces, Watchie lost sight of his diminished self and the puzzlement which had been with him since his meetings with Anthony Clarke and which had been roused further at the time of his fixing of the traction-engine, when he had known more through intuition of the mechanism of a metal beast he had never seen before that day than of a kitchen cwean with a pleasant smile. Watchie had not the time nor the will to ask what was the matter that Kirsty had become so sullen, not at this moment, for there was the striking train to be placed yet, and there would be time enough for asking tomorrow, after the work had been finished and the clock had spoken its hour, when he would know for certain if his work, and the work they had shared, had been to any purpose.

And yet there were still times when Kirsty could cause him to pause in his labours simply to look at her, such as when he was close to the striking train to observe the fitting of one of the wheels in its arbor, on his knees and with his jeweller's glass against his eye so that he might examine the detail of it, and it was only when he was straightened once again that he saw that for the first time Kirsty had chosen to sit on the barrel he had recovered from Johannes Dreimann's clock, the barrel which she had refused before for being too rusted for a cwean who knew the work of laundering clothes. She sat perfectly upright, and she was illuminated by the very faintest of their lanterns' casts so that a slight powder of gold was scattered over the image of her, and for that moment Watchie thought her the queen of time herself, settled on the most appropriate throne from which to command her subjects, a throne made from the core of the balance which drew to their height one weight and then another, favouring first this brass and then the next; but a strangely dejected queen she appeared to be, holding herself proudly and yet her face a submission to despair, and it was from this that Watchie began to understand the great toil which she had performed on his behalf, and to which he offered a word of what he considered to be encouragement,

Aye, he said, the clockie'll be ringin grand the morra, jist richt for the provost's dinner, and for Watchie this was encouragement: there was an end in sight that would be satisfactory for all, from which thought Watchie certainly took courage. Strange to his mind was the reply that she made to him, therefore, flat and without enthusiasm, hardly a reply at all, for it seemed to be an answer to a different question, a question in her own thoughts,

I'll hae tae gang tae the chapel the day efter,

and Watchie stood to walk to her side, interposing himself between Kirsty and the light which was dusting her and so throwing his shadow over her like a black sheet.

Ye can gang the neist week, can ye nae, gin ye canna gang on Sunday?

Though there was no light in the chamber that was able to shine in Kirsty's direction, there was the beginning of a ferocious blaze in the pupil of her eye as Watchie's ill-considered words struck a spark from her; but her voice was cold as she said, with a sense of injury and accusation,

Fit d'ye ken o' me, Wulliam? Fit d'ye ken o' my faith, that ye'd say thon tae me, fan jist missin the ane time o' a mass wid hae us gangin tae the deil in hell; nae ane o' yer Protestant faiths, that a man widna gang tae his kirk frae the stert o' the year tae the end o' it and still cry himsel a Christian.

Watchie understood then why it was every Sunday as far away as Banff for the O'Donnells; and why she had insisted that their work halt on a Sunday, that it was a matter of her soul and not the matter of preference he had supposed it to be. At first, his apology came to his lips, but the very sight of her stilled him, for the damage was done; and Watchie became more withdrawn during the rest of the evening's work, and thought back to when Kirsty first came to the chamber, how uncertain she had been, and how without his prompting she had opened out like a flower in the warmth, becoming as confident as to give out her sweet flow of song. Now, as the time approached for the clock's redemption in the life of the village, it was a matter of sorrow that Kirsty was becoming so remote from him, and as he said,

I widna hae said gin I'd kent, Kersty,

he told himself that tomorrow he would put it all right with his thanks, and then he would have to talk to the provost about his fee for the work, which he hoped would be enough for a young watchmaker to consider a rental on a shop, and then perhaps he might find himself in a proper position to pay Geordie O'Donnell and his elder daughter a visit at the croft, on which occasion he might be able to make up for these days of hard labour in full.

Kirsty and Watchie returned along the Cornhill Road together on this last night before the completion of their work, and it was a journey that, like the days previously, was conducted almost the entire length of it in silence. Once, however, the two of them reached Smallbrae, there was a realization on the part of Watchie that he had let another time pass in the company of Kirsty when he might have made known the truth of his feeling for her, an undeniable truth that grew by the day and which cast him in its shadow, and there had been times in the evenings gone by when they had parted before the path to Smallbrae at the end of the warm summer's days, when something great and almost magical flowed in the veins of the young clockmaker, as vital as blood and yet somehow as subtle as electricity, and there was a desire without name which drew him to the purest source of this sensation.

On this night, this last before a day of culminating labour, he stood before Kirsty O'Donnell as usual, and then he realized that there was a silence which neither of them had the will to end; and especially now, after he gave the matter as much thought as he was able, Watchie understood that there had come over Kirsty a gradual change in the weeks that she had been coming to the tower to give him food, and eventually to help, her eyes were now more comfortable with him, at her ease in his presence, as much as she was with her father and Mhairi in the croft. Though there was not always softness in the message of her eyes, it was still taken as a hopeful sign by Watchie that he might find himself becoming more important to her in the time to follow the healing of the clock, for now, as they stood in front of the farm under the last banner of the sun, now Watchie felt himself easy with the questioning of her eyes, the opening of a channel between them without the taint of words, a whole and complete cry from one to the other. It was through this channel that Watchie felt the tripping of mechanisms that were beyond his solitary ability to control, as if within him there had fallen a lever which had been holding back the power of a mainspring, wound to a tight and negligible point which told nothing of the potential it held; and a tripping there was in them each, for Watchie could sense that Kirsty was being drawn to him slowly as if each were no more than expressions of a single mechanism's united design, and Watchie thought of the Belgian clock in the possession of Mr Strachan, of how each of the players took their appointed promenade and met every hour on the hour; and it was then that Watchie looked away from Kirsty, and seized the lever that had brought them both so close together, asserting his free will and changing his movement into a stride forward and beyond her and wishing her a good-night, for now was not the proper time, he thought, not when the last work was to be done, and Kirsty nodded and said, I'll see ye the morra, Wulliam, and there was bitterness in her voice, and a scoring edge like that of uncut crystal, and Watchie carried with him into the house a great and crushing disappointment.

In the kitchen, there was his mother, drinking a last cup of tea before it was time for her to go to bed, and so Watchie asked Jeannie what it had been like when she was courting his father, and he was surprised to see that she looked to the ground, she appeared to be resigned to something or other, though he did not understand what, and she told him the story, of a young fiddler at the fair, called to play with the band of men on the floor, for he was known to play a fine song with it. He was handsome, she thought, sure of himself, his fingers never missed a note on the bridge, sawing away with the bow so confidently, and he asked her for a dance after he had finished, though she wished she could have heard him play for ever. She was Jeannie Richie then, and miles away from Smallbrae she lived with her parents, an only child of a sullen marriage; but Wullie Leckie rode the miles in the family gig to see her, and sometimes he would bring Johnnie, who had not yet gone to sea, though not always, and the elder son of the Leckies was gentle, and not at all assured when he hadn't the voice of the fiddle to tell his stories. She told it plainly to Watchie, making him a cup of tea as she did so, but she was restless as she told it, as if she were composing the tale as it was being told to Watchie, crafting a baroque design upon the facings of a wooden box which was holding secret a thing she would never look on by light of day; and strange to tell, from that day she had little to say about Kirsty O'Donnell, either good or bad, for if there was one thing that Jeannie Leckie needed few lessons about, it was the frailty of the heart.

The cock bird was riding the breeze high above Kirsty O'Donnell long before she came to the grove, seemingly planing along the tatters of scarlet remaining in the sky as if to lend its form to a motif in honour of the turning of the year. Now, with the back of the year broken across the solstice, the edges of the night were becoming tapered and bevelled, now no longer was there this promiscuous association of day and night, with sunset and dawn barely divisible by any time at all, but there was now a finality about the darkness which made Kirsty think of death and endings; for this was what Geordie O'Donnell had said to his daughters, when there was Ailsa by the fire and death was no enemy to them, that winter was the time of long death as trees lost their ornament of leaves and became thin and bony and entirely without cladding, and many creatures there were that died a wee bit in their lairs so that they might resurrect like Jesus come the spring, and this was the truth that Geordie told to Kirsty and Mhairi while Ailsa knitted and purled and shook her head, aye, there was Geordie away with his tales again and drawing the smoke from his pipe as he did so, even we're given a wee taste of what it's like to be dyin for good, so that we can make somethin out of the time that we're awake; and then there was the death of her mother, and Kirsty thought more on what her father had said during the long evenings when she took the seat by the fire, and knitted clothes for them as best she could with fingers that were not as agile as those of her mother, and it was there that she thought of winter as the year's slow dying, the year's pivoting on its fulcrum towards the victory of night, when the sun was hardly warm and then it was pinched out like a candle, and when the nights were as cold as turned the blood to very ice broth, and the chill of the mornings searched to the bone to find a weakness in the will and the fibre.

It was this familiar of Jamie Watts's that brought such thoughts to her, by changing her focus so that she was minded on the sky, and of the time of year, its own noon and midnight as it were, and of the passage of time itself, the trickle of the seconds through the clenched waist of the hourglass; and then, there was a terrible realization about her, that she was falling prey to a passion of the moment, the passion of anger which welled gradually from the slow wounds of Watchie's carelessness and indifference towards her during her time of helping. It was the rage that led her, pace by pace to the fast beating of her heart, back towards the croft, so that she had no words for the gardener who was standing in his accustomed place now waiting for her return to share with her the fiction of his existence, but, much to the astonishment that she never waited to see on his face, took the securing length of string from around the gatepost and let the gate fall closed behind her as she passed Jamie Watts by, declaring aloud,

Gin ye'd keep up wi me, Master Waatts, ye winna need tae stand aboot there like a tattie boodie, jist,

and then around the perimeter she went, rather than the straight path back to the crofting between the defining runnels left by the cart, not caring whether or not he was following in her steps. Behind her she heard Jamie Watts talking to the cock bird in his strange language of clucks and whistles, and she wondered if perhaps he were sending the bird away, like an unwanted crony from the alehouse, and then she heard his voice closer but still to the back of her,

Fit's a-dee wi ye, Kersty? Yon's nae like yersel,

and it was curious how readily she smiled to hear this, that there was one at least who understood that she was capable of differing from her apparent self, to whom she could express her impatience without it being questioned or ridiculed or considered as being more appropriate to another, or as being foreign to her nature. In the company of Jamie Watts, there was a freedom, a licence, to declare her anger, the fury which had sustained her since Watchie Leckie left her standing at Smallbrae like a fool, waiting for what she did not know; and it was a licence that she took with a will as she said,

Master Waatts, ken, ye're richt aboot thon clock, I'm thinkin, for an ill future it has afore it as weel as an ill past ahint it,

and though normally Jamie Watts was as stealthy in his actions as the poacher, he said,

As I tellt ye mysel, Kersty, though I'd ken jist fit made ye think it.

And so came the first of her night's betrayals, as she was later to come to think of them herself, when she told to Jamie Watts, as generously as if he were a brother to her, the indignity of her thankless labours, for so generous he had been himself in the telling of his own stories that as right it seemed to her as the telling of her faults and sins to the priest in his confessional, as if there were only himself and God to hear them. She told him of Watchie's thoughtlessness; and the more she told him the more bitterness she knew herself to have harboured.

Yon clock, she said, he's ca'in it efter a cwean, and he winna see ony ither thing aboot the place but it's yon clock,

and Jamie Watts shook his head by way of sympathy and declared,

Aye, an ill clock richt eneuch, Kersty, for fan the deil maks a fascination for a mannie, he winna see ony ither thing aboot him, gin the Laird himsel were tae cam doon tae him,

and on it went, Kirsty now alight and incandescent as if she had borrowed the touch of the lantern's flame, Jamie nodding encouragement, casting his kindling towards the fire of her so that she would not fall to rest, and together they walked the perimeter of the croft halfway round before Kirsty felt at the same time cleansed of her rage towards Watchie and yet vindicated in the substance of it, with no reason to regret nor be ashamed of the anger to which she had given refuge. In the medium distance were the lights of the croft one moment there and the next extinguished, like the lanterns of fishing boats as they fell away from the horizon, and Kirsty realized with their absence that so late had she been back all that week that she had never seen nor spoken to Geordie and Mhairi; and though she knew that Geordie would scarce be a one to blame Watchie for his application to his work, for hardly was he to be seen himself from morning until night when there was repairing work to be done, it was the futility of her time with the watchmaker loon that was so frustrating to her, as well as the conviction that Jamie Watts was perhaps right to see the clock as being possessed of an ill spirit, and maybe even that of Clootie the old cloven-hoof himself. In truth, the work of the clock had kept her from a matter that had been much on her mind of late, and though she had heard the story of how Geordie had met her mother on his journey to Ailsa's island home, aye, and a fine darlin woman there was lookin at me on the shore and me with me cart and ragged owl horse just across the water, though it was as familiar on her lips as a Hail Mary or the Misericordia, still she was wanting to ask her father just the one question, and that was how he had known that the woman looking at him would be his wife, for some time there was between the seeing and the wedding. Though there was enough evidence by which Kirsty could tell there had been happiness in the marriage, there were still the words of Ailsa on her last bed, when she had asked Geordie why she had taken her from her island, which now brought to Kirsty's mind the idea that there might be such a thing as a wrong marriage, a choice made through ignorance and impatience; and it seemed to her that she was thinking much about marriage, and she could only wonder why.

Ye'll hae tae ken, Jamie Waatts, I'm nae for trustin ony man fa'd tak me tae my door, said Kirsty O'Donnell as they went by the threading flow of the burn which ran gently along the tilt of the land, the source of the O'Donnells' drinking and washing and cooking water; for there was a comfort to be taken from the quarrelling of the currents, the way that the water played and pleated and which could only be seen in the way that its unholy rush tore apart the light from the lantern as if it were gold leaf, shredding it into rags. Jamie Watts walked alongside her away from the burn, and he said,

I widna hae ye trust ony man, Kersty, for we're a' sinners, o' ane kind nor ither,

and to this she nodded, as if she were privy to some secret knowledge of the duplicity of man and of men that it was a sweetness itself to hold, and which yet was onerous to her to have to carry, and this was noticed by Jamie, this knowledge which caused her lips to rise at the same time as it took her spirit down, for even as the smile came to her face there was a seriousness about the eyes that Jamie Watts knew must not be left to pass, and so nothing did he say to her that might alleviate the burden of this knowledge, no words did he speak at all but left her to grow weary with the unshared carrying of it, and kept up his staring, for if there was one thing that Jamie Watts had learned about her in his time at the croft it was how sensitive she was to the subtle pressures of the eyes. There was the sound of the flowing of the burn to their side, no confident surge of a torrent but the long and unending murmur of doubts and questions as it plied the land where it could; and for a moment, Kirsty O'Donnell closed her eyes in the darkness and appeared to be intuiting her footfalls as lithely as a cat, and she seemed to listen to the sound of the burn, its arguments and negotiations, as if it spoke to her as truly with the many bickering voices of amiable dissent, her best advisors in her father's croft and acres, and it was with a distant contempt for her faith that Jamie Watts observed this in her, no surprise was it to him that a faith so insistent on the worshipping of graven idols as if they were the very object of reverence themselves, with as many sainted men and women as there were false gods in the Roman pantheon that came before Catholicism, would make a cwean like Kirsty turn like the heathens of old to the trees and the streams for her advice in times of bother. In point of fact, it was the sound of the burn that was focusing the prayer of Kirsty to the Virgin Mary, cleansing her thoughts as if the waters themselves were draining through her, and so there was nothing idolatrous or animistic in her sudden concentration, and indeed the prayer in itself was a focus for her, a means by which she might make the best decision while the prayer itself was a blessing upon the decision once made; and finally her eyes opened, and she took a long breath and said,

Ye'll ken, Jamie Waatts, that there's mannies ye'd luik at and think're chiels; and there's mannies ye'll luik at and think're tae be respectit; and then there's mannies ye think're tae be respectit, but they're chiels in their herts.

For one moment, Jamie Watts knew himself what it was like to have a fist clenched about his middle; and in the midst of his sudden and abrupt breathing, he wondered if in fact she had done differently to his suppositions, and had told Watchie about his lodging at the croft. A curious experience it was for Jamie Watts, and one which he was able to accept with a certain detachment, that never had he thought so much about the consequences of an error in judgement as in this particular instance, as delicate a catch this was as the mesmerizing play of the fingers in the river that lulls the trout to slumber, and from there to a more embracing sleep; and now, there was the possibility that he had been as transparent as glass to her all along, even as he had passed on to her his false stories. There was that moment of fear, and though there was no chill to the summer's night, still he trembled under the penetrating cold of what she might know, and though he heard his own voice crying fit way feart am I, ane o' the Laird's elect? it was no voice that sprang to his lips, and which sang within himself as if bounding from the walls of a great cathedral, for though grandeur and ostentation were denied in the outward expression of his faith, there were no walls high enough to contain the splendour of his God-aggrandized self, unless they were walls that he himself might shake to their foundations.

Too long dissembling had Jamie Watts spent in his life to allow himself to be so readily hooked by his own bait, however. There would be no dropping to his knees to beg for the merciful judgement of her aggrieved innocence, for if there was one thing Jamie indulged himself with pride in the reckoning, it was in his understanding of the angers and jealousies that were the legacy of Adam's disobedience, and of Eve's temptations, and which were the devil's own workings in the heart of man, and of woman; and scarcely likely he thought it that she would tell him so much of Watchie Leckie's shortcomings only to present him with any knowledge she might have gleaned from Watchie in turn of the times when Jamie Watts had been forced to use the devil's means to enact the justice of the Lord in the favour of one of his elect. There were many reasons by which he knew this to be true; and the first, and most telling, was that she had chosen to confide in him, for had she been told of Jamie Watts's departure from Smallbrae, then no doubt she would have been further told that it had been a dismissal in ignominy, with no telling of Watts's humiliation by Cathie Loudon, nor of Wullie's taking the side of the kitchen cwean when all justice cried out for her to be brought low, and of all the other tiltings against him that called for reparation to be made, and so, hearing only the one side, she would never have trusted him with the fragile load of her troubled thoughts in such a way, and especially not when Watchie was her greatest concern. This was not to say that Watchie had been the wellspring of it, but few other people did she see during her working day, and hardly would any think that she needed to know the truth about Jamie Watts as a pressing matter, for careful had Jamie been to observe his Sabbath in another town, preferring to be seen by no one who would doubtless tell of his return, the widow Jamieson perhaps; and so Jamie Watts used his reason to calm his thinking, deciding whatever she meant, the situation was by no means irrecoverable, and said,

Kersty, a man's nae aye tae blame for a' he says nor does,

leaving himself a door to exit by should his fears in fact take substance.

Ye'll hae heard o' my faither frae Macandlish.

Jamie realized that now they were walking back towards the gate, though hardly any of the dyke or the road was there to be seen, and past the croft were they on the way down the forgiving slope of the hill which carried the water of the burn at such a leisurely spill. He said,

Aye, a wee bittie jist, his werk's thocht weel o' aboot the coonty, I'm tellt,

as disingenuously as he could, for indeed he had known of Geordie O'Donnell the tinsmith, never one to take the proper title of such a lowly trade but an honest worker with a reputation beyond his county, and had known of him for some time before he entered the employ of Macandlish. Kirsty nodded, of course Macandlish would tell his gardener of the man with whom he would be lodging, nothing less would she expect, and she said,

Aye, jist noo it is,

and then took in a long breath, and now it was time for Kirsty O'Donnell to tell Jamie Watts a story. For the length of it, Jamie Watts experienced such a relief that he had to restrain himself in case he laughed aloud, but a grave story it was, and not appropriate for laughter, and so out of respect for the matter of her tale, Jamie Watts held his peace, and breathed more easily now the fist had left him be, and listened, saying nothing.

XXXIX

Kirsty O'Donnell told Jamie Watts of a time after the death of her mother, and she told it with a strength and dignity Jamie found admirable in a woman, of how the land away from the croft which had once been cared for by Ailsa became once again strangled by the barbed ropes of thistles; but the plot was still tended to by Kirsty, as tenderly as she would have kept her mother's own grave had Geordie the inclination ever to pay it a visit. One day, with Mhairi's help, she took it upon herself to dig from the soil a root cellar, where the action of the winds and the moisture of the earth kept the vegetables as fresh as the day they were pulled up. Like a princess from her mother's stories, Kirsty had also grown with the years, into a fine handsome figure of a young woman; her hair was as black as the coal, her eyes rich and hazel, but peculiarly dead, in the manner of a wax simulacrum with eyes of glass, and the mysterious bruises she could not seem to help but gather were mapped on to a skin that took its weathering well, better than the slow perdition that damned the croft. Mhairi was also opening out into her adult form; her hair was as brown as her father's, but lean and awkward where her sister was assured and graceful, and often young Mhairi watched her sister closely, and after a long while of looking when her sister could not see, for Kirsty was unusually anxious over the intrusion of eyes, Mhairi decided that her sister had most grown to resemble the woman whom Geordie referred to as yer sainted mother. A curious transformation for Mhairi this was, for one day she seemed to be talking to her sister, a shy thing of spindles and thread, looking down to the ground whenever she could and away, and the next, seemingly come with the dawn, there once again was Ailsa, with hazel eyes both hard and soft at once; and all of a sudden the house was in the best order it had been since

Geordie's discovery of company and the bottle, the dirty clothes swept up in a morning. Kirsty stood over the tin bath with the clothes slumped pitifully beside her, and one by one she took them all, raising a fine lather from a white brick of soap and thrashing the dirt out of them across a corrugated washboard, leaving them to one side to drain on to the soil; her face was taut and almost hateful, as if the dirt she was punishing from the fibres were more than just simple grime, as if she were attacking a more profound malaise of the spirit whose outward form was the accretion of neglect and glaur.

At first Geordie, with his snout in a glass of whisky of an evening, with a bottle to look forward to when he returned, saw nothing for the extra money that Kirsty asked from him, no better meals, no new clothing; until one evening, as he rode Maisie back along the road after another evening in the company of Johnnie Deans, he heard a regular beat echoing from the hills, and strange he thought it was, until he came closer to the croft, and found that Kirsty was spread on the angle of the roof, finishing off the last repair to a tile of slate. Geordie clambered from the board of the cart, and went over on trembling legs to stand beside Mhairi, who stood holding the ladder, looking at him for a while then away to the overhang of the roof. He said,

Is that yer sister up there, fixin the tiles?

Mhairi kept looking to the sky, shrugged.

Aye, it is that.

Geordie laughed to himself for a moment, and said,

Sure, if only she'd had the patience to wait for a wee while longer, I'd've been doin it meself, so I would.

He entered the house. The sound of Kirsty's last blows on the hammer was a pulse in his ears, but Geordie only felt a profound exhaustion. He went over to his bed, and reached under, for his bottle of whisky, which he uncorked, and drank as if it were sufficient on its own to contain the thirst he felt in the cavern of his throat.

A while later, Geordie returned to another of Kirsty's repairs, for she had bought the planking with which to replace the rotted flooring, and she looked up when he came in, and returned to her work without so much as a pause. Geordie watched her for a moment, and then saw that his whisky was on the kitchen table, for Kirsty was repairing the floor under the bed; so he went over to it, and sat down on the benching, and reached out for it, draining a huge pull from it. He regarded her with some amusement, as if he were watching a child's game which had stepped over the frontiers of pretend, said,

What d'ye think ye're doin, lass?

Kirsty fixed a final nail with a decisive arc of the hammer, a concussion which pulled at the foundations of the croft. She stood up, clapped the sawdust from the linen of her skirt; still not looking at him directly, she said,

Fexin the floorin. It's been in need o't for a lang time.

Geordie's hand rested on his bottle, as if the very contact were a comfort.

Haven't I been meanin to do it for a while now? I said I'd get round to it, have ye not been listenin to a word I say?

Kirsty became taut. She said,

Aye, meanin tae, and yon's as far as ye'll gang, meanin tae.

Geordie sat upright on his bench, suddenly aware of the severity of the charges. He gathered as much dignity as he could to himself, said,

It isn't work for a lass like yerself, Kirsty, it's work for a man, and I said I'd do it, did ye not hear me?

Kirsty bent over to pick up the sprinkled nails on the floor, now restored to soundness, and the hammer. She looked at the blades of her hands, now thick with calluses, a second skin of insensitive leather grown over the delicate parchment underneath.

It was werk, fine d'ye ken, and it needed deein.

Geordie stared at her, but her black hair kept her eyes from his sight.

I told ye, lassie, I'll be doin it, or is that not to yer likin from yer own father?

Kirsty turned suddenly, which made Geordie fall back against the table, clutching at the bottle he almost capsized.

Aye, and fit way wid ye dee it, fan ye canna dee the werk ye're supposed tae dee for ithers?

Geordie's eyes widened at the defiance of his daughter. He held a finger pointed at her, sighted along it as if it were a child's finger pistol.

That's enough, Kirsty, I'll not be hearin any more from ye. How dare ye say a thing like that to the best worker in tin in the whole of Aberlevin?

Despite herself, Kirsty threw back her head and laughed, causing her hair to flood over the dams of her shoulders. For the first time Geordie saw the bruise, a wild crescent discoloration over her eye.

Aye, the best werker in tin, and d'ye ken fit a lang time it's been sin a'body said yon aboot ye?

A blade of ice bedded itself in Geordie's heart, causing a chill to run along with his blood. He scowled at his daughter,

What are they sayin, Kirsty? Tell me, what are they sayin?

Kirsty faced him, the bruise lurid above her eye even in the thin light of the oil lamps.

They're sayin, aye, yon's Geordie O'Donnell there, noo, mind he did guid werk a file ago, afore . . .

She stepped back. Geordie leapt to his feet, reeling at the suddenness of it.

What's in ye, lassie? What's in ye, Kirsty? I wouldn't have taken cheek like that, no, not even from yer mother. Hold yer tongue, I'm warnin ye now.

Kirsty was now laughing, for a pathetic empty balloon of a man her father was before her, now reduced to repeated threat and the gusting of a gale. She pressed on,

Aye, and fine d'ye ken fit way they're sayin thon aboot ye, Geordie O'Donnell, richt fine d'ye ken.

Geordie stood before her accusation, in a croft restored to the way it was before his wife died, now more than ever a proper mockery of his dissolution, for it was not his own hand that had restored it, but the hand of his daughter, and he stood and looked at her; and as he did so, a strange thing happened, for the harder he stared at her, she seemed to divide in two, losing his focus as the action of parallax presented him with a Kirsty to the left, a Kirsty to the right, and for one dismembered instant he fancied that this was not just Kirsty standing before him, not just one woman, but that he was faced by Kirsty and Ailsa together, that within Kirsty for all these years there had been nurtured a grain of Ailsa which had now divided and fruited in front of him, and it was such a shock that he held up his hands from it, as if before a source of light too fierce to look upon, their twin accusation turned upon him and casting shadows behind of the purest blackness,

D'ye ken fit way, I'm askin ye?

said his wife and daughter together, and Geordie cried out,

No, I don't know, I don't,

and in answer the Kirsty with the hammer swung out her hand as casually as a gesture, shattering the bottle of whisky resting on the table, spilling it over the floor. Geordie looked to the table, as if there the bottle would find itself reconstructed by a miracle, flying together and whole again as if in a glory of reversed time, the whisky seeping back as the fissures came together and healed themselves; but only Kirsty became whole again, and there was no Ailsa to be seen dealing upon him her accusation, only Kirsty fretting her bottom lip with her teeth, waiting for a movement from him. Mhairi, spectating in the corner, ran to her sister's side and pleaded for her, daddy, dinna hit her, she wisna richt aboot the heid, but Geordie plucked at her arm and threw her to one side, across the room.

The first two blows stung the flats of his hands. Kirsty's arms stayed by her side, not even raised to defend herself. His boots ground the glass underfoot; and then, stranger still, he saw a parade of scenes like magic-lantern slides bursting from a locked chest, suddenly springing open, burning upon the screen of his memory with all the force of forgotten deeds. Kirsty and Mhairi, huddled under the bed, crying and pleading. A leather belt folded double in his hands, snapped into one striking thong with a sound like the crack of a switch upon a horse's back. Kirsty running from the house, her hand seized around Mhairi's wrist, heading for the stables. They were the memories of another man, savage and bestial and quite without compassion; but they were memories seen through the lamps of his own eyes, played before him with more authority than the memories of another, and still Kirsty stood before him, tears leaking slowly from her eyes, Kirsty now, Kirsty taking his unjust punishment with the resignation of one used to it; his hand was raised above him in the attitude of swearing an oath before the court of the land, and Kirsty said,

I dinna ken fit way ye'd face oor mither, gin she was here tae see ye.

Geordie turned and walked out of the door to the croft. He walked a short distance, to the end of the vegetable plot, to where the thistles grew on the ruined, barren earth, until his knees were no longer able to support him, and he fell to the ground, in the attitude of forgiveness and prayer he remembered from the chapel. He looked back over his shoulder, to the croft, now whole once again, the way it had been when Ailsa was alive. He remembered his father, in the darkness of their room, raising a hand to his mother, the smell of his drinking perceptible over the distance; how his mother sacrificed herself to him, rather than have him give the children a leathering. Under the wide chapel of the sky, Geordie O'Donnell prayed a whole rosary and more besides; for his father, that he might be forgiven wherever he was for what his mother suffered to protect her bairns; for his mother, that she might be at rest by the side of the God she served with every thought and with great patience; for Ailsa, whom he took from her island to nothing but a grave beside a river; and for himself, that God might forgive him for what he had done this night.

XL

Kirsty O'Donnell finished her tale, and her head fell forward on to her chest as she recalled her father on that night, as if it had been the sheerest exertion for her, until at last she turned to Jamie and said,

Fit're ye like efter a drink yersel, Meester Waatts?

By now they were on their second round of the dyke's enclosure, and the flame of the lantern was burning hardly at all, a lean rim of dilute gold about the wick was all that was left as the story, and the walk, had dried the oil in its well. Hardly sooner had she spoken than Jamie Watts declared,

I dinna drink, Kersty, but I'm a bonnie fechter, and I'd gie ony man fa'd cam hame fu' o' the drink and fecht wi his ain fowk this for his trouble,

and held his fist up for Kirsty's inspection, for all the world as if his arm were a hough of ham from the butcher's, a cudgel offered for her protection, though neither was it broad nor brawny. Kirsty shook her head,

I'm nae in need o' the help of a'body, Meester Waatts, nae frae my ain faither,

but Jamie kept the arm upright as if its release were dependent upon a trigger, and said,

Mebbe ye'll hae the need o' it ane o' these fine days, Kersty,

and there was the trigger for it, his courteous offer, for all of a sudden he relaxed the fist and brought his arm down to be held away from his side, an invitation for her to rearrange the basket so that the arch of its handle was hooked on her arm and the lantern held in the same hand, and leaving her free on one side to take the arm which was offered, which she did; and this was how they walked for a while, and Kirsty began to wish that indeed she and her sister had had such a defender to subdue her father at a time when he might have been weaned from the suck of the bottle, when the fiery milk of it had turned him as wilful as a bairn and as strong as a horse in a burning byre, and though she could not see the expression on Jamie Watts's face, she knew that it would be level, and as strong as she would expect from one who had been in the regiments.

Jamie Watts took the basket from Kirsty at last while leaving her with the lantern by which to inform their footsteps, though it was the moon overhead which plated the road before them with more light. He told her of his severe mother and her death in her bed, and with such courage, Kirsty thought, for not once did his voice waver nor threaten to break as he described her in her bed, as fit as if she could have lived another lifetime, while Kirsty told of the sudden pain which had taken Ailsa,

Yon's fit way my faither wis drinkin, she said, he widna gin she wis livin,

and Jamie Watts nodded and then, just at the gate to the land, turned them both so that they were walking towards the croft and the stable, guiding her as if she were a horse at the plough, with slight and hardly noticed pressures upon her from his arm against hers. It was just as they were approaching the croft, seen only by the glitter of the moon against its slates that made it from a distance seem as if Geordie had roofed it with his patches of tin, that Jamie Watts began to muse about marriage, and he said to Kirsty,

Aye, a man's nae jist richt withoot a wife, my mither wis aye sayin tae me,

and Kirsty looked at him from the side, up and down, and replied,

Nae merriet yet, Meester Waatts? Fit'd yer mither say tae ye the noo?

and then thought how ill-mannered he must now think her, and had her apology all ready for him when she heard the sound of his laughter, as if struck from a barrel of desiccated wood, peculiarly humourless,

I dinna ken, Kersty, for I've nae cam across a wumman fa'd hae me.

Kirsty O'Donnell looked once again, and totalled him from top to bottom as best she could in the silver of the moon, to which her eyes were now becoming accustomed; but Jamie Watts would only look forward, to the road that they were on, as if certain that there was to be a false step, casting forward to the vale between the gouged oblongs of the vegetable plots which grew plentifully as if in green tribute to Ailsa, and all the while Jamie Watts was sure of the way that both of them trod upon, placing her feet almost as much as his own, so that Kirsty knew she was following his road, and that her steps were taken with his sight. It was then she became aware that she had allowed herself to be steered by him, as if she were newly coming to her senses after a long and curiously pleasant dream during which she had been guided over pastures and along by the threads of cool spun water, a counterfeit of which the waking truth was somehow more of a shabby copy than the fabrication itself; and though it was disturbing to Kirsty to find that she had surrendered so much of the responsibility she priced so dearly to the will of another, it was as if, preferring the dream, she allowed herself to fall once again into slumber, closing her eyes and wishing the same guide to return to her once more, for now it was her time in the tower which was the dream, a curiosity to be remembered at a distance, an imagined task from the ditches of damnation to which she had given her most earnest belief and which was now gone from her, a sentence with but a single day to its end.

Jamie Watts guided her to the end of the plot, and from there to the door of the stable which was his room as well as that of Maisie, and this she allowed, for here was the one who understood the torment of her days, and Kirsty thought back to the time when she had first seen Jamie Watts within her father's land as if he had been Macandlish himself and not just his servant, when she had considered the arrogance of the man quite breathtaking, when she had feared him for this self-possession of his, what she had then considered to be arrogance. She saw no light at the window of the croft, and from this concluded that her father and Mhairi had gone to their beds. It was

when Kirsty and Jamie approached the door of the stable that
Kirsty realized that all light was to be stolen from her, that
hardly would there be any means by which she might see, for it
was blind to the moon under the peak of the stable's roof, and
so for a moment she felt trepidation rise within her, and her
feet halted just on the shores of the blackness which was the edge
of the moon's silver influence, beyond which it would be blind
to them; but Jamie said,

Fit're ye feart for, Kersty, my cwean? Ye were deein grand
jist there,

and it was then she remembered her arm was through his, as
he stopped beside her and then guided her pace by pace into the
abysmal black, the last of her journey from the tower to here,
and his touch was understanding, as if he knew her fear to be
more than simply that of the night, and so it was with his help
that she came to a halt without properly knowing where she
was, but intuiting the shape of a door beside her, and there she
stood, unable in the blackness to see the expression of Jamie
Watts. For a long while she waited for Jamie to release her arm,
but he would not do so, and still she waited, not daring to take
it back herself, and not knowing whether this was a touch she
wanted to last; and then she heard Jamie from beside her, taking
in a long breath as if ready to speak, and quickly she said,

Ye ken, I've nae seen Maisie in far ower lang,

and then reached out into the darkness to take her arm away
from his clasp, knowing with her fingers where she would find
the bolts securing the door to the stable, and in hardly any time
at all and with no noise that might be heard from the croft, the
stable was open, and she was inside the threshold, in another
darkness, and with more room to draw breath than she had
outside.

Even without the least vestige of light, there were shapes that
were known to Kirsty; the vertical braces that held the roof
overhead, piercing the cage of the rafters, joining together like
bones; the stall which held Maisie with its single gate of horizon-
tals and crossed battens, with the shallow partitioning wall

giving the poor old mare a look at the cart it was her duty to haul.

So vivid was her imagination of the stable that she could almost place Jamie within its interior by the sound of his feet, going towards the upright in which she knew her father had fixed a hook of iron, and then she knew what he was about to do; for it was from this hook that the lantern which gave him light for the darker evenings was hung, and so now he did with the familiarity of ritual what he did every evening when the sun began to fail, remembering as if by rote the procession of it. First of all, Jamie raised the glass to expose the wick soaked in oil drawn from its well before taking the matchbox from his pocket and rousing a flame from the match after a number of strikes against the sandpaper, and it was this sound which turned Kirsty's head, to see a thing which at first startled her; the face it was of Jamie Watts, painted in all the leaping shades of living fire as he protected the leaf of gold on the end of the matchstick as if it had been born into his hands, and there to the sight of Kirsty he was dancing in the air without a body to hold him away from the floor, carrying the fire to the lamp as if he were a grim spirit charged with performing just this single task for all eternity as a penance for a living wrong. At length, the wick of the lamp took the flame after a while of kindling, and at once Kirsty's perception was sharpened as the interior of the stable was blessed with gold, a light which stammered like the unworthy brought to judgement, and in turn causing the shadows themselves to tremble as if in mortal fear before any force that could inspire such a terror in the majestic flame. Jamie settled the glass atop the crown of fire and then adjusted the protrusion of the wick to create a gentler and less intrusive light, more like the sun's first appearance of the day, blunting the edges of everything in the room so that Maisie reclining in her straw might have been a granite boulder of irregular shape bedded in soil, the wooden uprights tree-trunks in a spinney, quite unlike the clarity of the lamps which Watchie set to burning in the clock chamber, crisp and defining, a hungry and deceptive light this was to the preference of Jamie, and it was a light that Kirsty

471

somehow preferred herself to the stark glare that Watchie required for his work.

Many was the time that Kirsty could remember sharing Maisie's stall with Mhairi whenever the two of them fled for their lives from their father at the times when he was raging and full of the drink, and there was the old mare ready to take them in as if they were fillies of hers, bedding them alongside her and sharing her warmth with them no matter how sharp against the bone was the winter's night; and this she told to Jamie Watts,

Aye, Maisie brocht us here tae oor croft, she ended, and Maisie wis a guid freen tae mysel and my sester, for a' that my mither thocht she wis siller gangin tae waste,

and she stood and went to the stall's gate, and waited for Jamie Watts to stand aside to let her by; but for a long time he studied her, and hardly was Kirsty surprised when he raised his hands together and took her face in them as if the better to study her, and not at all did she encourage him to have the kiss for which he was evidently thirsting, and not at all did she refuse him when he drew nearer to her, but stood before him as if she were mesmerized, and closed her eyes as he touched her lips with his, fondly, as a brother might a sister at first, and wondered what about her story of the mare's affections would make him think of coming to her in such a way.

At first, Jamie Watts cupped her head in his hands as if raising a vessel of delicate ceramic to take a drink from it, but for a while he simply brushed dry lips against hers, as Kirsty stood with her hands by her side, and a pity she thought it that Mr Watts should now ruin in this way his reputation as a gentleman, though flattering of course that it had been dashed to pieces before her feet, and then she thought of her earlier parting from Watchie, how she had stood there almost as if in opposition to him across the frame of his bicycle, and how he had left her dry for the want of his slightest regard after he had let himself be captured by the look of her, after she had thought he might be drawn towards her, bound to her silent will. For a long time,

Watts touched his lips to hers in this way, like a finger drawing the song from a glass of crystal, and Kirsty's eyes remained closed, so that she might fashion the likeness of Watchie as if she were Johnnie Leckie carving a whale from its legacy of bone, and sinful indeed she thought herself as she saw Watchie and the tower's high chamber about them as bright as daylight, a sorry treachery it was to perpetrate on one who regarded her so, and she replied with a greater passion herself, opening gates that had previously been locked against him, for natural it seemed that they should mesh like this, almost as if crafted, and then the breath swelled within her and she seemed to be under the influence of the laudanum which had taken the sense away from Watchie, drugged so that she could no longer trust her feet, towards Watts she swayed as if borne by a current.

Jamie Watts released her suddenly as if ashamed of what he had done, as if the implications of it had only just reached him, and it became cold against Kirsty's cheeks with the absence of his hands, which he placed by his side; and casting his eyes to the floor, he said,

I dinna ken fit deil's ta'en me, Kersty.

It was such a look of defeat, claimed he had been by desires he had no right to possess, that Kirsty reached down and took his restless hands in hers, and said,

Then the deil's ta'en us baith, Jamie,

and abruptly he looked up and into her steady eyes. Certain she was that wherever he was minded to lead her, then she would follow with perfect faith, and Jamie said,

Mebbe a waanderin mannie like mysel's needin tae be settlet, ane day.

Kirsty heard the proposal implied in his words, and then, walking upon surer ground than ever she had with Watchie, raised the back of his hand to her lips as if she were the gentleman, he the fine lady, and placed a kiss there; and waited once again for him to lead her to the dance, brimming over with belief in him as if he would deliver her from the evil of her uncertainty.

★

Jamie Watts took her to his bed, a nest of straw he had built for himself alongside the cart, tall enough to keep him from the cold of the floorboards, and there he led her by the hand which she had kissed as if she were a child; and he felt through the length of her arm that she was trembling as if from the cold, though it wasn't the time of year for it. The cwean of Geordie O'Donnell was woman enough to be taken, delivering herself as if she were a lamb into the trust of a hungry shepherd, and so Jamie Watts made no sudden movements that might damage the spell of reluctance by which he had entrapped her, playing the charmed music that all her fickle kind of the Church of Rome would dance to, every one of them, falling for this trap of the flesh knowing that they could hurl themselves upon the mercy of the confessional, allowing themselves the forgiveness of the priest and imagining in their foolishness that it was the forgiveness of God himself they were receiving, when only damnation eternal was there waiting for them at the hind end of their days.

Jamie Watts took her down to kneel with him on the straw, and gently kissed her, alert to the times when she shied like a horse brought to the harness of a strange carriage, when he would speak into her ear, dinna be feart, I'll nae hairm ye, for she was hardly the first cwean of a damned communion from whom he had taken the maidenhood, and hardly would she be the last; but a rarer and more sensitive cwean she was than many of the others, taking more of his patience and a greater delicacy than he had at first thought would be necessary. It was almost in honour of this that Jamie took his time over the pleasuring of her rather than simply using her as if she were a brute, taking her down to lie beside him on the straw when he sensed that she would prefer to recline, settling her with a gentle insistence of his arms to which she readily surrendered into the pillow of quills; progressing by inches and degrees, until he was lying atop her and she had discovered for herself that more comfortable it would be if she were to part her legs to accommodate him better, restricted not at all by the width of her skirts, and Jamie slowly began to press his loins against hers, establish-

474

ing no rhythm as yet but causing Kirsty to catch her breath every so often, and so by listening to such tell-tales did he advance by stealth, a journey known by many such landmarks. Her eyes began to close, and as each drank the breath from the other, Jamie Watts thought he heard the name William from her lips, and it was then that he began to dare more, stripping the jacket from himself and casting it to one side, and releasing the buttons of his sark; and while he raised himself to do this, Kirsty held a hand against his chest to stop him, and engaged his eyes in a manner that made him afraid for a moment that she would plumb him to the depth of his intentions, and she said,

Wid ye mairry a cwean like mysel, fa'd gie ye fit ye're efter?

Jamie Watts looked at her, and felt the demand of his lust pressing against the weave that held it.

Jamie Watts stared earnestly at her in return,

Aye, my cwean, I wid that,

he said, and reached to unbuckle the fastening of his belt.

XLI

On the morning of the final working day, that is the day which would culminate in the clock's first telling of true time for a hundred years, Kirsty O'Donnell woke with a curious feeling of great contentment, such as might follow a night of restful dreaming; and so she arose before the rest of the house was wakened, clambering away from her sister, who was nearest the wall, having been the sooner to bed, placing herself delicately so as not to waken her father. Fastidiously Kirsty set to washing herself at the stand of varnished and restored mahogany, pouring enough water from the jug of porcelain with its fading glaze and its wide orchid's lip into the complementary basin, scooping out chilled water by the handful with which to refresh her face and open her eyes before she gave the rest of her body a cat's wash to take away from it the scent of the night before. If there was one thing that Ailsa had dinned into her bairns before they were very old, it was that they had as much reason to keep themselves clean as the lairds in their grand houses, for all the airs they put on with their expensively cut coats and the wives with their flamboyant hats and their crinolines which rendered them unfit for work, and therefore as ornamental as roses. Not that Kirsty considered herself to be any blossom, for she had not the conceit about her to be continually seeing her face in her father's shaving glass, the only mirror about the croft; but a pride she took in her appearance whenever circumstances forced her away from the croft and into Aberlevin itself, for Kirsty O'Donnell understood deep in her very bones that the whole family, herself and Mhairi but her father more minutely than any of them, would be seen by the villagers such as the widow Jamieson and others of her communion, quick to stand in high judgement for any sign of laxity about them, observant of their smallest misdemeanours, and so no insult would she encourage to Ailsa's lasting memorial of home, by having any O'Donnell seen ill-kempt or dressed in rags, when well the cwean knew that her mother would never have allowed any of them to leave the croft, Geordie included, without a good brush and a polishing so that the world would choke on the very utterance of the word tinker.

Kirsty O'Donnell dressed herself behind the opaque curtain, as she assumed layer upon layer of modesty and linen until she was a creature of concentric shells protecting a mystery at the heart, the mystery she had revealed to Jamie Watts for his kindness and consideration; and then, as she set a new fire of peat and kindling in the grate to heat a cauldron for her porridge, she began to remember the words of the lodger, perhaps it was the fire that reminded her of his eyes, aye, my cwean, ye're a wumman the nicht, and sooner I'm certain ye'd hae a man for yer hisband than a man fa'd fex the deil's clocks for him. As she looked into the gape of the cauldron to see the oatmeal become thicker, she thought more about it, having no one to distract her, and wondered what had possessed Watchie Leckie to shake hands with a descendant of the reiving Macpherson, of whom it was said, God forgive her for thinking ill of anyone not around to speak in their own defence, that the brigand's ways still ran richly in his merchant's veins, with the fortunes he charged for his boots and shoes. She thought of what her man of the gloaming had said as if it had been trawled from the depths of the good book itself, brought to light for her to see, and surely there was truth in what he said, surely wickedness was better left to die without celebration and headstones in its memory, and now she began to wonder about her own role in the restoration of the clock; but she had made her promise of her own free will, and this was what bound her not to the clock but to the welfare of Watchie Leckie, a friend he still was after all, for promises were not to be broken so lightly, a lesson she remembered from her father for he was always saying it to her.

In the contemplative quiet of an early summer morning, warmed by the fire in its hearth at a time when the sun had blessed the earth with its light while not yet gracing it with its heat, Kirsty O'Donnell ate her porridge and thought more on the words of Jamie Watts, and thought ill of her beautiful, mechanical rival; for now she fancied that she could see the harlot in the clock that had seduced Watchie Leckie away from her, and quite in a crisis was Kirsty over what should be done, for the clock claimed all of Watchie's attention with this wrong with it and that wrong with it, and only flesh and blood was Kirsty. No demands did she ever make upon Watchie's craft with her imperfect machinery of bone and muscle and her living tendency to disease and decay and her vulnerability to the leathering processes of ageing, no interest was there for him in a thing he had not crafted for himself, she considered in a moment of rage and sadness, no mirror was she to his own ingenuity, the image of his own driven self in reflection. As she finished her porridge, and washed her bowl in the basin so as to give less work to her sister, she heard the closing of the stable door, and the throwing of its bolt, and there, through the window above Geordie's bed, the window he had put himself into the blind granite, she saw Jamie Watts, the back of him only, striding with purpose from his humble lodging, much faster than Kirsty could hope to keep up with, so that in a curious way it could be said that it was the modesty of the times which prevented her from dropping the bowl into the tin basin and following him as far as until their roads parted. Rarely had Kirsty seen a man who expressed himself so vividly in his manner of locomotion, a dance in itself it was, and for a moment Kirsty was swept by an illusion that he was standing in place and was driving the earth around under his feet as if his legs were pistons for turning the world, and she wondered if he knew that he was being seen from the croft, for not a glance behind him did he cast, and before long he was away from sight on his way to the laird Macandlish's property, hidden behind the grove. Kirsty found herself wondering when next she would see him, and it was his drive that inspired her, she must fill herself with a similar sense of purpose, and now she felt the cold touch of determination stiffen her spine as if the very marrow of it had set into a rod of ice the better to tell Watchie that she would present him with this day's labours as a gift to their friendship, but that she would be taking a husband soon, for it was only but right after what had happened, and the promises that had been made.

She left the croft with care, closing the door over gently so that Geordie and Mhairi would not be wakened by her, and on her way to the village she thought of many ways to tell the news to Watchie, but there was not a single way that did not fill her with dread, and so faster she went in her agitation. Pace after pace she took the road, and anyone seeing her from a distance would have sworn that it was the widow Jamieson herself, for a fair head of steam could the widow achieve in the midst of a good dudgeon, although never did the widow carry a pannier nor a lantern fully charged with oil on her arm like unwieldy jewellery. The more Kirsty O'Donnell rehearsed her words to Watchie, the more her step lightened out of the sheerest relief, for she could hear herself declaim as clearly as a town crier all the dissatisfactions which had preyed upon her thoughts the day before, and there she saw Watchie in front of her in this imagined chamber, dumbfoundered by her new confidence, as radiant as the lantern at night she was, making a pile of all of her grievances and setting them there before him, there y'are, Master Leckie, but thon's the truth, we'd nae mak an affa guid couple. Kirsty O'Donnell began to sing on her road, without words, for words would only have been crystals among the flow of it, and only the purest sweetness was tapped from her for the moment as she asserted herself in her own solitary thoughts.

Under determined feet, and driven by the song which made the Cornhill Road into a path of feathers, Kirsty mounted the rise which led to her first sight of Aberlevin proper, and this was when the resolve of distance first began to turn like two-day milk, for there before she knew it was the tower, it was as if her boots had been transformed into weights and shells of lead, and there she knew was Watchie at the top of it, working hard already if she knew anything about him, and now it was as if his presence there made the tower into a lighthouse, a beacon of industry and diligence which cast around the whole village, and there she was with her petty considerings caught in the beam of it, casting behind her a sleek, black, treacherous shadow, and there the music died in her throat before it could be coined. She took the rim of the hill at a good pace, for prepared she felt herself to be for even this, but the abrupt ending of her song told the truth of it, and now she passed through the streets as Kirsty O'Donnell, the cwean of Geordie the tinker, by degrees her head fell like an unwatered flower from the searching of so many eyes, here one and there one whose look held a memory of the tinker's fall into the pit of contempt, so that by the time she came to the shadow of the tower, it was as if her omniscient God were throned at the head of it, with ancient eyes long used to peering into the abyss of the penitent soul. At the mouth of the tower, with the door left ajar to welcome her in, Kirsty took a pause to draw in a long breath, for she knew that she would need the courage of that moment's rest before going on; and once her heart was beating to its proper time, only then did she take her first steps up the rise which drew her by inches to Watchie, and there was the final kindling of her resolve, her knowledge that now was the time to tell him that she was to be his helpmeet and not the pack mule of the damnable clock, now was the time and she blew on the slight flame with each one of her ascending steps. But the voice which had been so quick to celebrate her decision was now held behind dry and tortured gates, now enfeebled in the light of proximity, and then she was recognizing the patterns of wear on the stones of the wall, slants and vortices where many hands had trusted to its guide in the darkness, and then she knew that she was close to the chamber itself, no beast of burden would she be for another day; and then she was at the mouth of the chamber, and then she saw Watchie, and her heart fell still.

Watchie Leckie was bent double over the metal framework, in an attitude identical to that of his previous strained posture when overwork had cut his wires for him, and once again not a sound was he uttering; and all the rehearsed fury that Kirsty

O'Donnell had ready to march upon him stood on her tongue with nowhere to go, in an immeasurable seed of an instant, and she allowed the pannier of soda bread and curd cheese that Mhairi had left for their food to drop from her arm and land softly on the flags; and it was this sound that caused Watchie's concentration on the meshing of the two mechanisms to break, for quite unaware had he been of any footsteps on the stairs and immediately he looked up and around, at the basket first of all and only then at Kirsty, to the first cause of the sound, and Kirsty O'Donnell had never been so relieved in her life. He smiled with no idea of what had caused the basket to fall from her hands and said,

Ready tae werk, Kersty, this fine morn?

Kirsty had no reply for him; but she nodded, and stooped to retrieve what had fallen from the pannier, the cheese in its waxed paper, the rounds of bread which had rolled like coins along the floor, and by the time everything was gathered, she had nothing to say to Watchie. She had the shawl from her shoulders and folded it into a fine triangle and placed it on the fusée barrel that Watchie had polished into a seat for her, and during her hard-working day she cursed the weakness in herself that would not speak plainly to him, as one man might to another. The more she worked, the more it was the fault of the clock, and then it was her own fault for the desertion of her nerve, and then last of all it was the fault of Watchie for being so infatuated with his brass and iron hizzie taking shape in front of him, that the shine of it could so blind him to the needs of others; but this was surely blaming Peter to exonerate Paul, when the times, and not the time, were to blame for stealing the music from Kirsty's throat, and the dissent from her will, when all she needed to do was to talk to him as an equal partner in labour, a position of strength if ever one there was.

XLII

As above, so below; the Memorial Hall and the clock tower which grew like a trunk from its root were parallel hives of activity that day, and while Watchie and Kirsty were together fixing the rope to the striking train and securing it to the walls to be fed to the belfry, the members of the council were working under the imperious aesthetic of the Provost Macpherson of Aberlevin to create festivity within the hall itself. Here he sent the baillies, those officials of the council who had either closed their shops for the day or had left them in the charge of their wives, to ornament the long chamber with bunting, and with the flags of both Scotland and the union on the dais at the head of the hall, and with the portrait of the late Queen Victoria which the Provost had generously donated to the occasion hung prominently on the oak panelling over the dais; there he sent the servitors, the young sons and daughters and some of the councillors' wives, to prepare the tables for the evening's feast, causing a clatter of ramshackle wood as folding tables were set to four square and placed in front of the dais in the pattern of a trident, with the tines of it facing away from the queen and towards the hall's main door; and there stood Macpherson among it all, smelling the success of the day as the hall assumed the shape of its later celebration, seeing the seats filling already in time for the midnight bells.

No one had heard the like of the noise which signalled the arrival of Lord Gordon of Aberlevin's cook, Mrs Kelvin, for she rode in the back of a thing that no one had ever seen, and that was the first horseless carriage ever to arrive in the village, though the villagers took the sight of it in stride, of course they had heard of it, even if none of them as yet owned one. It was a well-cared-for motor car, polished like a shoe to a mirrored gloss, open to the kind elements, and Mrs Kelvin sat in the back of it while the lord's chauffeur, one Bertie Lorne, drove it at a safe and sedate trot through the streets, and the growling that it made turned all the heads and drew from the houses an attendant gaggle of children, who stood to gape at the shiny beast as it came to a stop in front of the Memorial Hall. While Mrs Kelvin left to make her arrival known to the provost, leaving a carpet bag of culinary instruments in the back, Bertie Lorne rolled himself a fat cigarette and had a smile to himself as the children ran their eyes over the creature's silken bodywork, from the rounded haunches of the mudguards to the clenched teeth of the radiator, a proud panther of metal, at the moment left in a sleep. Also quickly on the scene was the widow Jamieson, at a safe distance across the pavement, an iron pin drawn by the magnetism of blasphemy as well as the commotion, and when she saw what was causing such a stir she was pushed to contain her venom; the stink of it came to her notice at the same time as the beast itself, a sharp razor of a stink with an edge which brought the water to her mouth as if she had just swallowed a draught of vinegar, it even smelled of evil, never mind the look of it, and the fascination of the children declared it as clearly as its shape as a monster to be expelled from God's green earth; but there was little she could do about its presence except loathe it down to the very marrow of her bones, which she could just as easily do from a distance, and indeed preferred to, as if the motor car carried in its metal system the incurable virus of modernity against which she would fight to her final breath. Before she turned to make her way back to her house, to its antiseptic impeccable walls which were her best protection against such rot, there was a voice beside her, a woman tempted into a walk to the shops by the sound outside, carrying a wicker basket on her arm, and she said,

Affa queer luikin beastie, is't nae?

The widow gathered the folds of her dudgeon about her, a garment impervious to the chill of uncertainty, and said,

Fauch! yon's nae beastie, Mrs Imrie, it hisnae a mither nor a faither, and I'll say the noo, it fair hisnae the Laird for a faither neether, and with this Parthian shot left the scene, to the protection of her home, where she would be spared from the sight of such ill sculptures given the unholy breath of poison, such a stink it exhaled, reeking of the pits of hell itself.

The moment she arrived, Mrs Kelvin made it clear to the Provost Macpherson that he was not the Provost of the hall's kitchen; crackling with starch, she asked about the delivery of the ingredients she had demanded, and found it to be in order, then asked to be shown her place of work, and found it to be the most disorderly pantry she had ever been called upon to supervise. She found herself none too impressed with this figure of a provost standing in front of her, or rather to her side as she stood face on to the worktop, waiting as far as Mrs Kelvin could see to no end or conceivable purpose other than to give himself the feeling of command and involvement that he had embossed upon the rest of the preparation; to the eye which she fancied had been finely tuned by years of meeting and talking to the silvered visitors of the Lord Gordon's home, the Provost was bombastic and vulgar, and she knew that he would have no consideration that the work of the stove was indeed work and a craft, for it was the work of wives and therefore the sheerest product of magic, to his forlorn sensibilities, and so she was as brusque with him as she thought he deserved, and raised her head one fatal degree and sighted along the barrel of her nose, and said,

Will ye be wanting anything from the kitchen, Mr Macpherson? For if ye will, ye'd best take it the now, and show me to the ingredients of the evening's meal, for there won't be time while I'm at my work,

and thus was the hierarchy of the kitchen established, Mrs Kelvin incontrovertibly at the helm of it, while the Provost led her meekly to the cupboard which was bricked to the ceiling with tea chests spilling with vegetables, and at which she nodded, prodding the huge haunch of dark red venison with a clean forefinger, before returning to the motor car for her carpet bag of culinary implements. As she left the side door to the hall, Macpherson said,

I'll lee ye tae yer cuikin, Mrs Kelvin, for I dinna ken a'thin aboot it mysel, I widna be efter disturbin ye,

and away he went, thinking of the sweet taste of the haunch of venison, and of its doubtful provenance.

Watchie and Kirsty were still at the bell tower when the musicians came to the village, and they had the best view of the countryside surrounding them, the same view, though neither had the slightest notion, as the baillie who had ensured that the hanging proceeded with dispatch, and thereby also ensuring the clock's fall from trust with the villagers, and thus its consequent destruction. Watchie had told Kirsty many weeks previously, even before his accident, that the going train was connected to the striking train, and the striking train pulled on the bell rope, and through a canny series of trips the rope was connected to the pivot, and in this way did the bell sing the hour, a perfectly sound bell was Dreimann's original, unmolested by its long exposure to the elements and in Watchie's opinion perfectly adequate still for the job. But as much as Kirsty accepted the word of Watchie that such a thing had to be done, she had awful visions, had had for many weeks, that there would be Watchie on the unguarded platform high above the village, performing the intricate task of knotting and spooling the rope through the eyes in the woodwork, thread for the needles, when there would be a gust of wind, anything to overthrow the balance, and there would be Watchie, cast down from the height of it by an unseen punch, with only the hard pavement or the peak of the hall's roof to land on, she would hear about it afterward when she came for her visit, and this she determined would never happen, she would be there when the job needed to be done. And now she was wondering about her right to hold such concerns for a loon she had betrayed as surely as Peter had Christ three times before the crow of the rooster, while Watchie was already in something of a small hurry, almost as if the urgency of the preparations below had risen through the trunk of the tower like sap, charging the clock chamber itself. At first she had clambered on to the platform with her eyes closed, after Watchie, though she opened them when he took her forearm in his hand and helped her to raise herself; there was no wind, which made her feel a bit more stable as she stretched her legs to their fullest, finally trusting that the platform would not be buckling under them; and there in front of her was the bell itself, an upended cup of sullen metal, not nearly as large as she had imagined, and she was confident enough to look where Watchie was pointing, not to the planking floor but into the rafters of the cone above them, to the family of bats she had forgotten about in her greater fear of the height. Their tiny claws were roots in the wood of the pivot, and their wings were wrapped around their eyes as if they were children huddled underneath the blankets on a cold morning, and Watchie said,

I dinna ken gin they'll flee awa efter the bell's ringin; I wid hopena,

and now Kirsty lost her fear of them altogether, and saw that they were just as Watchie had described them, mice with wings, nothing more, certainly nothing to be frightened of in the light of day, though she would not reach out to stroke them. She thought they looked peaceful enough, and thought, curiously, of Watchie in his bed after she had brought him back from the tower, sleeping off his exhaustion. She thought that bats must find their night-times as taxing as we do our daytimes, she saw the bat bairns at their rest, not yet grown to maturity, unripe black fruit on the bough of the pivot, and now she thought that she could not despise them no matter how hard she tried, having seen them in their families, having seen the vulnerable young and knowing that soon they would be adult flittermice. They were roused not in the least by Watchie's drilling into the timber of the frame, a slight disturbance to their sleep and no more, perhaps adjusting their wings like curtains over the window. Then, for the first time, Kirsty had her look at the street below, at the curious impulses which drove the miniature villagers from place to place, and she quite forgot how high she was above them, and there was a giddy sense of power about it, the feeling which had overcome the baillie who had stood in her place the century before, that a hand before the eye could obliterate one of the figures from view, that a reach could lift a house from its foundations on the periphery of the village and bring it closer to her; she saw the distant trees and the house of Lord Gordon of Aberlevin at the core of them, not recognizing it as such, only seeing its topmost crown, but she could see over the rim of the dish in which Aberlevin was served, and there she saw the Deil's Shieling, that single rump within sight of Watchie's own house and over the loch from the Lord Gordon's. She saw far and wide, and the only thing which returned her to a narrower perspective was the sound of Watchie's drill bit in the wood. Then they heard the rattling of hooves on the cobbles below, and Kirsty pulled on Watchie's sleeve and pointed. Now it was her turn to show him something, the quartet of mannies in serge coats riding in the open gig, three of them with curiously shaped and lumpen baggage clutched to themselves, the fourth free and unencumbered to look around, and if they could have seen his expression from that height, they would have seen that his face was pinched in perfect disgust at the variety of smells he had endured on his way to North Street, the odours of dung and the earth which had travelled with the gig to the village so that he felt saturated with their presence, and a refined nose he turned this way and that to catch a trailing wind which might carry the odours away from him.

Yon's a case for a big melodion,

said Watchie, pointing to one of the men; and Kirsty's eyes caught light as she realized that here were the men to make the evening's music; perhaps later, when there was little work left to be done, she would be able to hear them play.

The smell of cooking writhed from the cupboard kitchen like a serpent, putting Macpherson in mind of his own lunch, and right delicious it was, so it seemed, though he respected Mrs Kelvin's dominance over the realm of the stove, and forebore from entering. The tables were coated in linens as white as purity, unblemished and with envelope triangles draped over the edges, and on top of them the cutlery was symmetrically ordered on either side and above the plates and bowls of pure white china, and every so often along the arrangement there were small cut-glass vases from which sprouted three white roses each, and their fragrance was a sweet liquor which blended grudgingly with the smells of the kitchen. All was pleasing to the Provost; he looked and saw that it was all good. Soon he would have to take himself to his house and prepare himself for the evening, but before he did, he went to the tower and made his halting journey to the top of the stairs, there to find Watchie.

When he finally gained the chamber, he saw that it was empty, that is empty of Watchie and Kirsty, both of whom he had seen arriving for work earlier that day; the bag of Watchie's tools was in the corner, on the opposite side from the mechanism in its framework, in what state of completion the Provost had no idea, though he trusted that everything was in readiness as Watchie had assured him it would be. Then he heard voices from the open hatchway, and these drew him to the slanted ladder; he could hear footfalls on the wood of the ceiling, and so with difficulty he grasped the rungs and hauled himself through the hatch by inches, harder work it was for him than mounting the stairs, and raised his head until it appeared as if it had been severed from its carriage, his plenteous chin resting on the floor of the platform a little away from the booted feet of Kirsty, who at first never saw him, and gave a small cry of alarm as the Provost coughed, more an expression of discomfort at the exertion rather than a device to catch the eye. Watchie barely looked away from his drilling and hammering, only to acknowledge the presence of Macpherson, and said,

Fine day tae ye, Mr Macpherson. It winna be ower lang till yer denner, will it nae?

Macpherson felt his pose on the ladder to be a precarious one, and said,

Aye, weel, an oor or twa at the least, I've nae been luikin.

There was a long time of silence, for Watchie was evidently

engrossed in his work and had not the time to be talking, while Kirsty was also busy hammering eyelets into the upright of the wood, capturing the rope in the loops. Macpherson coughed once again, and said,

Jist, I cam up tae ask ye fit time yer clockie'll be ready, gin ye ken, gin ye're able tae taal me . . .

Watchie kept his concentration focused on the bit of the drill, and answered offhandedly,

It'll strike at midnicht, Mr Macpherson, dinna fash yersel.

Macpherson lifted his shoulders over the parapet of the hatchway, so that he looked now like a bust of himself. He said,

Jist, fan ye've done wi it, ye ken, fan ye've done a' ye're able tae dee, I've tellt Mrs Kelvin, yon's the cuik, ye ken, the wumman fa's cuikin the nicht's denner, that ye've tae hae a feed tae yersel frae the ketchen, the baith o' ye. Roast venison, Master Leckie, a feed for a king, a' tae yersels!

and so much did his enthusiasm take him that he quite forgot that he was uneasily balanced on the rungs of the ladder, and so was forced to grasp it afresh, though he had only a little distance to fall; Watchie nodded, still concentrating on the drilling, and said,

Weel, thanks affa kindly, Mr Macpherson, but I'll nae tak lang ower it, I've a wee bit fexin tae dee yit.

Macpherson's brows soared to crescents when he heard this.

Mair fexin, Master Leckie? But it'll be feenished for the nicht, will it nae?

Watchie gathered his patience, the patience that was the gift from his mother, and said,

Aye, Mr Macpherson, it'll be feenished for the nicht, ye've nae a thing tae fear, wee things jist.

Macpherson's relief was obvious, and he said,

Capital, Master Leckie, jist capital. I'll lee ye be, and gang awa doon the noo. Dinna forget tae tak yer denner fan ye're ready for it,

and then he was on his way down the stairs, and Kirsty and Watchie both could hear his stumbling gait on the easier journey, the ragged footfalls as if he were a doll being walked down a toy staircase by a child's hand. Kirsty turned to Watchie, and said,

Coorse mannie that he is; fan'll ye hae the clock done, faugh!

but Watchie was by now drilling a new hole in the wood-work, saying over his shoulder,

Affa decent o' him, giein us oor denner like yon,

and once again Kirsty was stopped in her tracks by the loon, taken by surprise by this generosity that never seemed to fail him; and thought herself more fallen, even more of a dismal sinner, for what she would have to do to him later.

There was a time when the hall below was calm, when all that needed to be done was done, except of course in the kitchen, where Mrs Kelvin laboured in her preparations of the huge hillock of meat that was crackling in the tin alongside an escort of roasting potatoes; the musicians had returned to their room in the hotel, the women who had been employed for the evening from households all over the village were preparing their plainest and least obtrusive dresses, with a promise of a share in the dinner as a part of their fee; by and large they were indifferent to the grandeur of the occasion, simply one more excuse, they reasoned, for the lairds and the shopkeepers to drink and eat their fill. There was none the less a sense of festivity among those not invited to the dance, a willingness to grasp ahold of the skirts of the celebration, to turn it volte-face from the hands of the great and the good, and to celebrate the day as they wished; mindful they were that the man who was hanged was no friend of the council's in his time, and this was enough reason to enter the celeb-rations with a good heart. Fiddles, not violins, were wiped down, melodions removed from their cases, and the air of the early evening was alive with the tuning of songs in waiting; it chimed with bottles of whisky full to the lips taken from cupboards; households were open to all and Katie Maclennan's alehouse was boiling with the language of Babel, with those who wished to drink an early toast, and the toast was Macpherson, God bless him, and if the shade of Macpherson was abroad that night, then it would have wept a little, and not for the blustering tribute of his bastard removed offspring, but for the honest goodwill of those who had never known him, who wished him a peaceful rest in the sleep of the ages, and who were marking his long-ago passage in a manner he would have approved of himself.

XLIII

The bell was connected to the train and swinging to Watchie's satisfaction not long before the first guests came to the hall, and so there only remained the finer details to be attended to, the wee bit he had spoken of to the provost, and this was the oiling of the parts and a final scrutiny through his watchmaker's lens. It was engaging work, and required the most intense concentration of all, for he was examining each tooth and arbor one by one, wiping away the freckling of dust with his cloth of chamois. This was work that Kirsty could not help with, being the specialist's domain, and so she grew bored with standing outside the frame and not being talked to, and began to pace the cell in a variety of ways to give vent to her agitation as she wondered if this were the time that he should be told. First of all, she walked plainly around, her normal gait, and this took her many circles until she began to measure the floor by the length of her foot, toe to heel, and found it to be twenty-five shoe lengths by twenty-five shoe lengths, a discovery which interested her not in the slightest; as Watchie wiped down the wheels with rottenstone oil, giving them the faintest sheen of lubrication under the lantern light, she chose a line of the flagging stones and walked it like a tightrope, concentrating all of her attention on her balance and leaving Watchie to it, but despite the concentration which it cost her, she still had enough thought in reserve to mull over the thing which troubled her the most about Watchie, and that was his obsession with the clock, and in general with the world of mechanism, how he seemed to be slaved to the clock, drawing nourishment from it. It was a blowsy creature of leisure absorbing him so completely within its influence, within the caging of its frame, that Kirsty thought for a moment of a fat laird on his oxblood throne, calling for a flunkey to fill up his glass with wine, and she once again felt the swelling of resentment against it, and felt ridiculous, no sense in despising a thing which could retain no feeling for herself. Watchie was bent low over the wheels, bound to the creature by cords of concern, and she was trying to find some interest in what he was doing, knowing that it was of importance to him; but there was no escaping the fact that soon enough he would have to know of her decision of the previous night, but not yet, not while her thoughts were so disorderly, and so she turned and said,

I'll awa doon file ye're at yer werk,

and Watchie actually broke away from his wiping and scanning to look round at her, his inflamed single lens of an eye disconcerting to her and as large as the moon in the sky, so big that she could see the deep blackness of the pupil at the centre, and the blue rim which surrounded it, and he smiled at her, the best apology he could muster for her, and said,

Richt y'are, Kersty,

and then turned back to it, leaving Kirsty to take the stairs at a slow pace, the pace of one with nothing better to do and all the time in the world in which to do it. Far from being hurt at Watchie's apparent swiftness in accepting her intention to depart, she was relieved to be away, for the lens had revealed to her a strange light in Watchie's open eye, something she had never seen before, though she might have recognized it had she seen him at the fixing of Peter Millar's traction-engine; a beacon catching the first heat of the torch which ignites it, a charging with furious uncertain power, a yearning to know what lies ahead, and the intensity of that light cast the darkest shadow behind her, and she could not bear to be near for the now, not while Watchie was brought to his knees by the last finicky work of preparation, though she would be there for the end of it, when she would be needed, and not a word of discontent would she speak until the Lord had given him his success.

On her way down the stairs, without a lantern in her hand but by now needing no light, Kirsty heard the music of the orchestra clearly in her ears as if she were being followed by the musicians; and she felt herself resonate with the music, the kind which her father called high class with tongue in cheek, so sweet and delicate it sounded to her. She plucked it from the air as if it were fruit, and how good she found the taste of it, slowing the heart in her breast and bringing tranquillity to her for the first time since she had left the croft early that morning, when she had thought herself courageous enough to tell the truth to Watchie. There were aromas in the air as well, the round savour of meats she had never smelled before, a smell of luxury which seemed to expand around the hall, which along with the music opened her like a bottle and poured within her a draught of pleasure which made her think of the night before, when she had known her first release and contentment in her time as a cwean.

The smell of a good meal like none she had ever held in her mouth and the melody from pure instruments mesmerized her towards the door of the tower, left partly open, she noticed, by the provost, and the night was spreading its dark cloth over the sky, showing the lateness of the hour, and once out on to the street there were other scents to be gathered, the heavy liquor of flowers from many gardens, for growing and nurturing was in the blood and there was no escaping it; there was the trail of stink left by Lord Gordon's motor car which she had never seen, a slight edge of acid which made her frown, knowing nothing of the cause of it, and there was the freshness of pollen on the air from the grasses and drifting from the cornfields. Such a fine brew, so unlike the close and musty atmosphere of the chamber, that she thought she would grow drunk on it; and there was still the aroma of meat, and there was still the song, muted by the granite, but she knew where to follow it, she was a hound on the scent, drawn along by the thread of it which tugged her through the door to the hall.

She was in a wide vestibule, the floor stone-flagged in the same way as the chamber, and there was a single door in the centre of the facing granite wall, and to one side of the door was a framed notice-board lined with felt as green as a well-kept lawn, and tacked to the felt were a number of squares and oblongs of paper, bills she could not read, though she understood that they must contain information of importance to someone. She heard the music, her music, welling out of the door, the door with its single pane of stippled glass, and through the glass she could see nothing distinct, as if the picture to be seen from inside the room had been broken and fixed imperfectly together. She approached the door as one who had no right to be there, steering around the window, and before she could bring herself short she had opened the door to release the music, and there it was, crisp and polished, and she closed her eyes so that she might not be distracted; and as little as she knew of Vivaldi, she knew that what she was listening to was the sheerest delight, though how curious it sounded with the breathless tenor voice of the accordion and its need to take a drink of air every several bars. No matter to Kirsty, caught in the web of it, but after a while of listening she realized that there was another sound distracting her, a counter-rhythm played on a strange percussion instrument indeed, an industrious clicking and clacking sometimes like the chime of a bell, sometimes dull and with no ring to it, never at rest, and this made her squint inside the hall to see where it was coming from. Through the narrow slice which the door carved out of the entire scene within, she could see a number of lairds who were known to her, landowners of differing reputations for generosity or sloth, Macandlish among them, she noted, and their wives in pastel gowns seated beside them, as well as a number of shopkeepers who had served her not a while back, and their wives in much dowdier prints, and all the men had this in common, excepting the Revd Lyle, who sat at the head of the table next to the provost; they each were dressed in the drape of the kilt, its bounty of fabric spilling over their seats like the cloths on the tables, and she had never seen so many legs exposed so prominently in her life before, legs bulging with meat and spindly legs like the cabriole legs of a chair, she found herself quite moved to laughter which she contained with an open hand seized across her lips, and now she could see that the sound was caused by the many knives and forks playing upon the china of the plates, some striking the rims and some driven through the venison, some herding a cluster of peas to be dashed to pulp against the meat they had carved and some spearing an odd vegetable Kirsty had never seen before, lacquered with butter and in appearance like a white carrot. The manners of the lairds and their wives were beyond reproach, wiping their mouths with the corners of their napkins, taking slight sips from their goblets of deep claret wine; the shopkeepers treated it with no more respect than they would a glass of malt, draining their glasses faster than the women serving could keep up with, much to the chagrin, an appropriate term for such an elevated sense of discomfort, of the lairds. For his part, the Provost was downing his meal with a will, hardly one piece of the hide sent on its way than another was being chewed, and Kirsty closed the door so that she might laugh until she was content at the gross appetite of the first citizen of the village of Aberlevin, all the grace of his office forgotten in the satisfaction of desire. But the laughter failed in her throat, for the door to the vestibule opened, and there stood Jamie Watts, as if he had received a late-posted invitation to the affair.

XLIV

Kirsty's heart began to leap to a rhythm that was quite unlike that of the welling song beyond the door, the beat of the hammer in the smithy, the pulse that she heard from within her father's shed as he fixed patches of tin to a leaking vessel. It was the first time that she had seen him in the proper light, the burning of oil-lamps held away from the narrow walls on brass standards curved in mimicry of organic growth, as if burgeoning naturally into tulip cups of bright incandescent gold; and curious it was to her to see how tall he was, though this she should have known from their walks, as little light as there had been for the length of them. Jamie was wearing a gardener's leather apron over good clothing, a thick and shining hide of chestnut brown to protect him from those plants and flowers which grew barbs in their defence, and in each of the twinned pouches of leather which bowed forward from the belly of the apron there was a leather gauntlet, but his hands with their slender fingers were held on either side of him, too seemingly pale and wan for such a robust skin, like a pair of thin and scuttling creatures under a great shield of a shell. He saw that she stood away from him, and that she was looking at the clothing of his profession in some astonishment, and so he said to her,

The flooers for the tables were ta'en frae Macandlish's gairden, Kersty, I've been peckin flooers a' day and takkin the thorns frae them.

Not since the morning had Kirsty O'Donnell seen Jamie Watts, and now she could think of no words she might say to him, for none were important enough, nor substantial enough. She studied him in the light of the vestibule as if it were the first time she had ever seen him, and with a shock as sudden as if she had absently held her hand in a flame, as if only now realizing that this pain suffusing her arm belonged to her, she understood that this was the first time she had seen him properly, and so brightly, and now she saw that his mouth was held in an habitual rictus of irony, not indeed a smile but an expression she imagined might persist in him after his death, and that the eyes which had released the light they had taken so generously in the darkness were wide and greedy, feasting, open like the beaks of hatchlings, tearing light away in rags as if it were bread, resting on nothing for long, and the eyes were shaded under the peak of a flat cap, which he now removed, as was only politeness. The hair underneath was correctly short, this she knew for the silver of the moon had sparked from it as if it had been a cap of short metallic fibres beaten into shape, and there was a parting as straight and as clean as a furrow on the right as she looked at him, which meant that he had combed his hair that day thoroughly and often before placing the cap on top of it, so for all he had said to her, that appearance was the least of the man and that the Lord was there to judge the soul without its garments, even the intimate garment of flesh, his hair it was that gave the lie to it all, and Kirsty began to wonder how confident he was himself in the words he spoke, how much was truth held dearly, how much was mere blather.

No matter; for Kirsty spoke at first clearly and with the conviction of one who believed absolutely in her right to be heard, and she tilted her head upright so as to hold herself more proudly, and she said,

Ye've nae reason tae be here the noo, Jamie Waatts, for the flooers're on the tables, and ye're nae invitet tae the deenner . . .

Jamie's lips canted, and had Kirsty but known it, it was the same look as Watchie had seen himself after Watts had come from the fireside talk with Wullie resulting in the dismissal of Dodie Mearns.

Aye, weel, invitet in a manner o' speakin, Kersty, for I wisna jist here tae gie them their roses, but Meester Macandlish thocht I'd be o' sairvice ahint the ketchen, tae sheft casks o' wine and the like. Nae invitet y'are yersel, is yon nae a fact?

The petulance of a cwean rose within Kirsty at this, though she was ashamed of the words that came to her lips,

I am as weel invitet, the provost tellt me himsel I was.

Jamie laughed as if she were a plough horse kicking against the leash, with nowhere else to go if she escaped from him, an impotent dash which would end back where it started, with the only comfort and security it knew and understood.

Aye, he said, invitet wi the serving cweans and the like o' mysel at the hin' end o' the ha', awa frae the carousin, is yon nae it?

Kirsty was silent, for to say otherwise would have been a lie, and so she cast down her eyes to the flagging, and looked for a refuge in the study of the repeated lozenge patterns. She spoke, and it was as if she were speaking to the floor, as if she were talking to a presence which she knew to be without actual substance.

Fit way're ye here, Jamie? she said, did I nae say I'd see ye efter the nicht?

When she looked up Jamie Watts was still there, no mirage called into being by her own imagination, and now his face was as serious as it was able to be. The perfume of roses came to her just then, and Kirsty realized that it was a perfume from Jamie himself, a fragrance borrowed from the petals of the roses he had clipped for the sake of decoration, light upon the rich smell of worn leather.

I was tae be here onyway, Kersty, and I winna see ye haein ither thochts aboot it.

Kirsty shook her head emphatically, dared to take a step forward against him, staring fully and courageously into his eyes; and now into the broth of smells there came the thick and black spectres of vapour burned away by the lamps, and conducted away and into the air by the open cups of their globes, a mixture that caused Kirsty to cough discreetly into her hand. She said,

Ye ken I winna say the noo, I tellt ye thon . . .

and the smoke from the lamps it was that pierced Kirsty's eyes and brought the first moisture to the corners of them, not the crying of a sorry cwean, she told herself, as natural as dew in the morning, only to be expected in such a close room as this. Jamie Watts took her by the arm, and using no force other than that of his persuasive voice and the insistence of a gentle grasp, led her towards the door to the vestibule, and said,

Cam awa ootside, Kersty, for it's nae richt guid for ye staanin aroon in here.

Jamie asked her if her eyes were any better for the cooler breeze of the street, and she nodded and said aye, a good wipe away with the handkerchief she had secreted in her sleeve and no more did they bother her, but she found little to please her in his company, and this she said to him, and from time to time she glanced over her shoulder and up towards the tower, to the cap of the belfry, where she saw the flight of the bats at the top of it, like midges puzzling a grazing cow they seemed from so far away; but Jamie understood her anxiety, and said,

He'll nae hear nor see ye frae here, Kersty, he's nae like the Laird,

with an edge of steel to it, and Kirsty brought her head back around and gave Jamie a smile; she had been caught in a moment of timidity and superstitious dread and now he was a father to her uncertain wee cwean, a man more than ten years her senior, and now meekly she went beside him, asking him,

Far aboots are we gangin?

Jamie Watts said,

Tae far aboots I'll be sheftin the wine casks. Ye can wait ootside til I'm done wi them.

Along the side of the hall Jamie Watts took her, past the illuminated windows, all the while complaining to the air that his employer had no Christian decency about him, to command one such as himself to be nothing more than a porter to the droughty throats of the county's sinners, and then, at the rear door to the hall, he told her to stand and wait for him, for he wouldn't have a woman among the drink, faith he wouldn't be there himself were it not for the silver being paid to him to quieten his tongue; and then he was gone inside, among a swelling of heat and a spill of the aroma from the kitchen, the roasting of Mrs Kelvin's venison, before the door was closed and Kirsty was left in darkness. While Kirsty waited for him to perform the devil's work, as he had called it before the door closed behind him, she cast glances overhead, knowing well enough that she could be seen from the belfry of the tower, if Watchie were conducting any further repairs to the rope which led from the bell to the striking train. She tried not to look over her shoulders, and with a smile to herself she realized that she did not know which of them she feared the most, Watchie for the judgement he might pass upon her, or Jamie for the lash of his tongue; and yet, for no reason she could tell, she felt free of them both, transgressing both their wishes as she was just then, there she was with Jamie when she had promised her time with Watchie, and here she was thinking of Watchie with concern while she was walking with Jamie; suspended between them both, she was independent of them, for neither of them possessed her entire, and a great feeling of freedom came to her as she considered it, though no more free she was than a woman falling, belonging neither to cliff nor to shingle but rather to gravity, calling her slavery to this unseen force liberation.

At last, after what seemed to be hours of listening to the bounding and rolling of the great fat barrels along the narrow corridors, she heard the rear door open, and there was Jamie, with the leather gauntlets of his gardening profession serving to protect his hands from the thorns and splinters and the gravid weight of the casks. He stood before Kirsty, not in the least exerted by the work he had done, and when he shelled the gauntlets from his hands to return them to their pouches, it was with distaste at the ullage of a breached cask, a mark like that of blood, which he would not even touch. Kirsty said,

Ye shidna hae cam the nicht, Jamie.

The music now had the power and the drive to emerge from the hall, for no longer was Provost Macpherson's orchestra playing chamber pieces to aid the digestion, but during Kirsty's wait the meal had been finished and a dancing floor cleared for the celebrations approaching the telling hour, and not a sight of it need Kirsty see but the story was told in the spin of the music. Jamie Watts cocked his head to hear the melody better, and then his eyes filled with pity as if he were caught in the silver wire of it, an insect in an exquisite web, struggling for his very freedom, and at last, he deigned to answer Kirsty, his eyes now as large as lanterns, as if he were now appealing to her for pity, as if she were the spider at the heart of the web of song, and he said,

I'll hae tae ken, Kersty, it's jist fair and richt.

Kirsty leaned back upon the door, her breath now properly in rhythm with her pulse, and she shied away from even the promise of his touch.

I canna, Jamie, I dinna ken mysel,

she said, and now she would not allow herself to look at him, as if there were a snare in just the sight of him; he came round before her so as to present himself to her gaze, but she turned her head to one side to avoid him, and this caused her hair to lash around suddenly with the movement, the binding of it at the back of her scalp made loose and the adjustment made necessary by the slide of the bun, all the gathering and tightening and subjecting to the bite of the clasp, became her reason for not looking at Jamie, no matter how immovably he stood before her. At last Kirsty's hair was fixed to her satisfaction, once again as close to her as she could almost feel it as a weight drawing back her head, but down she insisted on looking still, to the caps of her boots which shone as roundly as the cobbles of the path which girded the hall about; and directly opposite her feet were his, shod in boots that were almost a source of light in themselves, so scrupulously had they been polished that day. There was nothing more that she would say to him, and so she waited for him to understand this and then step back and away from her; but then, suddenly, Jamie Watts grasped her by the forearm, not painfully at first, and so like a sudden bolt it was that Kirsty pulled away from the hold, resisting against him and so causing him to tighten his grip to retain it, and the sheer brazenness of his action made her fasten her eyes upon his, if only to fire the fullest broadside of her anger at him, a warning that this she would not stand for, and the moment she did so, Jamie began to laugh and then gave her the arm back, and how much like a fool, a gullible child, did she feel just then in the presence of this older man who knew more wisely than she did herself. Amused he was at first, but now, kindly she thought after his trickery had claimed her attention, Jamie Watts said, quietly,

Cam wi me, and we'll see the ceilidh frae ootside,

and then he went past her and around the side of the hall, seemingly not at all bothered whether or not she was following him; and silently she damned him for knowing that she would.

The provost's orchestra had struck up a Dashing White Sergeant, a promiscuous jig in which partners were exchanged with careless abandon, certainly no dance for the sober, for it caused a spin to the kilts and the skirts which made the fabric fly around like the vortex of a catherine wheel, and Kirsty laughed in the knowledge that none inside would hear her for the music, for surely these would have been no friends to the brigand of old, sacks of fine living and indulgence every one of them, hardly their feet to be seen for their bellies. But there was Jamie by her side to point to such and such a one he remembered from his days farming near here, to Tommy Macdade of Macdade's the grocer's who played out a fine pantomime of moderation, draining his glass so swiftly that only one with the detached perspective of God might see the quickness of it, and then, with the sleight of a conjuror, Tommy Macdade had the glass back on the drinks table as fast as you'd blink, and then a little way from it he walked as if the glass were none of his concern, until along came a serving lass, an elder daughter of one of the guests perhaps under the provost's generous instructions that no glass should be seen to be empty for the duration of the ceilidh, and lo and behold there was Tommy Macdade's glass replenished with a dram of the Glenlevin, while the first was warming him through with its miraculous radiance, and so for long enough he held the whisky, aye, jist the ane'll dee me for the nicht, and so he would declare while his eyes closed and the drink fell from his hand, aye, jist ane for the nicht, and the day after there he would be at the counter of the shop, his nose alight and his cheeks raw and writhing, and still he would declare to his customers who inquired after his health, I dinna ken jist fit happened, for I had jist the ane a' nicht, and this was the reason why you would never see the widow Jamieson going anywhere but Henderson's for her groceries, for at least Mr Henderson was no liar before God, and no drunkard was he either.

This was not to say that Macdade was the only one that Jamie brought to Kirsty's notice, for indeed they had the next best perspective to God's, that of the unseen observer, and it was from this honoured vantage that they were able to see the gathered wealth of Aberlevin, such as it was, sporting itself for its own pleasure. There were the women in their varied outfits for the evening, some as sober as angels, here for the sake of their husbands, and some as frivolous as cweans, wrapped in frills and trimmings of lace, the blowsy petals of a flower promising to open, there at the occasion as much to display their husbands' wealth and taste as to celebrate the clock's repair for their own satisfaction; but there was one woman among them, whom Jamie pointed out among the excesses of the gilded rabble who had raised Macpherson to the highest office of the village, who was partnered by no one, and who had been invited solely for the honour of her father's memory, and that was Nan Cairney, the owner of the haberdasher's shop, qualified to vote for a provost as a ratepayer, denied her franchise because of her sex. Often enough Kirsty had bought cloth from her to make repairs to Geordie's working coat and to make new garments for herself and Mhairi, and thought the spinster Cairney a fine and handsome woman, not deserving of her solitude; but there she was at the provost's dance, and scarcely welcome at all she seemed to be, for she was seated in the corner, as alone as she was in her shop of a day, but it was only when Kirsty looked more carefully that she realized the spinster was wearing a dress unlike any she had seen before. It was a gown made of a silk as cool and as blue as the sky seen through the glass of an icicle, gathered at the waist and then flared like a bell, and with a trimming of white lace on the high collar and about the waist.

Kirsty thought she had never seen a woman so bonny in her life, nor heard tell of in any of her father's stories of queens or princesses, for it had the extravagance of a joyful display of craft, and yet there seemed to Kirsty to be a notion behind it, the silk expressing the glistening fluency of water in a burn, the lace as the foam risen by the breaking of the burn's thin torrent, quite the spirit of grace in motion was the spinster and a gown of her own making it was in Kirsty's opinion, for a singular design it was and so different from those of the dowdier or more aggressive women present. And yet, despite the beauty of the frock, despite the fact that there was none to match her in the hall, there she sat in the corner nearest to the orchestra, as upright as a lady and with her hands pleated in her lap as if conducting a silent prayer, her hair bound as tightly as Kirsty's as if for fear that accidental release would show the profligacy of it, for a fabric it was in itself, grown steadily since she was a cwean, the volume of it gathered behind her; a burn she was without direction, for demurely she sat, and patiently, looking around at the spinning festivities, and those who saw her there in her seat said to themselves or to others, Nan Cairney noo, thinks she's ower grand for the likes o' us, fit way did she cam here at a'? But there was Kirsty O'Donnell who saw the hall all around from the diamond grid of the window, and she thought that of all the women at the celebration, it was Nan Cairney who most carried herself with dignity.

Just as Jamie Watts suggested that they should leave, Kirsty saw that the provost was looking in the direction of the spinster, and so Kirsty held up her hand and said nae yit, Jamie, in a meenit, for she was wondering what was to happen now, and quite pleased she was to stay and see the business of the evening, such a power had never been granted to her before, that of the presence effaced, hardly was this spying at all. Now she saw the approach of Macpherson to the corner, for some reason she felt threatened almost on Miss Cairney's behalf, for she had always thought there was something faintly predatory about the little Provost, and yet pitiable, like a tom cat fed his favourite meat whenever he cried out for it, master of his territory but scarcely master over his own wants and desires. In the event, however, Kirsty's concern for the spinster proved unnecessary, for the Provost merely stood by her side and brought himself lower so that he might speak in her ear, to be heard above the playing of his orchestra; her fear swelled again as Miss Cairney took the arm of the Provost as it was offered to her, and Jamie Watts breathed,

Aye, Sodom and Gomorrah it is richt eneuch, for his wife's jist awa at the ither end o' the ha'!

but Kirsty understood that it was only what a gentleman should do to lead a lady across a dance floor, and told Jamie to wheesht as if a lapse in her concentration would end the drama; and sure enough, the little Provost seemed just as glad to be seen leading her by the arm, for nothing improper would he have done so boldly, as much as Jamie with a characteristic lack of generosity would have preferred it to be so.

It was to the Revd Lyle, standing on his own at the hall's opposite corner nearest the door and letting a foot rise and fall to the pulse of the music, so that it might not be thought that he was unaffected by the evening's spell of levity and brightness, that the Provost brought Miss Cairney, and then, releasing her arm, opened his own abbreviated arms wide as if he were joining them in the sight of this congregation of revellers, and then away he went to the table with the drinks, returning with a goblet of wine for the spinster and a watered whisky for the Reverend, for this was an evening when the Provost could perform any miracles in the name of the Macpherson, and Kirsty said,

Yon's affa guid o' the Provost,

but Jamie Watts was not to be deluded, the entire evening had not met with his approval.

Aye, he said, ca'in thegither a cwean fa's a' dressed for the cuikin pot, and an aal feel fa's minded tae be pluckin her feathers.

Jamie Watts smiled at Kirsty's frown as if it were the most generous tribute she could give him, and Kirsty thought of Watchie, how in his pain he had been able to invert the truth so that agony was a matter fit for laughter; a belittling of himself such laughter had been, to render his suffering a matter of no consequence.

Jamie turned away from her,

I'm awa back roon,

he said, and again did not wait for her.

They stood in front of the hall, and from the streets came the sounds of honest celebration, singing and the music that poured like wild honey from the fiddle, and there was an iron expectation in the air, the charge that gathers before the thrashing of the storm, and Kirsty knew that there would not be long now until the clock was due to ring. Jamie Watts, taller than her, taller than anyone she had known since her days as a cwean, stood before her like the tower behind him, and so diminished by them both she was, for by changing the focus of her eyes, first the tower and then Jamie became defined in her sight, both imperfectly seen by the light of the moon. When first she lost her focus upon Jamie, there was the face of the clock, the single eye of blue glass with the gilt numerals and hands, and behind it she knew was Watchie, and though she could not see him she knew that he would be working there until the last minute before midnight, with no need for her presence, for scarce had he needed it other than for work; but the fact that he was not present in front of her, not there to be seen by her, made it easier for her to consider what she had not before, that perhaps Watchie Leckie held no feelings for her other than those he might hold for his sister; and then, her focus on Jamie Watts returned, and there he was, more real to her though less certain of him she was, a man who professed to fear the Lord while able to cause her much confusion and turbulence but whom she could reach out to and touch with her hands, there in a way that Watchie was not, spiritually and fundamentally aware of her in ways that Watchie could not begin to understand, and so when Jamie Watts said to her,

Weel, Kersty, wid ye be merriet tae me? For I'll fecht for ye, gin ye'd hae me dee it, she remembered what her mother had said, a long time ago, or so it seemed, mind lassie, whan comes the time tae merry, ye'll no aye hae the chance tae be merriet tae the man ye'd like, but jist see the guid in him, and yon'll do ye.

Kirsty looked up towards the tower once more, and found herself uttering a prayer, almost as if she were praying to the tower itself.

XLV

While Kirsty had been away on her walk, Watchie had finished his remaining oiling of the wheels, and more than that, with frequent looks at his father's watch, he had decided that the mechanism should be first engaged at precisely half-past eleven, so that any problems which might arise could be solved in the time before the clock was due to strike; and so this was done, the lever was thrown and the clock set in motion, but not before Watchie suffered the most profound doubts within, for there had risen within him the fear that all his work had been hurried and shoddy, and what a disgrace to the memory of the old clock he considered himself, to be barely completed the work when he was starting this never-tried mechanism, it was unthinkable for a craftsman with any pride about him, and he wondered what old Mr Strachan would have to say if he had been here to see such a thing, nae an affa fine bittie o' timin, Master Leckie, eh? Then there were the fears that something unforeseen by him might bring the whole rotation to a stop, a bad casting perhaps, a flaw that was not apparent to even the closest examination but which would show itself as a chasm at the first strain upon it; so much there was to go wrong that he suffered the paralysis of doubt with his hands on the engaging lever for quite a while, and it was only when he realized that he must be precise with the starting of the clock, timing it to the very second, that he found the means to resist the leaden anchor which dragged along the very depths of him, and at last the whole great engine of it was off and running. A powerful sound it gave out like the pulse of a giant contented heart, and all the parts were spinning smoothly, some scurrying around at speed and some gentle and stately, and Watchie Leckie then began to wonder where Kirsty had gone for so long, for now he wanted to share with her the feeling of elation, as he would have wanted her there if the mechanism had tumbled in wreckage.

When Watchie heard the footsteps on the darkened stairs, then he felt a sense of great relief that Kirsty had come back in time for the clock to strike, with fifteen minutes to spare in fact, which he could tell from his father's watch, open in his hand like a scallop at high tide. There was so little he could do now that the clock was to be left to its own devices, falling towards the hour of midnight, that he would be grateful for Kirsty's presence, and the reassurance that he might draw from her well of patient strength, for despite his solitary nature, he had such a need to reach beyond the chamber, outwith the dimensions of this constricting workshop, as close as an egg in which he might imagine himself to be the only power in creation, this shell of granite behind which he was bringing time back to the village. The footfalls came closer, a pitiful ticking on their own next to the monstrous beat of the mechanism; and now that Watchie was listening to them properly, they were not the reticent landings upon the stairs that were Kirsty's signature, for her footsteps would not have been heard above the din of the workings, but as steady and as confident as Macpherson's they were, and yet they were not his either, not slow enough to be his, like a reasoned argument they came to the head of the tower, the steps of one who was sure and canny in the dark, committing each lift with absolute care but not afraid to do so, reaching the chamber of light at the top of the stairs in good time and without fear.

The man who submitted himself to the doubled light from Watchie's and Kirsty's lanterns was taller than Watchie, and wore a strange outfit that the watchmaker loon could not imagine belonging to any occupation in particular, with the apron of leather that was settled over the neck and fastened behind the man's lean waist, and the gauntlets inside their pouches, and Watchie knew that he could not be a guest at the dinner below, and so wondered what his business was in coming here, for the man, now that he was in the light, walked about the chamber with the deliberation and arrogance of the worst kind of visitor to a museum, holding no curiosity for the pieces on display other than as foreign or exotic artifacts only serving to confirm his belief in the makers' savagery, and from the man's leisured and quite cursory examination of the mechanism behind its cage, Watchie took the notion that even had there been labels to explain the functioning of the clock's many parts, he would have refused to read them, for it was not the man's intention to know the machine but simply to look at it. As far as the man was concerned, Watchie might as well have been a mouse in a toy box, for his eyes were wholly filled by the mechanism that burned with the lanterns, and it was this possessive tour about the clock which caused the hackles of Watchie to rise, as slow as he was ordinarily to rouse to anger; but just as he was about to step forward to ask what the man's business might be, the man stopped by the wall of the chamber opposite the entrance, and slipped his hands into the pouches of the apron, nesting them beside the gauntlets, which gesture caused his arms to bend away from his torso as if each were a bow waiting to be strung, and declared,

Nae bad werk, Master Leckie, mendin the deil's clock for him! And nae lang it's ta'en ye neether, I've heard,

examining the workings in motion now as if they were an item of sculpture, with a distant eye. Watchie crossed his arms over his chest, and stared at the man as the man stared in his turn upon the mechanism, and then, quite unable to stop himself, he laughed as he heard properly what the interloper in leather had said.

And fit way'd ye cry it the deil's clock, noo, meester na'body, fan the deil hisna a'thin a–dee wi it?

The man strode towards the iron frame, two paces, and then stopped, still taken by the movements within as if mesmerized despite himself.

Meester na'body, is't? Aye, there's truth in thon, for it's the saul o' man that'll be judged at the end o' his days, richt eneuch.

It seemed curious to Watchie that though the man had declared it the devil's clock, how much he was captured by the sight of it, as if he were considering taking credit himself for its making; and so, when finally he did acknowledge Watchie, it was with a faint look to the side that hardly brushed Watchie's outline, as if he could not imagine such a mighty collaboration of brass to be within Watchie's capabilities.

The deil's clock I says it wis, Master Leckie, and yon's fit I meant, as certain I am o' it as gin he'd peyed ye the siller himsel,

said mister nobody; and now Watchie's rising anger became laughter in much the same way as his pain had while in Kirsty's arms weeks before, as if he were better able to express his anger if it were to be changed into a sensation as harmless as vapour, of no substance or consequence, and he said,

I ken, ye're thinkin the brigand's best nae minded on at a', is yon it? Aye, but can ye nae see it's guid for the toun tae hae a clock for fowk tae ken the time . . .

Mister nobody hacked off Watchie's attempt at reasoning brutally,

I'm meanin, Master Leckie, that the brigand belanged tae the deil, and thon clock's been stertit tae mind us on Macpherson, and yon maks it the deil's ain clock, and yon's nae ees for ony toun.

To hear it said in this manner brought a frown to Watchie's brow, a very slight cowling over his eyes; but mister nobody was still gazing into the frame with great admiration and loathing, and now it was as if he could scarcely hold back from reaching inside to the trains, to experience with his own sense of touch this creation of Watchie's, as fascinated with the machinations of sin as anyone who considered themselves upright before the Lord. Watchie said,

This toun's needed a clock e'er sin the aal ane was torn doon,

no longer prepared to deal pleasantly with this mister nobody who would dare to come into a man's place of work at a vital time and assail him with ill manners, but neither was he discourteous until the man replied,

Fit ees is a clock, man; a clock's nae ees tae a toun, wid ye nae say yersel?

Watchie knew that he was being goaded as if he were no more than a mule being thrashed along a difficult road, and he looked at the open fob in his hand, and knew that he had little time for such aggravations; but once again he frowned, more deeply, for there was something familiar about the profile that the man presented to him, but nothing came, and he said,

A clock'll tak fowk oot o' their beds at the same time ilka morn, and pit them tae their beds at the same time ilka nicht, yon's fit ees a clock is tae a toun.

The man stood away from the workings at last, and turned from Watchie's sight, pacing towards the back of the chamber now.

Yon's nae ees at a', man, for yon ye've dawn and sunsit, and gin ye'd nae clocks, fit need wid ye hae o' clockmakkers? I'm tellin ye as weel, clockmakkers are nae ees neether, wid ye nae say?

If Watchie had not been so agitated by the meaning of the approaching hour, and by the fact that he had just succumbed to Mr Strachan's old argument concerning the utility of clocks, then he might have more clearly heard the resonance of the man's words; but misdirected he was by his confusion, and he spun so that he looked after the man, who stood with his back turned to Watchie, wearing the shadow that Watchie cast from the nearest of the lanterns as his own garment, almost perfectly did it fit him, and Watchie said,

But there is sic a thing as clocks in the warld, ye hae need o' clockmakkers, ken.

The man spoke to the wall, as if it were keener of understanding than the loon behind him.

Then it's yersel that's nae ees; ye're nae ees, man man, nae ees at a',

said Jamie Watts; and then turned to face Watchie, and wore the paper-twist smile that Watchie remembered meant the leaving of Dodie Mearns from Smallbrae, and that he had carried with him after he had made Wullie Leckie count every farthing of his leaving purse, for the sight of the blood draining from the young clockmaker's face upon recognizing his old taskmaster was surely a pleasure that the vengeful Lord who deserved Jamie's worship gave only to those he had elected to save.

★

Jamie Watts was no longer as tall as Watchie remembered him in his imagination, for there was Watts in all of Watchie's cold and thankless labours, and Watchie minded on how the thought of his father's former orra loon had come to him just before his exhaustion had caused him to fall double over the bracings of the mechanism, for then the shade of Watts had assumed the size of the tower itself, and Watchie wondered, for a rare and superstitious moment in his life if the cry of his pain and impotence had somehow reached Watts, that he should come now at this time of Watchie's testing. Still he stood above Watchie, for he had been tall for a young man and had not stopped sprouting, but only a head above Watchie he was, and from this Watchie took some comfort, that the older man was unable to threaten by dint of seniority, for this chamber was Watchie's charge, the clock was of his craft and making, and so little reason was there for Watts to be here; but as bold was Watts as if the chamber were his own to claim, his shoulders were thrown back and his head was held raised upon the stalk of his neck, and this Watchie remembered of him most vividly, that his head was always too heavy for the strings of the neck to retain; and behind his old employer's son he looked fixedly, as if the mechanism were the trophy for which Watts was prepared to fight, and he said,

Are ye a proud faither o' yon muckle bairn, Master Leckie?

Watchie laughed, defensively, an attempt to turn aside the stealthy attack.

Fit a dampt feel y'are, Jamie Waatts; ony feel kens it's neether flesh nor blude.

Watts's smile was a gash upon his face, his lips now withdrawn.

Na, nae feel, Master Leckie; a feel's a'body as wid dee fit anither says, like rid the shite frae a byre.

Watchie coloured to be minded on his days of slavery to Watts, and suddenly he felt himself, quite without reason, to have been diminished by this memory, as if the very act of bringing it to mind were enough to bring back also the old relation between them, that of drudge to Jamie Watts's whim.

Watts was now relaxed and swelling with power, as if he had come to tell the king of time that his city was fallen, to stand aside for the usurper; and he said,

I dinna ken fit way the Laird has suffert yer clock tae be makt hale, Master Leckie, for mebbe I'm sent tae stop it, and mebbe the Laird meant for ye tae fex it jist for him tae tak it doon, like the Tour o' Babel. But yon's nae fit way I cam tae yer tour, jist.

Watchie was now trembling where he stood, unaware of the passage of significant minutes, his arms folded over, standing like a sentinel in front of the workings.

And fit way did ye cam, Jamie Waatts?

Watts took a pace forward, shrugging off the garment of Watchie's shadow, so that now the light which revealed him seemed to have been shed by himself, luminous and challenging, casting a shadow of Watchie in turn.

I cam tae the tour tae gie ye my thanks, Master Leckie.

Watchie's attempt at a rigid and determined posture fell slightly to hear this.

Fit wid ye be thankin me for?

Watts drilled Watchie through with his eyes,

For plou'in the field for a better man than yersel tae be sowin.

Watchie shook his head, said,

I'm nae a fairmer, Jamie Waatts.

Watts did not release the clockmaker loon from his eyes.

Nor am I mysel noo, Master Leckie, but a gairdner, werkin for Meester Macandlish. For the noo, he hasna the quaarters tae keep me, so I says tae him, Meester Macandlish, have ye nae a wee croftin nae affa far frae the toun, that ye sellt tae a tinker mannie a filie back? Yon'd dee for me. And d'ye ken, Master Leckie, but for the hale tinker tribe o' them bein papists, and it bein sae simple tae tempt them tae their damnation, they're nae affa bad comp'ny for the likes o' me.

And then Jamie Watts stood plainly in front of the young maker of this shrieking and squalling bairn of a mechanism, how it put out such a cry as that Watts would never know, and saw that the piercing of Watchie's eyes had caused understanding to come to him, and Watts had only seen a thing like this once, when his mother had lain on her bed, wearing the shape of consummate well-being but for the emptiness of the eyes, glass which showed her to be gouged out like a fallen log; and though Jamie Watts had felt as flat and as steely as a loch in drear autumn then, now there was a lightness around him, elation and a rapture as fulfilling as that of any papist saint, for while the Lord might have decided that the clock should be mended, surely it was not his intention that this godless maker should be left to prosper by the fixing of it. In this way, Jamie Watts served many purposes, his own as well as those of the Lord, though as he was one of the elect what difference was there between the two? For down at long long last came the son of his despised employer, a thing that Jamie Watts's Lord would certainly look upon with approval: if there was anything that Watts despised himself, it was the man or indeed the woman who was never done making things, for the shabbiest of mimics their attempts at craft inevitably were, these cuckoos in the nest of true creation, for there was Wullie Leckie and his joinering, surely the man who had given Watchie this will to be making through the blood, and no good would come of stealing the act of creating from God whose only right it was by his right as the first cause. If it could be said that Jamie Watts created anything, then it was discord among those he considered to be the enemies of the Lord, and therefore of righteousness, and therefore of himself, and the name he gave to this was justice, with not the slightest compunction about his means, and so drank sweetly from the well of his enemy's misery.

The chamber around Watchie Leckie became as wanting in depth as the pattern on a tapestry the more he contemplated this disclosure of Jamie Watts's, excluding all sound, and by the glimmering of the lantern's flame reflected from the wide open eyes of the man before him, Watchie knew there to be some truth in Jamie's words, though how much there was no telling. He said,
  Ye tellt the widda Jamieson a hillock o' lies aboot oor fairm, Jamie Waatts; fit way wid I ken the truth frae ye the noo?

Watts shrugged, casually.

Aye, ye're nae an affa trustin saul, Master Leckie. There's three fowk I'd hae ye ask gin I'm tellin the truth: Meester Macandlish, yon aal drunkard Geordie O'Donnell, and his fine dochter, aye, by heaven, affa fine!

From behind him, Watchie heard the beat of the clock, and a grateful pulse he heard, almost as if to remind him; and then Watts looked around himself at the chamber, and said,

Gin ye'd tak comfort frae it, I'll taal ye the noo, Master Leckie, she wis cryin oot yer name files she wis wi me, and yon's a fact,

and then there was a sharp pain in Watchie's hand, which he realized as he looked down upon it was the hand in which he had been holding his father's watch, for it had been inside a fist that had been tightening the longer he listened to Jamie, and only now did he feel the bite of it after its silver shell had closed upon the ham of his thumb, so sudden was it that the watch fell from his hand and dropped to the flags, and Watchie saw it turn in the air and then fall with the shell agape, landing on the glass. No blood had been drawn from his hand, but there was a risen crescent of bruised flesh, mottled the colour of spilled wine; but little was he thinking of his own injuries as he bent to inspect the watch at his feet, and sure enough, as he had suspected and feared, though hardly any light there was by which to see the proper damage, there was a constellation on the flags as if it had been drawn down from the clear night sky beyond the belfry, and only when he went on to his knees for a proper look did he see that the glass had indeed broken, and worse still, as he picked the watch from the ground, the facing with its round of roman numerals had worked free to show the raw matter of time itself within the oyster shell; and then from the opened case came spilling all the wheels he had worked upon those many years ago, as if the very presence of Jamie Watts were unravelling the work of his life. Wheel after wheel fell until Watchie could no longer tell whether it was happening in the present or simply part of his dream. Quickly he turned the casing upright and then closed it over so that there would be no more escapes, and placed the watch into the pocket of his dungarees, and to the sound of the mechanism on one side and Watts's laughter on the other, Watchie grubbed around the flags for the lost wheels, and a curious thing at that moment, suddenly he felt a strange crisis of perspective: for weeks he had overseen and constructed by himself the immense machinery to his left as he knelt, vast and bloated wheels that you might imagine were the very clockwork that powered the whole of creation, the rising and falling of the sun and the moon, the cogs of an orrery whose influence permeated all earthly and celestial being, so that not just the planets in their courses but also the growth and flourishing of everything within sight of the tower and beyond depended upon this pulse, this turning of vast forces; and so long now had he been working on such a size of a beast, that the wheels from his father's watch lay on the floor where they had fallen, and all but invisible they were to Watchie, unrecognizable to him as being kin to the great millstones which ground the raw hour into finer particles, making little more sense to him than sparks as they threw the lanterns' fire pitilessly back to him, hardly different they were to the needles and angles of the glass. Now Watchie grasped everything that shone from the flagging, like a beggar newly seeing the boots of the constable, taking a scattering of coins from the ground before him, caring not whether it was glass or parts of the mechanism he was picking up and dropping into his pockets, for he had little time to care which it was, and he said in reply to Jamie Watts,

Aye, ye didna tak her hert, Waatts,

attacking now, for he knew that he was in the posture of admitting defeat, and so now was the time for defiance, to show that perhaps he was on his knees but his spirit stood against his attacker; but in truth, he had little further to fall himself, and this Watts's instinct told him was the last bleeding of a punctured vessel, and so Jamie Watts said,

Dampt feel that y'are yersel, Master Leckie! Fit way wid I tak for saxpence fit I could tak for a farthin?

Watchie had collected all the shards of light that he could see on the flags, and on his hands there were more wounds now, blood drawn by the points and edges of the glass, lines that had been scrawled and beads from a piercing tip, so that it looked under the fading lantern gold that he had a handful of rubies. He stood upright at last, and from this better vantage said,

Then fit were ye efter, Waatts?

in genuine rage and confusion. Watts shrugged, carelessly.

Mair werth than a farthin I wis efter, Master Leckie, for a favour I've done ye, though ye winna think it.

Watchie's eyes widened; the gardener, as he now was, continued.

Aye, a favour, Master Leckie. Noo ye ken yer papists for fit they're like, sleekit sinners fa'd sooner dee ill and taal it tae their meenisters efter the deed than live the proper life o' a Christian; and twice damnt yon cwean is the noo, for bein o' the faith she professes, the hoor o' Babylon, and for bein a hoor hersel, for yon her ain faith winna even have.

Jamie Watts approached, so that he stood in front of Watchie, not tilting his head but looking down upon the watchmaker, challenging him by the fact of his presence.

Fit way, said Watts, wid I be efter her hert, Master Leckie, fan ane o' her ilk'd gie me her saul for a' the days o' time?

Watchie Leckie was shaking, hardly able to contain the mixture within him, heated and held just at the point of combustion. He said, quietly,

Ye're the deil himsel, Jamie Waatts.

Watts smiled.

Na na, Waatchie Leckie, I'm nae the deil. God-fearing I am richt eneuch, and I'll prove it tae ye; for I widna dee ither than the Bible says, and lie wi the beasts o' the fields fane'er the need taks me.

XLVI

At first, neither of the men heard the sound of footsteps from the darkness beyond the portal, for there was the grind of the machinery over all sounds but their own voices, but it was Watchie who heard the ticking out of rhythm before Watts, and so looked around to see the source of it. It took Kirsty a while to come into the fullness of the light, for she had been standing around the last turn of the spiral for a while now, since she had been displaced from the vestibule by the provost's announcement that it was time for the guests to leave the hall to see the clock salute its first midnight in one hundred years; and so she had run to the well of the clock tower and had closed the door behind her, where she could not be found by the crowds. It was there that she heard some among the guests declaring that the clock was not telling the right time they were reading from their fob watches, and Kirsty sensed with some outrage that here was the council preparing for yet another betrayal, this time attempting to devalue the price of Watchie's labour, until the Revd Lyle told them that Watchie had set the clock by a watch which had in turn been set that morning from the kirk's sundial, lighting the candle of the hour from the best and most accurate of flames, that of the sun itself, unless, the reverend went on drily, you're accusing the Lord of setting the sun wrongly, Mr Henderson, and even the old miser Henderson would not presume to argue with a minister. It was this that had caused Kirsty to turn her eyes above her, to the well into which the weights dipped and fell by scarcely noticeable increments every second, and though there was utter blackness about her, there was the chamber blazing with the false gold of brass as the lights of her lantern and Watchie's touched fire to the arrangement of the wheels, and there was a vibration deep within the stone of the tower that Kirsty knew to be the rotation of the wheels, and a curious feeling of pride surged through her as if conducted within the granite, her rightful share of the power that was being generated by the heart of time. There was nothing to be heard above the mechanism, no voices belonging to either of them, and with the door to the tower closed behind her, there was nothing to be seen except for the promise of warmth above her, the light the colour of honey in a jar struck through by the sun, a translucent and welcoming light which was almost strained through the intricate transformations of the wheels as if this light itself were the very juice of the hour, and for a moment she suffered the same illusion that had touched the men from the pantechnicon, that she was looking into a well of the golden fluid rather than up into a spill of it slathering the rounded walls; and then she was taken by a desire to go to the head of the tower that was hardly unnatural, since no more would it be than a submission to gravity, a fall rather than a climb, and so she set off as if she were drawn, as if there were nothing to distinguish between instinct and her own volition, until there was no light to be her guide.

During her climb, she wondered if this had been the sensation which had taken her mother upon leaving the confines of the flesh, this rising within a passage of darkness towards a light distantly seen, and now also, perhaps because of this reminder of death, and of the way that Ailsa had left Geordie a man excoriated by a last thoughtlessness, Kirsty became determined, and this she had thought while she waited for Jamie in the vestibule, that she should be kind to Watchie in the parting. The more she gave consideration to it, the more she knew that allowing Jamie to tell Watchie of their talk of marriage had been a dreadful act of cowardice, but then the arrival of Jamie Watts, at a time when Kirsty had begged him to leave Watchie during his day of success, meant that Jamie had succeeded in dominating her judgement by the force of his presence, and the call upon her memory of the night gone by, for hardly would she oppose the man who had brought her to her first understanding of desire, who had raised the passions of a woman from within the heart of a cwean as naturally as if they had been there since the day of her birth. Coming nearer to the chamber, she found herself wondering if ever Watchie would have kissed her in the same way as Jamie, and she remembered Geordie tapping this reluctant affection from Ailsa, outraged was Kirsty's mother that Geordie should have the ill manners to display himself like a greedy beast before the children, but always a laugh had come tumbling from her wide open mouth as if her pleasure had more weight than her sense of propriety, and a whisper she would put into Geordie's ear away from the hearing of the cweans; and it had been the night before when Kirsty had thought this as well, her arm linked to the gardener's as they walked towards the croft, when she thought of Watchie and of the betrayal she had just committed, and of what betrayals might yet come. Now, as she approached the head of the tower, Kirsty was prepared to face Watchie as earnestly as she hoped she would face the Lord himself on the hour of her death, with the truth on her lips and ready to stand before the proper judgement of one with the right to judge her most harshly, for this meeting would be her penance, and no priest, and scarcely even the Lord himself, had more of a right to cast her to damnation, or to condemn her to a lifetime of self-ordained purgatory, than the watchmaker loon in his tower, whose regard for her she had betrayed as surely as if she had been the Iscariot.

It was only when Kirsty gained the last turn of the spiral, where the light crept around the wider wall like a child in a nightgown, and when she heard clearly the voices of Watchie and Jamie over the pulse of the mechanism, that she stopped with her feet on different steps, and pressed herself against the inner of the spiral's walls. Now a sharp and sudden breath came to her, and she felt her resolve evaporate with all sense of self in the darkness, though she held her hand before the fringe of the light and saw its shape in the absence as if to remind her once again of her physical being after such a long climb. Kirsty held the breath once taken for as long as she could, as if to prepare herself more thoroughly for her duty, and so composed in her thoughts the action she would take upon approaching the chamber; first of all asking Jamie if he would oblige her by leaving her alone with Watchie, which request surely he could not refuse, and then she would offer her explanations as far as she was able, and accept his puzzlement and anger as the price for the flightiness of her heart, for little else, she thought as she stood away from the chamber, was she worthy of.

It was only as she went closer to the portal of the chamber that she heard what it was that Watts and Watchie were saying to each other; and the longer she listened, the more she wished that the stairs under her feet would turn as insubstantial as smoke, so that she might fall straight to the appropriate punishment for those who would heed their vanity before their common sense. She felt the swelling of tears in her eyes, but would not let them gather enough to fall; instead she swallowed down her misery, until with Watts's last words she could listen to no more, and then it was she chose to come into the light, having heard much of spite and malice but nothing of love or regard, and immediately went to stand by Watchie's side.

The moment she took her place beside Watchie, she passed her arm through his, not from any misplaced attempt to show him too late her affection, which had spoiled like game over time into a meal fit for one such as Watts, a rotten feast for twisted palates; but she had seen from as far as the doorway Watchie's arm growing tense, the fingers closing to make a solid fist, and so now as she stood beside him she became the post to which his gate was latched, a firm and secure support that none the less was not for allowing him to swing in the winds of his own passion, for she would not have him blackening his soul with the sin of violence for her sake, nor even for his own. Jamie Watts's face altered the moment he saw her.

Kersty, he said, fine pleased I am tae see ye here! Ye widna ken jist fit I've heared frae him fan I tellt him aboot oor mairriage, venom, jist! Aye, venom pourin oot his mooth, that a guid Chrestian shidna hae tae tak . . .

It was the eyes of Kirsty O'Donnell, eyes he had fooled for so long in darkness, which told Jamie that he could hide no more, for as tall the light within them climbed as if she had been fired from the lanterns, she said,

Nae sic a beast I am as I widna ken ye for a serpent yersel, Master Waatts,

and held Watchie more tightly by the arm, not daring to look him in the eye but sharing her strength with him through their touching, as strong as Watchie was himself but stronger still, for she was the one who contained Watchie's gathering rage; she said to him as if he were a bull in a byre ablaze, na na, ye're a' richt, dinna ye mind, holding him back from the fullest expression of his fury, until Watchie stood firmly where he was, so solidly he placed himself that Kirsty knew he would not be moving, and said,

Awa tae hell wi ye, Jamie Waatts, afore I tak ye tae the belfry and send ye there mysel.

Watts stood in his place for as long as it took for it to be known that he would go to the portal only when it pleased him, and not because of any threat that might have been issued; once he knew that Kirsty would hold Watchie from swinging a fist, only then did he turn at the portal and say,

Ye can hae the wee hoor, Master Leckie, for I'm done wi her noo, but I'm thinkin ye'll hae cause tae gie me thaanks, gin ye can stand tae luik at her.

And then he was taken into the throat of the tower, away from them both, and it was all that Kirsty could do to hold Watchie from pursuing him. She held him around with her arms, as if he were inert and rooted like the trunk of a tree, and this in itself slowed him until he had breasted the rise of his fury, and then as pliant as a tattie boodie he went in her arms from sudden exhaustion, a profound tiredness of the spirit which came upon him as he realized that many things were over as well as his work on the clock. He allowed Kirsty to hold him in place for a while, and it felt to him as if without her he would slump to the floor like a bag of laundry, the contents slack and loosened by too long a wearing, but as much as he willed it he could not bring his own arms around her. His face was leaning into the gathering of her hair, with the grace and volume of a pillow, stroking his cheek, and he rested against her for a moment, his ears filled with the pulse of the engine which was rolling behind him, turning to the insistence of the falling weights, caring nothing for the states of the watchmaker and the cwean who together had given it motion.

The engaging of the going and striking trains together sounded like the slow stirring of a giant asleep, taking in the first breath of the day, yawning as it readied itself to begin its work, as if here it had been all along, curled in slumber like a bairn in the chamber's cold granite womb, waiting the long hundred years for the one who might break the spell which had sent it to rest and cut out its tongue; and now time stretched with a grin of pleasure and rose to fill the whole of the village. Now the hour was given speech and song, and the old bell shook on its pivots and frightened to the air those pipistrels which had returned to their silent roost to enjoy the struggling feast of a moth captured on the wing, and there it was, the first ring of the hour in the hundred years.

The sound of it deafened Kirsty and Watchie in the tower, and caused them to fly apart to protect their ears with their flattened hands, but down on the street doors opened and manners were forgotten in the memory of the brigand, and voices cried, tae Macpherson, and the cries reached the pompous little Provost, who filled with air like a balloon and thought how kind were the simple folk of the village to remember him in their celebrations. Suddenly there was more than one orchestra at play in the village, not the refined melody of the chamber quartet, but the sound of many fiddles lashed until the music ran from them as rare as blood, and if there was a voice you would liken them to it would not be the tenor on his stage lifted above the multitude in rapture, but a gathering instead of the generations, elders who sang from deep down in throats cured by a lifetime of rolled cigarettes or pipes, pouring from themselves notes like barley wine strained through leather, younger voices striking the song as precisely as if cutting crystal, instruments not yet made blunt by age and disillusion, and those between, with a power to the lungs granted by the striving years, not yet dulled by the fear of their approaching winter. In front of the tower, there were the merchants and all the privilege of Aberlevin, some as drunk as the lords they imagined themselves to be, and some practising temperance despite the evening, for some there had been near ruined by a liking for the whisky, saved by Christ or the understanding of their spouses, and who now expressed their great admiration for the clock's return to voice by a polite tapping together of their hands, where the drinkers set up a rowdy cheer and a dance whereabouts they stood. Now the monument which had been raised to challenge the sky all those many years ago had had its meaning restored to it, now no longer merely a civic ornament, a grave marker to the ambition of a previous council, but a living giant it was, bringing the century's unfurling progress to the notice of all, even to those who would sooner that it were not heard; and just as the clock was restored to meaning, so also did the many who heard its first song in a hundred years find their own meaning in the occasion. For the Revd James Lyle, who had proposed the young watchmaker at the first suggestion of the council, it was a sermon in itself, a reminder that God had placed as a seed within his creation the will to create joyfully, as well as a reminder by the hour that the time sent by God was irreplaceable, and he knew that his sermon for later in the day would start with chapter three of Ecclesiastes, to every thing there is a season, and a time to every purpose under the heaven. For the Provost, it was the sound of a pardon coming a century late, but arriving never the less, so that he might be elevated by the name of his honoured ancestor, and as each of the chimes sounded, a slow procession of beats as if the hour were pondering the number it should ring after so long a quiet, he allowed the manly tears to swell and shine in his eyes. For the widow Jamieson, who, not possessing a clock, was taken by surprise at the first of the chimes before she was able to raise her hands to shield her ears as if she were as near to the bell as Watchie and Kirsty, it was the first evening of hell's reign in the village, when the devil would make good his promise of over two hundred years past, that twenty miles around where he then stood would be his to claim as his kingdom and further than this, for the first time the widow began to consider if she might need a clock for her mantle so that she might tell the approach of the hour, a clock without the indulgence of a chime of course, for she would be damned if she would listen to the din put out by the work of Wullie Leckie's son when she could be warned in good time to protect her hearing from it; and for the Revd Goodbody in the refuge of the kirk, it was a time for defeat, and for dropping his head in memory of the just departed that the Lord had taken into heaven.

The last of the chimes sounded in the tower, and Watchie and Kirsty released their ears. Kirsty summoned a smile as the final ring soaked into the stone, and she stood before him and said,

Yer clock rang, Wulliam, my loon!

and then she took his shoulders in her hands, and pushed herself towards him on the soles of her feet, as light as a dancer, and kissed his cheek, withdrawing so quickly that Watchie could not be certain she had kissed him at all, that it was not just the touch of thistledown. It was the kiss of a cwean to a brother, and Watchie put his fingers to his cheek and rubbed where she had kissed, as if to erase the sensation of it, while Kirsty looked to the floor, ashamed and forgetful.

Watchie Leckie gathered up his things as briskly as any worker with pride should, first of all taking his lantern from where he had suspended it, on one of the juts of the frame, and then used it to illuminate his procedure as he put his bottles of oil and his chamois leathers into the cloth bag of tools. Kirsty chattered like a child in a game as she too went about the chamber gathering items to be placed under the cloth of the pannier.

Aye, ye're richt eneuch, Wulliam, we'd sooner be gangin awa frae here, nae sense in hingin aboot fan the werk's a' done,

527

and then, taking her own lantern back from where Watchie had asked her to put it, on the opposite side of the frame from his, she went to stand beside him at the lip of the portal. For a moment, Watchie turned to look over his shoulder, at the chamber which had been his solitary work for so long, and which, he realized, had been so even with Kirsty there as his help; how it had been another womb for him as well as for sleeping time, for as much as he had given substance to the clock, so had it given substance to him, shape and form and courage in his accomplishment, taking form with it, until he could dare to think of asking Kirsty for her hand. The mechanism turned confidently in its anchors, and Watchie smiled faintly at his bairn for all that he was dull and insensible, for his bairn it was regardless, the flesh of his design, and Watchie thought of what the Revd Lyle had said before sending him to old man Strachan, that the watchmaker's work was the work of God himself.

The lanterns of Watchie and Kirsty together gilded the stone of the spiral, and on the way down, Watchie told Kirsty of how Watts had come to their farm as an orra loon many years ago, and of how Wullie had released him for his lies against the family, and Kirsty frowned, and shook her head, and said to him,

Ye widna believe a' he's tellt ye, then?

Watchie shook his head,

Nae half o' it, and scarce half o' fit's left,

but the rest of the spiral was taken in silence by them both, and Watchie could hardly wait to be away from the gathering at the door of the tower, among them the Reverend, who took Watchie by the hand and said he knew that God would be with the loon, and the Provost, blowing his nose and hardly able to speak, but to say his thanks, and to give those of his ancestor in his unconsecrated grave. He was offered a drink in the hall, for there would be a while yet of the celebration, but he declined, and went for his bicycle in the well of the tower; and while he was there, the Reverend came behind him and said quietly,

Was there any reason for the man who came out about two minutes before the bell rang to be in the tower?

Watchie hooked the lantern on the handlebar, and put his cloth bag into the carrier basket at the prow.

Nae reason at a', Reverend.

Lyle nodded.

Forgive me for prying, William, but he looked like someone I knew.

Watchie shook his head,

Aye, looked, jist,

and steered the bicycle out of the tower, and for the last time produced the key from his pocket and locked the door for the night. In silence, Watchie and Kirsty went the length of North Street, past many who were capering on the pavements in defiance of the widow's sabbath, and some who recognized Watchie and cried weel fexed my loon! but Watchie only smiled and went by; and that was how it was for the journey along the Cornhill Road, when the village was left behind, not a word went between them except for when they came to Smallbrae, when Watchie thanked Kirsty for all her help, and wondered would she come in to have a cup of tea. Kirsty shook her head no, she would have to wake up early in the morning to go with her family to the chapel at Banff, and Watchie nodded and said that he understood, remembering only then that the day was now Sunday.

In Watchie's house, the moment he walked through the door of the kitchen, there was genial pandemonium, and everyone was there; the chaumer had emptied into the house for the evening, and though it was now Sunday the drink had started to pour, and would pour for a while yet as long as Aal Wullie had the charge of the bottle, though in moderation as long as Peggy had charge of Aal Wullie. Jeannie had cut slices of Nana Richie's fruit cake as thick and as heavy as grave markers, and passed them around on a fine plate, and Wullie had fiddle and bow in his hand, and led the dance next door to the drawing-room. He was proud of his son now that the work was complete and now that the bell had been heard by all in a good circle about the village. Watchie stayed for as long as he felt was right to reward the expectation of the gathering, and took one drink of the whisky to oblige Aal Wullie, aye, ye're aal eneuch noo, Waatchie, I was twalve fan yer great-graandfaither gied me a fisky, and ate a slice of the cake for his mother, ye'll eat proper noo, I'll see tae thon, and Cathie Loudon stopped before him and held out her hand and said, fit way's a handsome mannie like yersel settin wi naebody for a partner? and so Watchie stood and danced with her, his feet as dull as lead while hers were as fleet as the deer's; and when Wullie drew the signature under the dance with a last trail of the bow over the strings of the fiddle, Watchie thanked Cathie, and then thanked everyone for staying up so late, and quietly excused himself to go to bed.

It was Wullie who first began to wonder why Kirsty had not come into the house with Watchie, for certain he had been that Watchie had been gathering together all his determination for some purpose in the week approaching this occasion. However, hardly fit matter it was for discussion in front of everyone, and so Wullie resolved to leave it until the morrow, with all the time to consider if perhaps the courage of his son had fallen before the vastness of his feelings, as had happened to the loon more than just once, and a stubborn wee bugger he could be once he had a secret which needed keeping to himself in any event, and with affection Wullie remembered his son in his bed after he had cracked open the bike of wasps, never would he tell the truth of what had made him cast the stone at it.

Kirsty O'Donnell stayed by the window of Smallbrae for long enough to hear the music from Wullie Leckie's fiddle starting, and heard as much as would tell her that he could draw the song from it as sweetly as the milk from a heifer. The curtains were closed snugly together, and try as she might, Kirsty could see nothing through them, but heard the tramping in rhythm of feet on the boards, softened by the placing of rugs, and there was laughing, and she even heard a raucous old voice clambering tunelessly above all the others, and knew whose it was. She heard all the sounds of joy in Watchie's achievement, and knew that it would not be long before he would return to his clocks and his work with Strachan, with his heart mended as if he had taken it from his chest and conducted the repair himself, and no longer would he need help by his side, for he would doubtless never work on a clock as sizeable again.

Kirsty O'Donnell took to the road home, to her croft, and wondered how far ahead of her was Jamie Watts. The Cornhill Road was laid like a burn, accommodating all the kinks and cambers of the thread of flat ground which settled between the oceanic roll and swell of the hills, and so after a rise and a long leftwards turn, she had lost the sight of Smallbrae; and it was then that she heard above her a sound like paper stolen from the grasp in the wind, a sound she had not heard all day, she wondered how long she had been followed by the cock bird before now hearing it, and then the tears she had not allowed herself in the tower began to flow, away from the sight of both men.

XLVII

Of Jamie Watts on his Sabbath there was no sign, and while Geordie thought this to be because he was consumed by his study of the hand-sized black Bible which he flaunted without fail while Geordie and Mhairi were at their grace, as had been the case on every other Sabbath of his stay, Kirsty knew there to be another reason, and sat quietly in her seat in front of the fire, and let no one see her face nor engage her sight.

Geordie wakened Kirsty from a dark and seemingly perpetual sleep, during which she thought she remembered meeting her mother; her hand was pressed against the middle of her chest when she wakened, where she had seen Ailsa nursing her own pain. Geordie's face was above her as she lay, which made her uneasy without her knowing the reason for it, and Mhairi was up already, and Kirsty knew how deeply she must have slept if Mhairi's climbing over her had not caused her to waken. Geordie said,

Up, lass, up, for we've mass to be goin to,

and kindly he was about it, Kirsty's midwife into the light of God's day, pulling the curtain to give her leave to be washed and dressed for Sunday in private. No breakfast was there for them, for no food was to pass their lips until the spiritual food of the host was in them, and indeed most of the day before Kirsty had declined the food that Mhairi had given her for Watchie; and to the stable it was for Geordie to harness Maisie to the cart and be off on the road to Banff, while Kirsty and Mhairi stayed in the croft so that their Sunday clothes might not be soiled. Mhairi sat on the bench at the kitchen table which faced her away from her sister sitting in the stool in front of the dead fire, and she said,

Ye werena wi Wulliam for affa lang efter the clock was fexed, and her fingers were around the enamel mug of water that would be her only meal for a while, resting on top of the table. Kirsty stared into the ashen remains of last night's burnt peat, took the fire's poker from its place by the side of the hearth, disturbed the ashes with the point of it as if she were expecting to find precious metals that had been formed in the now-cold furnace. Mhairi waited to hear an answer, and then, when none came, said,

Oor faither thocht Wulliam'd cam hame wi ye.

She dipped her finger into the water, drew out a pearl of it, let it drop into her mouth; and she wondered if her sister were looking at her, for she would not look round to see. Kirsty would not have noticed if she had, still casting about the hearth to no purpose; until Mhairi said at last,

And there wisna hide nor hair o' thon ludger of oors a' day lang,

and then Kirsty looked up from her task, to see that Mhairi was turned away from her and was playing with her drink of water as if she were a cwean, and she was about to tell her sister to hold her tongue when into the croft came their father, with a drawstring purse in the palm of his hand, and the look on him was one of open surprise,

The right amount, he said, down to the farthin, and not another thing to be found of him in the stable,

and so the sisters mounted the board of the cart while Geordie locked the door of the croft behind them.

Wullie knew that something was wrong with his son when he realized that he was seeing another Watchie, in his room and at his book when he was not at his work with Strachan or at the table with his family; and fine well did Wullie know this to be the way that all the Leckies dealt with whatever was troubling them, Aal Wullie and his drinking, Johnnie and his escape to the ocean, himself and his temperamental silences, they each of them had their own cocoons into which they would withdraw, and Wullie knew without ever having seen it before now that this was his son's. Watchie's absences were a worry to Jeannie, who found herself looking at a different cloth of withdrawal from the one which he had worn many years ago as a solitary loon, for now there was barely a smile to him, and no more could she break his isolation by sending him into the yard with the Laird.

It's thon Romish cwean,

she said to Wullie and the others one evening as they sat around a hearth, which was consuming just enough coal and peat to warm the room and no more, for it was summer and there was hardly the need for the fire; her knitting needles clicked furiously together, and she declared,

She'll hae the pair loon in an early grave, thon's fit it'll be, heed ye weel fit I'm sayin.

Wullie behind his newspaper growled,

Wheesht, wumman, ye dinna ken yon,

but Jeannie gave an insolent little snort, a telling punctuation accusing Wullie of complicity, and when he lowered the paper he saw that while Jeannie was spending all of her concentration on the coming and going of the needles, everyone else seated about the fire, apart from his daughter, freeing the wool for her mother to knit, was looking at him as if he were wearing a dummy's hat seen plainly by all but himself, and it occurred to him then that perhaps he had spent so long with sword in hand on the cwean's behalf that he was no longer able to see the blame in her, and so after a decent time he folded the paper and put it on the arm of the chair, and stood up from it to quietly leave the room.

Watchie was sitting upright at his desk when Wullie entered his room, careful only to do so after knocking and being invited. The oil-lamp cast a great ring of light around from its minaret, and there was Watchie with the book that Wullie had given him as a diversion during his convalescence from the wasp stings, still the oldest and least confusing of his friends; and there was the rest of the room in darkness, so that to Wullie's eyes it was as if he might step over the threshold and into a deep plummet without end. Only when he entered fully was he able to see the tallboy to one side, with Watchie's remaining clock

cases that he had not taken in for Strachan to see, and Johnnie
Leckie's present of a conch shell, and the bone whale with its
sprig of carved water blown from the top of its head. He went
closer to Watchie, until he could see over Watchie's shoulder,
and saw that the loon was looking at a curious engine on the
page which appeared to Wullie to be steam driven, though little
he knew of it.

Fit is't?

he said quietly. Watchie was silent for a while, and then, as if
it were his first, drew in a long breath.

It's a waater pump,

he said, and appeared to be tracing its connections, from here
to there, with a finger on the page. He seemed to be doing it
idly, almost without his entire attention on the diagram, and
Wullie said,

Yer uncle Johnnie tellt me ye gied him a luik at thon verra
same thing, the nicht he came for yer sester's christnin.

Watchie looked over his shoulder at his father.

He tellt me as weel . . .

Wullie nodded,

I ken fit he tellt ye, for he said it tae me as weel as yersel. The
loon'll nae graa a fairmer, he says tae me, though ye'd weesh it
til the end o' yer days.

Watchie slumped over the book, all of a sudden seeming
older than his years, and weary.

Ye widna listen tae yer ain brither.

Wullie stood as upright as Watchie had been in his chair
when Wullie had entered his room, as if his back had fused into
one hard supporting bone.

Aye, and fit way wid I dee thon, fan I'm the elder o' us?

Watchie turned suddenly to look at his father, and saw in the
clear light of the lamp the glitter of amusement in Wullie's eye
and, a rare thing in these last few weeks, a smile came to
Watchie's face, briefly, gone before it could settle. Wullie came
around the desk and stood in front of the window, to Watchie's
side, and turned so that he was looking down upon Watchie's
head, at the height it had been when as a wee boy he had

535

cleaned the inside of his first watch. Now Wullie looked down from a father's height above his son, as he had not been able to do in some time, and saw that Watchie would not raise his head to look at him; and so he took the repaired watch from his fob pocket, opened it in front of Watchie as if to consult it, over which he made great show, and Watchie's eyes lifted from the page to the mirrored coin that was raised by the lamp, which struck him in the eye, the engraved casing of the watch's shell, looking at it as if it were a totem to him, representing more than the worth of its material being.

Aye, werkin grand, is yer waatch the noo, said Wullie. Ye were aye guid at mendin fite'er was broken, Waatchie.

Watchie looked down, not to the book but to the wood of the desk, as if to escape the garish light of his father's excessive praise.

Yon's the geft I was gied,

he said, simply, to give the credit where he felt it was more properly due. Wullie nodded.

Aye, weel, yon's as mebbe, he said, but it's a geft ye can yaise, ony time ye're in need o' it. Nae jist for waatches, ken fit I'm sayin?

Watchie looked up at his father, now feeling as small as a loon, not understanding.

Waatches are fit I mend, he said. And clocks.

Aye, and traaction-engines as weel, though naebody tellt ye the way; is thon nae richt eneuch?

Watchie nodded, it was true.

Weel, there y'are, said Wullie. And gin ye'll mend a muckle great bull o' a thing like yon, there's nae a'thin ye canna mend.

Watchie laced his hands in front of himself, on top of the desk, and looked into the hollow of them, as if there had appeared the motive for Wullie's secretive conversation. He smiled, knowledgeably, and said,

I widna mend some things gin they were cryin oot for it, for ye dinna ken gin they'll jist break on ye some ither day.

Wullie Leckie nodded, slowly, and closed over his twice-mended watch, replacing it into its pocket. Fine well did he

Mnow that Watchie would do his own will no matter what he counselled, but at the very least he might have started Watchie along a path that he eventually would mistake for one he had chosen himself; and when all was said and done, perhaps that was the only way that one Leckie might ever influence another, for calling his brother all the fools in creation had not stopped Johnnie from going upon the mercy of the ocean. Wullie bid his son a good-night, and then went down the stairs to take his place in front of the fire, saying nothing to any of them, and opened his paper to read the news from Europe, the pages almost pressed against his face under the sustained gazing of them all.

Watchie had long since returned to his work at Strachan's, and about the only place it was that he was treated no differently than at home, a great relief was this work to him, for without it his days would have been long vacancies of contemplation and melancholy. Strachan was fine pleased to see the return of his pupil, and told Watchie that the Revd Lyle had given him high praise for his dedication, especially after his injury, and Watchie thanked the old man for saying so; but it was the last he heard of it before, aye, and afore yer heid graas ower big for the doorway, we'll hae tae get ye baack tae dee yer proper werk, eh, Master Waatchie, said Strachan, his eyes opaque as his glasses reflected from the spirit lamps, and Watchie nodded gratefully and sat on his stool in the workshop, ready to be distracted by his vocation. For days on end, Watchie came to the shop and performed the repairs he was given, and at first he was as bewildered by the reduction in scale as he had been when he had searched the floor of the chamber for the wheels of his father's watch, from raising wheels that could be fixed to the axle of a cart to pinching on the points of tweezers wheels that could barely be fixed to a chariot in a flea circus, and all within a few weeks; but so simple were the repairs that he was called upon to do, that Strachan looked upon his absent work almost with concern, and said,

Nae that I'm unhappy wi yer werk, Master Waatchie, but

ye're affa lik thon loonie on the clock wi his cweanie, are ye
nae? For yer hert disna seem like it's in it,

but Watchie shook his head in denial.

Na na, Meester Strachan, there's nae a thing wrang wi me,

and though Strachan had heard of his apprentice's stubbornness in the tower, the watches and clocks were being repaired,
and so no further inquiry did he make.

It was when he saw the ruination that had been visited upon
a watch that had been given to Strachan to be fixed several
weeks into his return that Watchie first found himself moved
by a repair, for he pitied the watch as much as he had pitied the
village clock at the first sight of it, as if it were a beast bearing
the scars of cruelty; for inside the watch's shell of the rarest gold
was a mechanism which had been pocketed by the shoddiest
arrangement of wheels in their arbors that Watchie had ever
seen in such a fine casing, and he almost recoiled to see it, for
while it was a common enough complaint in the tin oysters that
Geordie O'Donnell had given to him, there was no excuse for
such lax workmanship in any watch, let alone one that would
claim such a price. It was a fault that would worsen during all
the years of the watch's life, and it was a fault that Watchie had
been especially careful to ensure would not happen in his clock,
until the wheels' teeth were eroded to nothing by the irregular
centring of their spin, and all because of a hurried or careless
beginning to the work of assembly, small flaws that would
bring the mechanism to a halt as certainly as if a hammer had
been brought upon it. Watchie took it to Mr Strachan to see,
and Strachan held it up to his eyes, with the watchmaker's lens
in the empty spectacles doubled over his real glasses, to see
inside the golden casing, and he said,

Faith, fit an affa mess, Master Waatchie! Weel seein it didna
cam frae this shoppie, eh?

and Watchie smiled, for neither it had, and said,

It's nae jist the ane feel that's pocketed, either, Meester
Strachan, see.

Strachan held it towards the fierce light of the spirit-lamp,
and looked more closely inside.

Richt y'are, Master Waatchie, I've nae seen the like o' it afore; aye, ye'll hae yer werk cut oot for ye.

Watchie assembled replacements of the appropriate size from a number of drawers on the shelf at eye height, placing them with the pincers upon his cloth of velvet, while Strachan returned to his other repair, and it was just as he was sorting them that the old man said, almost idly,

Ye ken, yon's the way fan ye dinna stert richt, Master Waatchie. Yer ills aye mount up, and mount up, until nae a thing'll gang richt efter a filie, and ye've tae hae it fexed, is yon nae true?

Watchie frowned, and put on his own lens in its frame, for it had been one of his earliest lessons as an apprentice. Beside his cloth of velvet was a container of spirits of wine, in which the new wheels would steep for a time to remove any moisture that might be on their surface. He said aye to Strachan, idly, for he was busy for the moment; but as he dropped the wheels into the container, Strachan continued,

And fan it a' mounts up, ye'll see it's nae jist the fault o' the ane pairt o' the waatch, ye ken, but there's twa tae mak a fault in the werkins, wid ye nae say, eh, Master Waatchie?

Watchie said aye Meester Strachan as he took the damaged wheels from the casing, and wondered what had possessed his old employer to repeat to him what he had already been taught as his first lesson; and then, after he had soaked the fresh wheels and cleaned them of the spirits, he put the new workings together with great care and attention, and when at last he looked up from his work, he saw Strachan smiling over him, and then going to the stove to start the flame for another pot of tea.

XLVIII

On the Friday evening, five weeks after the first sounding of
Aberlevin's village clock, came the mighty knocking on the
kitchen door which prised Jeannie Leckie from her seat with an
ill grace, for all the family were seated at the table and halfway
through their dinner of stew, and under her breath she uttered,

Fa'd be camin fan maist fowk're at their denner?

When the door was opened, there were Geordie O'Donnell
and his cwean on the other side of it, and hardly could Jeannie
stop herself from recoiling from the very sight of the tinsmith
and the cap he wore like a lid to one of his fixed pans; but she
stood to one side and said not a word, giving the head of the
table a look of him as well, and though she did so silently there
was an unmistakable look of distaste on her, as if she had
opened the door to lepers, which Wullie ignored as he stood up
and said,

Geordie, it's yersel, and Kersty, fine pleased tae see ye, man,

and looked meaningfully beyond them and to his wife, a
broadside whose arc Geordie did not follow with his eyes, and
which warned Jeannie to respect the observances of hospitality
and set them a place at their table should they need them.
Wullie waved his hand, and said,

Cam awa ben, the baith o' ye,

and to Watchie he looked, expecting to see that the loon
would be up on his feet and smiling to see the O'Donnell
cwean, a welcome surely was there to be offered to the one
who had brought him back home after his injury; but as
Geordie and his daughter came fully into the kitchen, Wullie
knew for certain that something was the matter, for he had
never seen Geordie so stern in all his days of hawking for repairs
at the mart, and proud stood the tinsmith as he doffed his cap, a
man who would not cower but who was here for a purpose,

one that might be spoken before equals. More than simply Geordie's strength was there curious about this visit, for there was Kirsty as well, reticent she was before them all, her eyes as far cast to the floor as to be effectively closed, that Wullie thought Geordie's newly assumed height and dignity to have been transfused from her; and when Wullie looked at his own son seated at his right hand, a fork loaded with stew held above the plate but his own eyes suddenly tumbling away and fixing on nothing, then an unworthy suspicion began to form in Wullie's thoughts, though little would he let show of it at first.

Geordie held his cap at his waist in both hands as if it were buckling them in place, while Kirsty's hands were laced into a steeple before her, but though both struck the attitude of proper worship and respect, Geordie had no fear about him as he said,

The both of us have eaten, Wullie, thank ye kindly,

then, nodding to one side to acknowledge her supremacy in the kitchen,

Mrs Leckie, but we're not here to be takin the food from yer mouths, no indeed. I'm wondrin if I might have a word with yer boy, if ye wouldn't be mindin that, Wullie, and we'll wait next door so we won't be disturbin yer dinner.

Wullie heard the gravity behind the request, and his suspicion began to harden. Jeannie was still behind the door, and her outrage was plain to see, that a common tinker would dare to come into their kitchen, their own kitchen mark you well, and make demands of their son, as absurd a notion as the mice in the skirting-boards scuttling out of their holes and serving them their eviction; and so when Wullie pushed his seat to one side and went to the door of the kitchen to conduct Geordie and his daughter to the drawing-room, Jeannie's mouth fell, and hardly could she bring herself to close the door behind them as if for fear of sealing behind them all manner of infestations carried with them as naturally as hay on a cart. As she resumed her seat, Jeannie shook herself as if she were dislodging the lice and fleas she knew must have leapt upon her from the tinsmith's woollen jacket, surely a thing that his thieving hands must have taken from the back of a dead man, for such stories did she hear of tinkers, and she beat her clothes as if they were rugs on a line, while the others at the table looked on to the actions of this stranger until at last Watchie said,

Kersty does the laundry twa times a week, mither, jist like ye dee yersel,

and brought his fork to his mouth, looking humbly down at his plate; and though Jeannie always said that children should never speak against their elders, the generosity of her son quite brought her to humility, and she plunged her own fork into her stew, and would not look up as she ate.

Jeannie's respect for her husband's wishes kept her silent, if brooding, through the remainder of the meal, and it was when Wullie looked up from his stew and pronounced,

I'm thinkin oor visitors'd be affa gratefu for a wee cuppie o' tea in the draain-room wi Waatchie files we're at oor ain tea through here, wid ye nae say, Jeannie?

that she fell into a silence that settled like dust upon the table, grain by grain accumulating until you could plough a line through it with a finger, and not a one of them spoke for fear of raising Jeannie's anger further. An ill-tempered meal it became; and through the oppressive quiet, Watchie felt the eyes of his father upon him as if it were the unseen touch of a feather, and so he looked and sure enough there was Wullie staring frankly at his son with a bucket of a look which trawled him as if he were a well, down to the truth among the silt and the mire, but Watchie matched his father's intrusive stare for as long as it was necessary for no taint to emerge, and finally Wullie shook his head and went back to his meal, and a smile there was that Watchie remembered from the night that his father had come by the side of his bed to talk about the watch he had fixed, not exactly approval, wonderment perhaps.

At the end of dinner, Jessica darted around the table and collected the plates for her mother, and Peggy gave hers over and said,

Affa fine denner, Jeannie, jist grand,

and everyone agreed one after the other that it had indeed been fine, to which Jeannie gave them her thanks with a shallow smile, and then set her kettle on the range and began to spoon out the tea into the family pot, a willow pattern of recent acquisition; and all the while, Jeannie was like the governor in a steam engine, holding the pressure in the room and releasing it whenever she smiled to Jessica as the cwean brought all the dishes to the sink,

Guid werk, my cwean, there'll be hate waater eneuch in the kettle tae be waashin them,

and soon everyone in the kitchen became sensitive to her displeasure, knowing that the time to talk of Wullie's deliveries that day was when Jeannie was helping her daughter to sort the plates from the cutlery in the sink, and that the time to stop was when Jeannie brought the empty cups and saucers for Watchie and the visitors to the table, landing them harshly as if their breaking would be of little importance to her and filling them from the newly brewed pot as if she were the reluctant inheritor of a tearoom, minded to chase away the custom with her abrupt service so that she might give herself peace. At Peggy's suggestion, she brought from its cake tin Nana Richie's latest fruit cake, given to the family at Easter and not finished yet, but thin parings she took from it, such tissues that the light of day came golden through the raisins as if they were stained glass in a kirk window, carving the slices onto a plate and putting it on a tray with a jug of milk and a pot of sugar, lifting the tray and handing it over to Watchie.

For a loon whose heart had recently been beating as dull and as regular a time as a metronome, now Watchie felt it playing an unpredictable rhythm in his chest, like a pebble thrown by a child over the nap of a loch, bounding without reason, and he stood outside the door to the drawing-room for many a long second, his palms slippery on the brass handles of the tray, and readied himself for his first meeting with Kirsty since the morning of the clock's fixing. At last, he felt the breath come to him more easily, and just as he was wondering if he would have to let the tray on to the floor in order to open the door without creating a spill, the door opened seemingly on its own,

and there in his grandfather's seat by the side of the hearth was
Geordie O'Donnell – any old throne would do to establish a
court in exile – and as Watchie took the tray into the room, he
saw Kirsty standing by the door through the corner of the eye,
effacing herself from his sight as if she were a servant lass and
closing the door behind him, avoiding his eyes in her turn.
Watchie stood with the tray before the hearth, and just as he
was about to find a place to put the burden that was becoming
more difficult to hold, Geordie said,

Just a moment, please, Watchie,

and then began to knock the bowl of his pipe against the
inside cowling of the grate to shake loose the burnt dregs of a
previous smoke; and obediently, Watchie stood where he had
been told, and thought that he had never seen the tinsmith so
entirely commanding, so wanting in sociability and humour,
and now Watchie felt curiously unsettled, for it was as if he
were entering not a room in his father's house but the croft of
Geordie O'Donnell instead, and entering it as a stranger besides,
one unknown to this hearthside monarch who would command
him here and make him wait for his pleasure. Just as Geordie
was taking his leather pouch from the pocket of his jacket to
begin filling his pipe, suddenly Watchie became aware of the
tinsmith's daughter going towards the fiddle cabinet, and looked
in time to see her taking from the side of it the occasional table
of his father's construction and placing it in front of the hearth,
so that Watchie might rest the tray upon it, and so he did with
gratitude, letting it down with as little of a tremor of the
brimming cups as he could manage and preparing a smile of the
barest politeness to Kirsty for her small service, a smile for
which he had no need as,

Kirsty, darlin, don't be strainin yerself now,

said Geordie, replacing the pouch and indicating to his daughter with a lit match the empty chair opposite his own as if
guiding her by a torch, in which she sat as she was directed
while Geordie persuaded the fibres of tobacco to ignite by the
play of the match flame over them. The time it took Geordie to
achieve a good column of smoke from his pipe gave Watchie

the chance to look at Kirsty, a chance that she herself shirked, as if the old separation which had existed between them at the croft during Watchie's year of mending Geordie's tin watches had never been mended itself; but more than simply a memory of their past estrangement, it was as if his scrutiny would cause the tinsmith's cwean to shrivel within and leave only a cwean of paper behind, the merest sketch of herself with neither content nor dimension, the last petal of a desiccated flower, and so, evading his eyes by looking into the hearth, at the flame of the peat fire, she waited with respect for her father to finish his meal of smoke, and joined her hands together on her lap as if uttering a prayer within the private kirk of her head.

Geordie O'Donnell was lost in the clouds like the peak of a hill of modest height, and when he was certain that the fire had caught in the hearth of his pipe, he shook out the match and cast it into the peat to be incinerated. He drank a mouthful of the pale tea as if it were the finest of clarets and then, noticing that Watchie was still on his feet, waved him to Wullie's accustomed chair of spindles beside the elder's comfortable seat as generously as Wullie had waved him into the house, such largesse he dispensed in another's home, but as Watchie's elder in the room he was entitled to his respect, and so Watchie took the chair and placed it so that it was opposite the occasional table and at right angles to both father and daughter, and then sat down, reaching for his own cup of tea.

And how's yerself, Watchie?

said Geordie suddenly, lifting a slice of cake to give it an inspection and then raising the plate to press upon Kirsty, who shook her head.

I'm fine, Meester O'Donnell; and yersel, and Kersty?

Geordie took another sip of tea and swallowed it over, put the cup on to the tray and then took the stalk of his pipe into his mouth, suckling it gently as if Watchie's pleasantry were capable of all manner of interpretations, a proposition to be considered at length, and all the while he did not rest his eyes upon Watchie, but instead looked at Kirsty, who was looking into her cup of tea, as if to see her own portrait there in sepia. Finally he said,

It's very kind of ye to ask after us both, Watchie, sure and it is, and I'm thinkin that such thoughtfulness is deservin of the fullest answerin that I'm able to give to ye. Now, then; ye're askin after meself first of all, and so I'd have to be tellin ye tis fine I am about the body, what a learned man like yerself'd be callin the mortal coil; ah, but now, if I were lookin about for a word to be tellin ye how I am in the heart, that's a different matter altogether now, and I'd have to say the word I'm thinkin of is perturbed, as a learned man like yerself might be callin it, Watchie.

Watchie almost felt the need to clutch the arms of his chair to stop himself from being cast downstream by Geordie in spate, for though hardly a word could the tinsmith read aside from his own name, a sharp memory he had for the way that words sounded, and never did he fail to ask the meaning of a word he had not heard before. Geordie now looked at him as if to hear what he had to say, and so Watchie said,

I'm richt sorry tae hear thon, Meester O'Donnell; and fit way're ye perturbed, like?

In all the time that Watchie had known Geordie, he had never felt so much that the tinsmith was appraising him for his honesty, and finding him wanting. Geordie stared at the loon fixedly for a long time while he had a sup of his pipe, and then sat back into the chair, nesting himself properly.

Ah, well now, young Watchie, said Geordie, it's not for meself I'm perturbed, ye see, and now ye're bringin me to answerin the second part o' yer thoughtful question; for as fine as I am meself, I'm sorry to say that me daughter isn't at all well, though I suppose ye'd be sayin at the same time that she's as fine as could be expected, takin all things into consideration.

Immediately Watchie said,

I'm affa sorry tae hear ye're nae weel, Kersty,

and then began to frown as he heard properly the riddle as the tinsmith had uttered it, not at all well yet as fine as could be expected, like a puzzle rhyme it was of the kind that Aal Wullie took great pleasure in defeating him with when he was a child, when a common object would be dressed up in verse as intricate as lace and with its most curious contradictions cast into relief. He looked to her steadily, and for once her eyes touched his before she brought up her hands to draw over her them like doubled shutters across a window, and then she seemed to be miming the washing of her face, rubbing her eyes as if to waken herself after a shocking dream. Geordie floated a long feather of smoke across the room, away from Watchie, and looked at the embers in the bowl of his pipe.

Ye see, Watchie, before she passed away, me darlin wife gave me two beautiful daughters, one of whom ye're knowin particularly well yerself seein as how ye've hardly been out of each other's sight for the past months, and so I'm hopin ye'll understand what it is I'm sayin when I tell ye that I know what it means when a woman's not well of a mornin, only nature takin her course so it is, and that's how Kirsty can be not well and yet right as rain at one and the same time, for that's what happens to a woman in a certain state, if ye're hearin right what I'm sayin to ye.

The news meant nothing to Watchie at first, merely a repeat of Geordie's previous conundrum, this time with a hint; for as he looked from one to the other, from Geordie with his look of wonderment at either Watchie's ignorance or his obduracy, to Kirsty with her arms now crossed over her and staring only at the open mouth of her teacup as it rested on the tray, he knew that it was meant to be his responsibility, at least so it seemed by the combative tone of Geordie's voice. Then the puzzle fell together, and Watchie sat as upright as his father's arthritic chair would let him, the joints crying in outrage in a way that Watchie could not, and his mouth worked impotently for a moment, labouring like the mouth of a fish brought to the bank. Watchie felt the surge of a denial rise to his lips as naturally as sap, but somehow the words were slow to come to bud, and after a number of attempts he stopped to think, for here if anything was proof that for once Jamie Watts had not uttered a word of a lie, at least in the matter of their coupling, this was how Watchie thought of it, like the mounting which had brought a calf to Lady those many years ago. His next thought was that Geordie seemed convinced beyond reason that he was responsible for the malaise of his daughter, and he wondered how much of a struggle Kirsty had put up against her father's misunderstanding, or if indeed she had struggled against it at all, if perhaps she had fostered it sooner than admit how foolishly she had cast her respect before the feet of a man who treated her gift as if it were fit only for treading into the dirt. The more that Watchie gave his thought to it, the more he fell back into his seat, taken by a great weariness that coiled within him like a worm, nourishing itself on the goodness that it deprived him of, thinning his blood until it had no more substance than slops or gruel; and once again he looked towards Kirsty, without knowing what would be the purpose of it, whether to judge her or to regard her as if she were a diary, closed against the curiosity of strangers by a fastening of string.

I ken, efter fit's jist been said, Meester O'Donnell, that ye'll be minded tae say na tae me; but I'd be affa gratefu tae ye gin ye'd allow Kersty tae gang for a waalk wi me, and further gratefu I'd be gin ye'd permit us tae gang awa in private thegither.

Geordie took a long milk of his pipe, and then sent the smoke thoughtfully around his mouth as if it were a visitor to a museum. First of all, he searched his daughter for any sign of treachery after his disappointment with her, and found only a plea different in quality from that she had sent to Watchie, begging as if to remind him that she was still after all his daughter, and therefore deserving of some trust for her years of obedience in spite of her one act of will; and then he turned his scrutiny on Watchie, and this was a proper beacon of a look at the loon who had spoiled the first child of his marriage, bright and cold as the light from mercury vapour, a light which scared the shadows into hiding. For a long time Watchie endured the balancing that Geordie made of it on the one mouthful of smoke, his daughter here and the young goat, that beast of excess, on his other side, until at last Geordie sent the smoke away from him in a tail like a horse's, and had a cough to himself, and after swallowing over the product of it had this to say,

Bearin in mind that all this started when yez were both left on yer own, but takin into the account that I'm sure ye'll both be mindful of the fact that I'll be here when ye'll be comin back, I've decided to grant ye the time together, for ye'll both be wantin the chance for a word with none of us about, I'd be reckonin.

Watchie nodded, and said,

Thanks for yer trust, Meester O'Donnell.

Geordie looked into the bowl of his pipe to the embers as they roasted slowly to the end, and then shook his head sadly.

I'm trustin the loon that came to me house to be fixin me watches, young Watchie, for I'm damned if I know what kind of bayst ye've became.

XLIX

Not a word did each say to the other as Watchie allowed Kirsty to lead them to the front door. It was a beautiful evening of late summer, and hopeful bees and wasps were haunting the decorative flowers that Jeannie had planted in the front garden, the cabbage roses and the Gloires de Dijon which made such a potion of the air, a sweetness that was roused by the breezes, and which reminded Kirsty of the times that she stopped here with Watchie before returning to the croft, the garden unseen in the night, spinning and blending its fragrances to trap her memory. As Watchie secured the door behind them, Kirsty went down the two steps and on to the path like a swimmer descending into water, to where the fragrance closed over her head as if to welcome her to her own drowning, and it was a refuge from her thoughts of the bairn within her, and of what Watchie was sure to say, and she found herself beginning to wish that this could be her end, that indeed the fragrance would be a fatal spirit, she might die with the sweetness of it, taking with her the seed of Jamie Watts, an ending she wished devoutly as she became aware of the presence of Watchie at her back, and still slowly she walked towards the wooden paling gate, taking the paving one stone at a time between the bedded roses and leaving Watchie to follow behind her. She said,

I weesh, wi a' my hert, I'd tellt ye fan ferst I'd met him,

for it was true, for all that to say so was to spit in fire. She saw nothing of Watchie but the black sprawl that his shadow made upon the ground alongside her own once they were parted from the house, and hardly could she bring herself to turn around to see the look on his face as she heard him take a breath, as if he too were drowning in the currents of the flowers' scent,

Fit way'd ye weesh thon, Kersty? Tae tak anither man fa wisna like him nor like me?

It was a cold stab, and in the back right enough, and Kirsty turned on her heel and crossed her arms over herself again, and said,

Aye, and mebbe tae tak a man fa widna sooner be merriet tae a clock than tae a wife!

and only then did she see how deeply Watchie had been hurt, and like an arrow loosed into flight what was said could not be retrieved until it had drawn its blood, causing his eyes to widen. Watchie's hands tightened, and the slender fingers curled into fists, and then, as if he were straining against their own will to action, he sheathed them inside his pockets, and said with effort,

The werst I've been hurt by a clock cam better.

Kirsty saw the look in his eyes, and thought of a horse she had seen once when Geordie took the family home from kirk one Sunday, many years before the death of Ailsa when she was a very young cwean; having slipped in mud, it had overturned the cart it had been drawing after a dancing attempt to regain its balance, and one of its back legs had broken like a branch, from which sight Ailsa turned away her daughters' eyes as its master knelt weeping alongside it, only bruised he was himself. As the horse tried to bring itself back to its hooves, it fought its agony as if it were pitted against an opponent with shearing claws; but its master held it by the head and whispered into its ear, na na, my loon, help's camin, dinna kick, and perhaps this was what gave it calm, and this was when Kirsty saw the great liquid eyes fill with a plea to its master to tear away the creature that was devouring it; and it was this memory that came to her now that she looked upon Watchie, and so she said,

I didna mean thon, Wulliam.

Fit ither way wid ye say it?

Kirsty shrugged, her arms still in front of her, turned to the side so that she was facing the roses on the border.

I didna waant Jamie Waatts . . .

Ye gied yersel tae him.

Kirsty brought her head around to look at Watchie.

He said he'd be a hisband tae me, and there wisna ony ither man offerin me yon, noo, wis there?

It was the small voice of justification, but hardly was Kirsty prepared to carry about with her the full weight of the blame for what had parted them. Watchie remembered the lessons of his repair at Strachan's, and looked to the ground, as if it were the plain that separated them. He said,

Fit way did ye taal yer faither a lie?

Kirsty let go of herself, reached to the height of her waist to stroke the petals of a Gloire de Dijon, as soft a fabric as she could imagine against her fingers.

I didna taal him a'thin, Wulliam, and thon's the truth. He thocht ye were the faither, and . . .

Watchie came around to the other side of Kirsty now, nearer to the gate, knowing that she was avoiding the look of him.

Ye'd lee him tae think me the faither o' yer bairn?

She would not turn to face him, but bent to draw the fragrance in as if it were a drug to her.

Sooner than hae him ken, aye.

Watchie stepped back from her a pace and stopped, as if another pace would take him over the lip of a precipice behind him.

Hell mend ye, Kersty, he said. Jist, hell mend ye.

Kirsty shook her head as if it were the judgement of the flowers.

Na na, Wulliam Leckie. In oor faith, purgatory mends ye. Hell's there for the likes o' Jamie Waatts.

She stood upright, and looked at Watchie, and a smile was on her lips, as if the scent of the flowers had stolen her reason, giving her into the possession of an inappropriate spirit of gaiety.

Far aboots are we gangin for a waalk?

she said, and away she was past him and out of the gate and into the Cornhill Road waiting for him before he could recover his senses, leaving him to follow her again.

For a while they went on the solid cobbles of the Cornhill Road, walking a little apart to avoid a collision even by accident and speaking not a word to each other; and then Watchie pointed to a path away from the road and through a gap in the hedging, where the plants were combed away on either side of a parting of bare earth, and there was where he led, and where Kirsty followed, not knowing why she should bother if he were to maintain this silence.

There were brambles and wild raspberries offering their fruit through a lash of defending thorns, inviting her to come and fetch them if only she dared, promising no immunity from scratches on the flesh of her hands, and she reached out and found that they were beyond her; but Watchie saw her thirsting for the sweetness of them, and so leaned beyond the fence of the dog roses with their inedible ruby hips and the teeth on their stems that curved wickedly back like the tip of a Saracen blade, tramping flat the nettles near the ground, so protective was the land of its treasures to be guarding them with such fierce weaponry. Watchie picked for her a handful of both brambles and raspberries, pulling first of all on the clustered fruit to see how easily they would come free from the bush and taking only those that gave up their hold without resistance, collecting those that consented to be picked in the palm of his hand until there were enough to spill across his doubled, cupped palms like the last water from a drying well, and it was then that, with his first backwards step, his hand brushed past the stem of a dog rose and caught on one of the hooks just at the web of the thumb, and he came to offer her the fruit as the blood began to leak from him and fell in drops, like the beads of the raspberry. Kirsty took a step forward, and bent down to look at the injury, but Watchie laughed again as she remembered from the clock tower, as if his pains were of small consequence in the scheme of broader suffering, and said,

Dinna ye mind on yon, tak yer raspberries and blaeberries,

even as Kirsty ignored him to touch the hand, and took away on the ends of her fingers a slight smear of blood, and Watchie looked at her with a sideways glance, see, there was no cause for worry at all. She said,

Hurtin yersel's nae for lauchin at, Wulliam; there'll cam a day fan ye'll nae be able for lauchin at it.

Watchie shook his head, and smiled.

I'm nae jist mindin my ain hurts, Kersty,

and held his doubled hands towards her as if it were a basket of fruit, insisting silently that she take what was reaped for her. Kirsty looked at him severely, but he would not let her help with his gash, and so she took from him a bramble in one hand and a raspberry in the other, and raised the raspberry to hold it in front of Watchie's lips, inviting him to take it from her. Watchie looked at her as if he were suspicious of the offering, and then shook his head,

I wisna efter ony for mysel,

and was about to take a step forward and away from her, when she stood deliberately in his way, refusing gently to let him by and holding the raspberry still to his mouth, closer if anything.

Fit way wid ye nae tak fit ye've gaithered fan it's in yer hands, Wulliam Leckie, and fan ye've jist hurt yersel tae gaither it?

Watchie opened his mouth to reply, and found that there were no end of answers, because he had gathered them for her, and not because he cared for them himself, because he could not feed himself with such a fortune of berries in his hands, because it would be greedy, after one of Jeannie's dinners, because he would not have her feeding him as if he were a bairn; but the longer he looked Kirsty in the eye, the more he found himself lost in a great hall of reflections, refractions, angled mirrors which sent him endlessly around as if he were nothing more than a solitary pin of light among them, and once more she pressed the raspberry towards him, making plain to him that she would not eat until he did. Watchie thought of horses taking oats from a pursed hand as he leaned towards her, but allowed her to put the berry into his mouth while she ate the bramble in her other hand, and on they went along Watchie's path, Kirsty eating the berries from Watchie's hands and when the last of them was finished all that was left were the stains on his palms, the mottled bruising left by the brambles and the blood of the raspberries, and Kirsty observed how little injury it took to draw the juice from them as Watchie rubbed his palms against each other in mirror image to clean them, and said nothing.

At length, the nature of the vegetation on either bank of the path began to change, from flat and spatulate to round like containers and beakers, the flowers becoming wider and blown about their stems like glass, while the bushes of thorns with their droplets of fruit fell back; and then, suddenly there was a parting of both banks, and for the first time Kirsty saw Loch Bannoch before her, swelling with each step she took like a great blossom of silver growing from the stem of the path, an illusion of perspective in itself, as the great source of it which kept and refreshed its waters was a burn, or at least as wide and as fast as a burn can be and not be considered a river, which followed a number of channels which the ages had scored with great subtlety in the land from a height some distance away which Kirsty knew to be called Macpherson's Rest, and which was as visible from her croft as the Deil's Shieling was from here. For a long while, Kirsty was held to the spot by the sight of it, from the swell of the Shieling Hill whose tale had been told to her by her father, who knew a good story to be passed on whenever he heard it, and where also she knew that the wifies of old had taken their corn to be winnowed by the Lord's discriminating winds before there were threshing mills to be sorting the wheat from the chaff, to the lochside forest of such density that there seemed to be no light within it, protecting the family seat of Lord Aberlevin from the eyes of casual trespassers, trees which had seen many lords of the title interred in the family graveyard, gambling lords, establishing lords, profiteering lords, lords returned from fields of battle and lords with no taste for risk of any kind, all been, all gone, and all of them welcomed into the soil by the elms and the sycamores that gave the forest height, and by the brotherhood of weeping willows that were recent transplants into the lochside earth, dropping their tresses into the waters as if hanging their heads in shame.

It was as if the loch and the forest, the belly of the hill and the sky which was ageing with the day had been painted on canvas in front of her; but then Kirsty realized Watchie had not been so stricken by awe that he had slowed down, and so, raising her skirts above her ankles in order to see better the placing of her feet, she said,

Dinna be in a hurry, Wulliam. I canna keep up wi ye!

and it was only then that Watchie turned to take notice of her, upon which she stopped immediately and let fall her skirts as if they were curtains, ashamed that he should have seen her so for even that little time, and went as gracefully as she could manage through the grasses which now gathered to efface the threadbare earth, stitched together in one seamless carpet of particularly luxurious pile, and came by Watchie's side. She passed a rebuke through her eyes towards him, and then, without a word, threaded her arm through his, and said,

Mebbe ye ken far aboots ye're gangin yersel, Wulliam Leckie, but I dinna ken,

and this was how they walked in the absence of a path, with Kirsty submitting to Watchie's guidance as he went towards the bleak, black forest.

Kirsty's uncertainty of step forced the pace for them both, and so Watchie told her of the memories that this place held for him, and of Anthony Clarke,

a loon that wis aye readin a buik, ne'er did I see him jist runnin aboot, ye ken,

and if he did not understand the irony of his own words then Kirsty certainly did, and she stared at him with the opaque shine to her eyes of a loch on a sullen day, turning back the grey of the sky, which Watchie quite missed in her. He showed her the places and was still able to name the flowers where he and Anthony had found them, marsh cinquefoil and bistort and dog violet, all the names still vibrant as the colours of their petals, but Kirsty laughed and said,

Yon's affa queer names,

for the way that they distorted Watchie's mouth, and he said,

Aye, Anthony widna taal me a'thin but their richt names, frae a buik, ye ken, and then showed her how they had migrated from their places in his memory, swept around the palette as if by the caprice of the artist's brush, and almost sad he appeared to be for them, Kirsty noted, as if they were the same blooms he remembered from then displaced and evicted without sentiment nor ceremony. Here was a place he would mind on most vividly, and often it was a flower or a spear of grass or the sight of a trout flying from the water that tore the seal from many keepsakes he had not unfolded in long enough, and then there was another place that would mind him on Anthony and his ways of an austere dominie, where Watchie could tell Kirsty word for word the judgement that Anthony had called upon the quality of his herder's intellect, and laughed as always when minding upon his hurts, and Kirsty said,

Yon loon and his faither, teacher or na, fit a pair o' skyellochs,

which brought a serious face to Watchie,

Ye're nae jist meant tae say yon aboot a teacher, they're learned fowk fa's been tae univairsties tae dee their werk, teachers.

Perhaps it was because Kirsty had never seen the chalky interior of a schoolroom in her life, and therefore learned no obedience of them through the exercise of discipline; but men and women teachers were in her eyes without privilege of station, and so,

Losh! she said, thon mannie Clarke, gin I met him on the street I'd think him touched gin he cairried on yon way as he did in yer class, well seein his loon's daft as weel,

and Watchie turned to look at her, and laughed this time for she had said what he would never dare to, what he had thought since the days of Pish-ma-breeks, though this he would never tell her.

After a while, as they came closer to the willows, Watchie let free Kirsty O'Donnell's arm and began to cast about like a dog, searching, and then suddenly his expression cleared as he went nearer to the shade of the willows, to where the trunks and branches constructed their vaults and alcoves, striking out away from the loch and leaving Kirsty to follow.

When Kirsty finally arrived by Watchie's side, she saw that he was standing in front of what seemed to be a forest in miniature; no sapling willows nor elms nor sycamores, but flowers she thought them which partook of the nature of trees, or trees which had fallen from grace with their maker and been reduced in stature for their humiliation – at first she had no means by which to tell. As she looked more closely into the dusk of shadow that the forest cast down at this time, she saw that their trunks were indeed stems upon which grew a fine bristling of hair, and that the branches were of even length and cast up to the sky tiny flowers in their white myriads to be shown to the sun, and all the trunks were of different heights, some as tall only as Kirsty's knees and several as high as her shoulders, though a few there were as tall as Jamie Watts and one at least was taller than that; and yet flimsier than trees they looked to her, as if their stems might not be as rigid as bone or wood, as if indeed they might be formed around air, and so curiously elevated and distorted flowers they seemed to her to be, and for some reason she was afraid of them, as if this forest of flowers were God's own proof that all things were possible to the maker, that he could even make one form imitate another, that here was a model of the greater forest which dwarfed and shadowed it, for Kirsty thought privately that it was certainly not their beauty which was their reason for existence. She looked to Watchie, and was about to ask him which they were, immense flowers or stunted trees, when she saw that Watchie's attention was claimed by this forest as if it were speaking to him in ways that she could not hear. For a while Watchie stood like this, as if these flowers, as she guessed they must be, were marking the spot of a death; and then he looked up at her, and then smiled, a smile which apologized for not attending sufficiently to her, disparaging himself for such a thoughtless withdrawal, and this made Kirsty frown in concern, taking his arm once again, though needing none of his guidance, and squeezing it gently as if to encourage him to speak, which he did, after a long breath.

Here they're here, jist far aboots we found them, Anthony and mysel.

He reached out a hand to touch the trunk of the nearest, the tallest of them, and a long time did he put off the last advance of his hand, as if afraid to find them simply fashioned out of the substance of all hopes and fears, the ghosts of his expectations; but there was indeed down under his fingers, a fine white hair on the green hide as thick as leather. Kirsty said,

Fit are they, Wulliam?

for though they were familiar enough to her as a sight among the hedges and the bushes, she had no name for them; and Watchie laughed, and shook his head in pity for the day that he had first seen them, and said,

Ah, noo, yon's nae jist sae easy tae say,

and so he told her of the disagreement between himself and the schoolmaster's loon, how each of them knew differently until there was no conceding, and all the while Kirsty shook her head as well in another kind of pity and when he was finished she said,

I winna ken fit way loons'll aye fecht ower the daftest things,

and then she heard her words as a stranger to them, as if another had spoken them aloud and caused the shared meaning between herself and Watchie to press her head forward, and so ashamed she was to be reminded of her state, forgotten in the sweetened air of the open, and she looked to the earth around the roots of the pluffers, hogweeds, either name was good enough for her, and waited for Watchie's judgement as impassively as she had her father's on the third day of her malaise, after he had counted for her symptom by symptom the ways in which this illness was similar to Ailsa's at the time of her conception and of Mhairi's. Watchie's voice began again, and to her surprise it was even, and not at all hurt,

Weel, ye widna jist say yer faither wis wrang, noo, wid ye?

Kirsty looked up, almost as suddenly as the time in the croft when her hair had sprung from its pin which now came to mind, and she said,

Ye wid yersel, Wulliam Leckie, fan yer faither'd've had ye as a fairmer as weel as a waatchmakker, mind ye thon?

but there was Watchie, ready and waiting for her with a tilted smile which caught her quite unawares, and which slackened her enough to smile in return. Gently he disengaged himself from Kirsty's arm, raising the latch which secured them together, and then went around the forest of pluffers slowly, to convince himself that they were not the same as those he had found with Anthony; and it was as if they had been grown and nourished upon this well of discord which had drenched the very soil, drinking it from the ground and distilling the spite from that day into the very elixir that burned the flesh, the milk which ran from stem to branches and which fed the flowers at the top. He walked all around them, and came to a stop at Kirsty once again, on the other side of her, and said,

My faither'll aye be my faither, Kersty.

Kirsty reached to the trunk of the pluffer that was nearest to her, as Watchie had done before, but could not bear to touch it, and brought her hand back to rest against her.

Jamie Waatts isna wi us ony mair.

Watchie looked to the height of the tallest of the pluffers, to the florets held up on the spokes that Anthony had taught him to call umbels, and which name he only remembered now that he was looking at them again.

Far aboots is he?

Kirsty stepped back a pace.

I'm nae luikin for him, Wulliam.

I'm askin, jist.

She shook her head.

My faither heared he wis lodgin wi Macandlish the noo, that he'd a place ready for him the day he left us.

Watchie nodded, still looking at the structure of the pluffer, as if in their use of driving uprights and the raising of their spindles to give sun to the florets at the head of them, there were some lesson to be learned in unity of purpose and design; and then, as suddenly as the farmer who leaps immediately from bed in the morning so as not to indulge his tiredness, he struck out once again in a curious change of direction, this time towards the forest proper, and Kirsty, knowing that she was being led, took up her skirts again and followed.

★

The forest was more alive with the light of the maturing sun than Kirsty would have thought from her look through its portals and pillars from the outside, for the branches above strained the darkening gold of it like honey through muslin, taking away the sharpness until it reminded her of the time around first light. Through this chamber of gloaming, Kirsty followed Watchie, and again the purpose to him was evident to see, for where she would have preferred to stop to trace the clue of a chirping or a crying of a hidden bird to the place from which it had been spun, there was no resting for Watchie, so that when she saw a red squirrel with its arrowed ears and alert eyes begging on its hind legs like a trained dog, he would not stop for her to tempt it by her side to pet it, but drawn forward he was as if by a lodestone, with no more will nor power to prevent his onward march than iron before an overwhelming current, and so forward she was pulled herself for fear of losing her way among the many passages and corridors defined by the trees, and all for the want of a sight of Watchie.

At last, Watchie came to a stop at the object of his determination; and it disappointed Kirsty to see that it was no more than just an old elm tree of no particular character, in front of which Watchie stood as if it were a shrine or a monument, with his head bowed in memory for a while as she came along by him, and then, oblivious to her presence, raised his head to the enveloped heaven above, as if in praise to a contained and imprisoned maker. Kirsty tilted her own head in puzzlement as she saw that Watchie was once again, as he had done at the pluffer forest, searching as if to find a distinctive flavouring threaded upon the air, which smelled to her thick and moist with decay; and then she saw more closely, that he was sighting along the tree towards the crown of it, to the uppermost of its branches, as close would he go to it without touching its bark as if the tree itself were as venomous as the laburnum, whose every part from root to twig was saturated in poison. If it was a thing in particular he was looking for in the branches, then he did not seem to find it, for there was a slight frustration about him as he turned to face Kirsty, and then he told her about the tumour which had been high in the branches many years ago, a mystery wrapped in what had seemed to be dry paper and which Anthony Clarke had told him it would be safe to bring down with a stone, and of what followed, and as much as the thought and the memory of it beat against Watchie, he stood as fast against it as a door, and presented Kirsty with the door's other face, sturdy and impassive. She remembered what Wullie Leckie had told her, over cake and tea in the drawing-room of the farmhouse, and like him before her reached through the years to take the stone from the young loon's hand, or at the very least to pick him up in her arms and take him away from the forest as fast as her legs could carry them both, so clearly could she see it as if Watchie and Anthony were there before her, and she said,

Yer faither tellt me ye were stung.

Aye, but he disna ken fit way tae this day, for I widna tell him at the time.

Kirsty frowned, and passed a hot coal of a look to Watchie, smouldering with indignity,

And fit way wid ye nae tell him?

and he reminded her of who Anthony's father was, and of the prohibition upon meeting other children placed upon the teacher's loon, and of Anthony's threat should he tell; all of which cast more fuel towards Kirsty, upon which she burned steadily for a thoughtful moment until she could contain herself no longer, and she said,

Yon's nae richt, tae haud yer tongue fan anither's at fault . . .

Watchie stared at her more evenly than ever he had met her eyes before, and said,

Aye, Kersty. Yon's nae richt, tae haud yer tongue fan anither's at fault. Mebbe ye'll ken fit way it's richt the noo, fan it wisna for a loon a' yon years ga'ed by.

Kirsty looked to the ground between them, the faint growth of grasses that were able to thrive on the little sunlight that was dripping into the wood like water through the fingers.

It's nae for an ill cause, Wulliam.

Watchie was as hard as the wood behind him, his eyes opaque, his posture rigid.

And fit cause wis it for, taal me?

She met his eyes again, pleading with him to understand as one who knew him capable of understanding.

The cause o' keepin my faither awa frae the drink efter a' his years o' nae drinkin, for gin he kent fa wis the faither o' the bairn, and gin he thocht I shid be merriet tae him, I dinna ken fit he'd dee tae himsel.

As Watchie looked at Kirsty, he saw that she was pleading not just for herself, that it was for many more folk; for her sister, whose years were all to come; for her father, that he should not bring himself to ruin for the sake of her thoughtlessness; and then, she brought her hands over her belly almost involuntarily, and Watchie thought last of all of the bairn, and the life before it with a mother thrown aside to be judged by a world forgetful of its own desires and indiscretions, and there he stood, with his back to the tree which marked the place where once he had been betrayed by a false friend, and knew that a decision would have to be made, and that it was only his to make.

The moment that Watchie Leckie came into the house with Kirsty, he asked her to wait in the hall, and there he found Geordie O'Donnell seated in the drawing-room still, with his father this time in the seat that was usually Peggy's, and while Wullie was having a small glass of the Glenlevin which was his indulgence at the end of a long week, Geordie was at another cup of tea, and Watchie nodded to see it, and then asked his father if he would be so good as to leave himself and Mr O'Donnell alone and in private for a while, to which Wullie readily enough agreed, taking his whisky with him and declaring that there was nothing to hurry them in whatever business needed such arrangements. It was boldly that Watchie went over to occupy the vacant seat opposite Geordie, and without waiting for the tinsmith to ask whereabouts his daughter was the now, Watchie leaned forward in the chair and said,

Mr O'Donnell, ye were richt tae cam here fan Kersty wis ill wi the stert o' a bairn, for I widna have had ye dee ony ither thing. I wid like tae mak richt fite'er ye feel I did wrang tae Kersty, and I'd say tae ye that I widna tak the honour o' a cwean I honour mysel, and that I'll be merriet tae her afore ye'd ken she had a bairn.

Geordie O'Donnell put the tea on to the tray, which was still placed on top of the occasional table; and then, a curious thing, let out a long breath, almost like a sigh which had been held for days on end, and immediately stood to invite Watchie to shake his hand,

Me boy, me boy, I knew ye'd do right by me daughter, I had faith in ye like I've faith in the Lord himself!

and always was Watchie suffering handshakes from those whose professions gave much power to their hands, first the provost Macpherson and now Geordie O'Donnell with even stronger hands, used to manipulating tin as if it were leather.

The next place that Watchie took the news was to the kitchen, where the family was gathered, and though sore disappointed they were in the loon, the best they made of it, though Jeannie would end her days with the notion that the cwean had taken her son's innocence; Wullie was the first to show how pleased he was to hear of the union, and then there was Peggy and Aal Wullie, who declared, aye weel, a man's tae live wi fit he's done, but she's nae affa bad a cwean, and then there was Jeannie, subdued Watchie thought, though she smiled and went to make another pot of tea, calling Jessica back to the kitchen to help and to explain why her brother's news was not to be wholly celebrated while the rest of the family poured through the door to meet the tinsmith and his daughter, soon to be family themselves. There they were, both of them, with Watchie in the drawing-room; standing now, for Geordie's court was adjourned, and no longer was he a father seeking a redress for his daughter's loss but a guest in another's house, pleased to see all of those who would soon be related to him in law, and shaking hands with Wullie.

Geordie O'Donnell, man, man, ye'll hae tae tak a dram wi us!

said the dairy farmer, for surely the merest smell of the

whisky that would colour the bottom of a glass would do no harm in his opinion, but still none of it would he have,

Not that I'd so soon refuse the hospitality o' the man to be another father to me daughter in such a short while,

said Geordie, but refuse he did with a hand held up to push aside the glass and the bottle that Wullie had not even found as of yet, and Wullie nodded, respecting his wish and the great confidence with which the tinsmith had declined, as if his determination had once again been made sound against all climates. It was when Wullie went to fetch his fiddle from the cabinet that Geordie O'Donnell declared that time it was for him to be going home, and Wullie turned to protest, on such an evening surely not, until he saw the overwhelming sadness in the eyes of the tinsmith, and Wullie Leckie remembered the funeral of Geordie's wife and thought a thing that he wouldn't have thought of before, that here Geordie was losing his daughter to the very sacrament that had been the wellspring from which had poured all his disillusion with the world, and so hardly would Wullie place the burden of laughter and company on one who had sentenced himself to solitude, and richt y'are then Geordie it was before Aal Wullie could use his own means of persuasion, and Kirsty said she would walk home with her father though Geordie told her he would not mind if she were to stay to be walked home later by her intended, as he said with a wink of the eye to Watchie; and before Kirsty left by the front door with her father, she turned to Watchie and took his hand in hers.

Not long after the door closed behind them, then Wullie asked that Jessica go to the chambering to bring the workers to the house, which hardly needed to be done on a Friday, and out of the cabinet came the fiddle and the bottle of the Glenlevin; and as Watchie waited for the arrival of Alistair and Cathie Loudon and the others, he thought of the way that Geordie had released the long breath upon hearing of Watchie's proposal, for this was how it seemed to Watchie the longer he thought of it, that Geordie had been as tense as one waiting for the result of a decision rather than sitting there, in the seat that Aal Wullie now claimed as his right, like one preparing to hear a confession. Once the workers came from the bothy, then there was no end to the shaking of hands and the congratulating that Watchie smiled to receive, for ill-mannered it would be to turn them aside, and even his mother came with her tray from the kitchen to offer her own best wishes, not wanting to call her son a weak-willed fool before the workers; but when the music of the fiddle started to give its spin to the evening, Watchie sat away from them all with a cup of tea in his hand, declining Aal Wullie's offered bottle and the cry of, aye soon tae be merriet but nae a drap o' fisky in his mou' yet! with a firmly raised hand, just like his father-in-law as would be, and wondered if the tinsmith had as much doubt over the paternity of the bairn in his daughter as he had faith in the watchmaker loon's will to set matters right.

L

The wedding was set before the child would show, but not until Watchie completed his instruction in Catholic doctrine at the chapel in Banff. There Watchie went with Kirsty to see Canon Collins, who was generous enough to make no mention of the circumstances of the coming marriage, who explained with patience the Stations of the Cross and the Beatitudes, the mystery of the rosary chain, the confession of sins and the sacraments; it was all so much to take in but he learned for the sake of Kirsty, who took his hand sometimes and squeezed it gently whenever he looked like failing in his memory. In truth, it was no harder to maintain than his own faith, that is the faith of his upbringing, though there was more mystery and ritual to it to be certain, and yet Watchie found that he was not grieving over this loss of the faith of his own fathers, it had come up in conversation one evening at Geordie's fireside, when Wullie had insisted in coming along in the gig and driving him there, despite it only being a brisk walk. The fire was cracking in the hearth, and Geordie refused Wullie's offer of a sociable whisky from the bottle which the farmer had brought; more to the point, Kirsty had refused for him, my faither disna tak fisky ony mair, and Geordie nodded and smiled a little regretfully, and had the tea she made instead, this causing a smile to pass between Kirsty and Watchie. Geordie made room in front of the hearth for them all, and Mhairi sat on the floor between his knees and curled herself on his lap like the family cat, having forgiven him long ago for the madness of the whisky, though hardly a smile did she give to Watchie, and Geordie, not without irony, lifted his enamel mug and toasted good health to them all, then said,

I've had a talk with the canon in Banff, ye might have heard o' the man, a fine man is Canon Collins, and he tells me the lad might have to convert to Kirsty's faith to make it easier to be wed, if ye're agreeable yerself, Watchie.

Watchie sat on a stool next to Kirsty, aware that the eyes of the room were upon him; he turned to his father, who shook his head, it was not his decision to be made, Wullie said,

I'll nae stand in yer way, Waatchie, but I'll hae tae hae a werd wi yer mither, ye ken fine.

For Watchie, there was no need for consideration; there was God almighty, the Revd Lyle's great watchmaker, and there was the worship of him, which mattered not where it was done nor by which formula of words; he turned to Kirsty, and there was no decision to be made. He said,

Gin yon's fit tae dee tae be merriet tae yer dauchter, Mr O'Donnell, I'll dee it,

and Wullie nodded slowly,

Then they'll be wed fan Waatchie's learnt fit way tae be a Catholic, Geordie, though I dinna ken mysel fit kind o' faith it is that'd mak ye dee sic a thing.

Geordie drank the thick liquor of the tea, and said,

Fools the lot o' them, Wullie, proper fools now, but Watchie's made up his mind,

and so every Tuesday and Thursday Wullie loaned his son the gig for the seven or so mile journey to the seaside village of Banff, days on which Jeannie looked upon her son as if he were a traitor, and his father more than this, for he could have spoken up and put an end to this papish rot while he had the chance. She sat sullenly in the kitchen and sometimes had a cry to herself while Peggy sat next to her as her consolation, sh my cwean, she said, gathering her daughter-in-law in her arms, being the pillar in her slowly cracking world, fit widna hae ye hae done tae be merriet tae Wulliam? And one day Jeannie told the truth of it to Peggy, he winna be needin me ony mair, Peggy, he'd dee onythin for thon cwean that he widna dee for me, and then Peggy knew the remedy for it, she said in as crisp and lacquered a voice as she could manage, dinna be sae daft, Jeannie Leckie, Jeannie Richie, ye're the loon's mither, ye're nae Kersty, and it was a help of a kind. Peggy took her in hand as she had done when the loon was to be born, easing her towards another birth, another loosening of the anchors of kin, and so Jeannie's wound gradually sealed itself, it grew over with the pale tissue of regret, was always visible, often hurt in the cold of abandonment.

Jeannie did not much care for having to invite the whole tinker tribe for a dinner, but Wullie insisted, and Peggy told her daughter-in-law what she had seen, the tinker cwean scraping the hair away from her son's forehead where the wind had disturbed it, all the signs which Jeannie remembered from the days when she placed her own markers upon the one she was minded to marry. She worked hard over the roasted beef for the meal, she was not having them think that her hospitality was in any way stinted for being grudged, and when they all arrived, precisely on time, it was because Watchie had set their clocks and watches for them so that his mother would not have the slightest excuse for complaint. Geordie approached Jeannie, and said,

How pleased to have me family at yer house on an occasion like this, Mrs Leckie, and especially such a well-kept house, I'm sure,

and she found herself charmed despite herself, he was neat and presentable against all her worst fears, shaven cleanly so that he might have been the mirror in which Aal Wullie could look at himself, so well tidied were they both, they sat to table and accepted the strange grace Wullie spoke over the meal and said amen at the finish of it. Mhairi passed messages across to Jessica with her eyes and seemed to promise a friendship. Everything went absurdly well and Jeannie felt the foundations of her thinking move underneath her as they spooned just the right amount of vegetables from the bowls on the table, not a greedy but a temperate amount. After the meal, there was laughter from the living-room, and Mhairi came through to help Jeannie with the dishes, drying them with the towel and putting them in their right places in the cupboard: and she smiled at Jeannie, a pleasure to see such a polite young cwean; then Wullie came through from the living-room with Kirsty, and said,

Aboot feenished, Jeannie? Jist that Kersty was efter haein a luik at the fairmyerd, and I thocht ye'd tak her aroon,

and so Jeannie was stuck with it, she sent such a look at her husband but he smiled as if impervious to it, and Kirsty looked to the floor aware of the trouble she was causing, but Jeannie was politeness itself as she took the tinker cwean around, yon's far the kye bide, yon's for the horses, yon's for the hens and yon's the chaumer, the light was fading but everything could be seen, and Kirsty smiled as Jeannie presented her with descriptions of all those who worked for the farm, what were their strengths and what were their weaknesses, she was gentle and affectionate and charitable with her tales of their carousing and the hard work they put in, and then there was a long silence, the well dried and they grew parched by the drought of it, and then Jeannie turned and for the first time looked into the eyes of Kirsty O'Donnell, Kirsty Leckie to be, and said,

Wid ye say yer Lord's Prayer for me, Kersty?

The question took Kirsty by surprise, but she gave a cough she did not need, and began,

Oor father, fa art in heaven, hallaed be thy name,

and Jeannie found that her own lips moved, in silence, to the same words, and lead us not intae temptation, but where Kirsty finished with amen, Jeannie continued, for thine is the kingdom, the power and the glory, forever and ever amen, and there was the only difference. Jeannie nodded slowly. The cows lowed in their byre, and there was the sound of sociable neighing in the stables, where Jess and Jonah were sharing their berth with Maisie; there was the peace of night about the farm, and Jeannie found a smile within herself for the cwean, and she took Kirsty's arm in her hand, and said,

They'll be at the fire, talkin aboot fit's in the newspaper, Kersty,

and led her into the house.

Jeannie compromised herself all the way to the chapel, where she sat and found that the ceremonies of the Catholic Church were not very different from her own, even if there was this strange abasement of genuflection which she thought of as something of a curiosity, even if she did feel obliged to comply with it. Wullie's arm came around the back of her as Watchie betrothed himself to the daughter of Geordie O'Donnell, and she wept a tear or two for the loss of her son and the thought that she would never see him again in the kirk at Aberlevin, and she remembered the trouble he had caused her on her lap, snatching at the hats of the fine ladies until she had learned how to stop him; but she was not the only one to weep, and she looked across the aisle at the distaff side of this doll's kirk, and there she saw empty Mhairi, on the eclipse side of her father, crying, thought Jeannie, for the loss of her sister. The ring, bought from Strachan's at a favourable price, was placed on Kirsty's hand, a modest circle of gold with the smallest chipping of a diamond, and then it was done; and Jeannie thought what a long affair was a papish wedding, what a strange thing it was to receive the body of Christ directly on the doorstep of the open mouth as if it were a ragged traveller seeking his lodging, and not long after that they were in the open salty air of the day and heading for Aberlevin, for home, where the reception was at Smallbrae, which was to be their home until Watchie could find a house for them with the twenty pounds that the council had given for payment.

Outside the lighted window, out of earshot of the rest of them, Mhairi and Jessica found companionship each in the company of the other, first playing games of chase which made them laugh, then sharing their passions, turning them over like cards in a game of chance, daring to reveal more, until Mhairi turned over the wildest card of all, causing Jessica's brows to raise to their fullest height. She pinned Mhairi on a glance, then laughed loud and hard, a song which never seemed to end, Mhairi appeared hurt, regretting what she had said, until Jessica found her breath,

Faith, Mhairi, have ye nae sense at a' in yer faimly? Ye'd think he was a hillock o' gowd, the pair o' ye fechtin like yon,

and Mhairi laughed as well; she was young and had a resilient heart, and laughing they returned to the farmhouse, where Aal

Wullie was full of the drink, where Wullie's fiddle and Andy MacGrath's jew's harp drove Kirsty and Watchie in their dance, and if there was one regret about the occasion it was that Johnnie Leckie could not be there, for he had gone to be a sailor in the king's navy, and they could not spare the time for him to see to family matters; but they made the best of it, the Richies were there as well though they had not made the wedding, it was an evening that Watchie would never have ended but for the impending dawn and their wish to be to bed, a wish respected by all.